Crumbs

DANIE
STIRLING

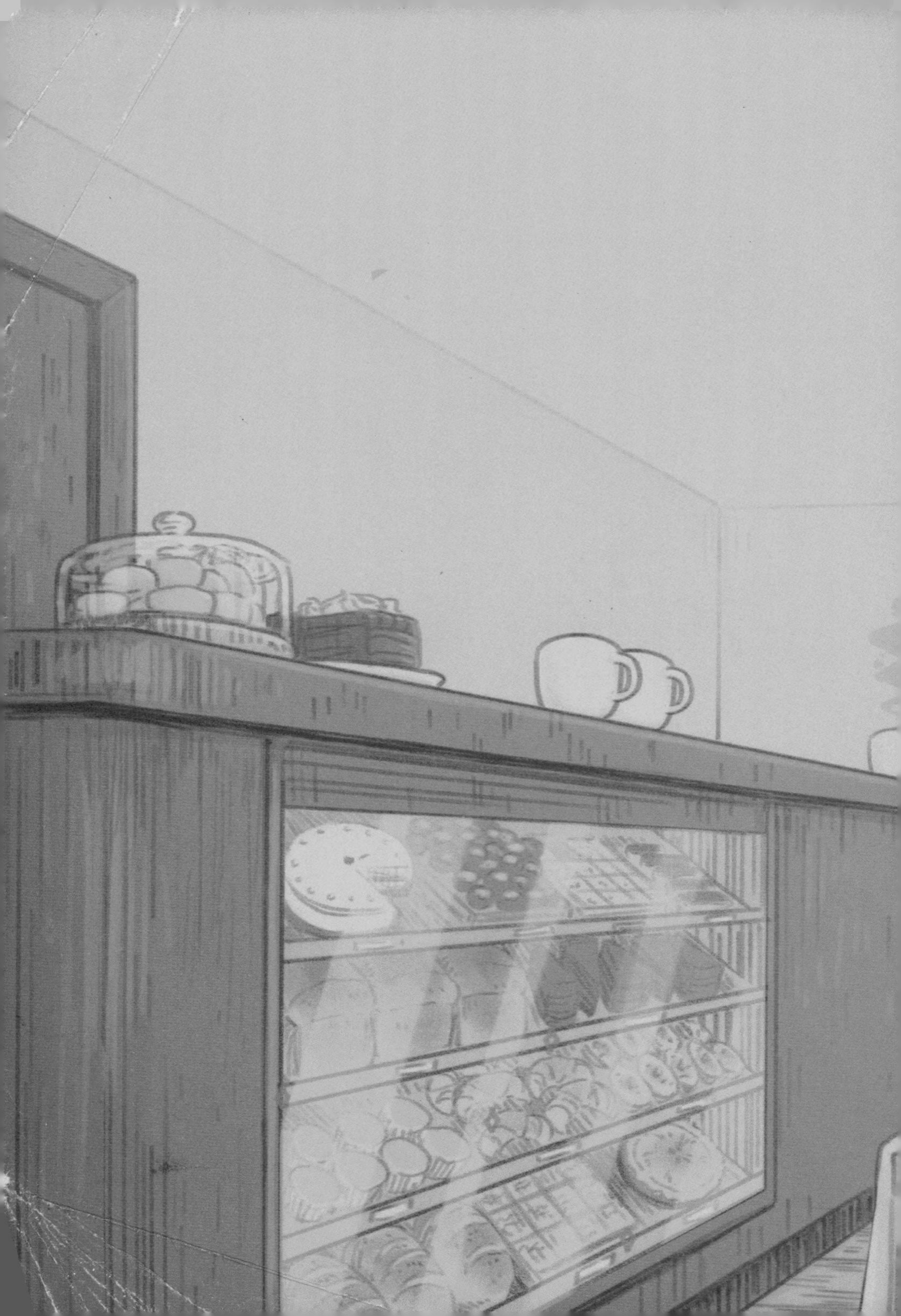

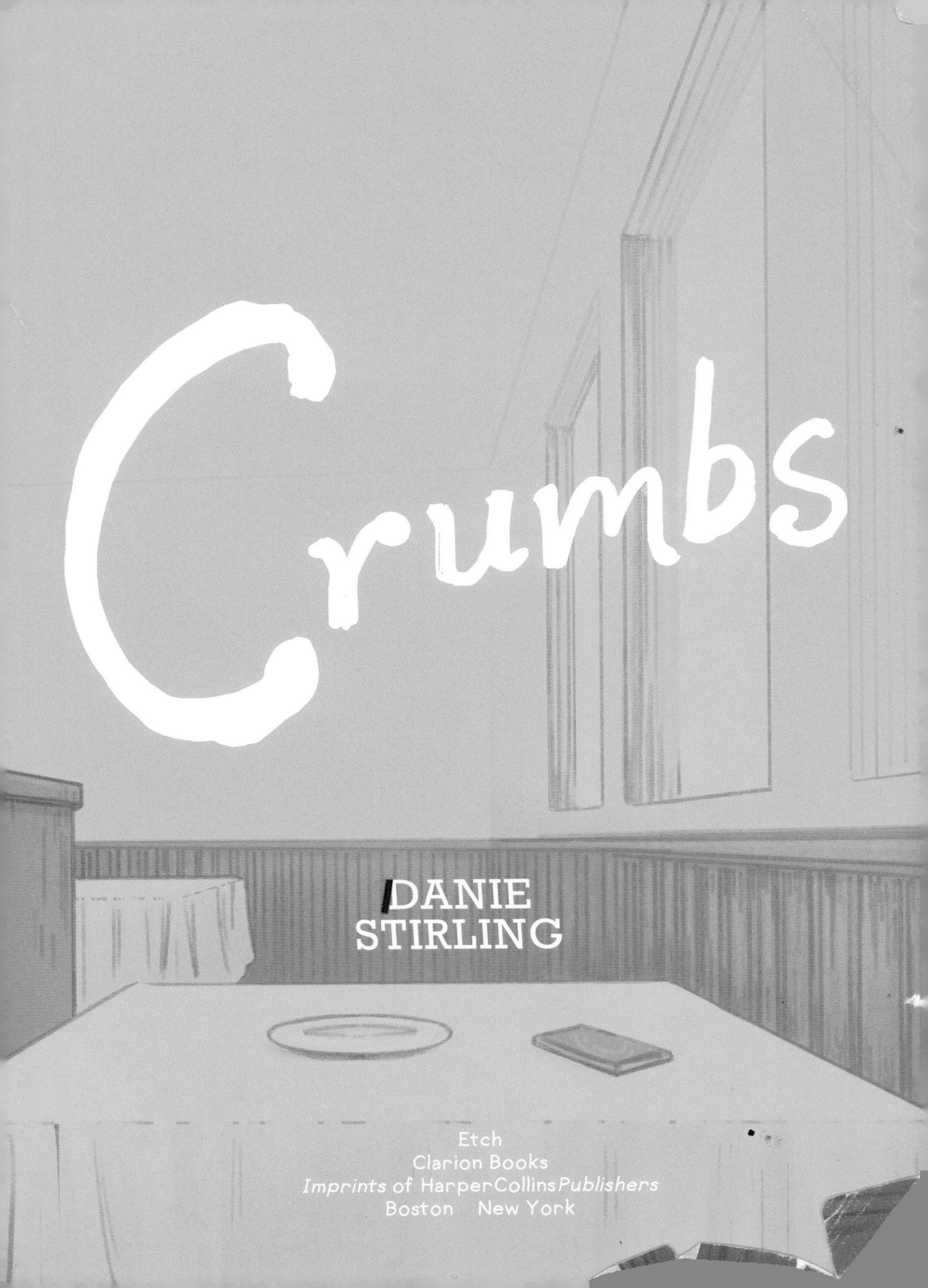

Crumbs

DANIE
STIRLING

Etch
Clarion Books
Imprints of HarperCollins*Publishers*
Boston New York

Etch and Clarion Books are imprints of HarperCollins Publishers.

clarionbooks.com

Library of Congress Cataloging-in-Publication Data has been applied for.

ISBN: 978-0-358-46779-3 hardcover
ISBN: 978-0-358-46781-6 paperback

The text was set in Gumball.

Manufactured in Spain
EP 10 9 8 7 6 5 4 3 2 1
4500844300

First Edition

A digital version of *Crumbs* was originally published on WEBTOON in 2020.

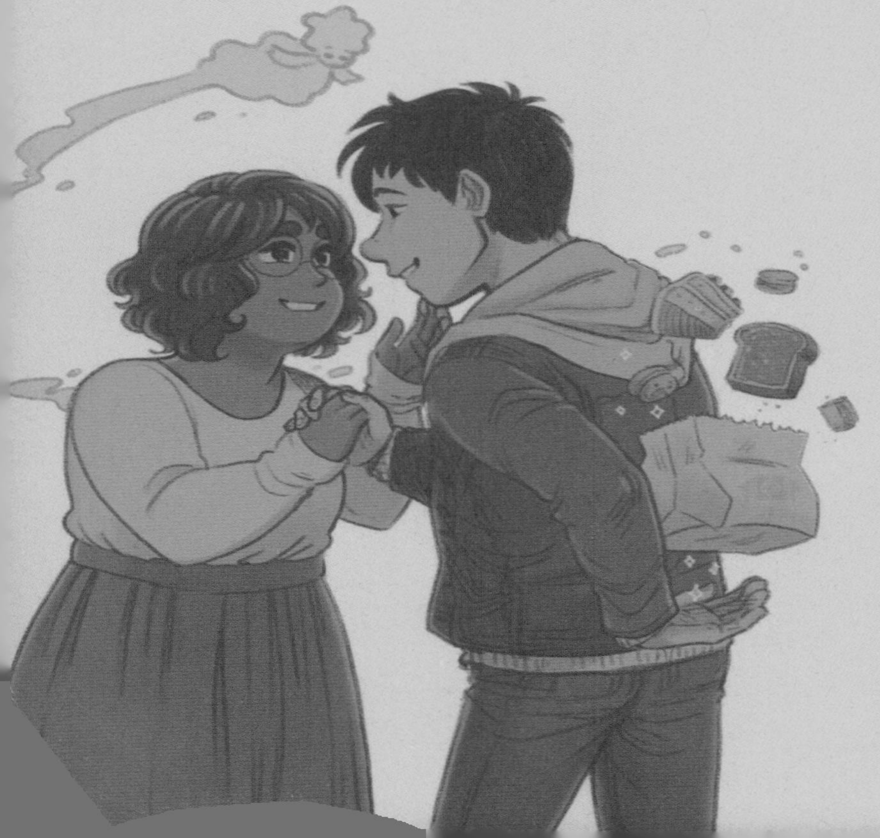

CHAPTER 1

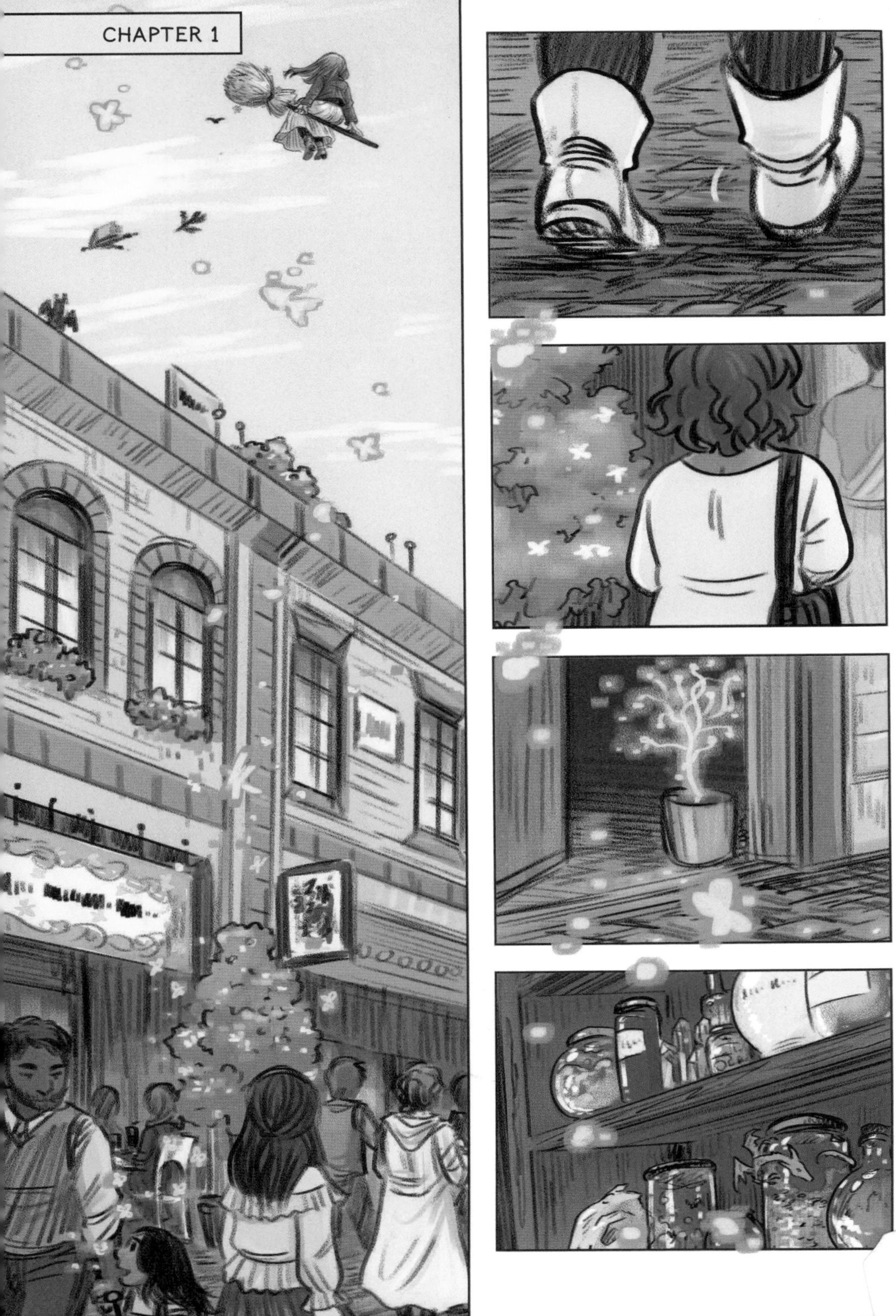

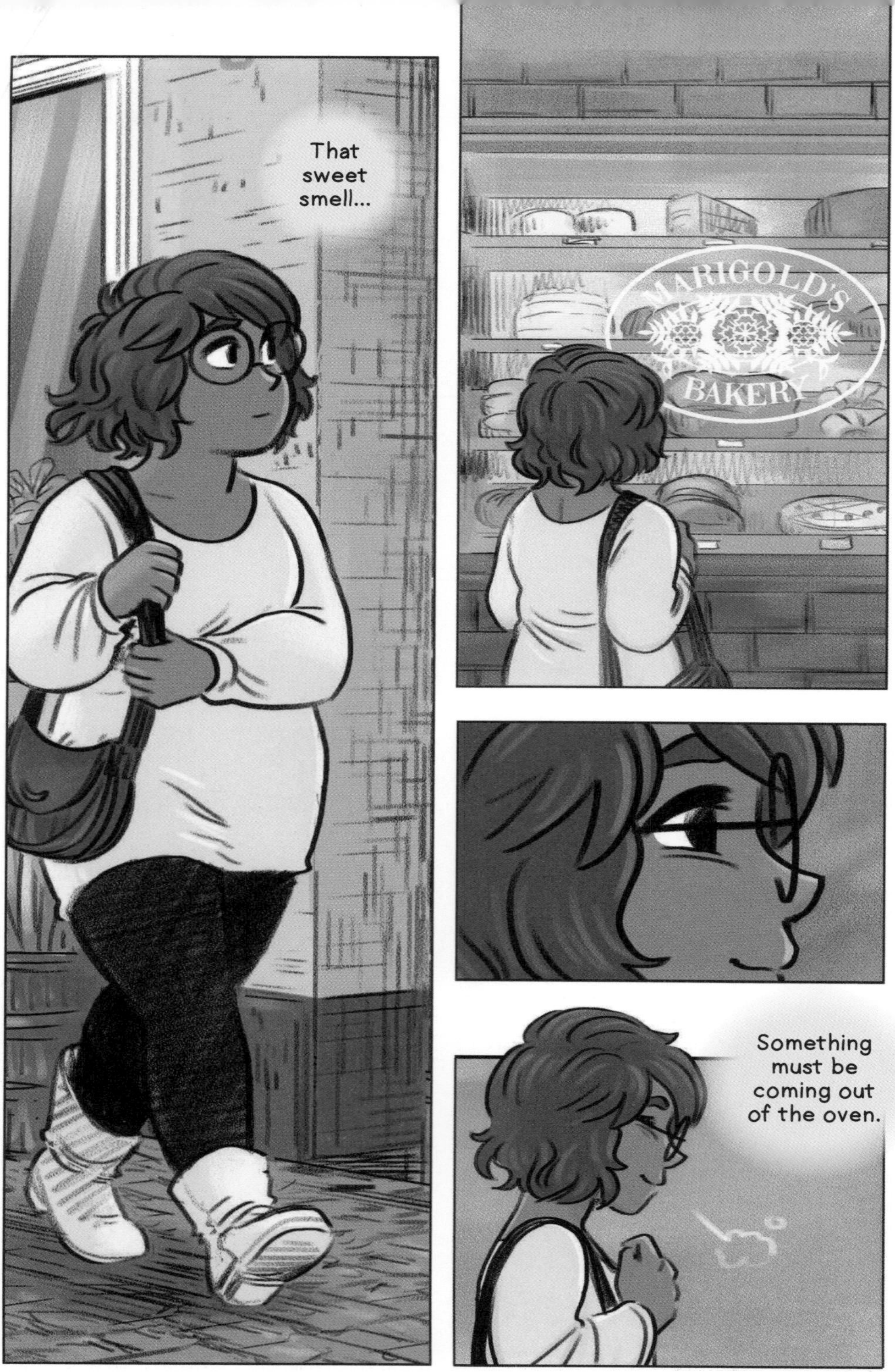
That sweet smell...
MARIGOLD'S BAKERY
Something must be coming out of the oven.

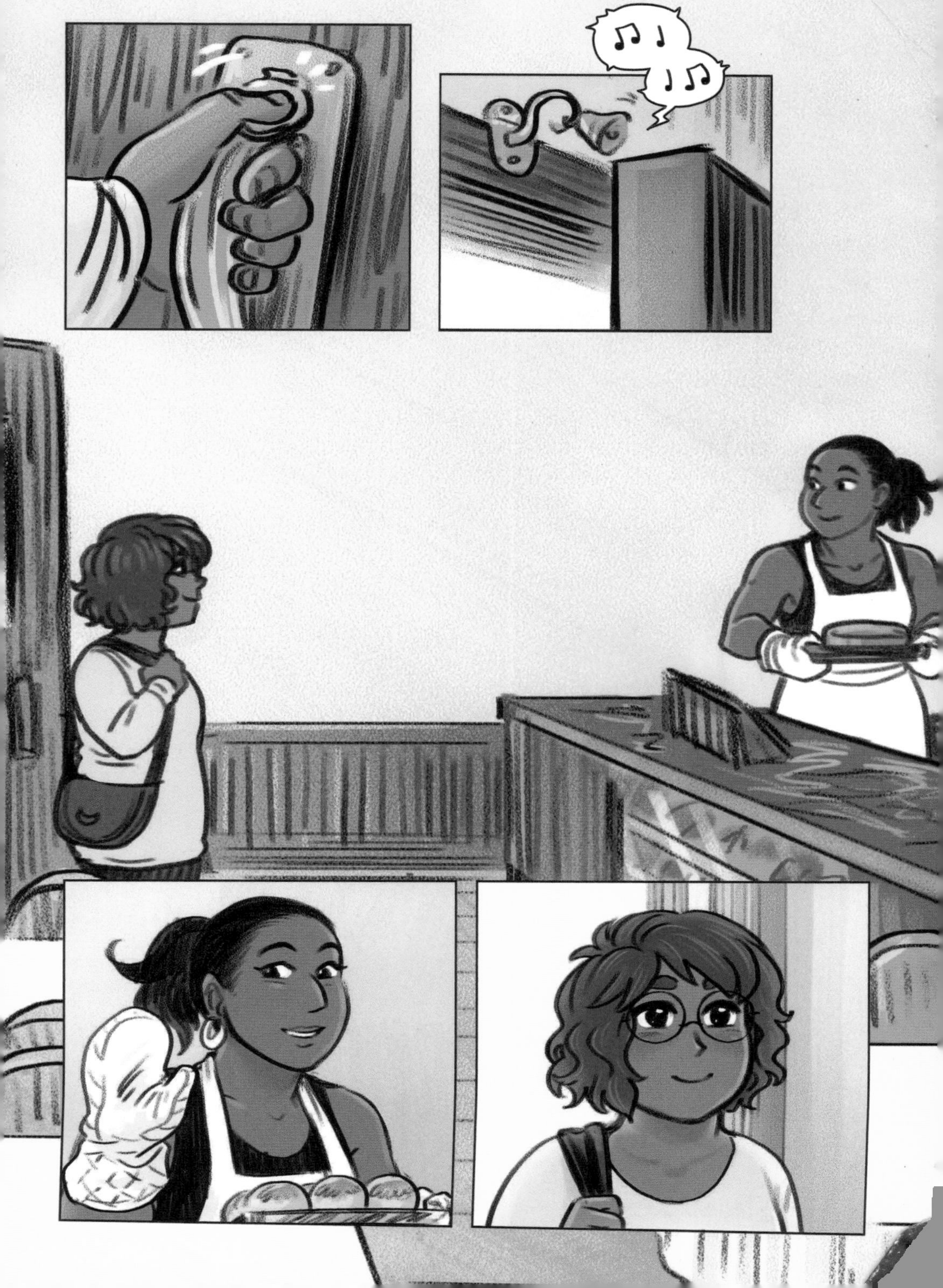

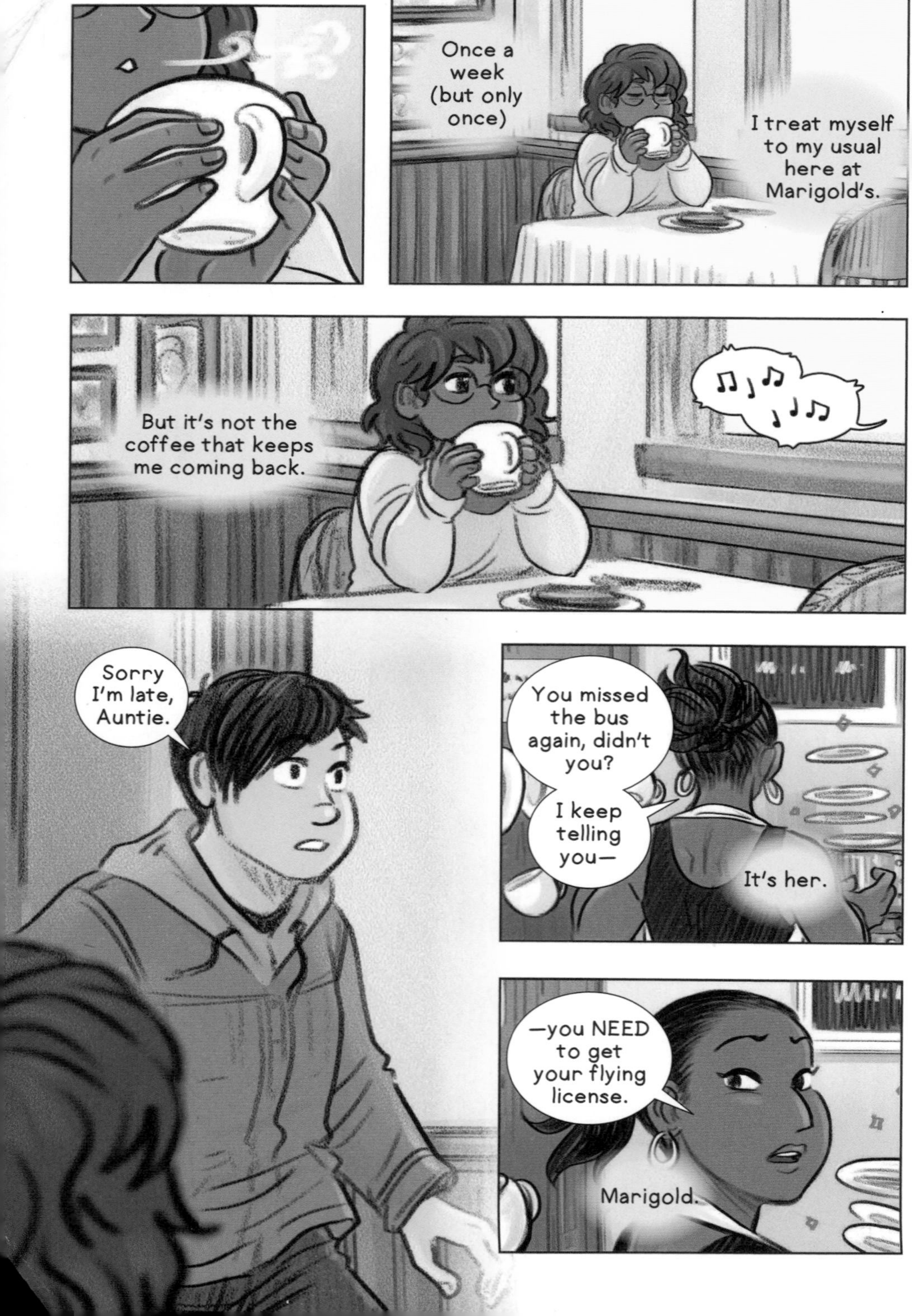
Once a week (but only once)
I treat myself to my usual here at Marigold's.
But it's not the coffee that keeps me coming back.
Sorry I'm late, Auntie.
You missed the bus again, didn't you?
I keep telling you—
It's her.
—you NEED to get your flying license.
Marigold.

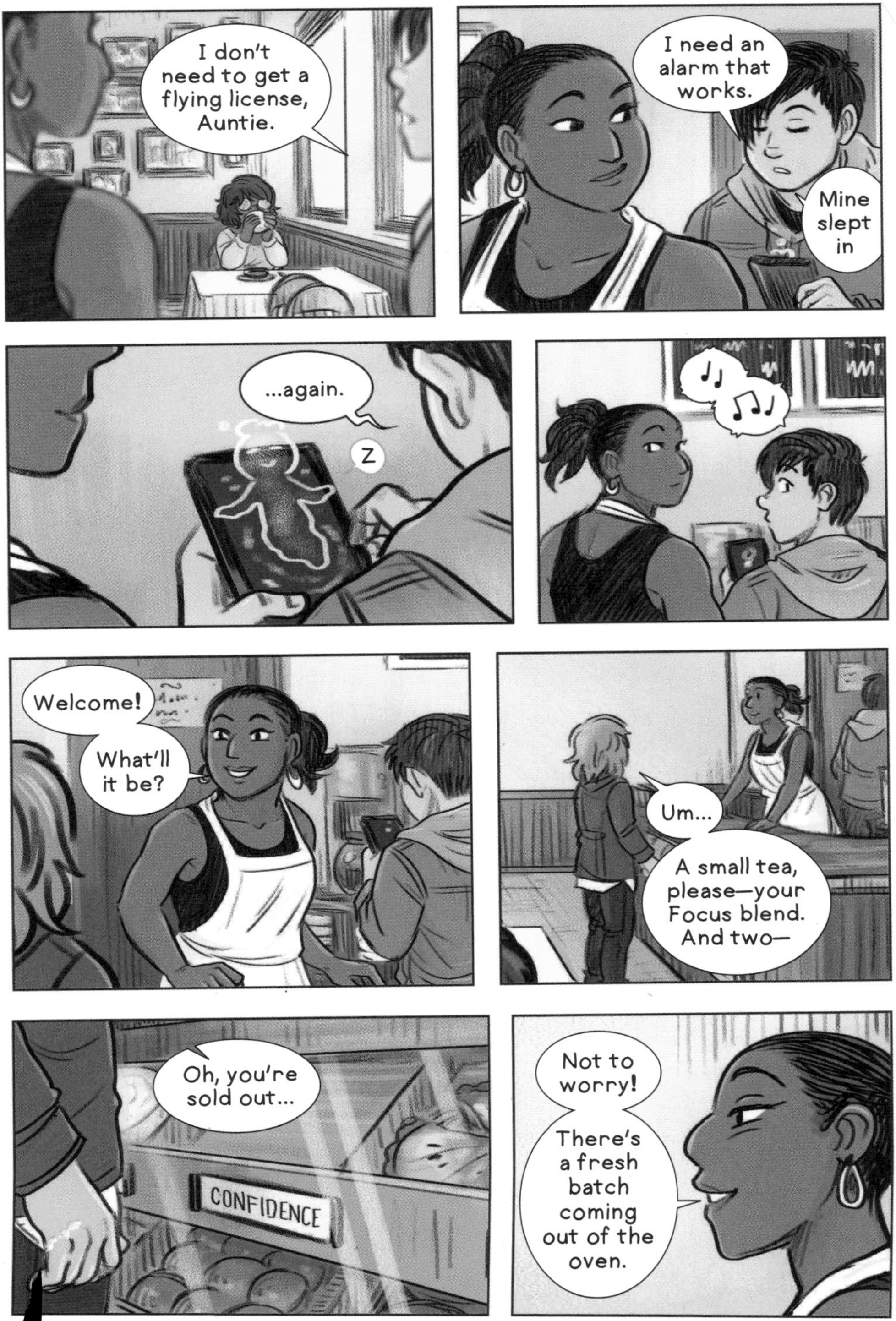
I don't need to get a flying license, Auntie.
I need an alarm that works.
Mine slept in
...again.
Z
Welcome!
What'll it be?
Um...
A small tea, please—your Focus blend. And two—
Oh, you're sold out...
CONFIDENCE
Not to worry!
There's a fresh batch coming out of the oven.

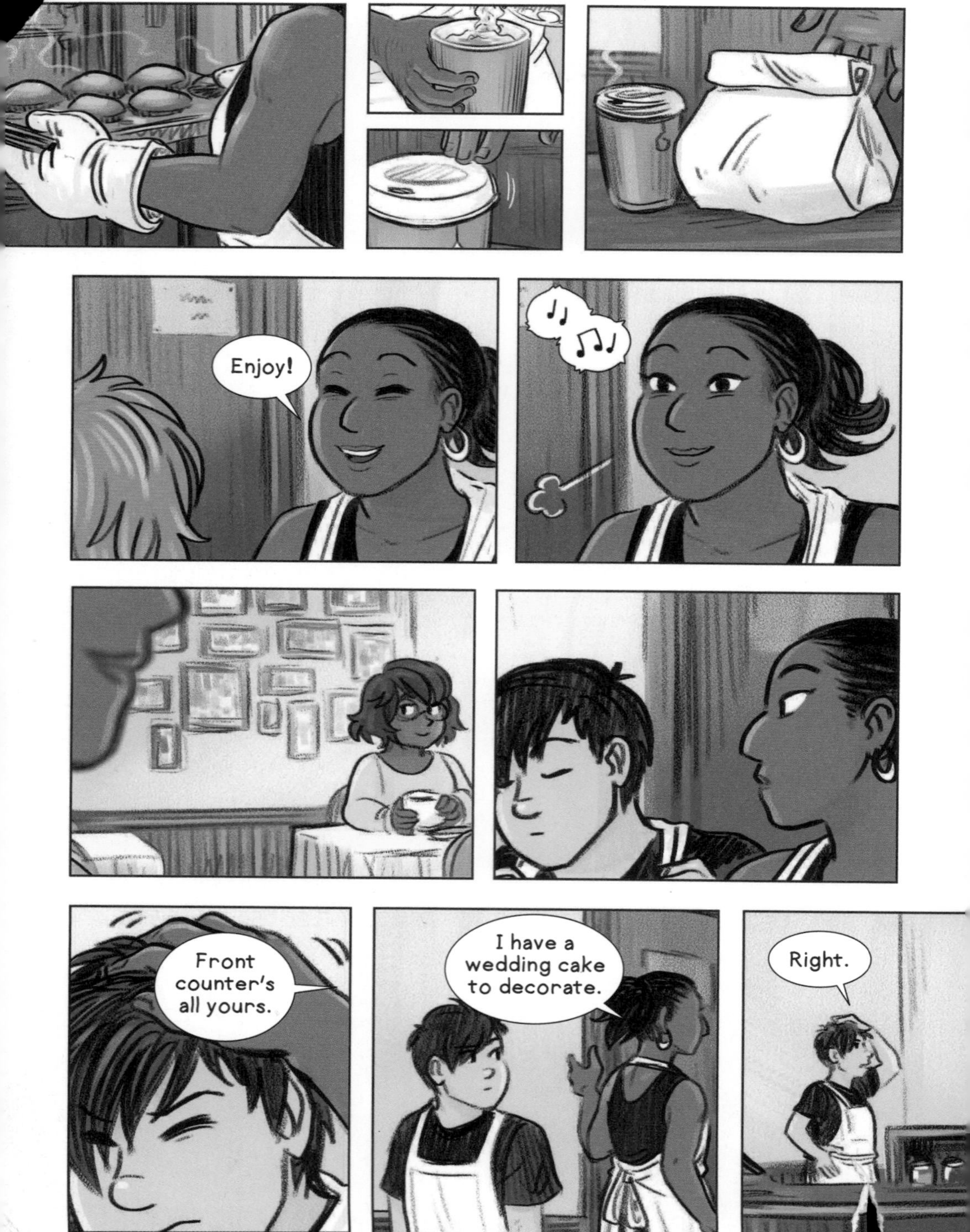
Enjoy!
Front counter's all yours.
I have a wedding cake to decorate.
Right.

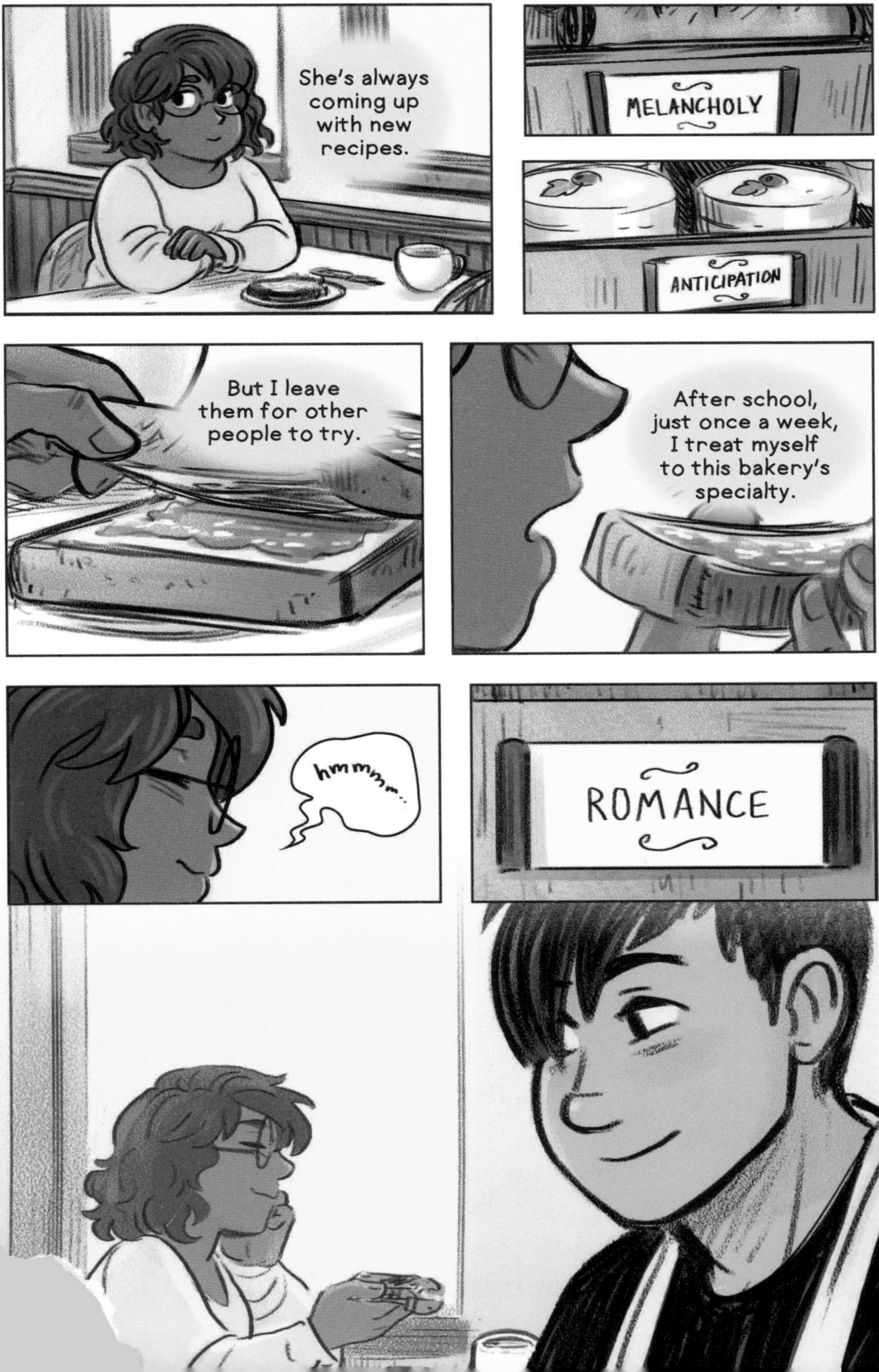

She's always coming up with new recipes.
MELANCHOLY
ANTICIPATION
But I leave them for other people to try.
After school, just once a week, I treat myself to this bakery's specialty.
hmmmm..
ROMANCE

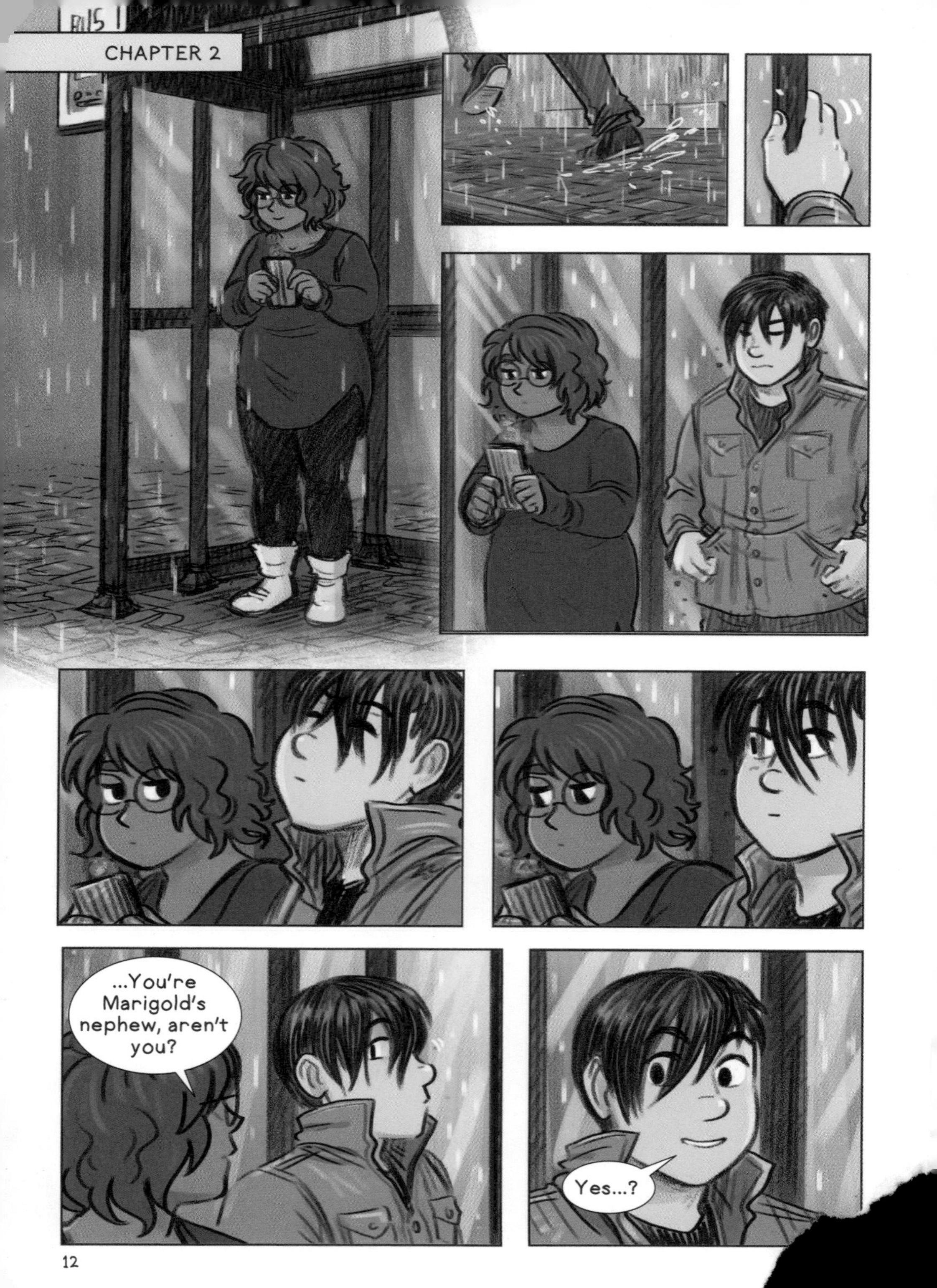
CHAPTER 2
...You're Marigold's nephew, aren't you?
Yes...?

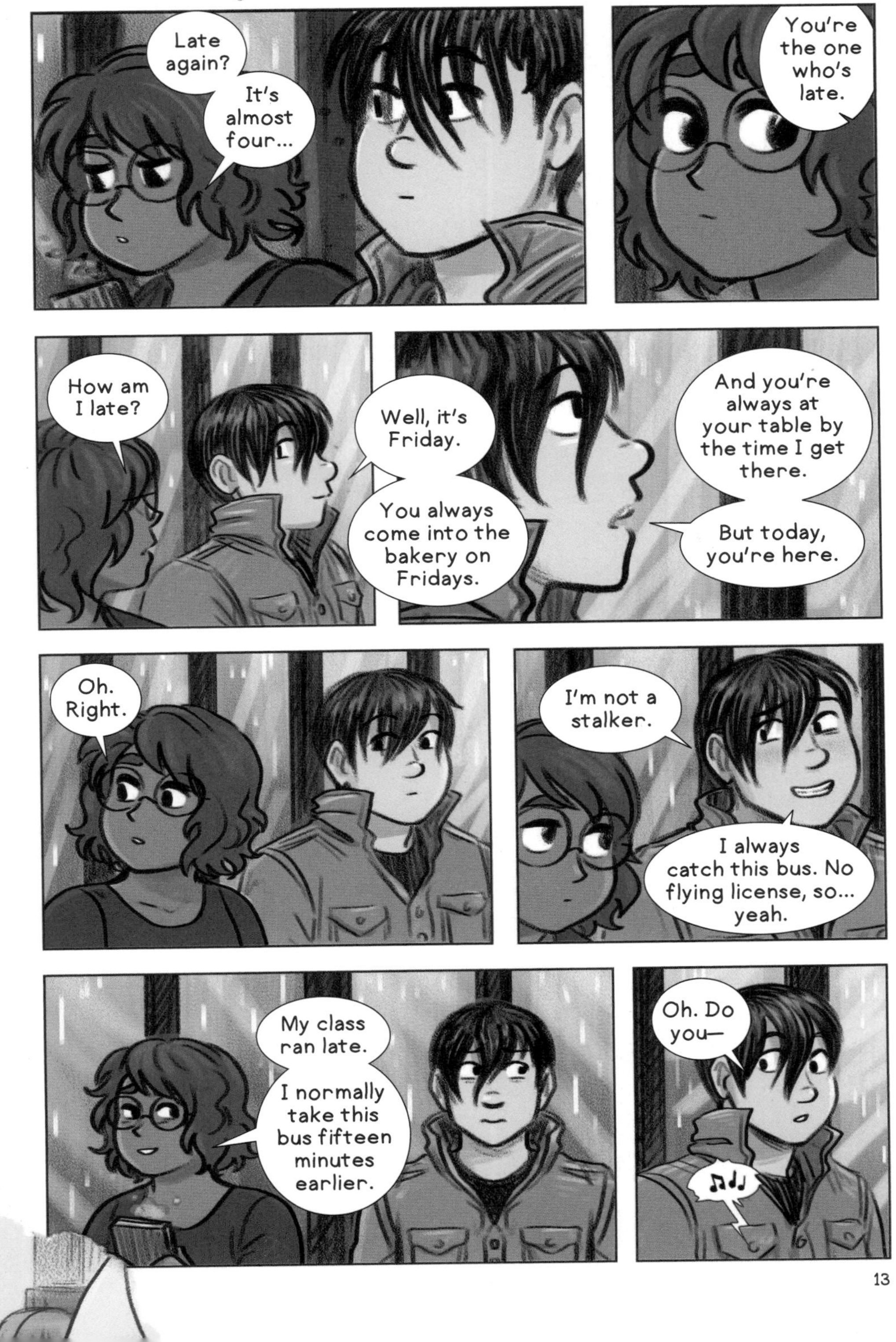
Late again?
It's almost four...
You're the one who's late.
How am I late?
Well, it's Friday.
You always come into the bakery on Fridays.
And you're always at your table by the time I get there.
But today, you're here.
Oh. Right.
I'm not a stalker.
I always catch this bus. No flying license, so... yeah.
My class ran late.
I normally take this bus fifteen minutes earlier.
Oh. Do you—

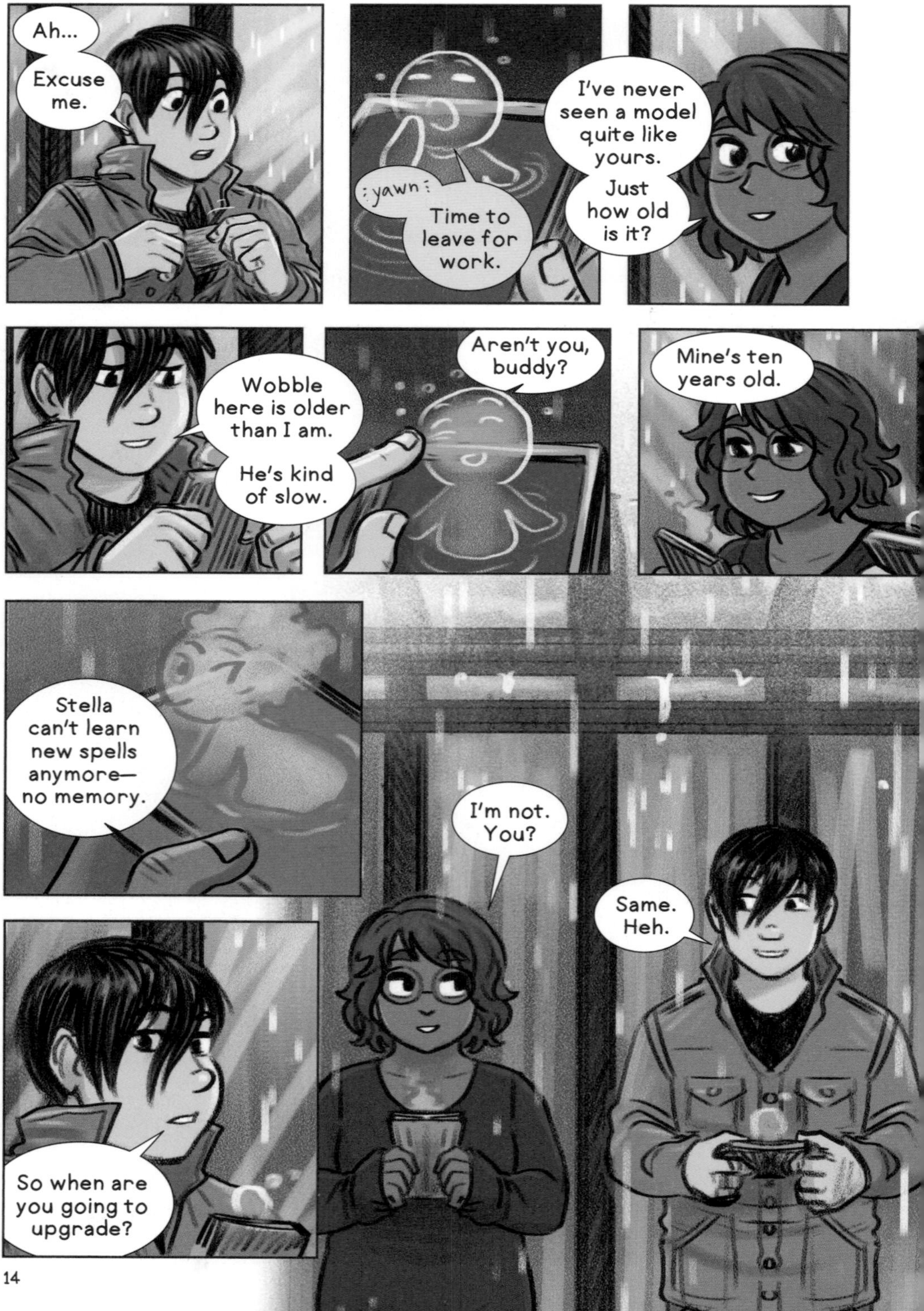
Ah...
Excuse me.
:yawn:
Time to leave for work.
I've never seen a model quite like yours.
Just how old is it?
Wobble here is older than I am.
He's kind of slow.
Aren't you, buddy?
Mine's ten years old.
Stella can't learn new spells anymore— no memory.
So when are you going to upgrade?
I'm not. You?
Same. Heh.

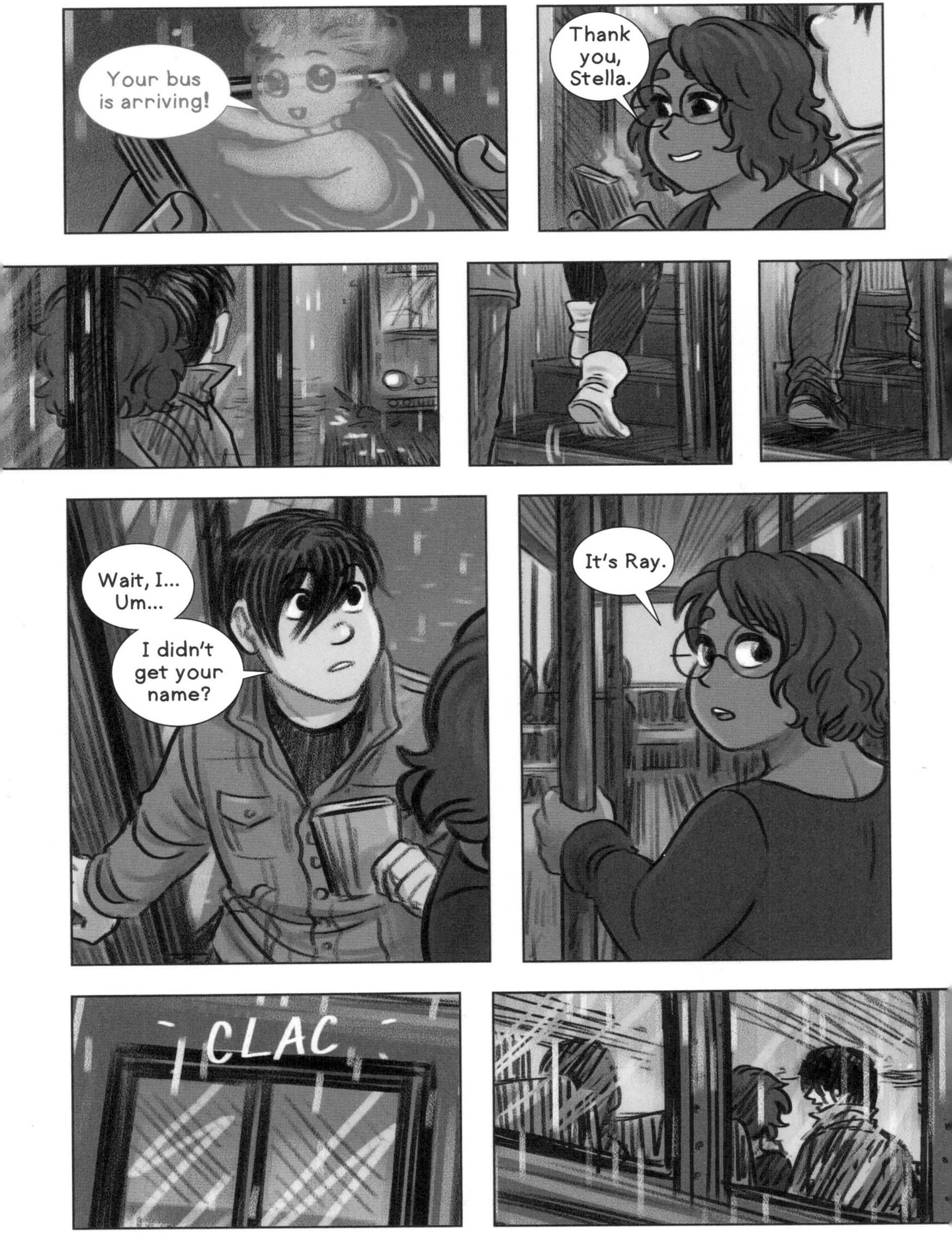
Your bus is arriving!
Thank you, Stella.
Wait, I... Um...
I didn't get your name?
It's Ray.
CLAC

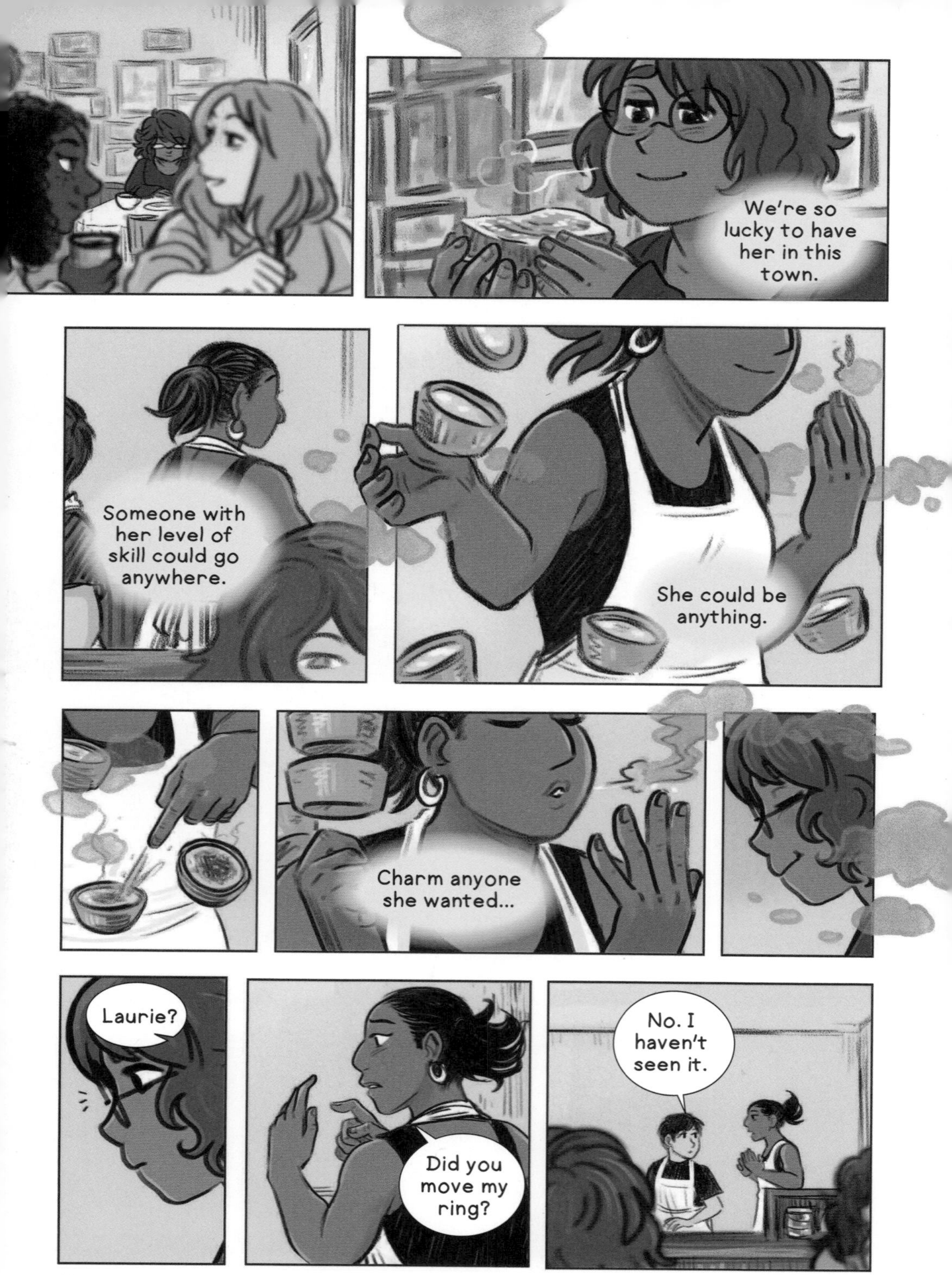
We're so lucky to have her in this town.
Someone with her level of skill could go anywhere.
She could be anything.
Charm anyone she wanted...
Laurie?
Did you move my ring?
No. I haven't seen it.

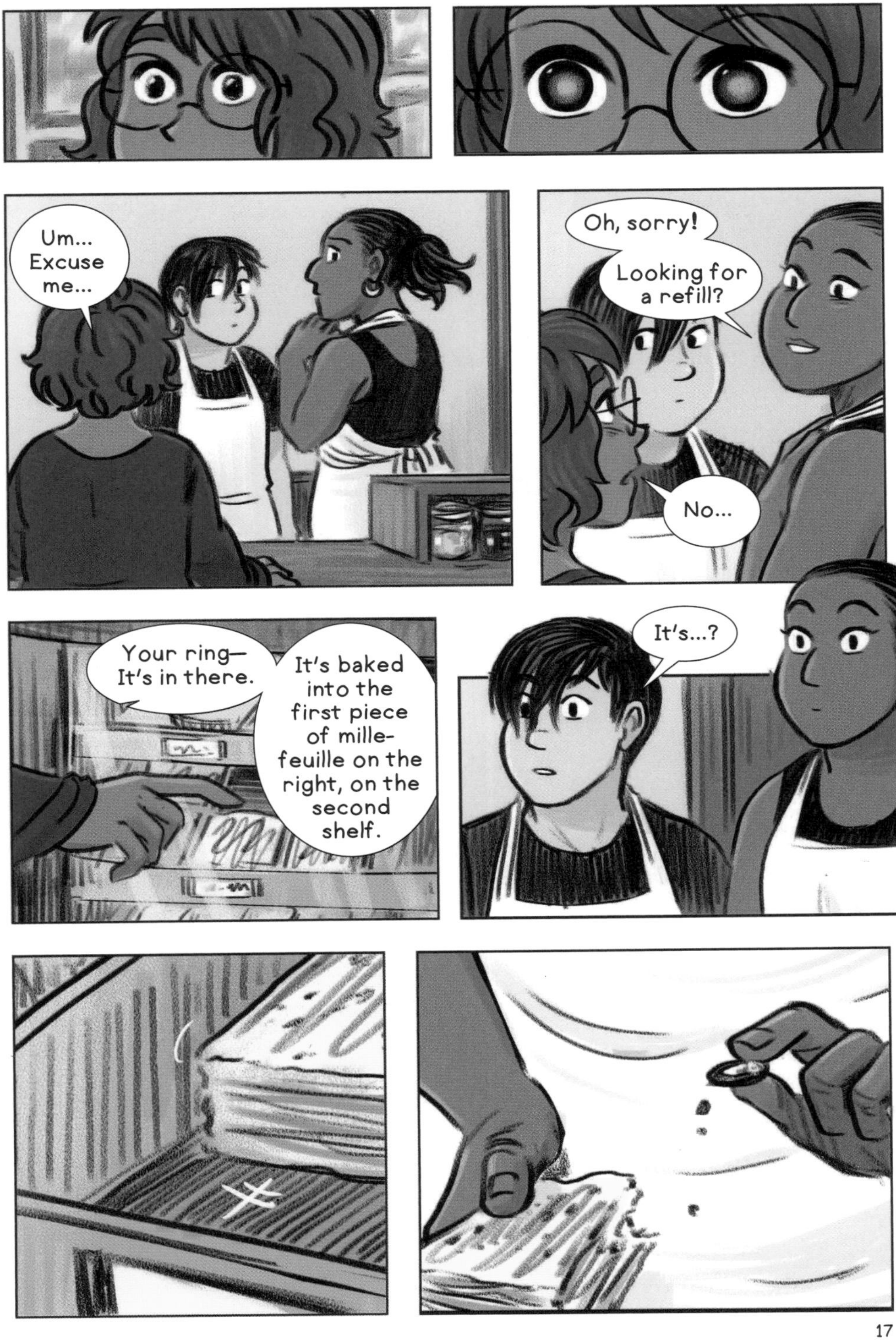
Um... Excuse me...
Oh, sorry!
Looking for a refill?
No...
Your ring— It's in there.
It's baked into the first piece of mille-feuille on the right, on the second shelf.
It's...?

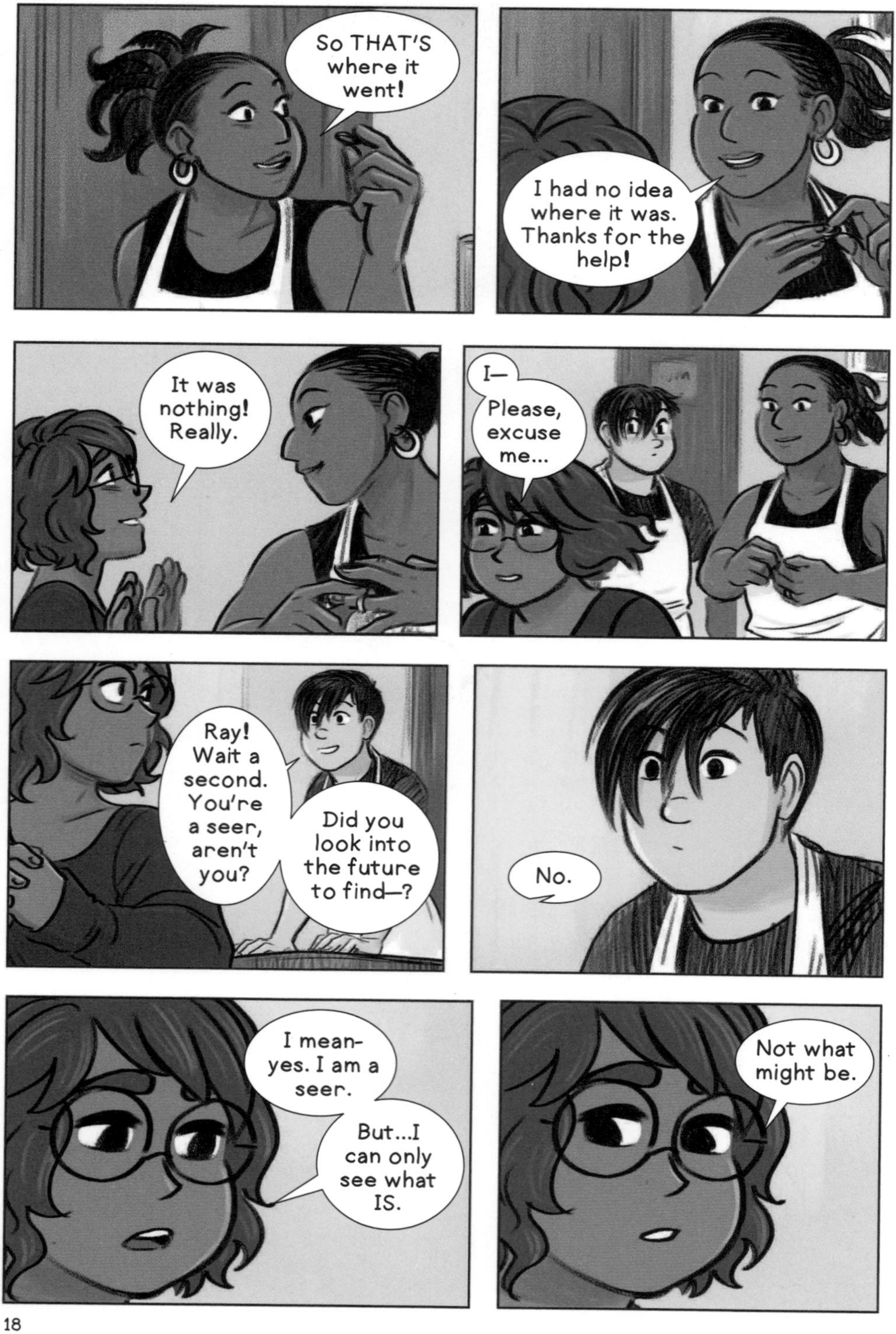

So THAT'S where it went!
I had no idea where it was. Thanks for the help!
It was nothing! Really.
I—
Please, excuse me...
Ray! Wait a second. You're a seer, aren't you?
Did you look into the future to find—?
No.
I mean- yes. I am a seer.
But...I can only see what IS.
Not what might be.

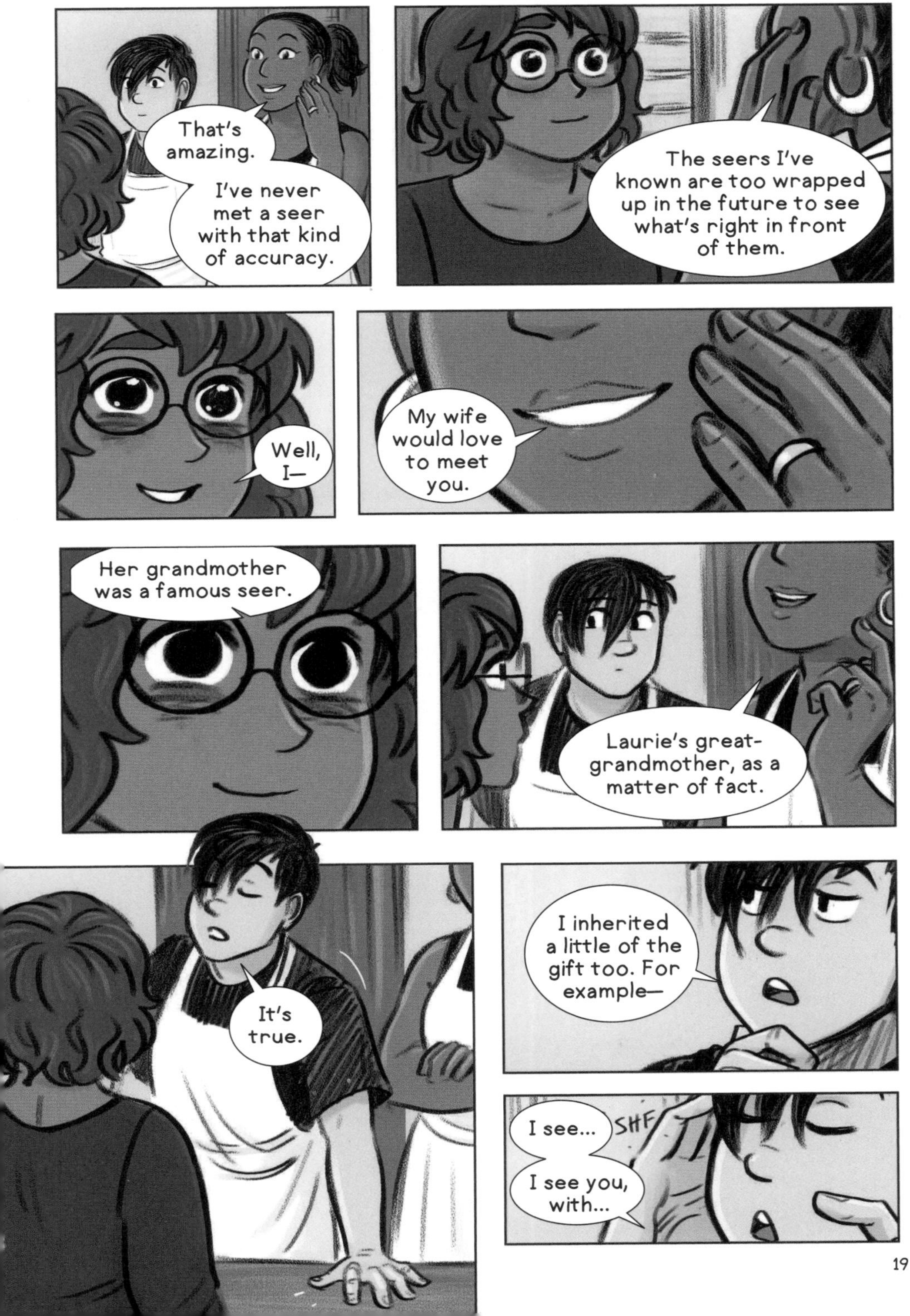
That's amazing.
I've never met a seer with that kind of accuracy.
The seers I've known are too wrapped up in the future to see what's right in front of them.
Well, I—
My wife would love to meet you.
Her grandmother was a famous seer.
Laurie's great-grandmother, as a matter of fact.
It's true.
I inherited a little of the gift too. For example—
I see...
SHF
I see you, with...

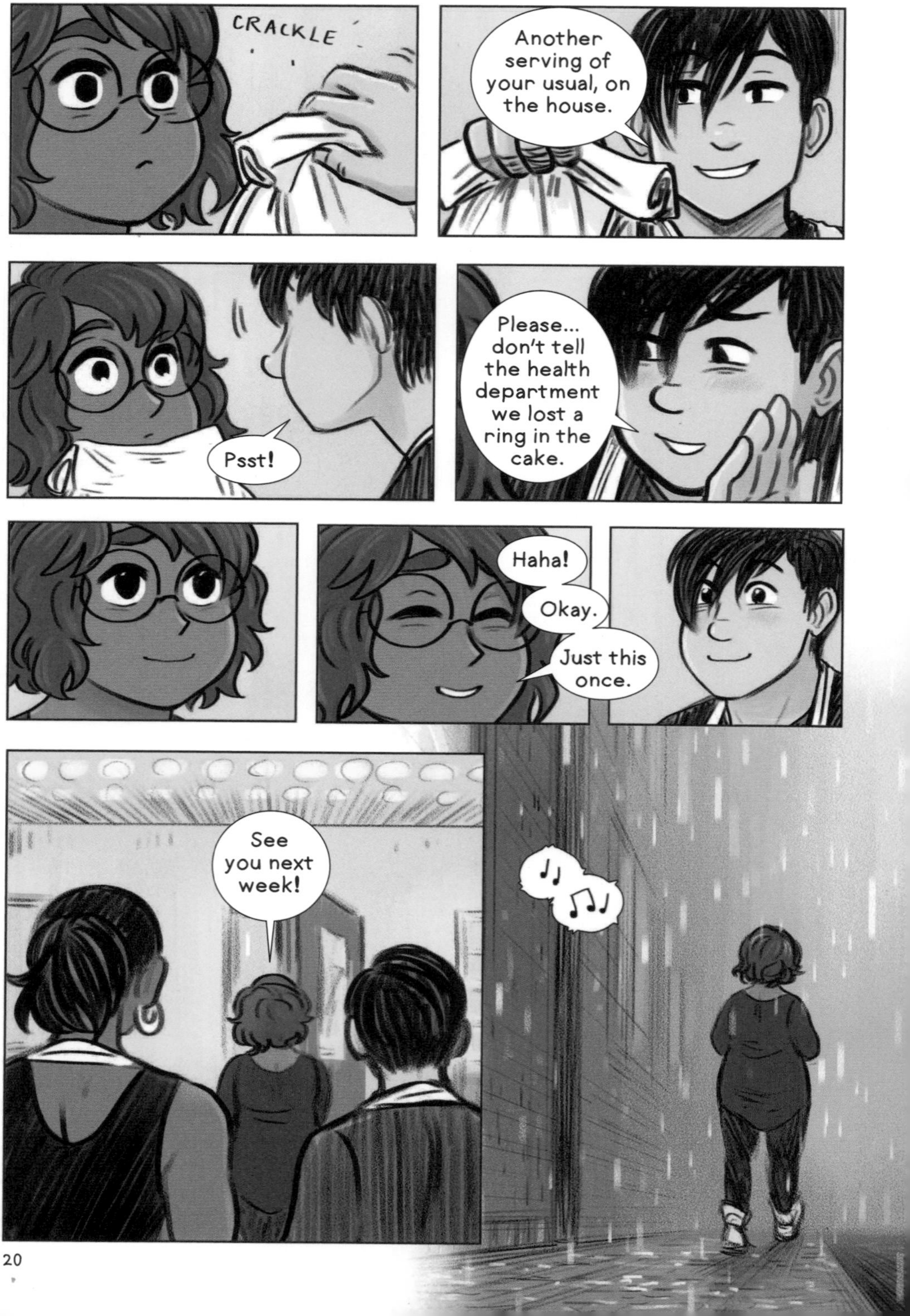

CRACKLE
Another serving of your usual, on the house.
Psst!
Please... don't tell the health department we lost a ring in the cake.
Haha!
Okay.
Just this once.
See you next week!

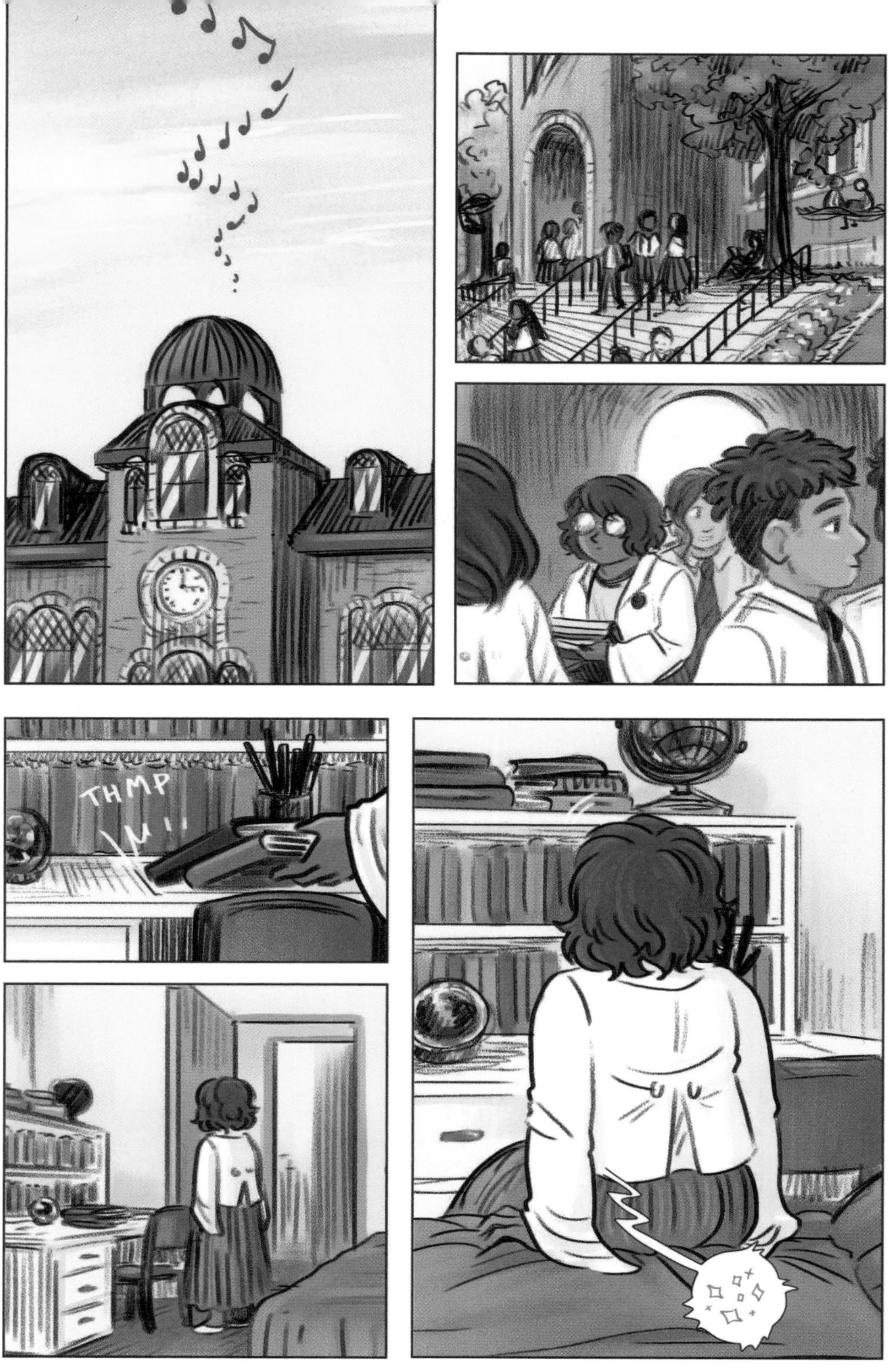
THMP

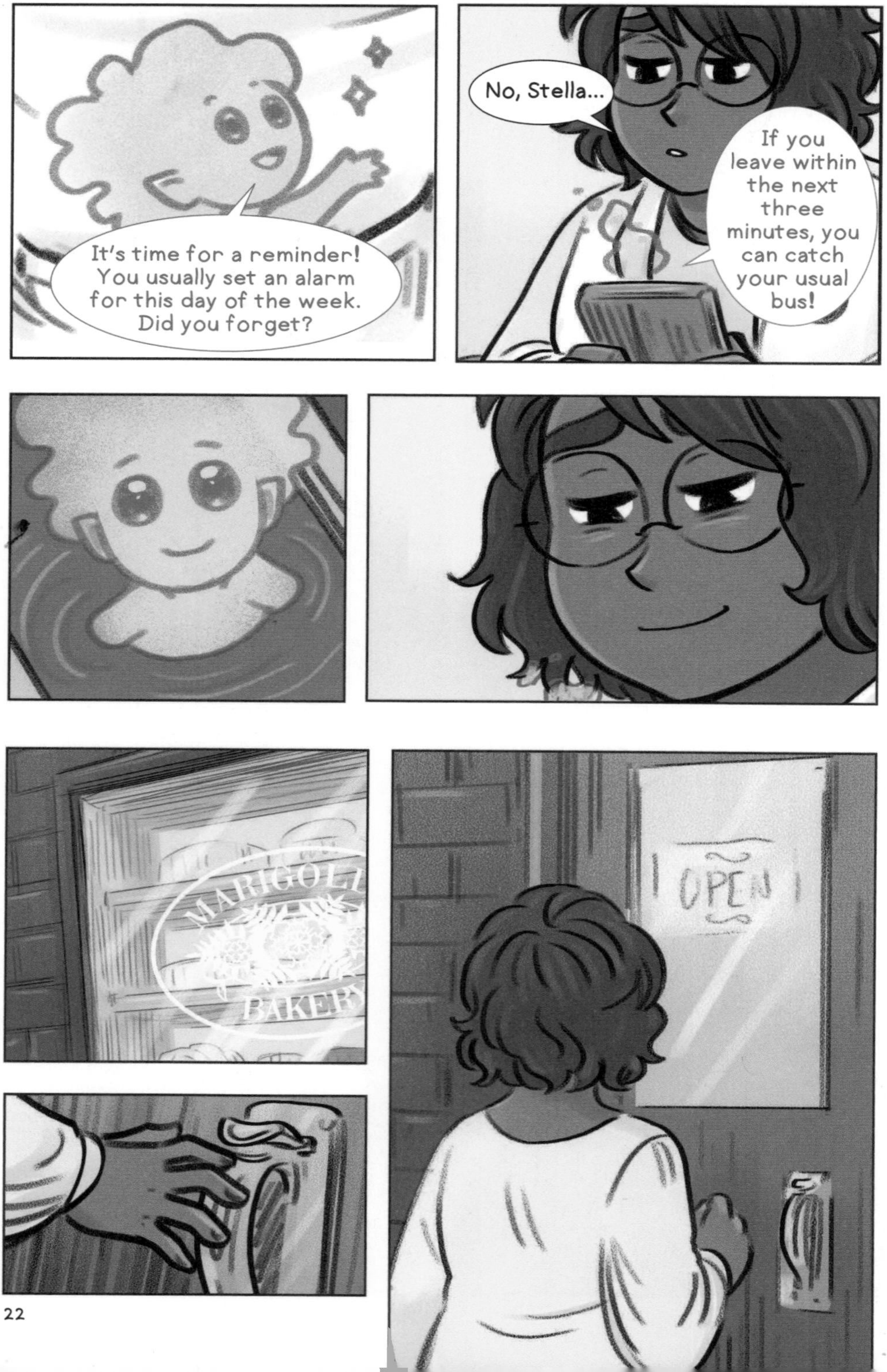
It's time for a reminder! You usually set an alarm for this day of the week. Did you forget?
No, Stella...
If you leave within the next three minutes, you can catch your usual bus!
MARIGOLD BAKERY
OPEN

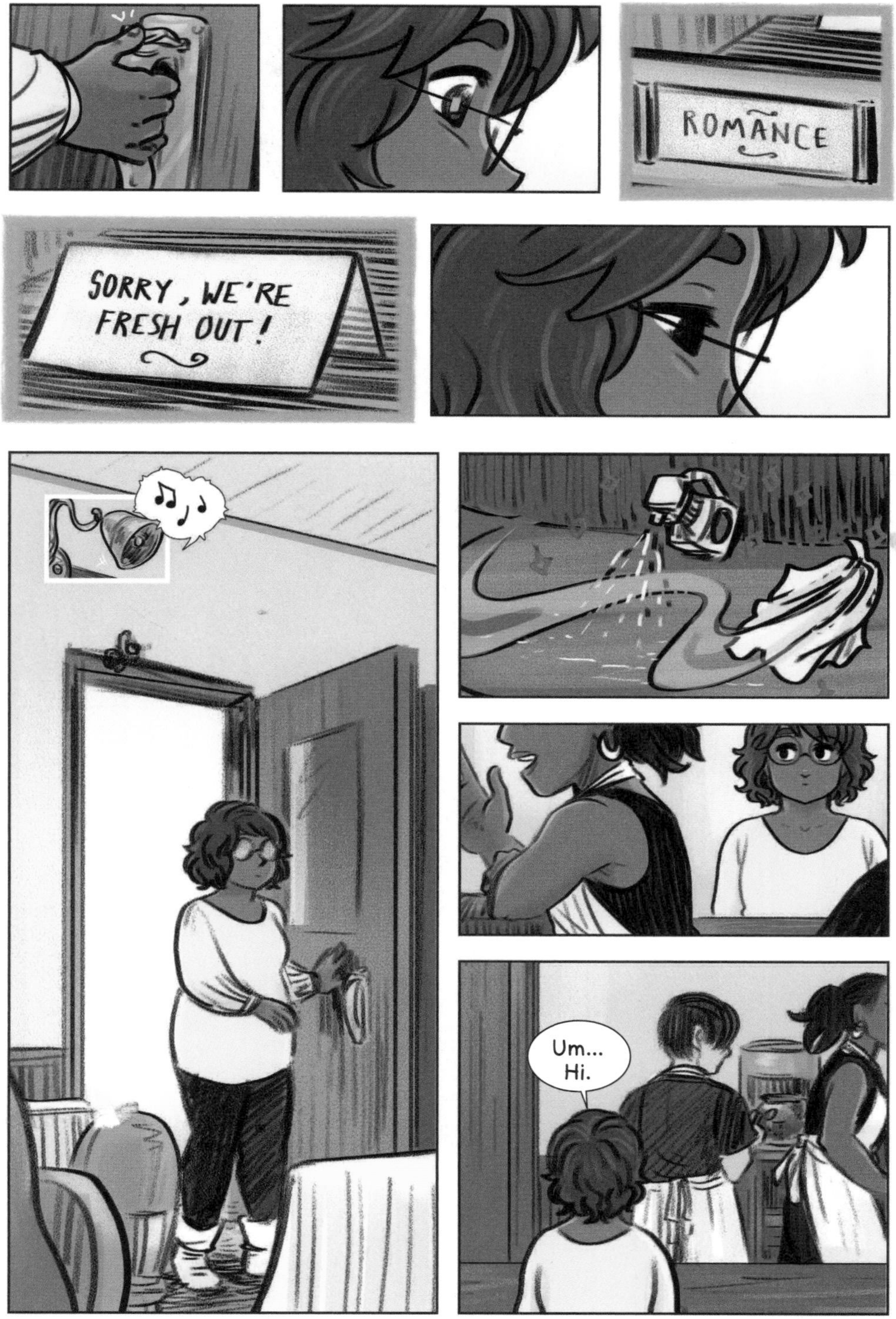
ROMANCE
SORRY, WE'RE FRESH OUT!
Um... Hi.

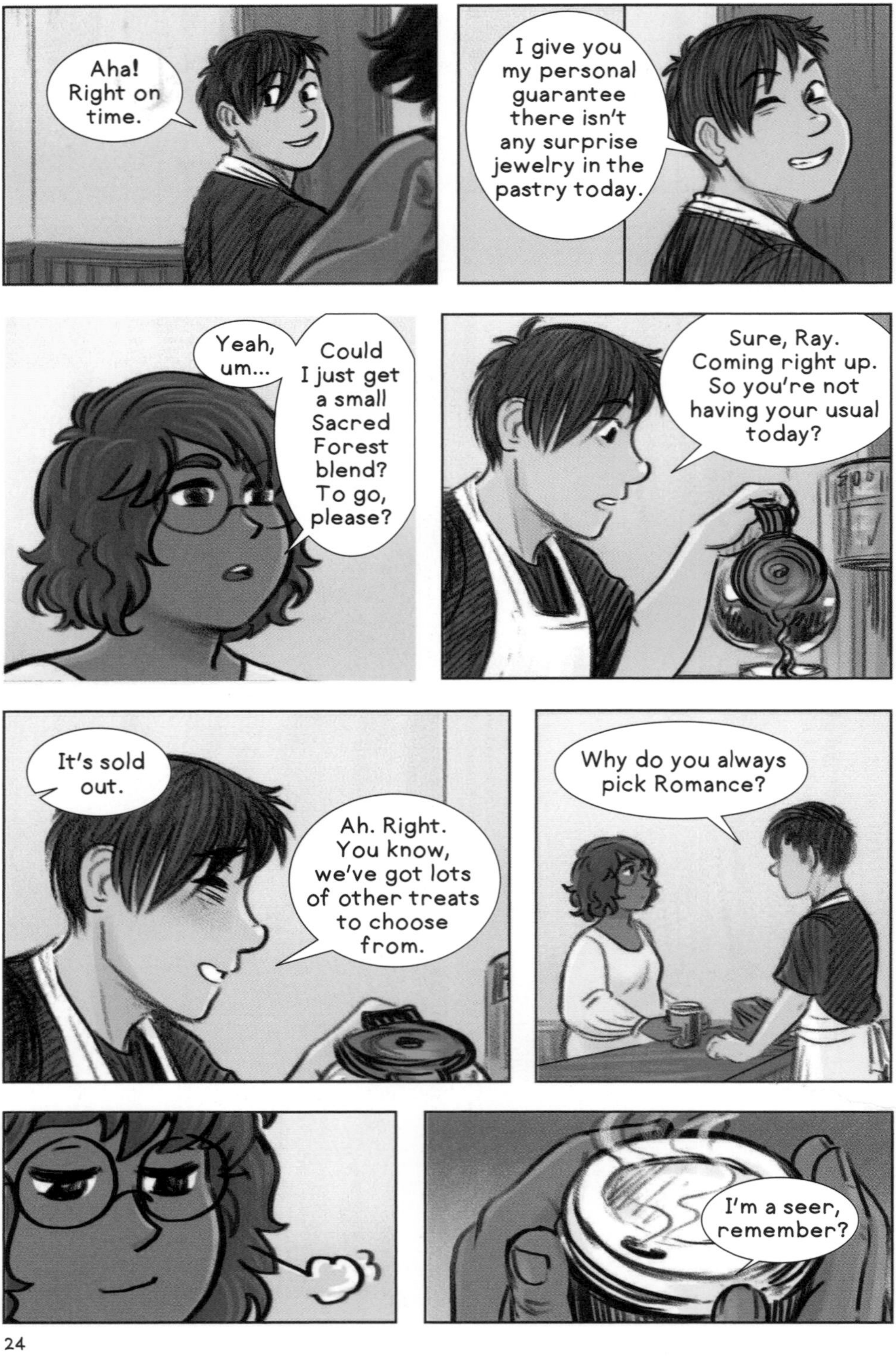
Aha! Right on time.
I give you my personal guarantee there isn't any surprise jewelry in the pastry today.
Yeah, um...
Could I just get a small Sacred Forest blend? To go, please?
Sure, Ray. Coming right up. So you're not having your usual today?
It's sold out.
Ah. Right. You know, we've got lots of other treats to choose from.
Why do you always pick Romance?
I'm a seer, remember?

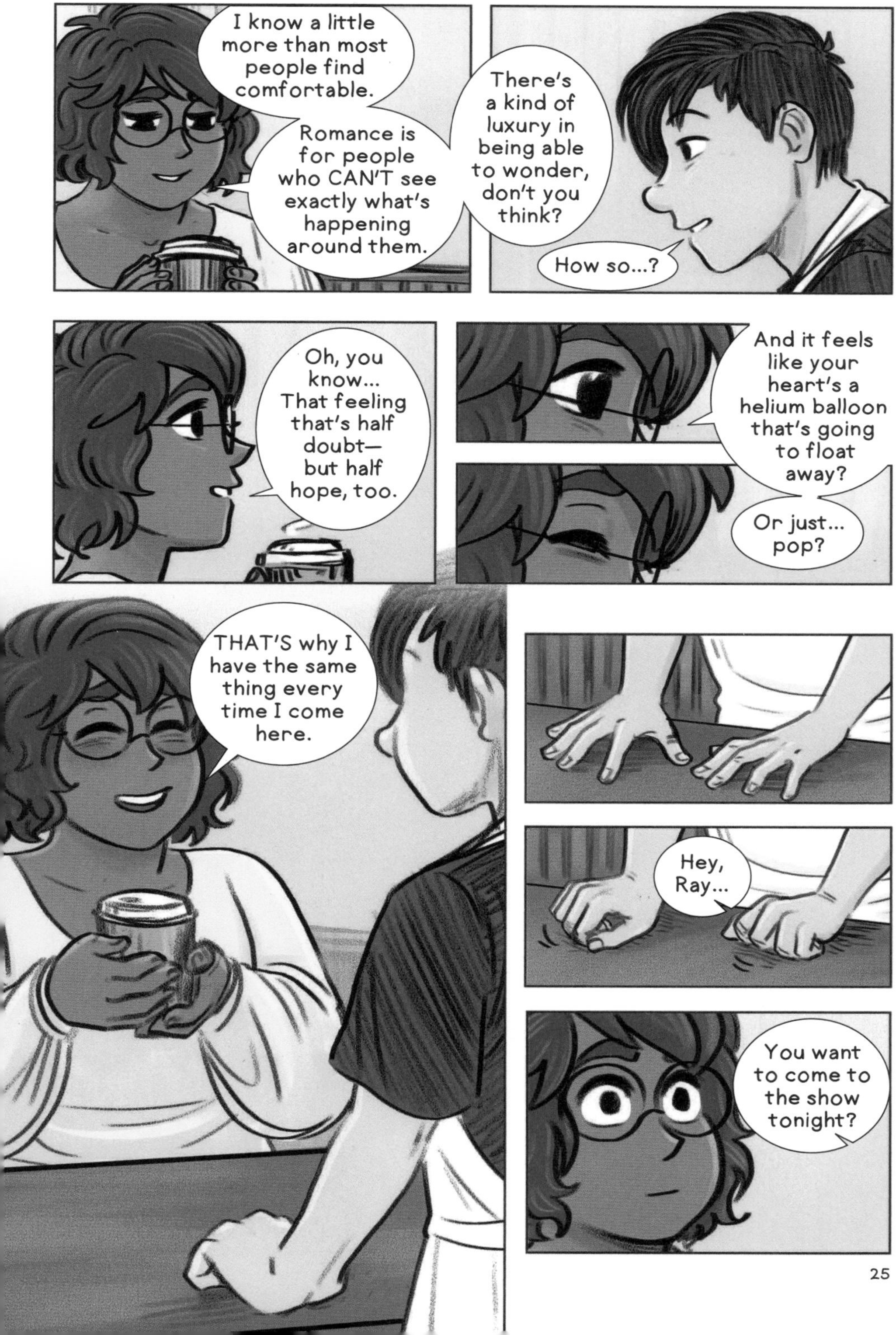
I know a little more than most people find comfortable.
Romance is for people who CAN'T see exactly what's happening around them.
There's a kind of luxury in being able to wonder, don't you think?
How so...?
Oh, you know... That feeling that's half doubt— but half hope, too.
And it feels like your heart's a helium balloon that's going to float away?
Or just... pop?
THAT'S why I have the same thing every time I come here.
Hey, Ray...
You want to come to the show tonight?

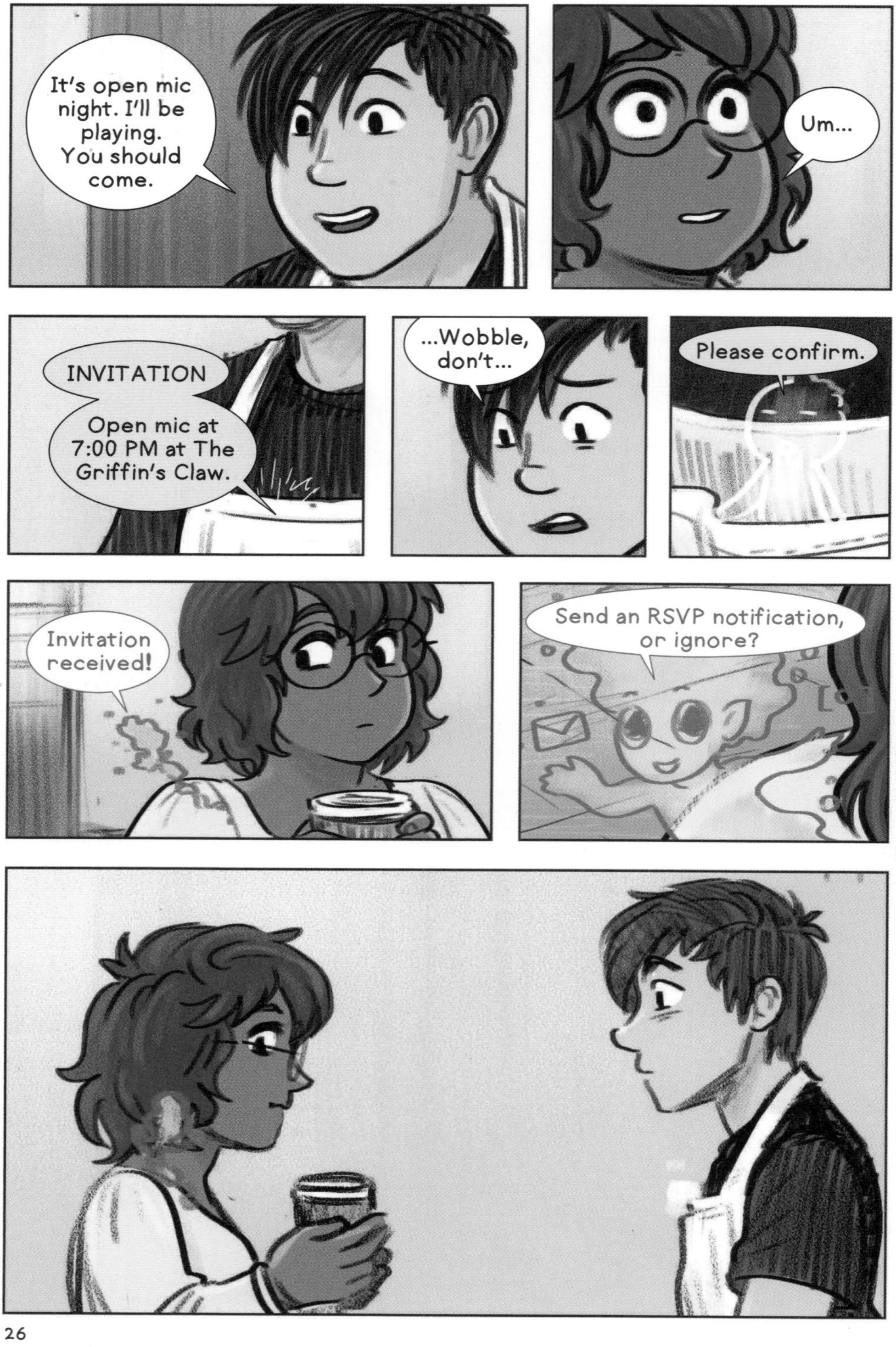
It's open mic night. I'll be playing. You should come.
Um...
INVITATION
Open mic at 7:00 PM at The Griffin's Claw.
...Wobble, don't...
Please confirm.
Invitation received!
Send an RSVP notification, or ignore?

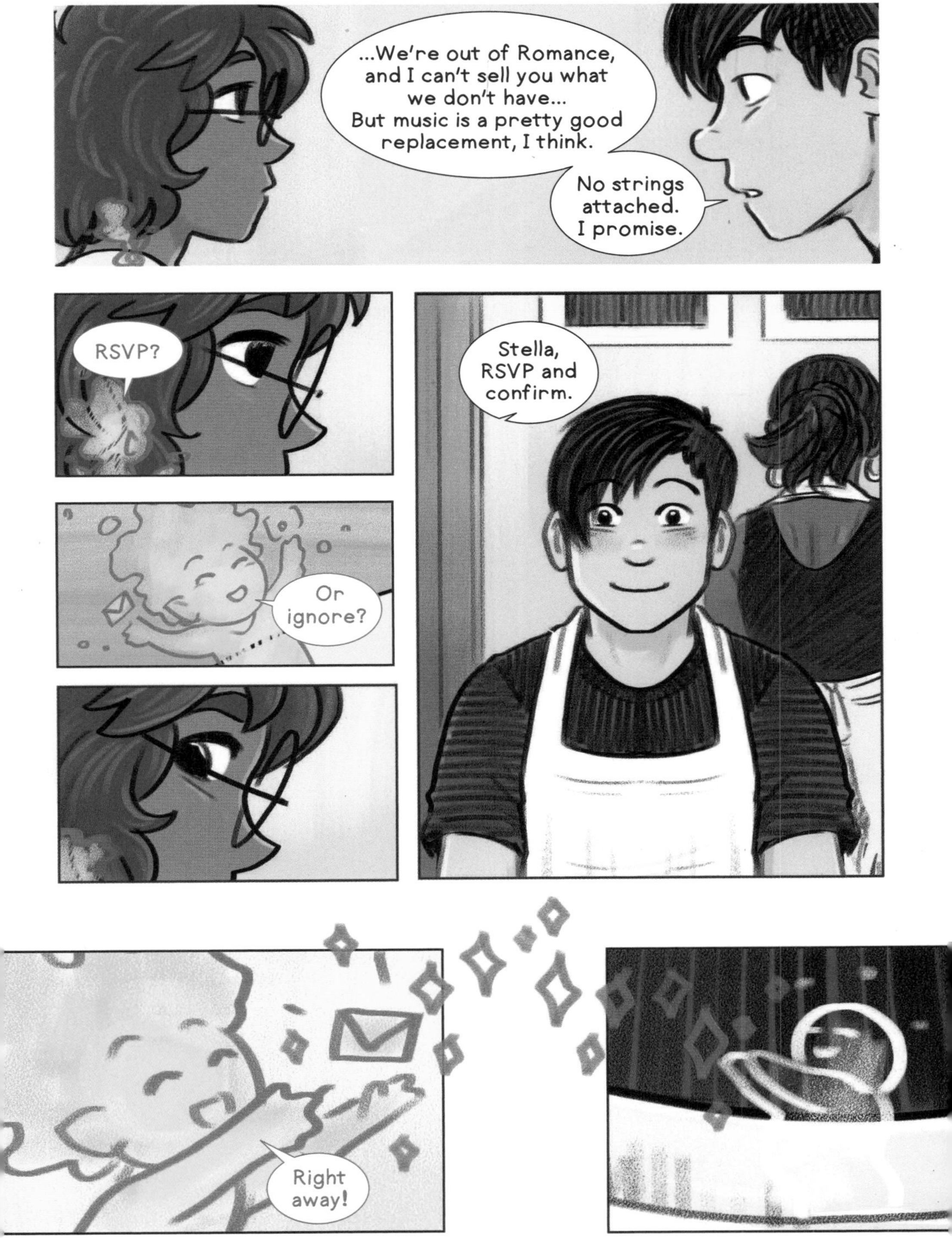
...We're out of Romance, and I can't sell you what we don't have... But music is a pretty good replacement, I think.
No strings attached. I promise.
RSVP?
Stella, RSVP and confirm.
Or ignore?
Right away!

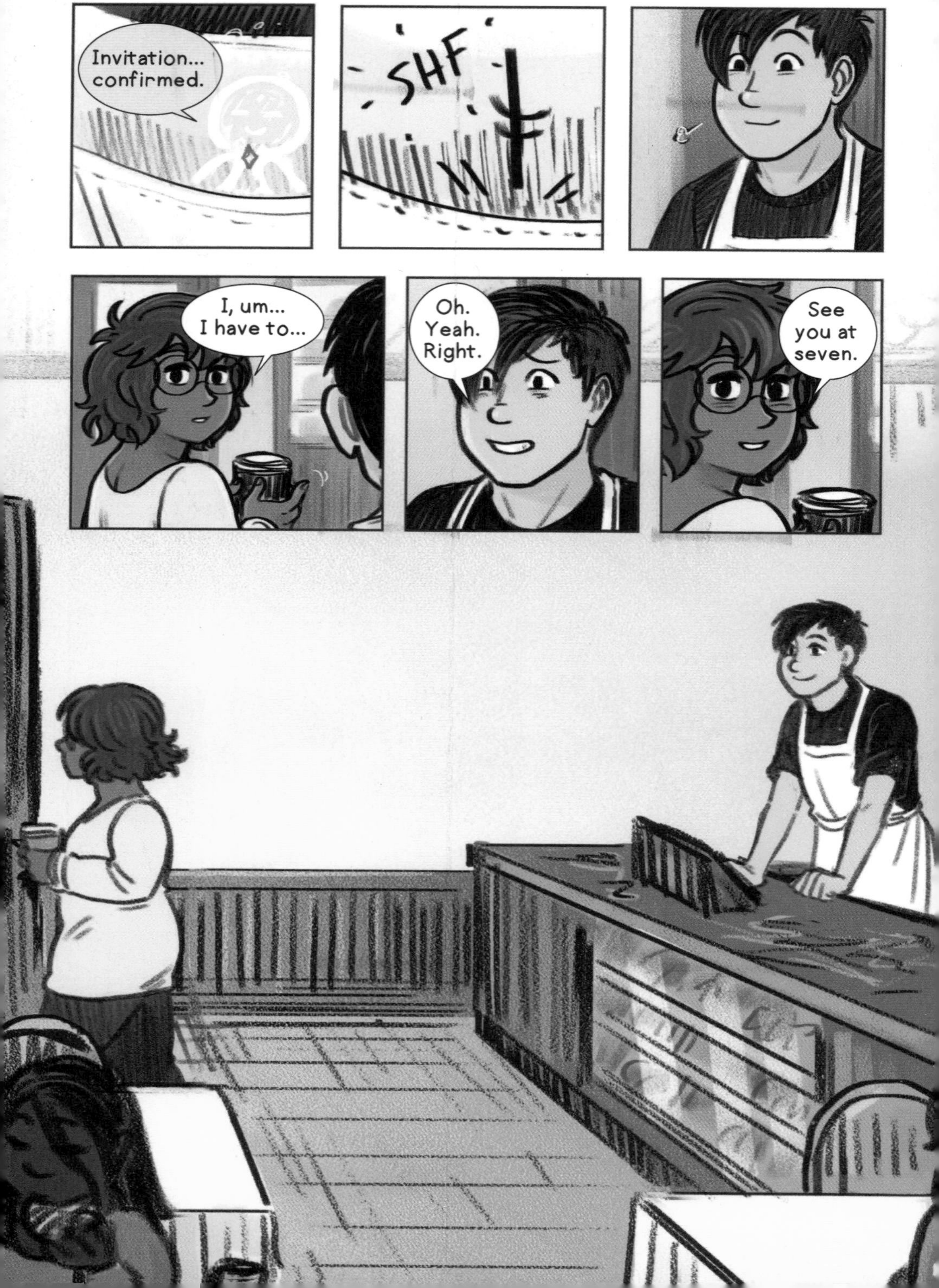
Invitation... confirmed.
SHF
I, um... I have to...
Oh. Yeah. Right.
See you at seven.

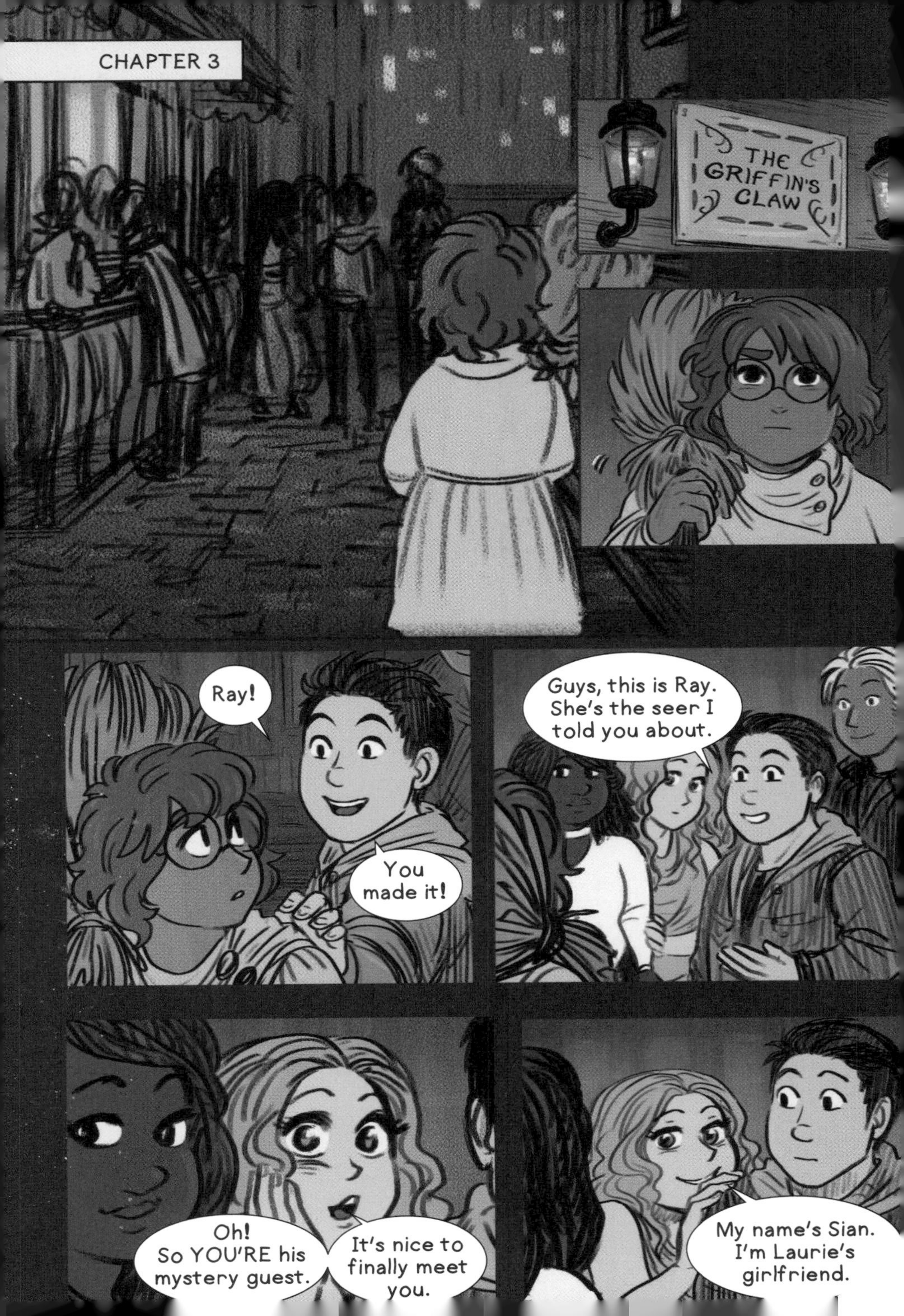
CHAPTER 3
THE GRIFFIN'S CLAW
Ray!
You made it!
Guys, this is Ray. She's the seer I told you about.
Oh! So YOU'RE his mystery guest.
It's nice to finally meet you.
My name's Sian. I'm Laurie's girlfriend.

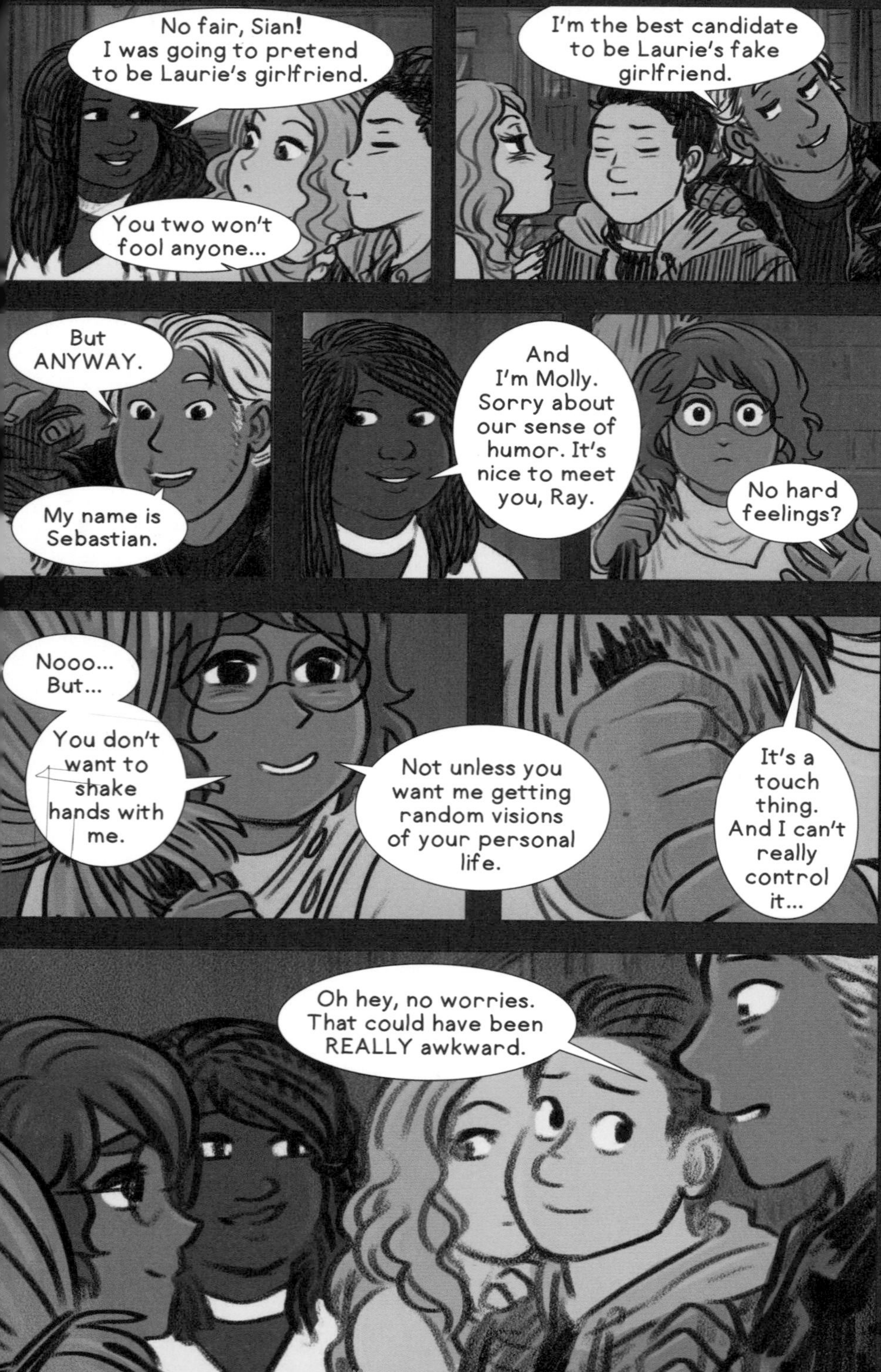
No fair, Sian! I was going to pretend to be Laurie's girlfriend.
You two won't fool anyone...
I'm the best candidate to be Laurie's fake girlfriend.
But ANYWAY.
My name is Sebastian.
And I'm Molly. Sorry about our sense of humor. It's nice to meet you, Ray.
No hard feelings?
Nooo... But...
You don't want to shake hands with me.
Not unless you want me getting random visions of your personal life.
It's a touch thing. And I can't really control it...
Oh hey, no worries. That could have been REALLY awkward.

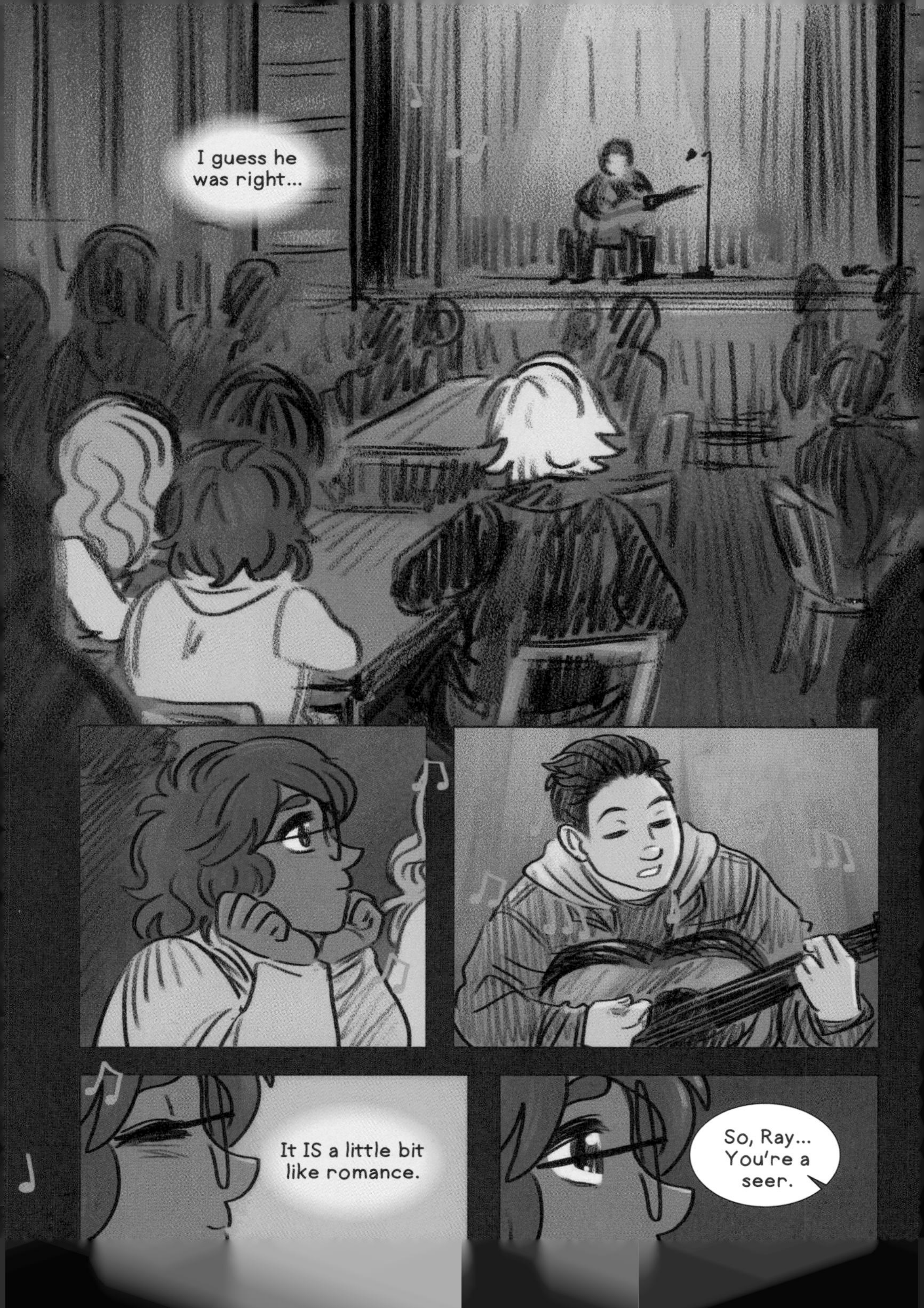
I guess he was right...
It IS a little bit like romance.
So, Ray... You're a seer.

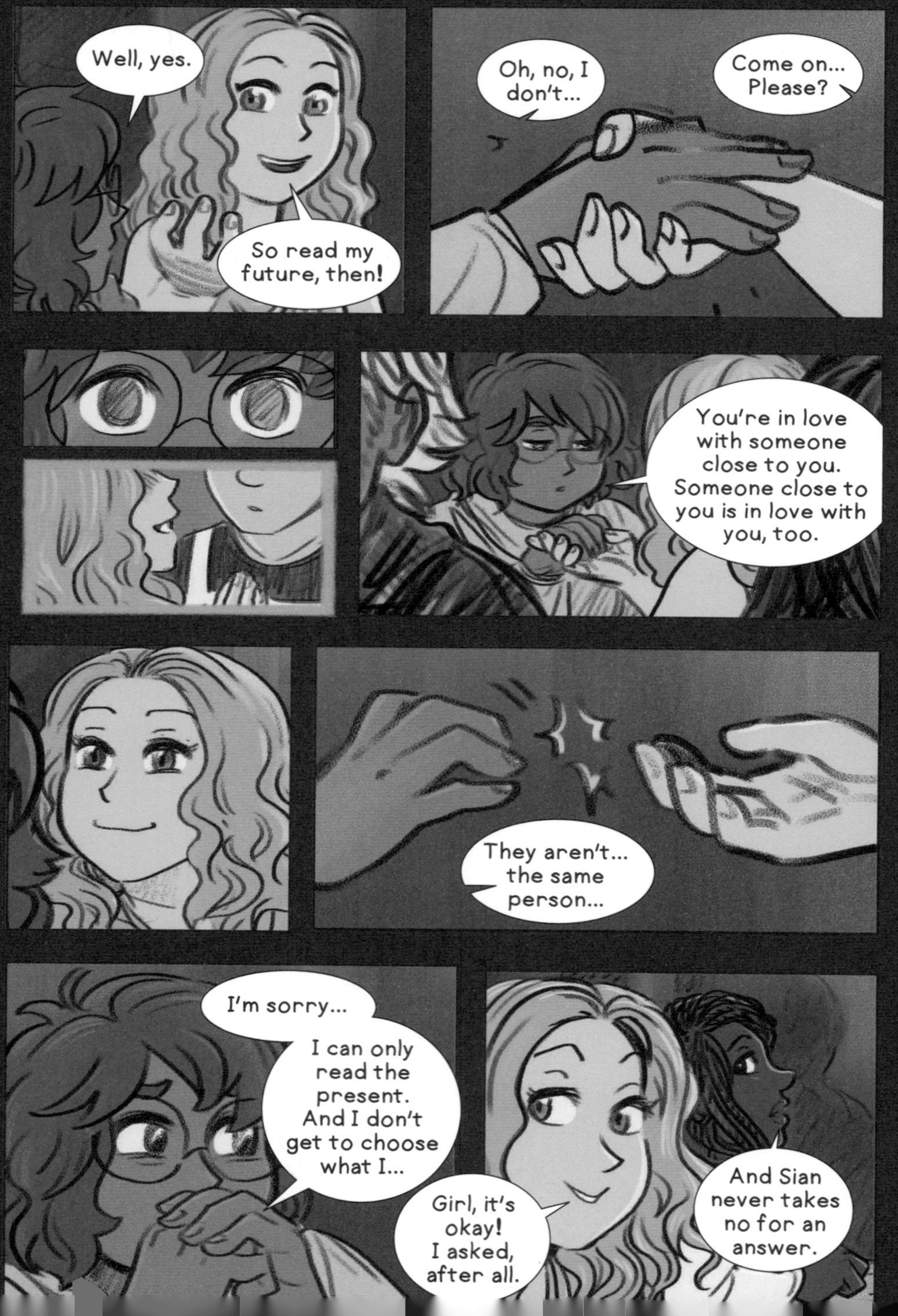
Well, yes.
So read my future, then!
Oh, no, I don't...
Come on... Please?
You're in love with someone close to you. Someone close to you is in love with you, too.
They aren't... the same person...
I'm sorry...
I can only read the present. And I don't get to choose what I...
Girl, it's okay! I asked, after all.
And Sian never takes no for an answer.

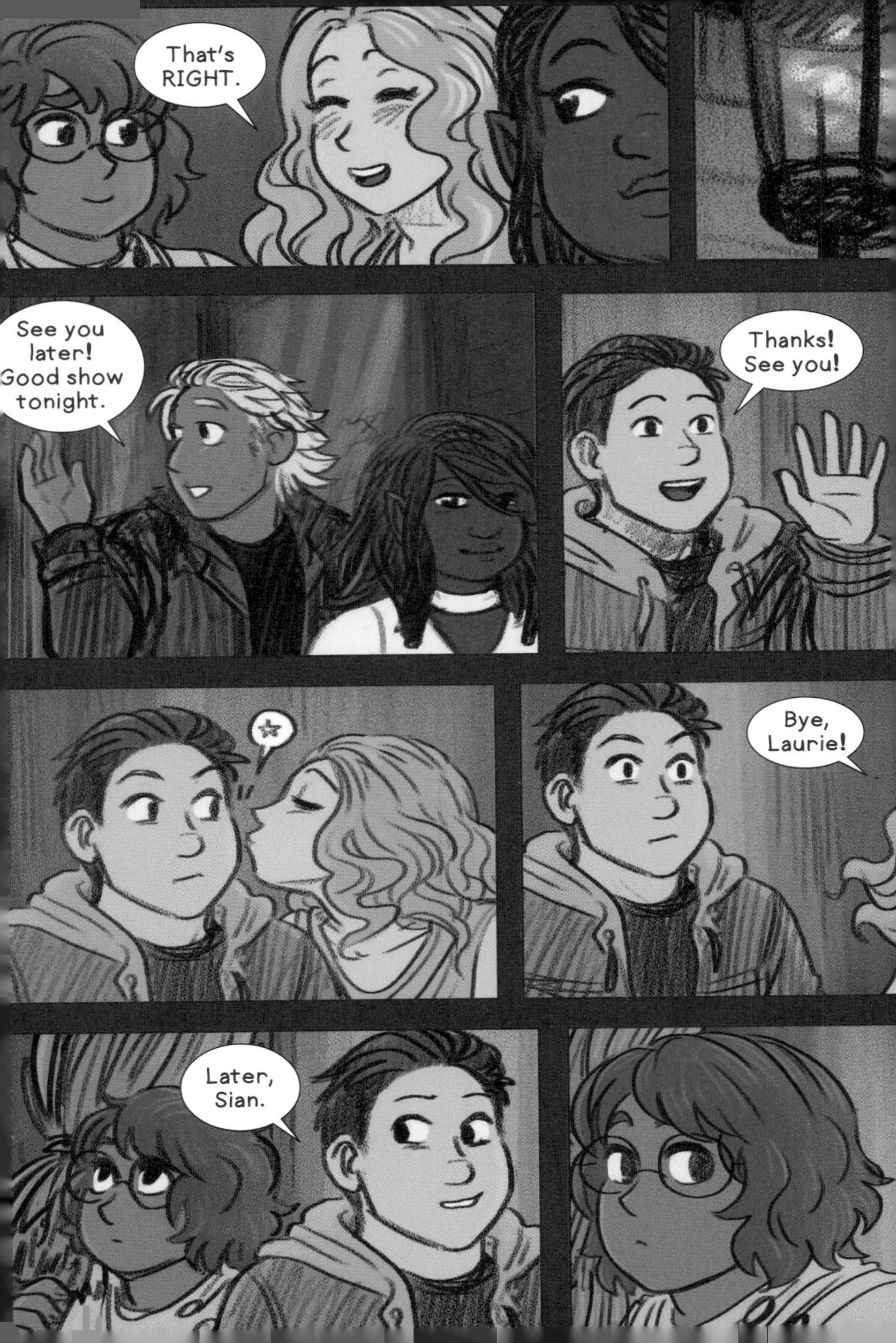
That's RIGHT.
See you later! Good show tonight.
Thanks! See you!
Bye, Laurie!
Later, Sian.

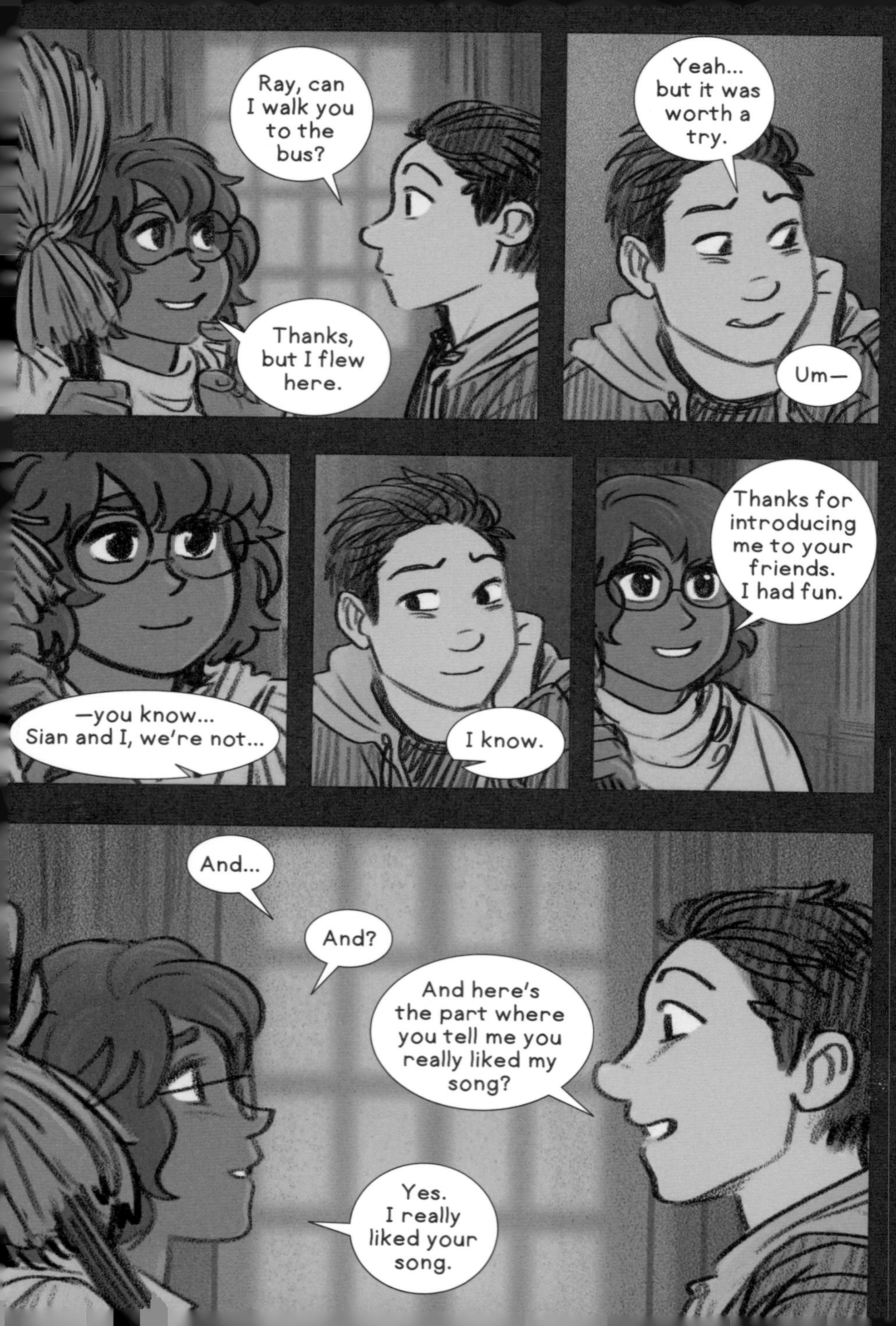
Ray, can I walk you to the bus?
Thanks, but I flew here.
Yeah... but it was worth a try.
Um—
—you know... Sian and I, we're not...
I know.
Thanks for introducing me to your friends. I had fun.
And...
And?
And here's the part where you tell me you really liked my song?
Yes. I really liked your song.

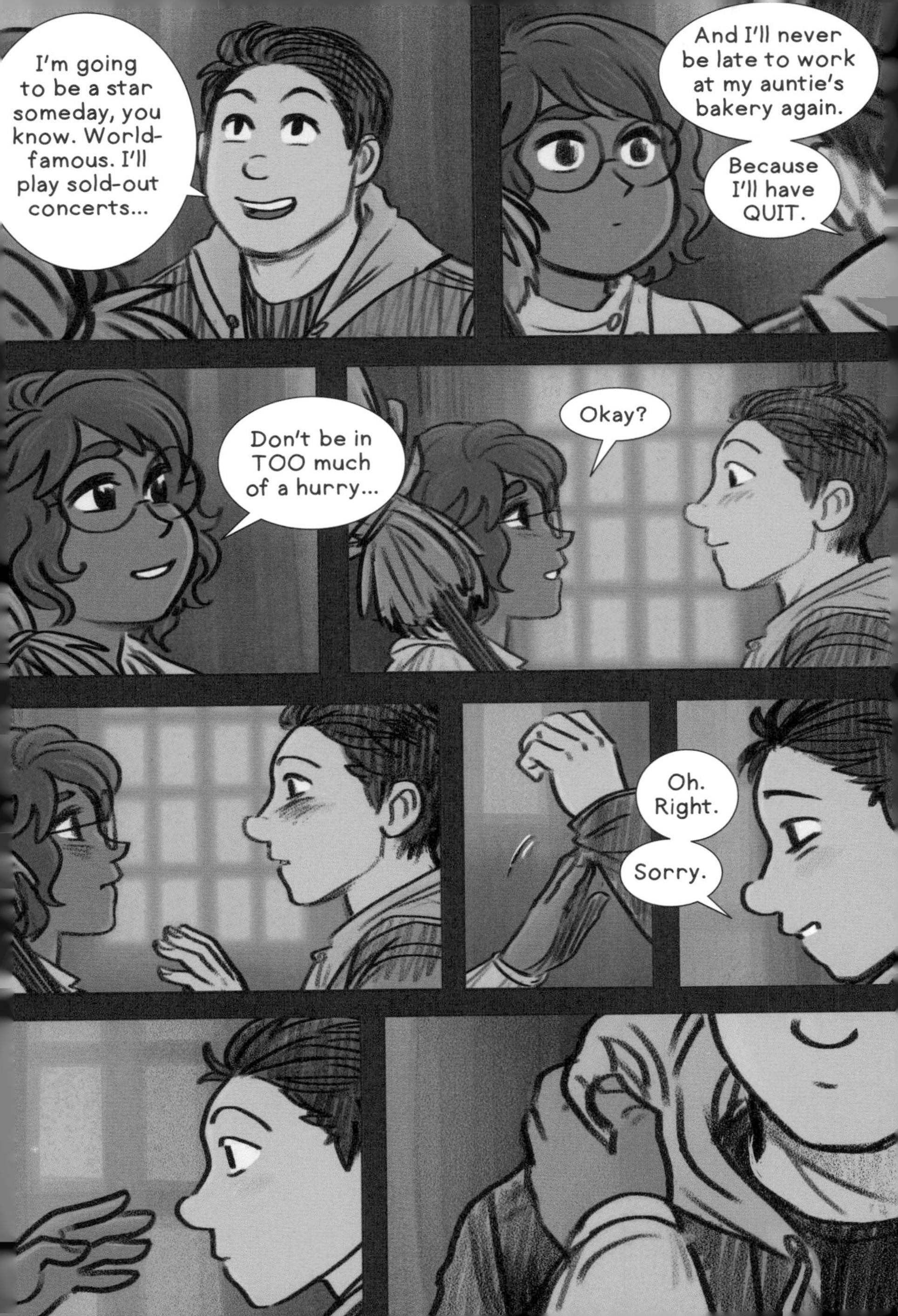
I'm going to be a star someday, you know. World-famous. I'll play sold-out concerts...
And I'll never be late to work at my auntie's bakery again.
Because I'll have QUIT.
Don't be in TOO much of a hurry...
Okay?
Oh. Right.
Sorry.

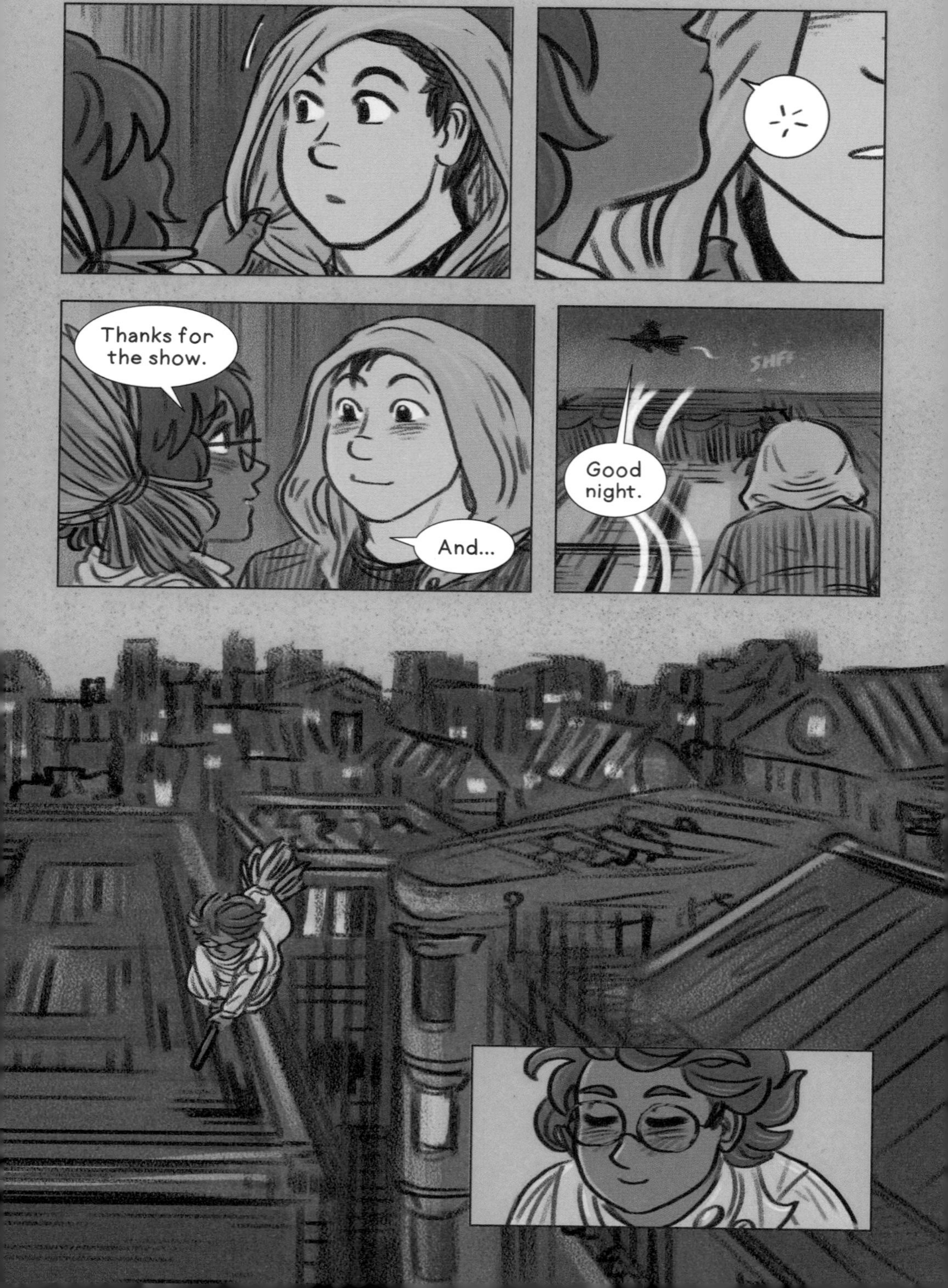
Thanks for the show.
And...
Good night.
SHF!

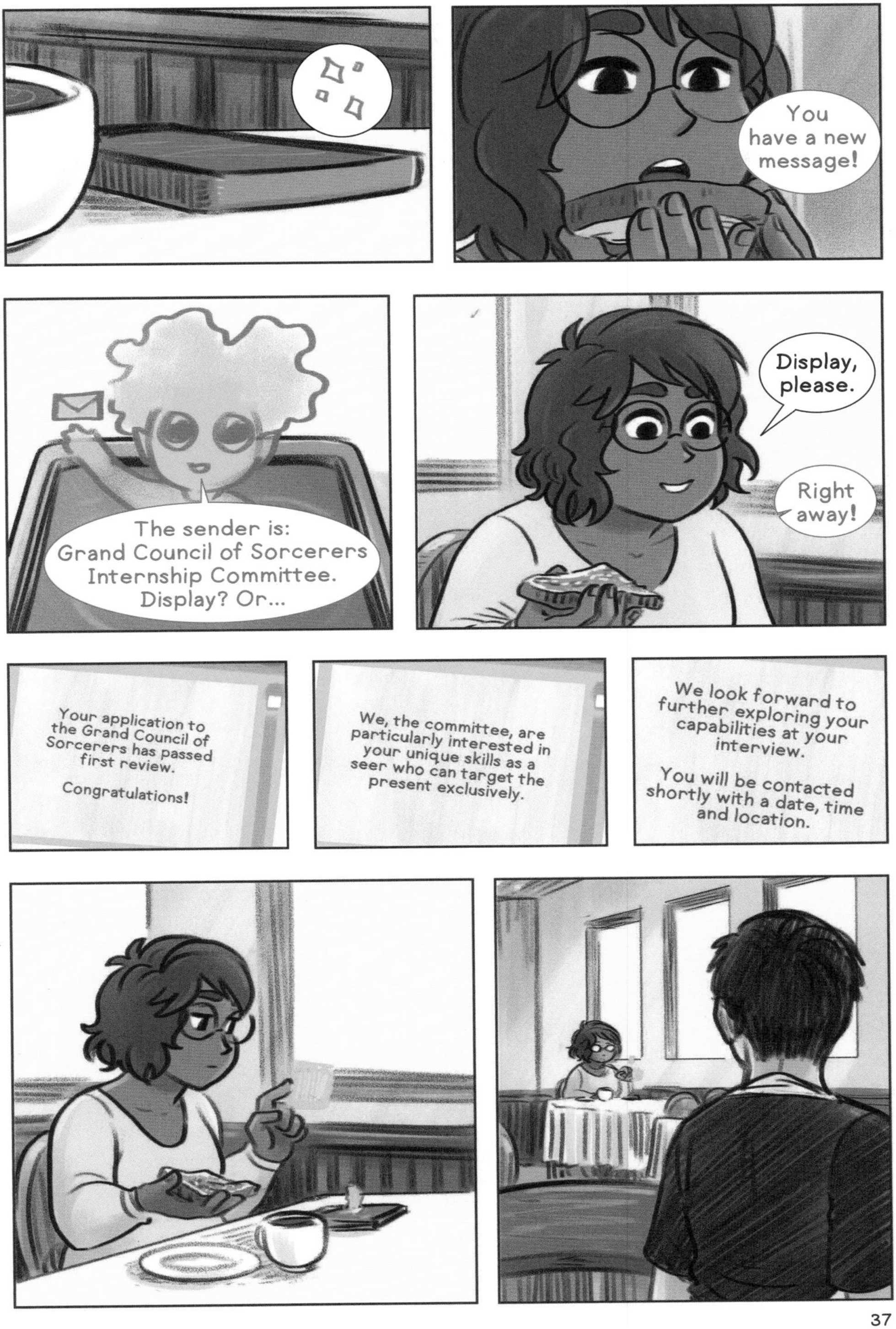
You have a new message!
The sender is: Grand Council of Sorcerers Internship Committee. Display? Or...
Display, please.
Right away!
Your application to the Grand Council of Sorcerers has passed first review.
Congratulations!
We, the committee, are particularly interested in your unique skills as a seer who can target the present exclusively.
We look forward to further exploring your capabilities at your interview.
You will be contacted shortly with a date, time and location.

"Interested in your unique skills as a seer," huh?

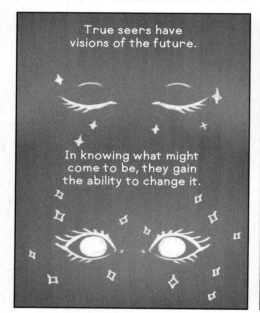

True seers have visions of the future.

In knowing what might come to be, they gain the ability to change it.

Any true seer will tell you that there's no such thing as fate: What they really see are possibilities.

I'm not a true seer.
I've only ever seen things exactly as they are.

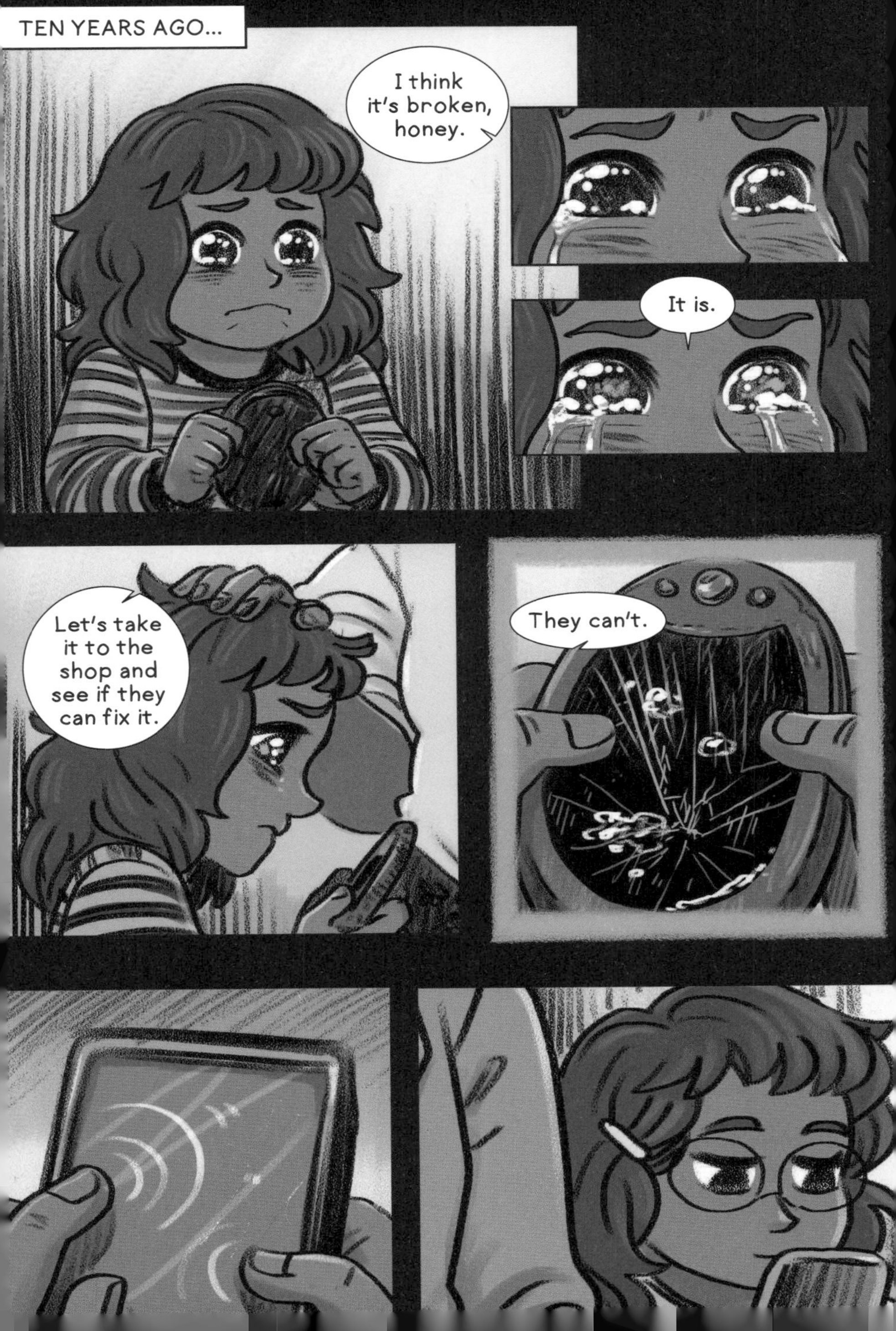
TEN YEARS AGO...
I think it's broken, honey.
It is.
Let's take it to the shop and see if they can fix it.
They can't.

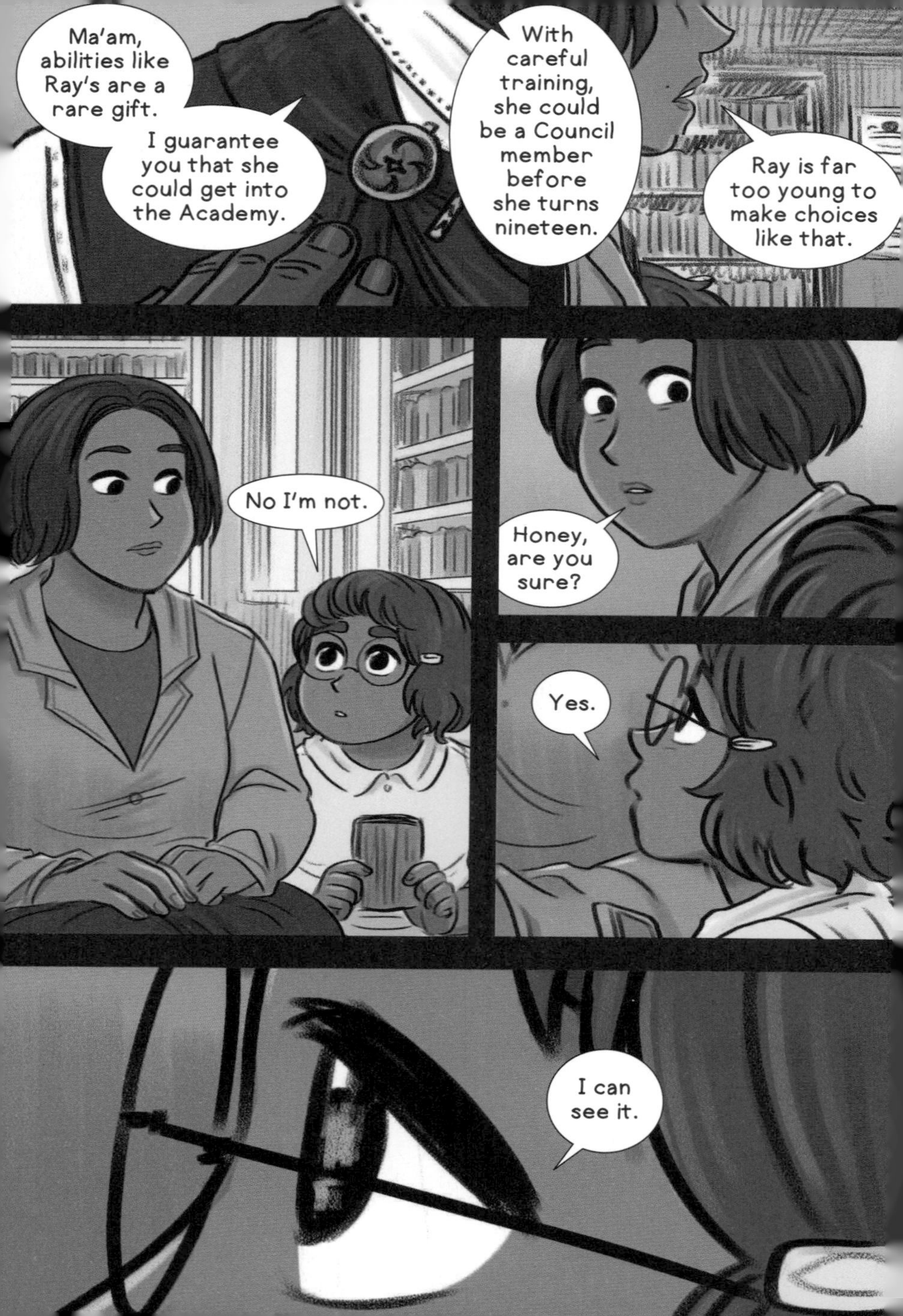
Ma'am, abilities like Ray's are a rare gift.
I guarantee you that she could get into the Academy.
With careful training, she could be a Council member before she turns nineteen.
Ray is far too young to make choices like that.
No I'm not.
Honey, are you sure?
Yes.
I can see it.

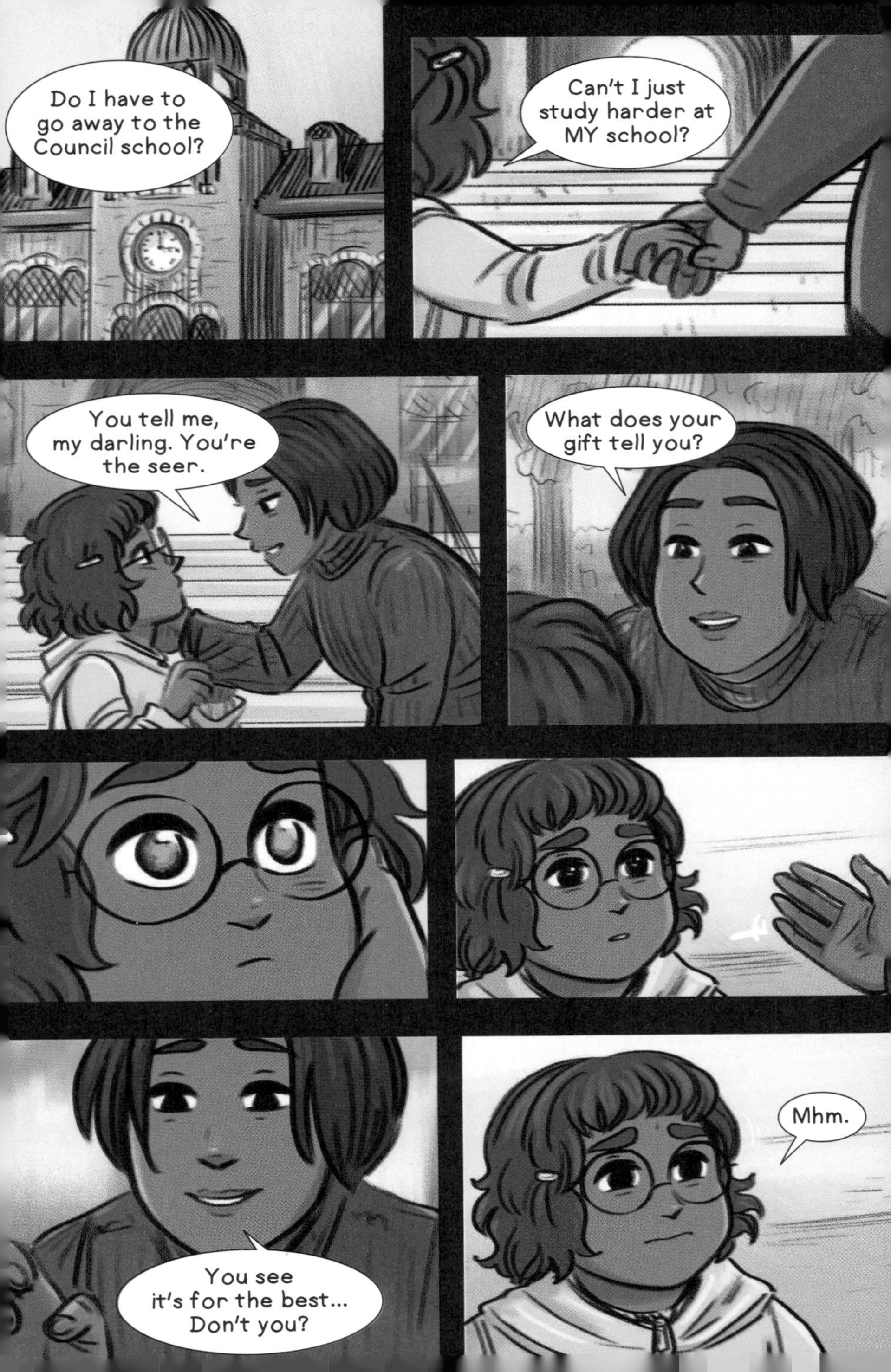
Do I have to go away to the Council school?
Can't I just study harder at MY school?
You tell me, my darling. You're the seer.
What does your gift tell you?
You see it's for the best... Don't you?
Mhm.

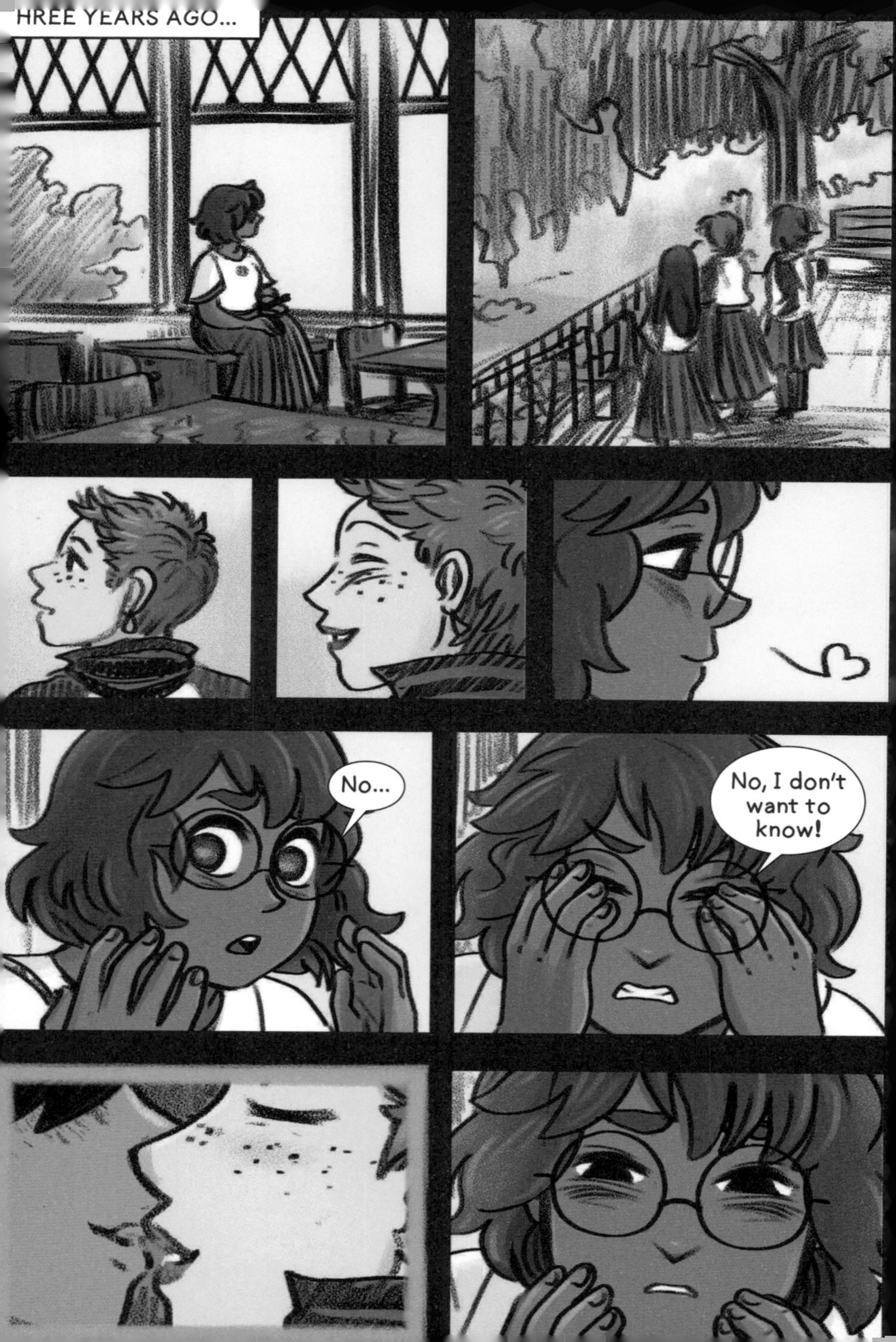
HREE YEARS AGO...
No...
No, I don't want to know!

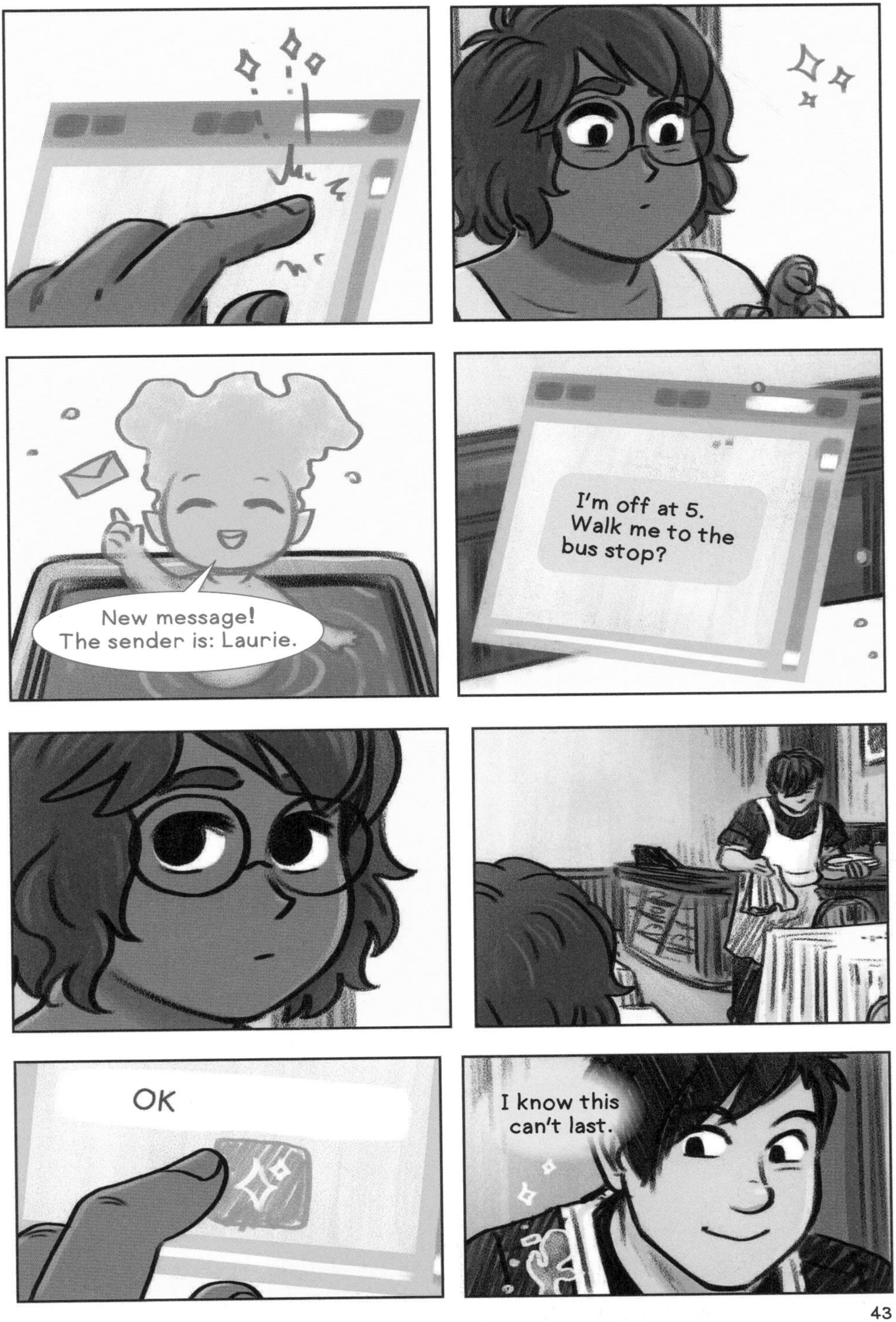
New message!
The sender is: Laurie.
I'm off at 5. Walk me to the bus stop?
OK
I know this can't last.

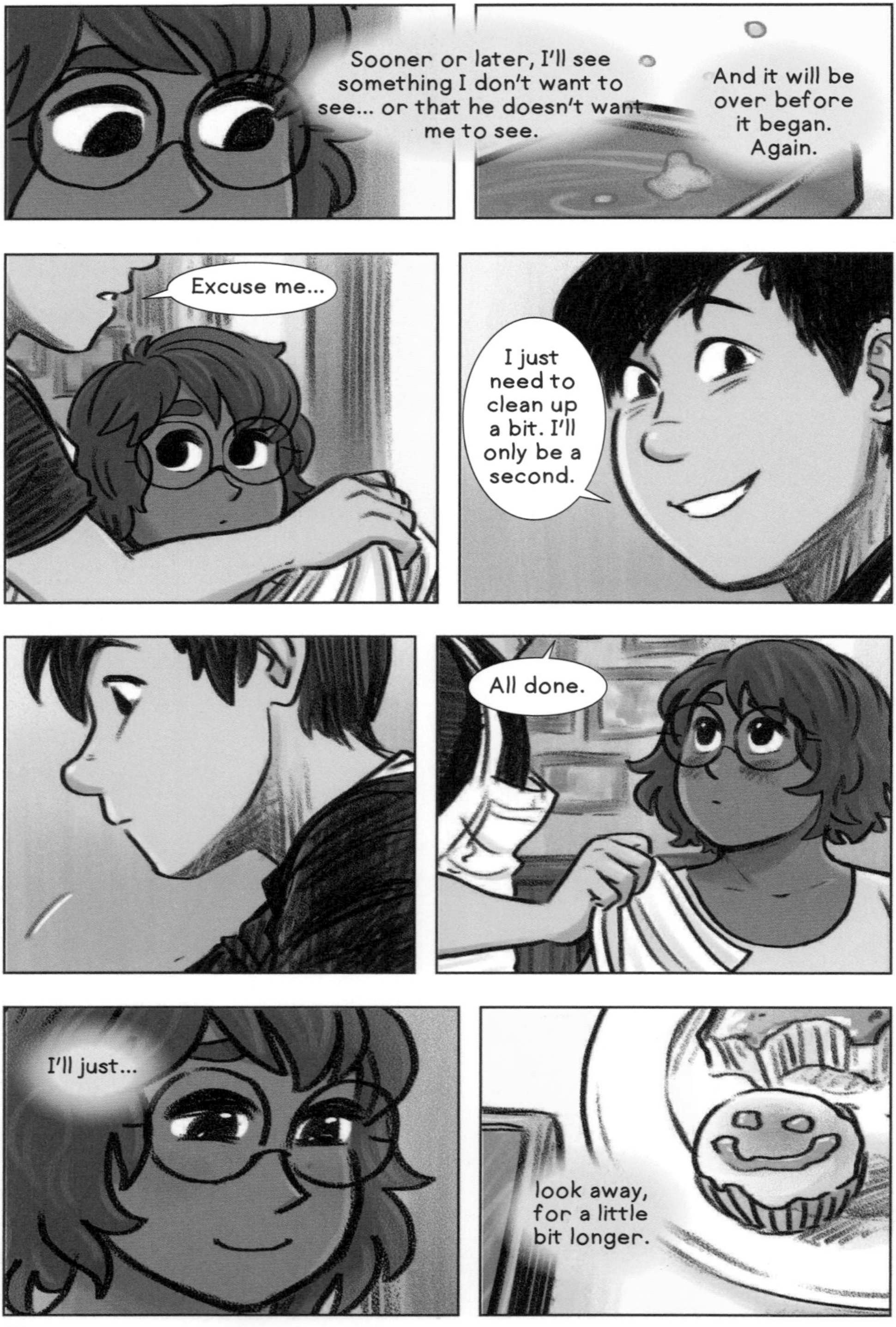
Sooner or later, I'll see something I don't want to see... or that he doesn't want me to see.
And it will be over before it began. Again.
Excuse me...
I just need to clean up a bit. I'll only be a second.
All done.
I'll just...
look away, for a little bit longer.

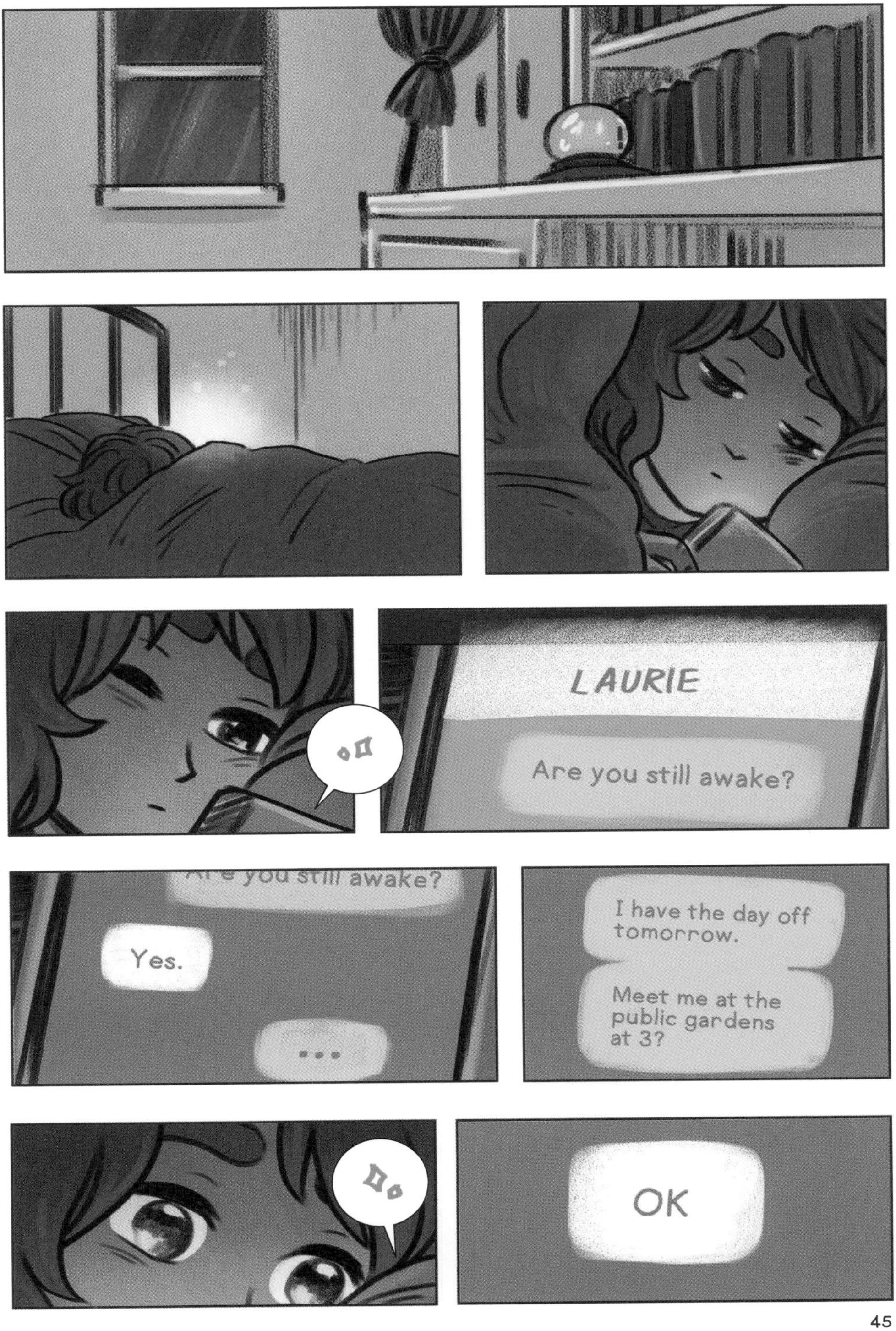
LAURIE
Are you still awake?
Are you still awake?
Yes.
...
I have the day off tomorrow.
Meet me at the public gardens at 3?
OK

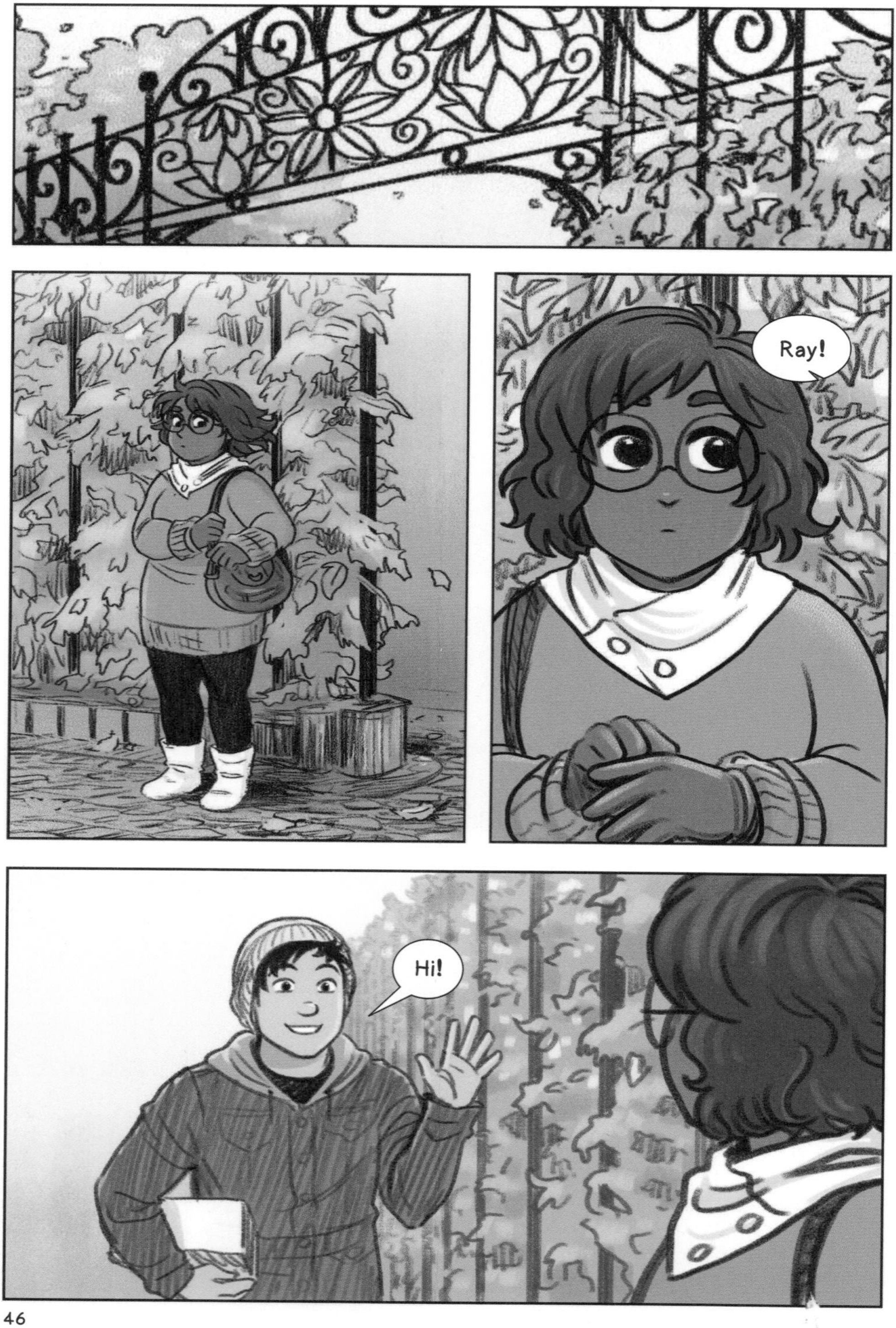
Ray!
Hi!

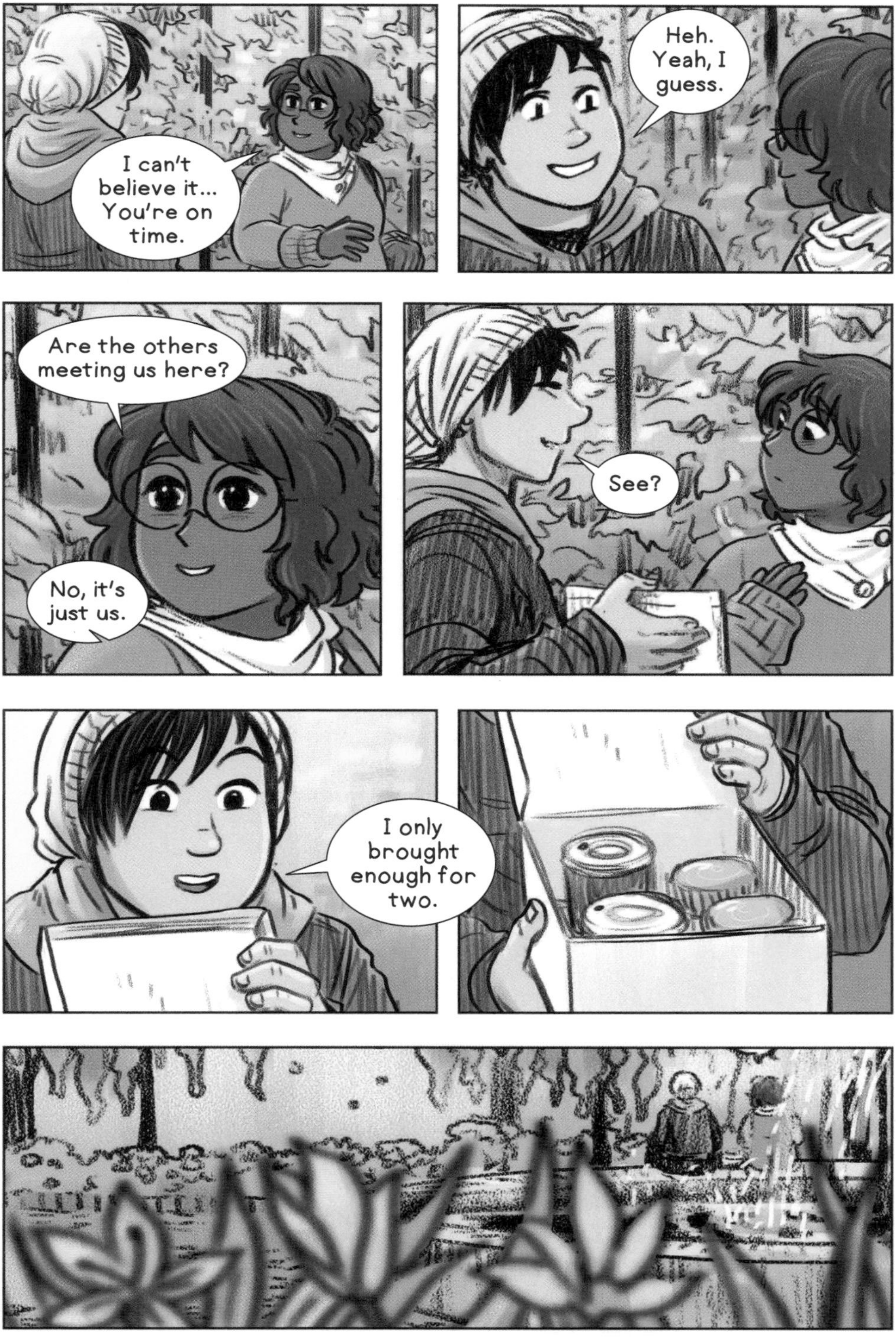
I can't believe it... You're on time.
Heh. Yeah, I guess.
Are the others meeting us here?
No, it's just us.
See?
I only brought enough for two.

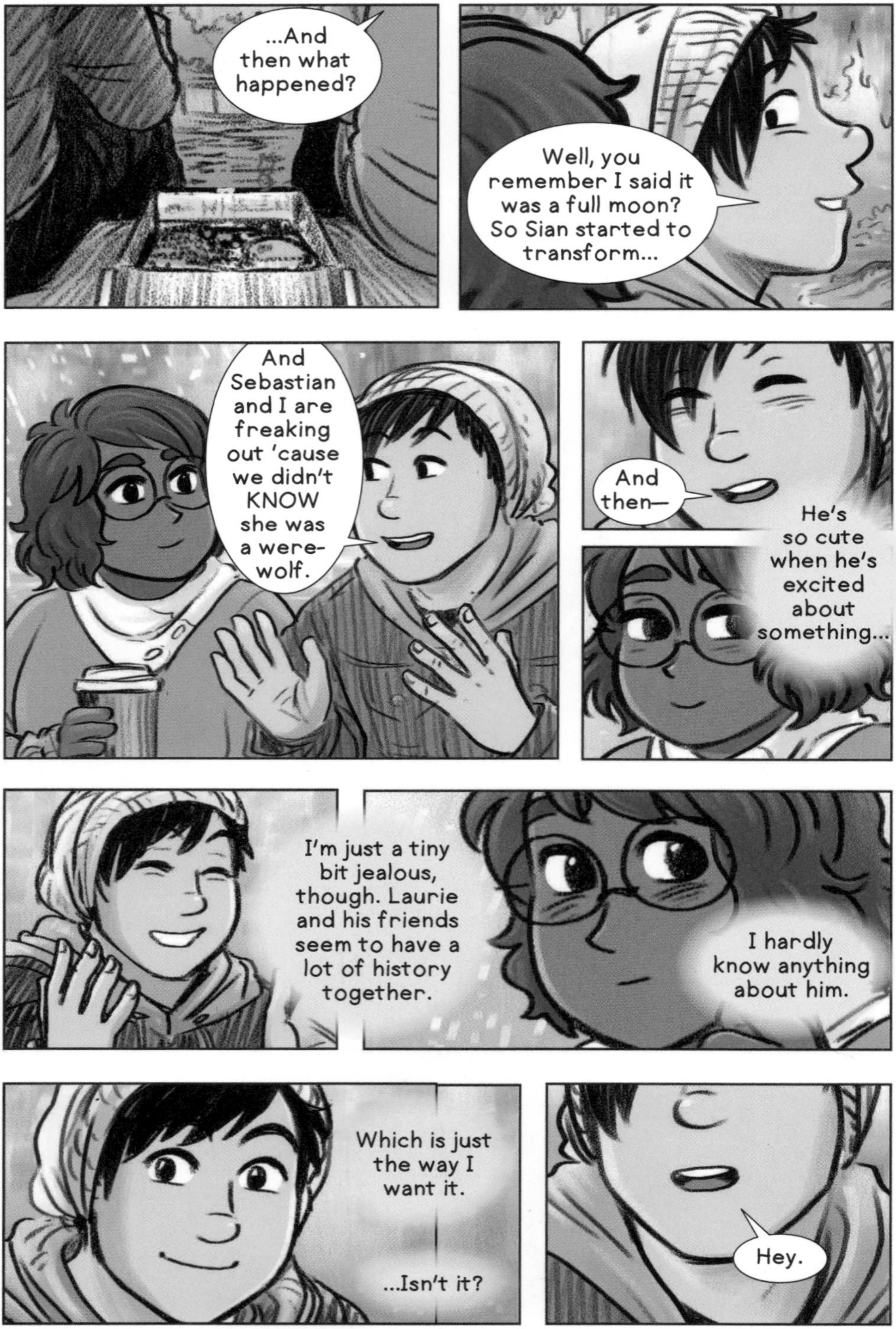
...And then what happened?
Well, you remember I said it was a full moon? So Sian started to transform...
And Sebastian and I are freaking out 'cause we didn't KNOW she was a were-wolf.
And then—
He's so cute when he's excited about something...
I'm just a tiny bit jealous, though. Laurie and his friends seem to have a lot of history together.
I hardly know anything about him.
Which is just the way I want it.
...Isn't it?
Hey.

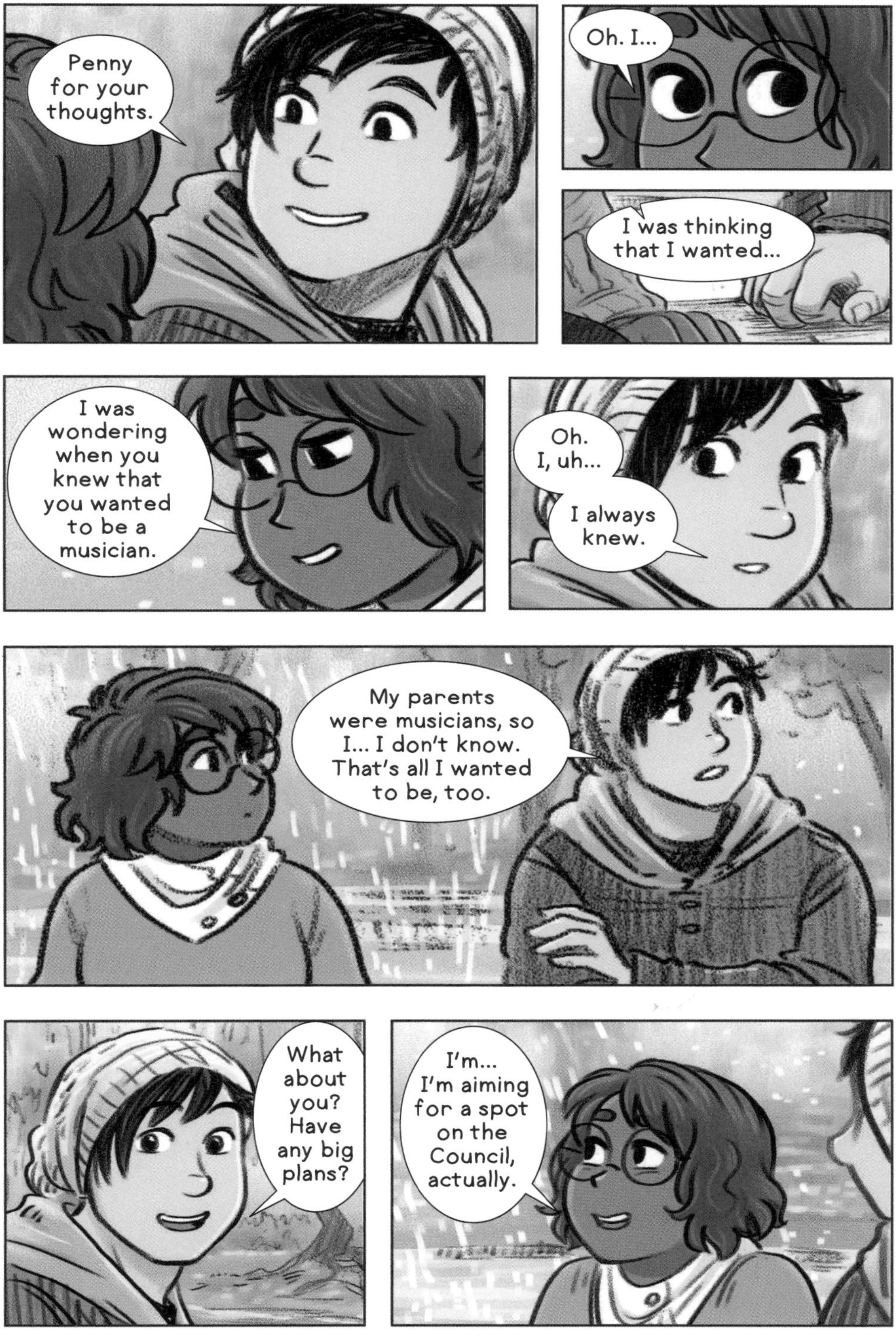

Penny for your thoughts.
Oh. I...
I was thinking that I wanted...
I was wondering when you knew that you wanted to be a musician.
Oh. I, uh...
I always knew.
My parents were musicians, so I... I don't know. That's all I wanted to be, too.
What about you? Have any big plans?
I'm... I'm aiming for a spot on the Council, actually.

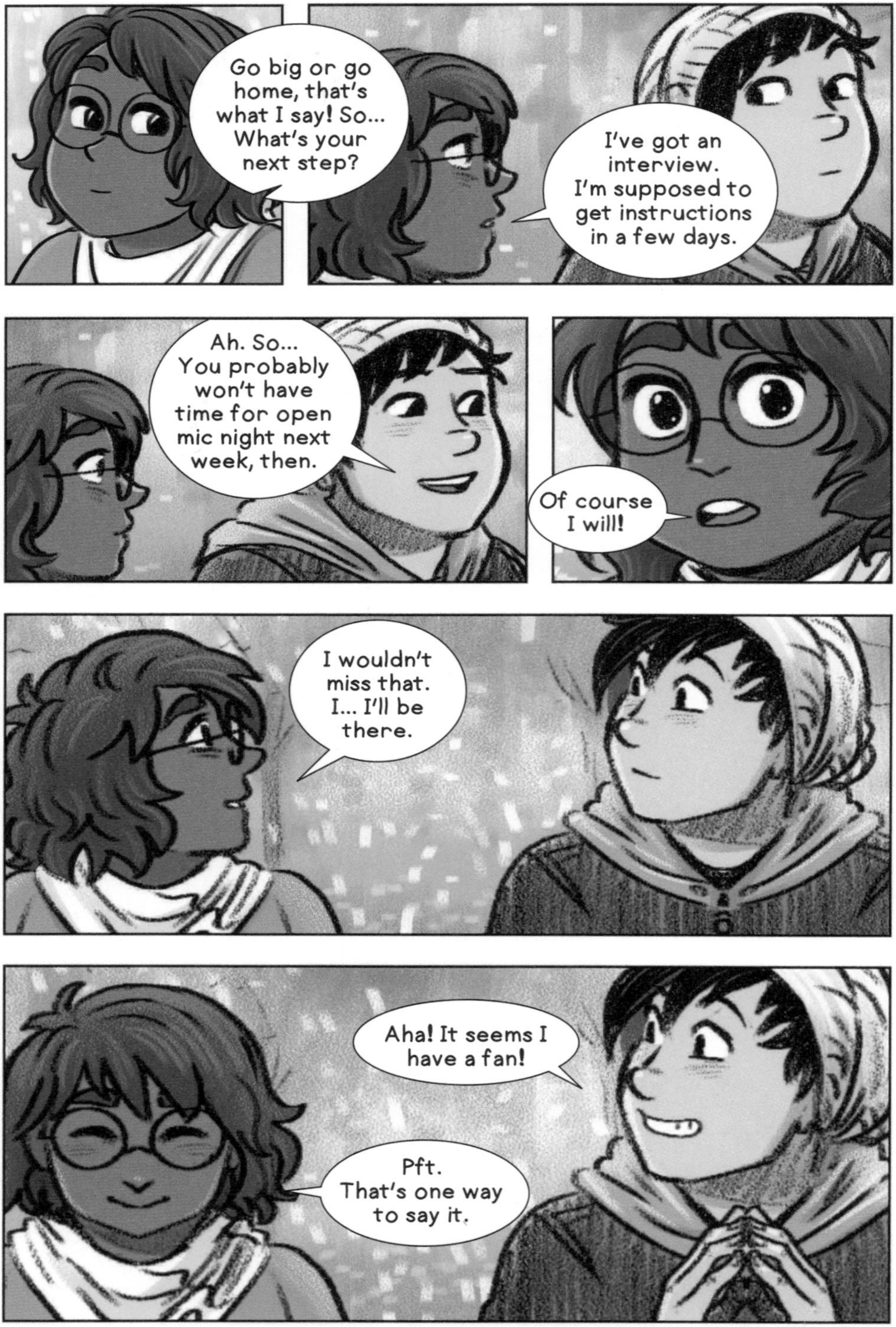
Go big or go home, that's what I say! So... What's your next step?
I've got an interview. I'm supposed to get instructions in a few days.
Ah. So... You probably won't have time for open mic night next week, then.
Of course I will!
I wouldn't miss that. I... I'll be there.
Aha! It seems I have a fan!
Pft. That's one way to say it.

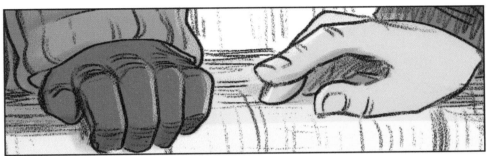

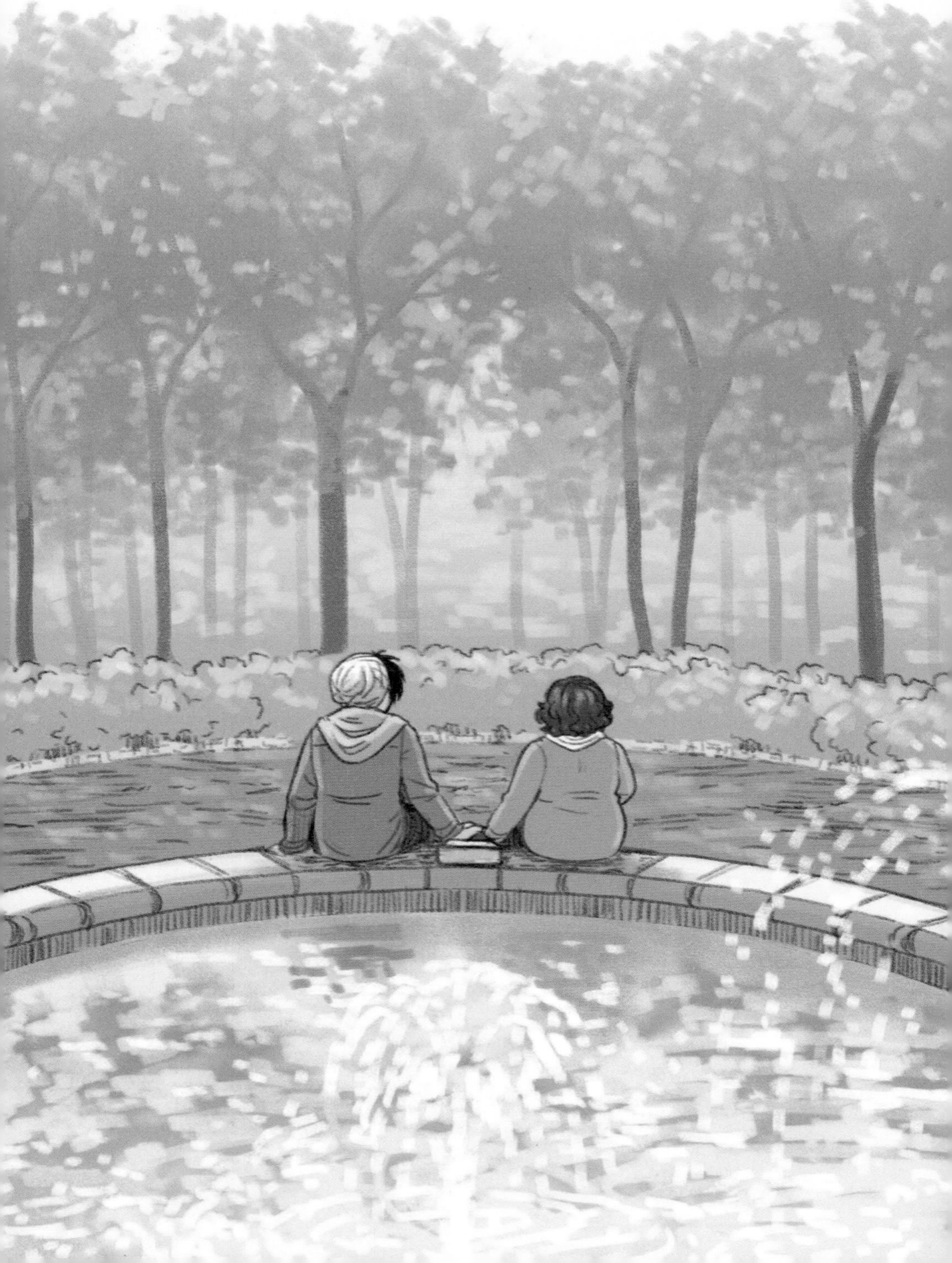

CHAPTER 4

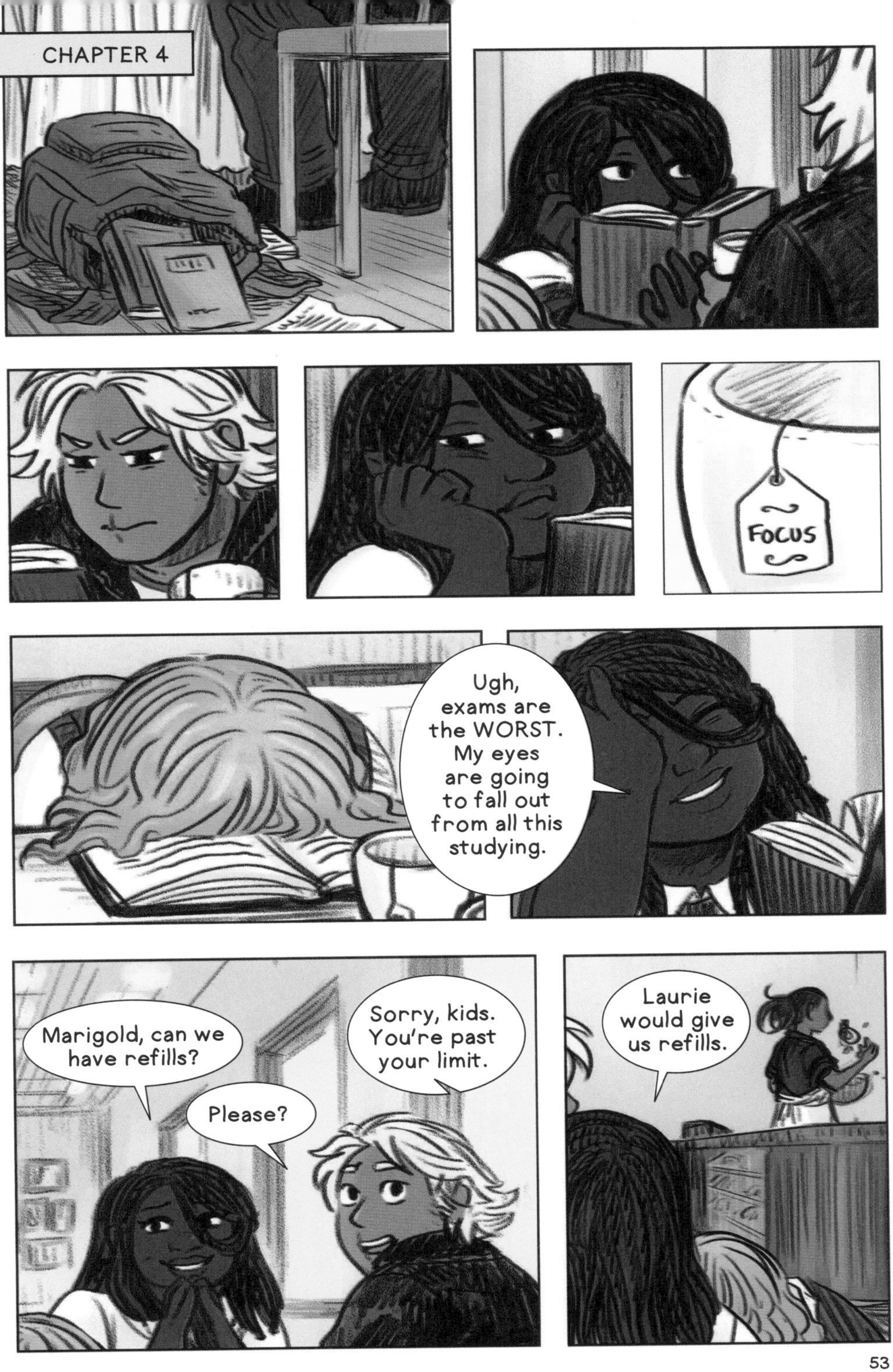
FOCUS
Ugh, exams are the WORST. My eyes are going to fall out from all this studying.
Marigold, can we have refills?
Please?
Sorry, kids. You're past your limit.
Laurie would give us refills.

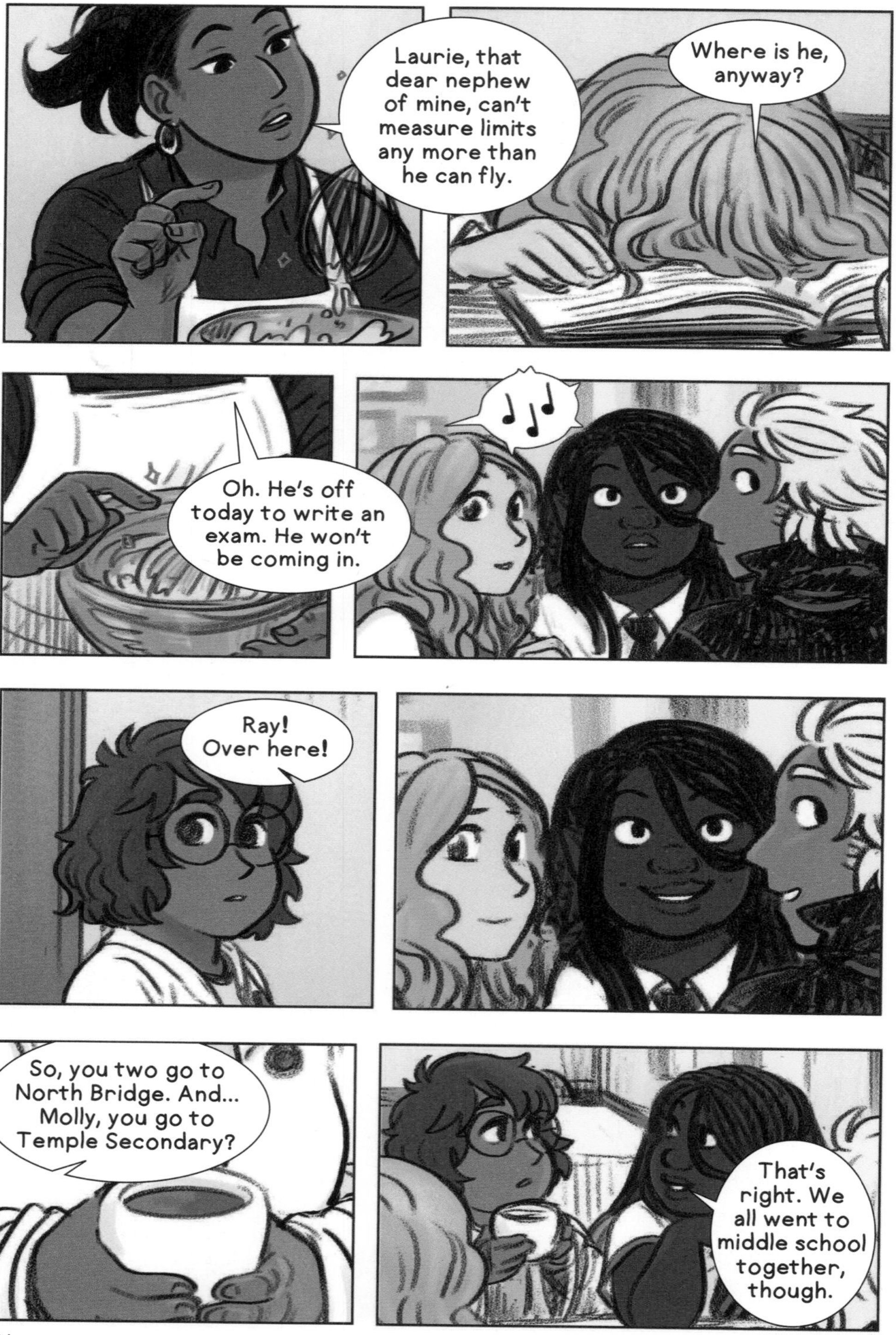
Laurie, that dear nephew of mine, can't measure limits any more than he can fly.
Where is he, anyway?
Oh. He's off today to write an exam. He won't be coming in.
Ray! Over here!
So, you two go to North Bridge. And... Molly, you go to Temple Secondary?
That's right. We all went to middle school together, though.

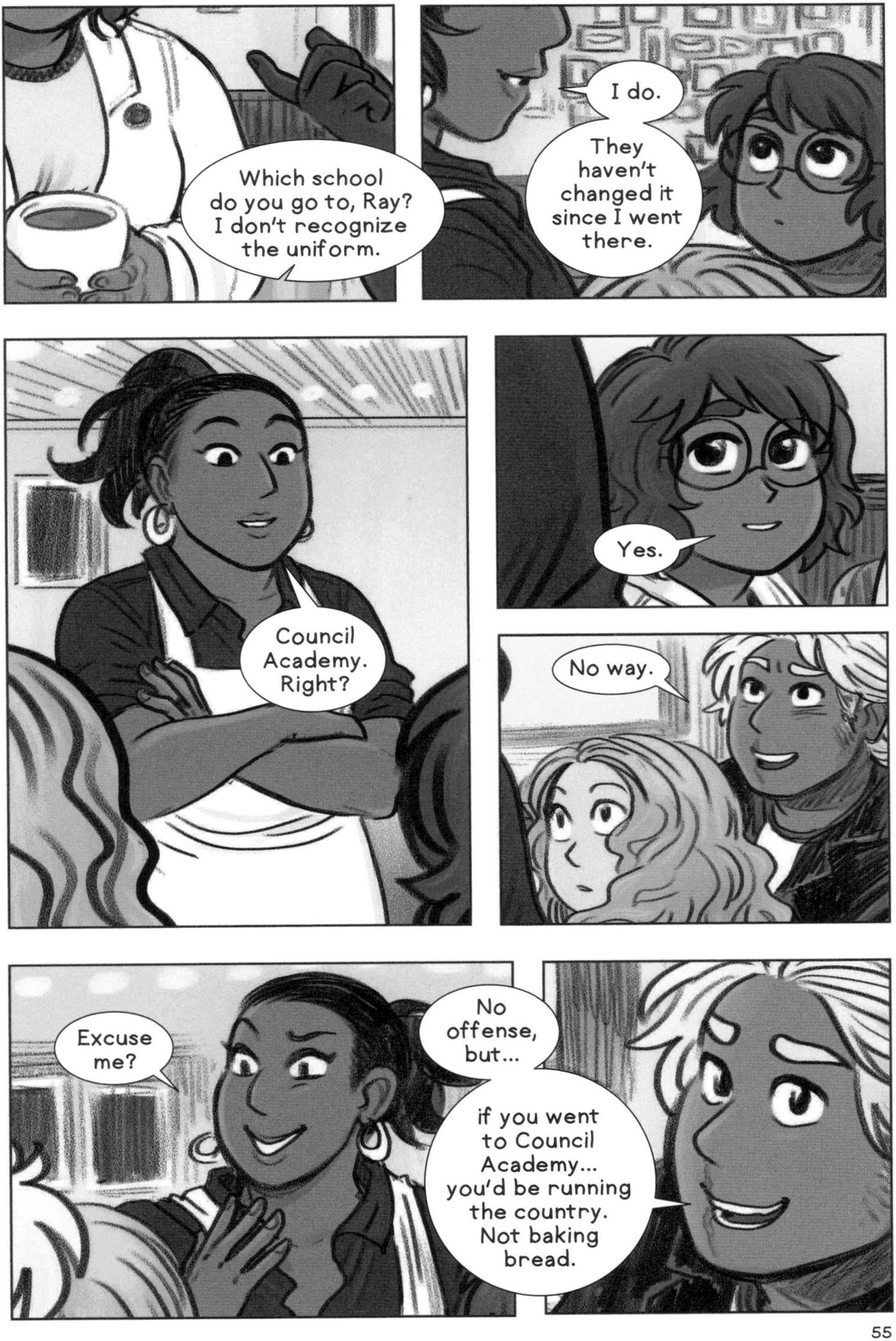
Which school do you go to, Ray? I don't recognize the uniform.
I do.
They haven't changed it since I went there.
Council Academy. Right?
Yes.
No way.
Excuse me?
No offense, but...
if you went to Council Academy... you'd be running the country. Not baking bread.

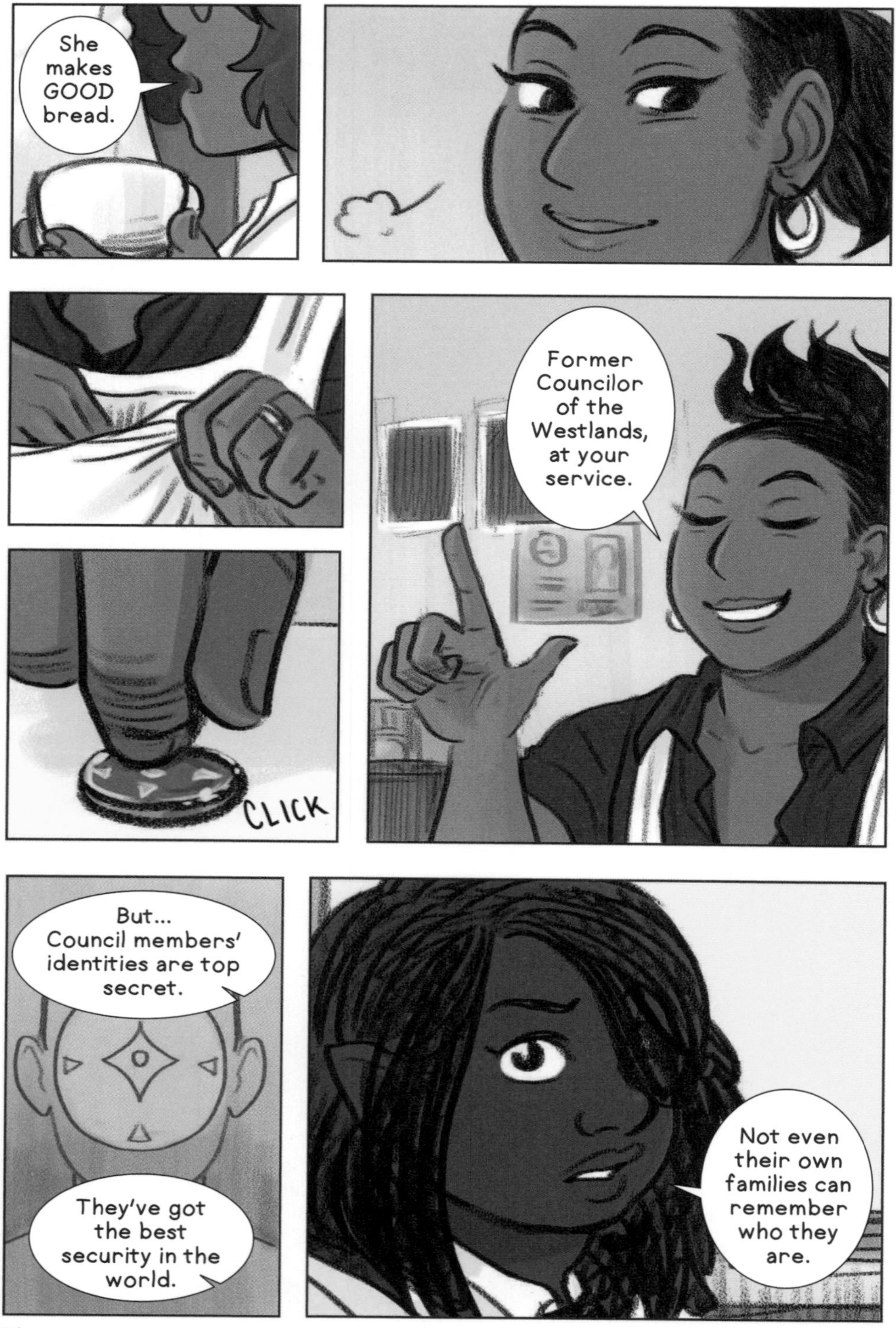
She makes GOOD bread.
Former Councilor of the Westlands, at your service.
CLICK
But... Council members' identities are top secret.
They've got the best security in the world.
Not even their own families can remember who they are.

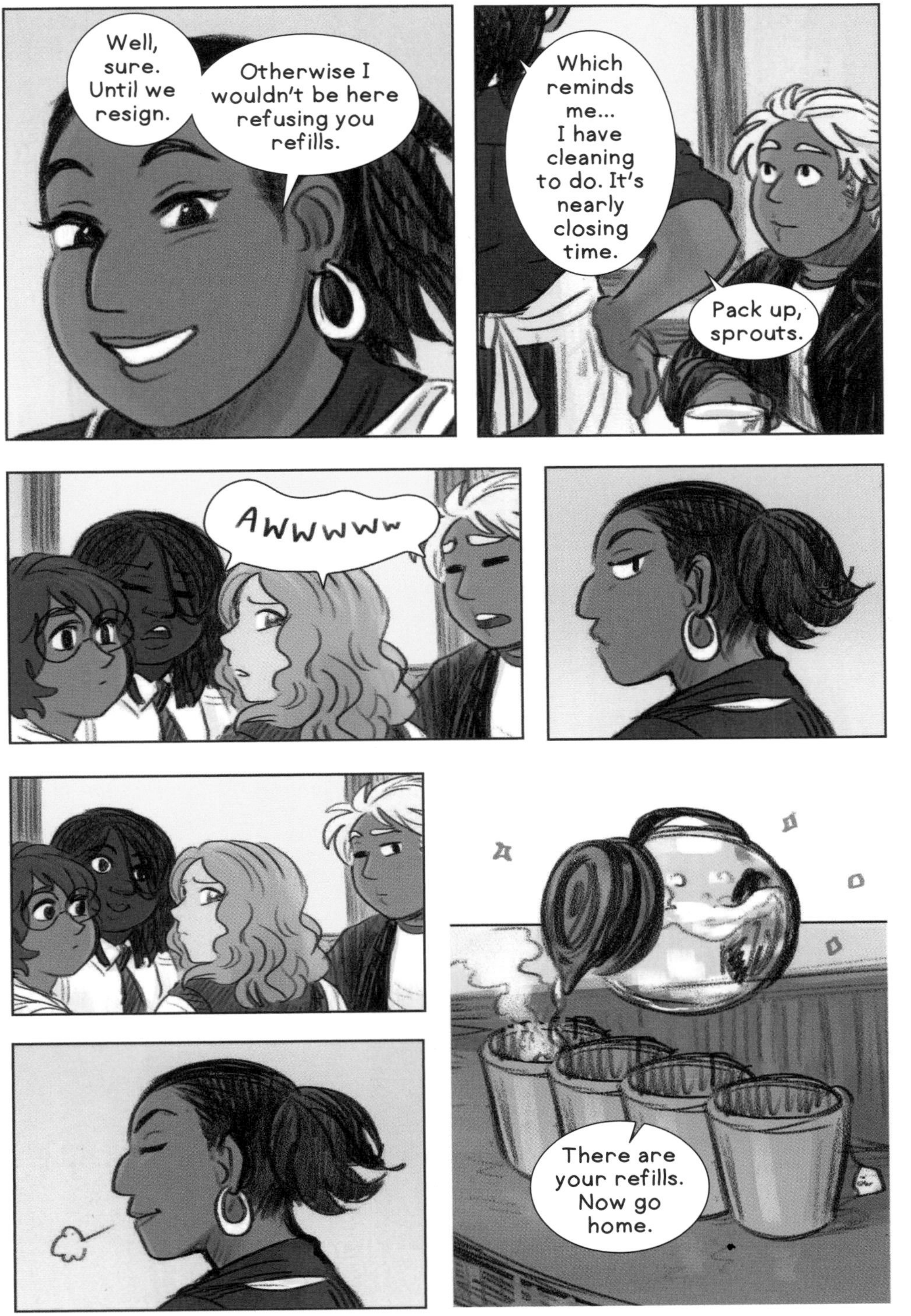
Well, sure. Until we resign.
Otherwise I wouldn't be here refusing you refills.
Which reminds me... I have cleaning to do. It's nearly closing time.
Pack up, sprouts.
AWWWWW
There are your refills. Now go home.

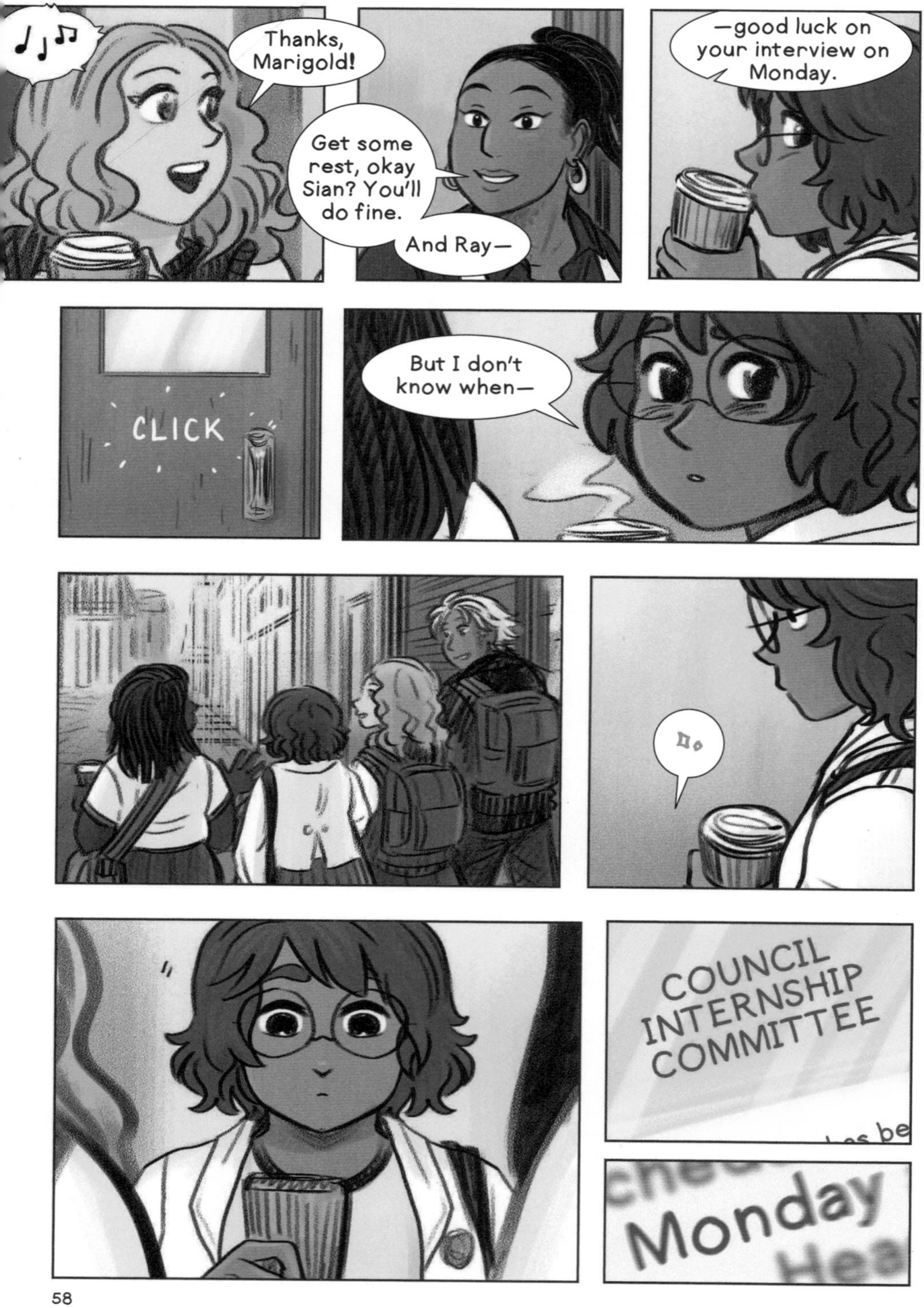

Thanks, Marigold!
Get some rest, okay Sian? You'll do fine.
And Ray—
—good luck on your interview on Monday.
CLICK
But I don't know when—
COUNCIL INTERNSHIP COMMITTEE
Monday

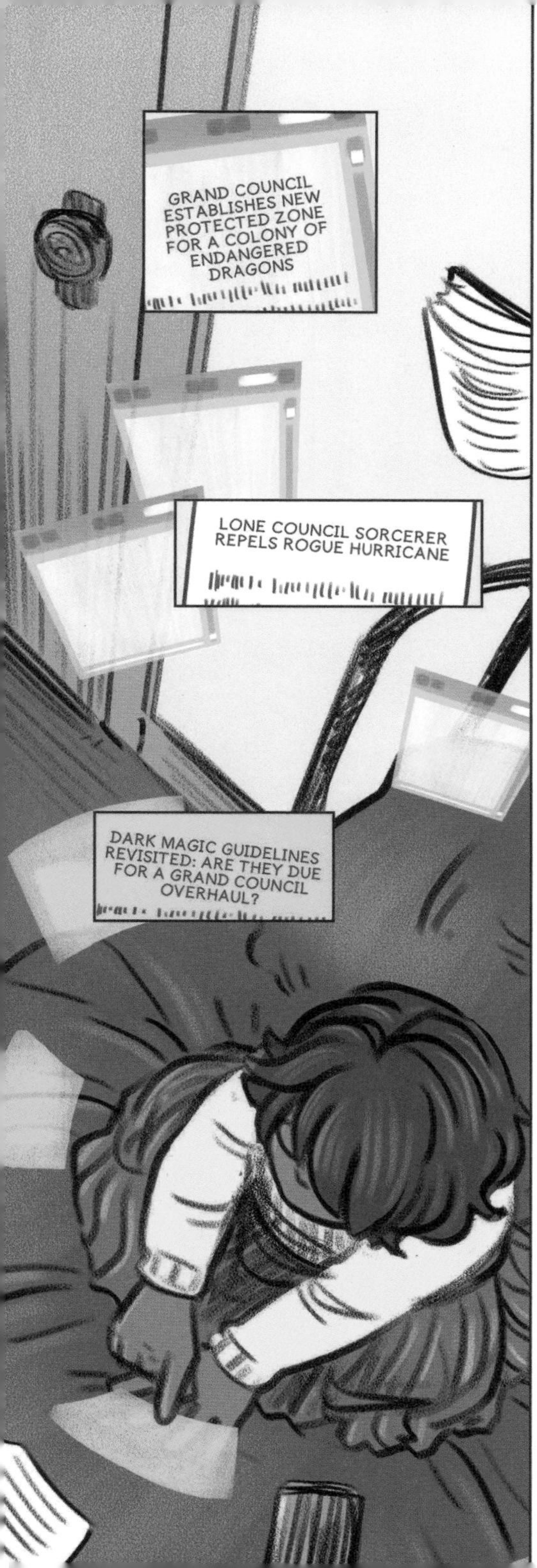
GRAND COUNCIL ESTABLISHES NEW PROTECTED ZONE FOR A COLONY OF ENDANGERED DRAGONS
LONE COUNCIL SORCERER REPELS ROGUE HURRICANE
DARK MAGIC GUIDELINES REVISITED: ARE THEY DUE FOR A GRAND COUNCIL OVERHAUL?

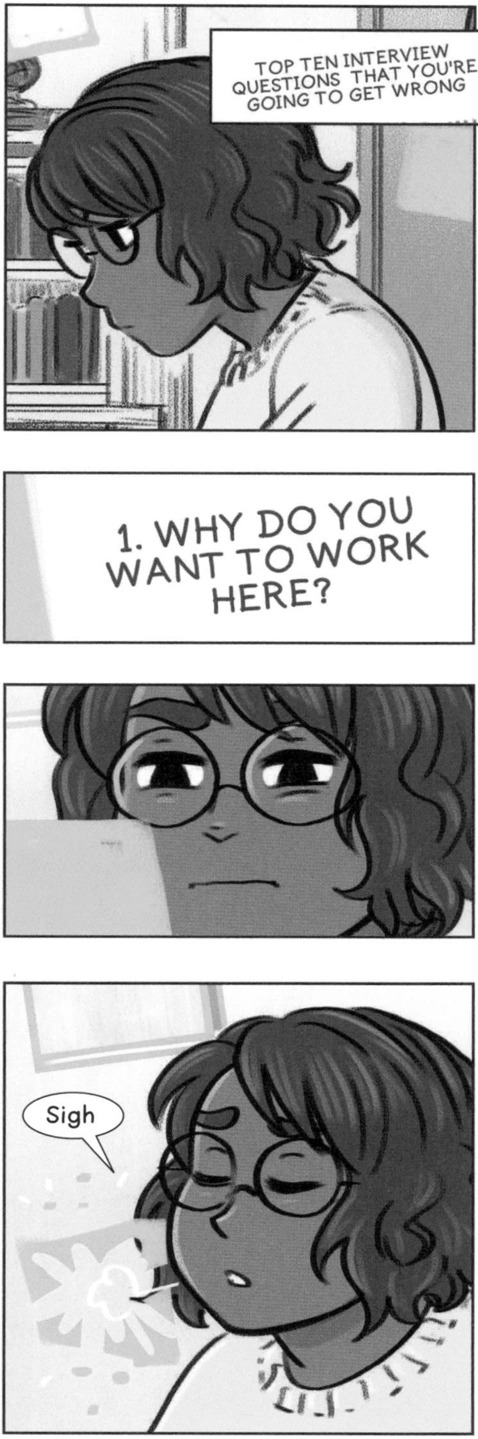
TOP TEN INTERVIEW QUESTIONS THAT YOU'RE GOING TO GET WRONG
1. WHY DO YOU WANT TO WORK HERE?
Sigh

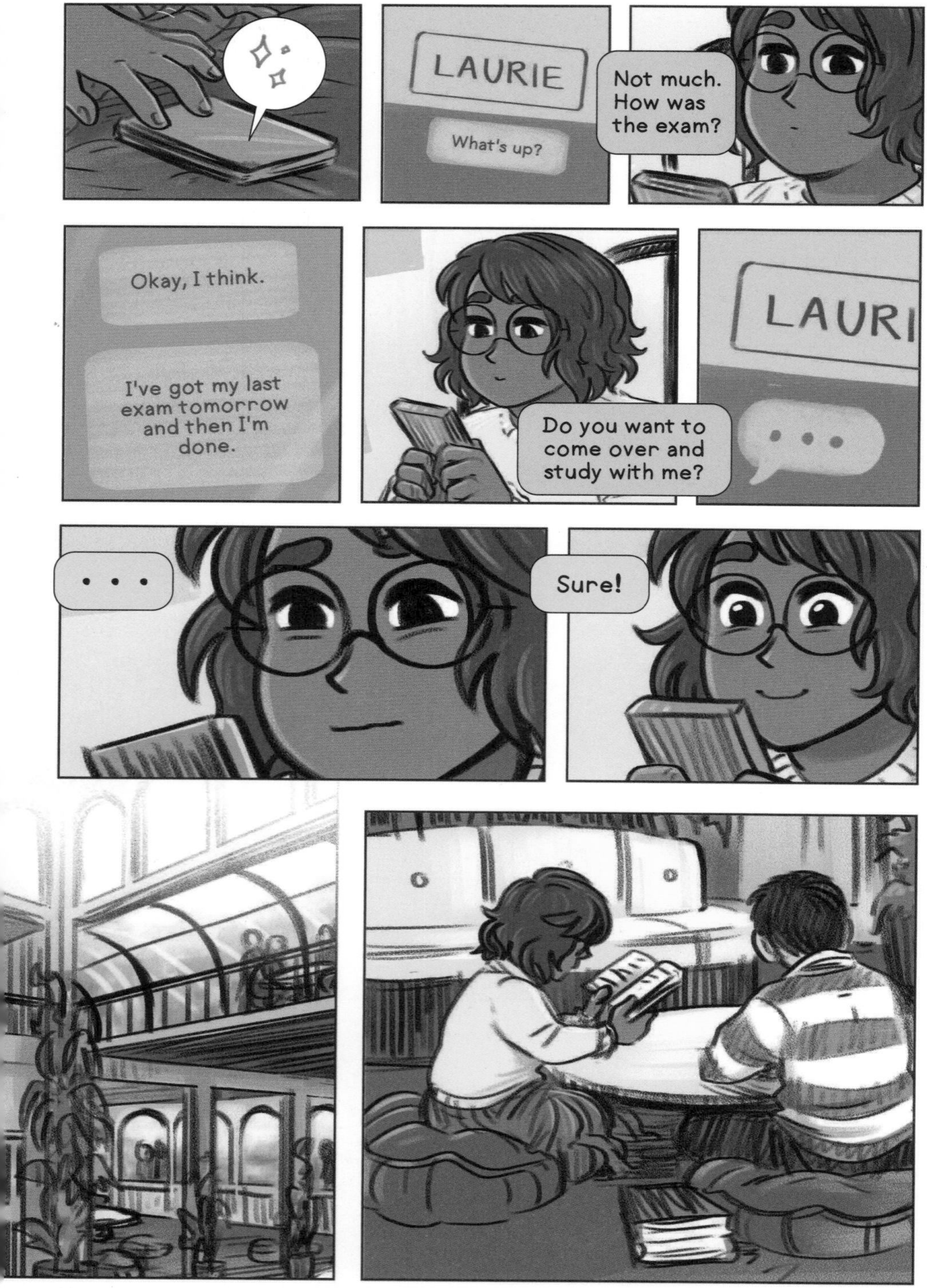
LAURIE
What's up?
Not much. How was the exam?
Okay, I think.
I've got my last exam tomorrow and then I'm done.
Do you want to come over and study with me?
LAURI
. . .
Sure!

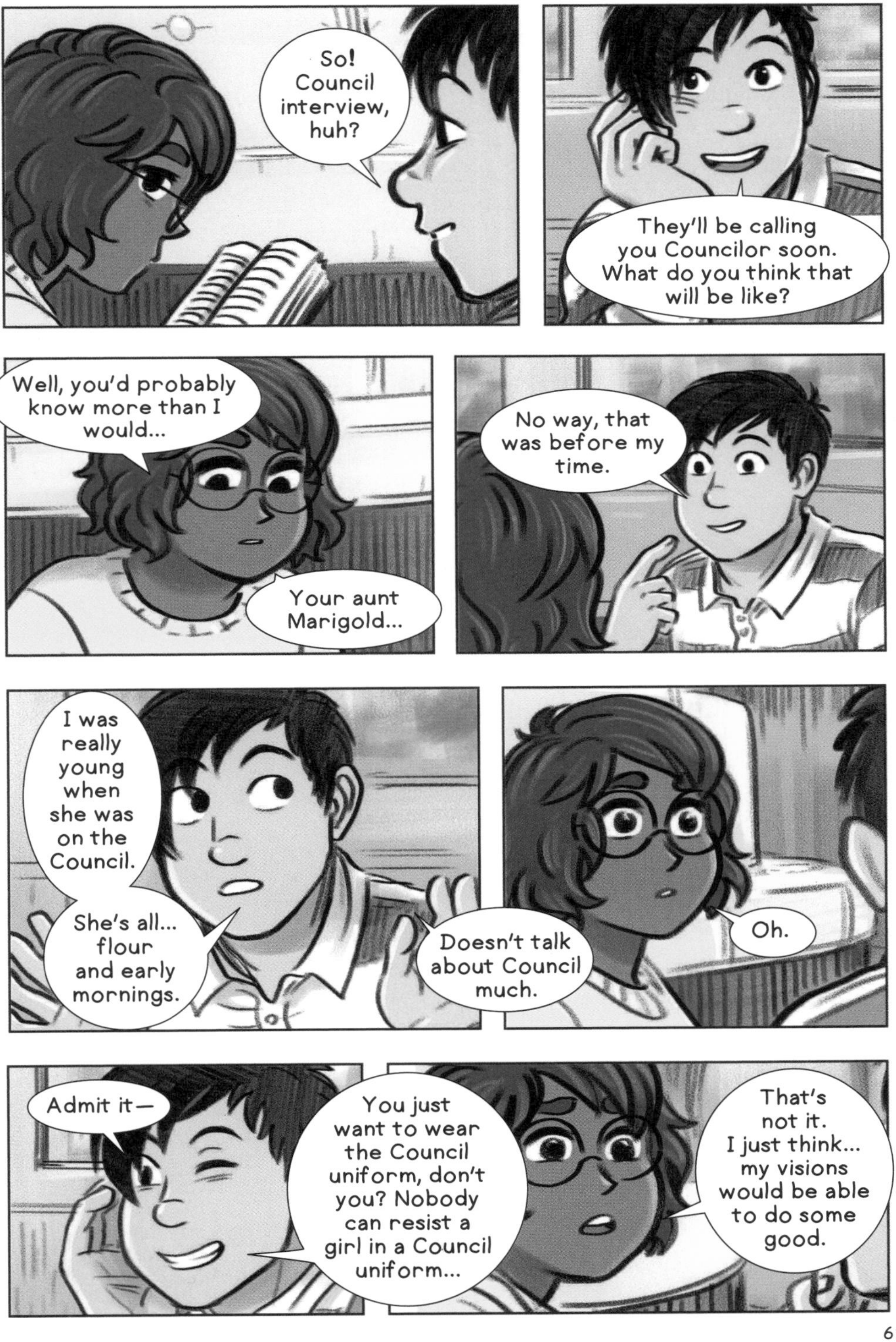
So! Council interview, huh?
They'll be calling you Councilor soon. What do you think that will be like?
Well, you'd probably know more than I would...
Your aunt Marigold...
No way, that was before my time.
I was really young when she was on the Council.
She's all... flour and early mornings.
Doesn't talk about Council much.
Oh.
Admit it—
You just want to wear the Council uniform, don't you? Nobody can resist a girl in a Council uniform...
That's not it. I just think... my visions would be able to do some good.

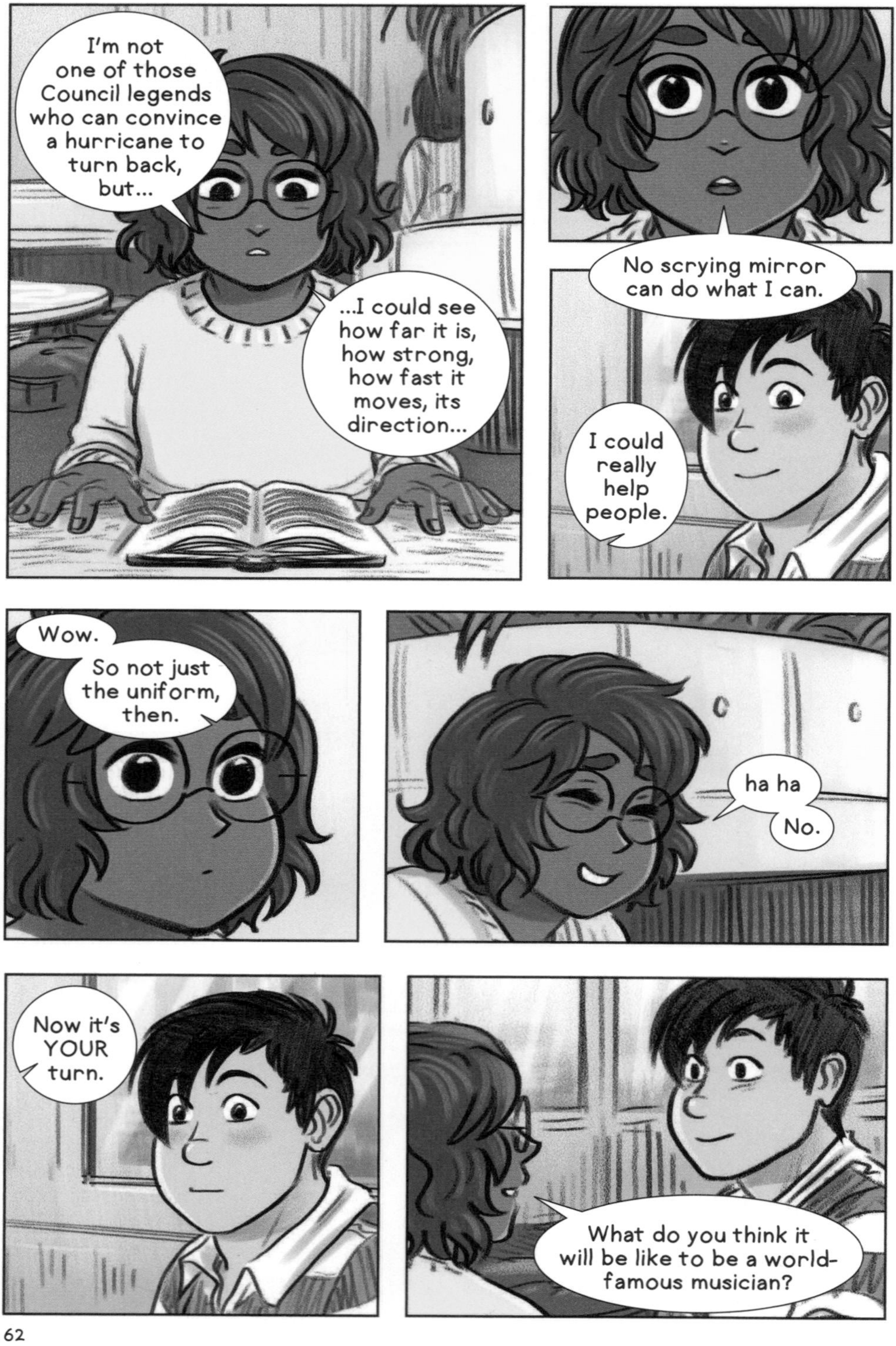
I'm not one of those Council legends who can convince a hurricane to turn back, but...
...I could see how far it is, how strong, how fast it moves, its direction...
No scrying mirror can do what I can.
I could really help people.
Wow.
So not just the uniform, then.
ha ha
No.
Now it's YOUR turn.
What do you think it will be like to be a world-famous musician?

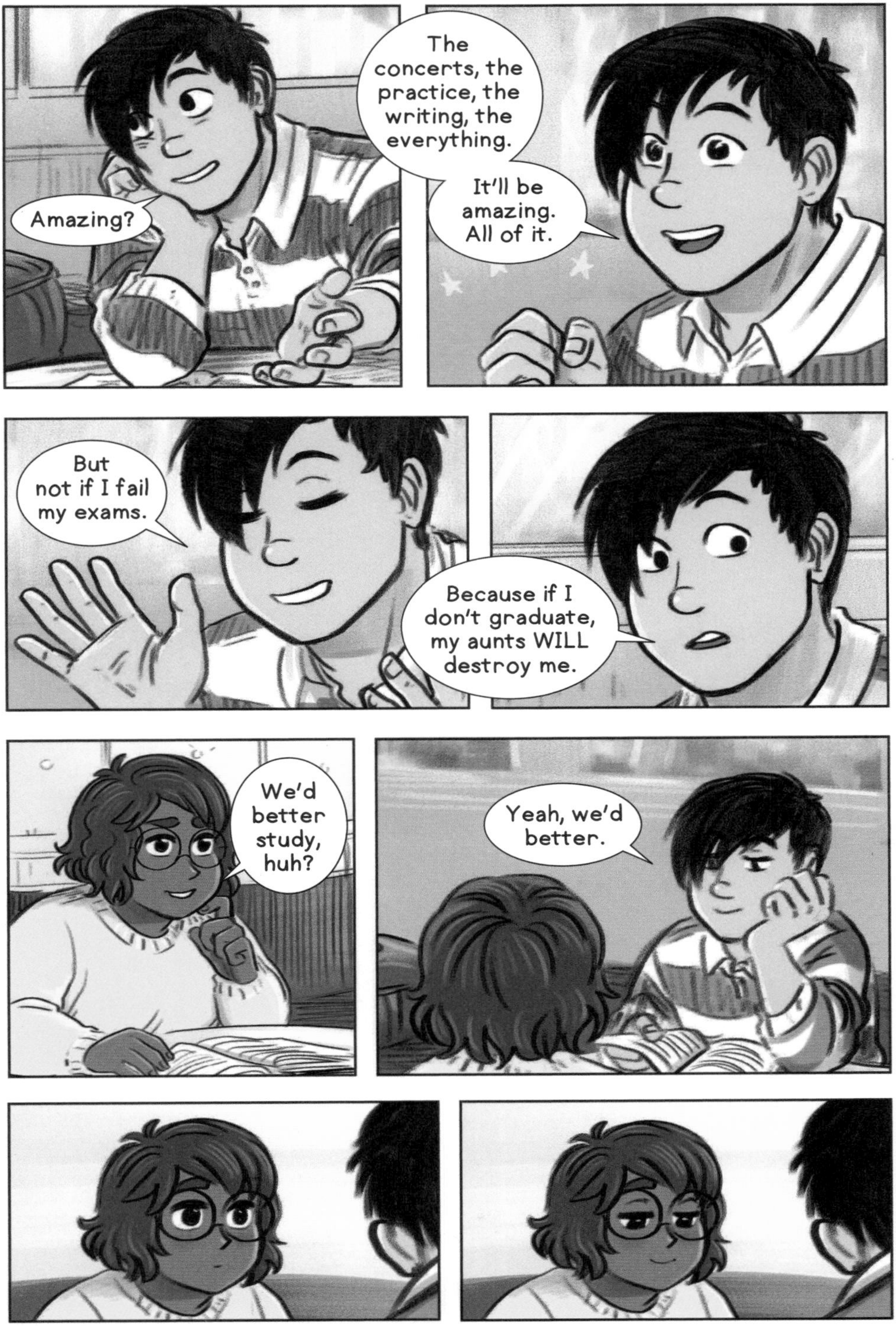

Amazing?
The concerts, the practice, the writing, the everything.
It'll be amazing. All of it.
But not if I fail my exams.
Because if I don't graduate, my aunts WILL destroy me.
We'd better study, huh?
Yeah, we'd better.

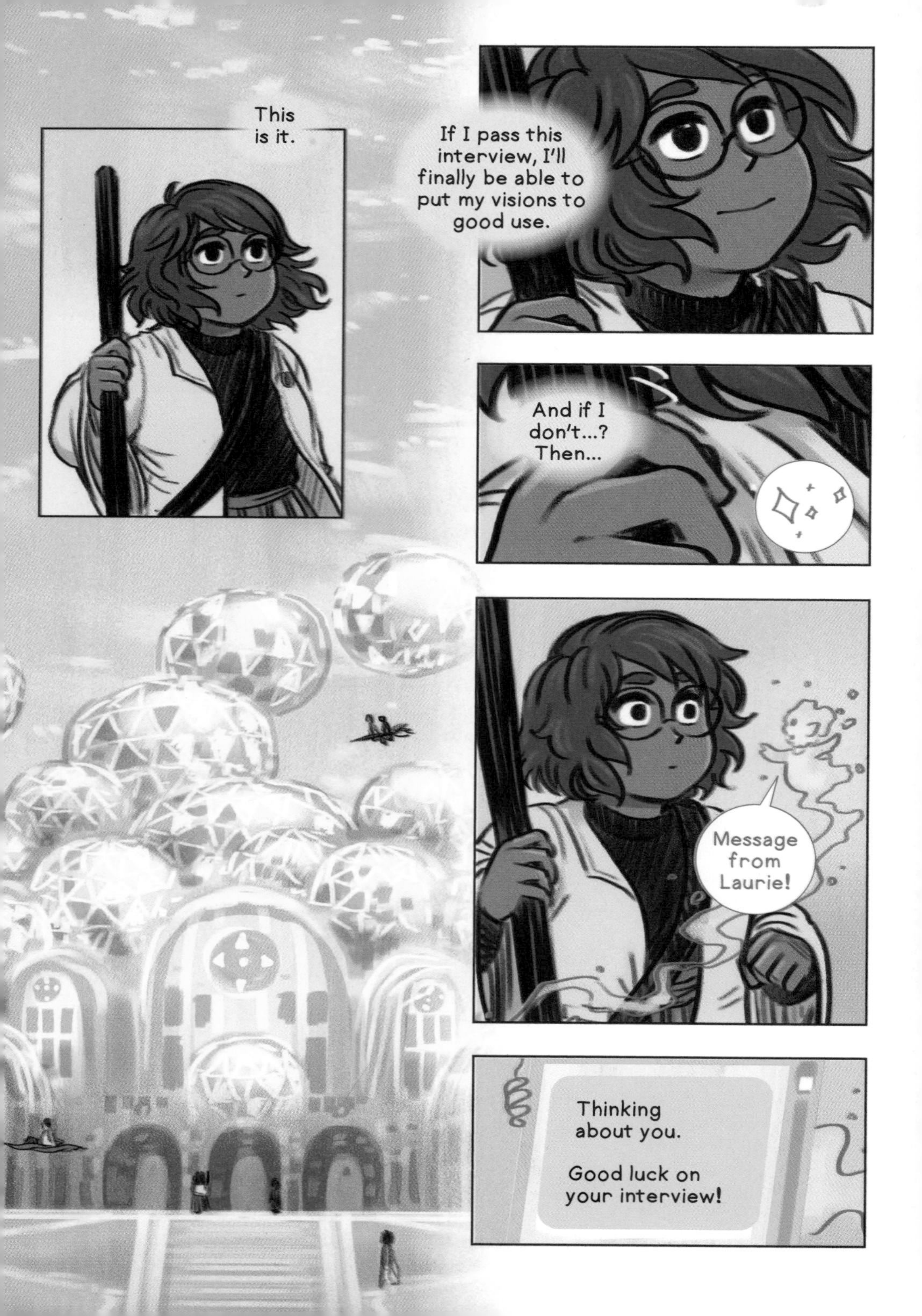
This is it.
If I pass this interview, I'll finally be able to put my visions to good use.
And if I don't...? Then...
Message from Laurie!
Thinking about you.
Good luck on your interview!

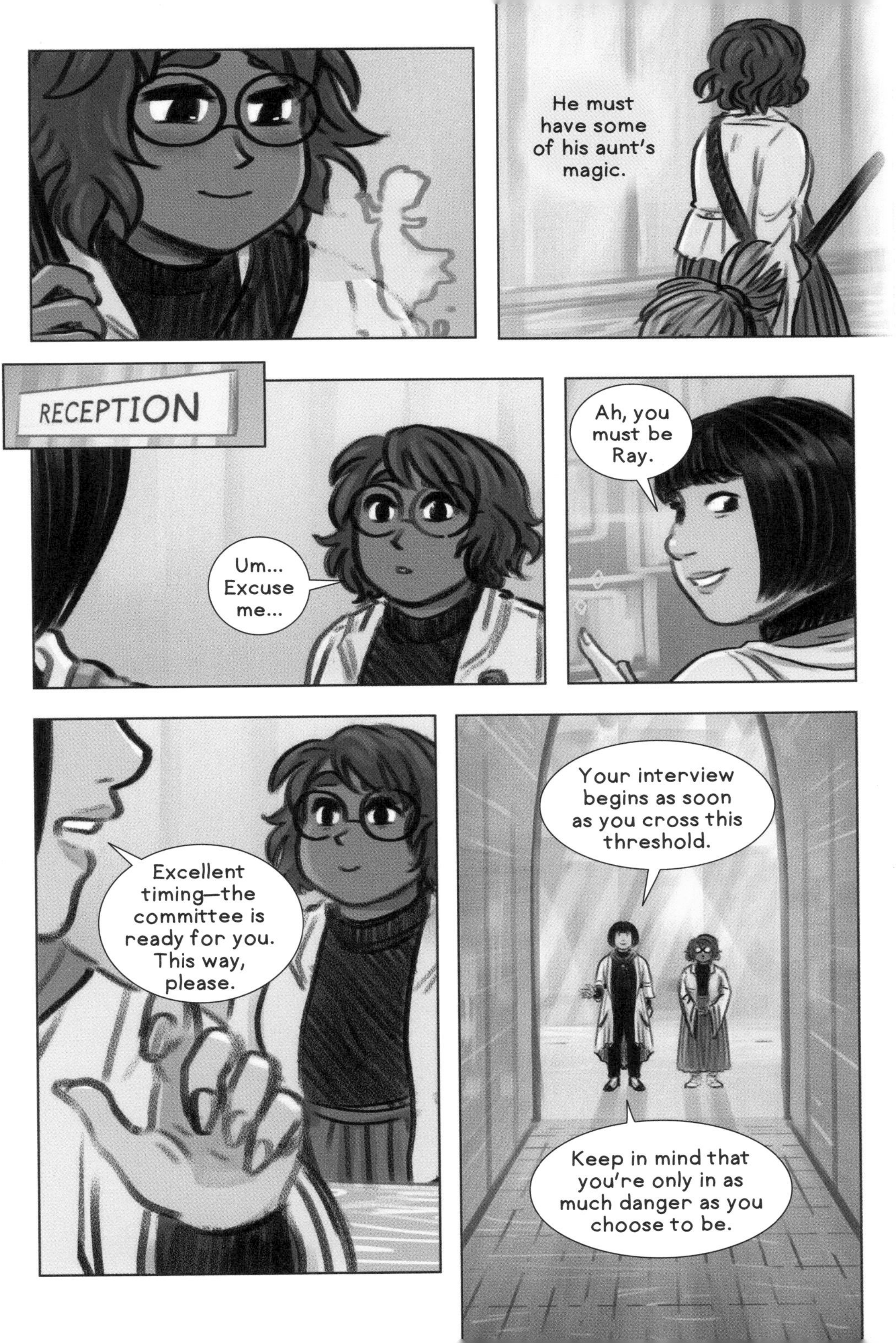
He must have some of his aunt's magic.
RECEPTION
Um... Excuse me...
Ah, you must be Ray.
Excellent timing—the committee is ready for you. This way, please.
Your interview begins as soon as you cross this threshold.
Keep in mind that you're only in as much danger as you choose to be.

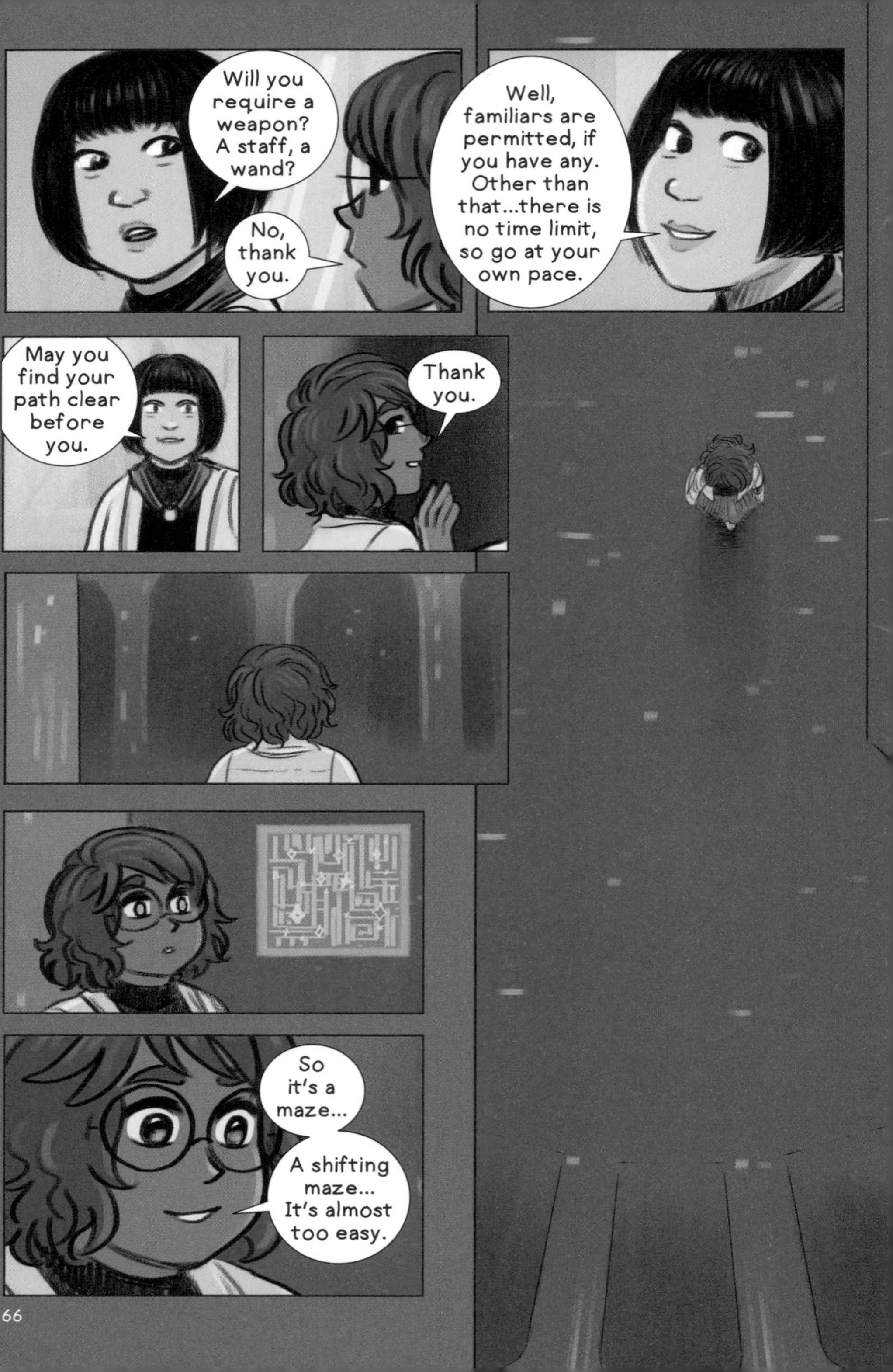

Will you require a weapon? A staff, a wand?
No, thank you.
Well, familiars are permitted, if you have any. Other than that...there is no time limit, so go at your own pace.
May you find your path clear before you.
Thank you.
So it's a maze...
A shifting maze... It's almost too easy.

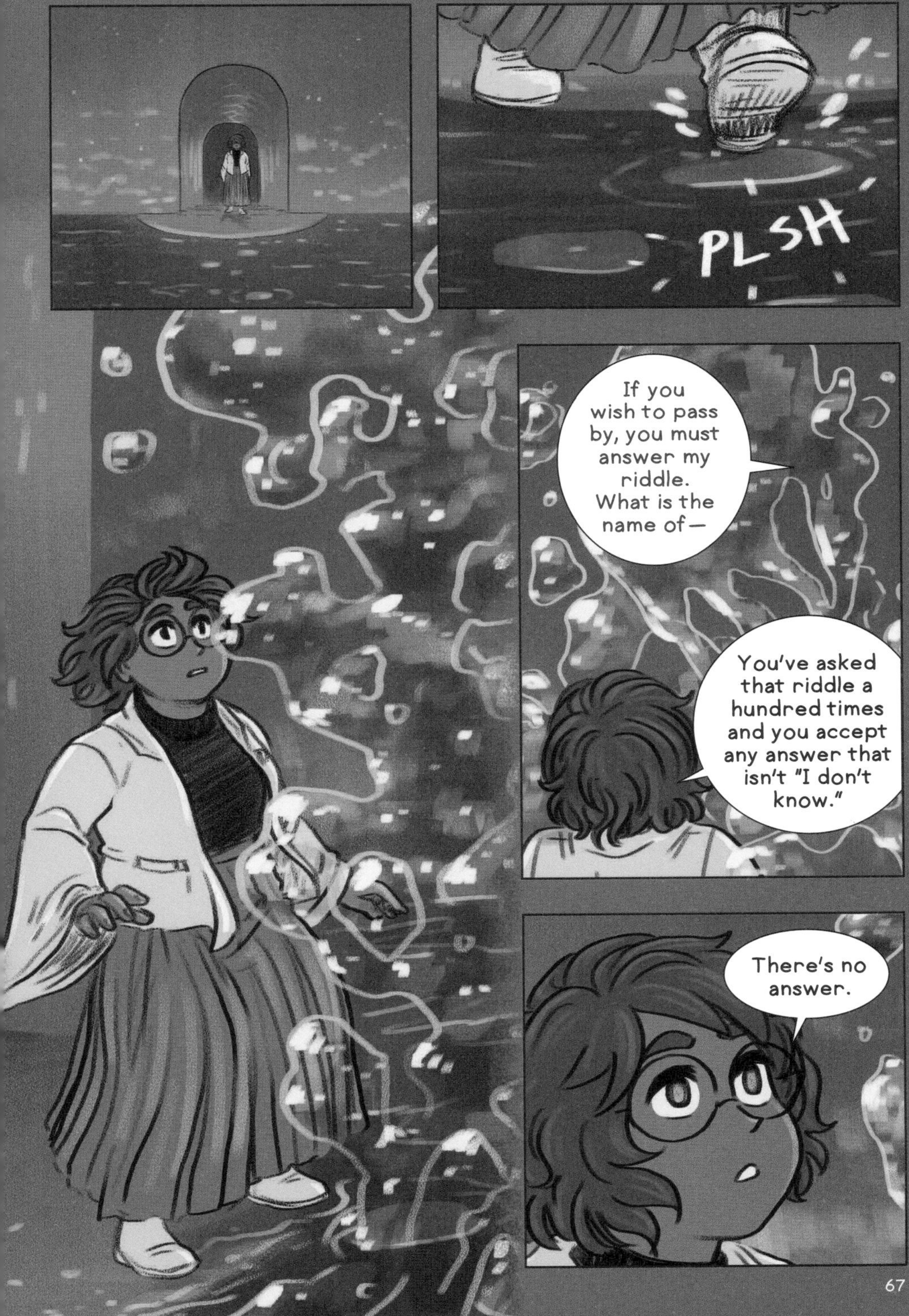
PLSH
If you wish to pass by, you must answer my riddle. What is the name of—
You've asked that riddle a hundred times and you accept any answer that isn't "I don't know."
There's no answer.

Isn't there?

PLSH

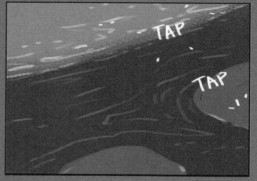

TAP

TAP

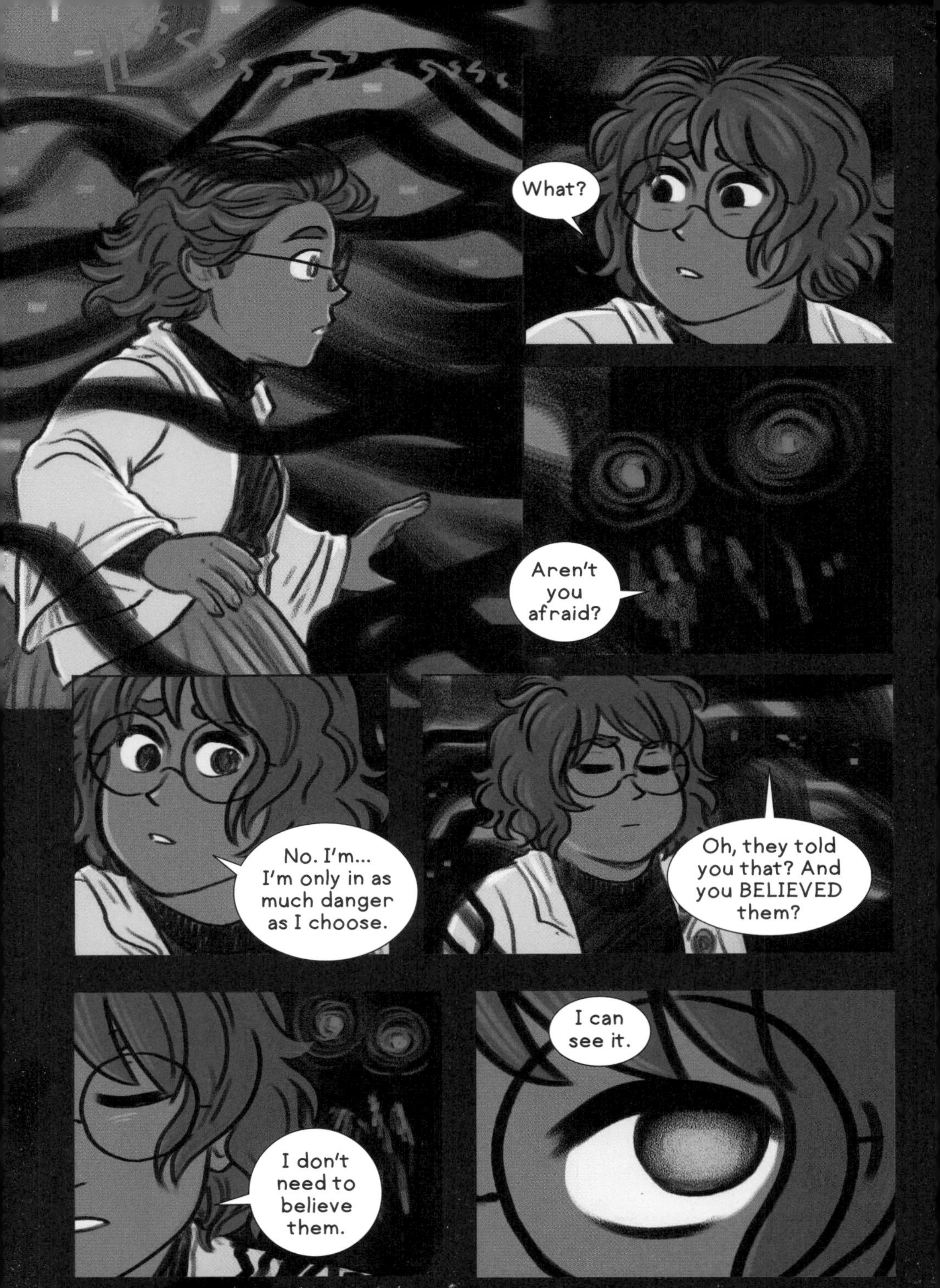

What?
Aren't you afraid?
No. I'm... I'm only in as much danger as I choose.
Oh, they told you that? And you BELIEVED them?
I don't need to believe them.
I can see it.

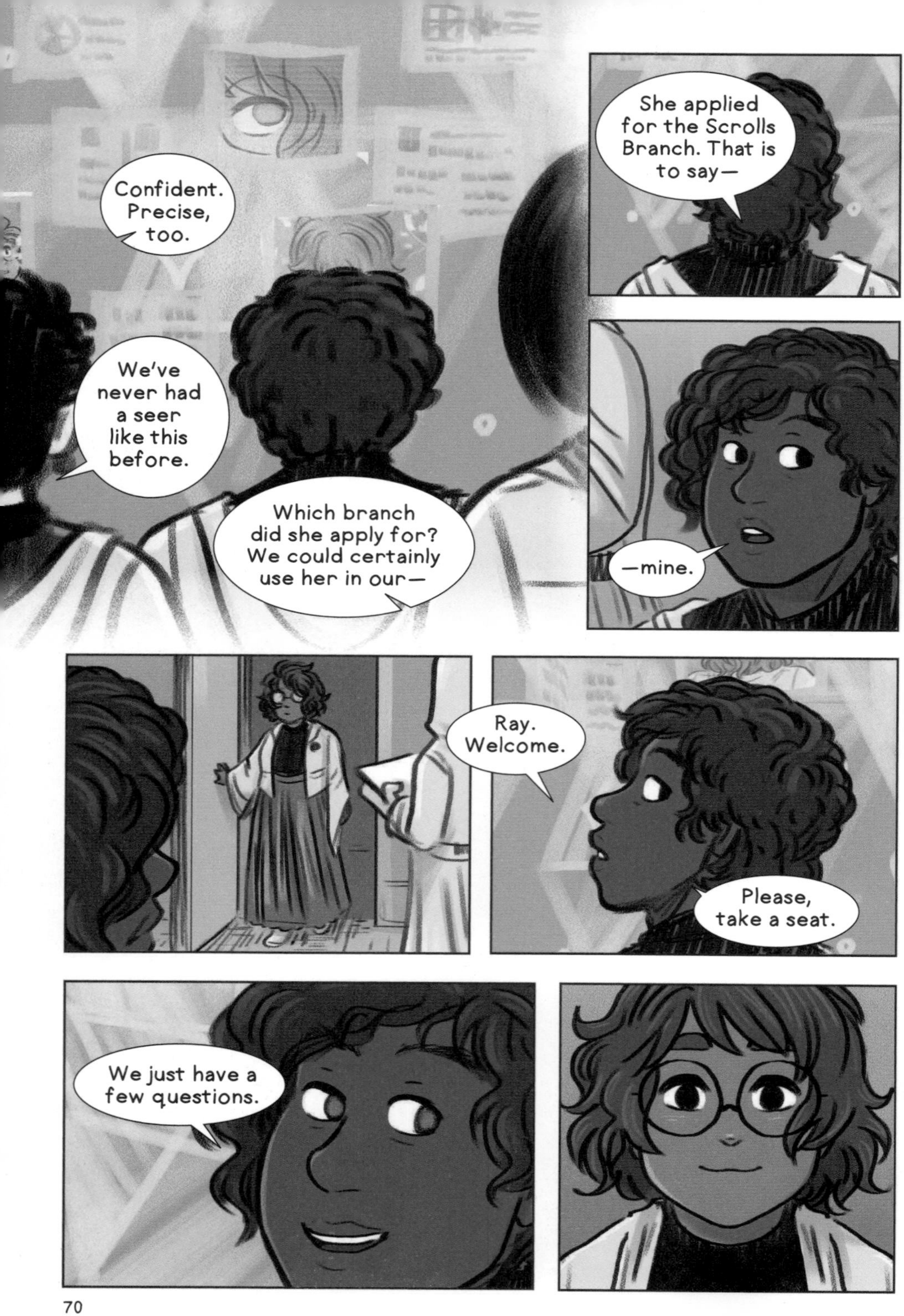
Confident. Precise, too.
We've never had a seer like this before.
Which branch did she apply for? We could certainly use her in our—
She applied for the Scrolls Branch. That is to say—
—mine.
Ray. Welcome.
Please, take a seat.
We just have a few questions.

CHAPTER 5

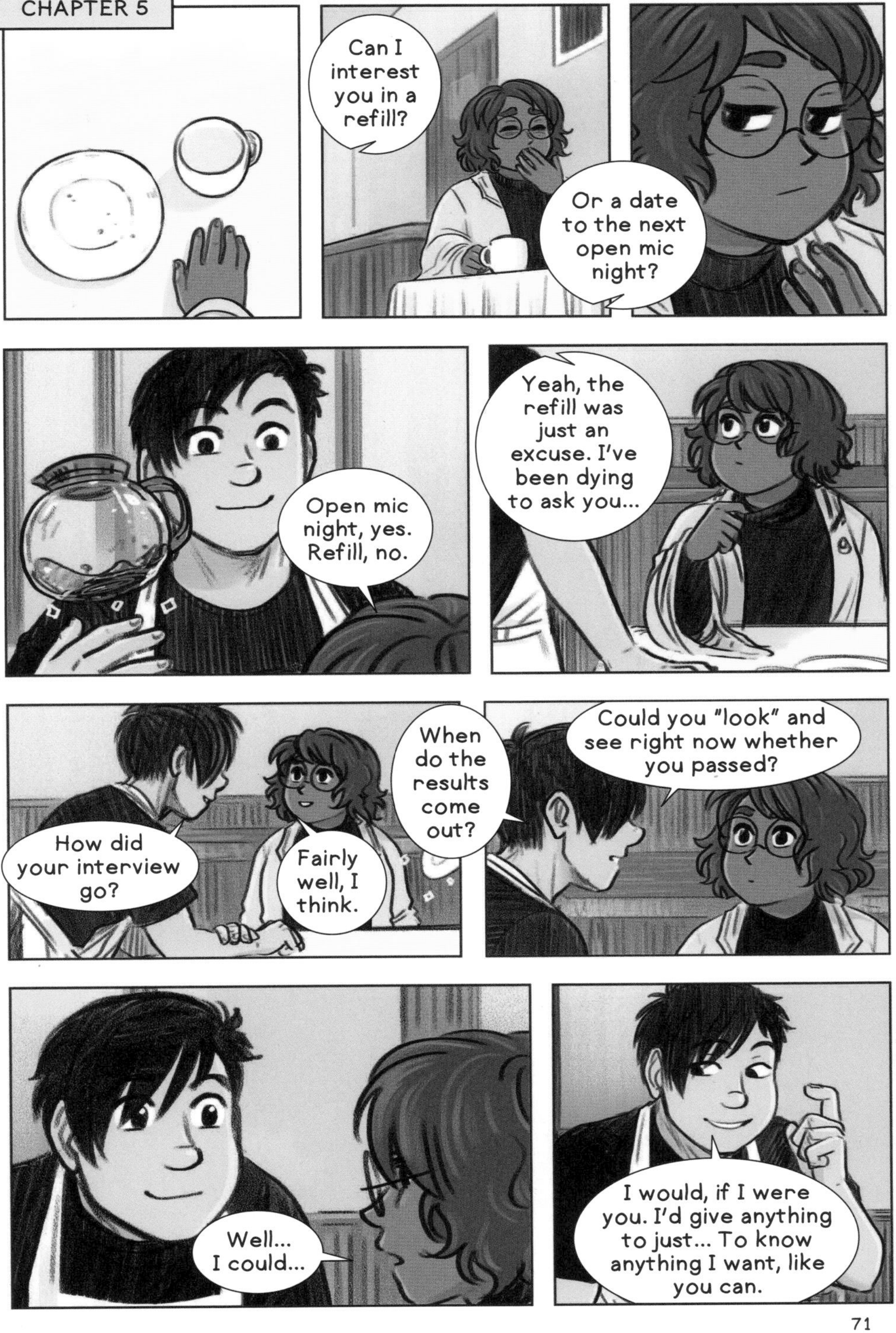
Can I interest you in a refill?
Or a date to the next open mic night?
Open mic night, yes. Refill, no.
Yeah, the refill was just an excuse. I've been dying to ask you...
How did your interview go?
Fairly well, I think.
When do the results come out?
Could you "look" and see right now whether you passed?
Well... I could...
I would, if I were you. I'd give anything to just... To know anything I want, like you can.

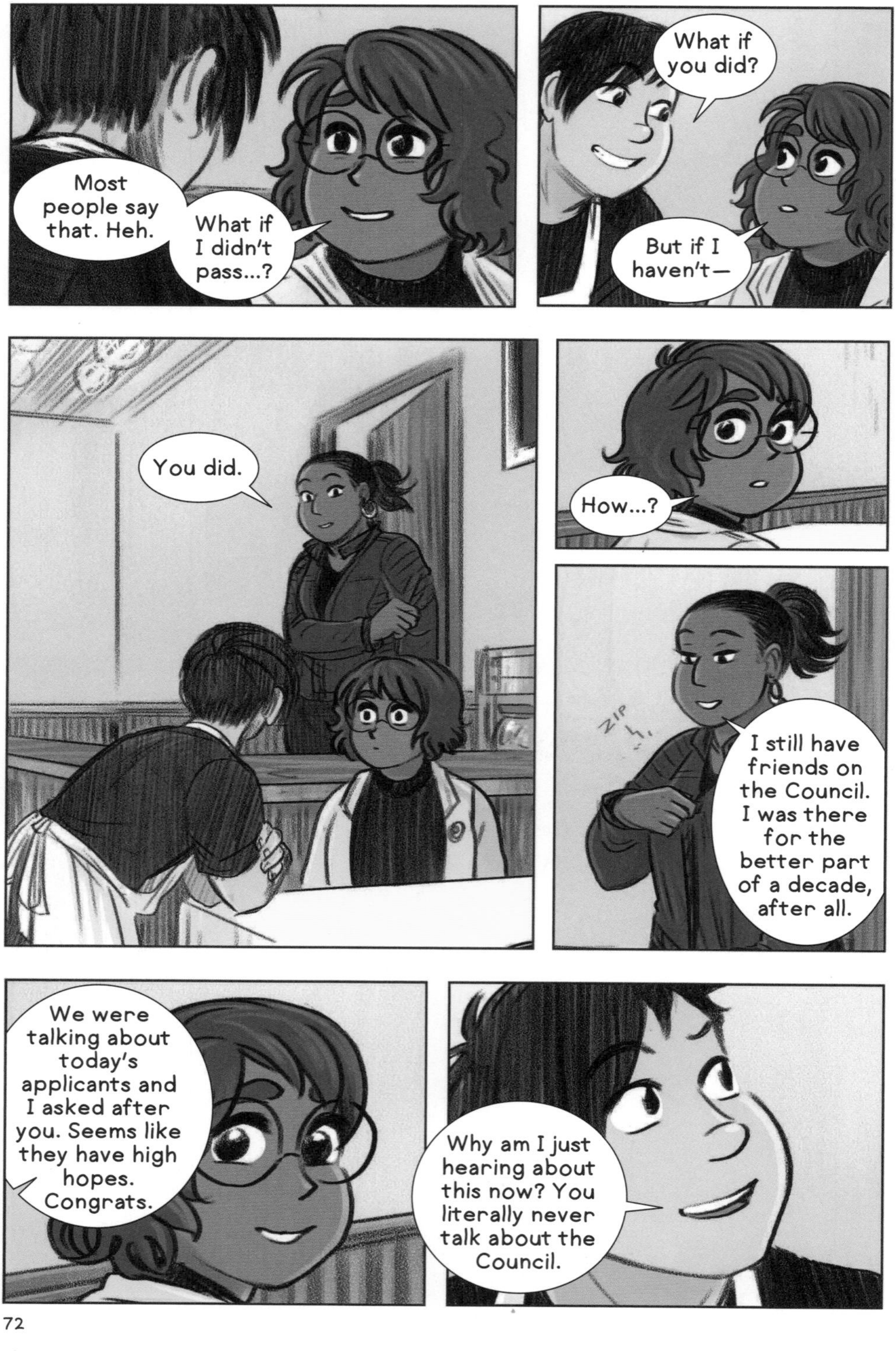

Most people say that. Heh.
What if I didn't pass...?
What if you did?
But if I haven't—
You did.
How...?
ZIP
I still have friends on the Council. I was there for the better part of a decade, after all.
We were talking about today's applicants and I asked after you. Seems like they have high hopes. Congrats.
Why am I just hearing about this now? You literally never talk about the Council.

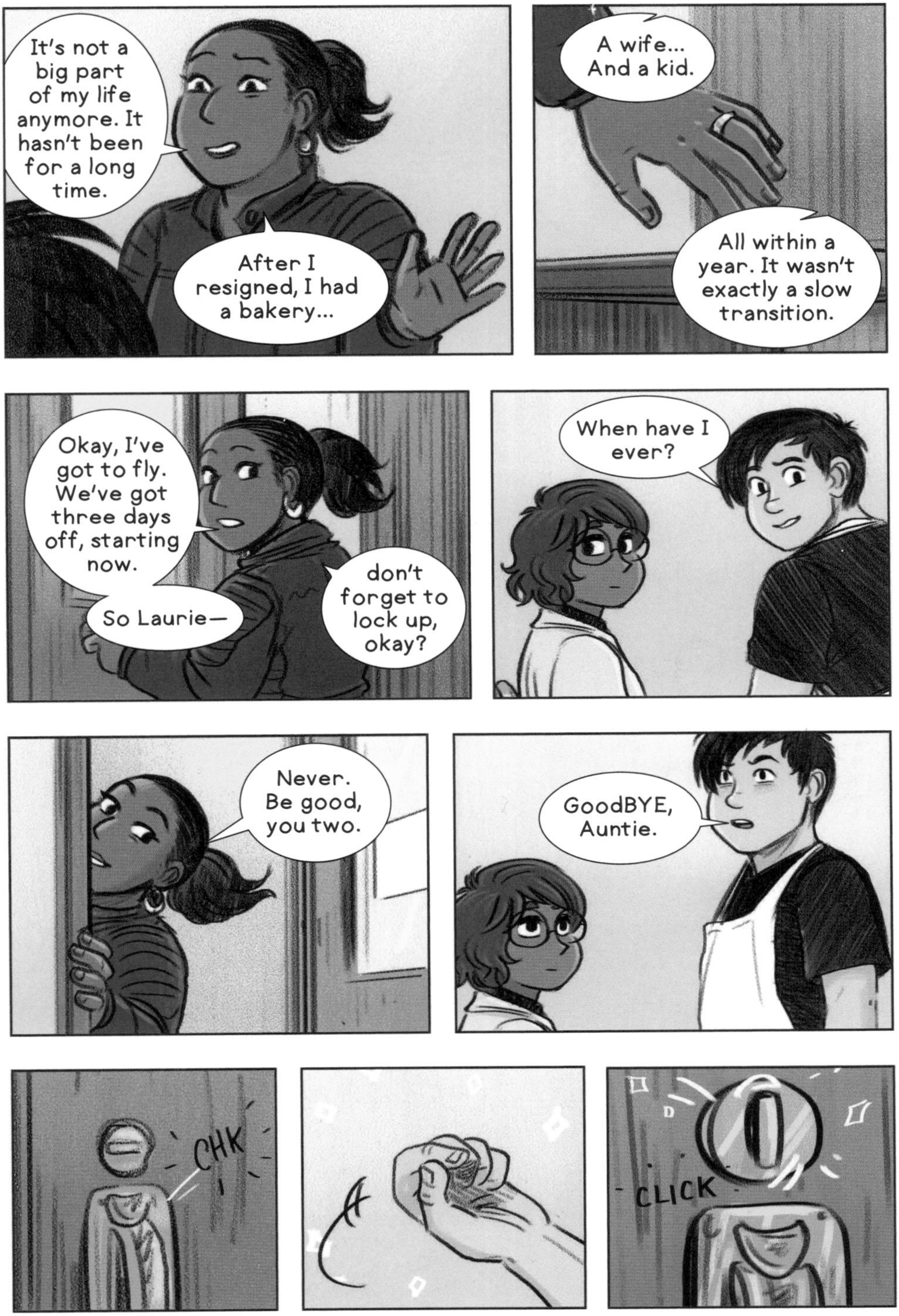
It's not a big part of my life anymore. It hasn't been for a long time.
After I resigned, I had a bakery...
A wife... And a kid.
All within a year. It wasn't exactly a slow transition.
Okay, I've got to fly. We've got three days off, starting now.
So Laurie—
don't forget to lock up, okay?
When have I ever?
Never. Be good, you two.
GoodBYE, Auntie.
CHK
CLICK

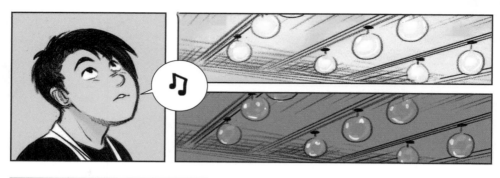

♪

Now I just need my jacket. Come on out back.

So this is where her magic happens.

You really admire her, don't you?

Of course! Your aunt—she makes incredible things. And she always looks so pleased to be doing it.

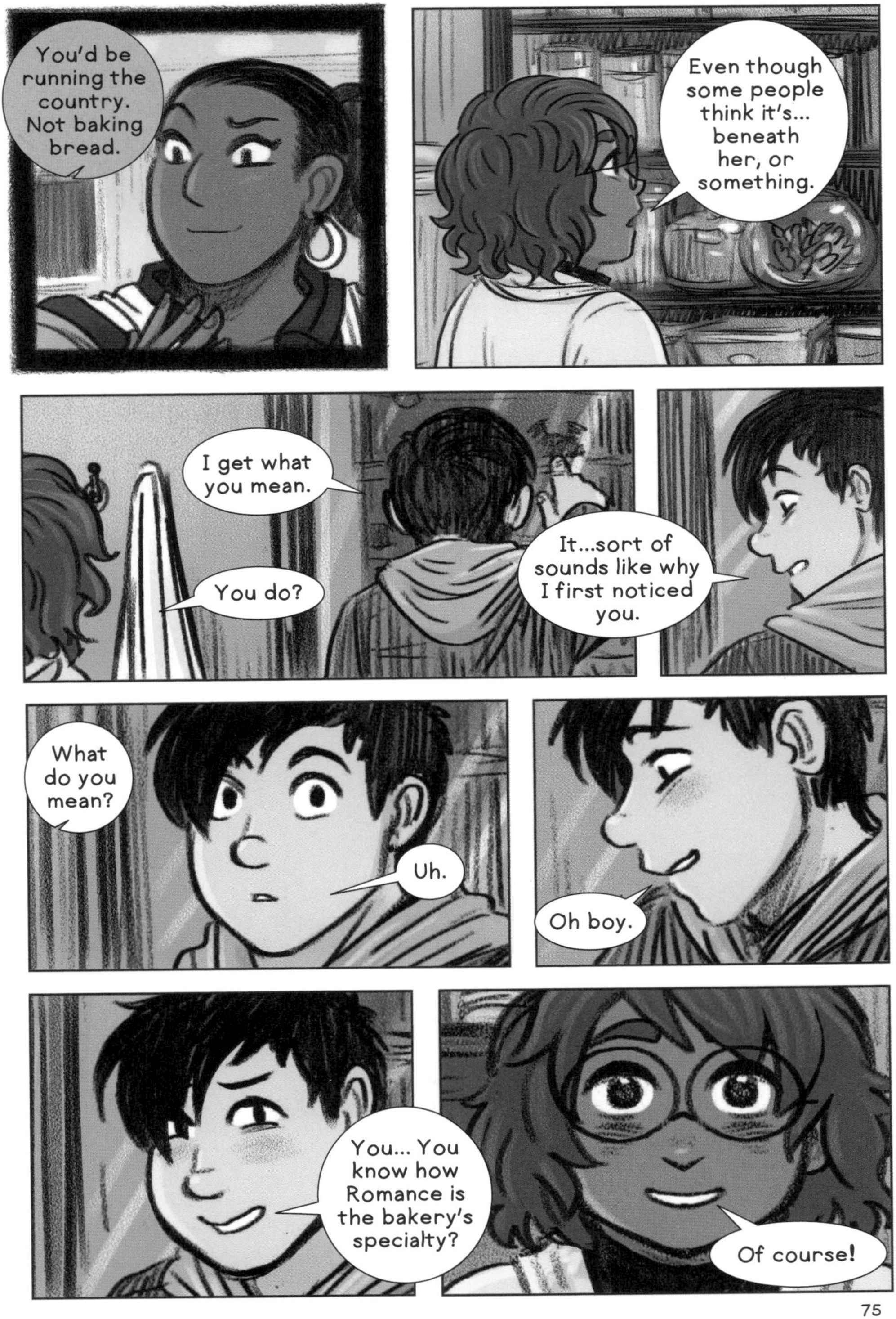
You'd be running the country. Not baking bread.
Even though some people think it's... beneath her, or something.
I get what you mean.
You do?
It...sort of sounds like why I first noticed you.
What do you mean?
Uh.
Oh boy.
You... You know how Romance is the bakery's specialty?
Of course!

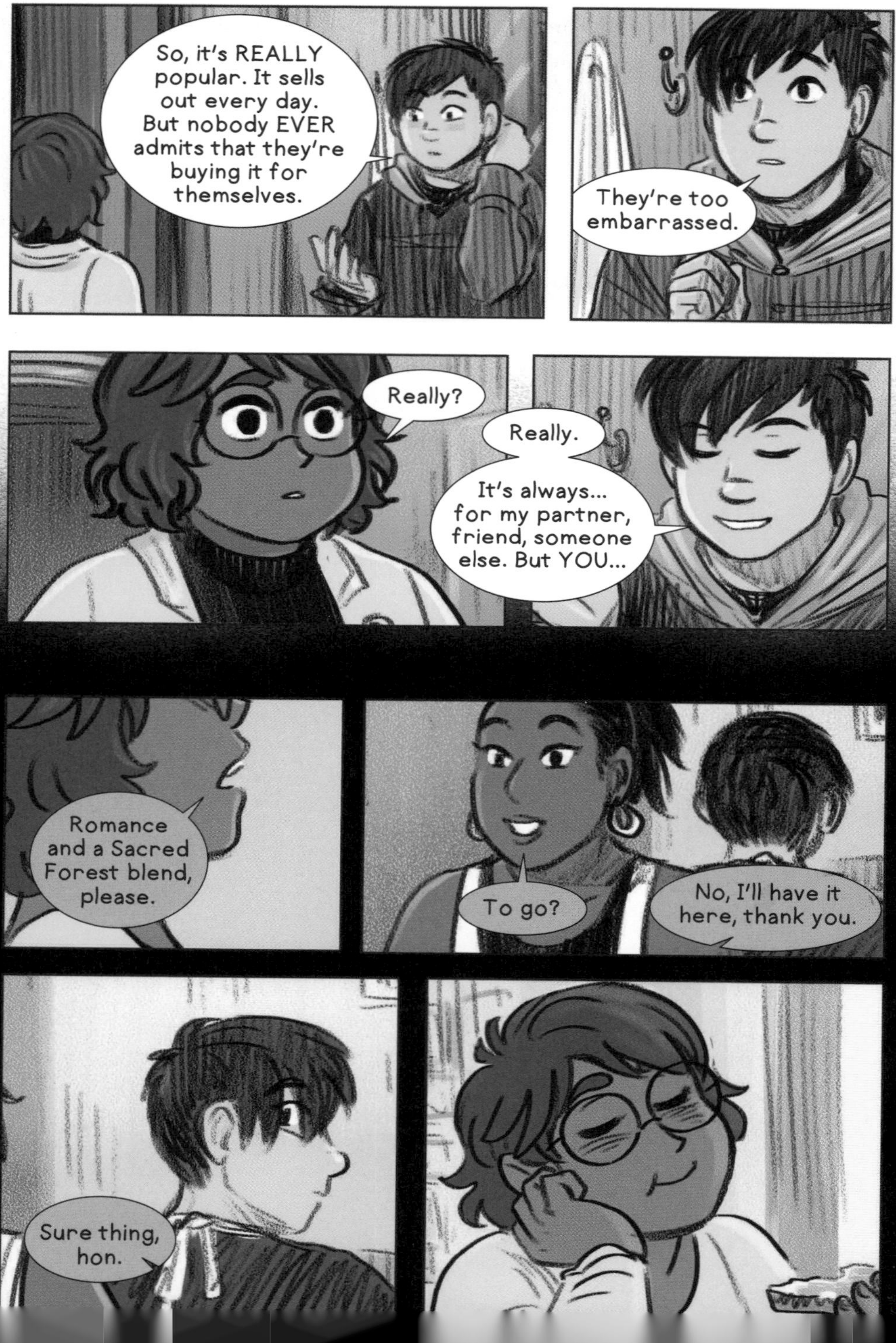
So, it's REALLY popular. It sells out every day. But nobody EVER admits that they're buying it for themselves.
They're too embarrassed.
Really?
Really.
It's always... for my partner, friend, someone else. But YOU...
Romance and a Sacred Forest blend, please.
To go?
No, I'll have it here, thank you.
Sure thing, hon.

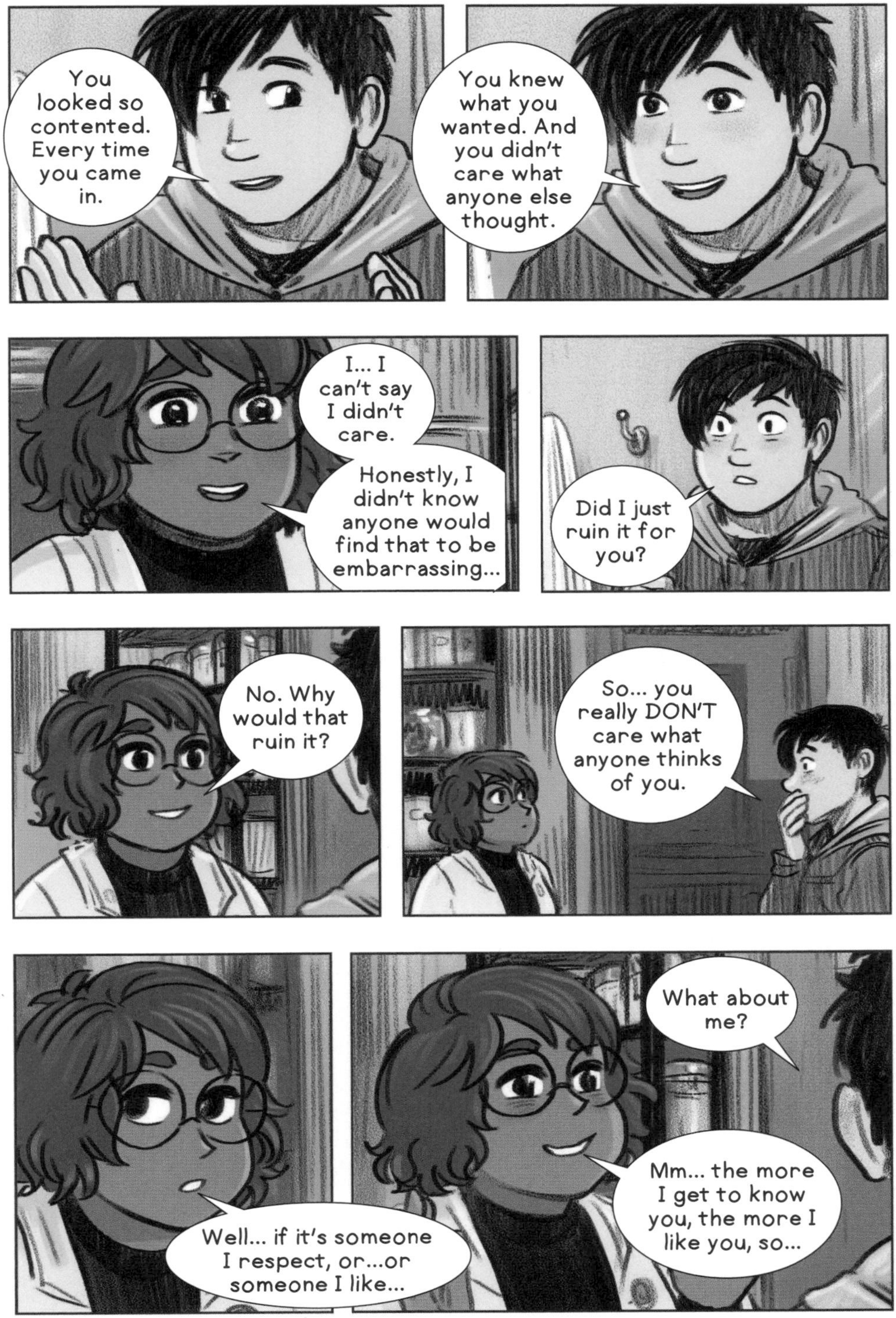

You looked so contented. Every time you came in.
You knew what you wanted. And you didn't care what anyone else thought.
I... I can't say I didn't care.
Honestly, I didn't know anyone would find that to be embarrassing...
Did I just ruin it for you?
No. Why would that ruin it?
So... you really DON'T care what anyone thinks of you.
Well... if it's someone I respect, or...or someone I like...
What about me?
Mm... the more I get to know you, the more I like you, so...

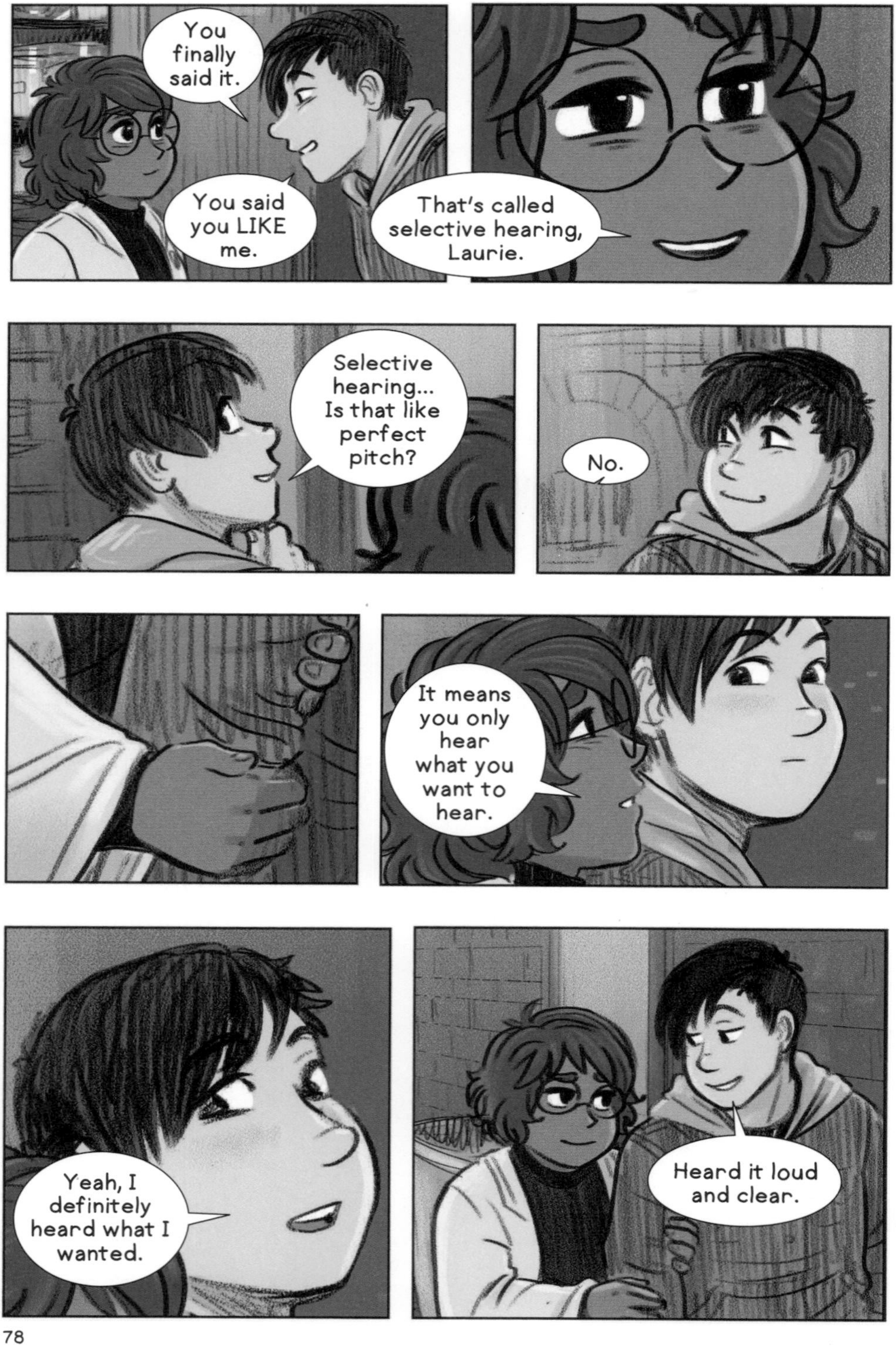
You finally said it.
You said you LIKE me.
That's called selective hearing, Laurie.
Selective hearing... Is that like perfect pitch?
No.
It means you only hear what you want to hear.
Yeah, I definitely heard what I wanted.
Heard it loud and clear.

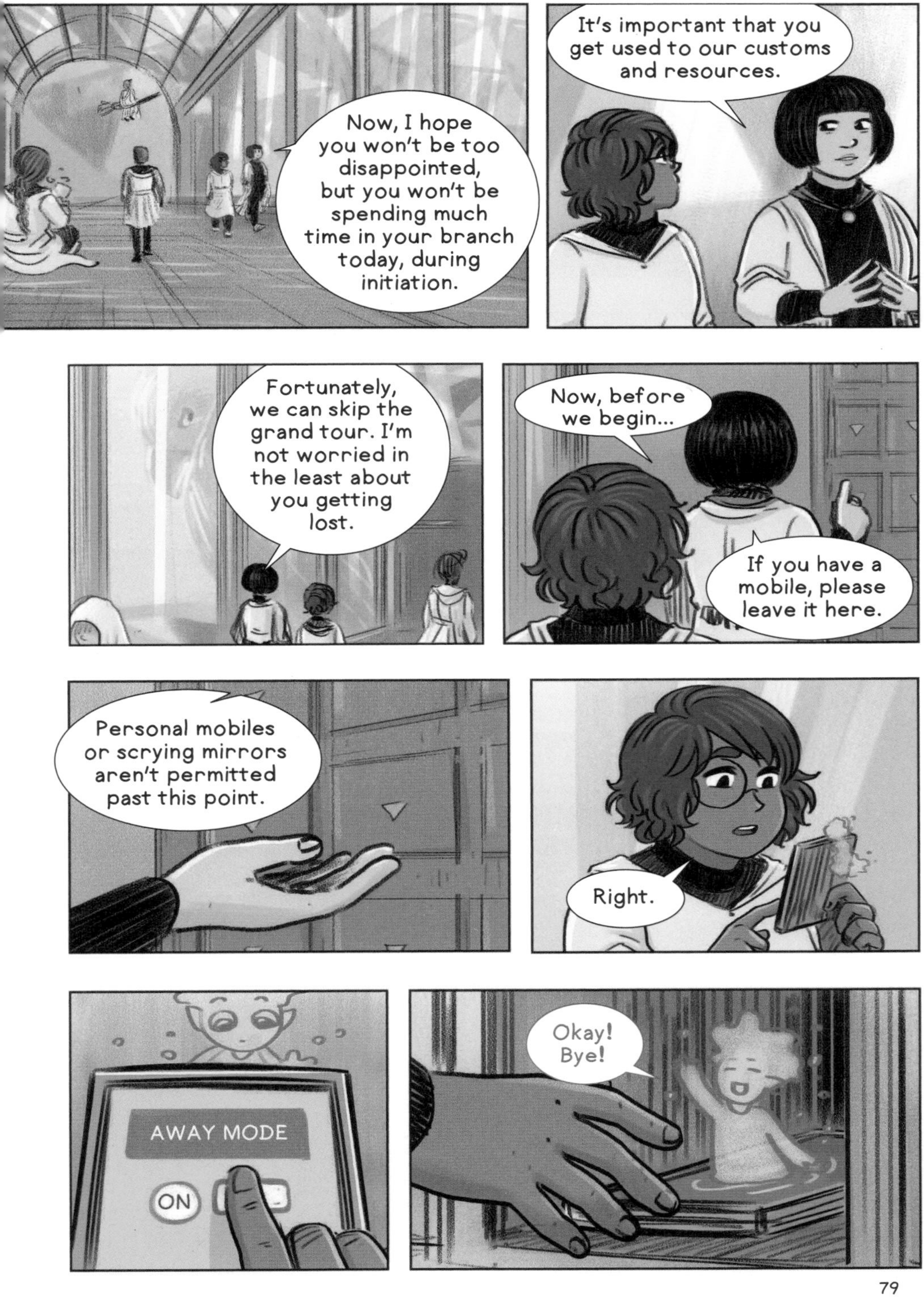
Now, I hope you won't be too disappointed, but you won't be spending much time in your branch today, during initiation.
It's important that you get used to our customs and resources.
Fortunately, we can skip the grand tour. I'm not worried in the least about you getting lost.
Now, before we begin...
If you have a mobile, please leave it here.
Personal mobiles or scrying mirrors aren't permitted past this point.
Right.
AWAY MODE
ON
Okay! Bye!

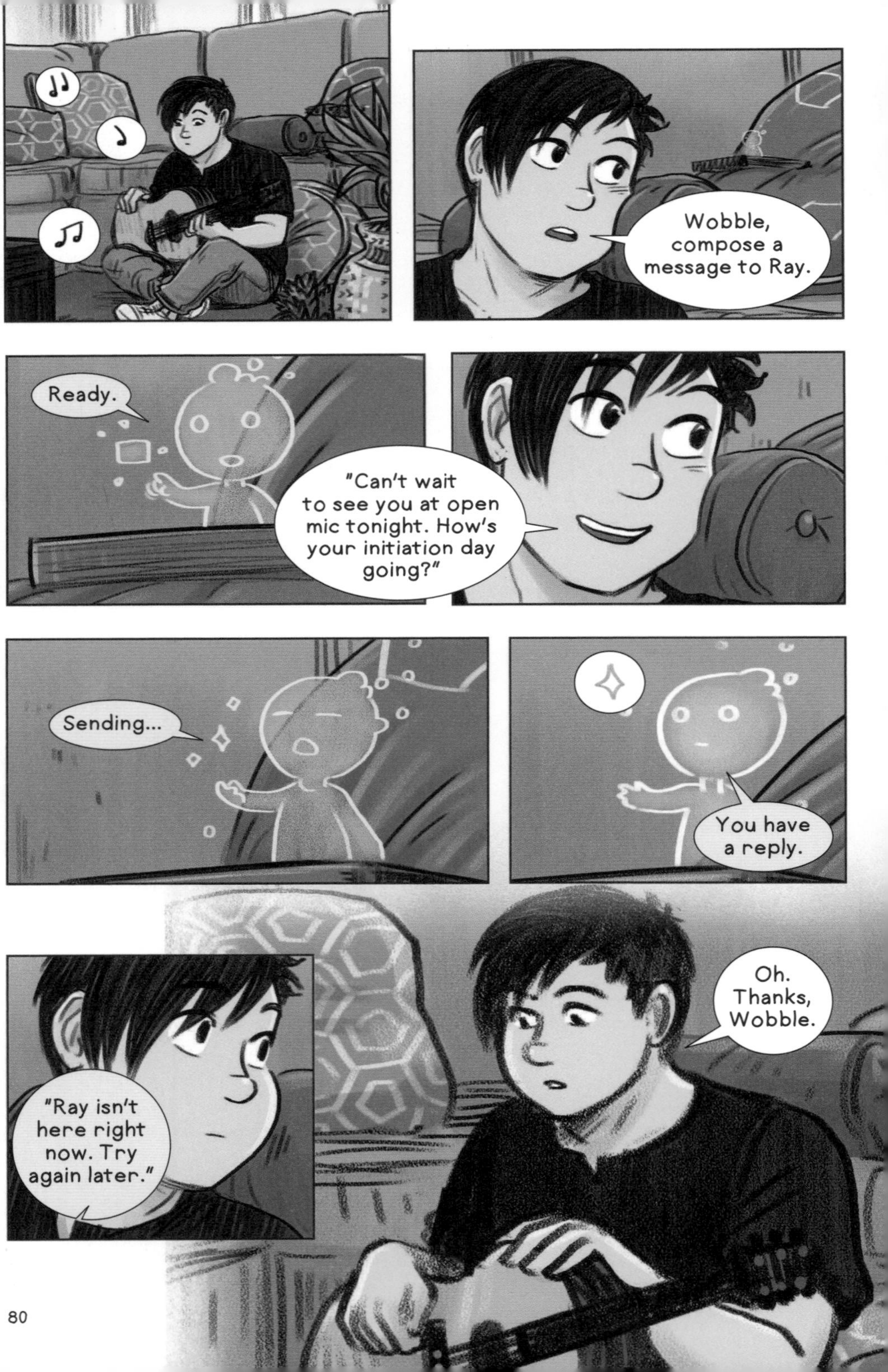
Wobble, compose a message to Ray.
Ready.
"Can't wait to see you at open mic tonight. How's your initiation day going?"
Sending...
You have a reply.
"Ray isn't here right now. Try again later."
Oh. Thanks, Wobble.

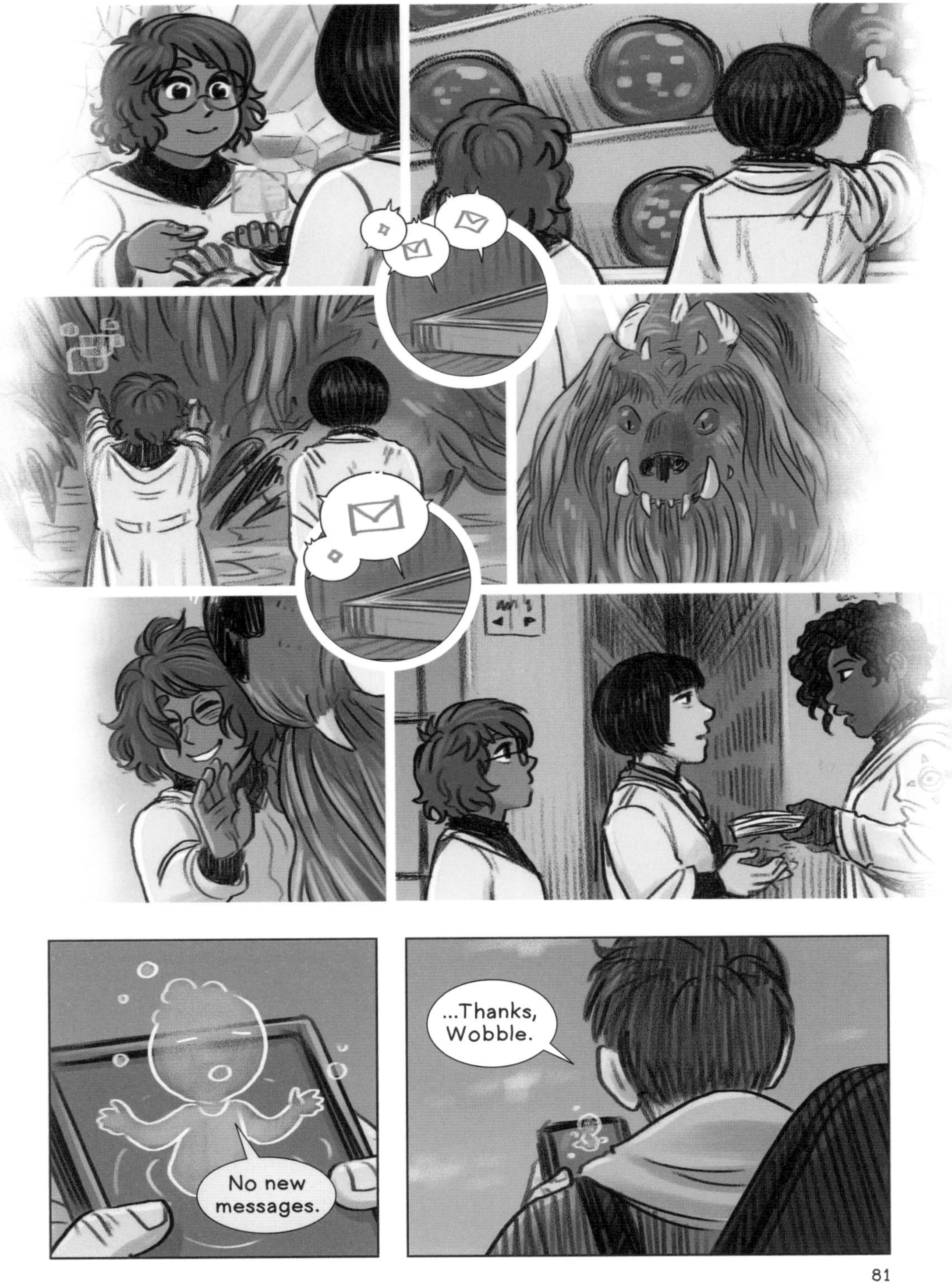
No new messages.
...Thanks, Wobble.

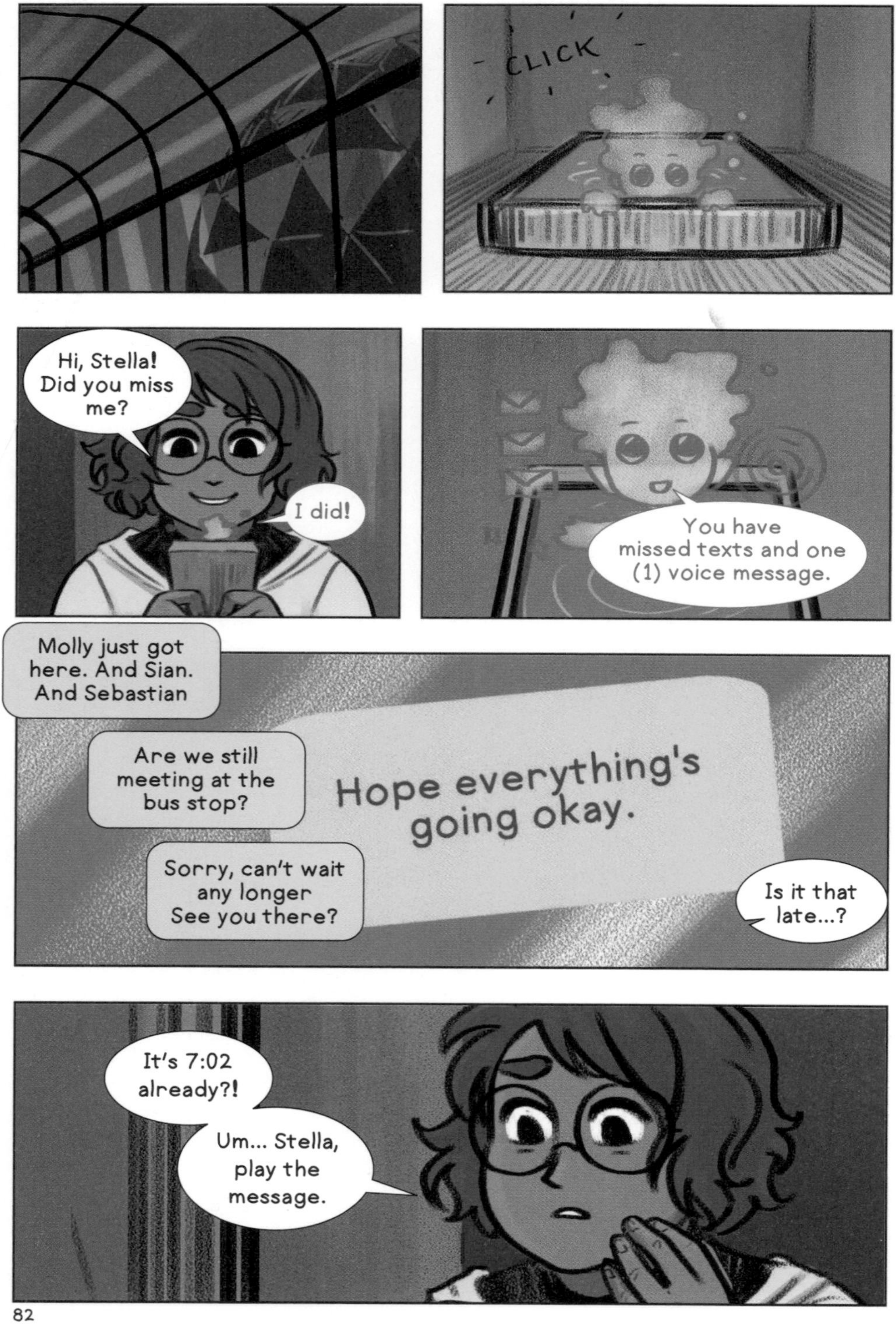
CLICK
Hi, Stella! Did you miss me?
I did!
You have missed texts and one (1) voice message.
Molly just got here. And Sian. And Sebastian
Are we still meeting at the bus stop?
Hope everything's going okay.
Sorry, can't wait any longer See you there?
Is it that late...?
It's 7:02 already?!
Um... Stella, play the message.

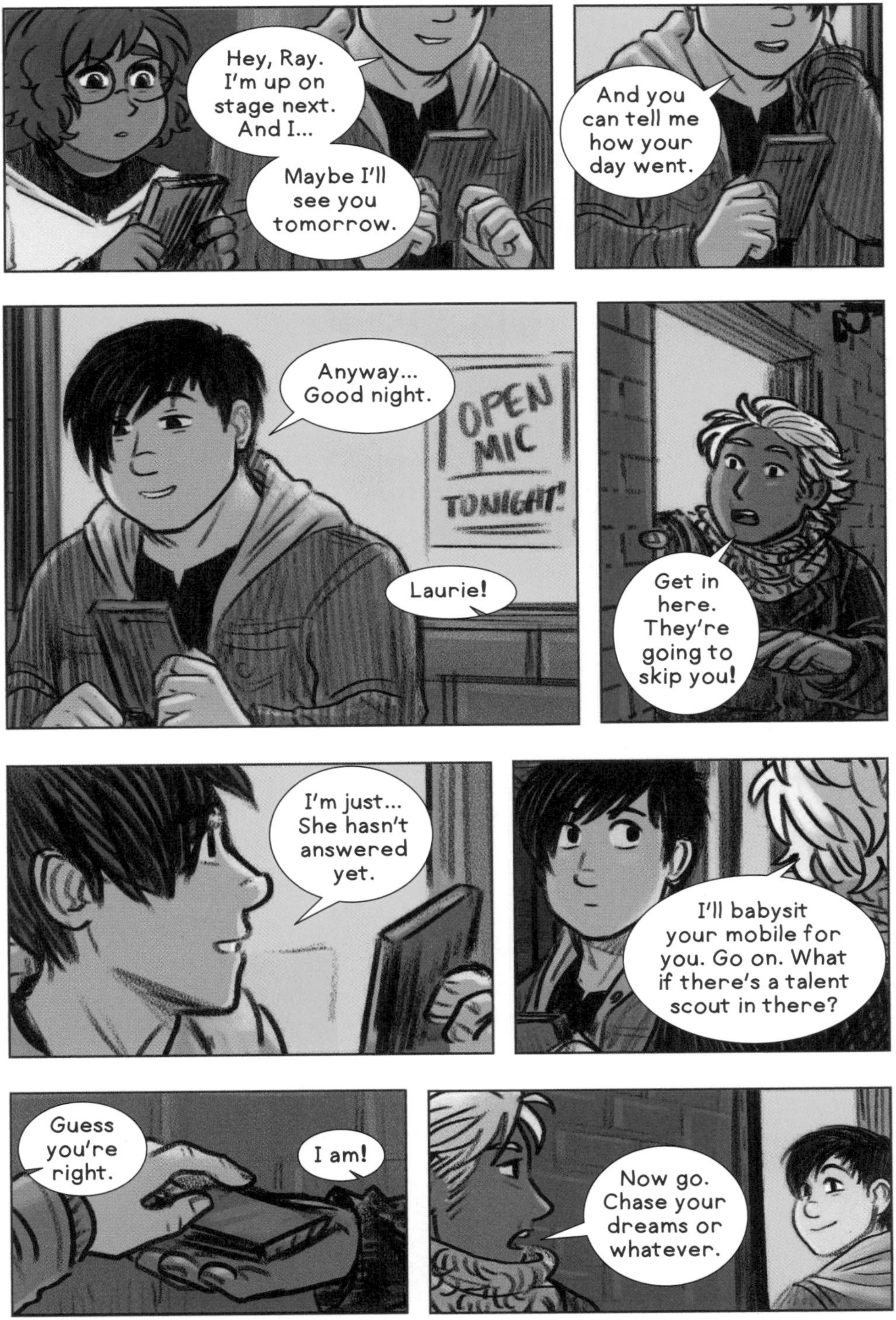
Hey, Ray. I'm up on stage next. And I...
Maybe I'll see you tomorrow.
And you can tell me how your day went.
Anyway... Good night.
OPEN MIC TONIGHT!
Laurie!
Get in here. They're going to skip you!
I'm just... She hasn't answered yet.
I'll babysit your mobile for you. Go on. What if there's a talent scout in there?
Guess you're right.
I am!
Now go. Chase your dreams or whatever.

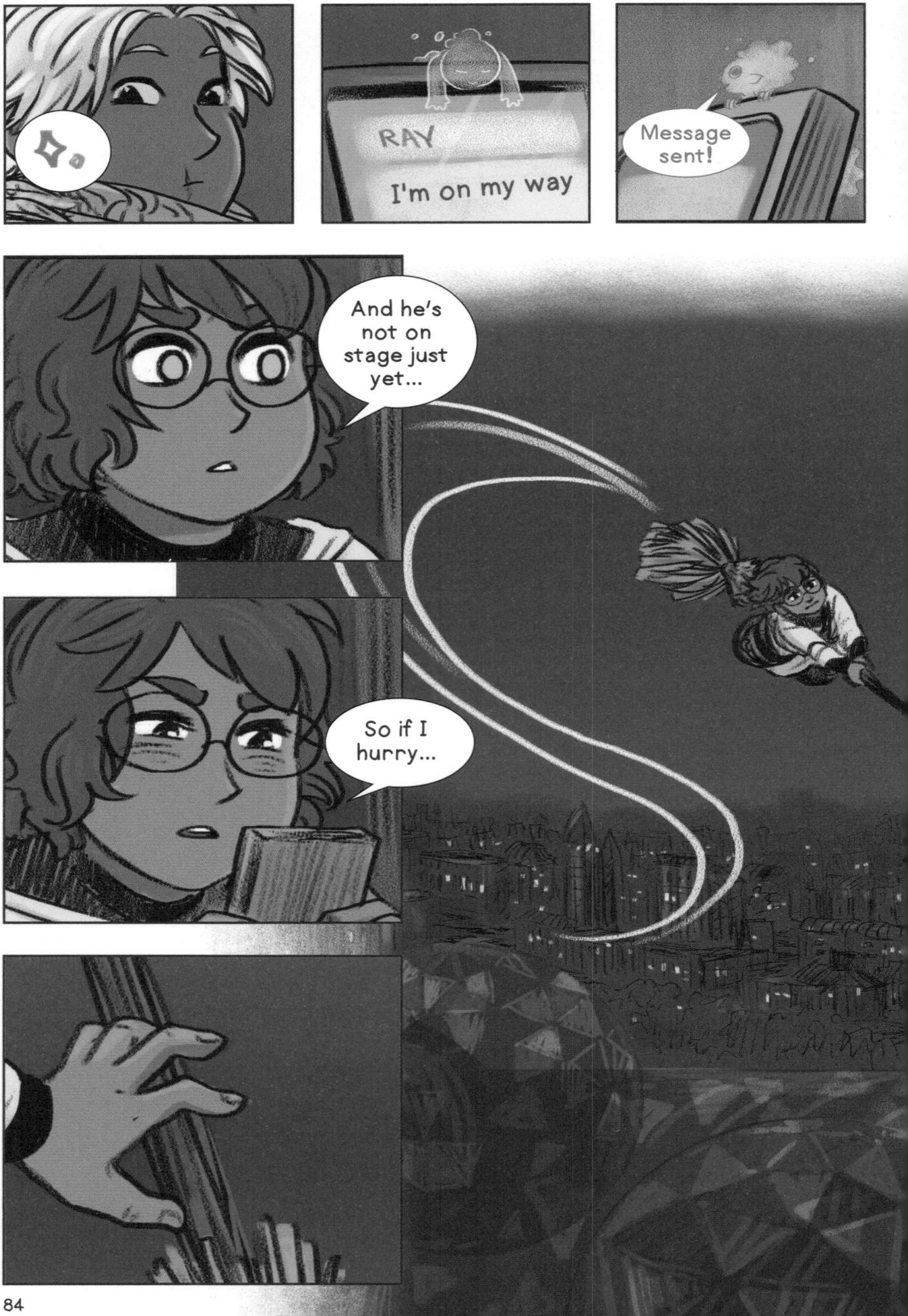
RAY
I'm on my way
Message sent!
And he's not on stage just yet...
So if I hurry...

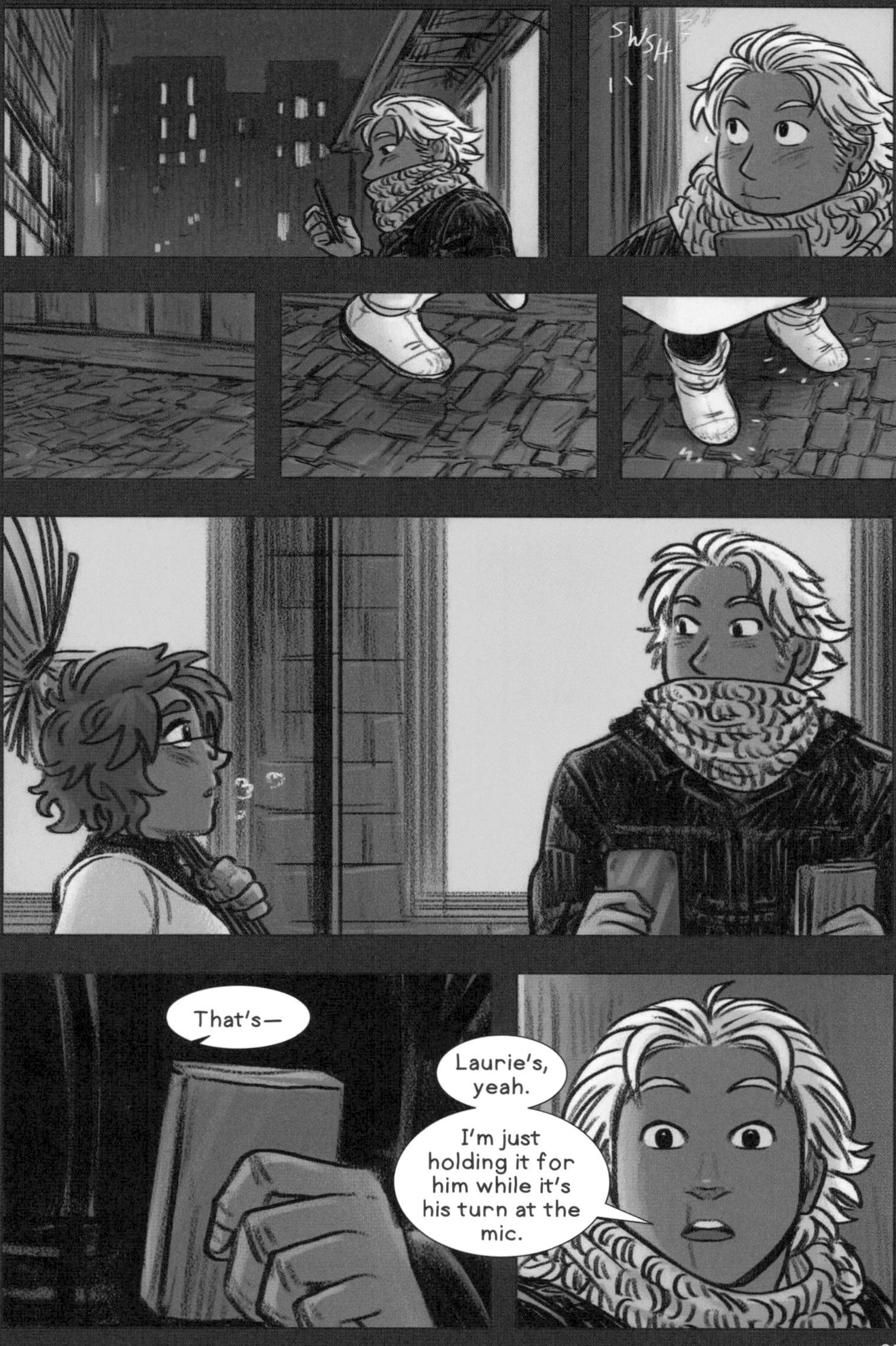
SWSH
That's—
Laurie's, yeah.
I'm just holding it for him while it's his turn at the mic.

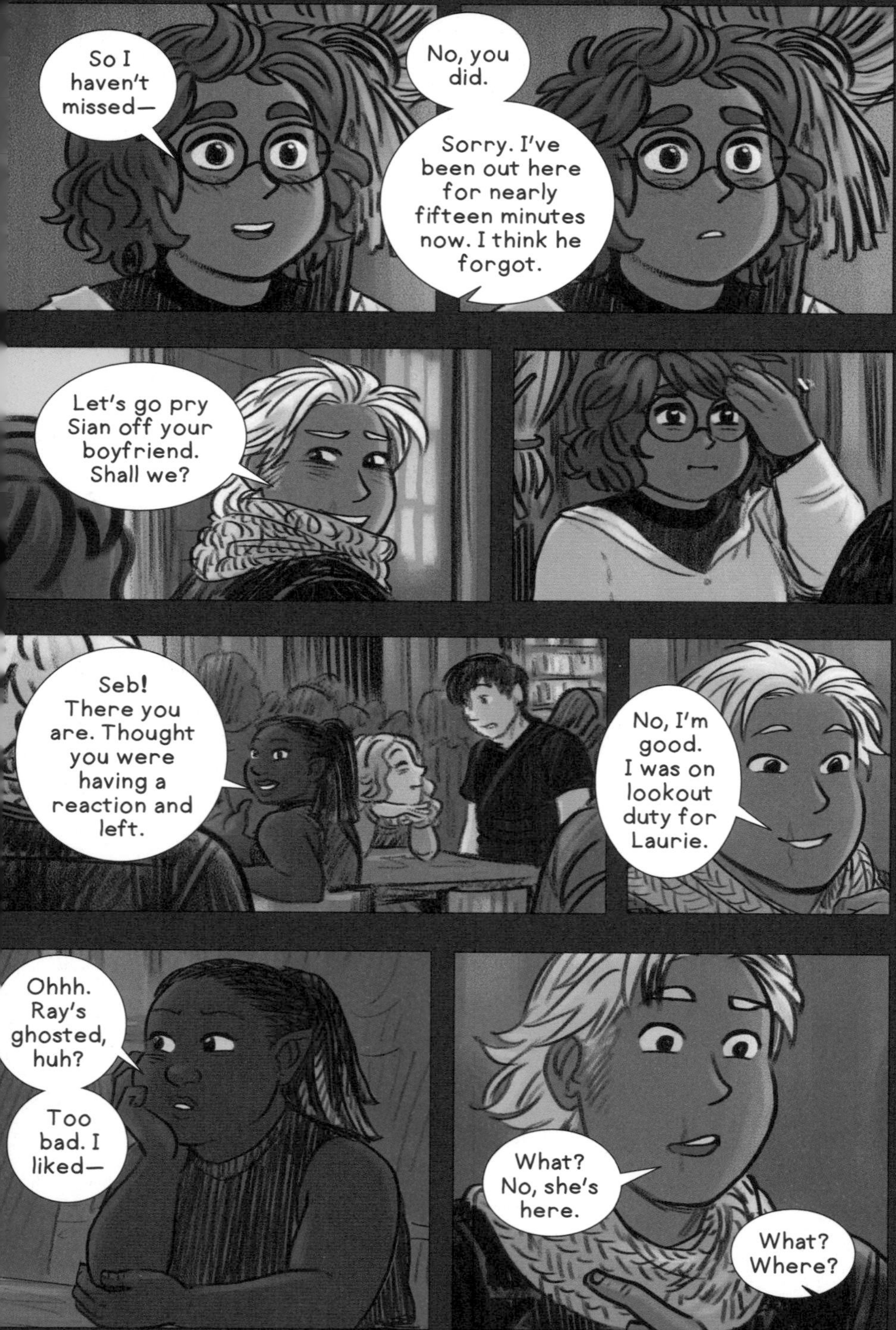
So I haven't missed—
No, you did.
Sorry. I've been out here for nearly fifteen minutes now. I think he forgot.
Let's go pry Sian off your boyfriend. Shall we?
Seb! There you are. Thought you were having a reaction and left.
No, I'm good. I was on lookout duty for Laurie.
Ohhh. Ray's ghosted, huh?
Too bad. I liked—
What? No, she's here.
What? Where?

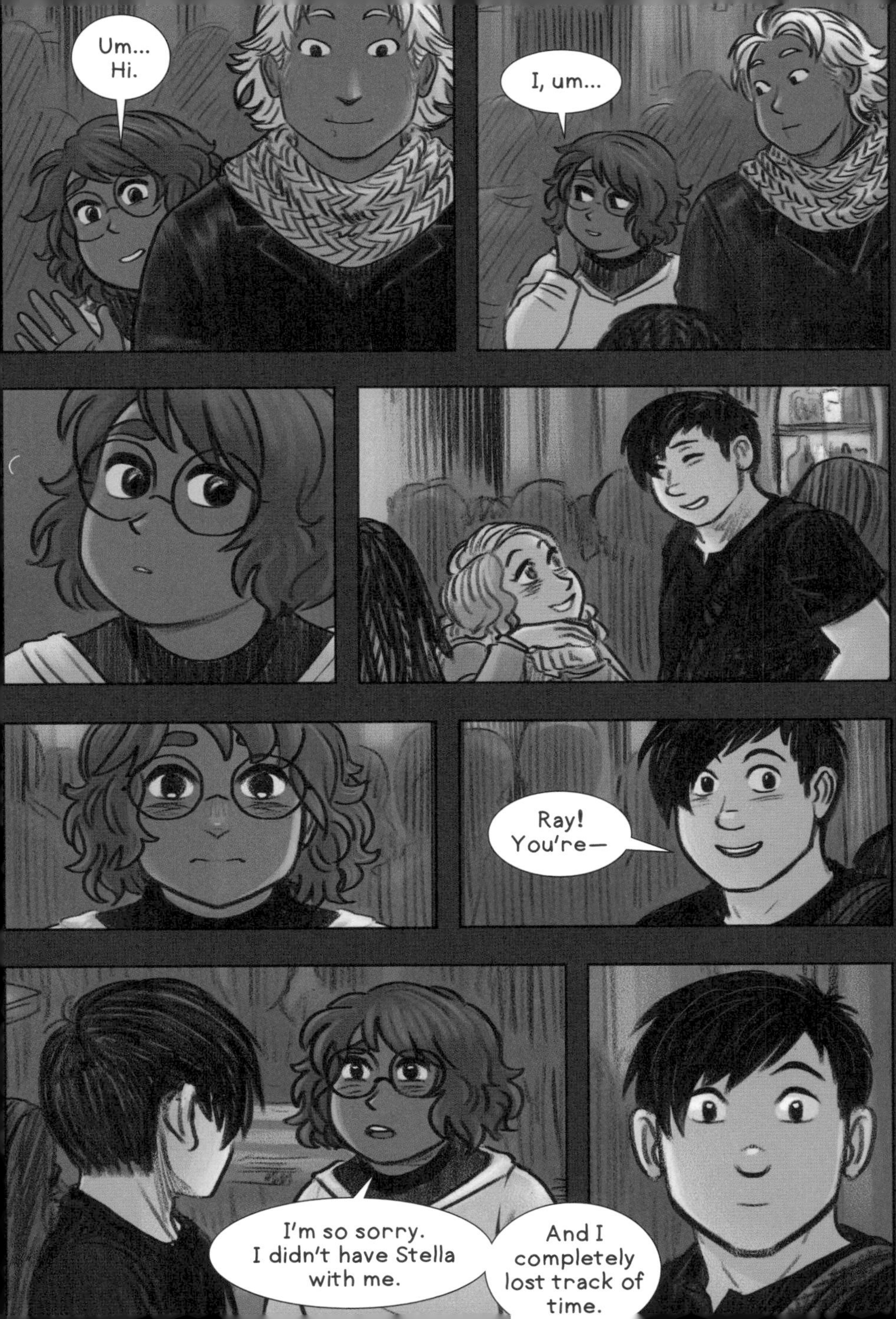
Um... Hi.
I, um...
Ray! You're—
I'm so sorry. I didn't have Stella with me.
And I completely lost track of time.

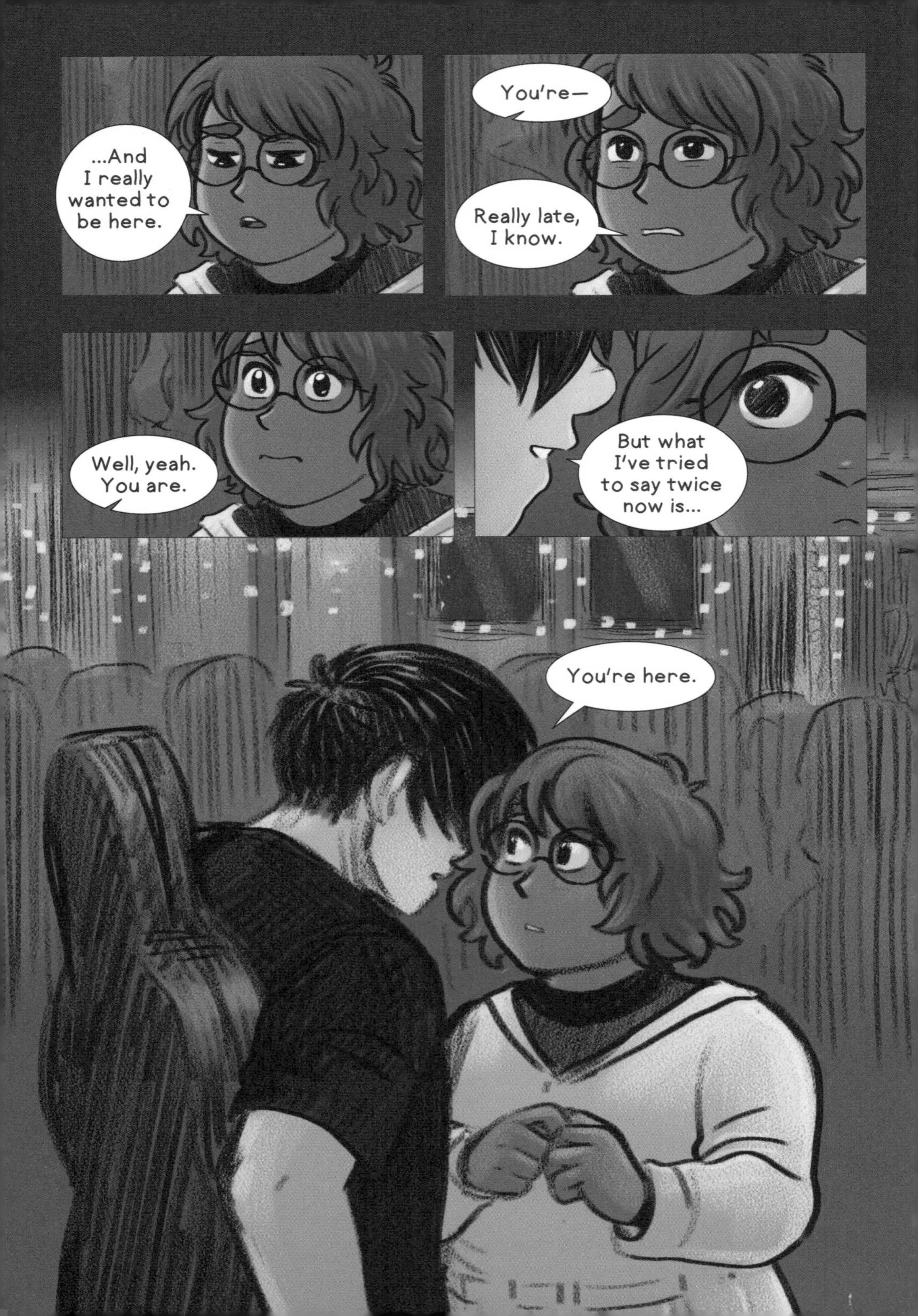
...And I really wanted to be here.
You're—
Really late, I know.
Well, yeah. You are.
But what I've tried to say twice now is...
You're here.

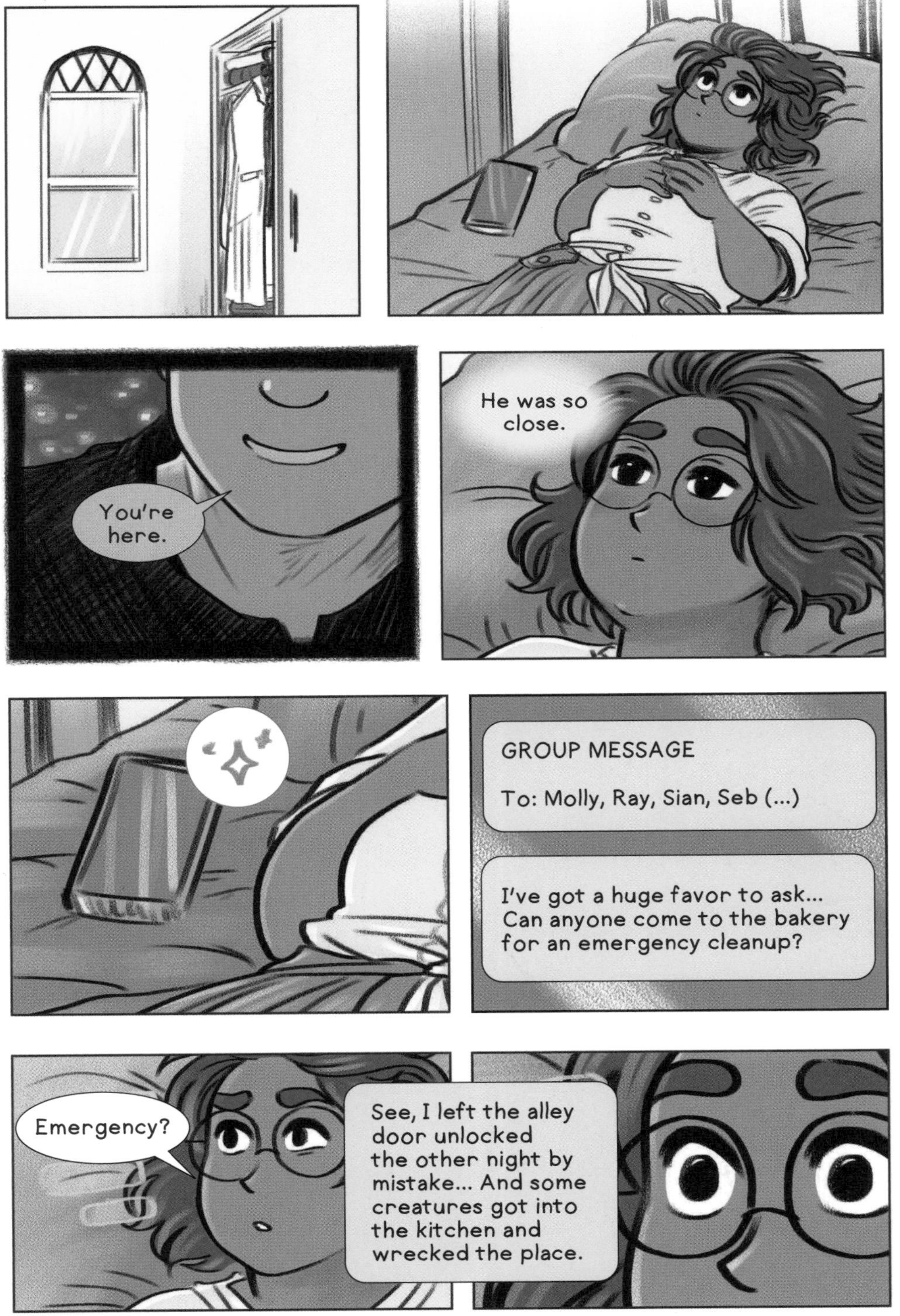

You're here.
He was so close.
GROUP MESSAGE
To: Molly, Ray, Sian, Seb (...)
I've got a huge favor to ask... Can anyone come to the bakery for an emergency cleanup?
Emergency?
See, I left the alley door unlocked the other night by mistake... And some creatures got into the kitchen and wrecked the place.

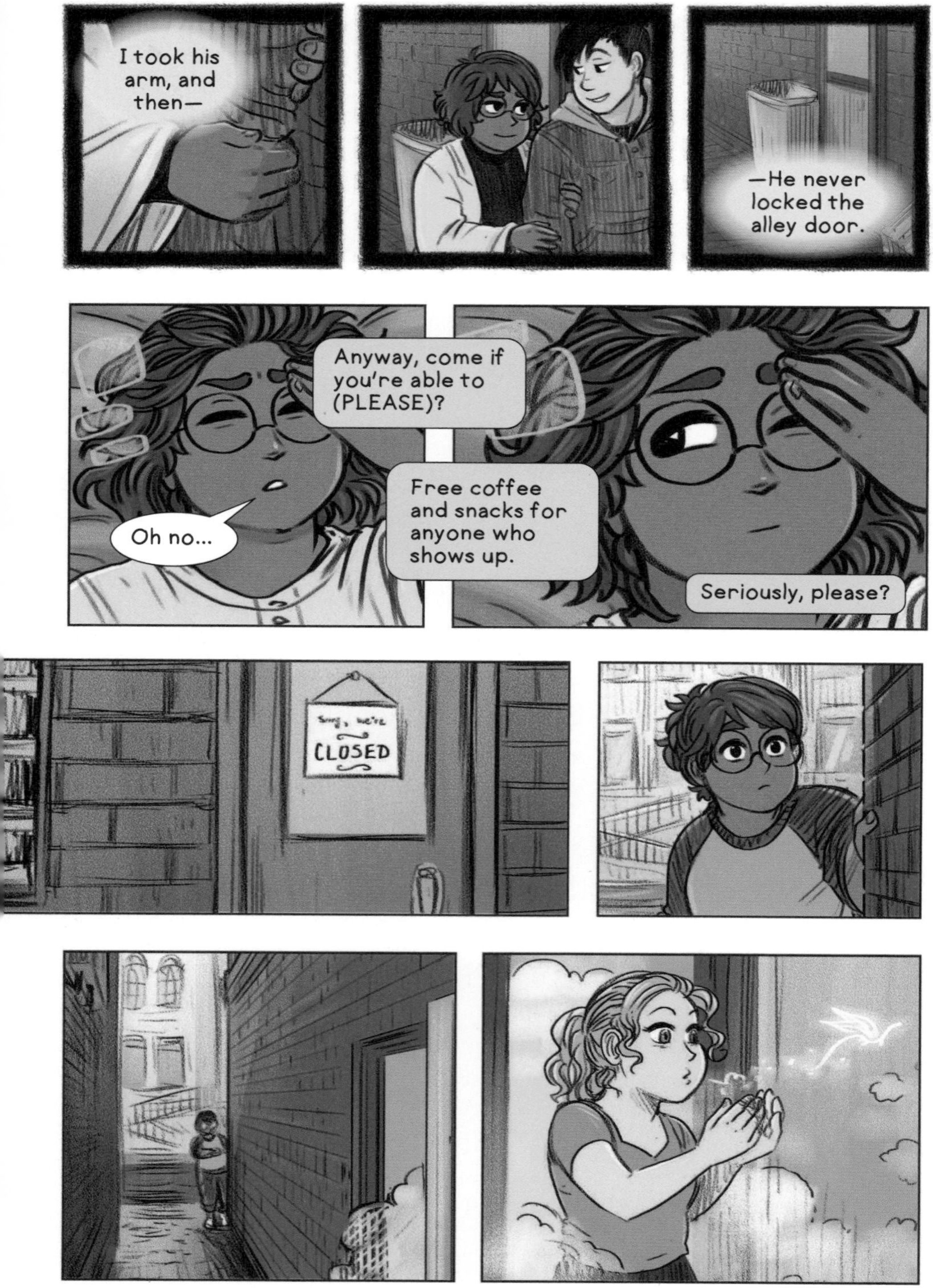
I took his arm, and then—
—He never locked the alley door.
Anyway, come if you're able to (PLEASE)?
Oh no...
Free coffee and snacks for anyone who shows up.
Seriously, please?
CLOSED

Marigold! We've got another pair of hands.

As you can see...

We can use all the help we can get.

Molly's gathering up the strays—

Can you trap them and then let them go outside?

Mm-hm!

Excellent. Thank you.

Ray, get ready to catch.

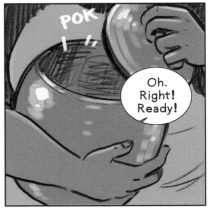

POK

Oh. Right! Ready!

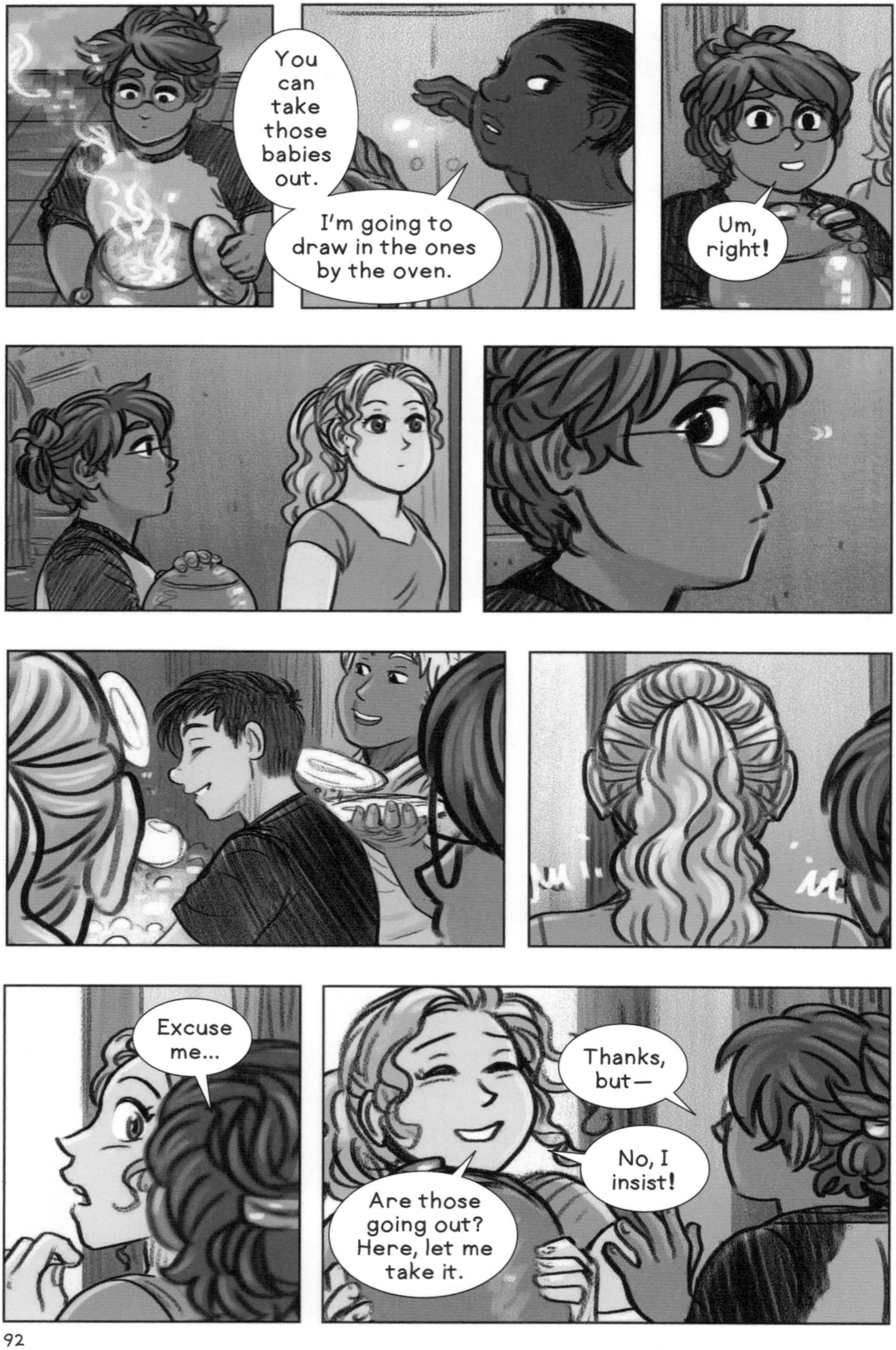
You can take those babies out.
I'm going to draw in the ones by the oven.
Um, right!
Excuse me...
Are those going out? Here, let me take it.
Thanks, but—
No, I insist!

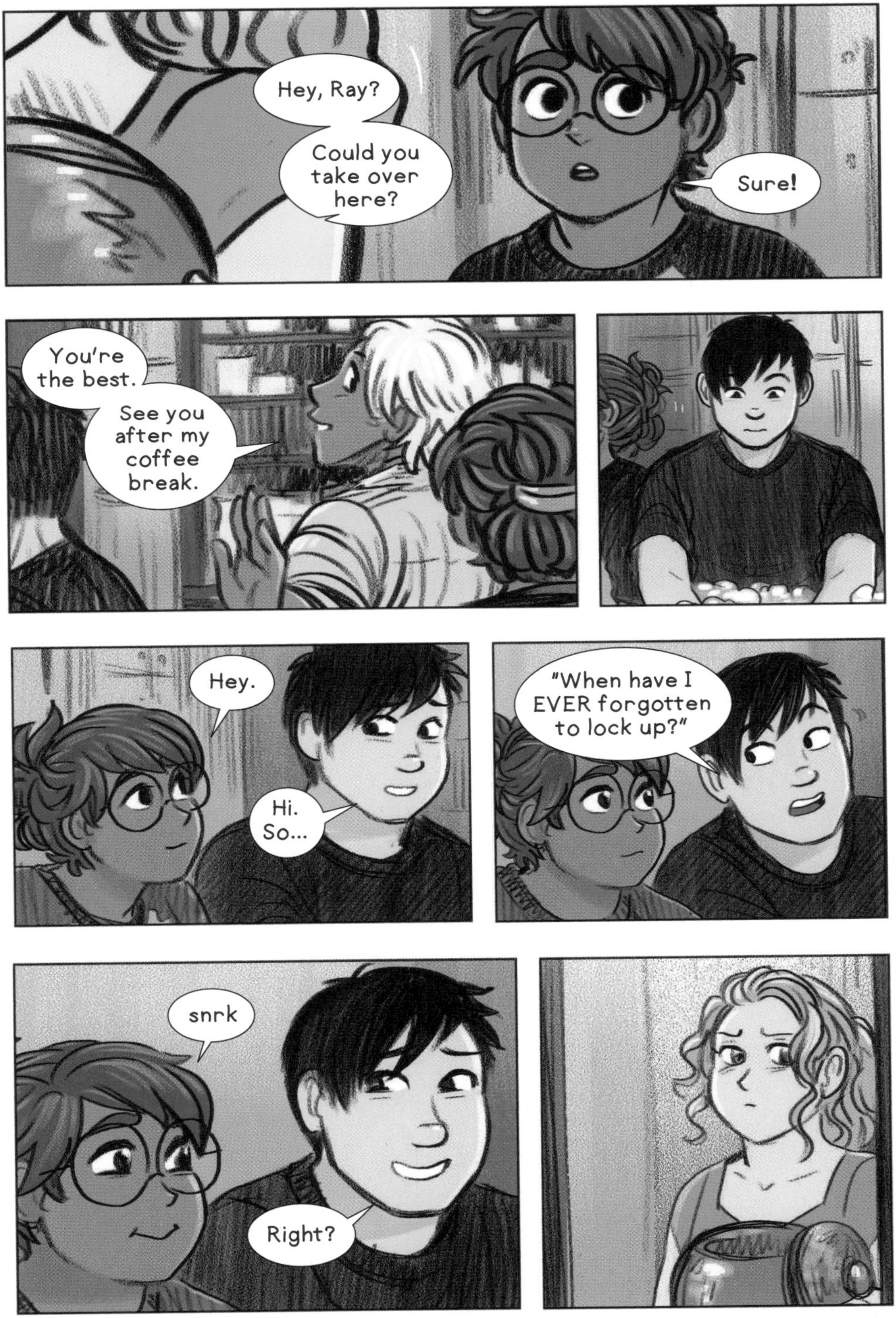
Hey, Ray?
Could you take over here?
Sure!
You're the best.
See you after my coffee break.
Hey.
Hi. So...
"When have I EVER forgotten to lock up?"
snrk
Right?

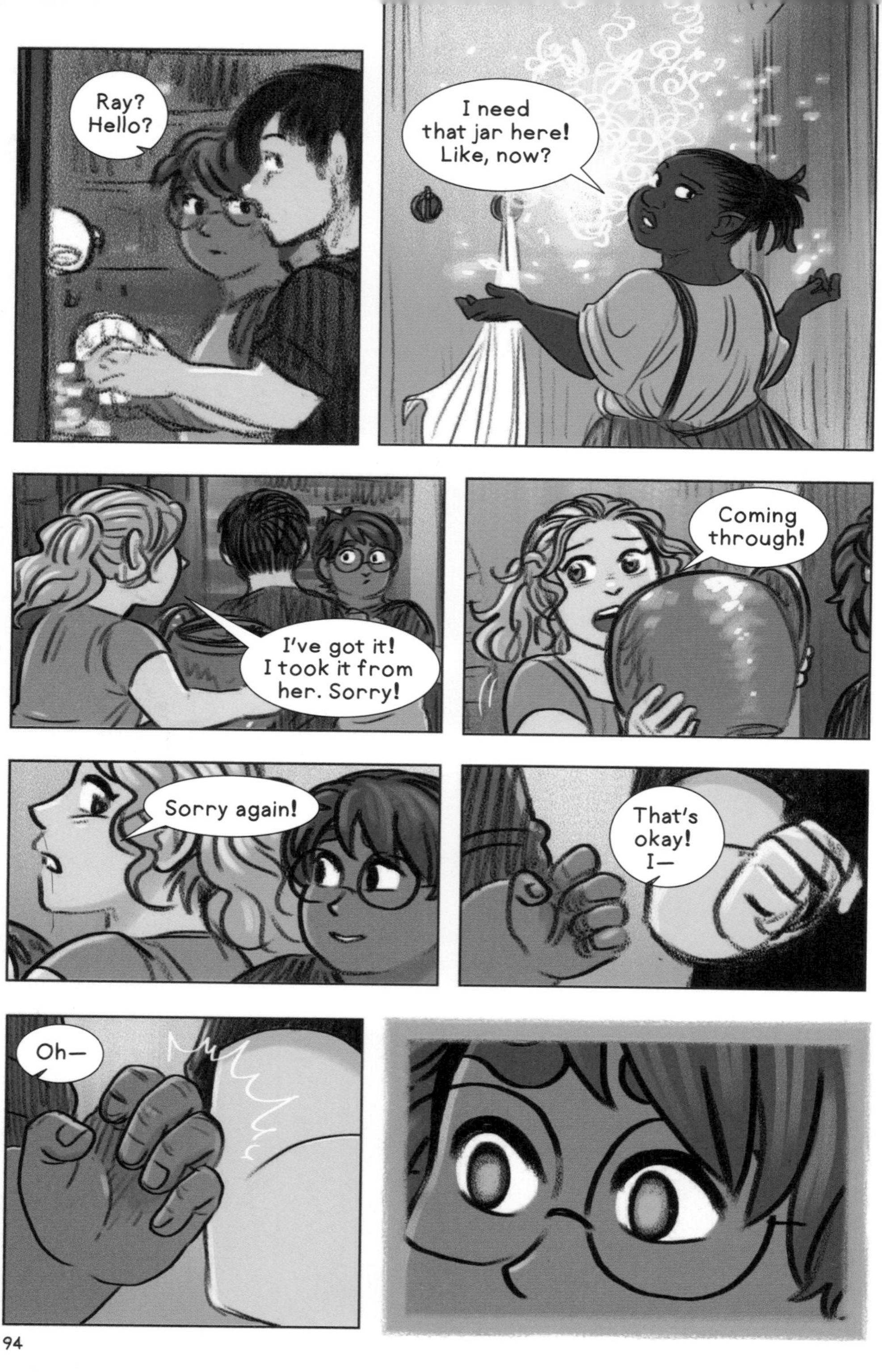
Ray?
Hello?
I need that jar here! Like, now?
I've got it! I took it from her. Sorry!
Coming through!
Sorry again!
That's okay! I—
Oh—

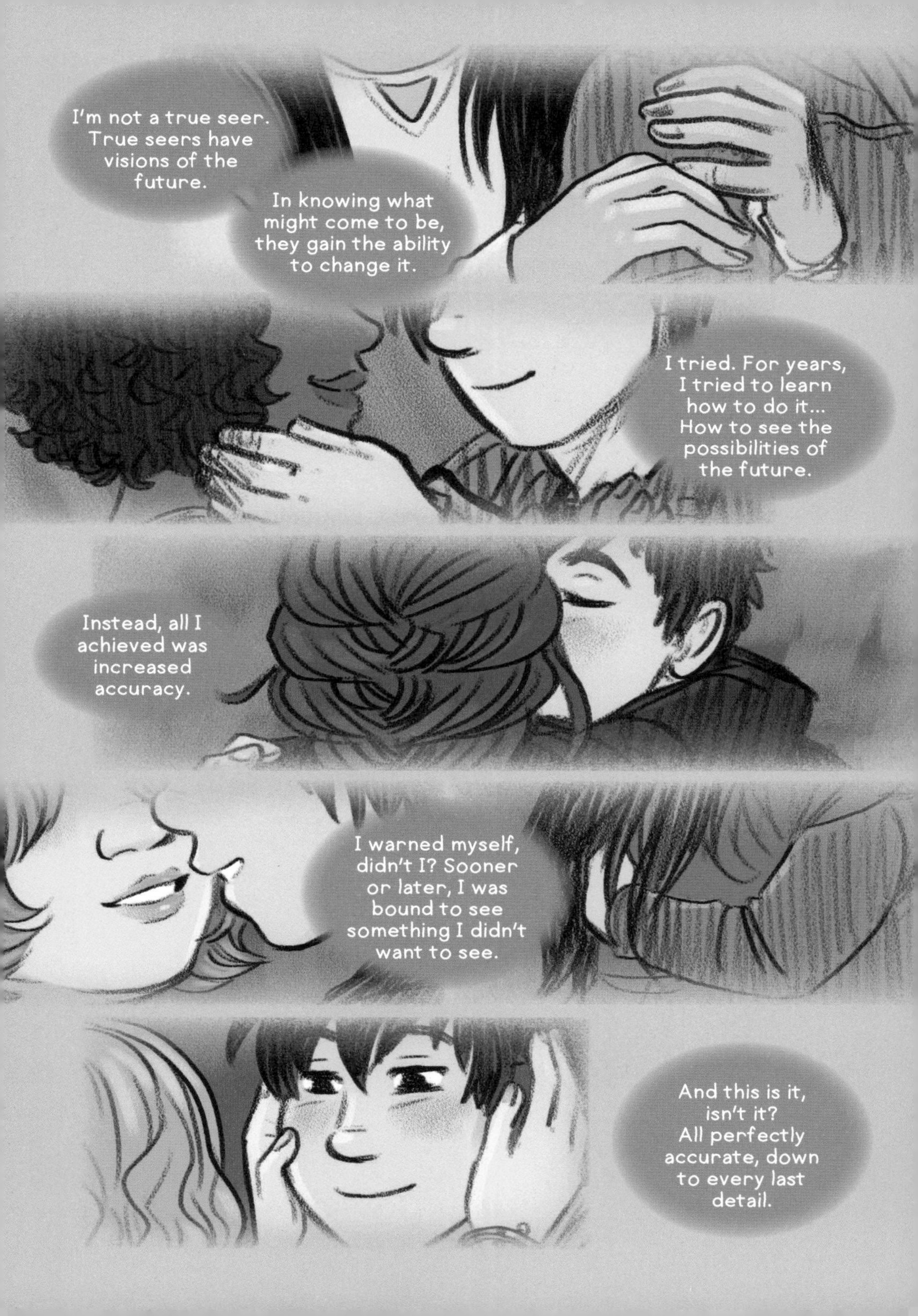
I'm not a true seer. True seers have visions of the future.
In knowing what might come to be, they gain the ability to change it.
I tried. For years, I tried to learn how to do it... How to see the possibilities of the future.
Instead, all I achieved was increased accuracy.
I warned myself, didn't I? Sooner or later, I was bound to see something I didn't want to see.
And this is it, isn't it? All perfectly accurate, down to every last detail.

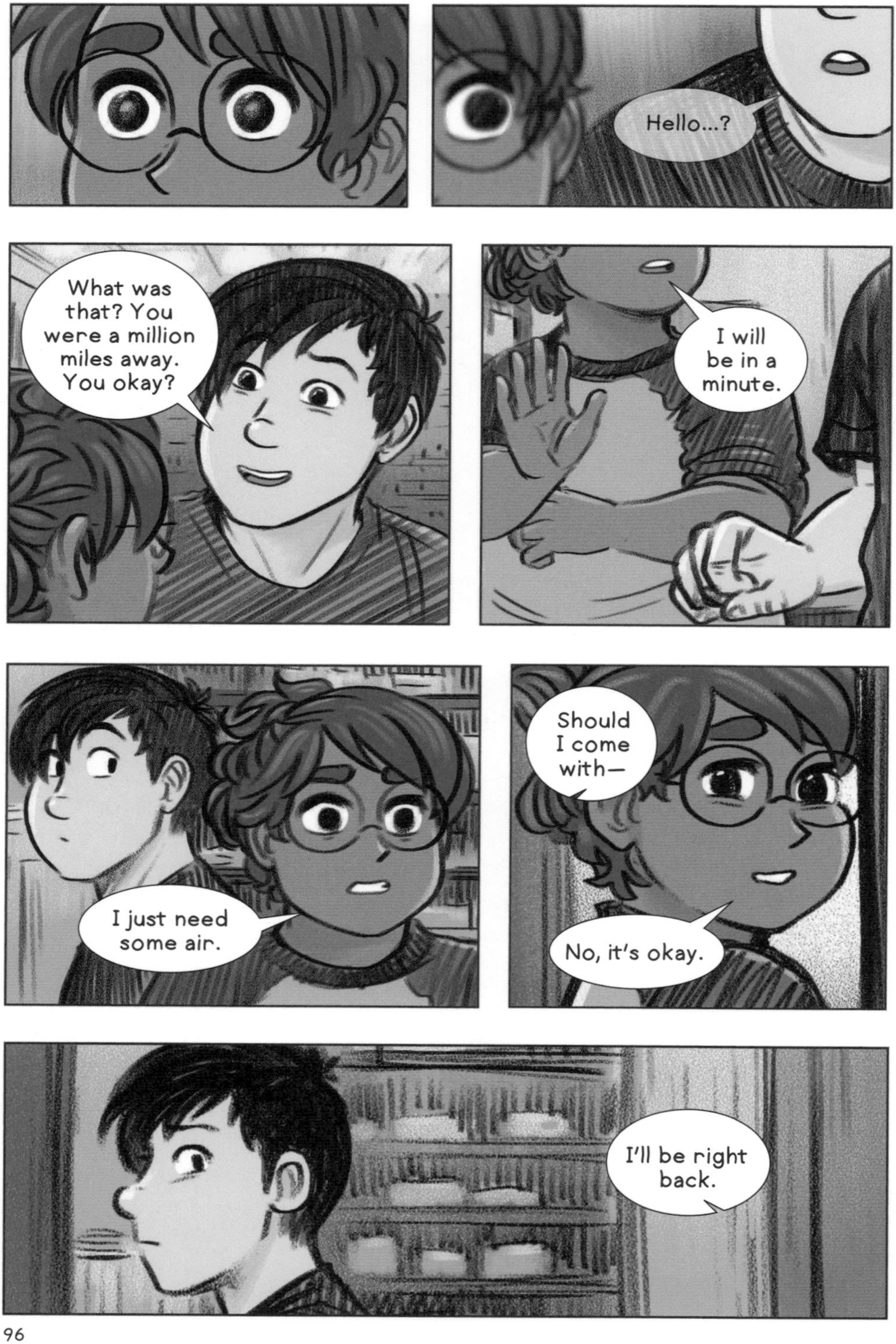
Hello...?
What was that? You were a million miles away. You okay?
I will be in a minute.
I just need some air.
Should I come with—
No, it's okay.
I'll be right back.

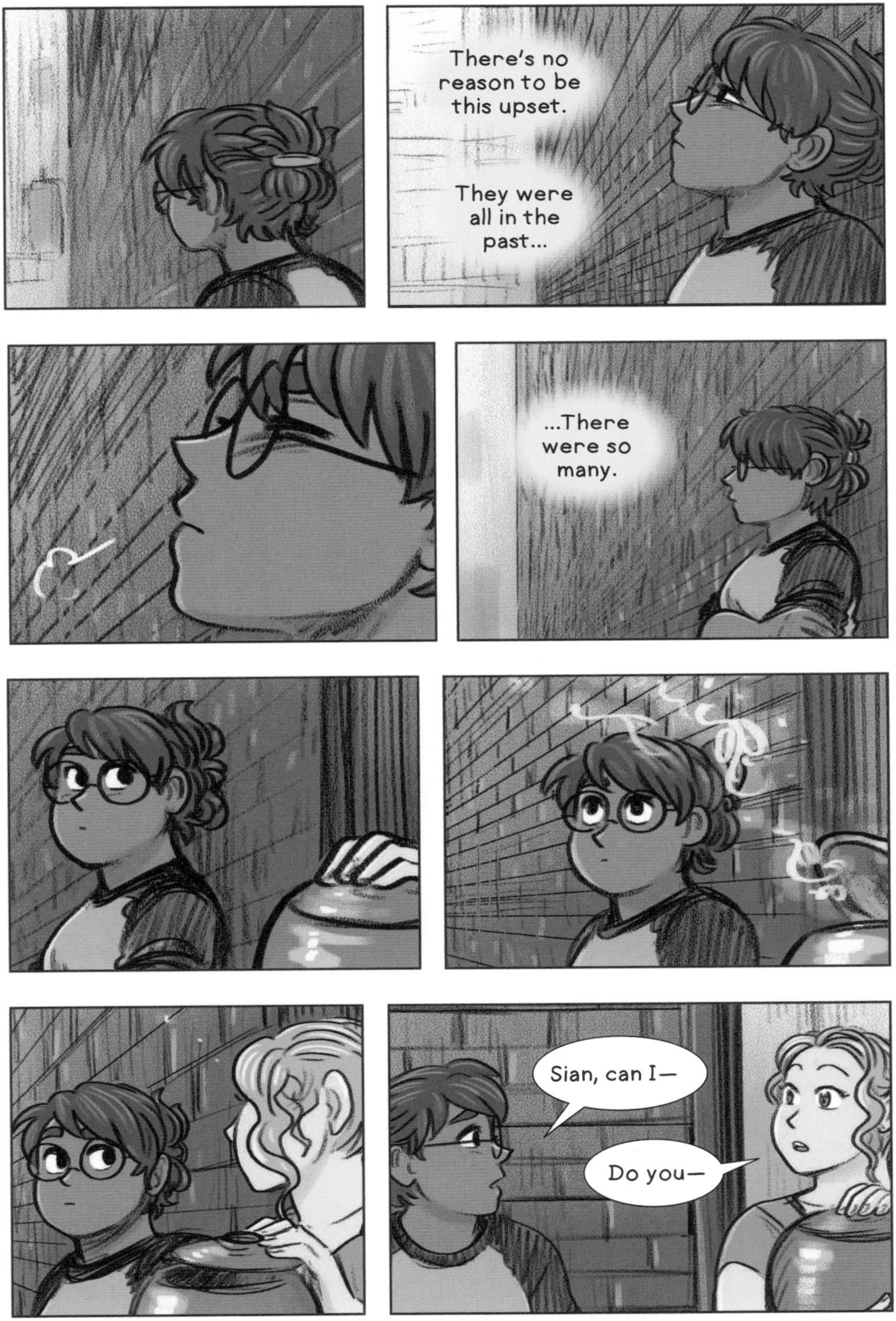
There's no reason to be this upset.
They were all in the past...
...There were so many.
Sian, can I—
Do you—

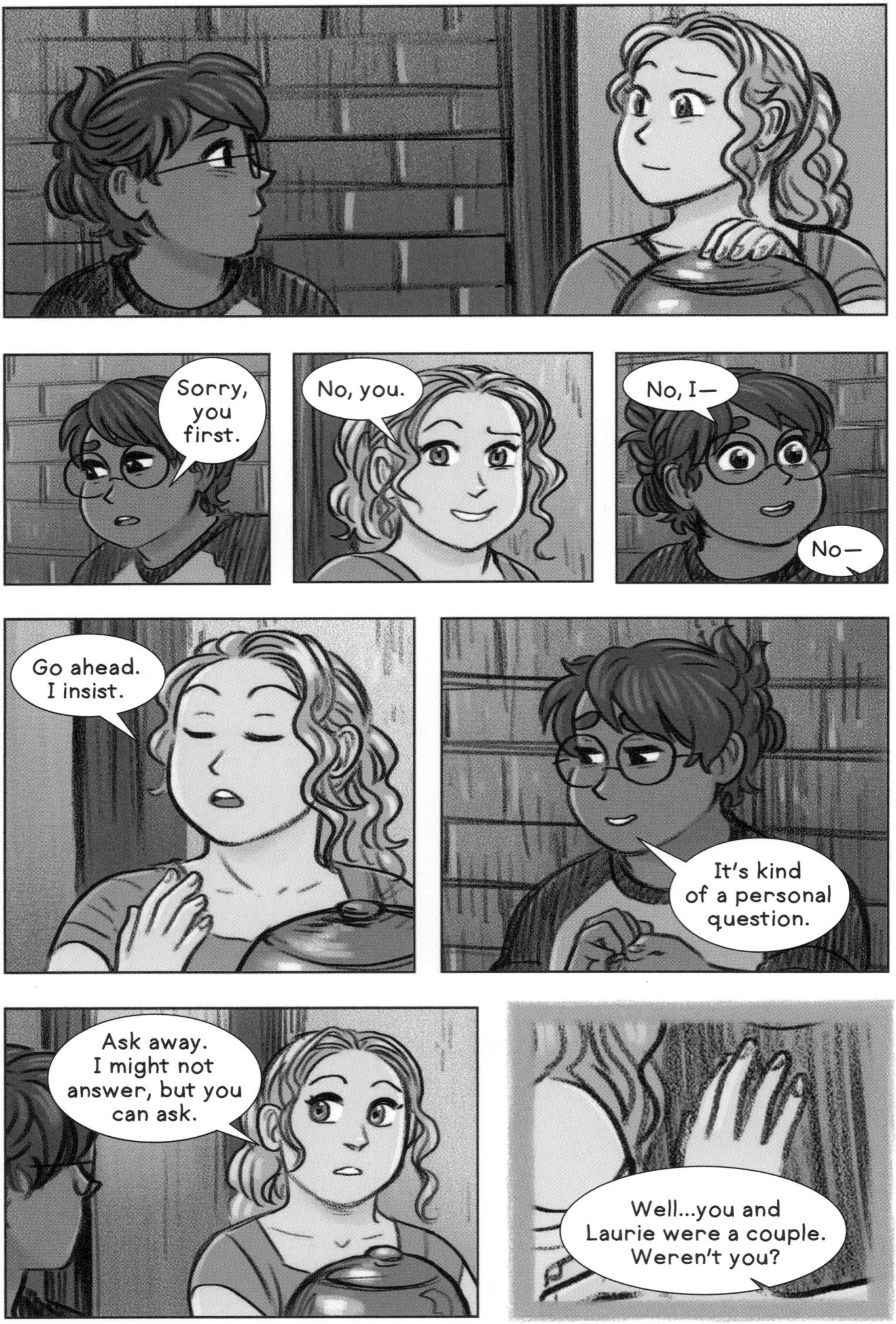
Sorry, you first.
No, you.
No, I—
No—
Go ahead. I insist.
It's kind of a personal question.
Ask away. I might not answer, but you can ask.
Well...you and Laurie were a couple. Weren't you?

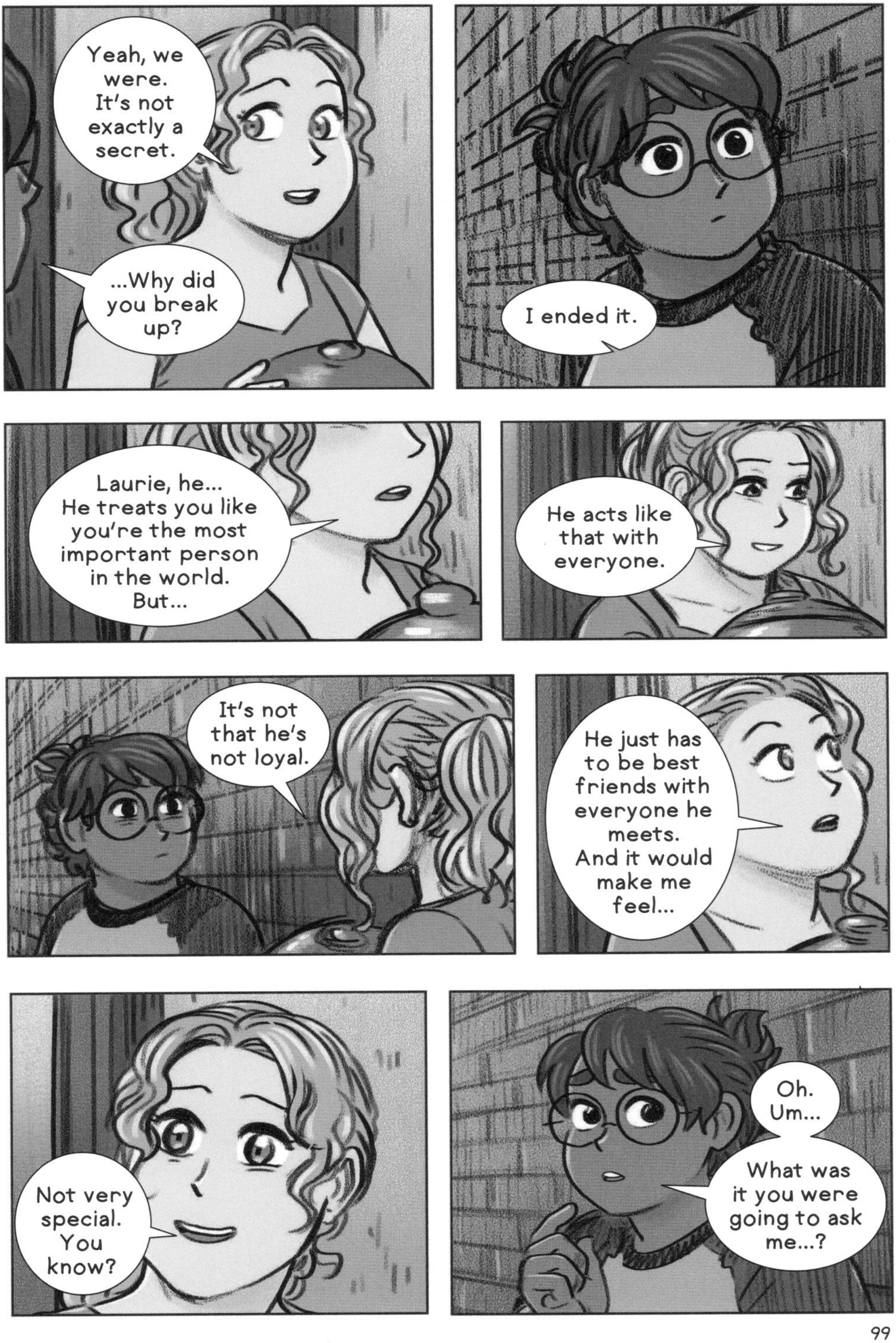
Yeah, we were. It's not exactly a secret.
...Why did you break up?
I ended it.
Laurie, he... He treats you like you're the most important person in the world. But...
He acts like that with everyone.
It's not that he's not loyal.
He just has to be best friends with everyone he meets. And it would make me feel...
Not very special. You know?
Oh. Um...
What was it you were going to ask me...?

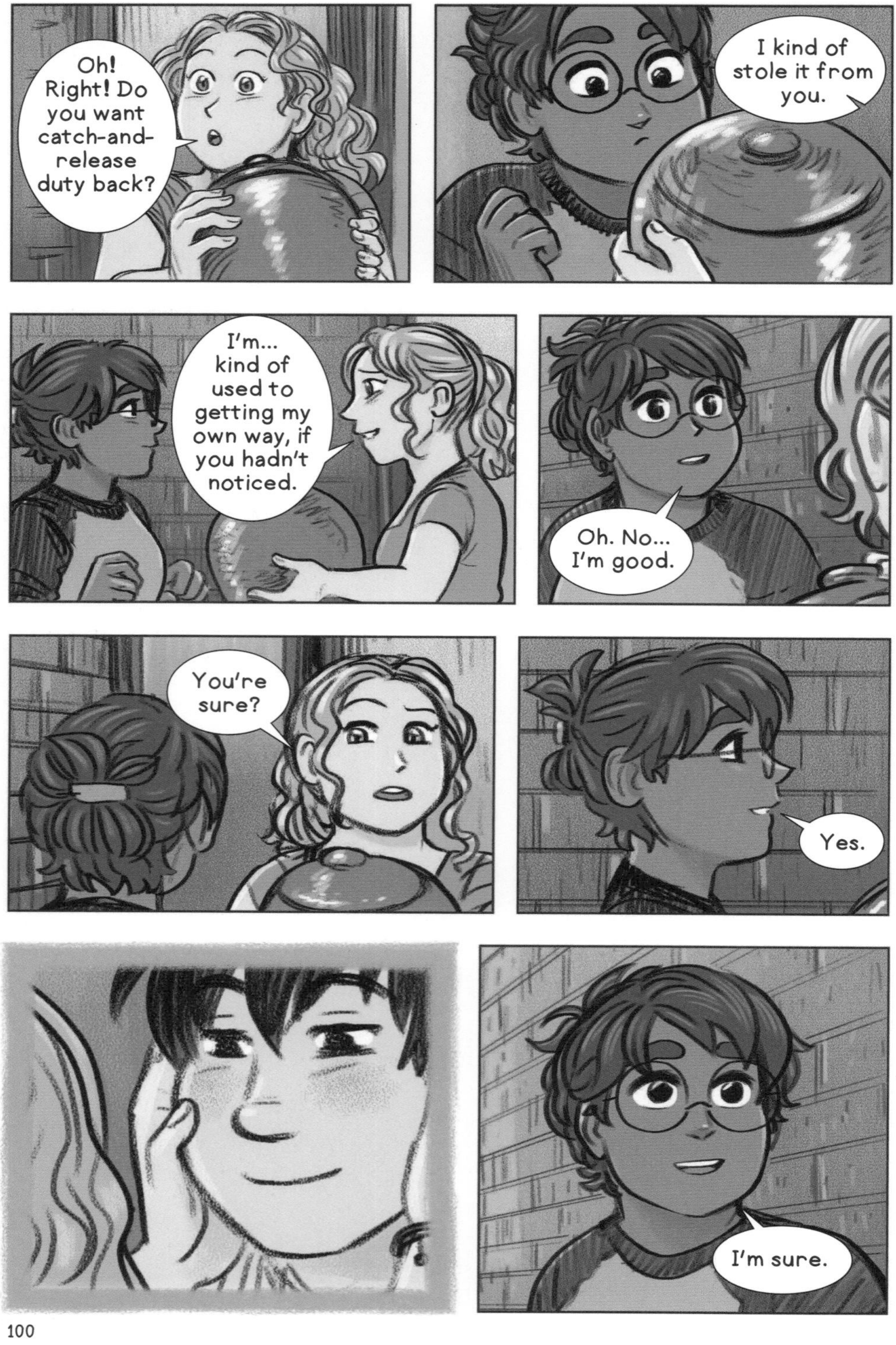
Oh! Right! Do you want catch-and-release duty back?
I kind of stole it from you.
I'm... kind of used to getting my own way, if you hadn't noticed.
Oh. No... I'm good.
You're sure?
Yes.
I'm sure.

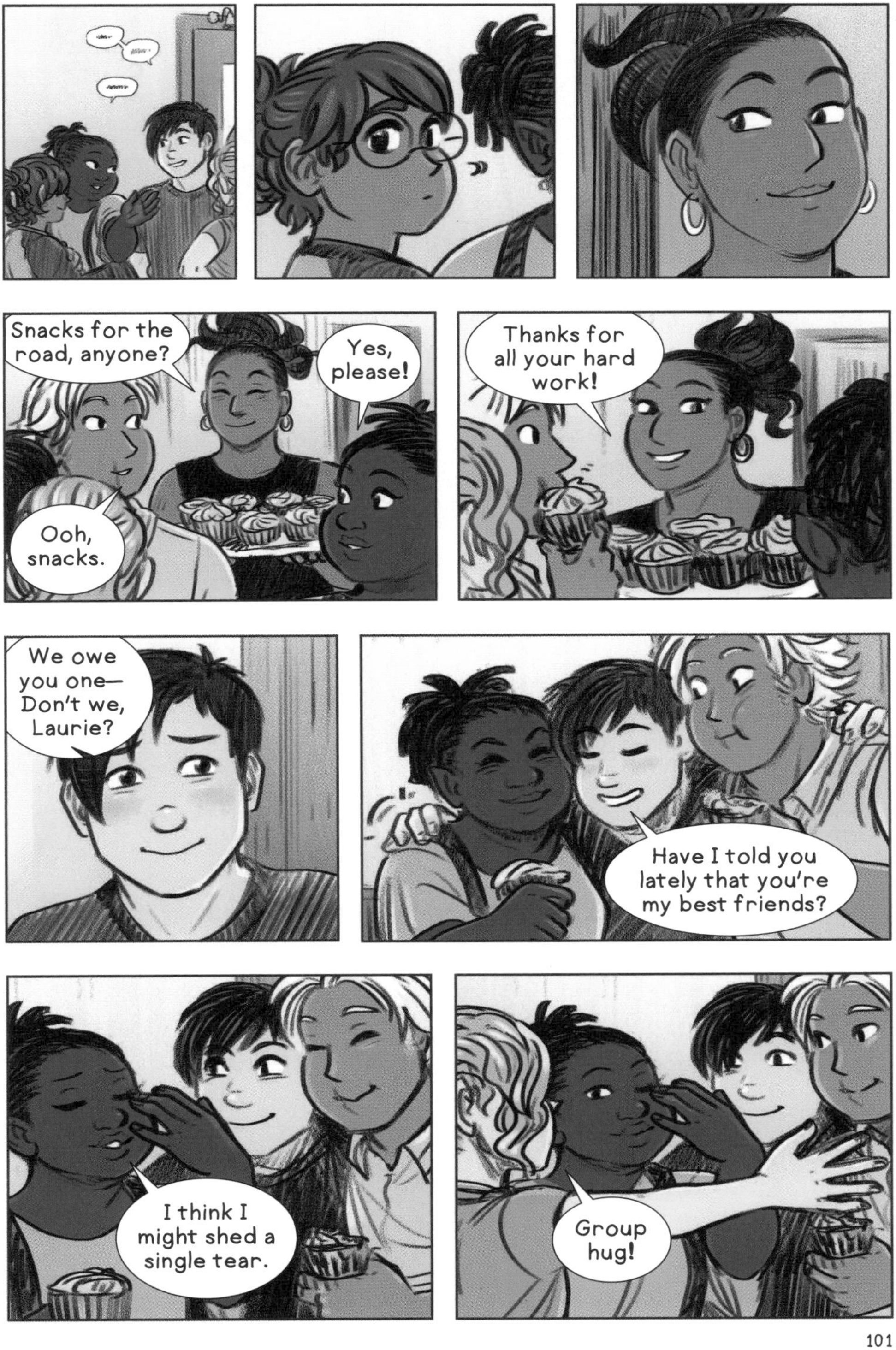
Snacks for the road, anyone?
Yes, please!
Ooh, snacks.
Thanks for all your hard work!
We owe you one— Don't we, Laurie?
Have I told you lately that you're my best friends?
I think I might shed a single tear.
Group hug!

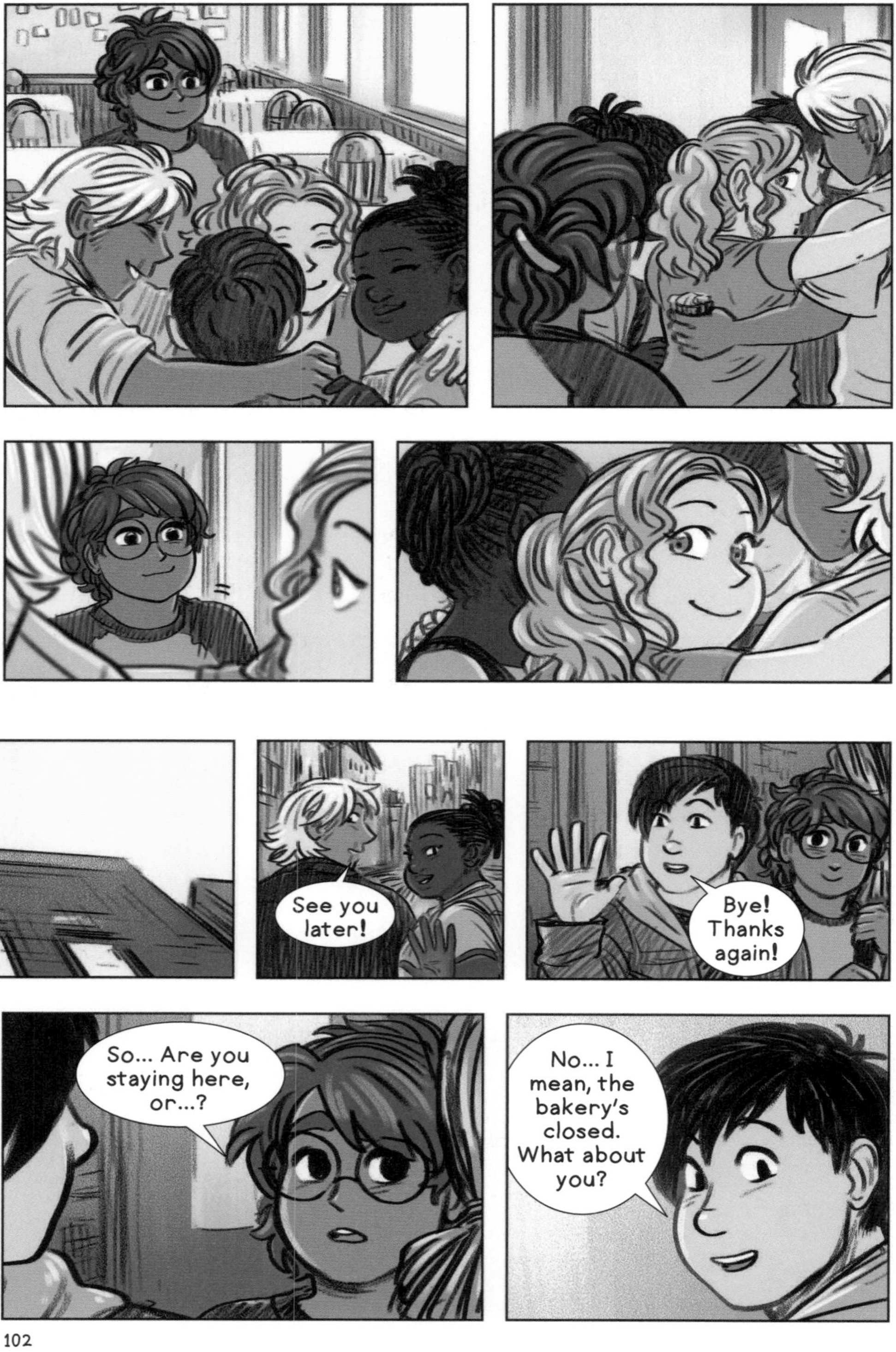
See you later!
Bye! Thanks again!
So... Are you staying here, or...?
No... I mean, the bakery's closed. What about you?

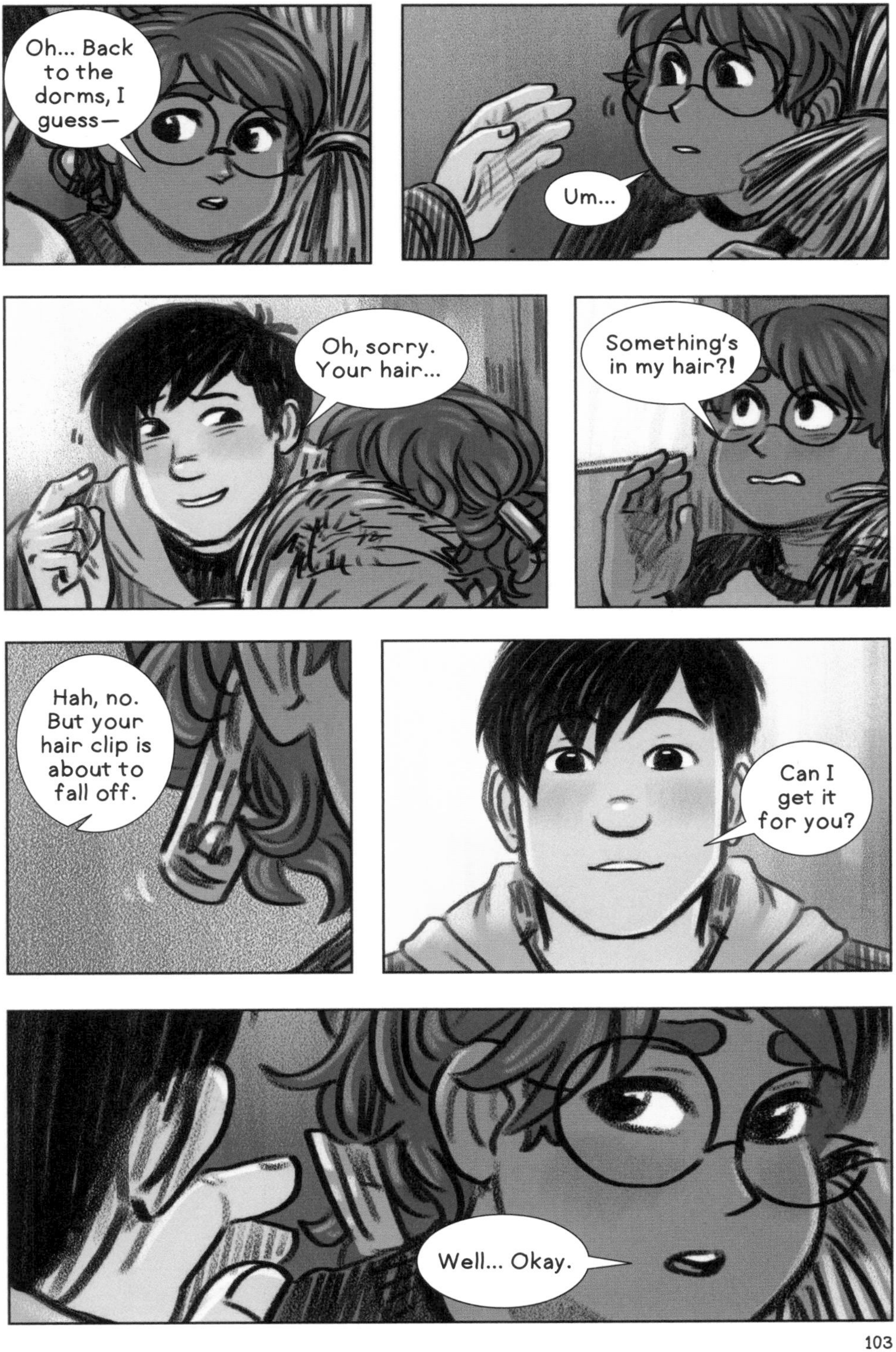
Oh... Back to the dorms, I guess—
Um...
Oh, sorry. Your hair...
Something's in my hair?!
Hah, no. But your hair clip is about to fall off.
Can I get it for you?
Well... Okay.

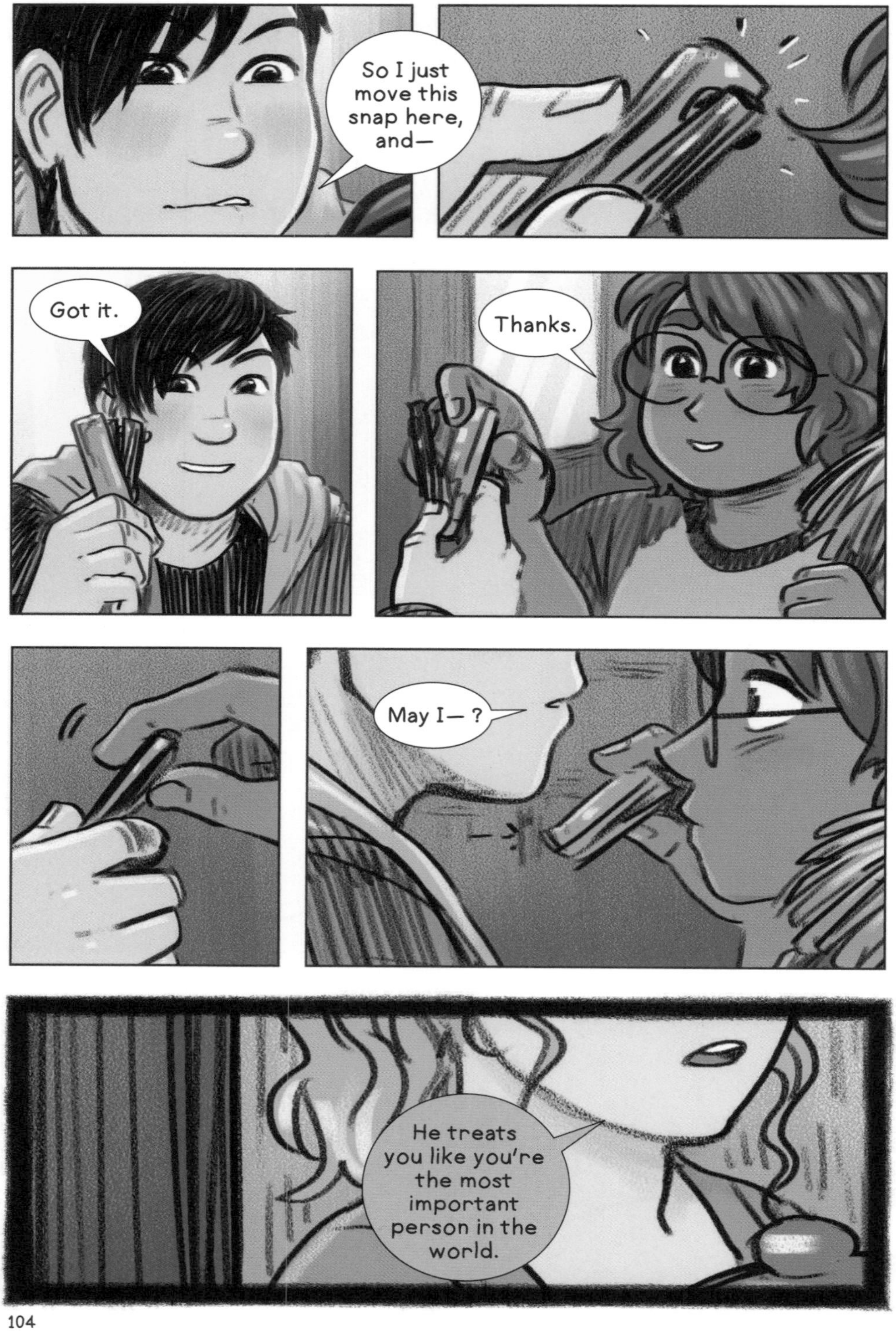
So I just move this snap here, and—
Got it.
Thanks.
May I— ?
He treats you like you're the most important person in the world.

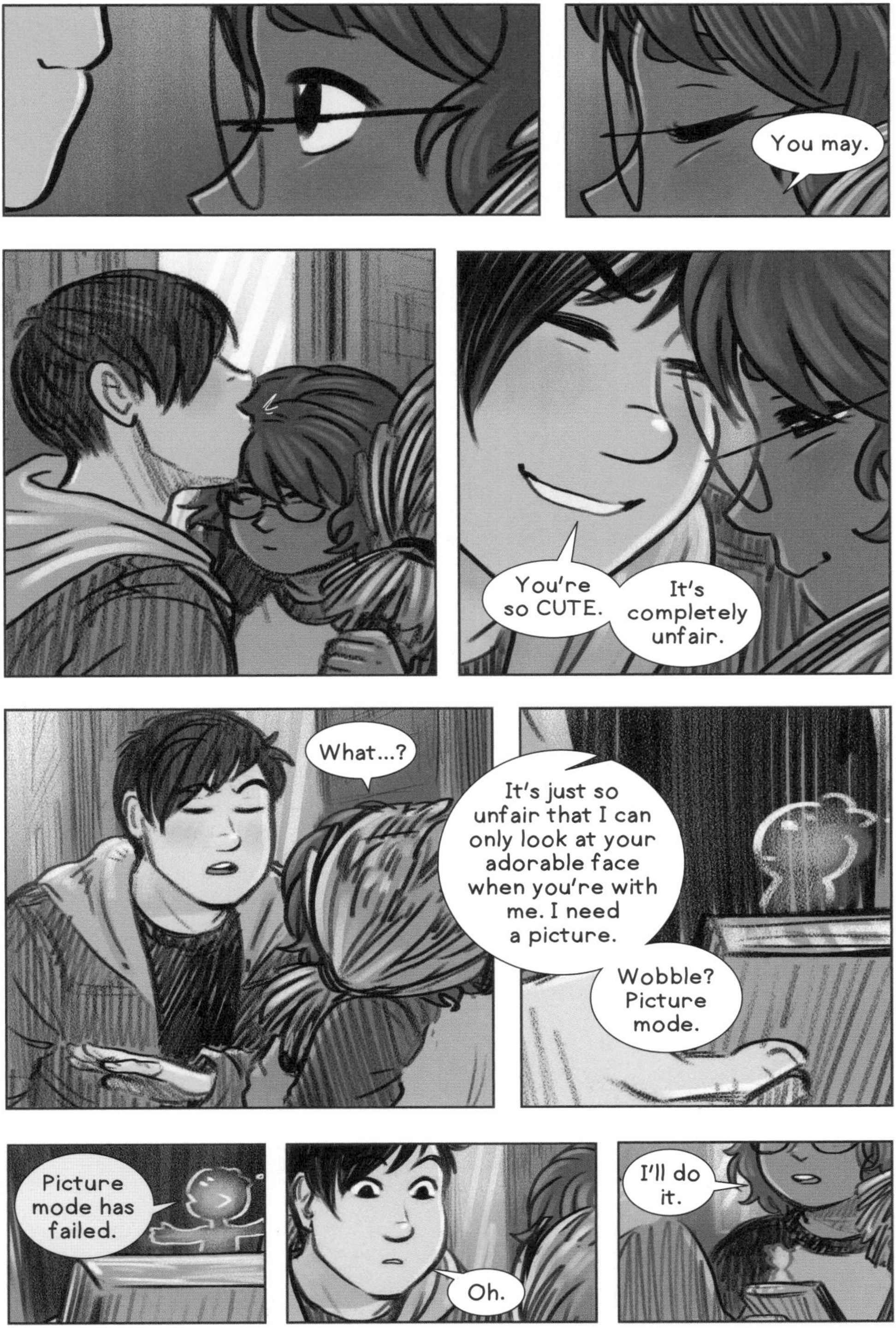
You may.
You're so CUTE.
It's completely unfair.
What...?
It's just so unfair that I can only look at your adorable face when you're with me. I need a picture.
Wobble? Picture mode.
Picture mode has failed.
Oh.
I'll do it.

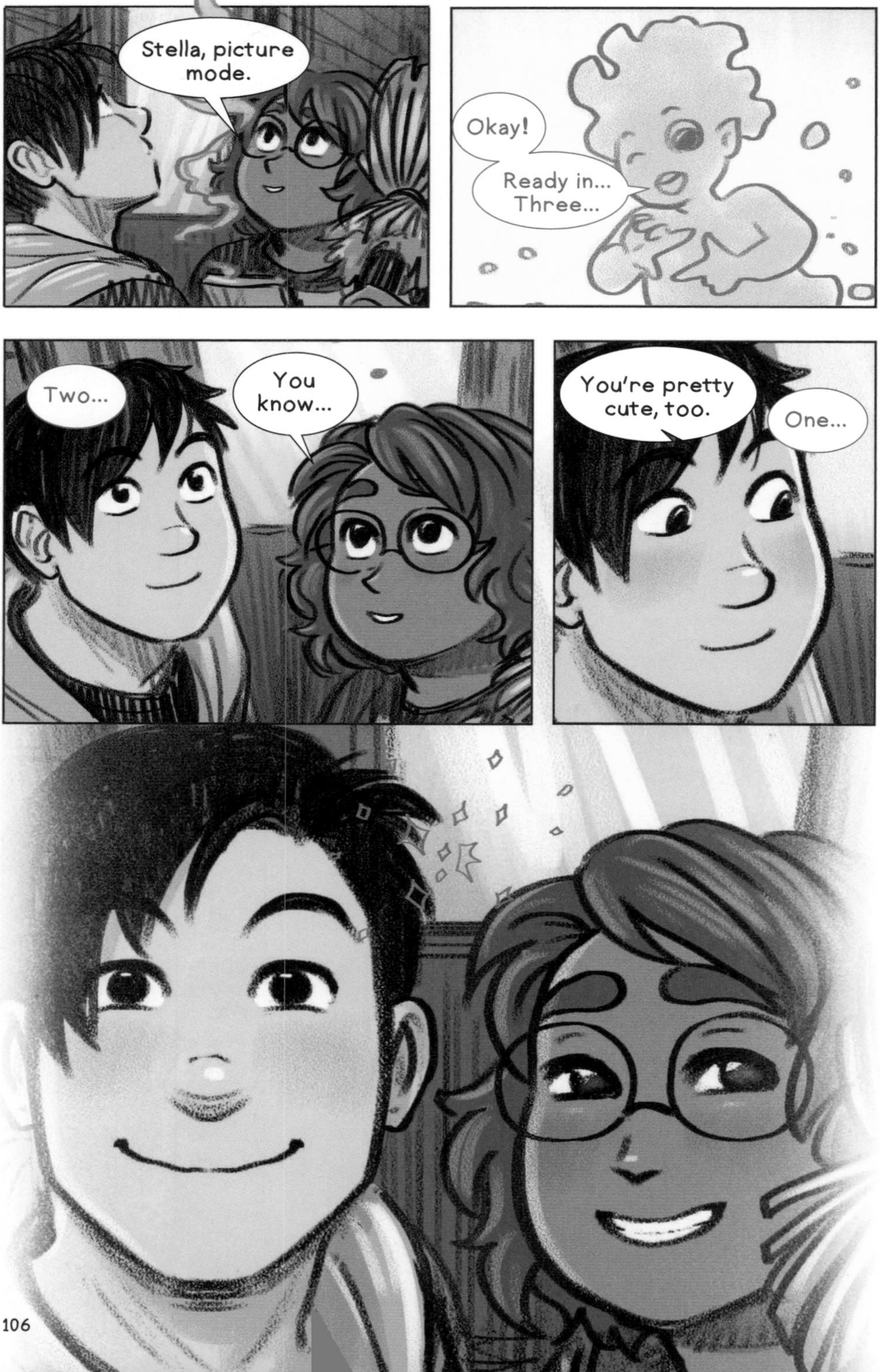
Stella, picture mode.
Okay!
Ready in... Three...
Two...
You know...
You're pretty cute, too.
One...

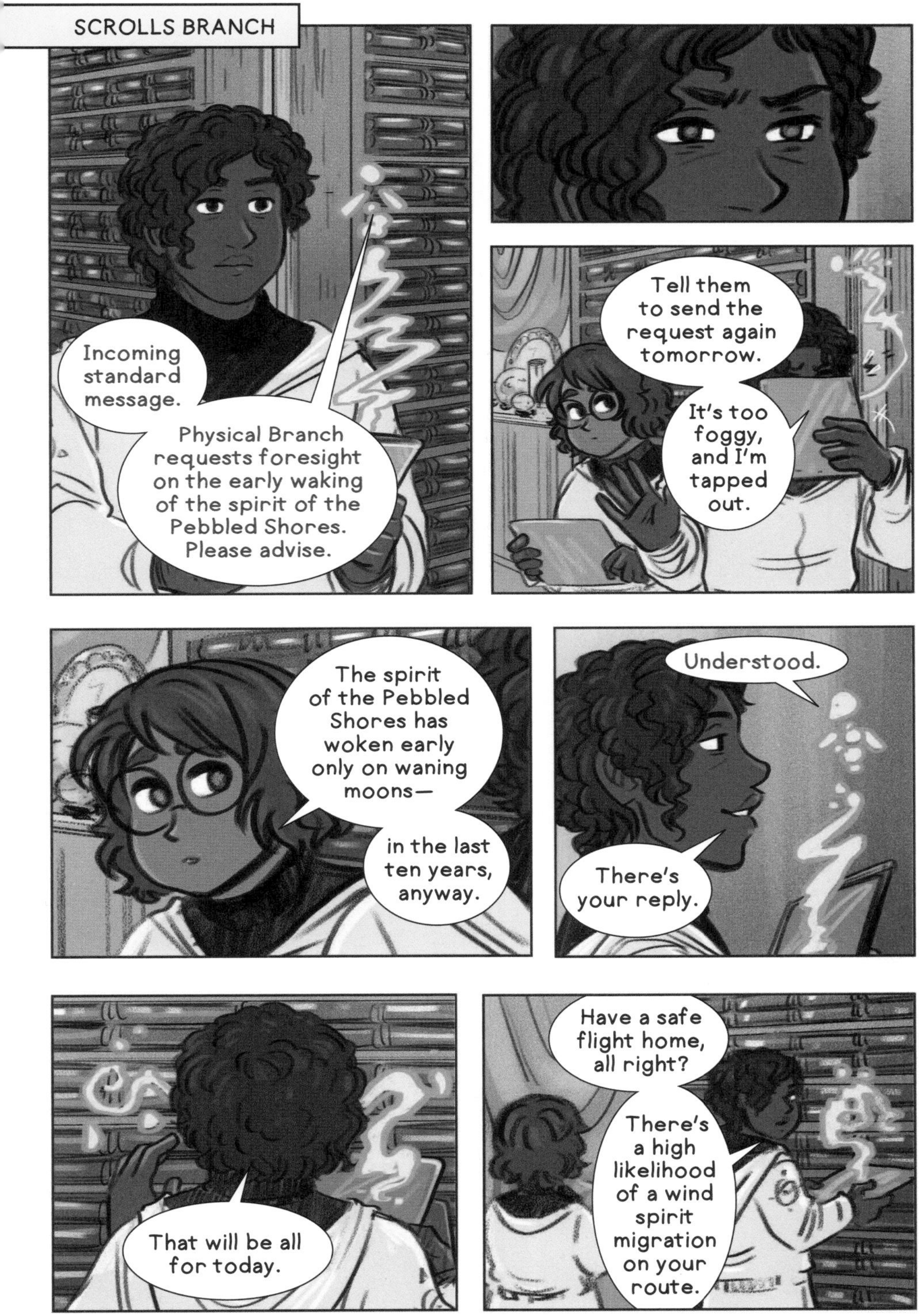
SCROLLS BRANCH
Incoming standard message.
Physical Branch requests foresight on the early waking of the spirit of the Pebbled Shores. Please advise.
Tell them to send the request again tomorrow.
It's too foggy, and I'm tapped out.
The spirit of the Pebbled Shores has woken early only on waning moons—
in the last ten years, anyway.
Understood.
There's your reply.
That will be all for today.
Have a safe flight home, all right?
There's a high likelihood of a wind spirit migration on your route.

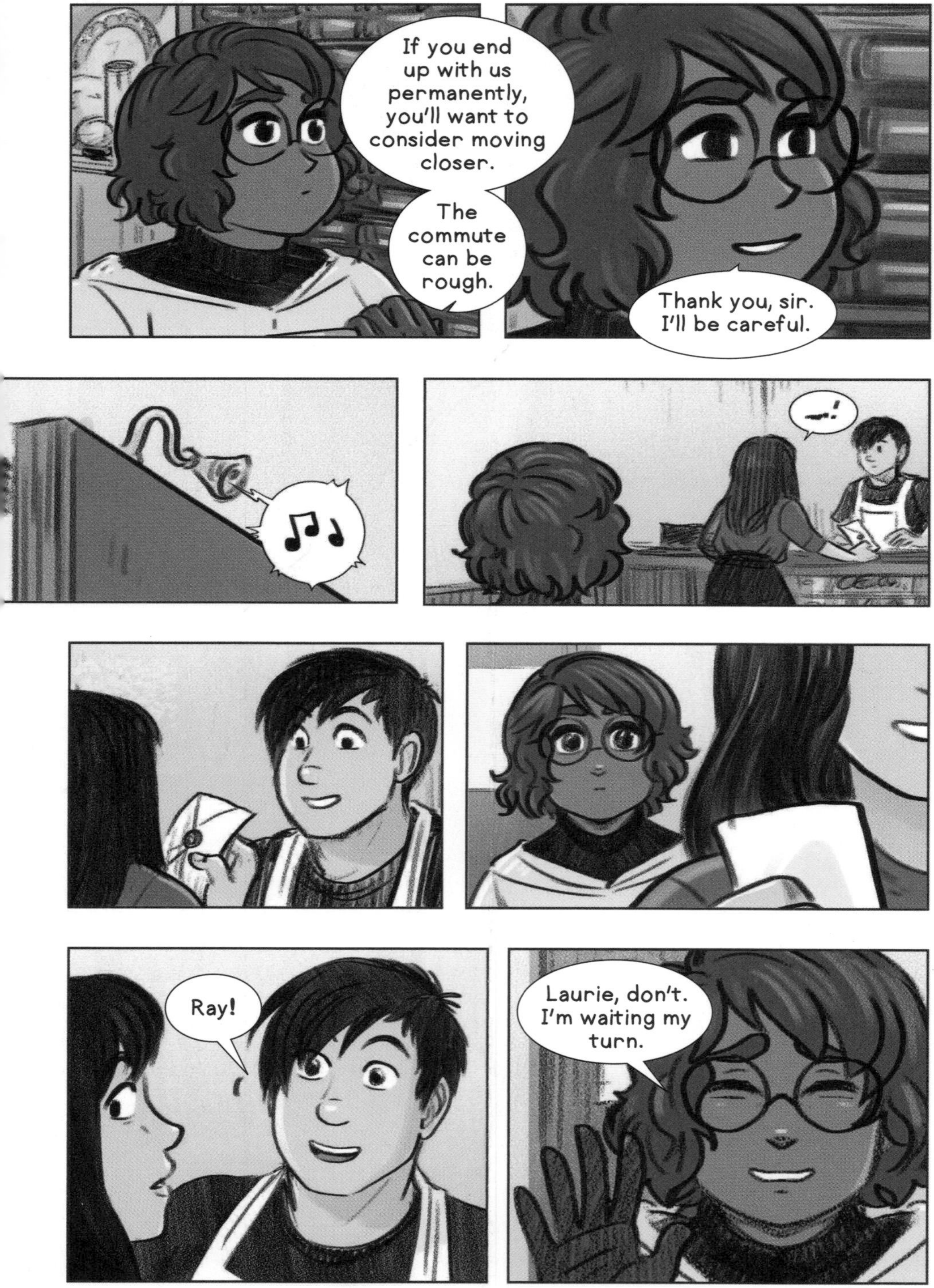
If you end up with us permanently, you'll want to consider moving closer.
The commute can be rough.
Thank you, sir. I'll be careful.
—!
Ray!
Laurie, don't. I'm waiting my turn.

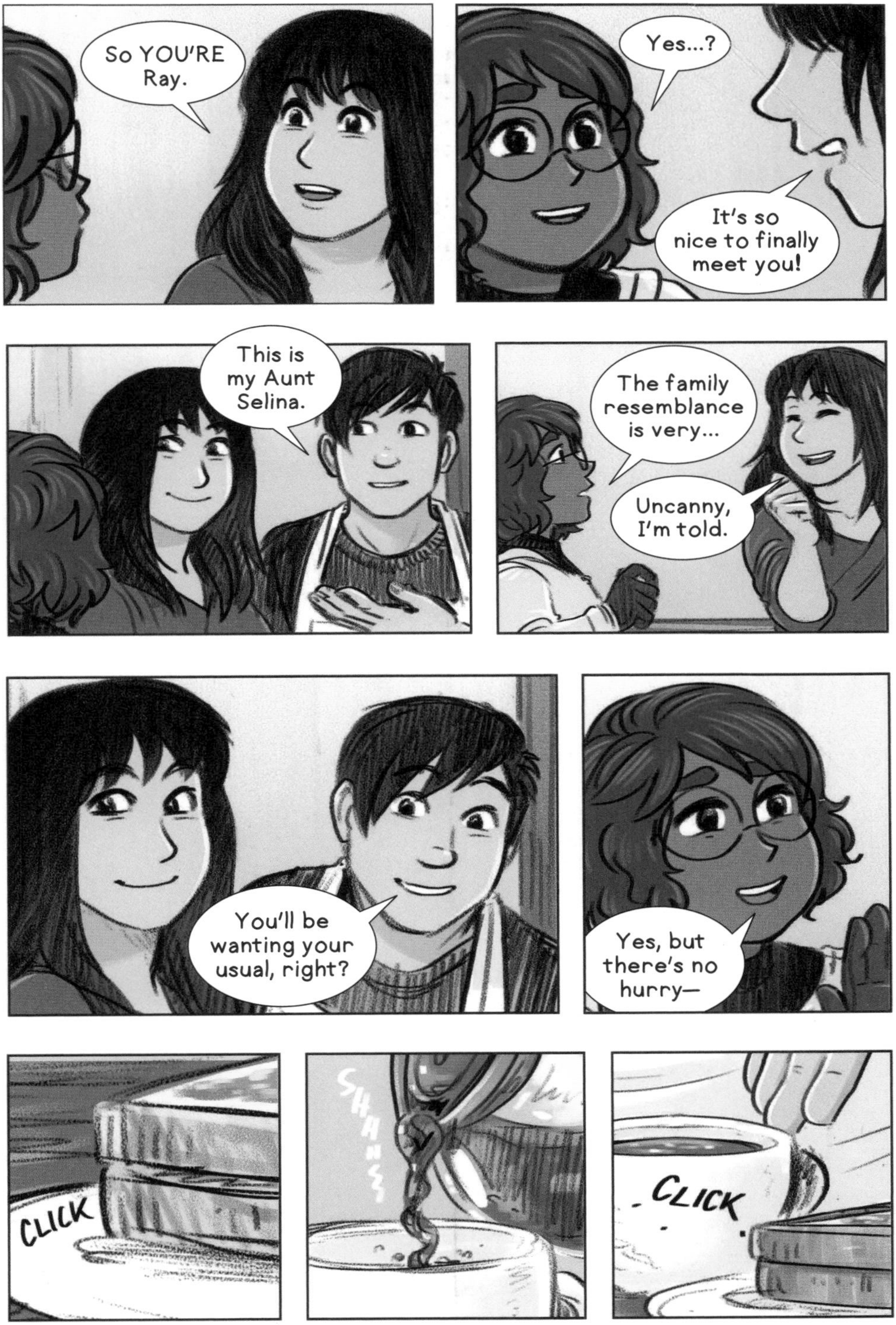
So YOU'RE Ray.
Yes...?
It's so nice to finally meet you!
This is my Aunt Selina.
The family resemblance is very...
Uncanny, I'm told.
You'll be wanting your usual, right?
Yes, but there's no hurry—
CLICK
SHHH
CLICK

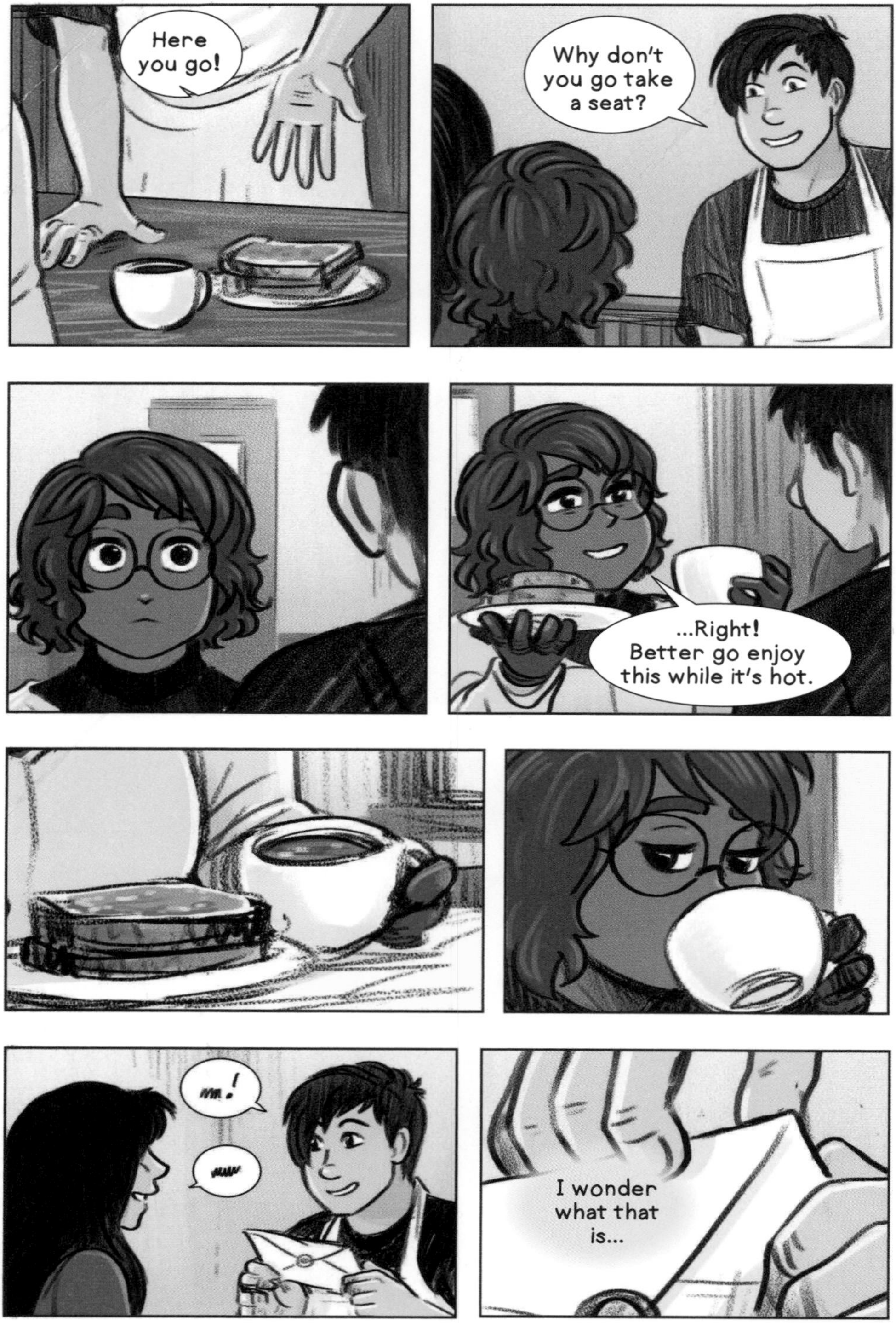
Here you go!
Why don't you go take a seat?
...Right! Better go enjoy this while it's hot.
I wonder what that is...

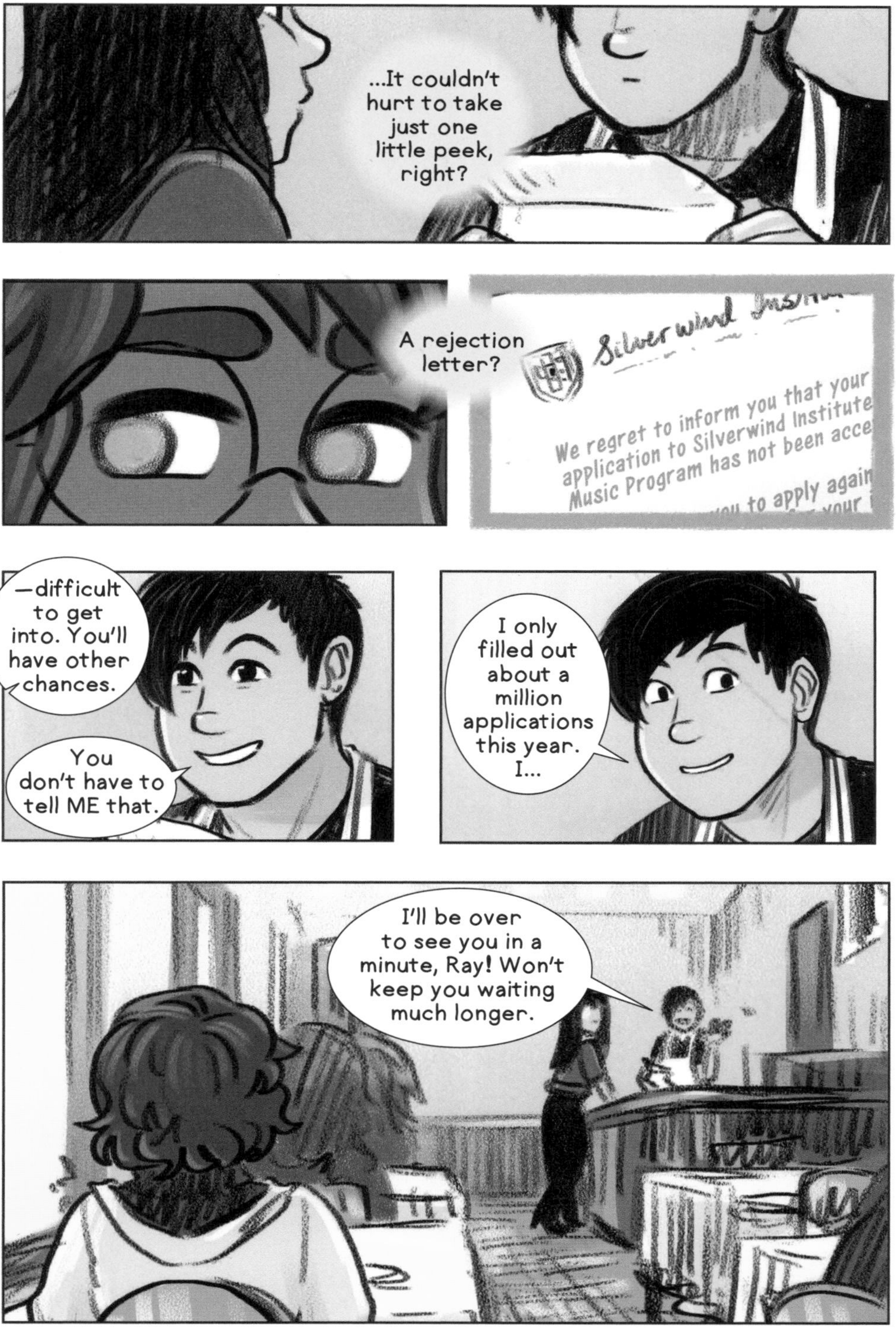
...It couldn't hurt to take just one little peek, right?
A rejection letter?
Silverwind Institute
We regret to inform you that your application to Silverwind Institute Music Program has not been acce
you to apply again
—difficult to get into. You'll have other chances.
You don't have to tell ME that.
I only filled out about a million applications this year. I...
I'll be over to see you in a minute, Ray! Won't keep you waiting much longer.

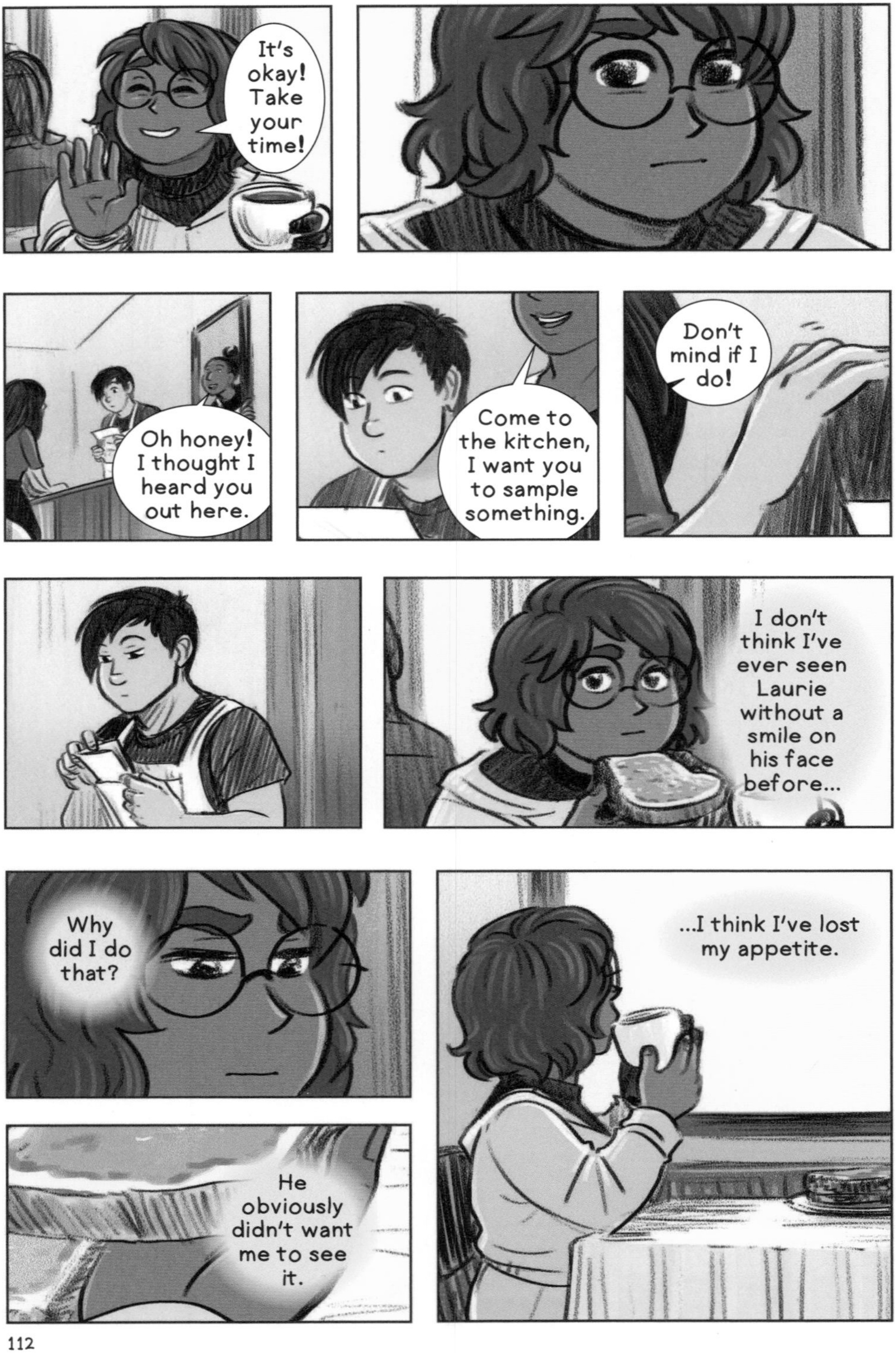
It's okay! Take your time!
Oh honey! I thought I heard you out here.
Come to the kitchen, I want you to sample something.
Don't mind if I do!
I don't think I've ever seen Laurie without a smile on his face before...
Why did I do that?
He obviously didn't want me to see it.
...I think I've lost my appetite.

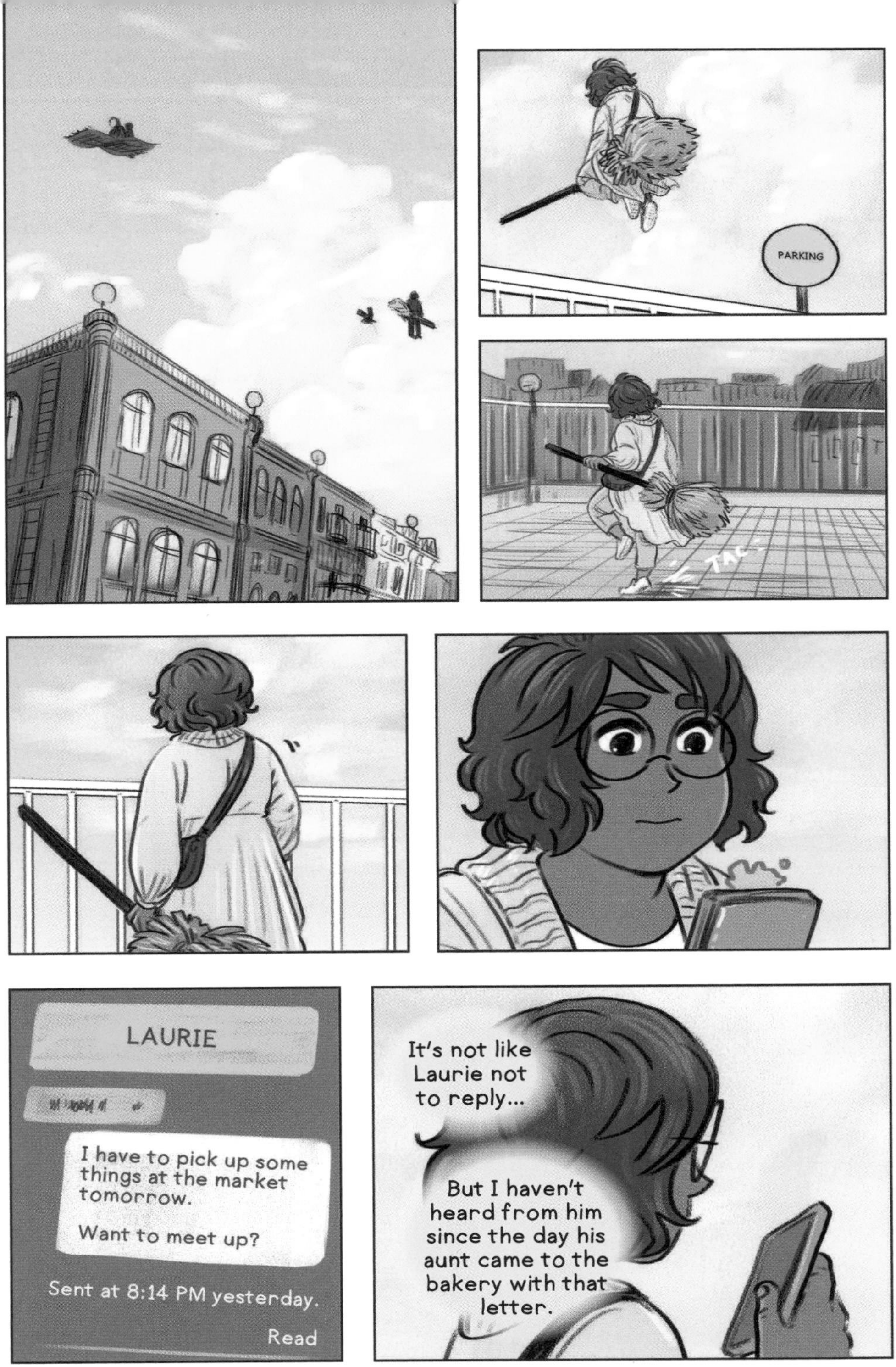
PARKING
TAC
LAURIE
I have to pick up some things at the market tomorrow.
Want to meet up?
Sent at 8:14 PM yesterday.
Read
It's not like Laurie not to reply...
But I haven't heard from him since the day his aunt came to the bakery with that letter.

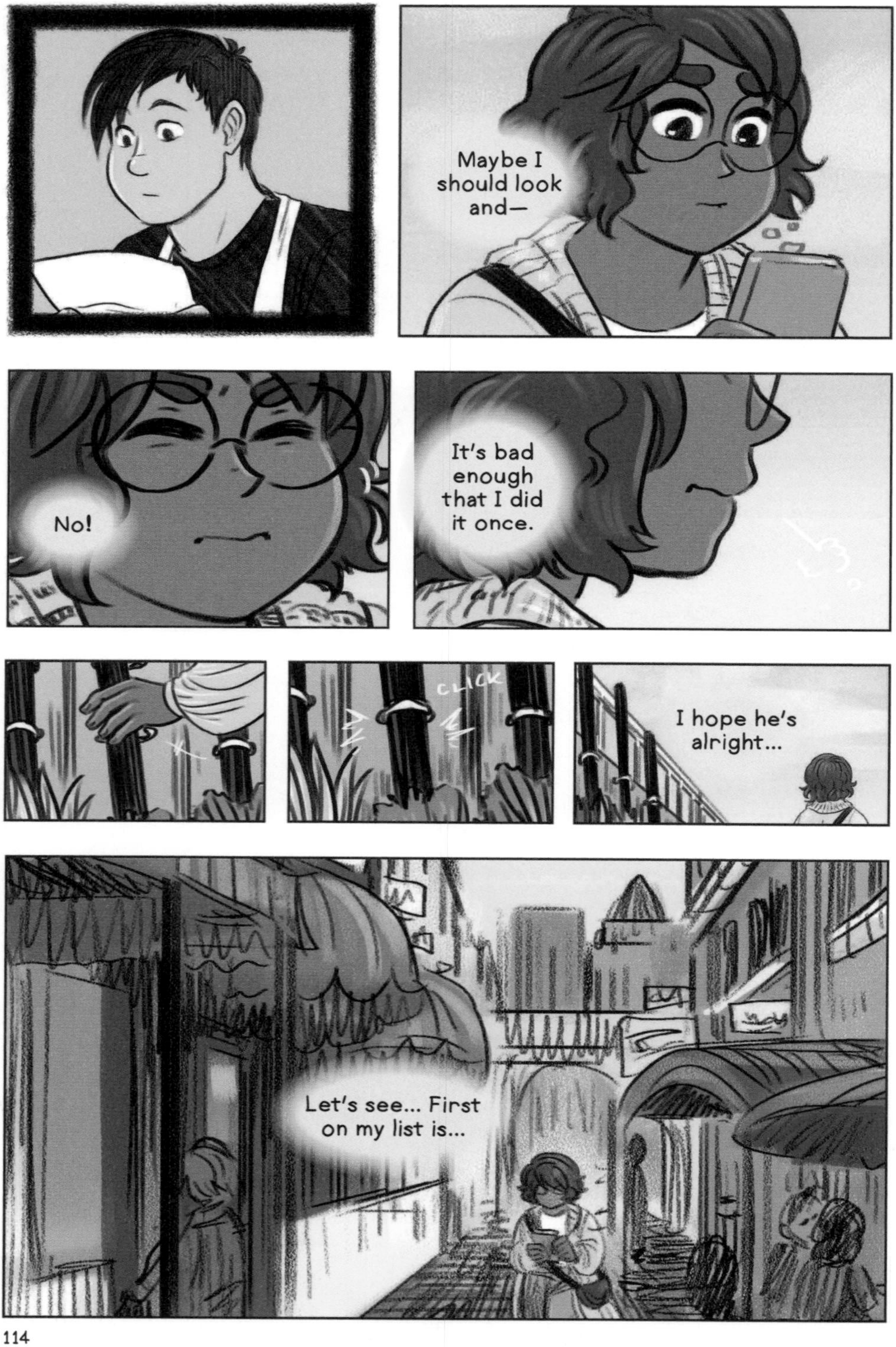
Maybe I should look and—
No!
It's bad enough that I did it once.
CLICK
I hope he's alright...
Let's see... First on my list is...

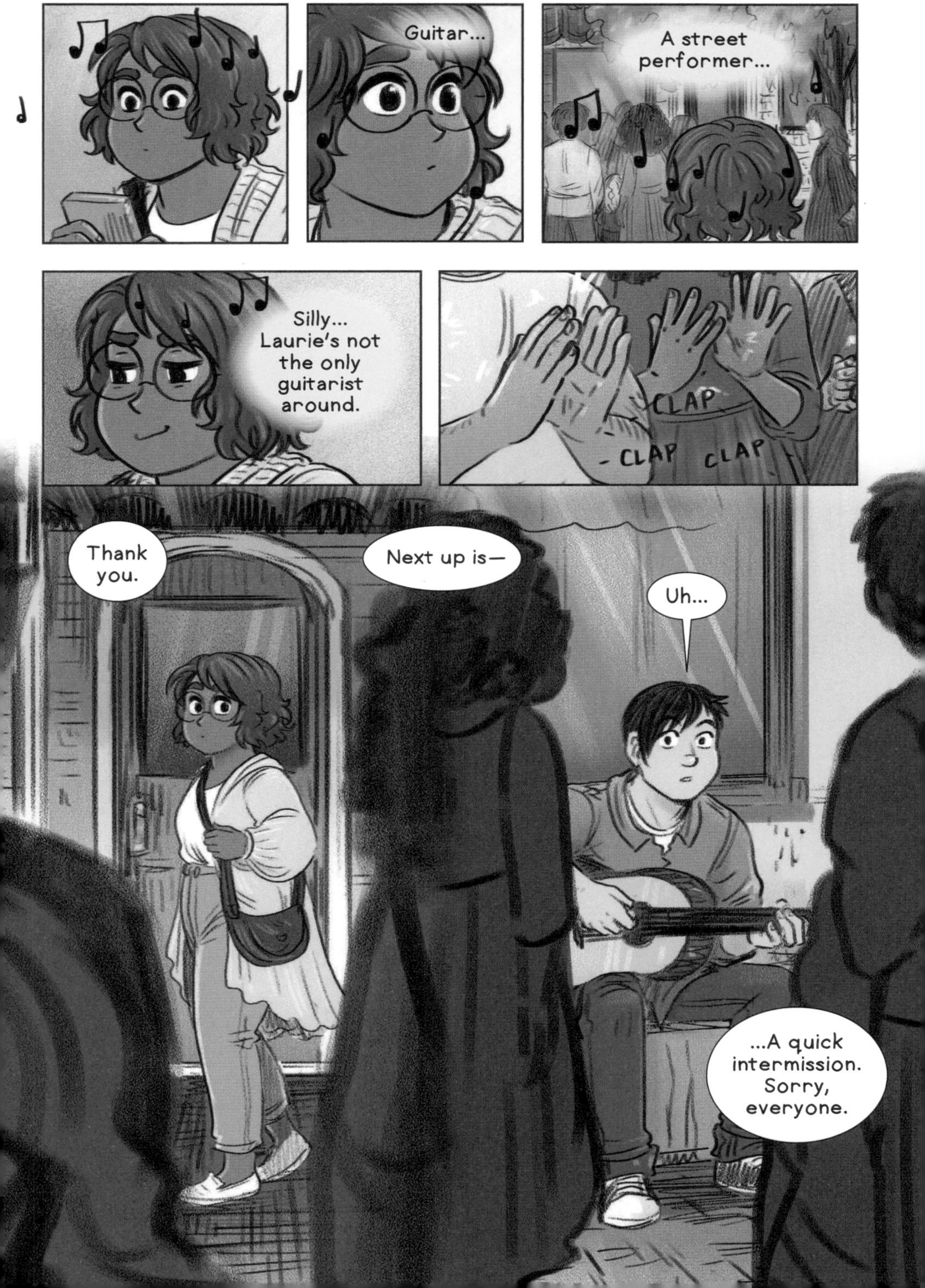
Guitar...
A street performer...
Silly... Laurie's not the only guitarist around.
CLAP
CLAP CLAP
Thank you.
Next up is—
Uh...
...A quick intermission. Sorry, everyone.

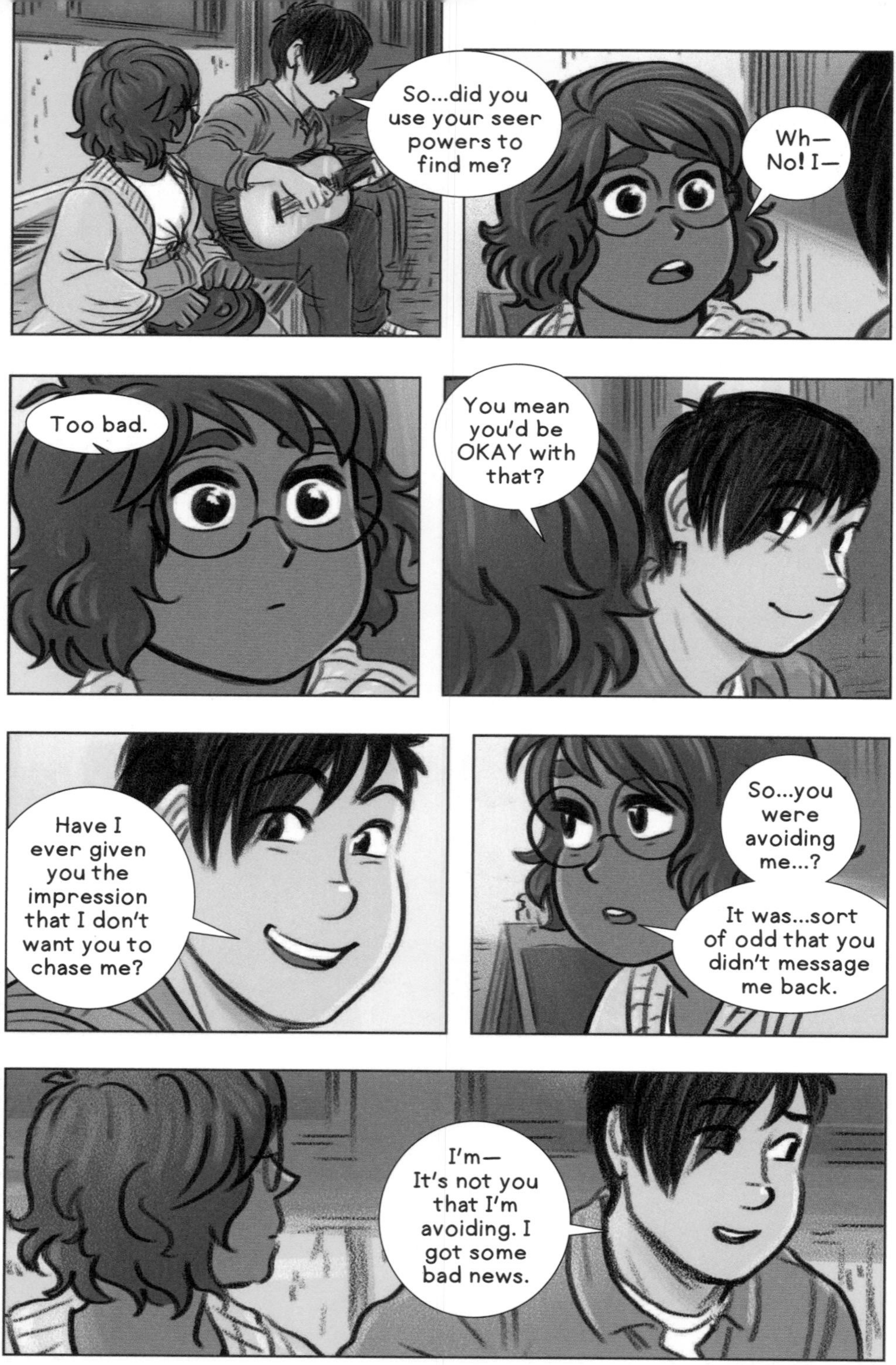
So...did you use your seer powers to find me?
Wh— No! I—
Too bad.
You mean you'd be OKAY with that?
Have I ever given you the impression that I don't want you to chase me?
So...you were avoiding me...?
It was...sort of odd that you didn't message me back.
I'm— It's not you that I'm avoiding. I got some bad news.

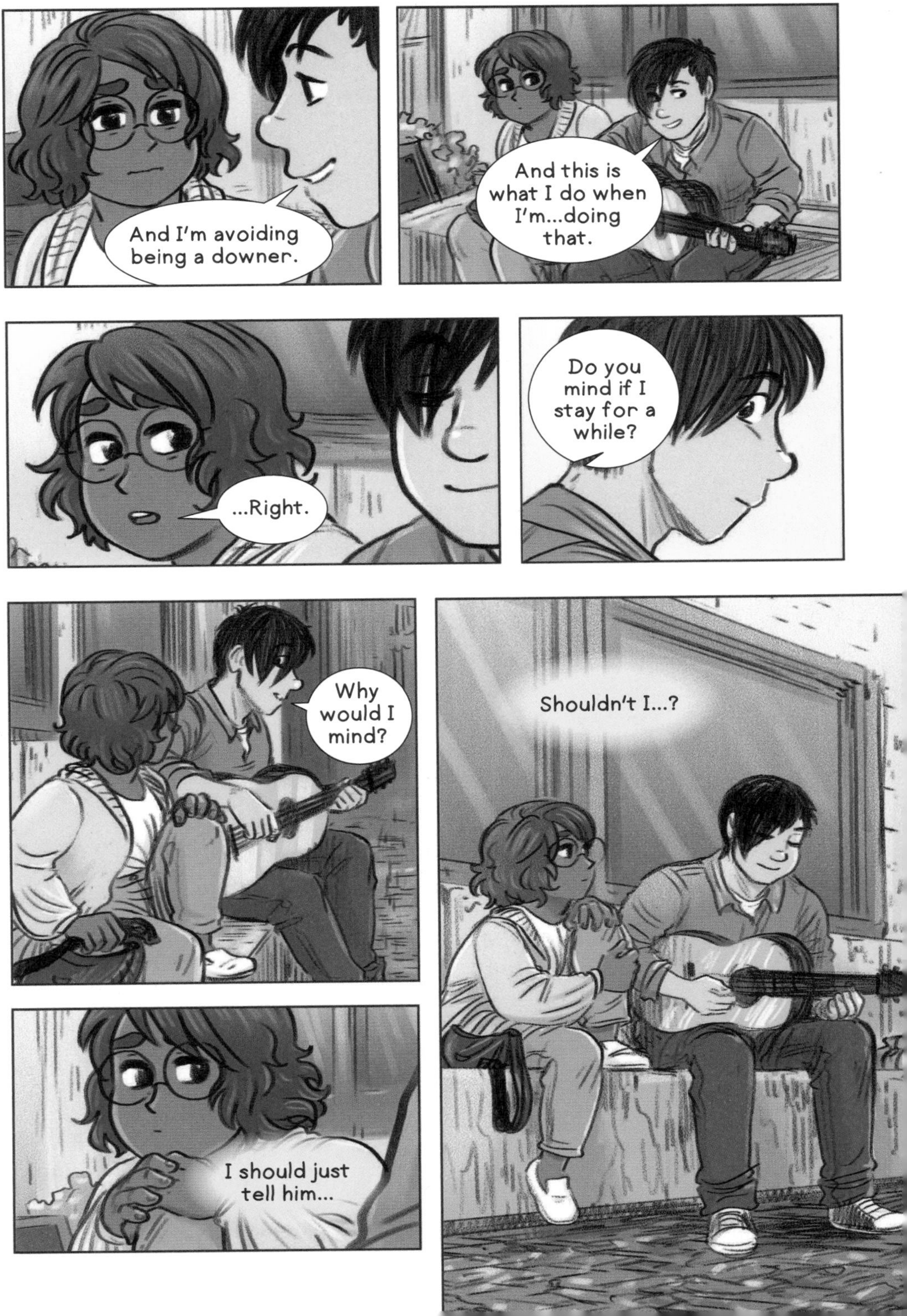
And I'm avoiding being a downer.
And this is what I do when I'm...doing that.
...Right.
Do you mind if I stay for a while?
Why would I mind?
I should just tell him...
Shouldn't I...?

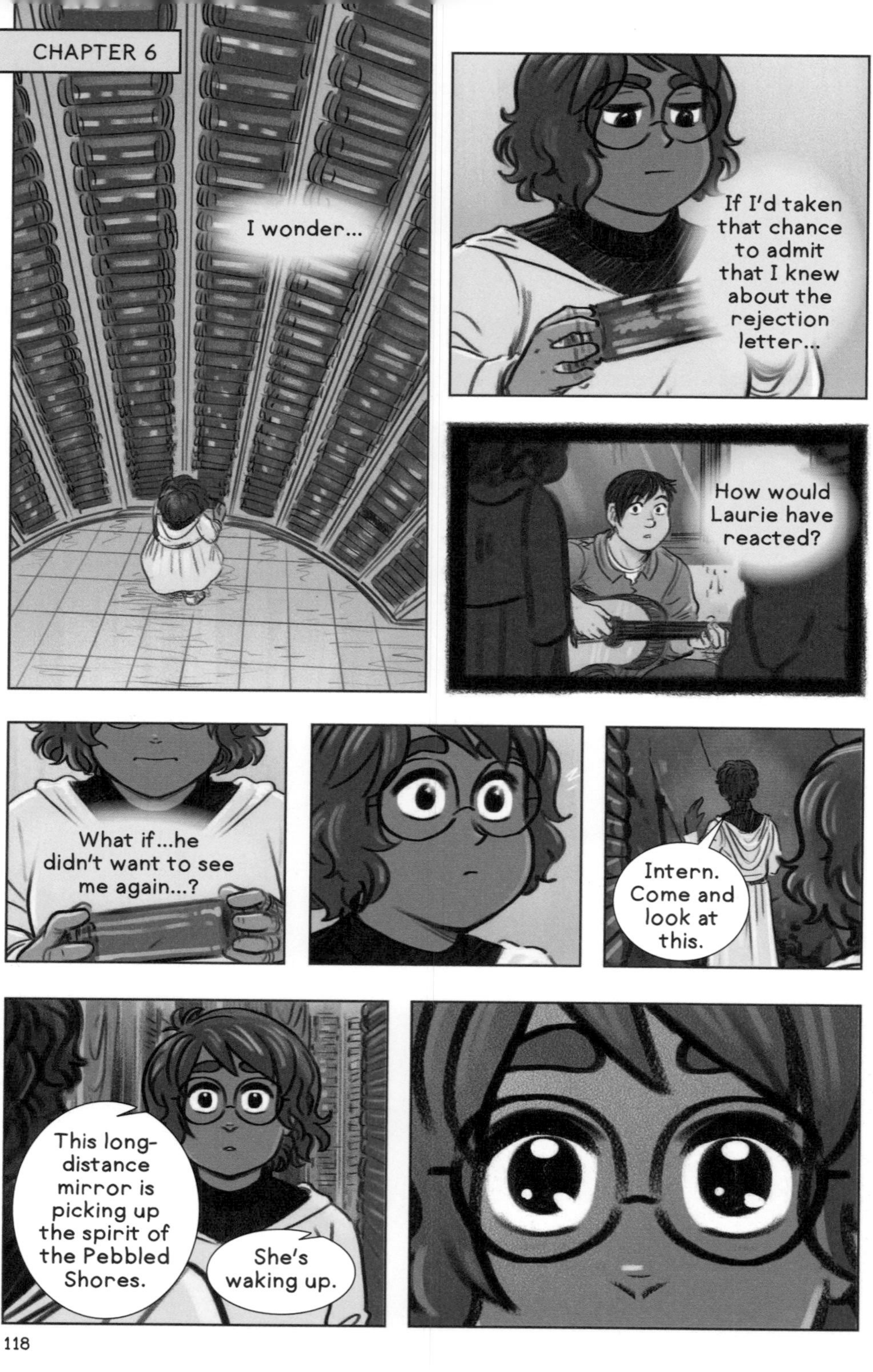
CHAPTER 6
I wonder...
If I'd taken that chance to admit that I knew about the rejection letter...
How would Laurie have reacted?
What if...he didn't want to see me again...?
Intern. Come and look at this.
This long-distance mirror is picking up the spirit of the Pebbled Shores.
She's waking up.

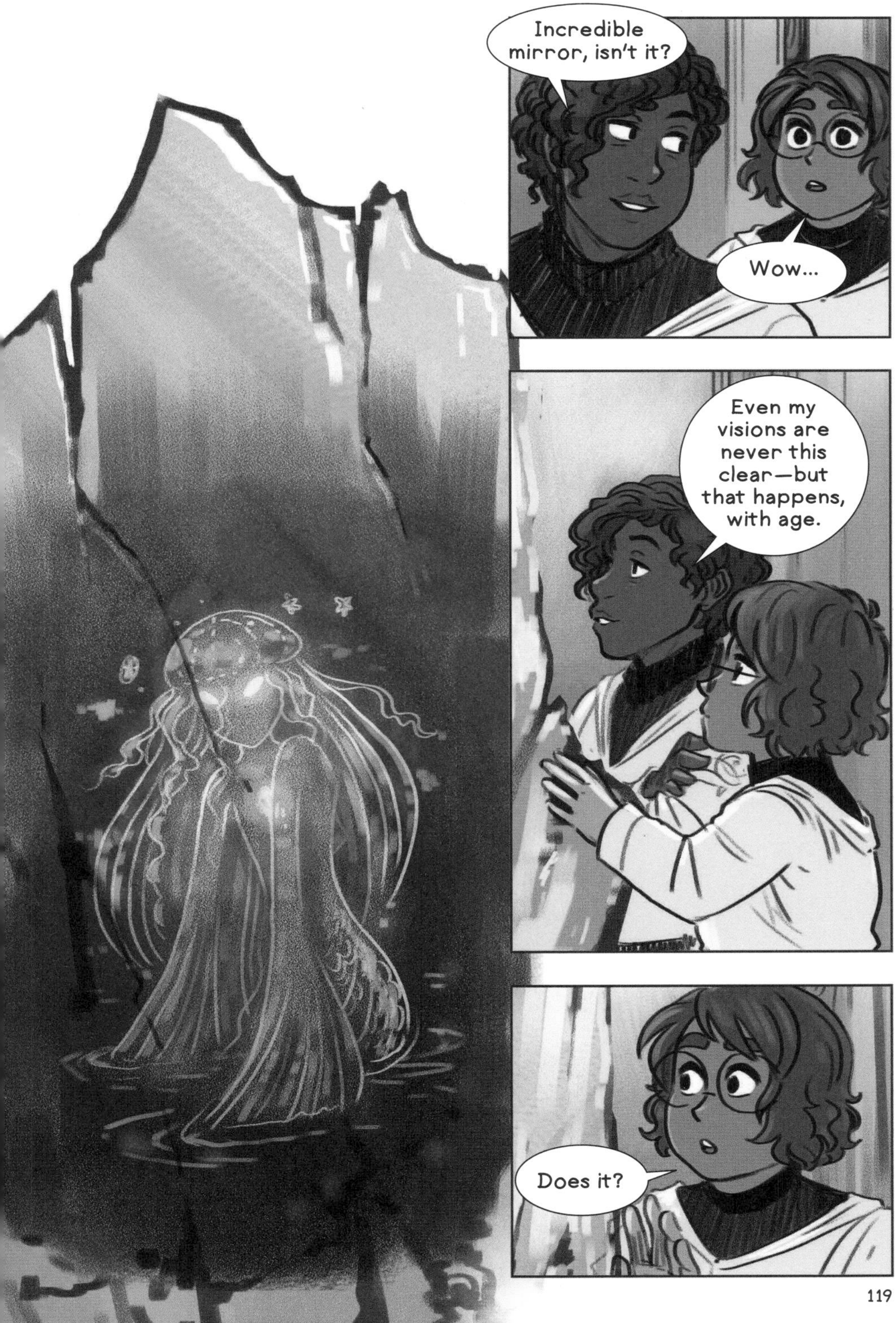
Incredible mirror, isn't it?
Wow...
Even my visions are never this clear—but that happens, with age.
Does it?

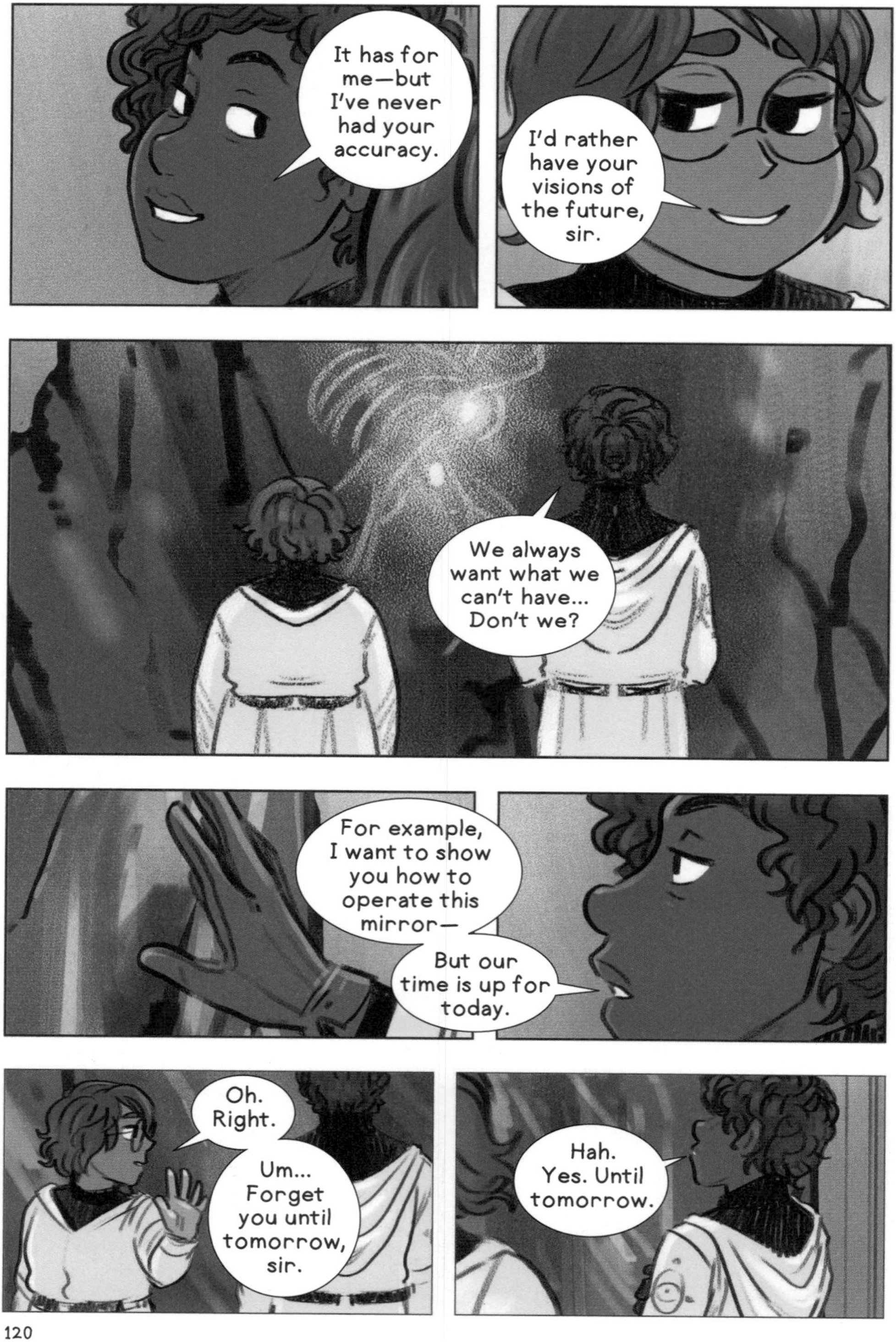

It has for me—but I've never had your accuracy.
I'd rather have your visions of the future, sir.
We always want what we can't have... Don't we?
For example, I want to show you how to operate this mirror—
But our time is up for today.
Oh. Right.
Um... Forget you until tomorrow, sir.
Hah. Yes. Until tomorrow.

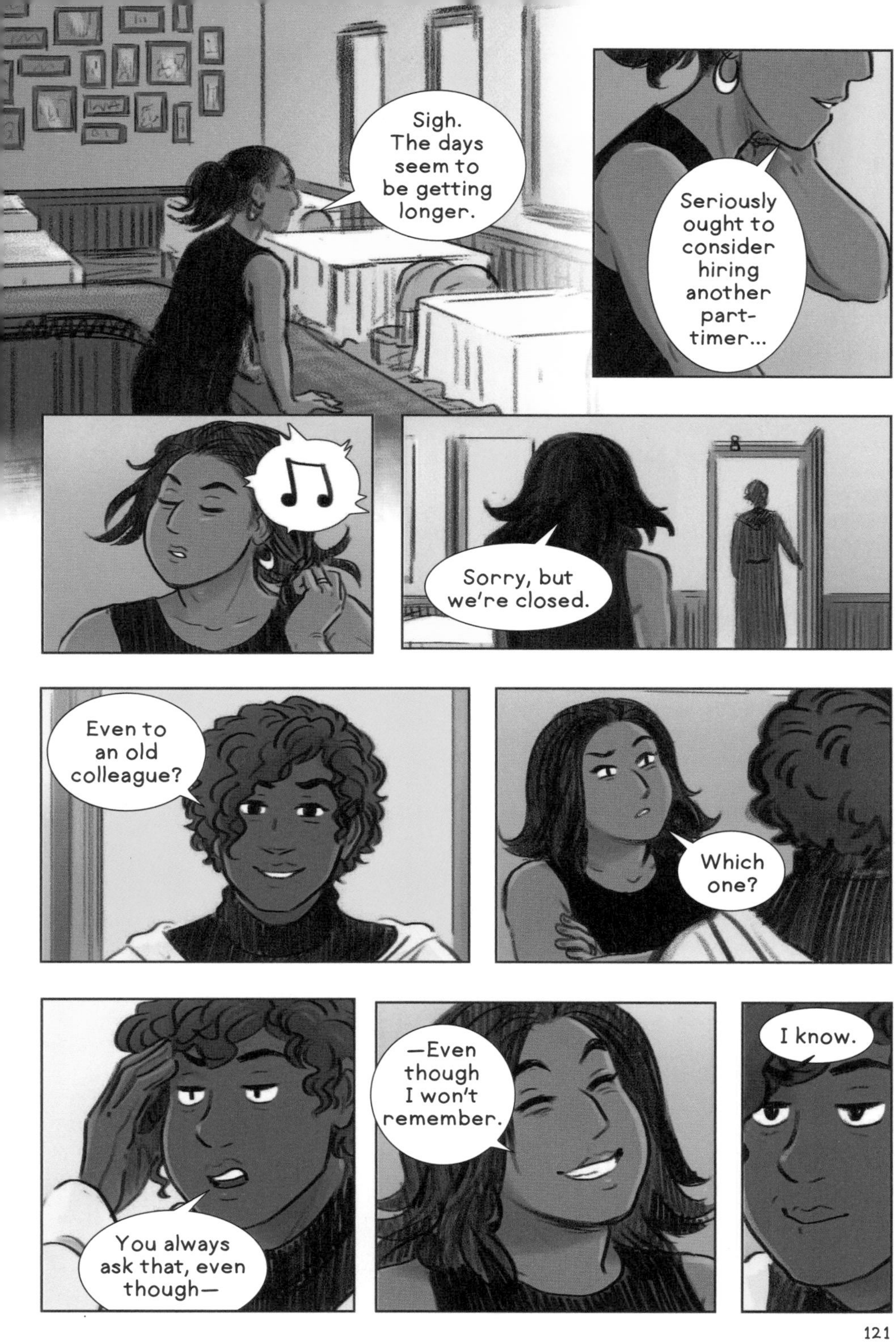
Sigh. The days seem to be getting longer.
Seriously ought to consider hiring another part-timer...
Sorry, but we're closed.
Even to an old colleague?
Which one?
You always ask that, even though—
—Even though I won't remember.
I know.

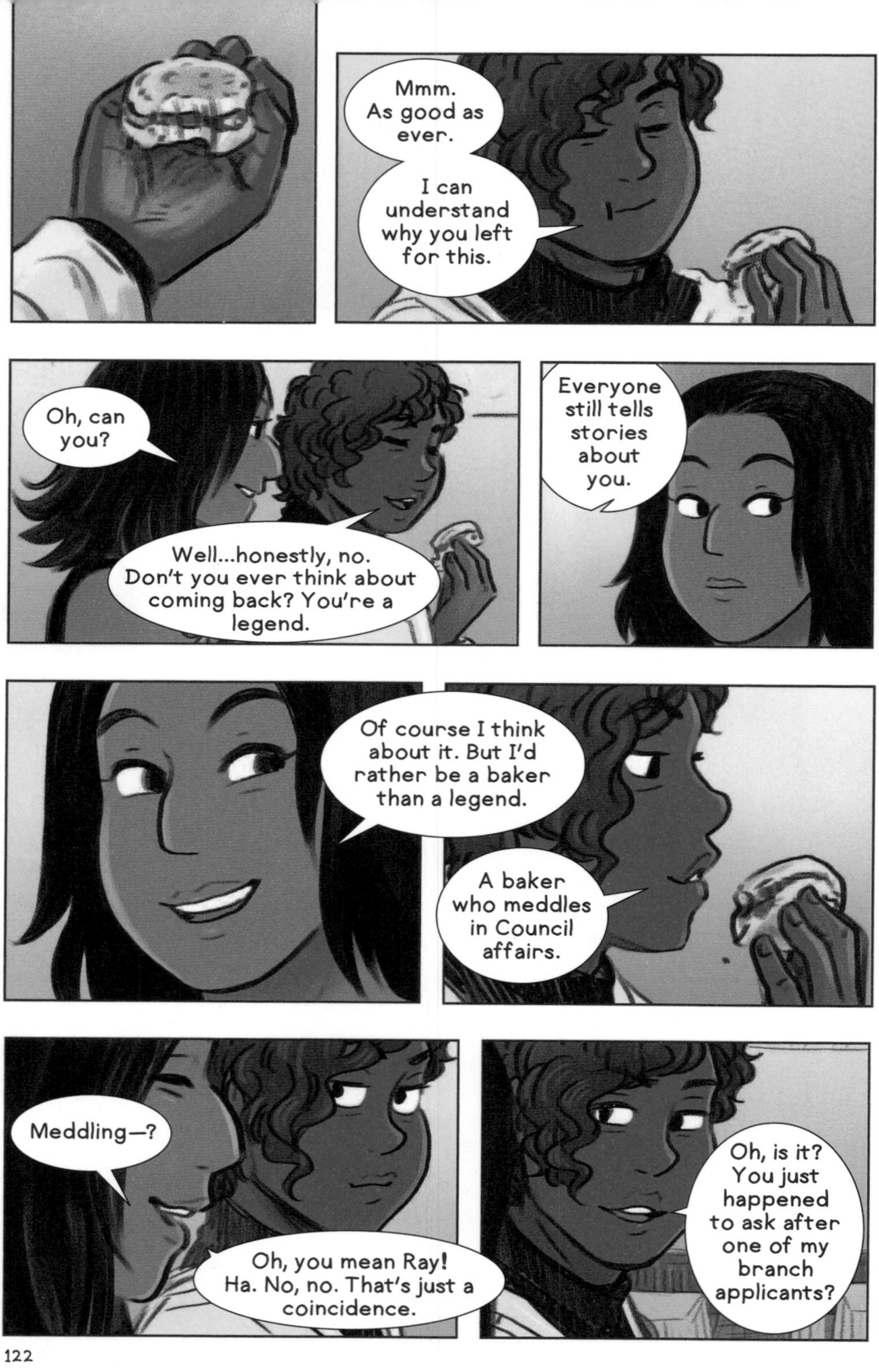
Mmm.
As good as ever.
I can understand why you left for this.
Oh, can you?
Well...honestly, no. Don't you ever think about coming back? You're a legend.
Everyone still tells stories about you.
Of course I think about it. But I'd rather be a baker than a legend.
A baker who meddles in Council affairs.
Meddling—?
Oh, you mean Ray! Ha. No, no. That's just a coincidence.
Oh, is it? You just happened to ask after one of my branch applicants?

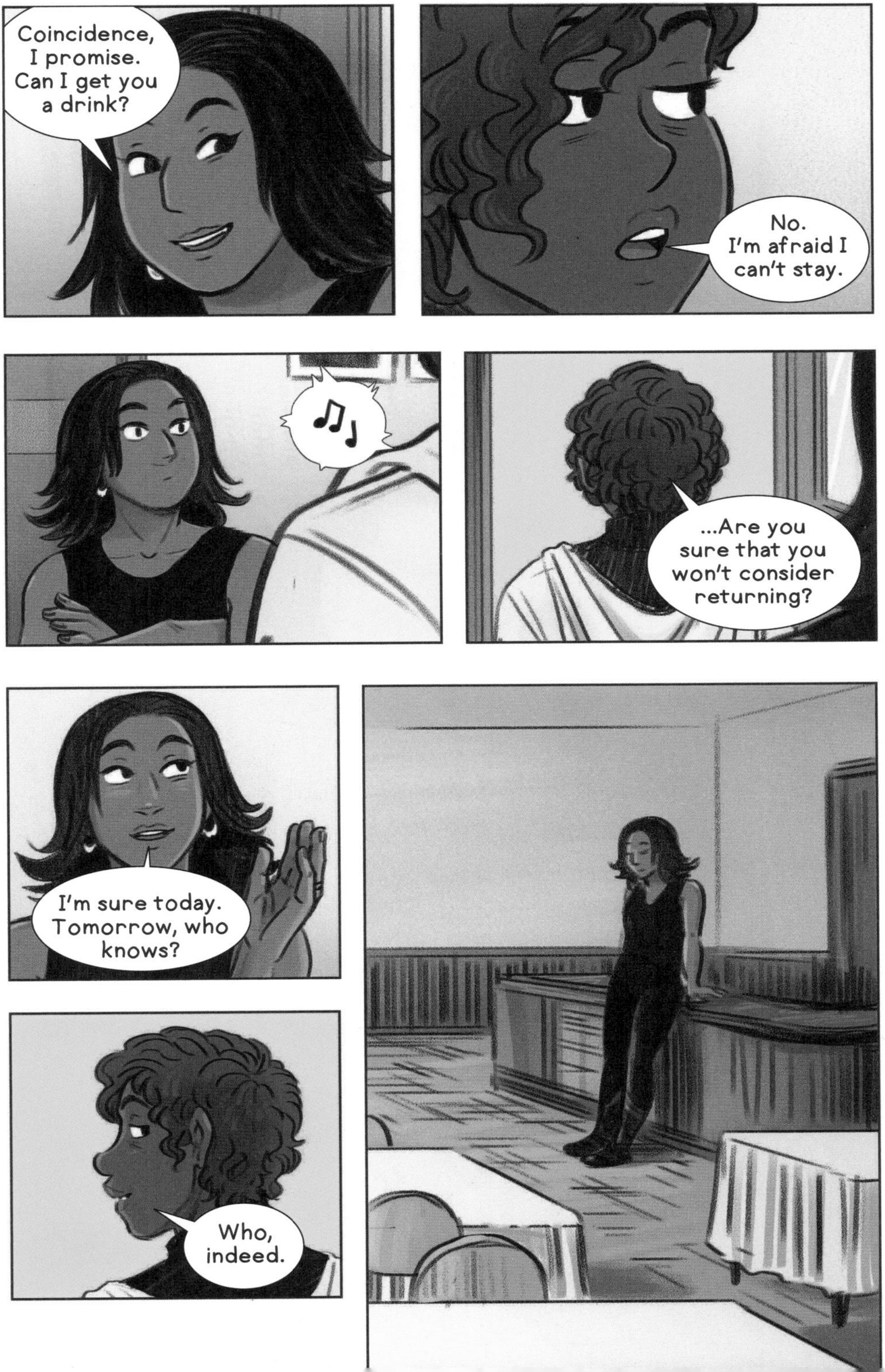
Coincidence, I promise. Can I get you a drink?
No. I'm afraid I can't stay.
...Are you sure that you won't consider returning?
I'm sure today. Tomorrow, who knows?
Who, indeed.

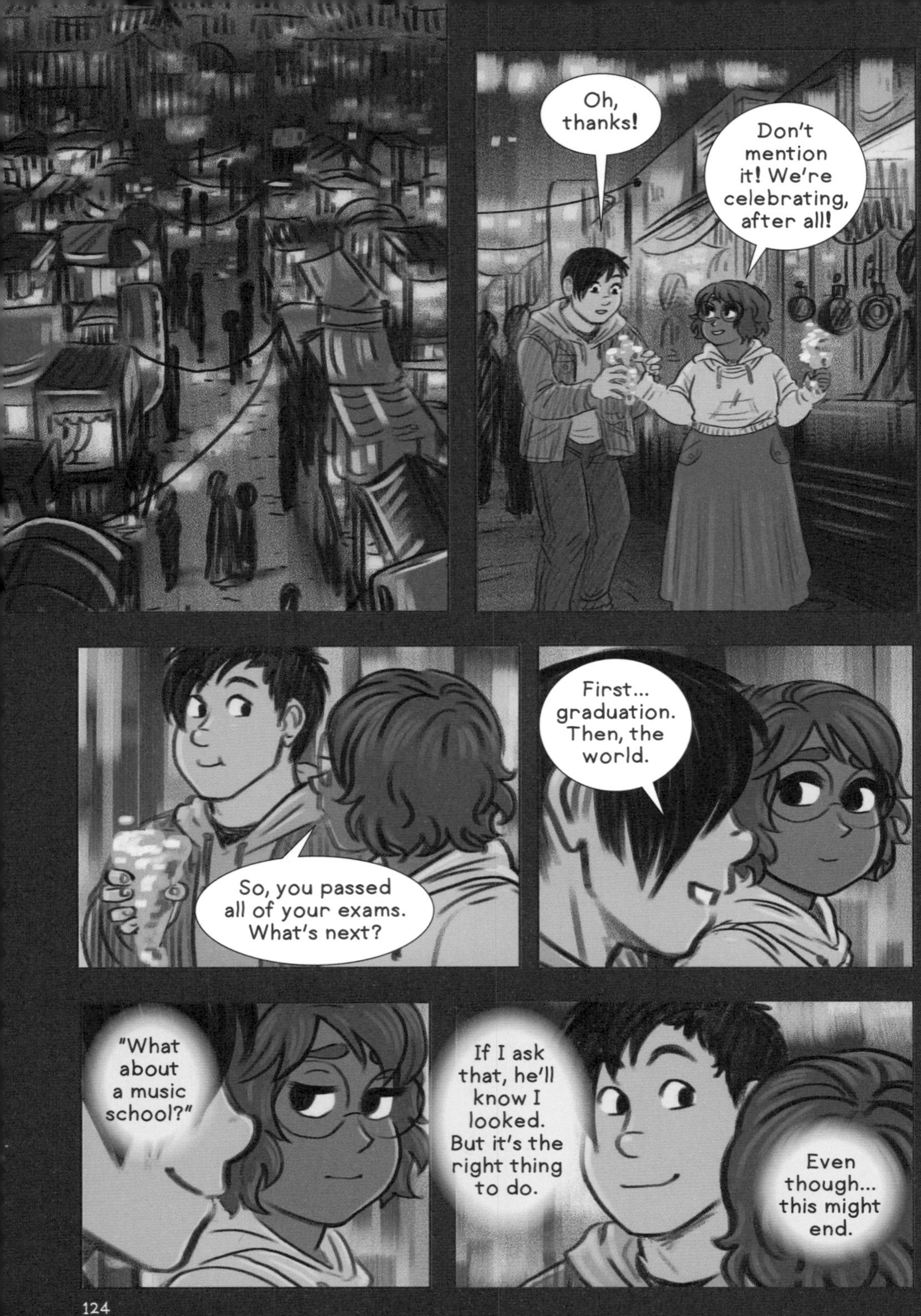
Oh, thanks!
Don't mention it! We're celebrating, after all!
So, you passed all of your exams. What's next?
First... graduation. Then, the world.
"What about a music school?"
If I ask that, he'll know I looked. But it's the right thing to do.
Even though... this might end.

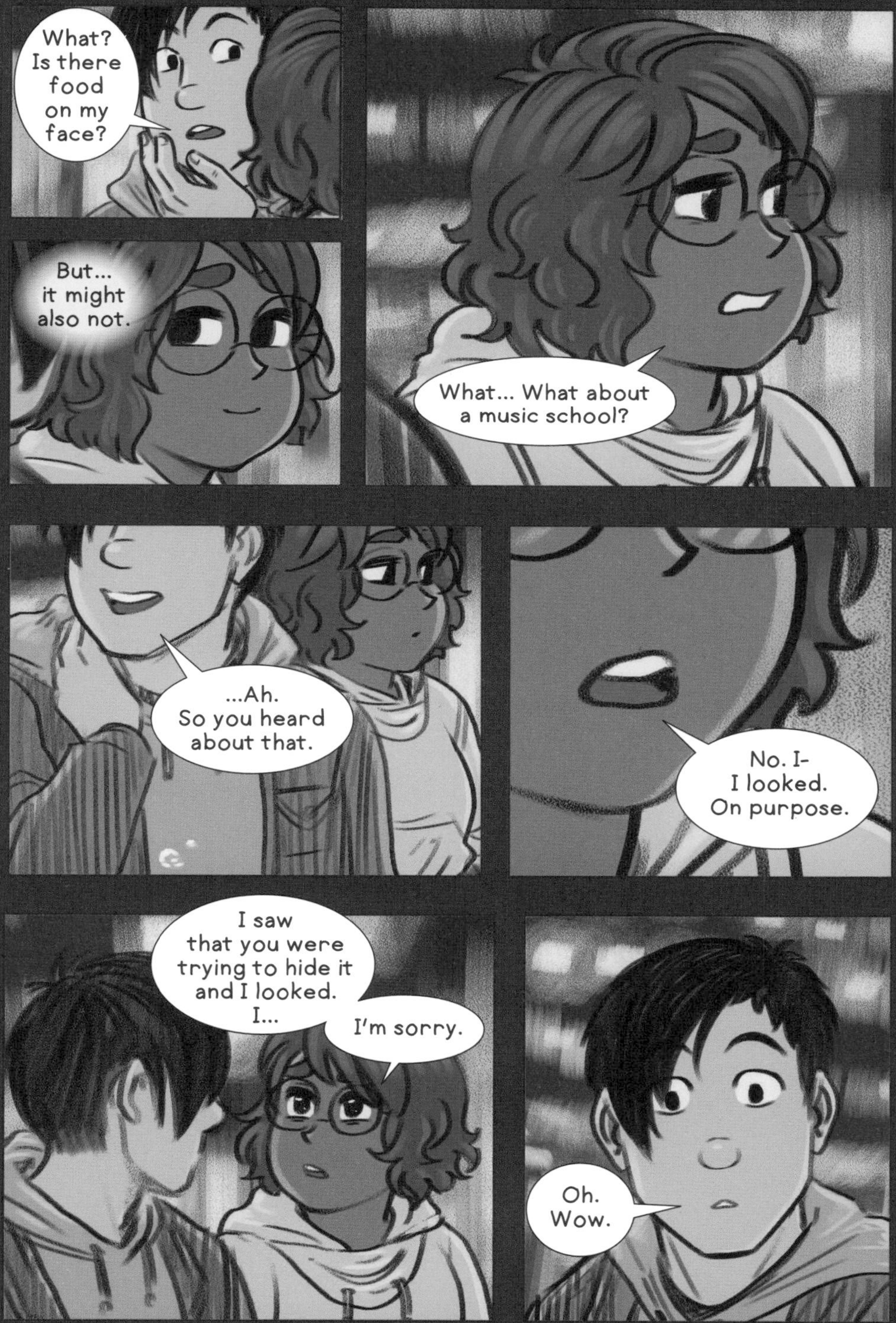
What? Is there food on my face?
But... it might also not.
What... What about a music school?
...Ah. So you heard about that.
No. I- I looked. On purpose.
I saw that you were trying to hide it and I looked. I...
I'm sorry.
Oh. Wow.

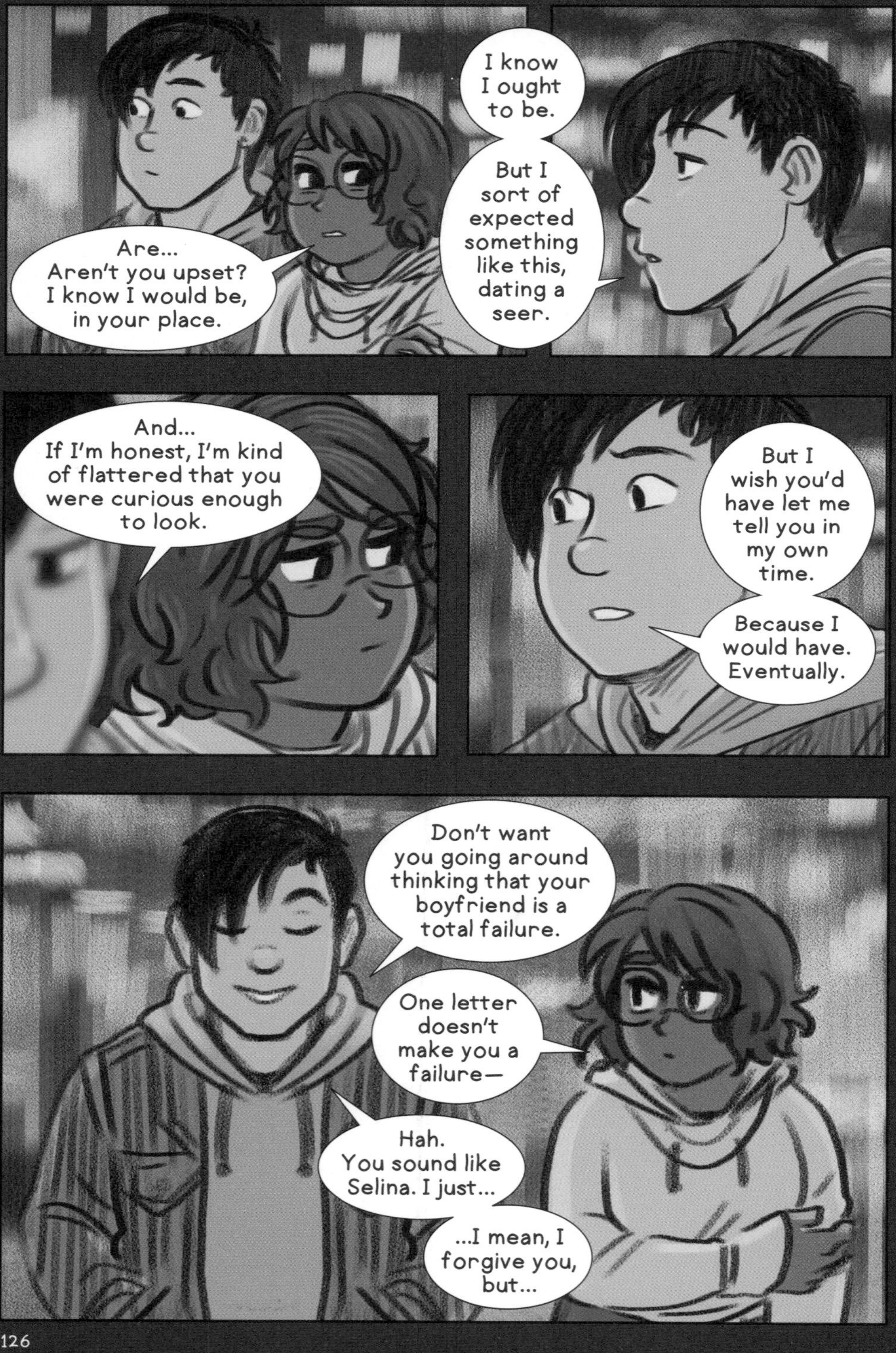
Are... Aren't you upset? I know I would be, in your place.
I know I ought to be.
But I sort of expected something like this, dating a seer.
And... If I'm honest, I'm kind of flattered that you were curious enough to look.
But I wish you'd have let me tell you in my own time.
Because I would have. Eventually.
Don't want you going around thinking that your boyfriend is a total failure.
One letter doesn't make you a failure—
Hah. You sound like Selina. I just...
...I mean, I forgive you, but...

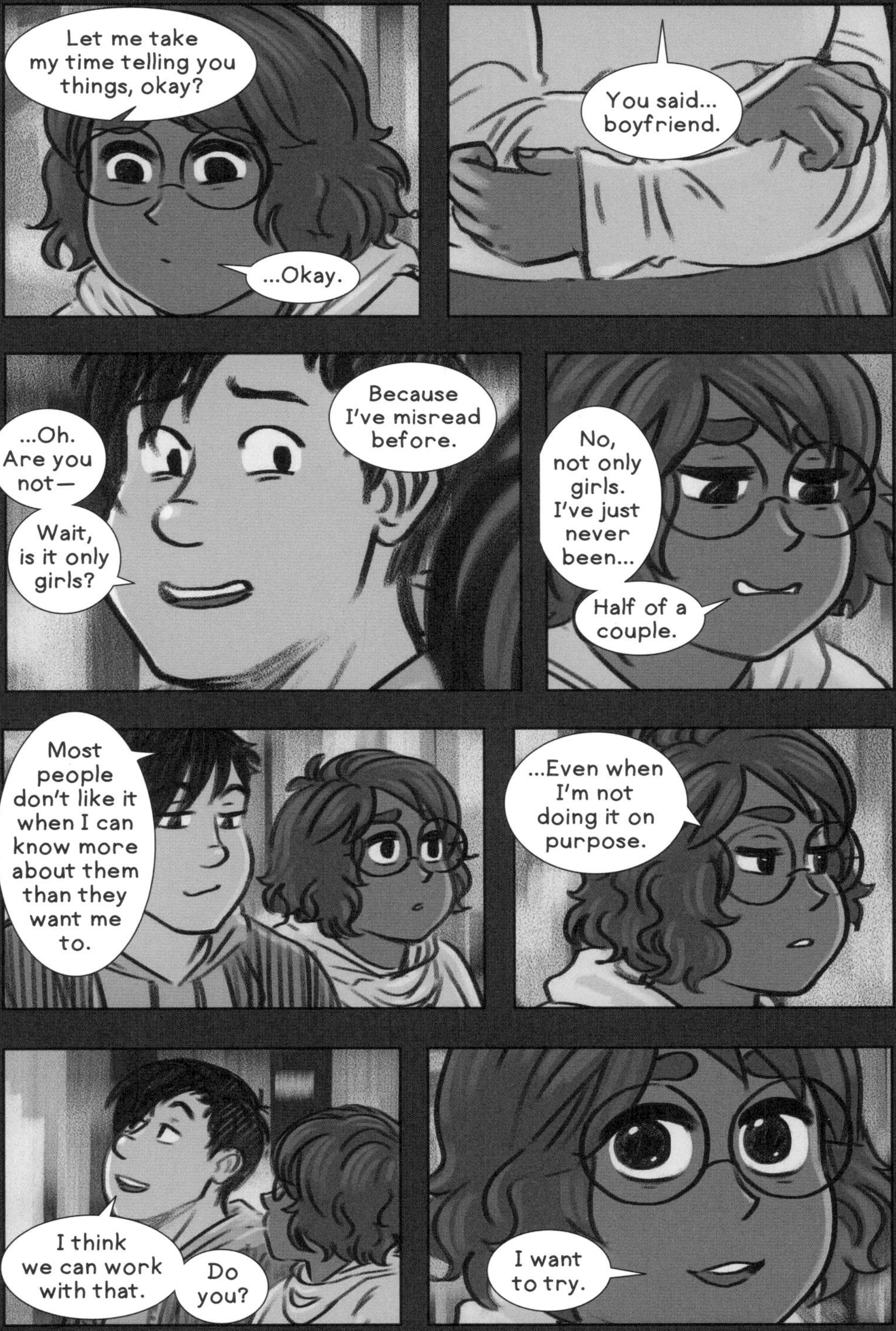

Let me take my time telling you things, okay?
...Okay.
You said... boyfriend.
...Oh. Are you not—
Wait, is it only girls?
Because I've misread before.
No, not only girls. I've just never been...
Half of a couple.
Most people don't like it when I can know more about them than they want me to.
...Even when I'm not doing it on purpose.
I think we can work with that.
Do you?
I want to try.

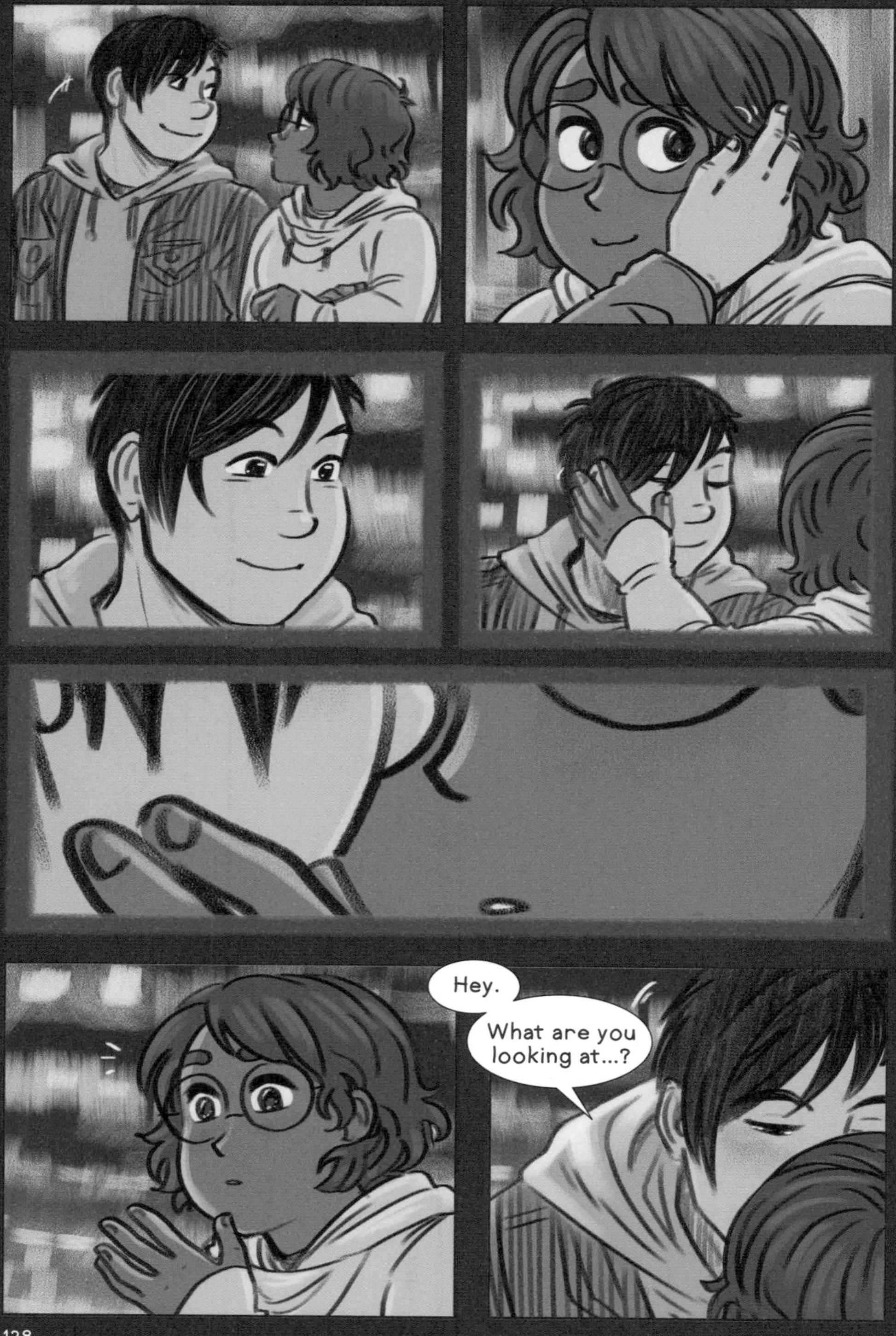
Hey.
What are you looking at...?

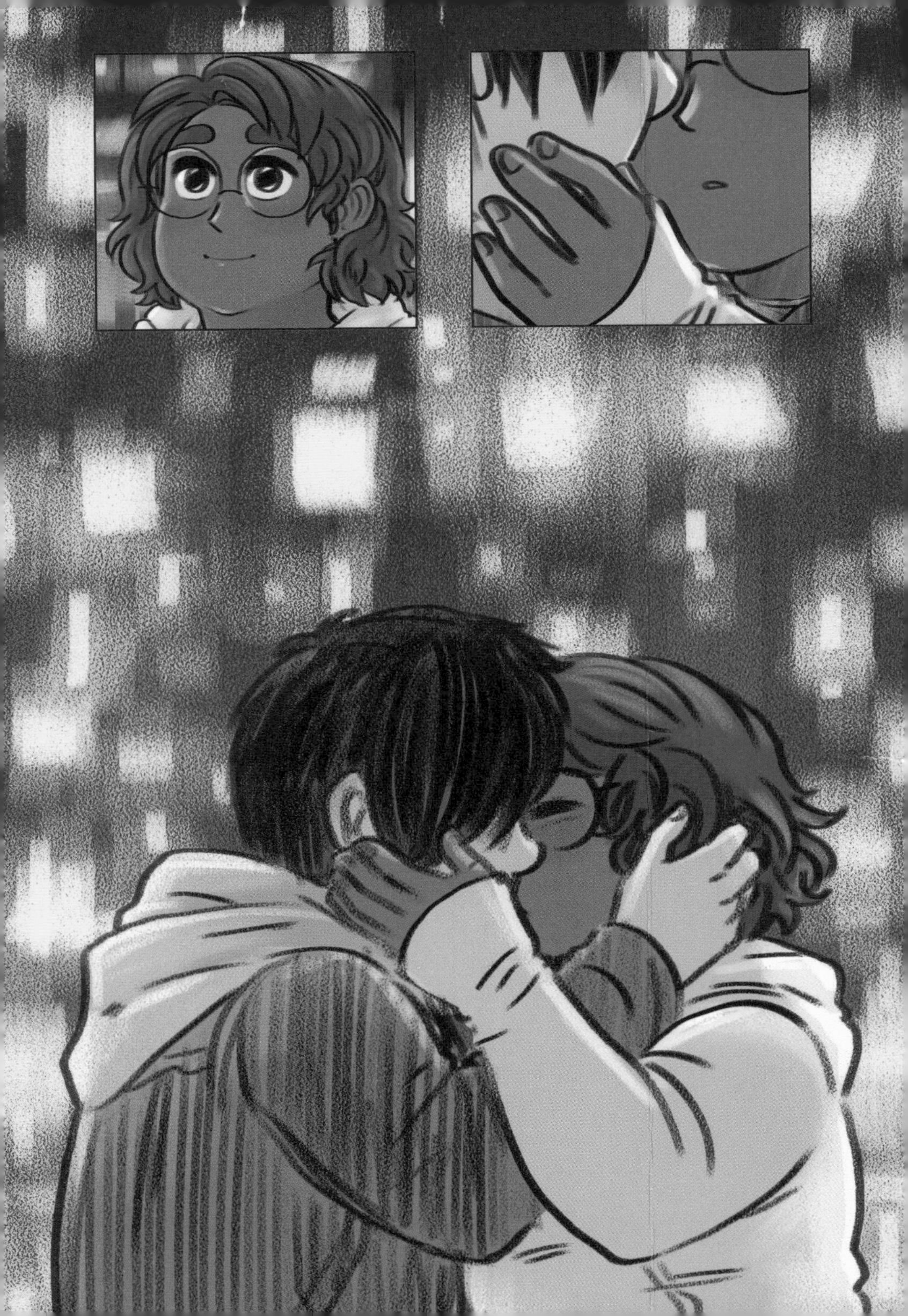

CHAPTER 7

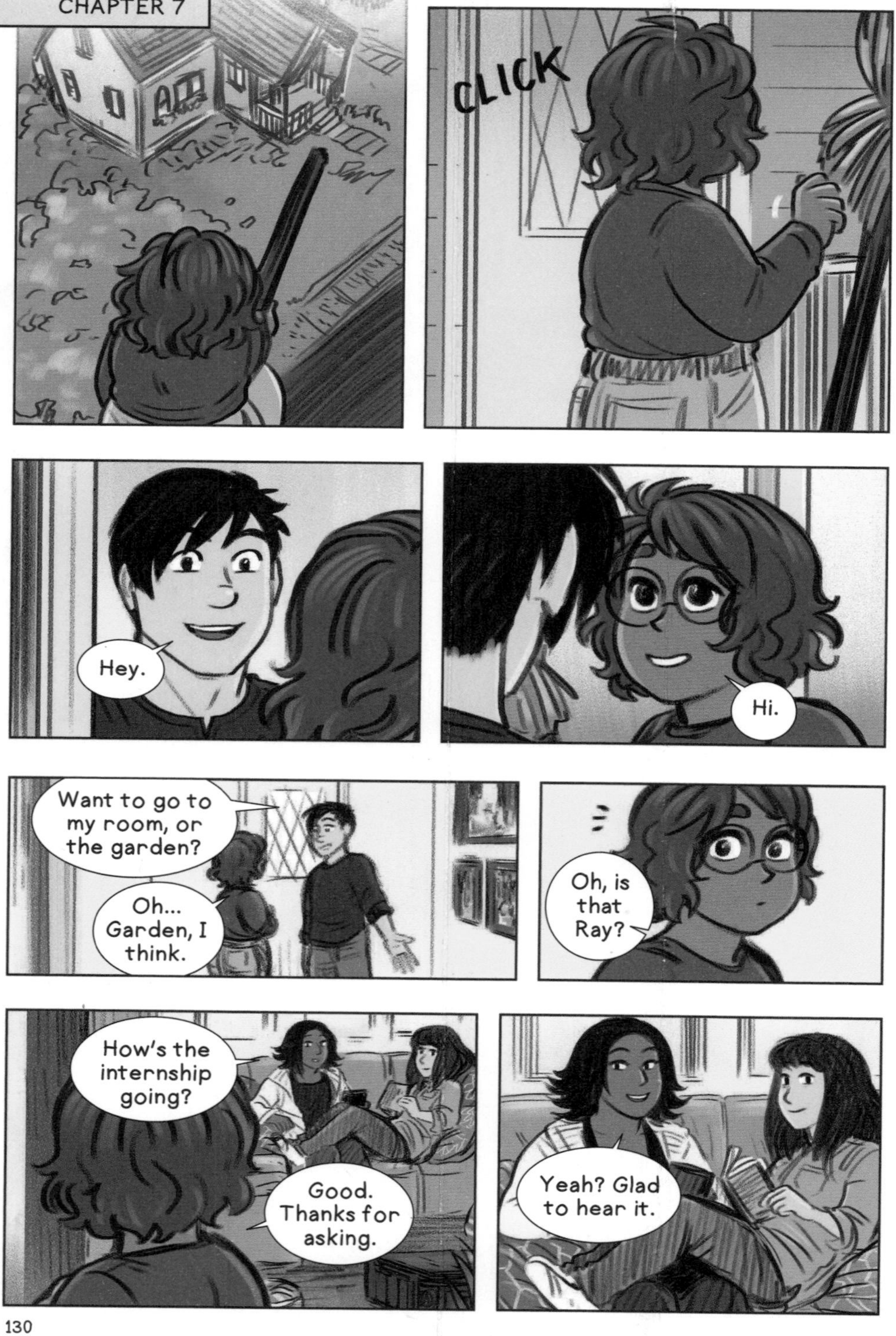
CLICK
Hey.
Hi.
Want to go to my room, or the garden?
Oh... Garden, I think.
Oh, is that Ray?
How's the internship going?
Good. Thanks for asking.
Yeah? Glad to hear it.

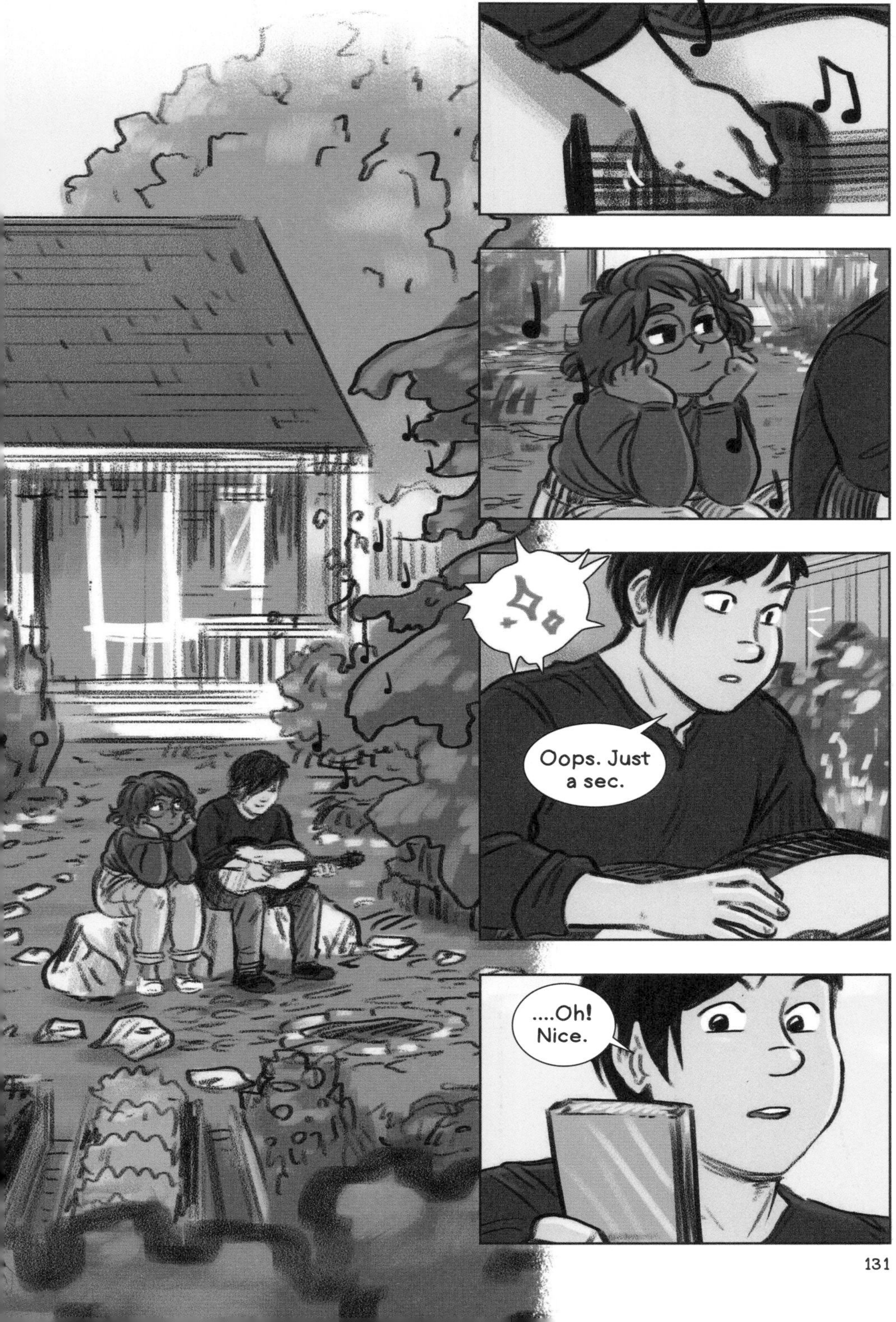
Oops. Just a sec.
....Oh! Nice.

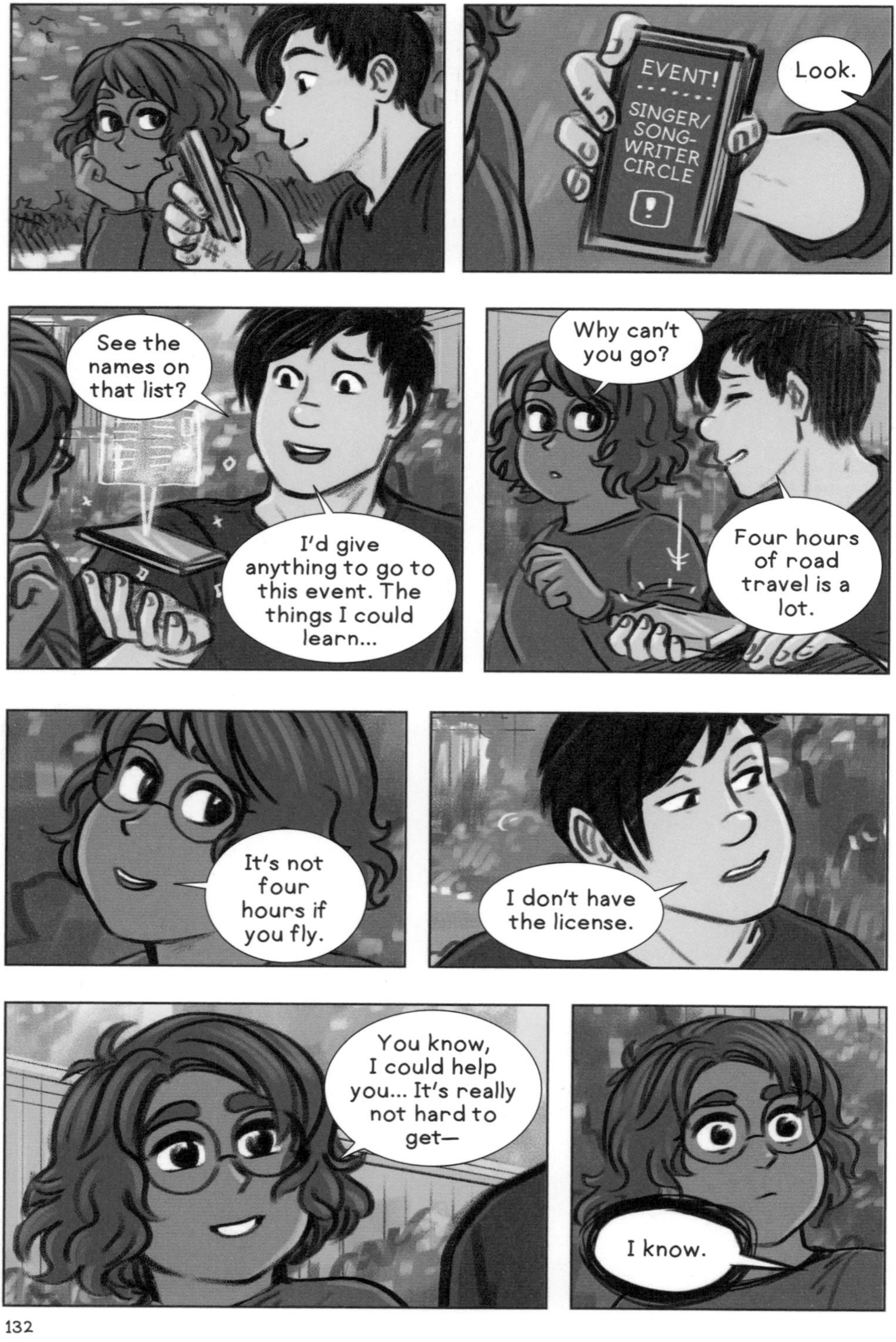
Look.
EVENT!
SINGER/ SONG-WRITER CIRCLE
See the names on that list?
I'd give anything to go to this event. The things I could learn...
Why can't you go?
Four hours of road travel is a lot.
It's not four hours if you fly.
I don't have the license.
You know, I could help you... It's really not hard to get—
I know.

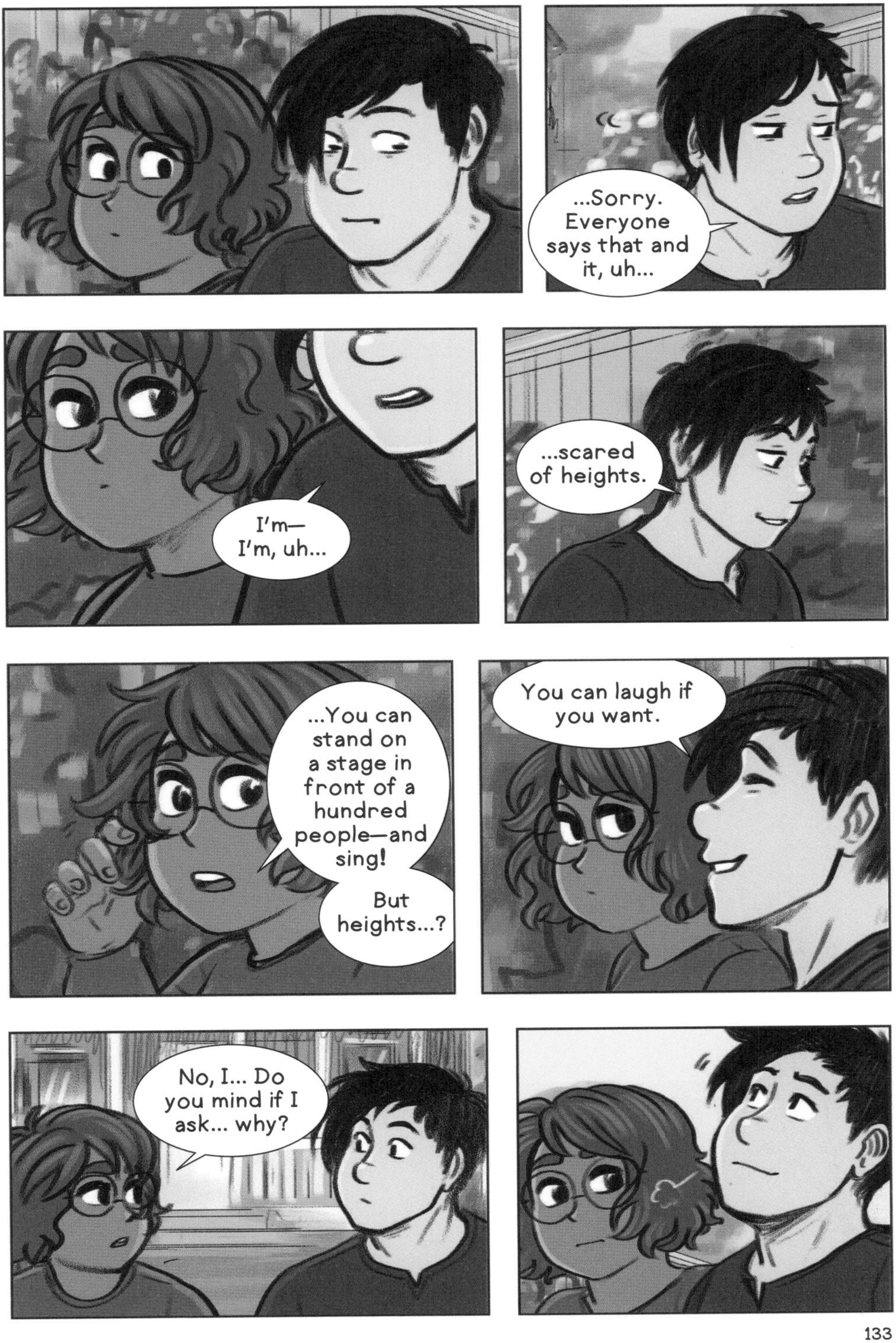
...Sorry. Everyone says that and it, uh...
I'm— I'm, uh...
...scared of heights.
...You can stand on a stage in front of a hundred people—and sing!
But heights...?
You can laugh if you want.
No, I... Do you mind if I ask... why?

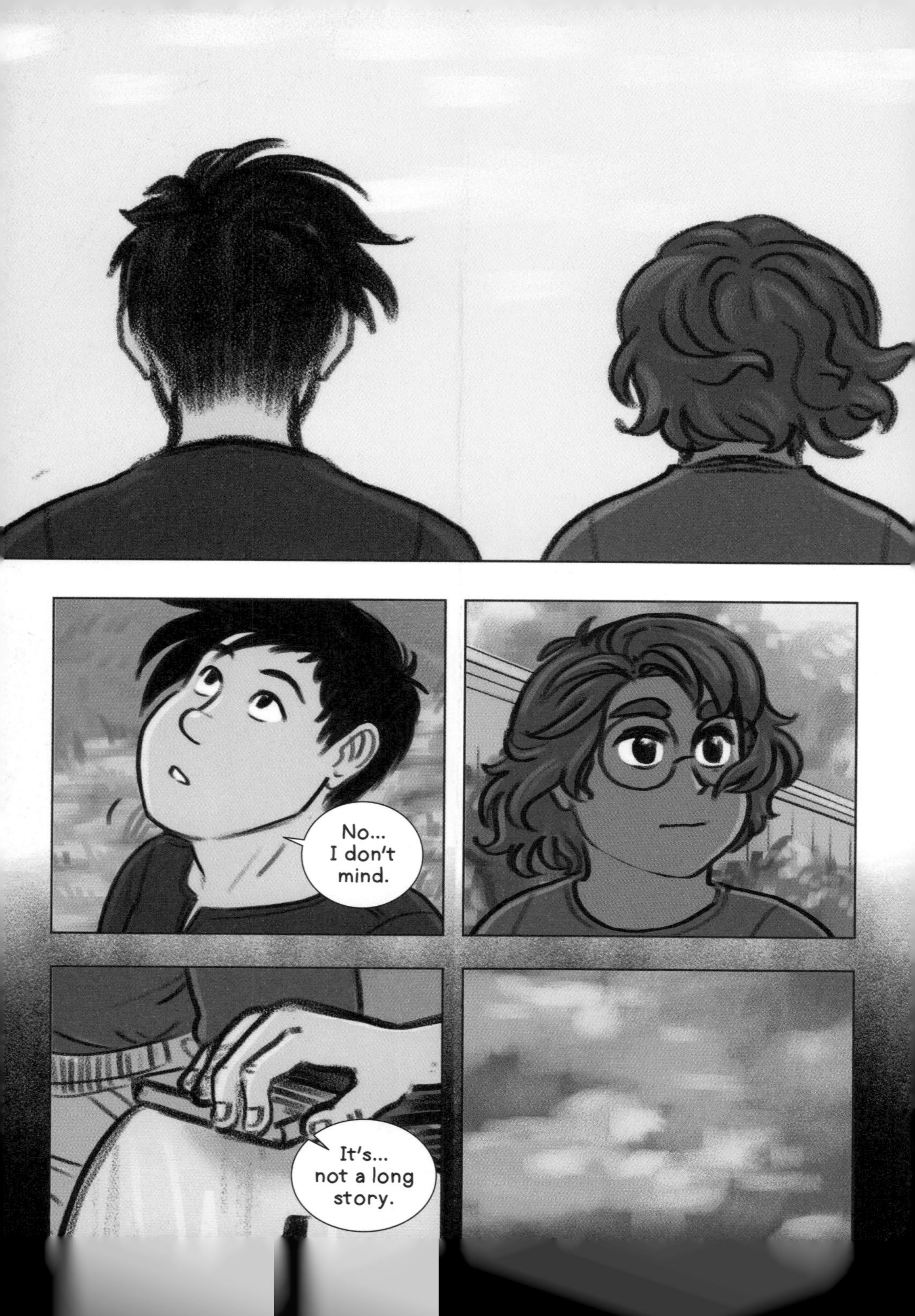
No... I don't mind.
It's... not a long story.

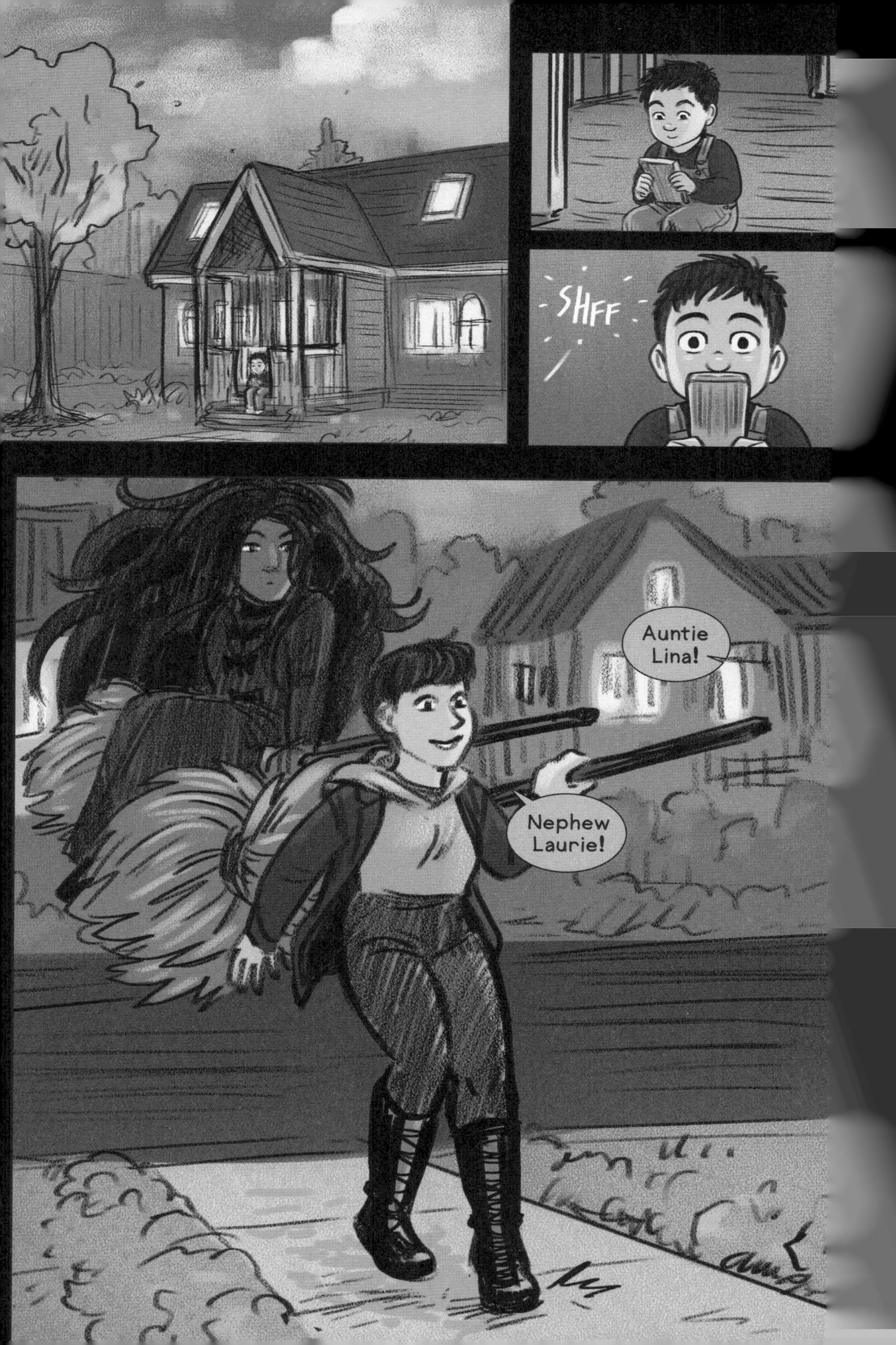
SHFF
Auntie Lina!
Nephew Laurie!

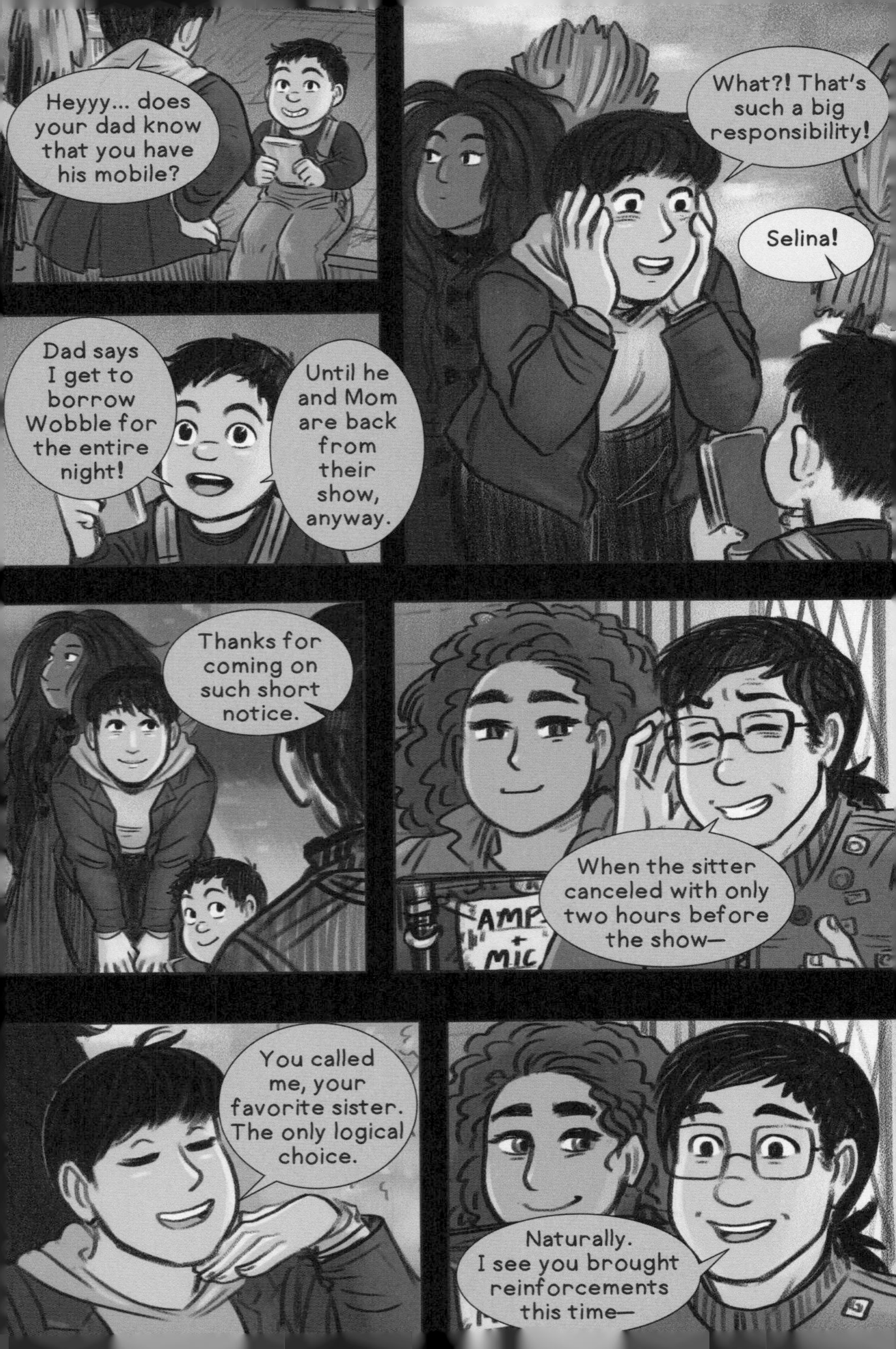

Heyyy... does your dad know that you have his mobile?
What?! That's such a big responsibility!
Selina!
Dad says I get to borrow Wobble for the entire night!
Until he and Mom are back from their show, anyway.
Thanks for coming on such short notice.
When the sitter canceled with only two hours before the show—
AMP + MIC
You called me, your favorite sister. The only logical choice.
Naturally. I see you brought reinforcements this time—

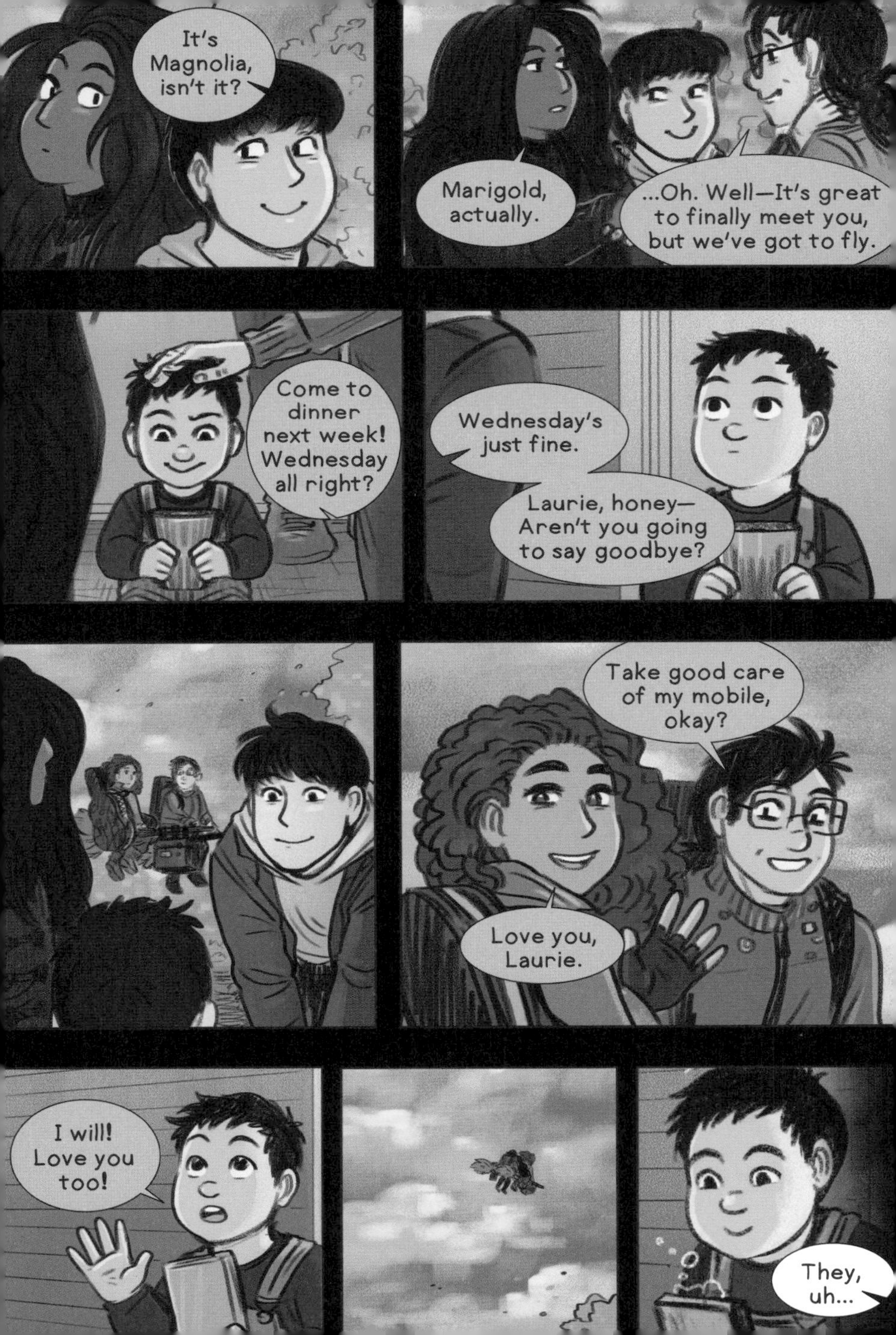
It's Magnolia, isn't it?
Marigold, actually.
...Oh. Well—It's great to finally meet you, but we've got to fly.
Come to dinner next week! Wednesday all right?
Wednesday's just fine.
Laurie, honey—Aren't you going to say goodbye?
Take good care of my mobile, okay?
Love you, Laurie.
I will! Love you too!
They, uh...

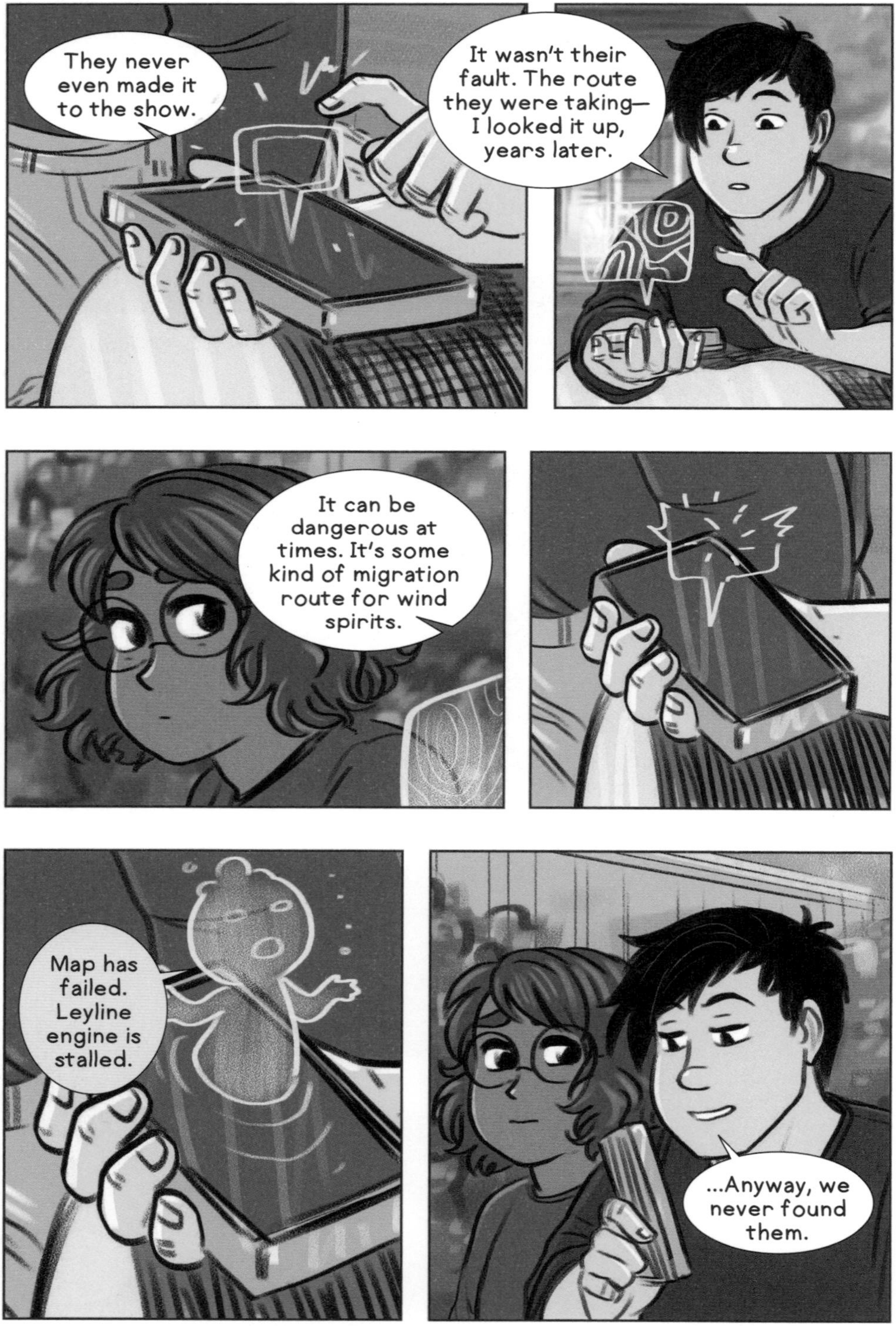
They never even made it to the show.
It wasn't their fault. The route they were taking— I looked it up, years later.
It can be dangerous at times. It's some kind of migration route for wind spirits.
Map has failed. Leyline engine is stalled.
...Anyway, we never found them.

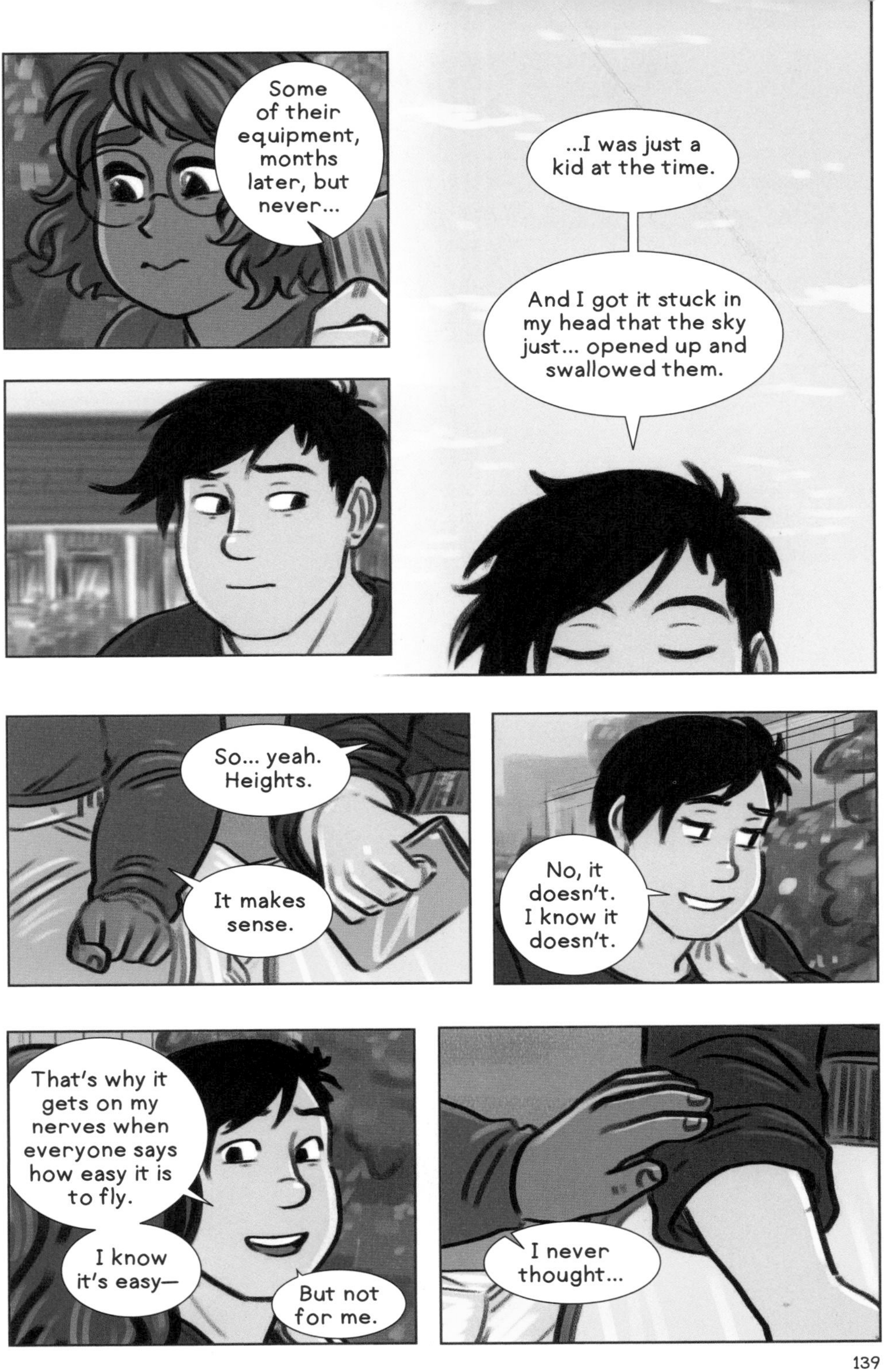
Some of their equipment, months later, but never...
...I was just a kid at the time.
And I got it stuck in my head that the sky just... opened up and swallowed them.
So... yeah. Heights.
It makes sense.
No, it doesn't. I know it doesn't.
That's why it gets on my nerves when everyone says how easy it is to fly.
I know it's easy—
But not for me.
I never thought...

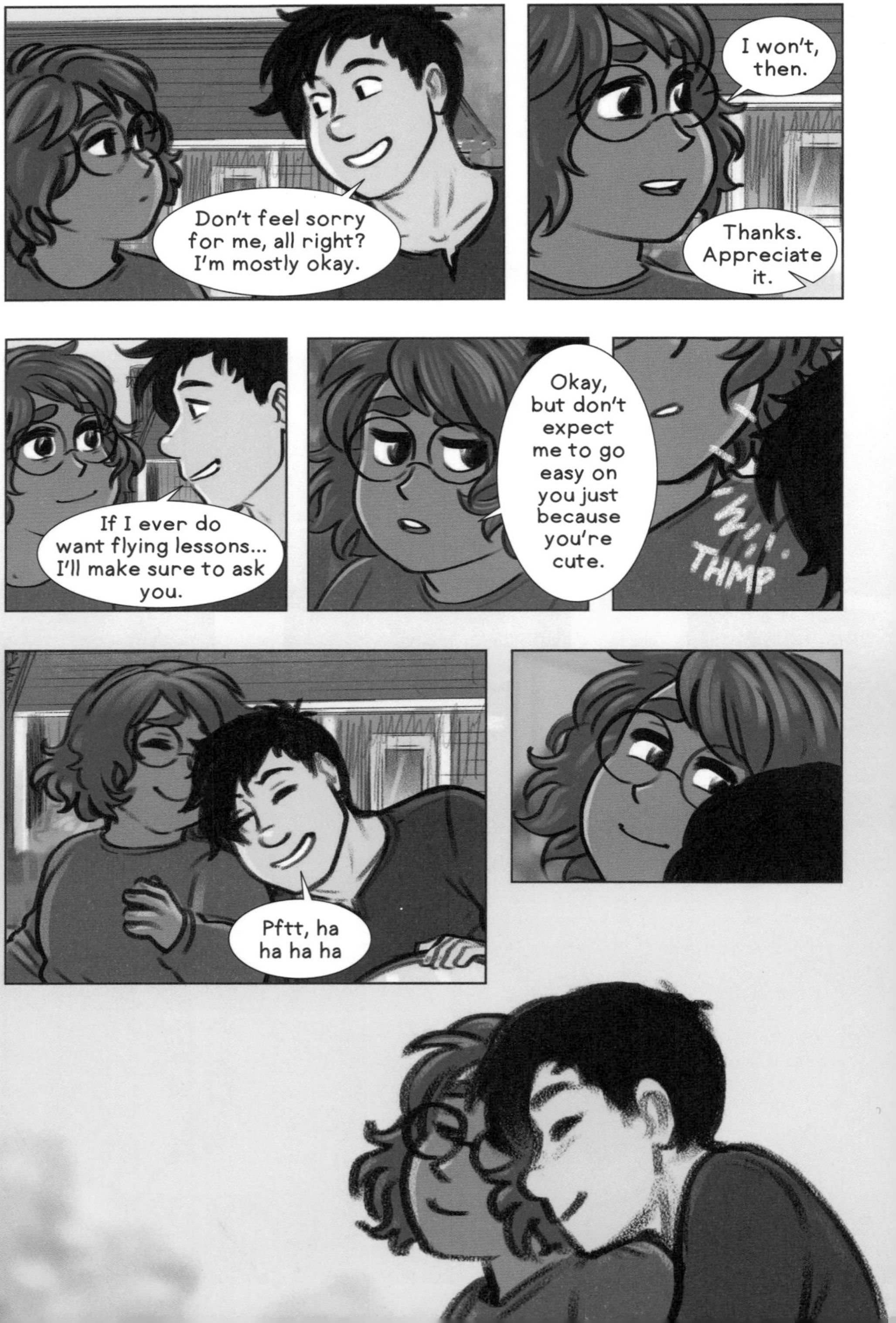
Don't feel sorry for me, all right? I'm mostly okay.
I won't, then.
Thanks. Appreciate it.
If I ever do want flying lessons... I'll make sure to ask you.
Okay, but don't expect me to go easy on you just because you're cute.
THMP
Pftt, ha ha ha ha

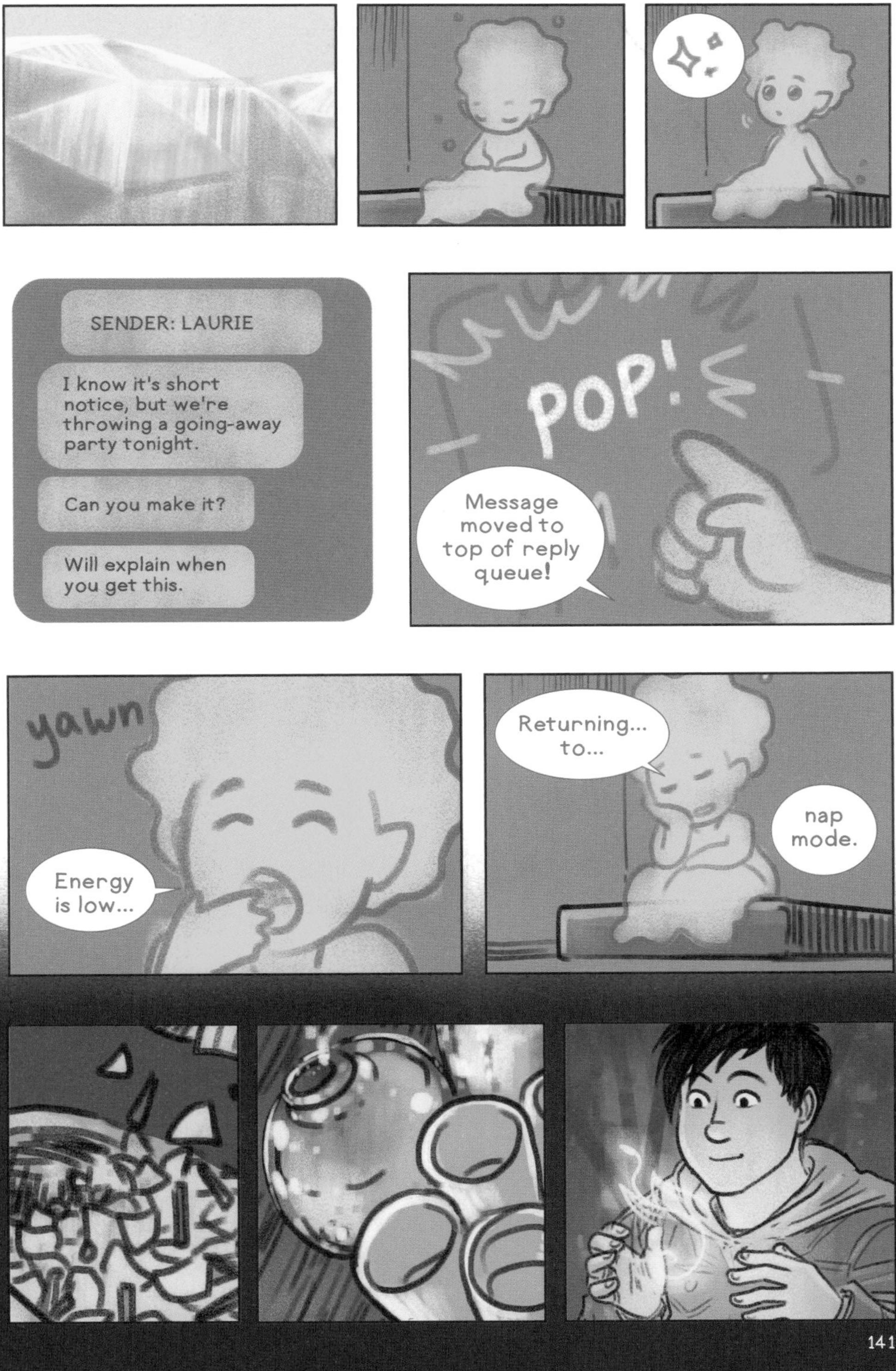
SENDER: LAURIE
I know it's short notice, but we're throwing a going-away party tonight.
Can you make it?
Will explain when you get this.
POP!
Message moved to top of reply queue!
yawn
Energy is low...
Returning... to...
nap mode.

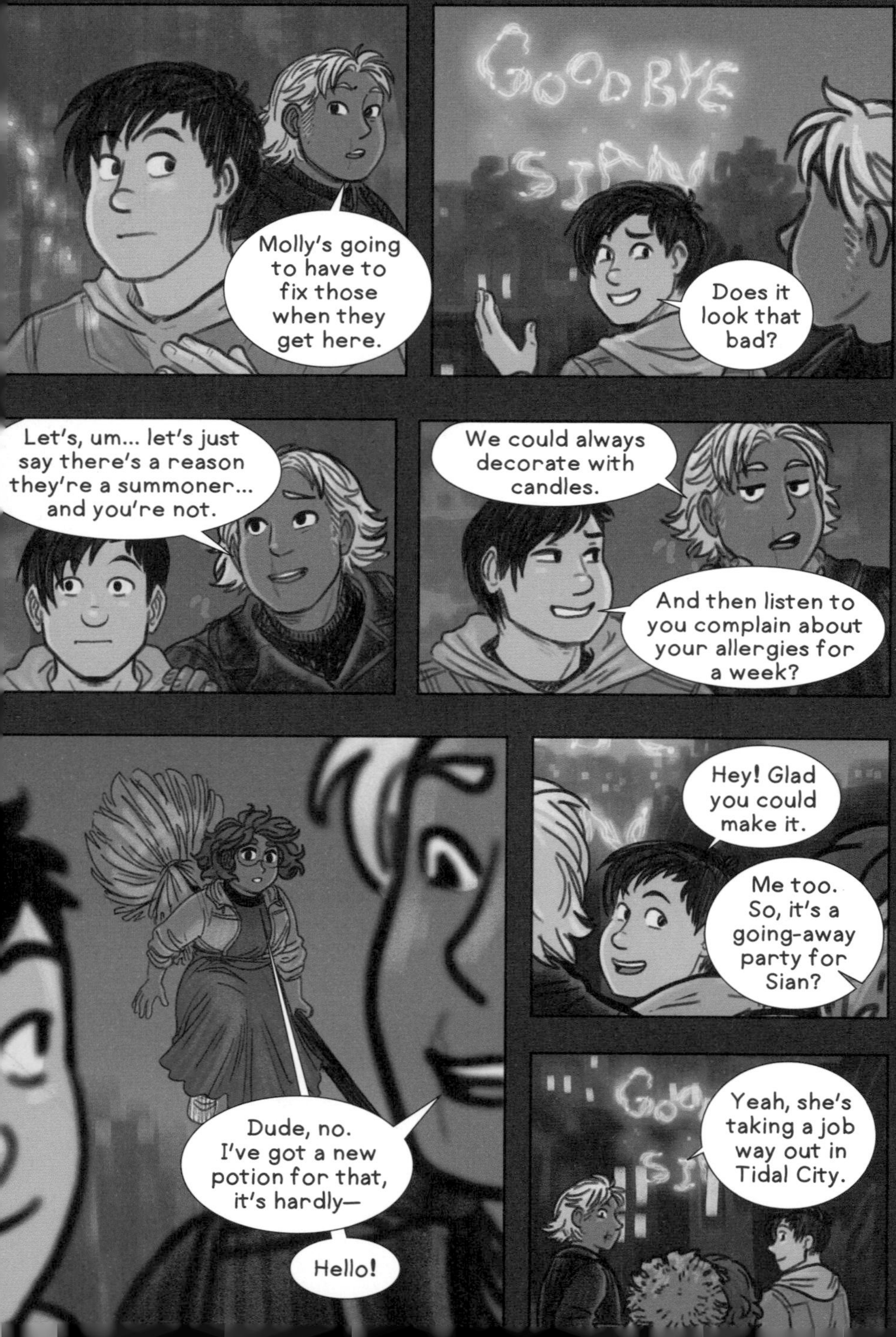

Molly's going to have to fix those when they get here.
Does it look that bad?
Let's, um... let's just say there's a reason they're a summoner... and you're not.
We could always decorate with candles.
And then listen to you complain about your allergies for a week?
Dude, no. I've got a new potion for that, it's hardly—
Hello!
Hey! Glad you could make it.
Me too. So, it's a going-away party for Sian?
Yeah, she's taking a job way out in Tidal City.

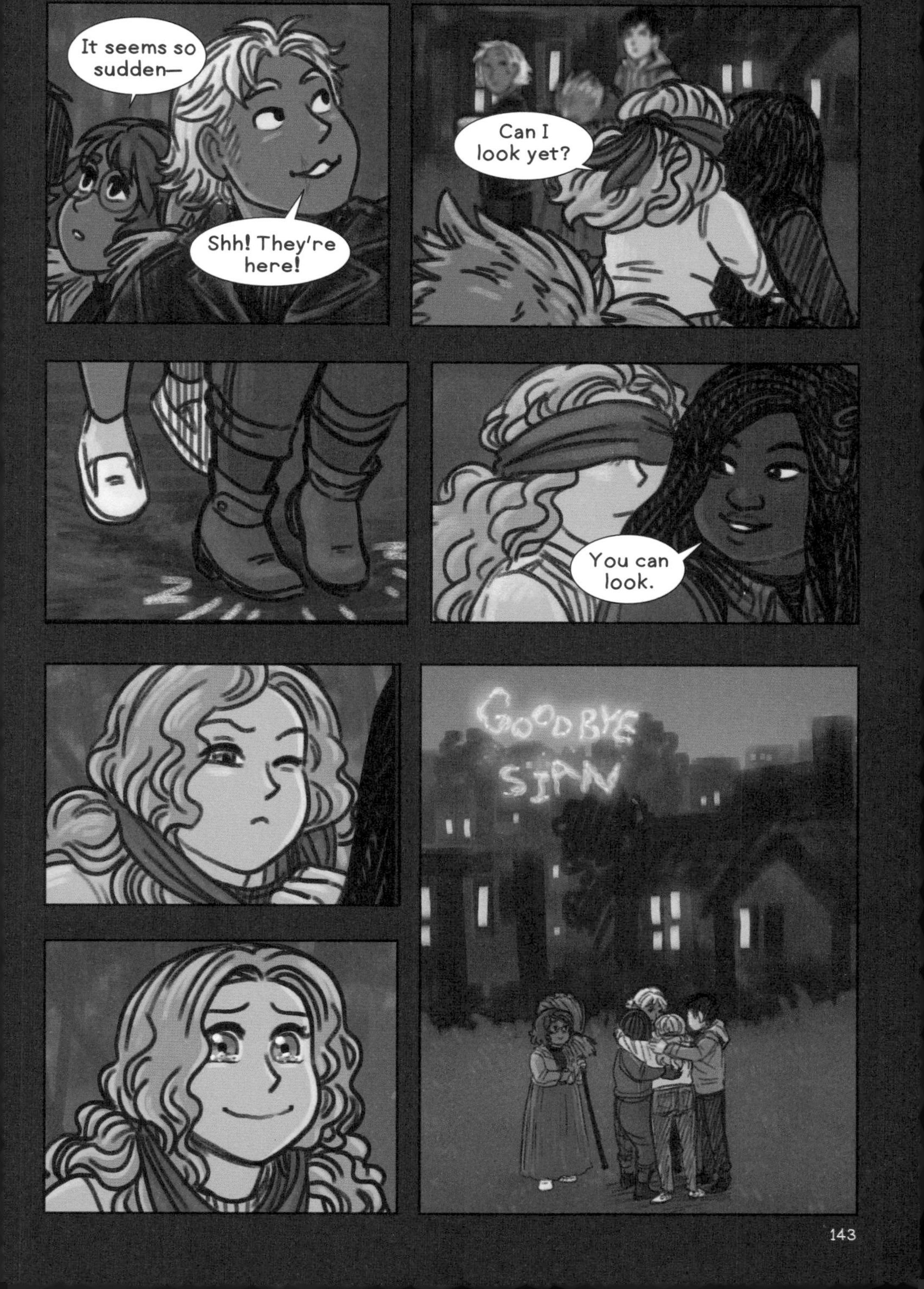
It seems so sudden—
Shh! They're here!
Can I look yet?
You can look.
GOODBYE SIAN

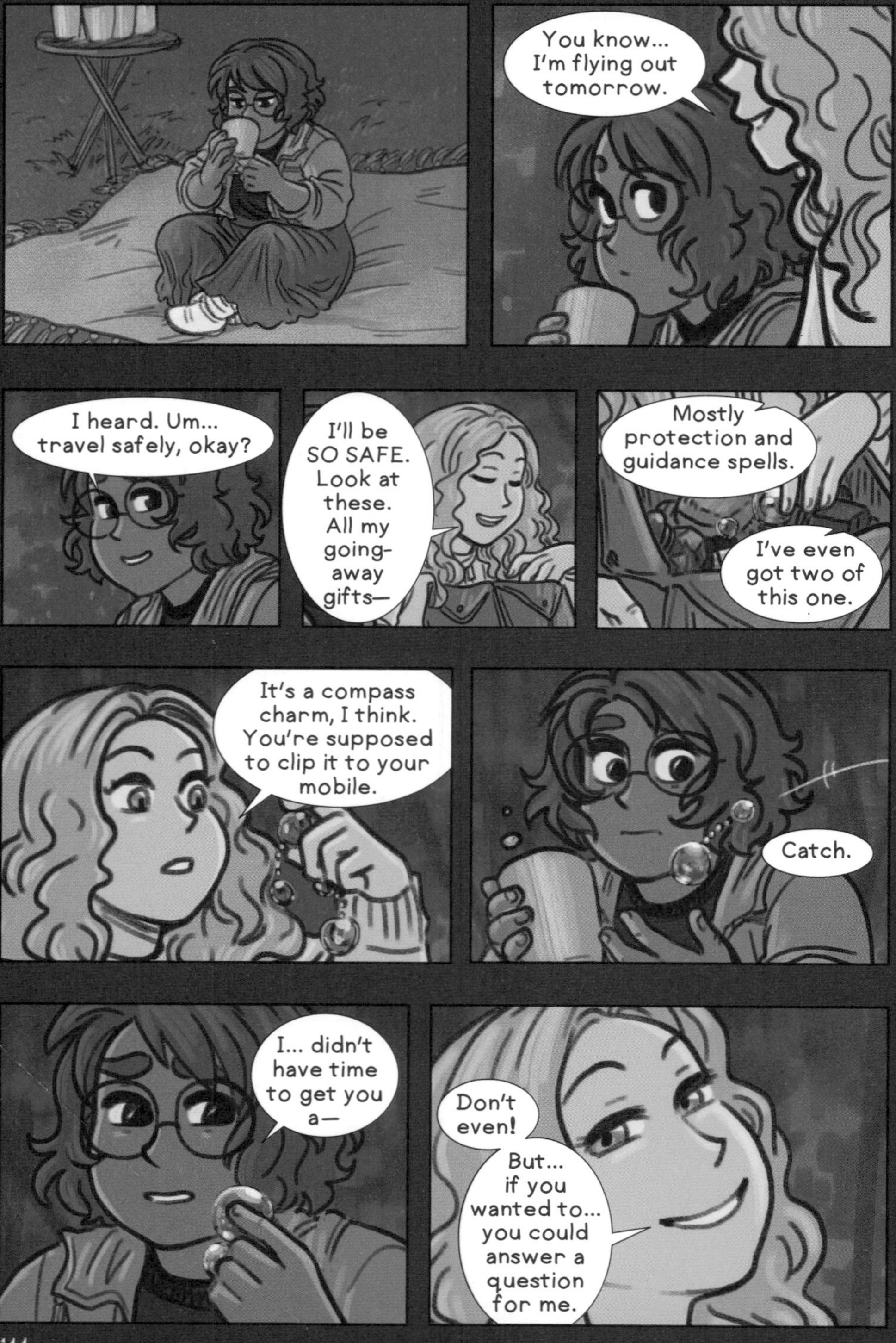
You know... I'm flying out tomorrow.
I heard. Um... travel safely, okay?
I'll be SO SAFE. Look at these. All my going-away gifts—
Mostly protection and guidance spells.
I've even got two of this one.
It's a compass charm, I think. You're supposed to clip it to your mobile.
Catch.
I... didn't have time to get you a—
Don't even!
But... if you wanted to... you could answer a question for me.

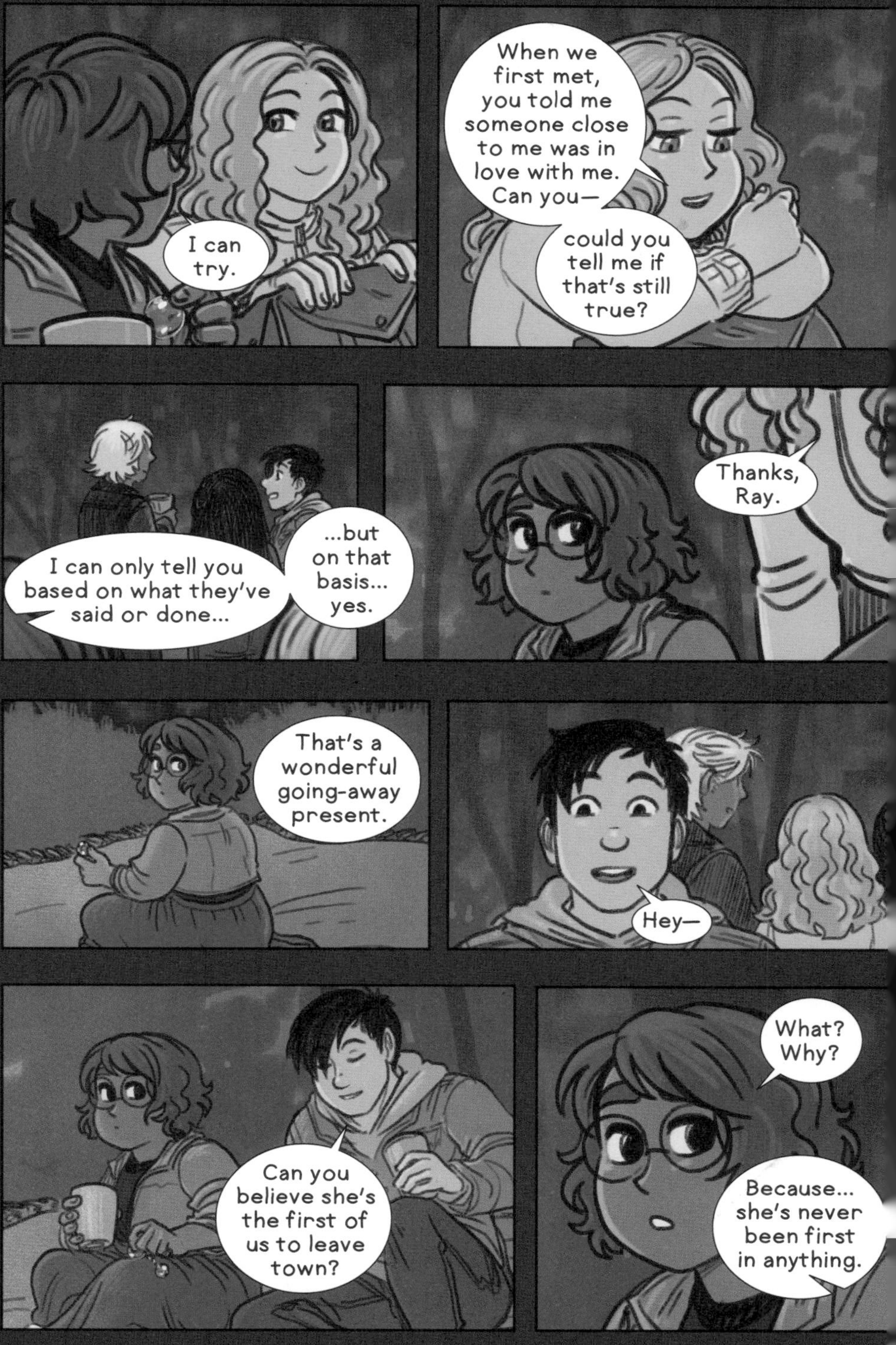
I can try.
When we first met, you told me someone close to me was in love with me. Can you—
could you tell me if that's still true?
I can only tell you based on what they've said or done...
...but on that basis... yes.
Thanks, Ray.
That's a wonderful going-away present.
Hey—
Can you believe she's the first of us to leave town?
What? Why?
Because... she's never been first in anything.

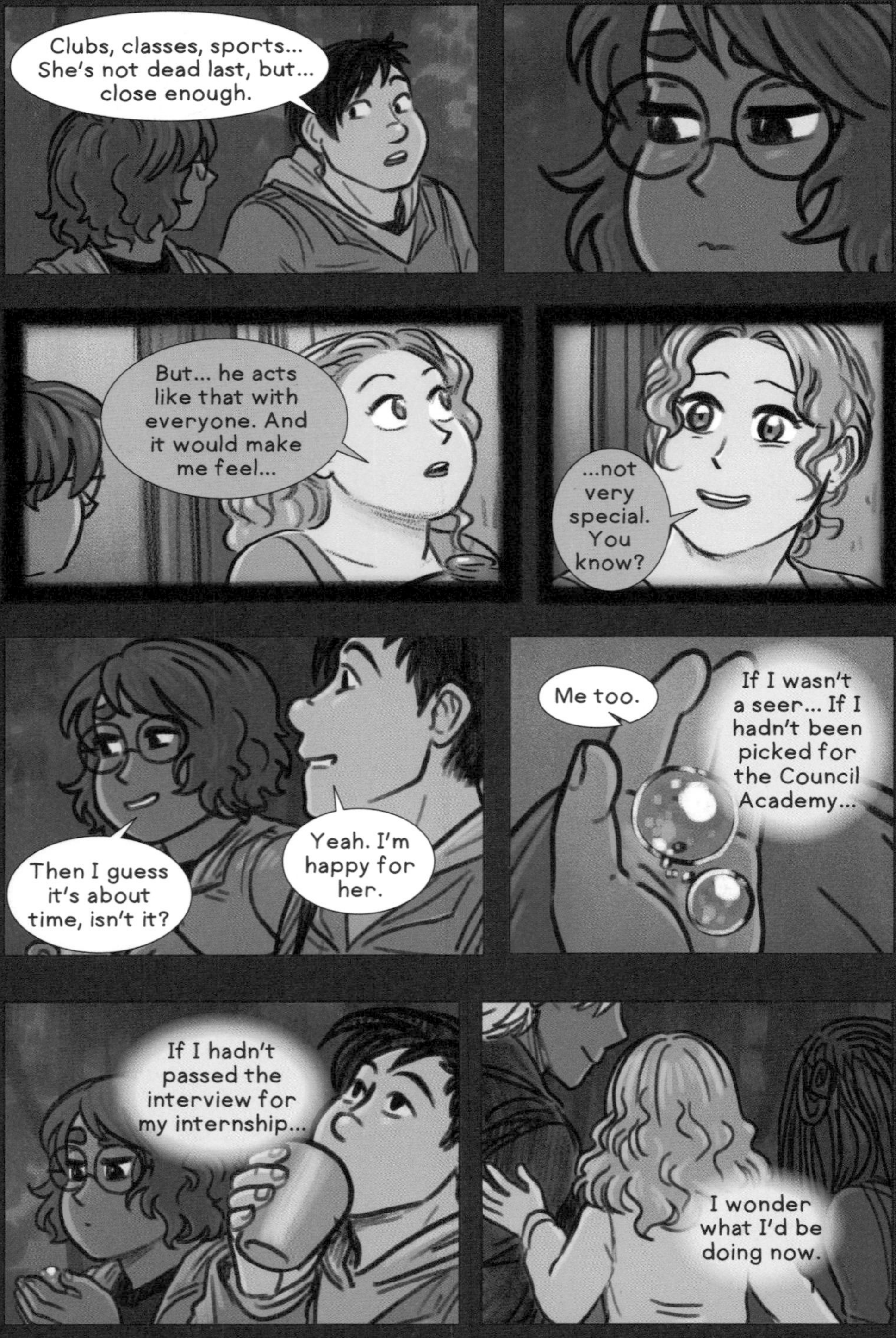
Clubs, classes, sports... She's not dead last, but... close enough.
But... he acts like that with everyone. And it would make me feel...
...not very special. You know?
Then I guess it's about time, isn't it?
Yeah. I'm happy for her.
Me too.
If I wasn't a seer... If I hadn't been picked for the Council Academy...
If I hadn't passed the interview for my internship...
I wonder what I'd be doing now.

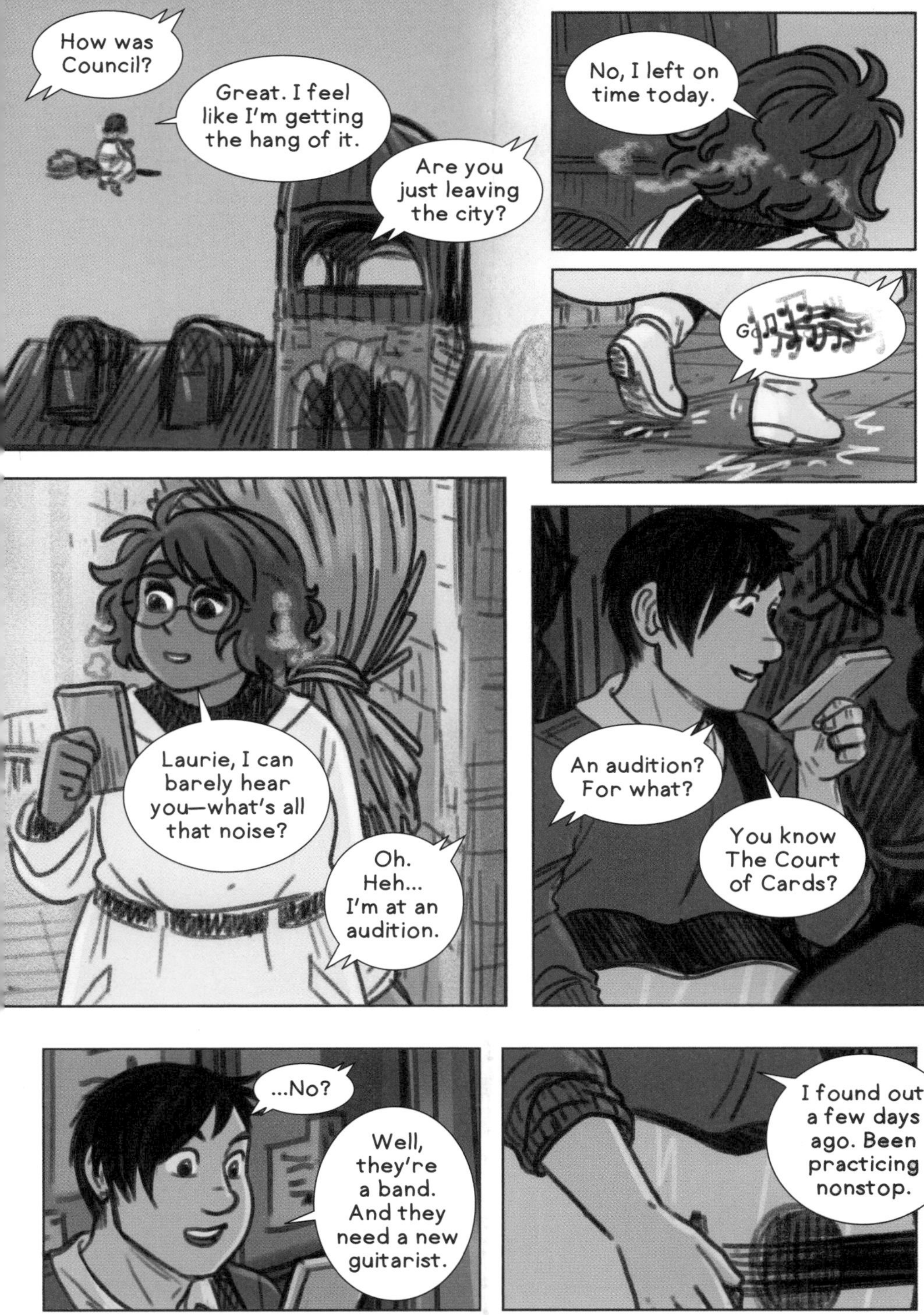
How was Council?
Great. I feel like I'm getting the hang of it.
Are you just leaving the city?
No, I left on time today.
Laurie, I can barely hear you—what's all that noise?
Oh. Heh... I'm at an audition.
An audition? For what?
You know The Court of Cards?
...No?
Well, they're a band. And they need a new guitarist.
I found out a few days ago. Been practicing nonstop.

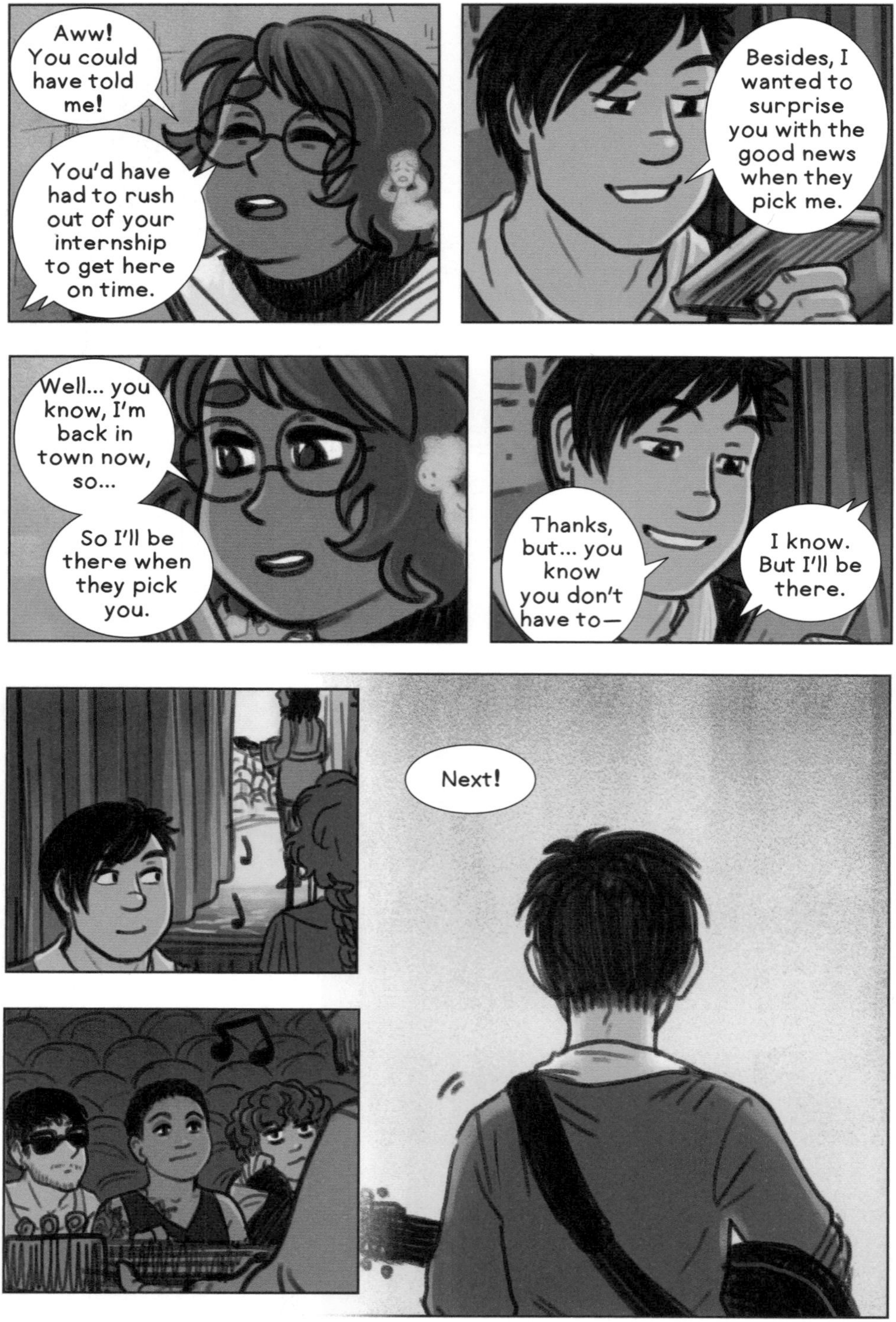
Aww! You could have told me!
You'd have had to rush out of your internship to get here on time.
Besides, I wanted to surprise you with the good news when they pick me.
Well... you know, I'm back in town now, so...
So I'll be there when they pick you.
Thanks, but... you know you don't have to—
I know. But I'll be there.
Next!

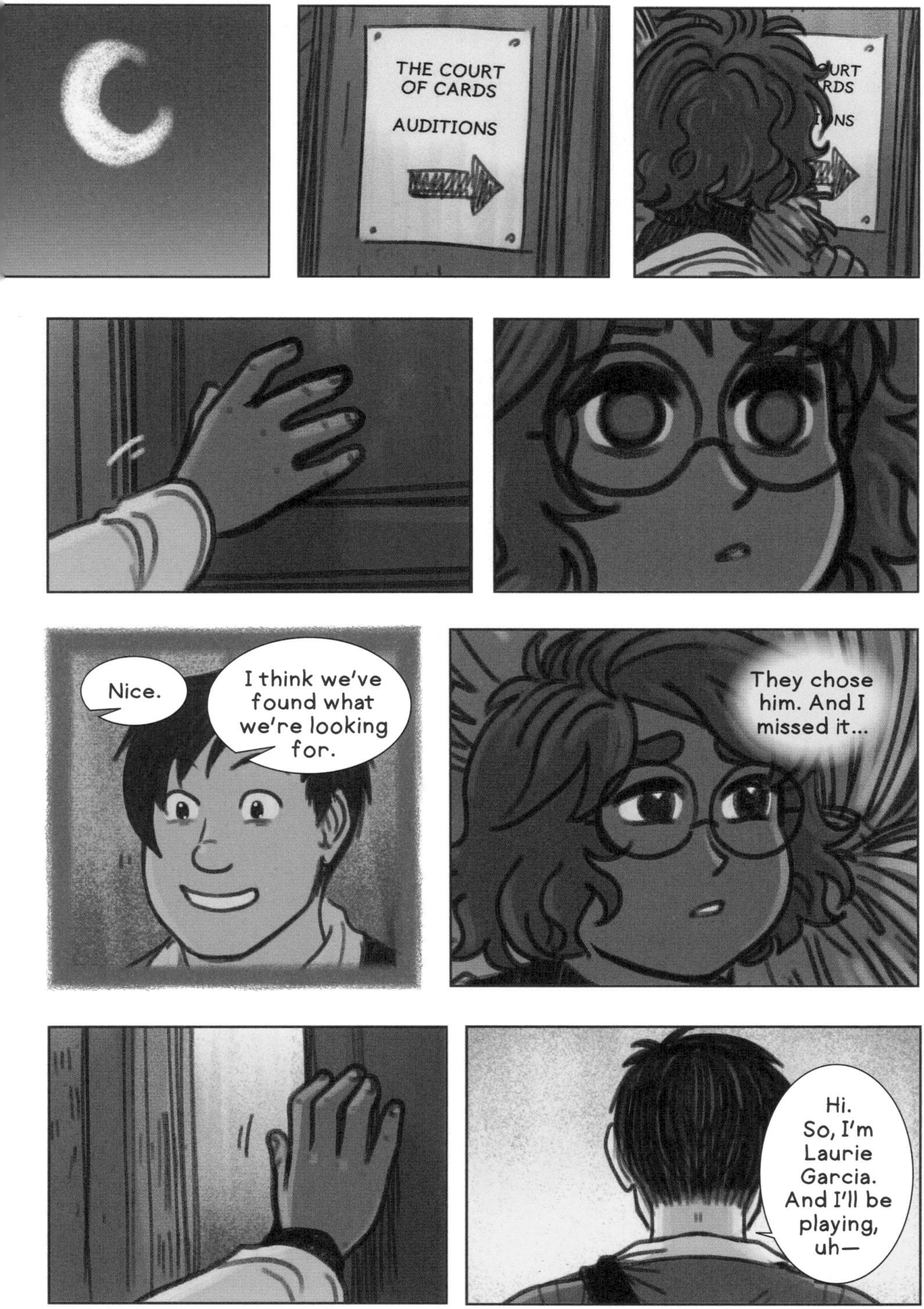
THE COURT
OF CARDS
AUDITIONS
Nice.
I think we've found what we're looking for.
They chose him. And I missed it...
Hi. So, I'm Laurie Garcia. And I'll be playing, uh—

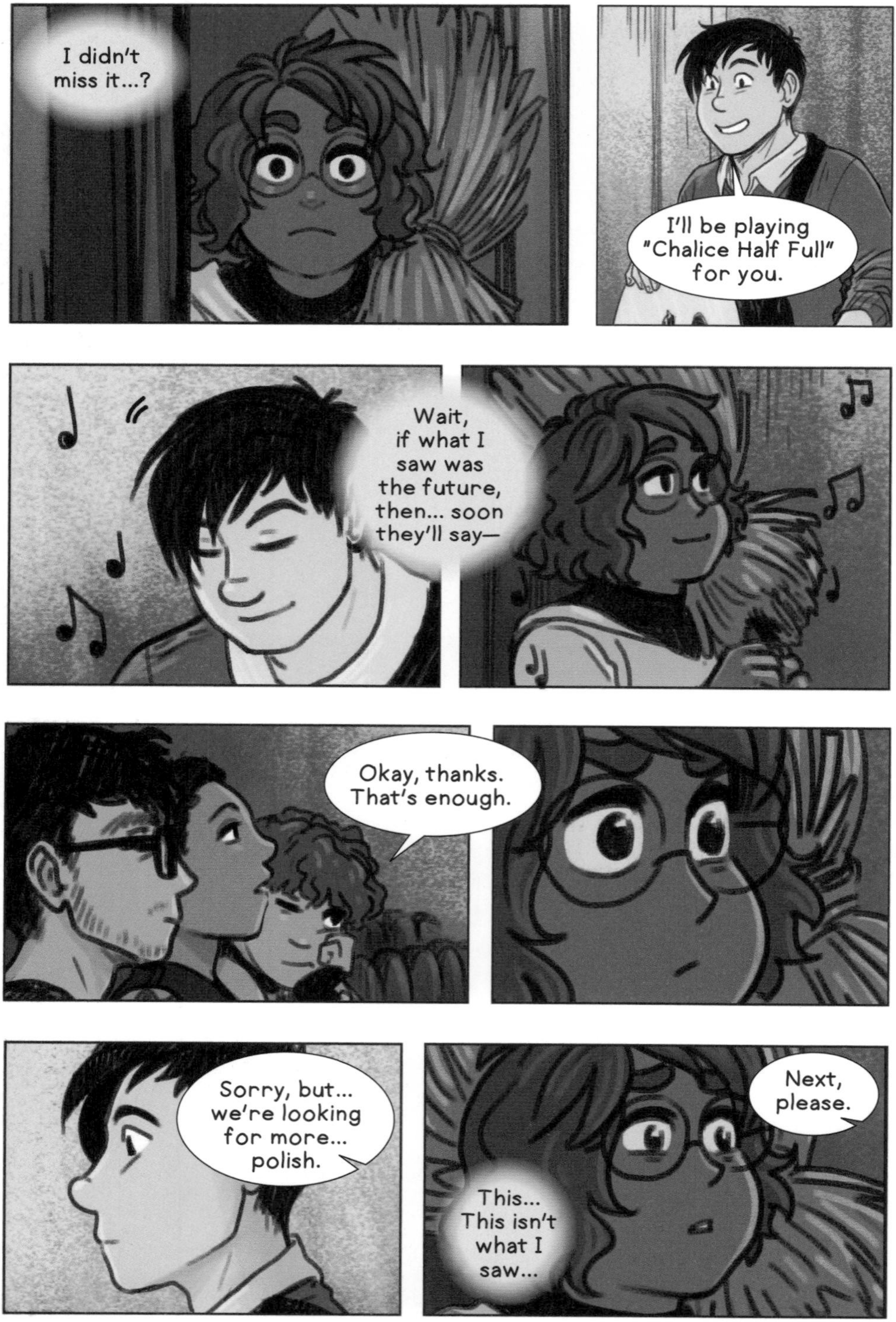
I didn't miss it...?
I'll be playing "Chalice Half Full" for you.
Wait, if what I saw was the future, then... soon they'll say—
Okay, thanks. That's enough.
Sorry, but... we're looking for more... polish.
Next, please.
This... This isn't what I saw...

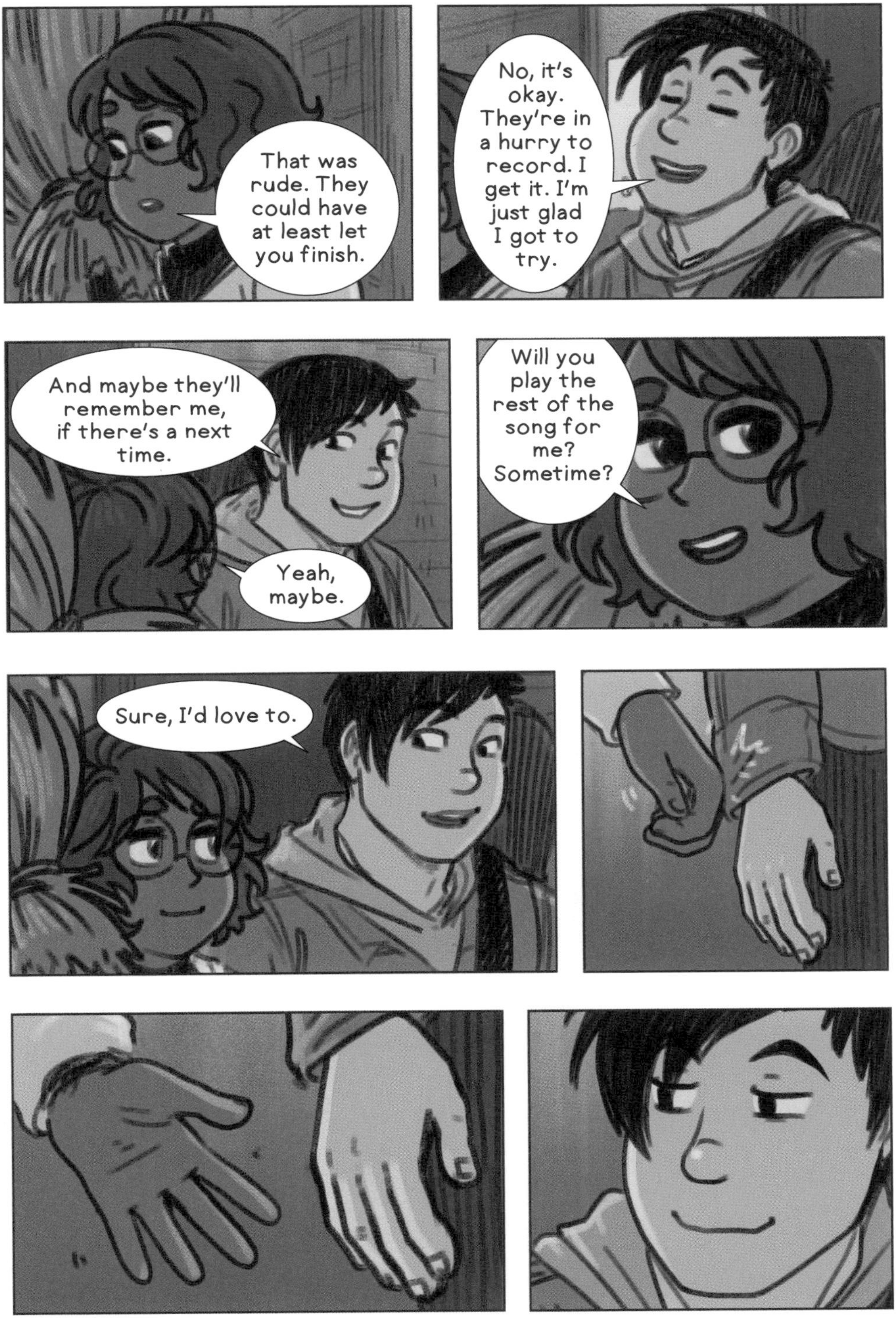
That was rude. They could have at least let you finish.
No, it's okay. They're in a hurry to record. I get it. I'm just glad I got to try.
And maybe they'll remember me, if there's a next time.
Yeah, maybe.
Will you play the rest of the song for me? Sometime?
Sure, I'd love to.

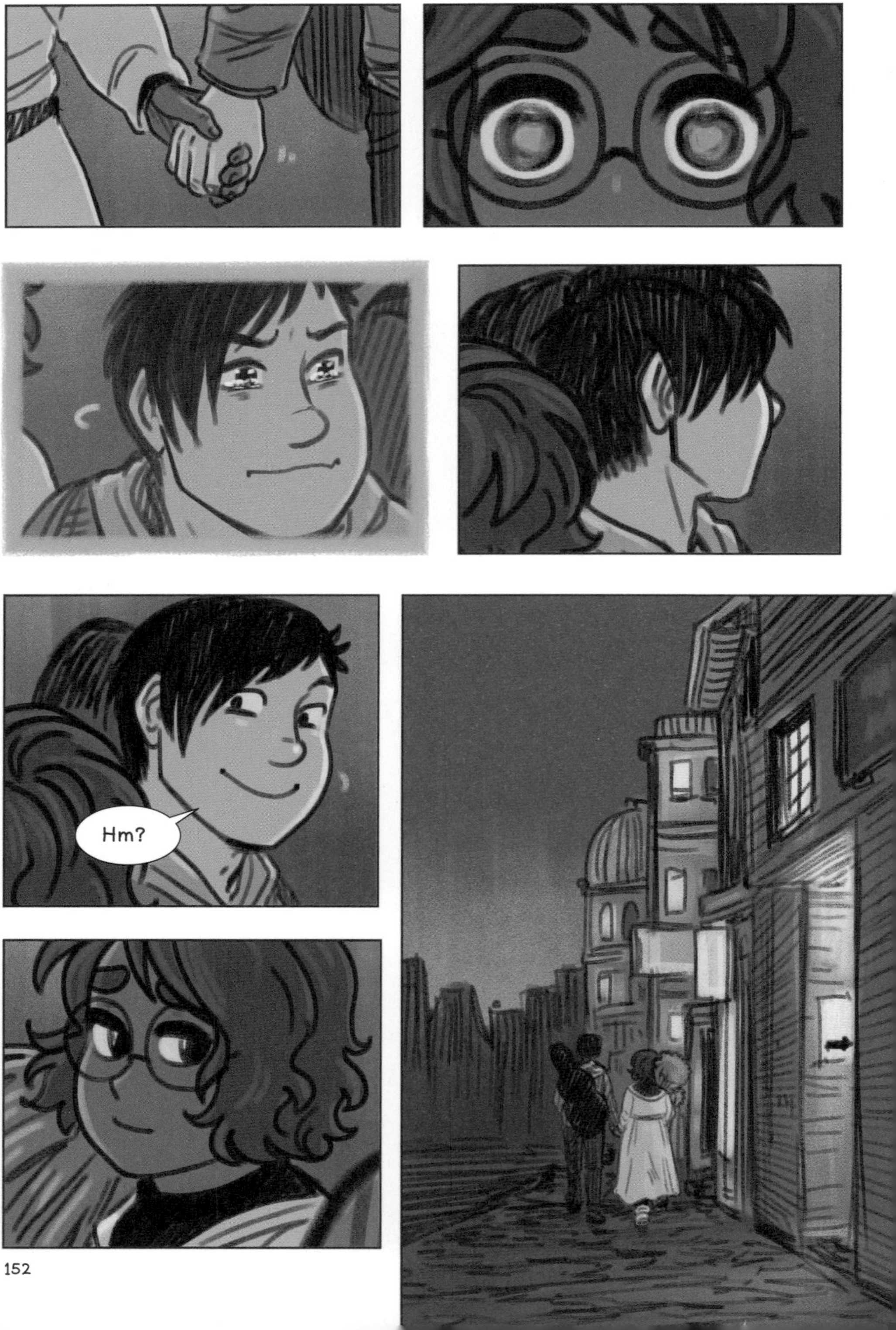
Hm?

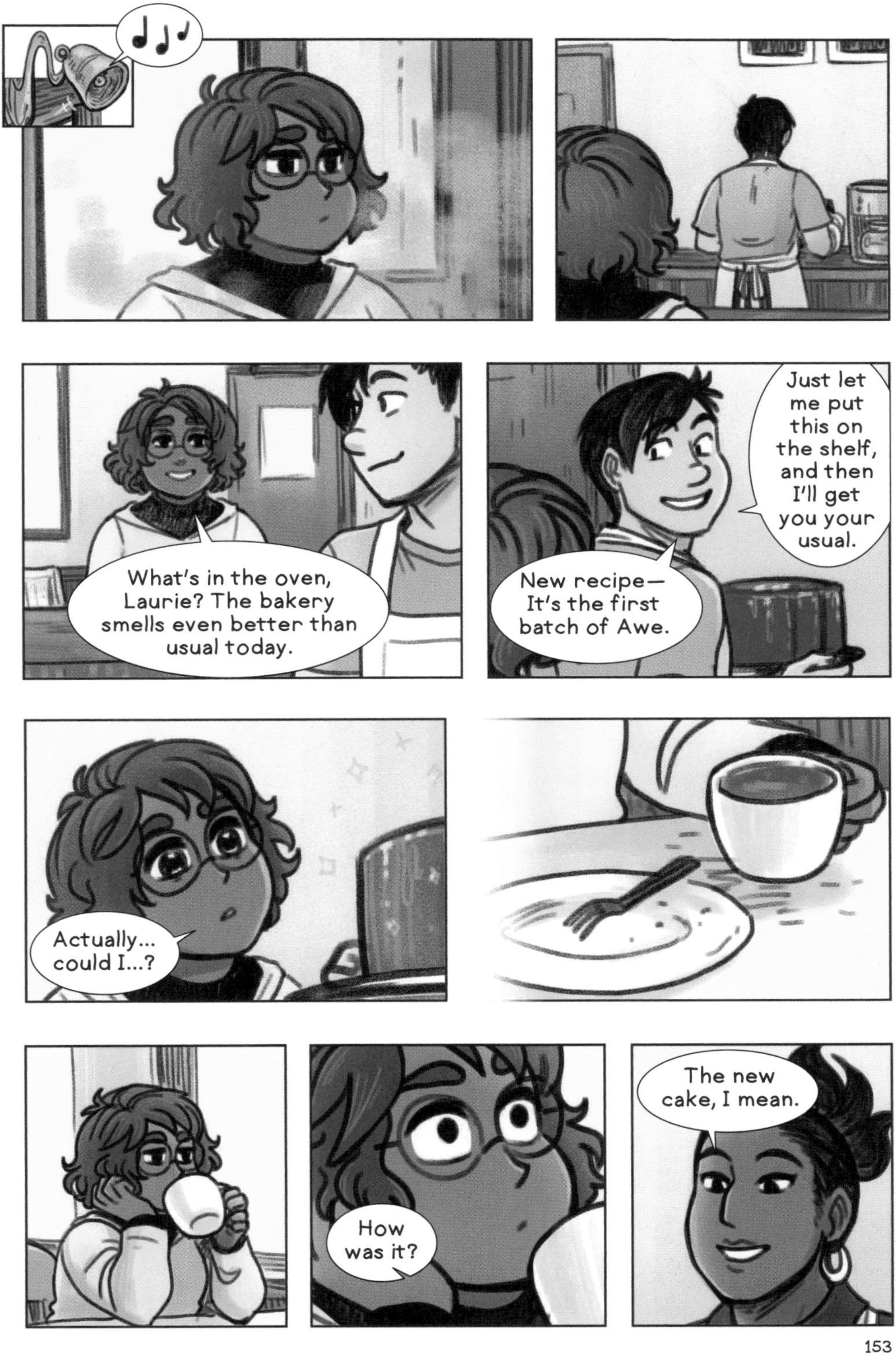
♩♩♩
What's in the oven, Laurie? The bakery smells even better than usual today.
New recipe— It's the first batch of Awe.
Just let me put this on the shelf, and then I'll get you your usual.
Actually... could I...?
How was it?
The new cake, I mean.

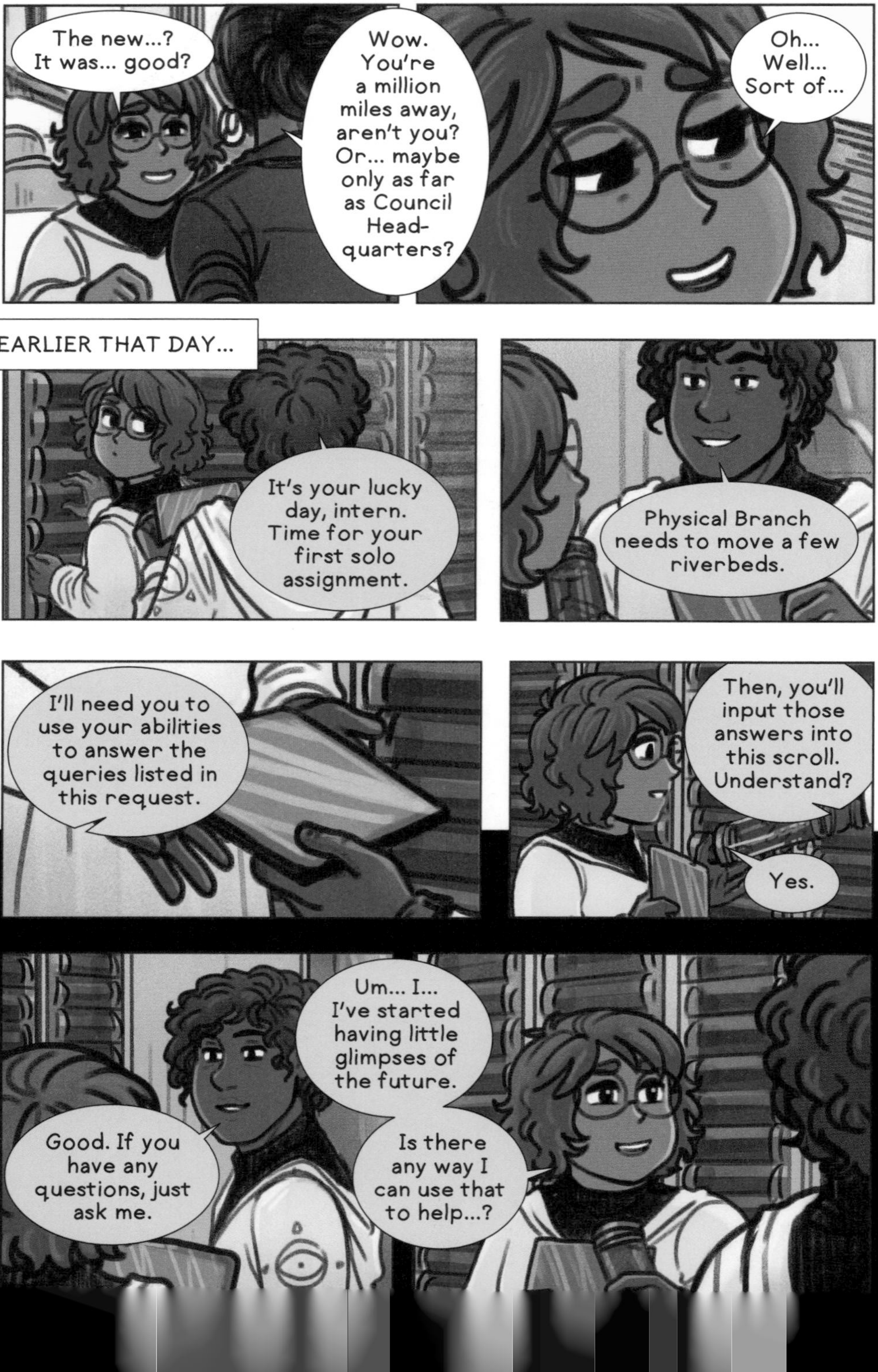
The new...? It was... good?
Wow. You're a million miles away, aren't you? Or... maybe only as far as Council Head-quarters?
Oh... Well... Sort of...
EARLIER THAT DAY...
It's your lucky day, intern. Time for your first solo assignment.
Physical Branch needs to move a few riverbeds.
I'll need you to use your abilities to answer the queries listed in this request.
Then, you'll input those answers into this scroll. Understand?
Yes.
Good. If you have any questions, just ask me.
Um... I... I've started having little glimpses of the future.
Is there any way I can use that to help...?

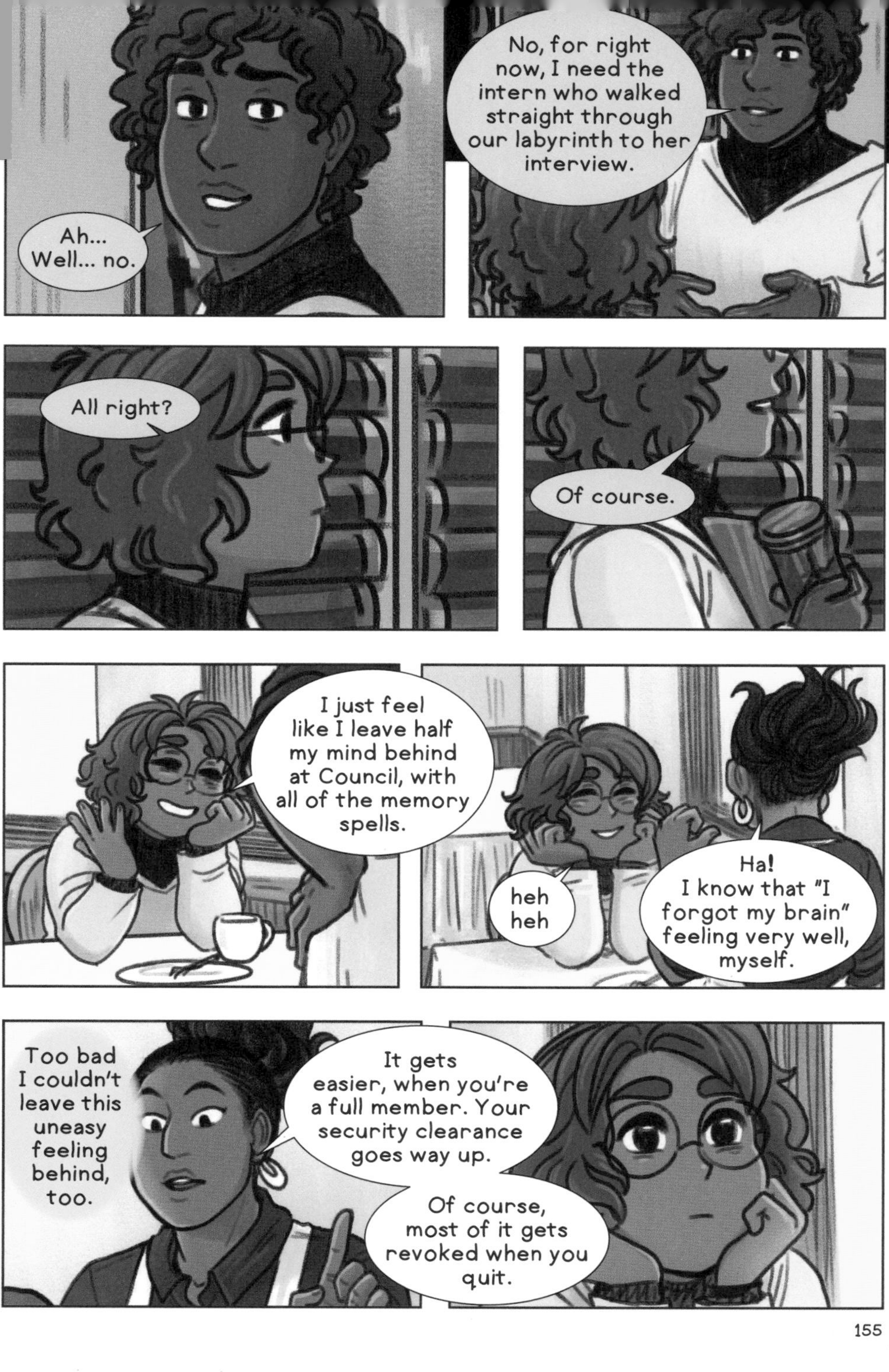
Ah...
Well... no.
No, for right now, I need the intern who walked straight through our labyrinth to her interview.
All right?
Of course.
I just feel like I leave half my mind behind at Council, with all of the memory spells.
heh heh
Ha! I know that "I forgot my brain" feeling very well, myself.
Too bad I couldn't leave this uneasy feeling behind, too.
It gets easier, when you're a full member. Your security clearance goes way up.
Of course, most of it gets revoked when you quit.

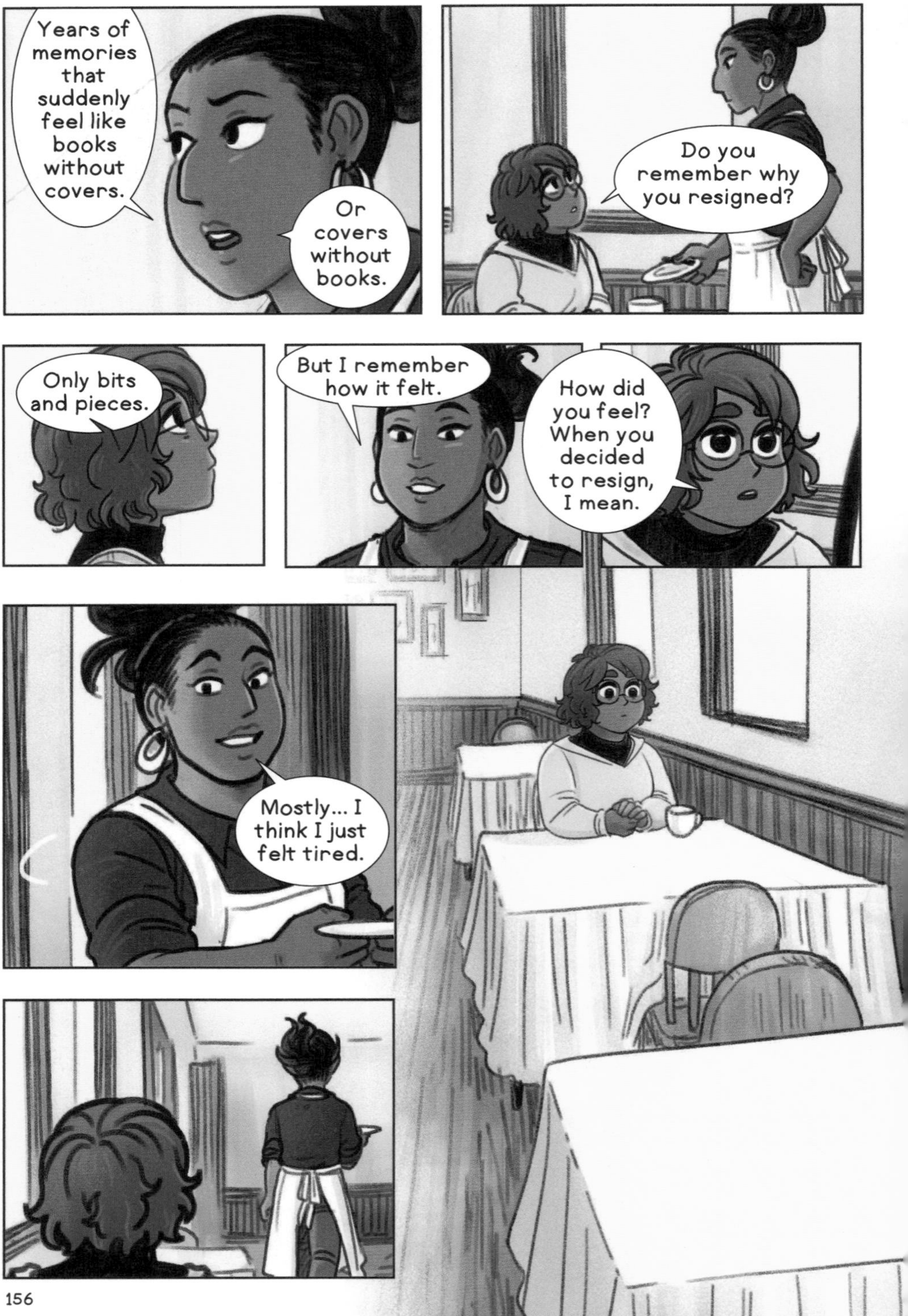
Years of memories that suddenly feel like books without covers.
Or covers without books.
Do you remember why you resigned?
Only bits and pieces.
But I remember how it felt.
How did you feel? When you decided to resign, I mean.
Mostly... I think I just felt tired.

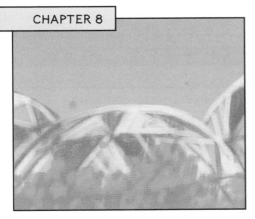

CHAPTER 8

REQUESTS
(FUTURE)

I can take these ones.

REQUESTS
(FUTURE)

I suppose you could, but...

REQUESTS (PRESENT)

REQUESTS (PRESENT)

REQUESTS (PRESENT)

You're the only one here who can reply to those.

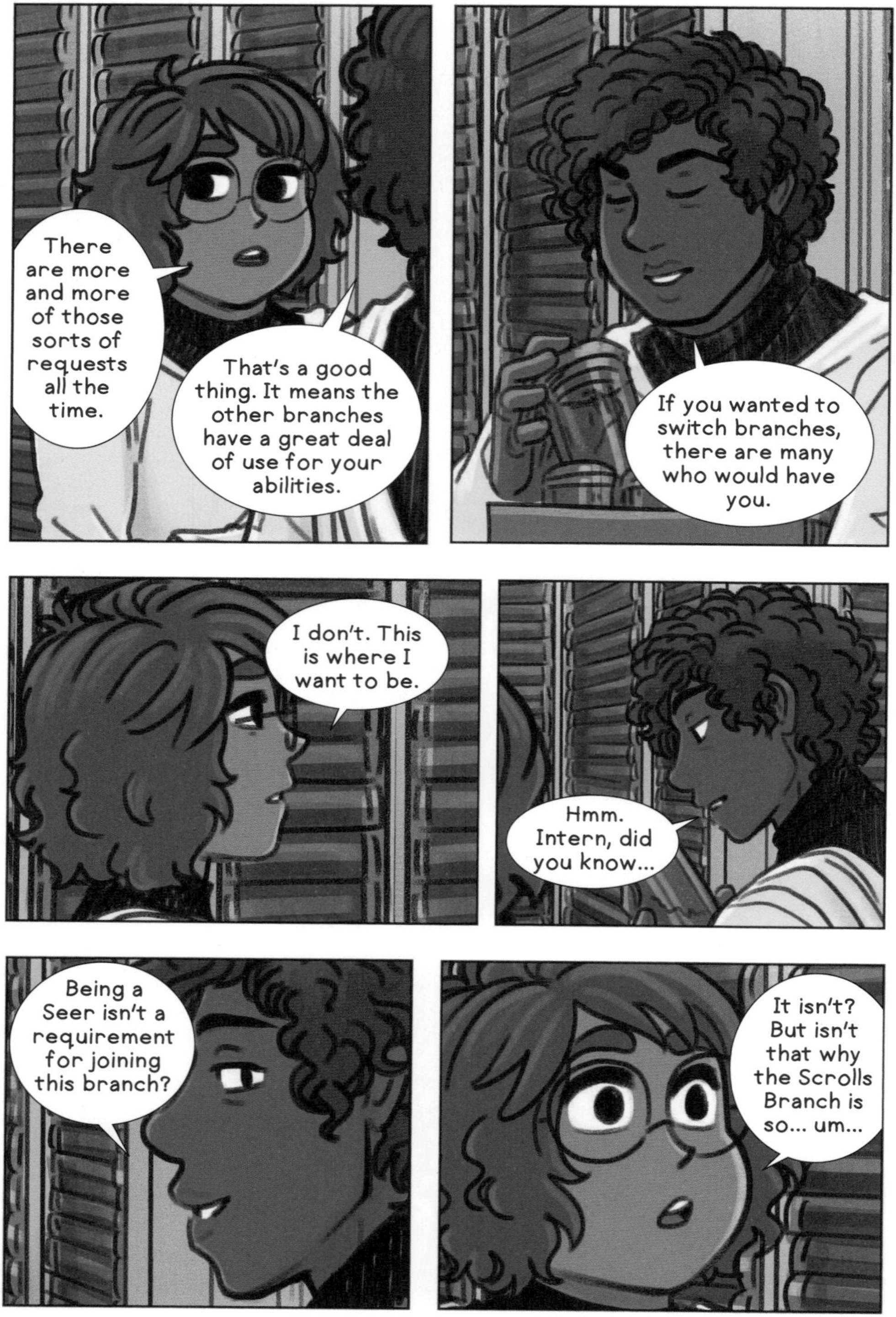
There are more and more of those sorts of requests all the time.
That's a good thing. It means the other branches have a great deal of use for your abilities.
If you wanted to switch branches, there are many who would have you.
I don't. This is where I want to be.
Hmm. Intern, did you know...
Being a Seer isn't a requirement for joining this branch?
It isn't? But isn't that why the Scrolls Branch is so... um...

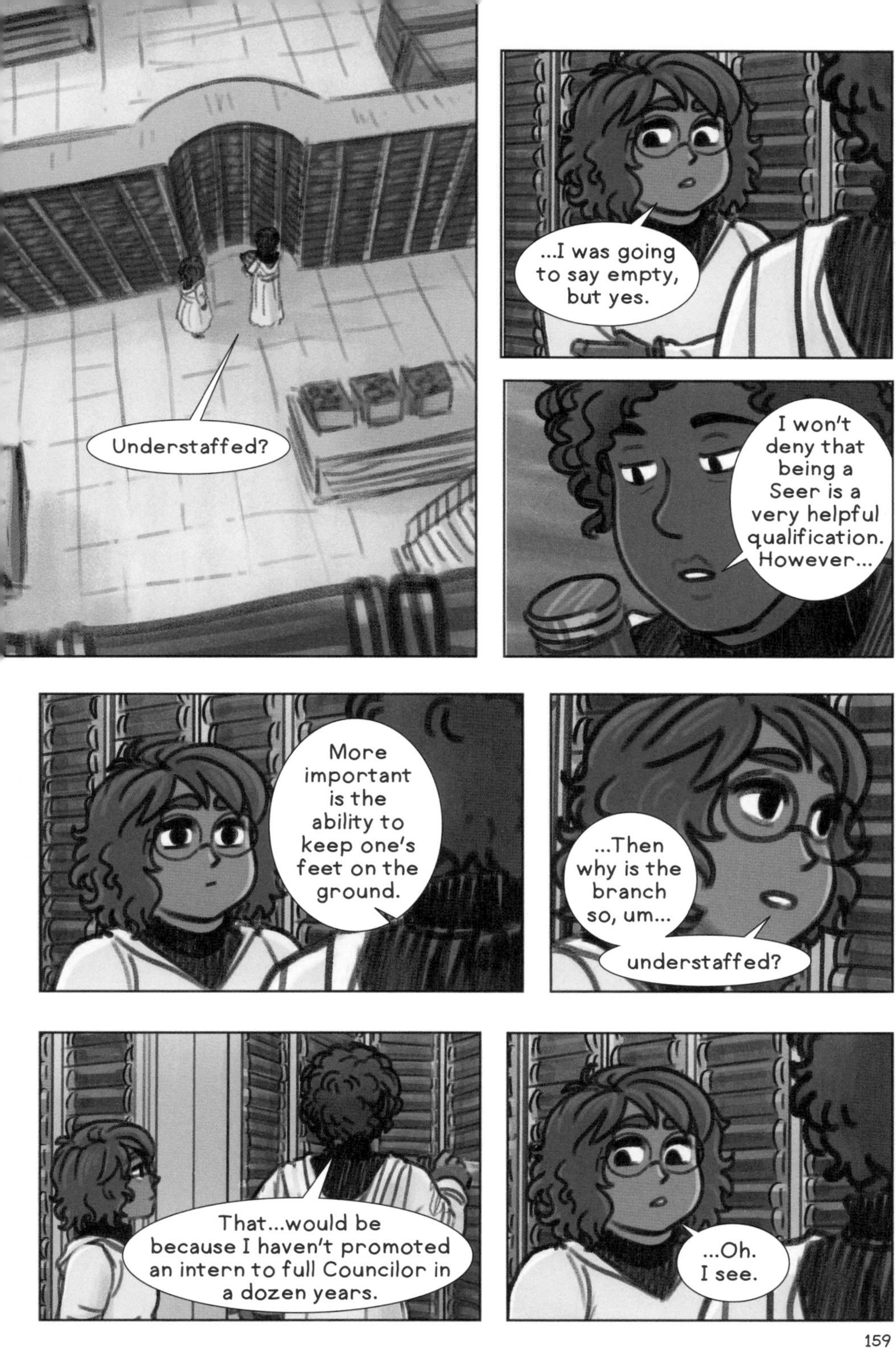
Understaffed?
...I was going to say empty, but yes.
I won't deny that being a Seer is a very helpful qualification. However...
More important is the ability to keep one's feet on the ground.
...Then why is the branch so, um...
understaffed?
That...would be because I haven't promoted an intern to full Councilor in a dozen years.
...Oh. I see.

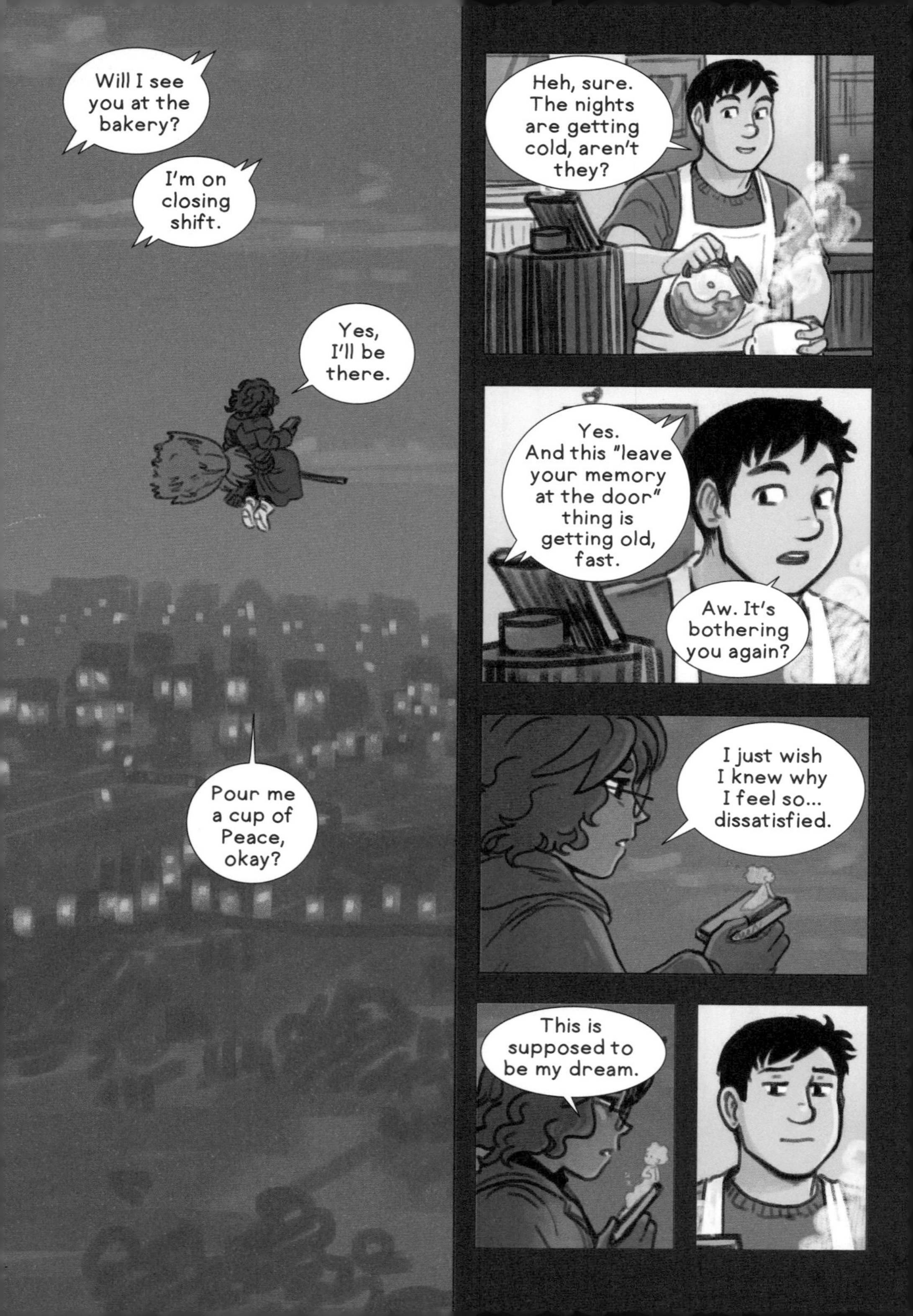
Will I see you at the bakery?
I'm on closing shift.
Yes, I'll be there.
Pour me a cup of Peace, okay?
Heh, sure. The nights are getting cold, aren't they?
Yes. And this "leave your memory at the door" thing is getting old, fast.
Aw. It's bothering you again?
I just wish I knew why I feel so... dissatisfied.
This is supposed to be my dream.

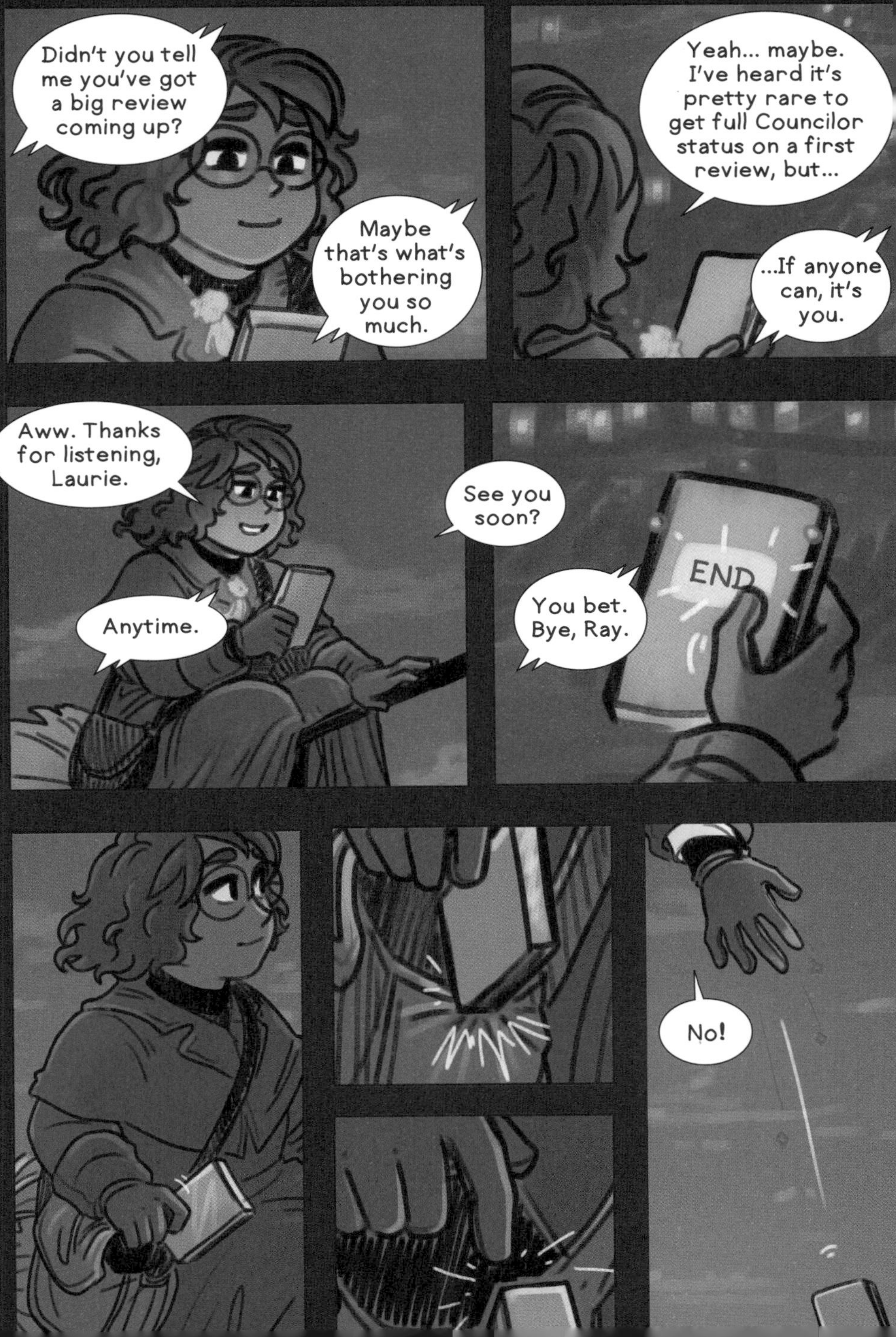

Didn't you tell me you've got a big review coming up?
Maybe that's what's bothering you so much.
Yeah... maybe. I've heard it's pretty rare to get full Councilor status on a first review, but...
...If anyone can, it's you.
Aww. Thanks for listening, Laurie.
Anytime.
See you soon?
END
You bet. Bye, Ray.
No!

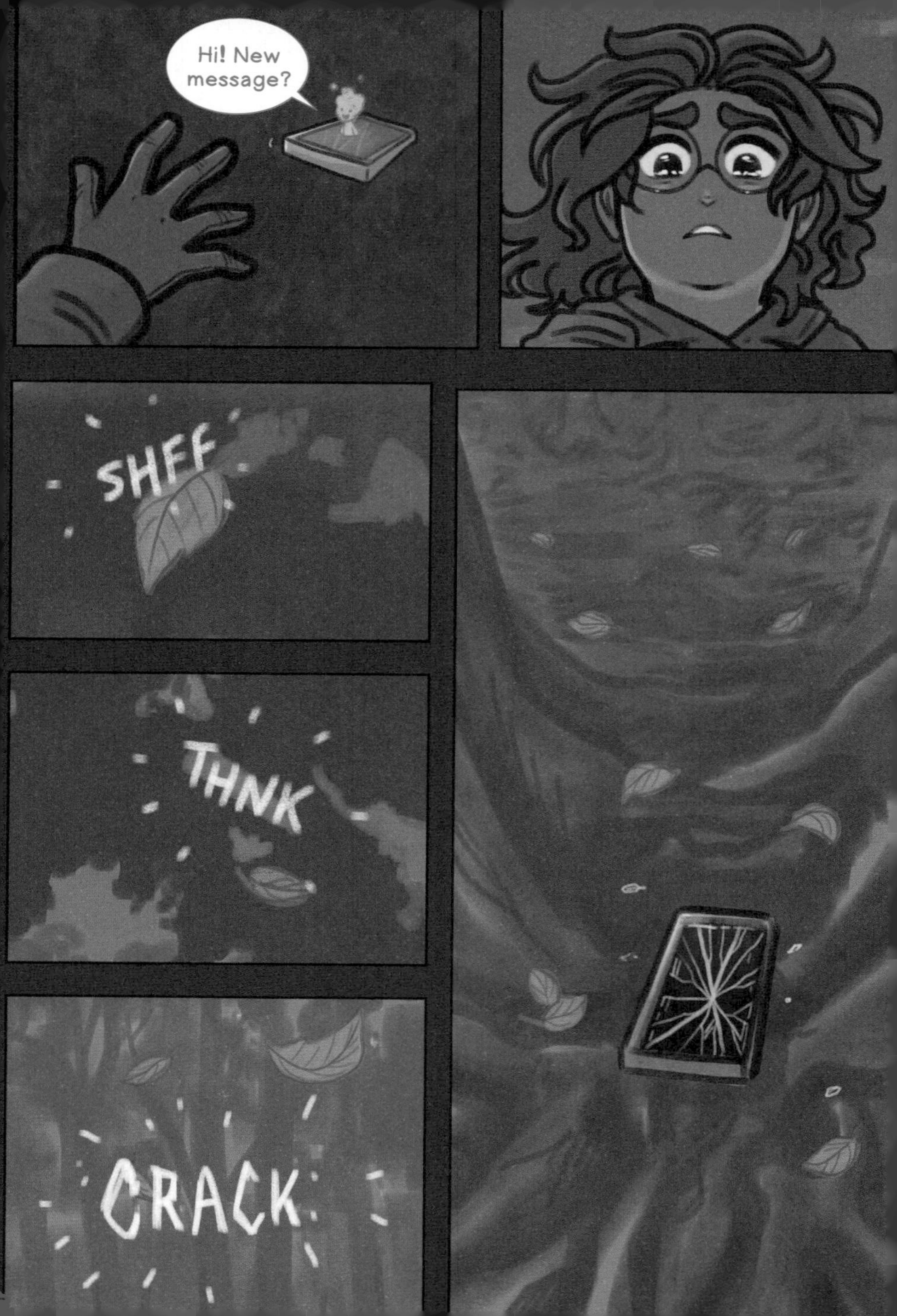
Hi! New message?
SHFF
THNK
CRACK

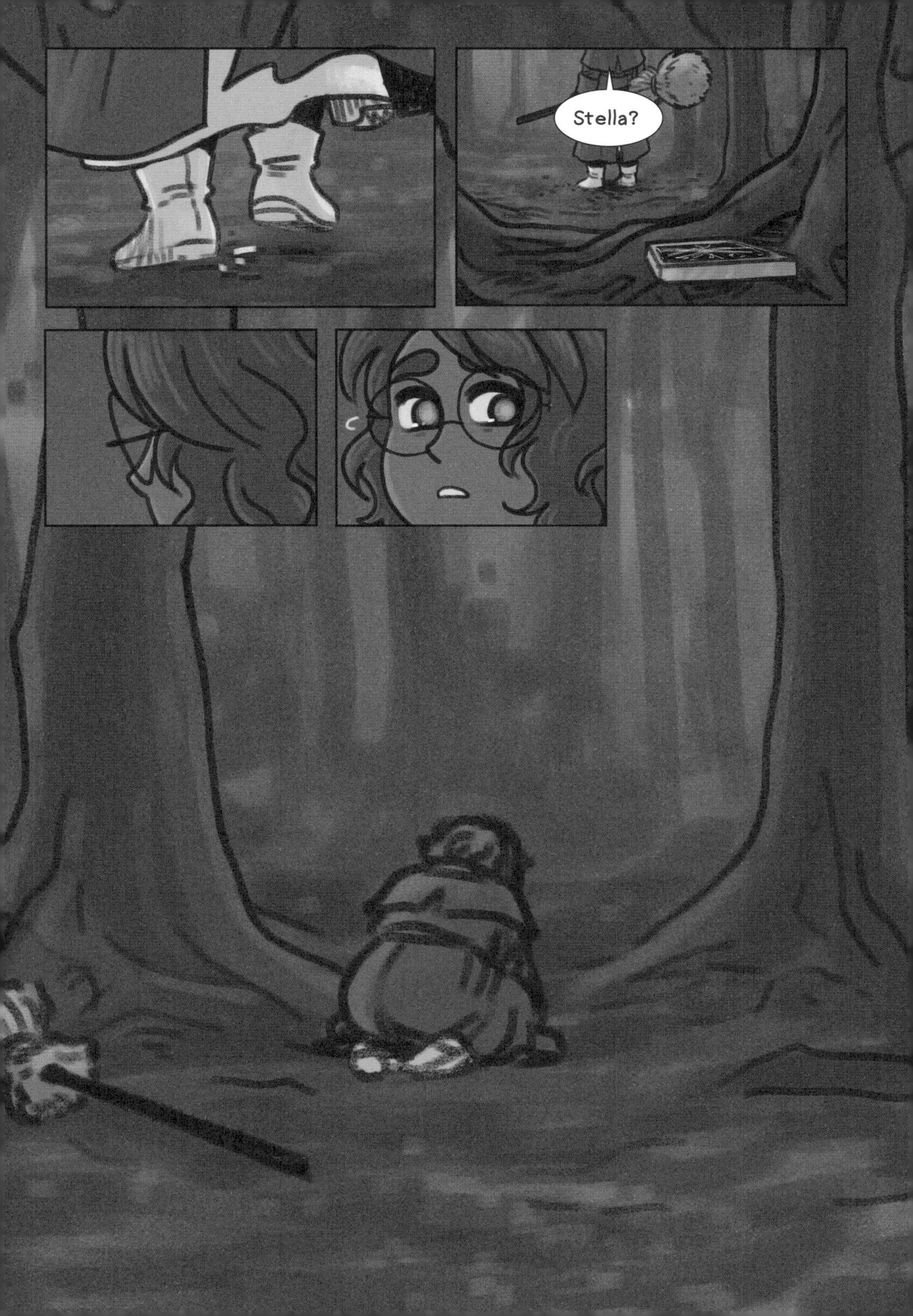
Stella?

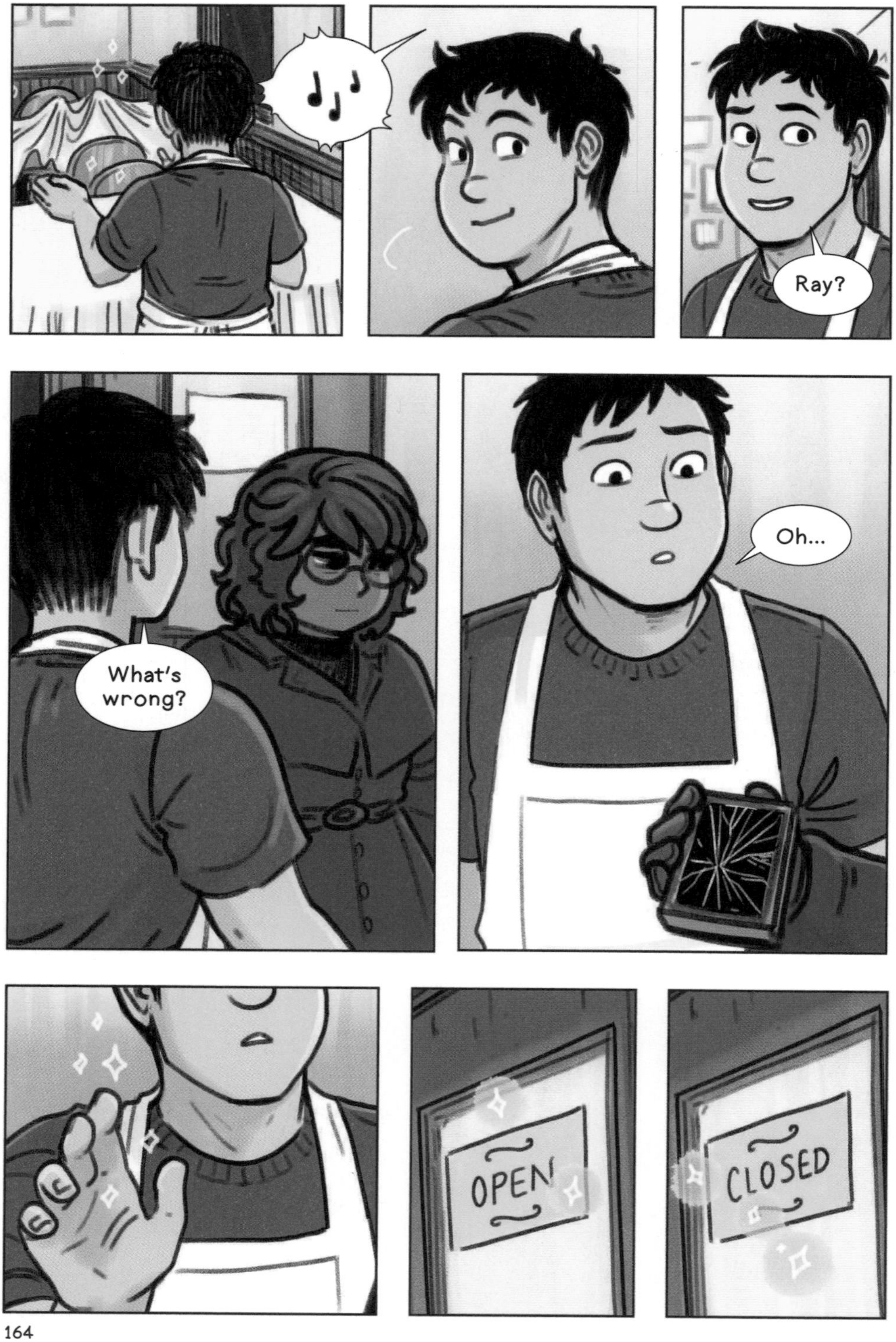
Ray?
What's wrong?
Oh...
OPEN
CLOSED

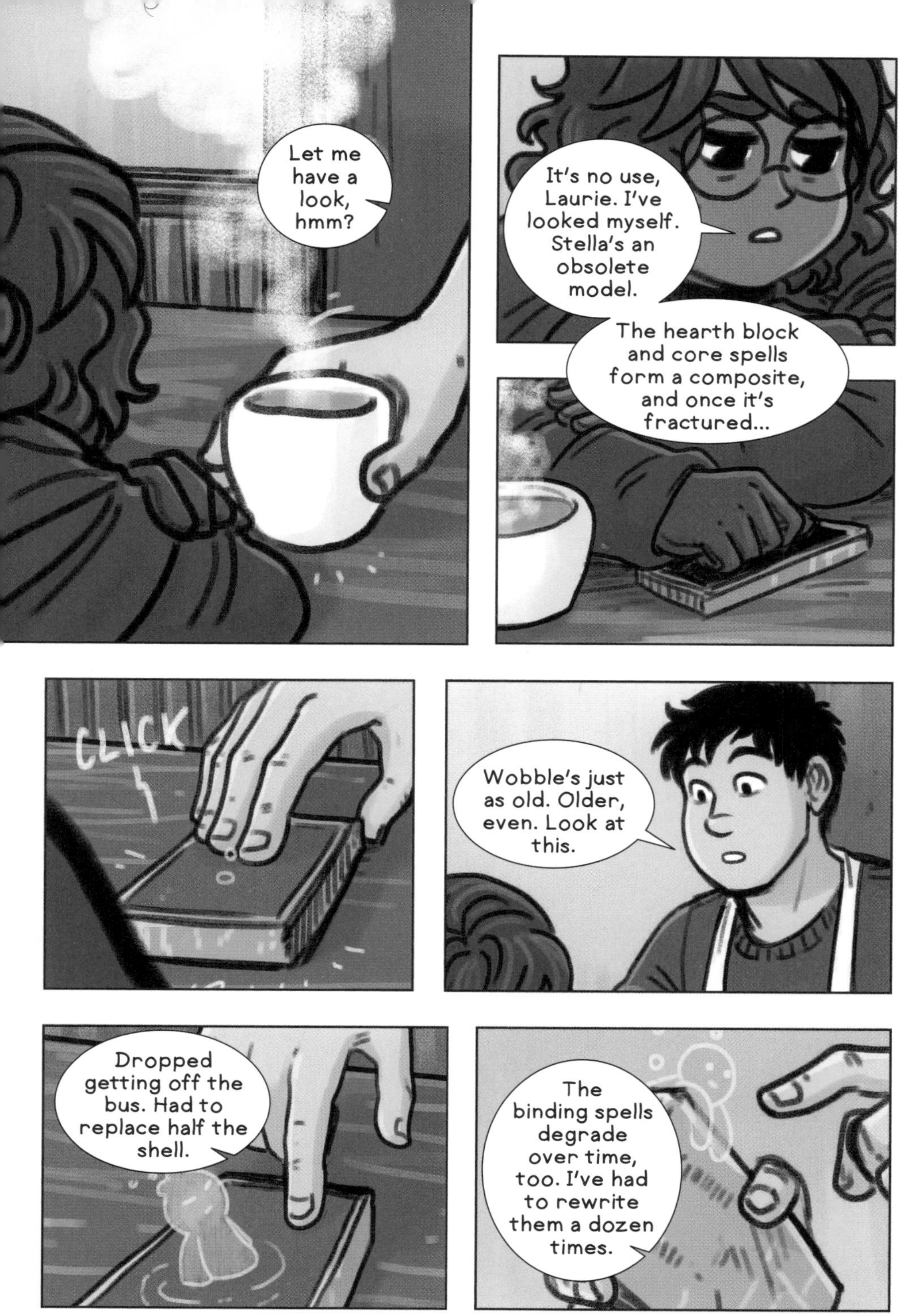
Let me have a look, hmm?
It's no use, Laurie. I've looked myself. Stella's an obsolete model.
The hearth block and core spells form a composite, and once it's fractured...
CLICK
Wobble's just as old. Older, even. Look at this.
Dropped getting off the bus. Had to replace half the shell.
The binding spells degrade over time, too. I've had to rewrite them a dozen times.

And this is from when I dropped him into a pond—

Laurie...

I know, they're not identical. Haven't dropped him out of the sky, but—

Laurie, I looked.

Stella's broken.

Sure, for now.

♪

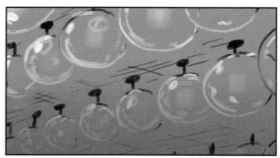

Come back to my place?

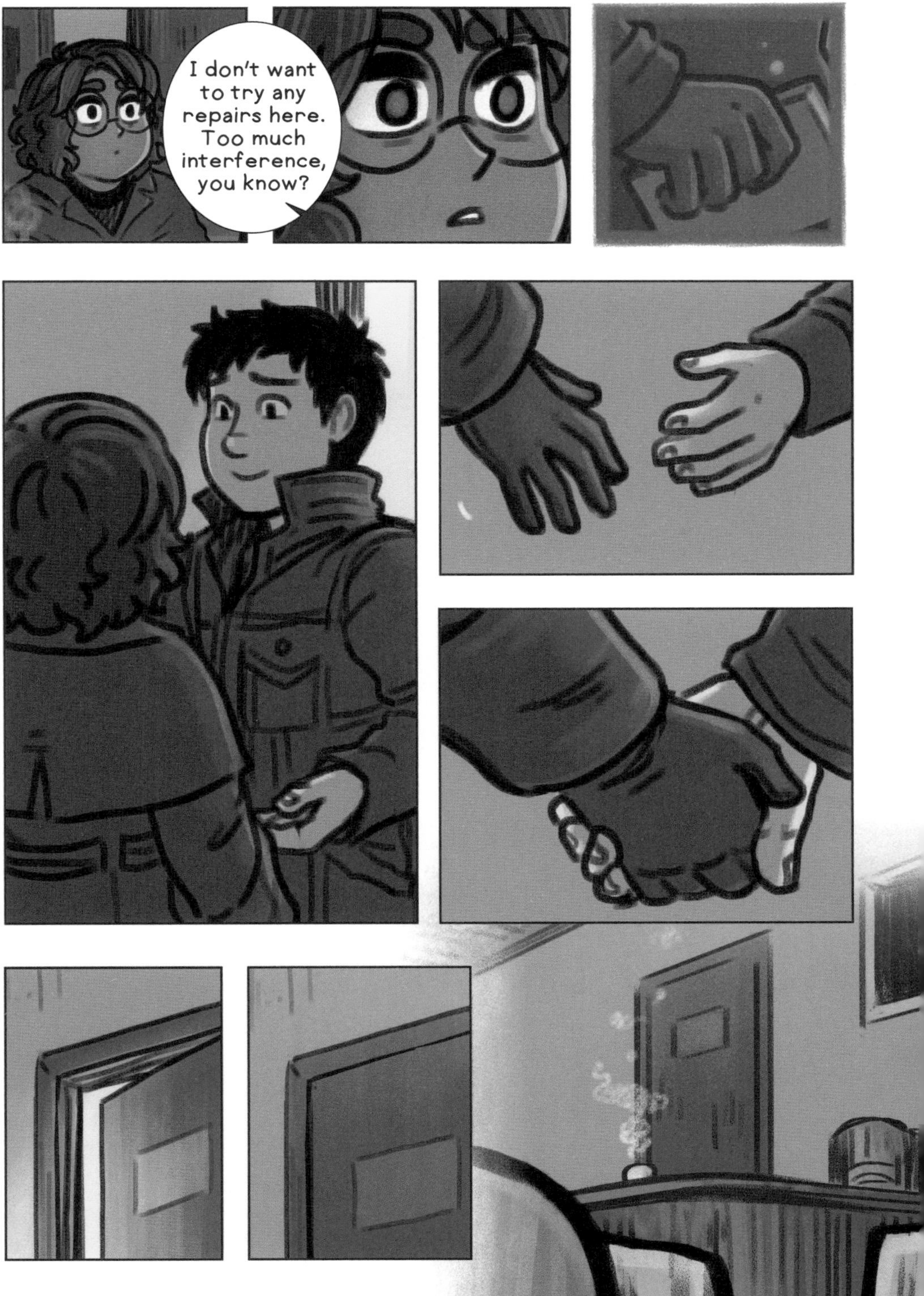
I don't want to try any repairs here. Too much interference, you know?

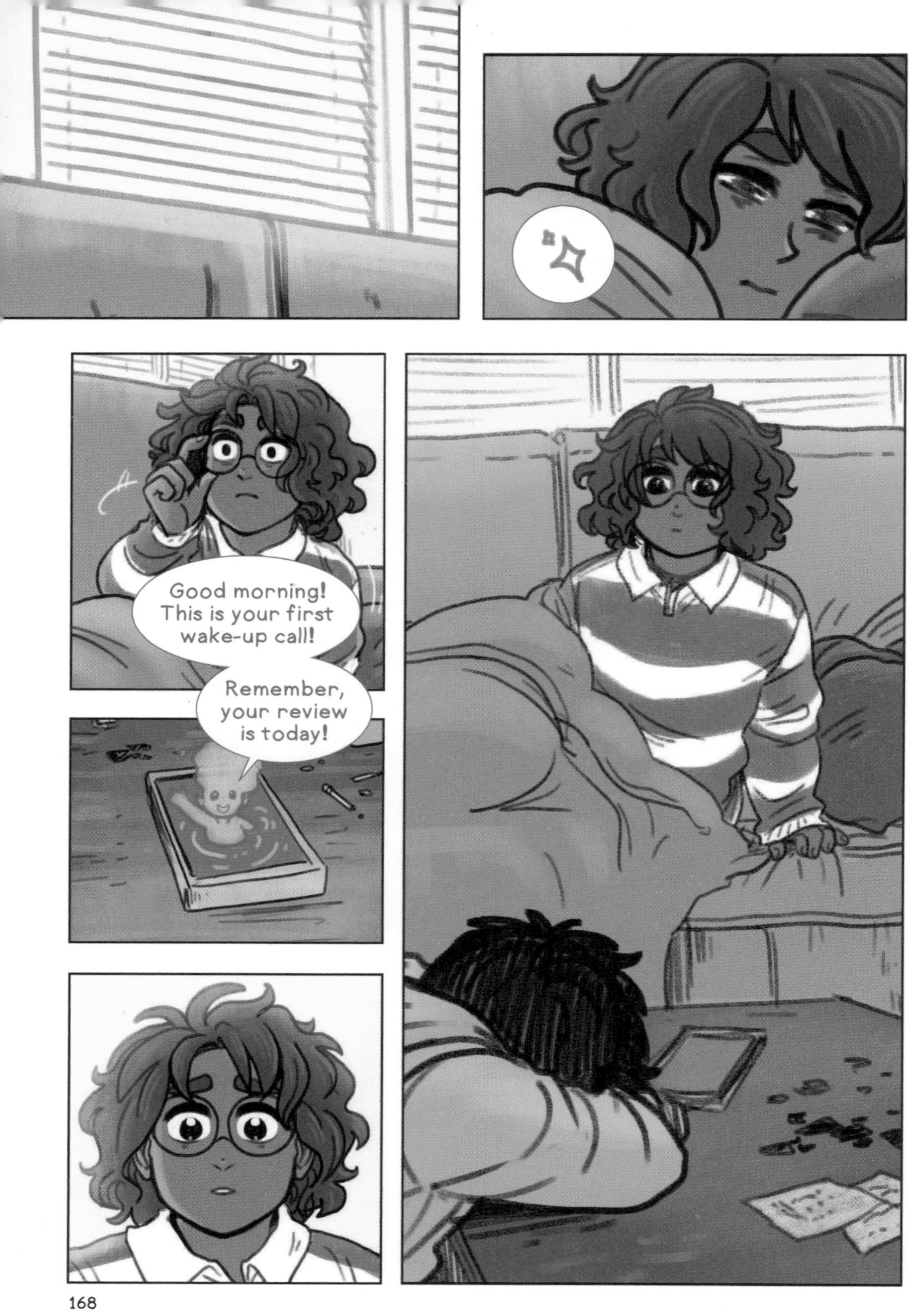
Good morning! This is your first wake-up call!
Remember, your review is today!

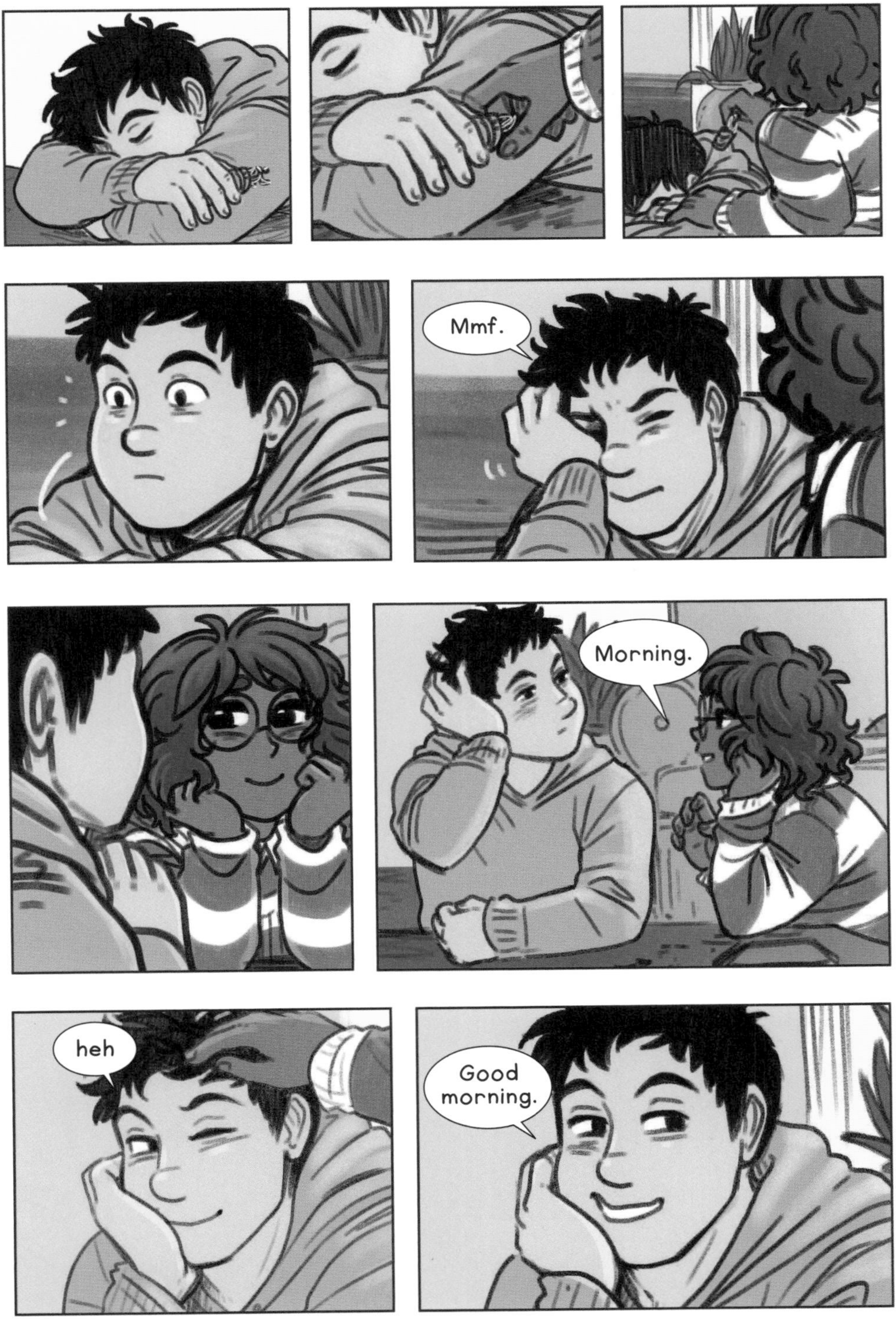
Mmf.
Morning.
heh
Good morning.

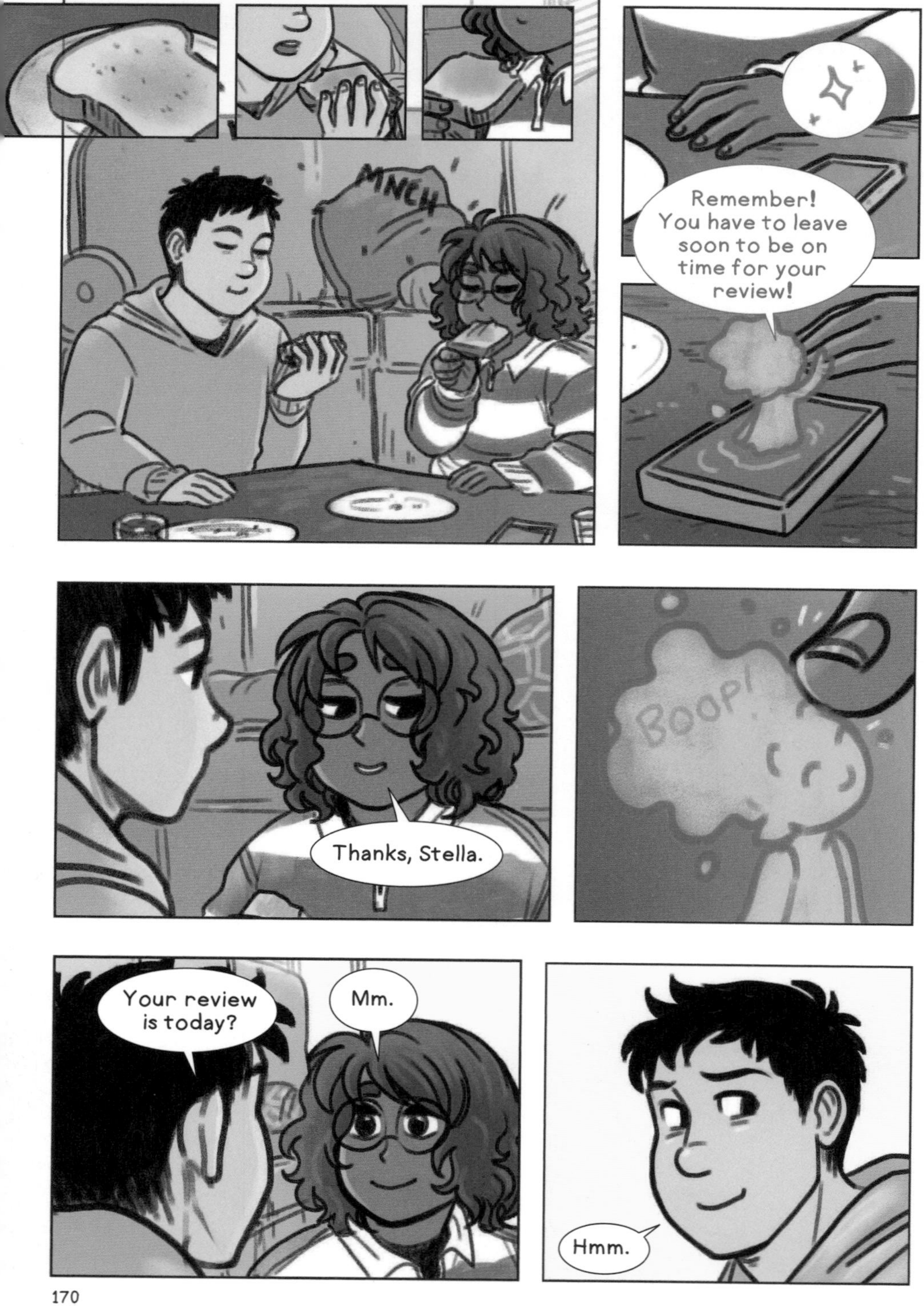
MNCH
Remember! You have to leave soon to be on time for your review!
Thanks, Stella.
BOOP!
Your review is today?
Mm.
Hmm.

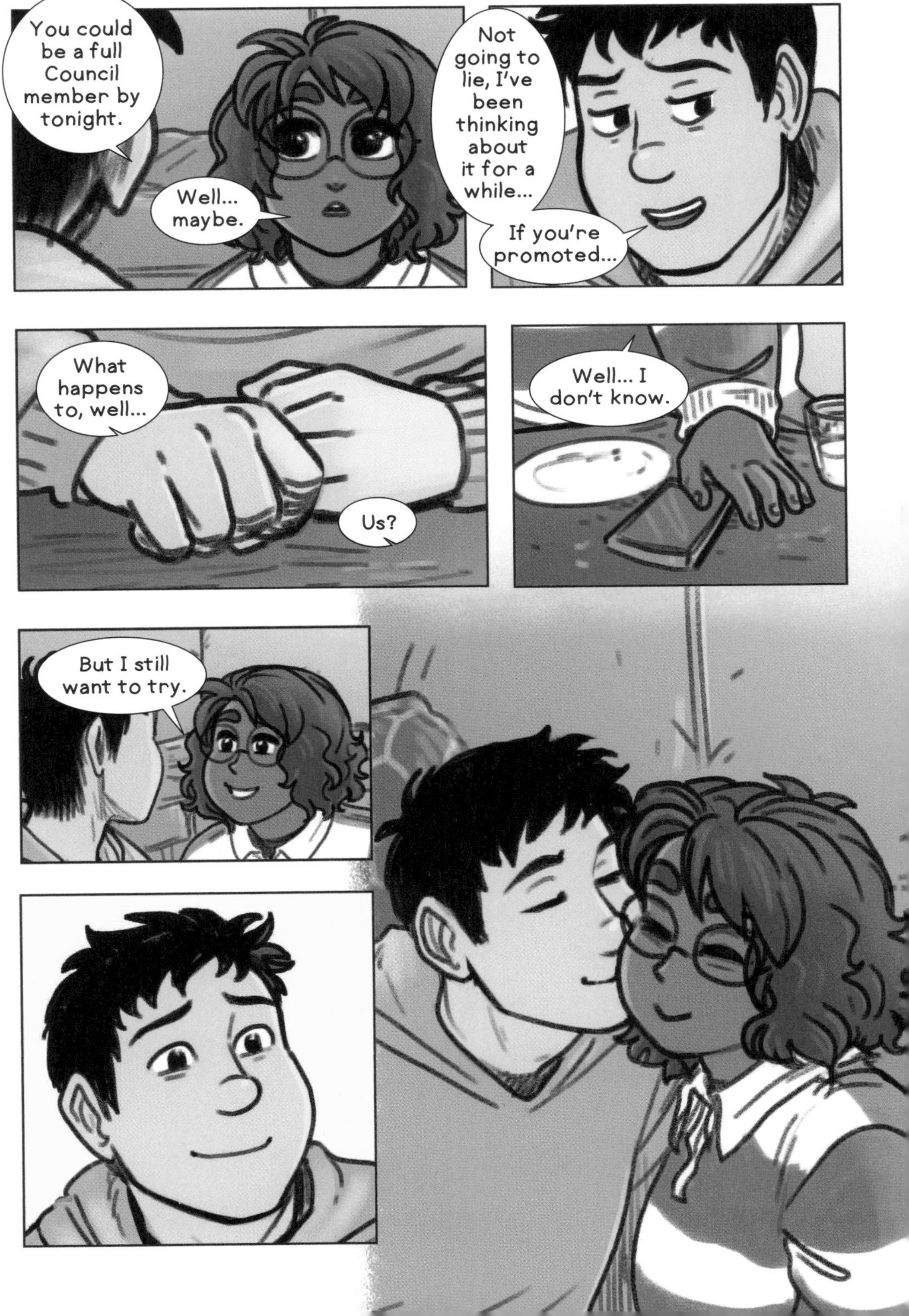
You could be a full Council member by tonight.
Well... maybe.
Not going to lie, I've been thinking about it for a while...
If you're promoted...
What happens to, well...
Us?
Well... I don't know.
But I still want to try.

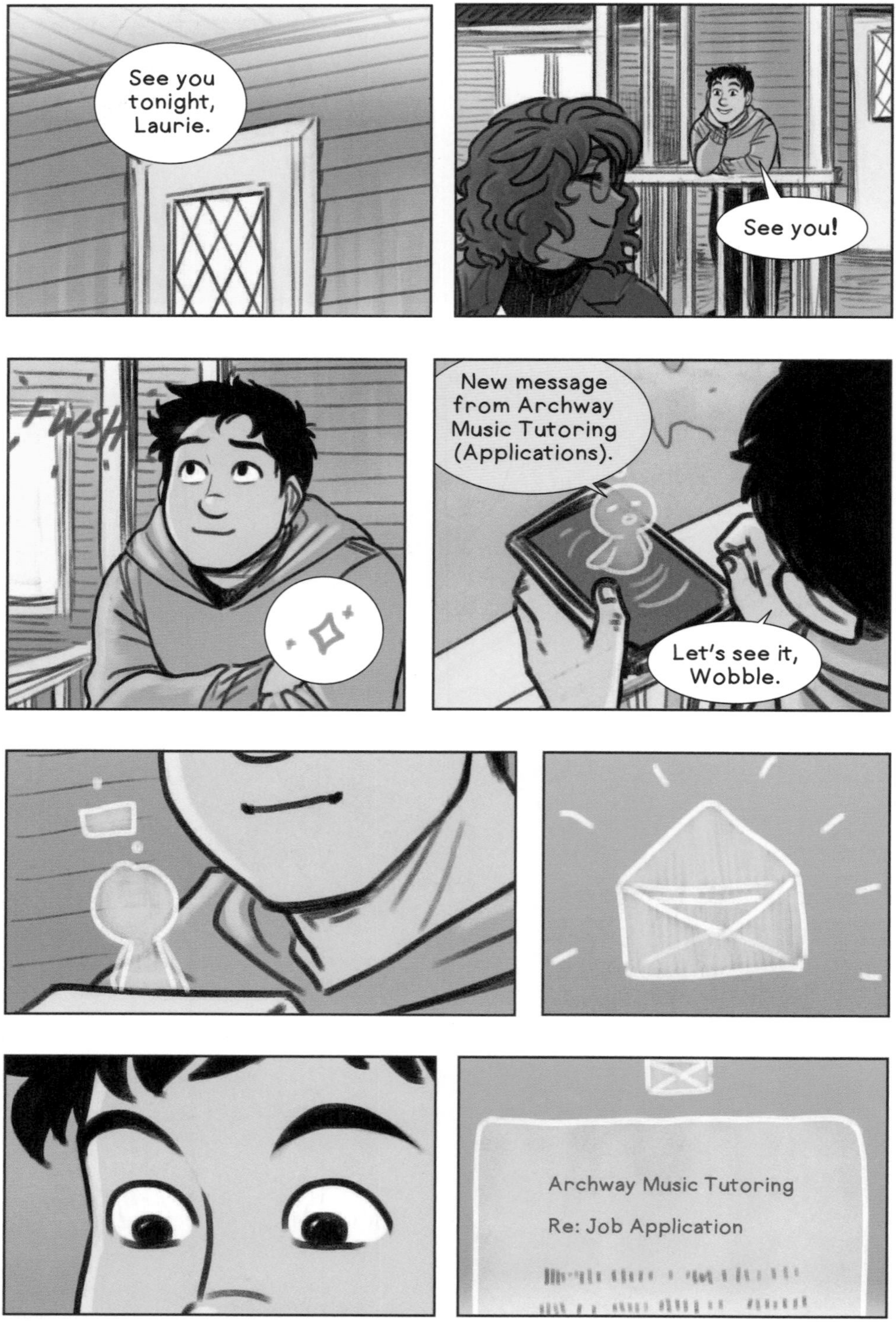
See you tonight, Laurie.
See you!
FWSH
New message from Archway Music Tutoring (Applications).
Let's see it, Wobble.
Archway Music Tutoring
Re: Job Application

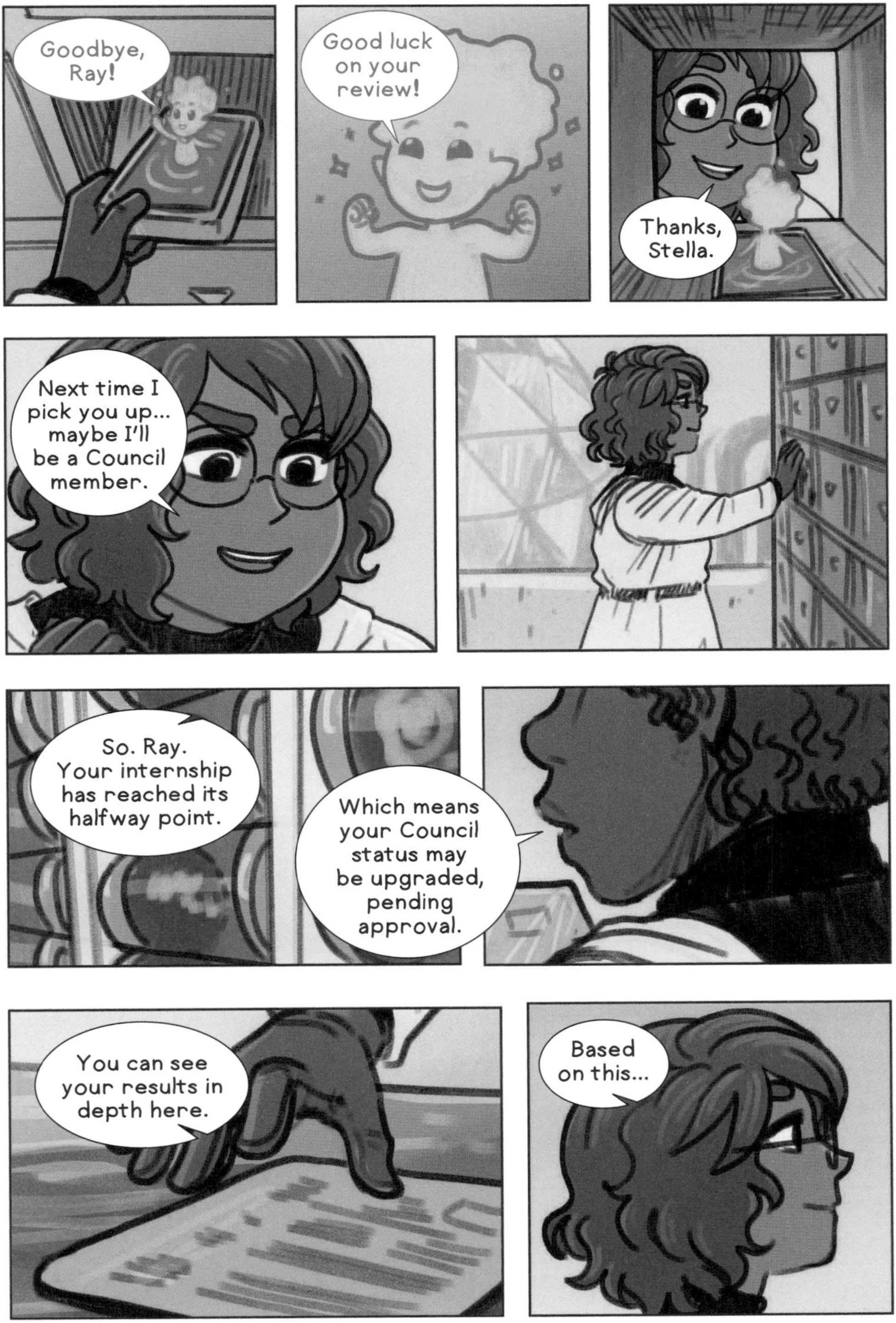

Goodbye, Ray!
Good luck on your review!
Thanks, Stella.
Next time I pick you up... maybe I'll be a Council member.
So. Ray. Your internship has reached its halfway point.
Which means your Council status may be upgraded, pending approval.
You can see your results in depth here.
Based on this...

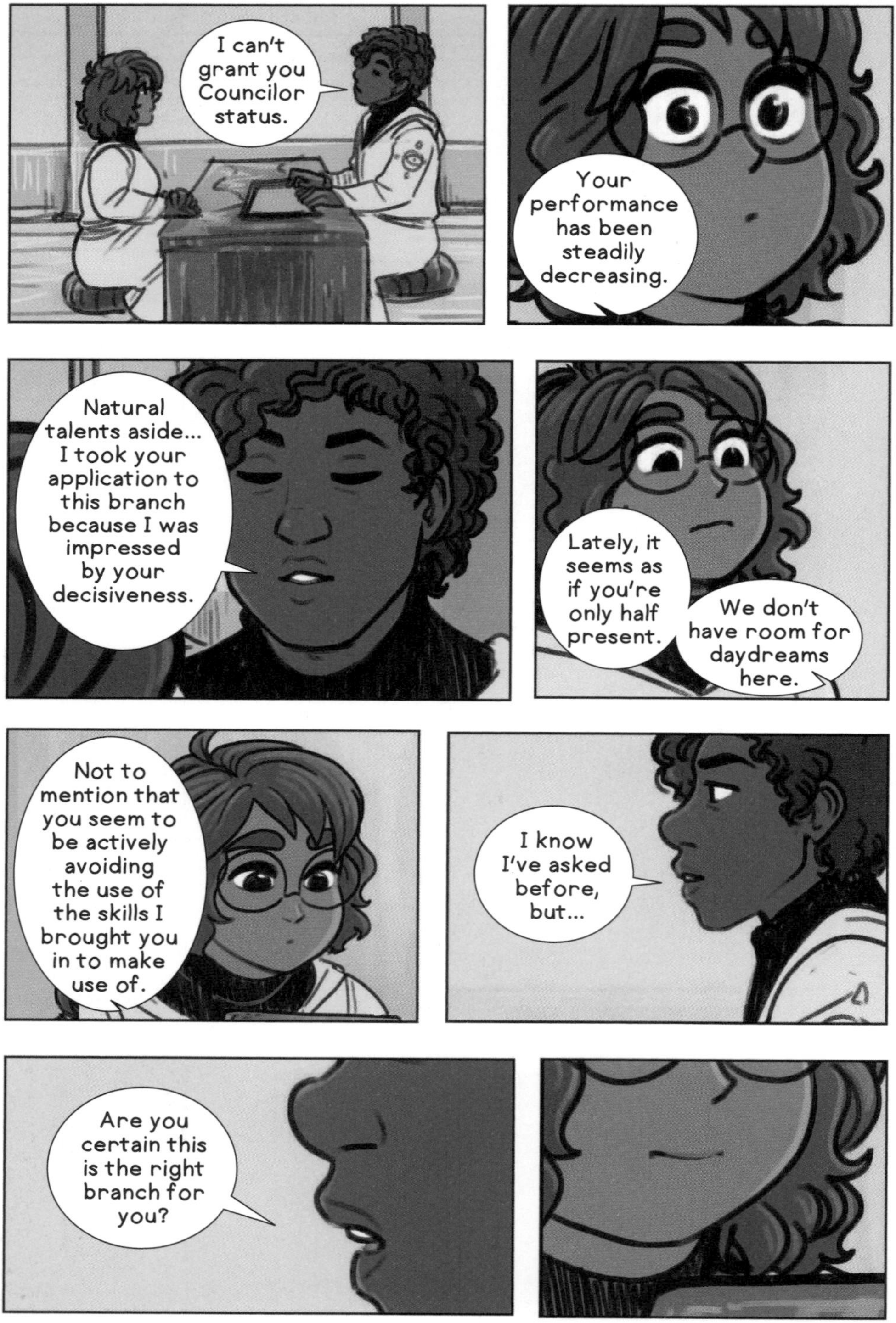
I can't grant you Councilor status.
Your performance has been steadily decreasing.
Natural talents aside... I took your application to this branch because I was impressed by your decisiveness.
Lately, it seems as if you're only half present.
We don't have room for daydreams here.
Not to mention that you seem to be actively avoiding the use of the skills I brought you in to make use of.
I know I've asked before, but...
Are you certain this is the right branch for you?

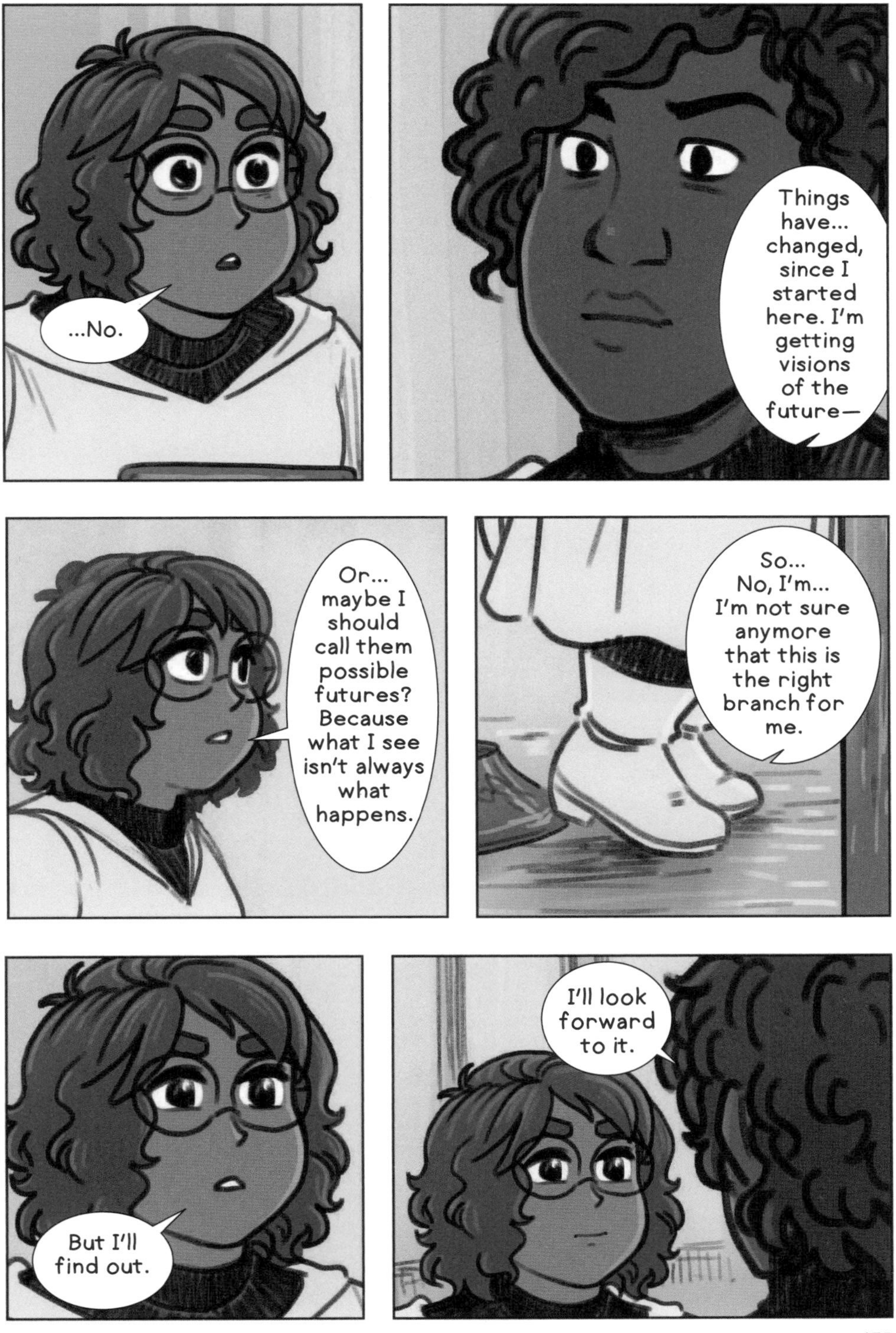
...No.
Things have... changed, since I started here. I'm getting visions of the future—
Or... maybe I should call them possible futures? Because what I see isn't always what happens.
So... No, I'm... I'm not sure anymore that this is the right branch for me.
But I'll find out.
I'll look forward to it.

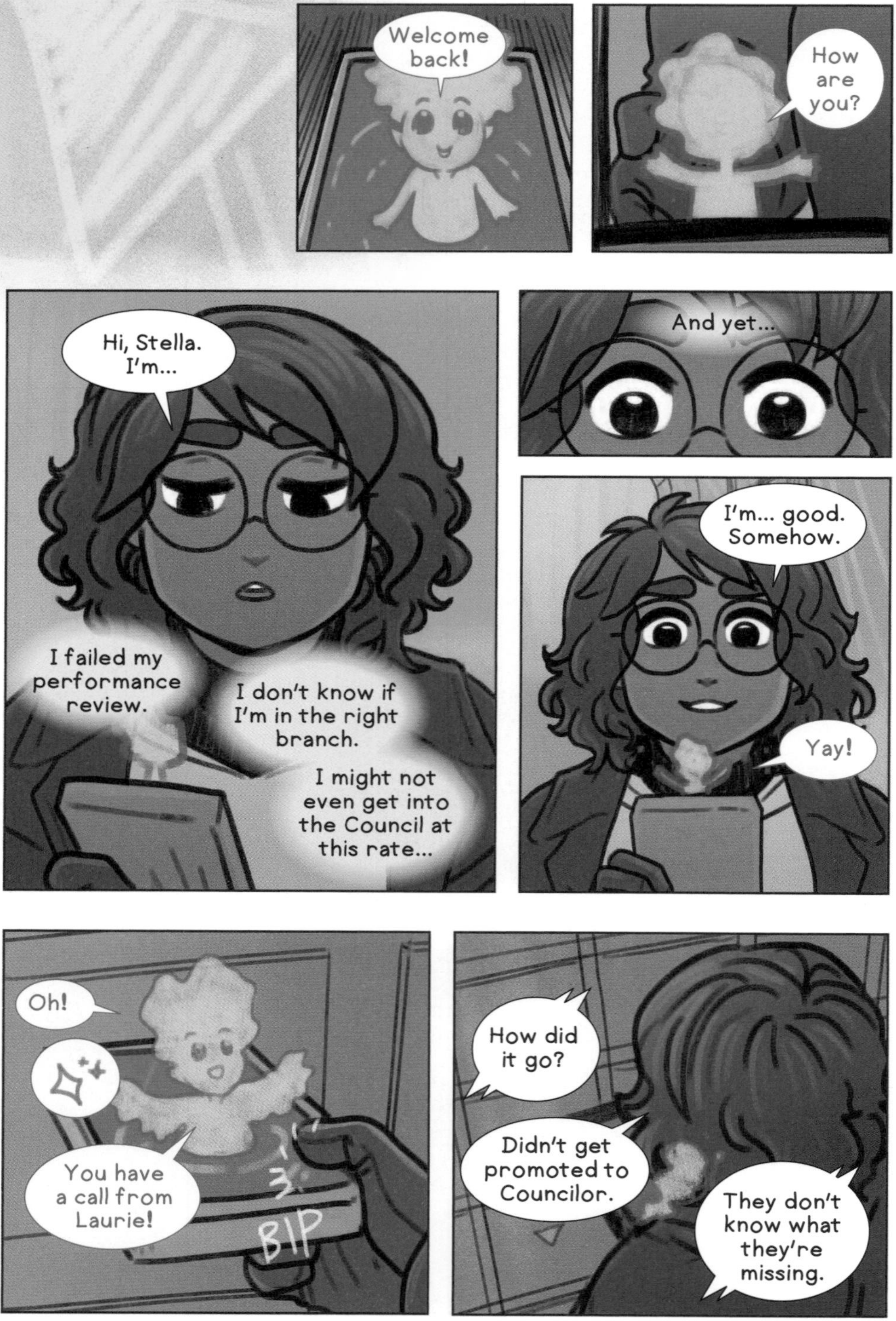
Welcome back!
How are you?
Hi, Stella. I'm...
I failed my performance review.
I don't know if I'm in the right branch.
I might not even get into the Council at this rate...
And yet...
I'm... good. Somehow.
Yay!
Oh!
You have a call from Laurie!
BIP
How did it go?
Didn't get promoted to Councilor.
They don't know what they're missing.

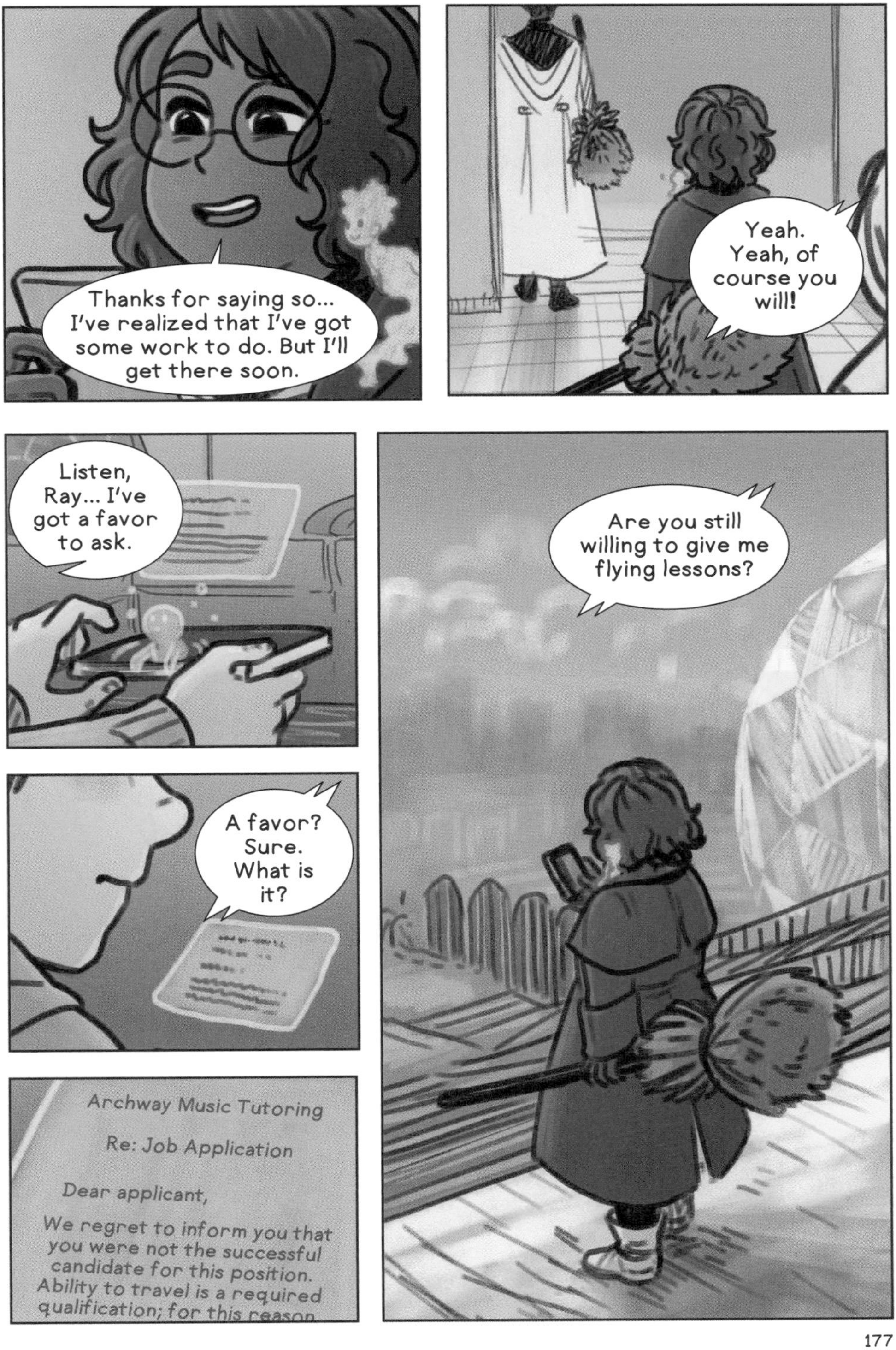
Thanks for saying so...
I've realized that I've got
some work to do. But I'll
get there soon.
Yeah.
Yeah, of
course you
will!
Listen,
Ray... I've
got a favor
to ask.
A favor?
Sure.
What is
it?
Archway Music Tutoring
Re: Job Application
Dear applicant,
We regret to inform you that
you were not the successful
candidate for this position.
Ability to travel is a required
qualification; for this reason
Are you still
willing to give me
flying lessons?

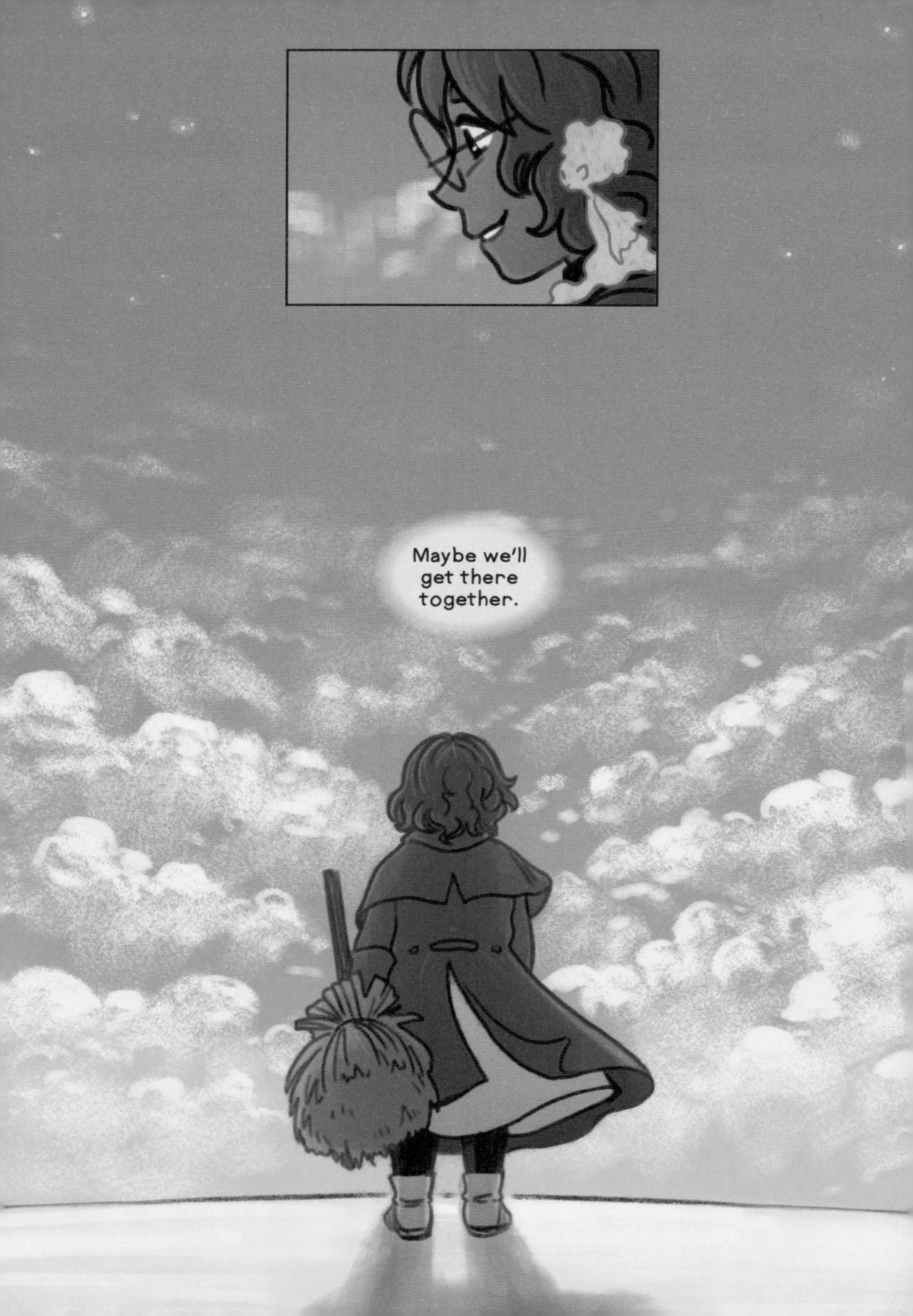
Maybe we'll get there together.

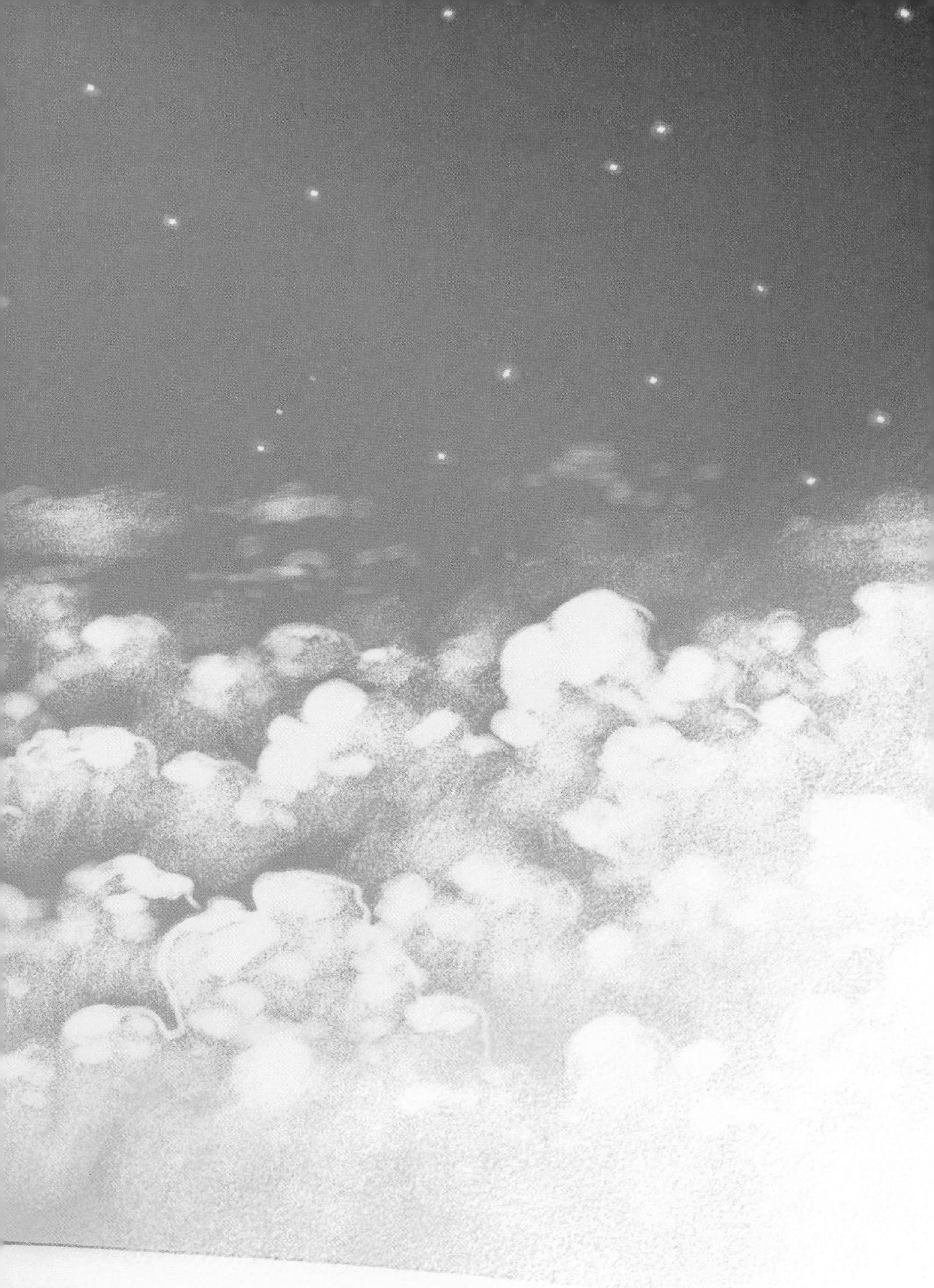

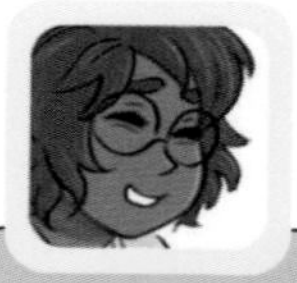

SEASON TWO

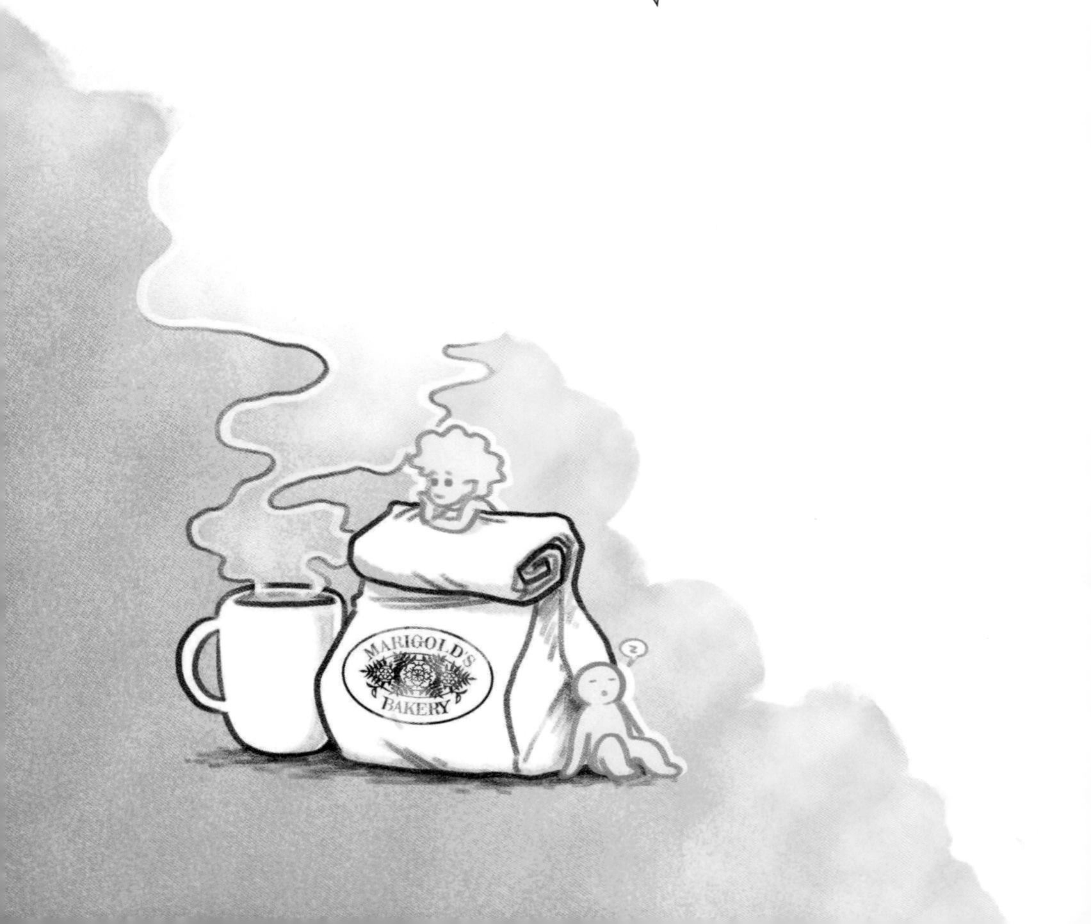
MARIGOLD'S
BAKERY

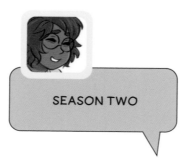

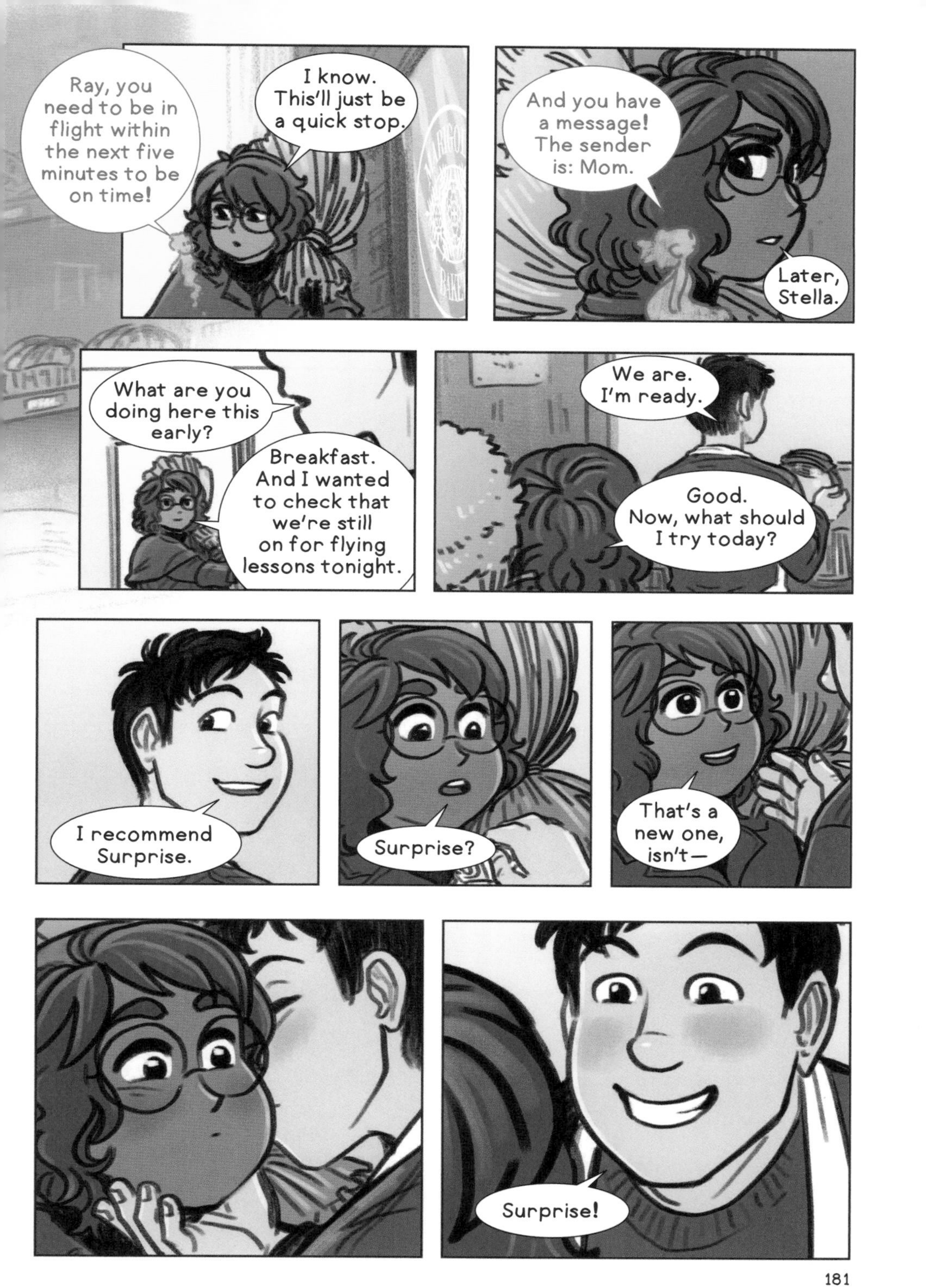
Ray, you need to be in flight within the next five minutes to be on time!
I know. This'll just be a quick stop.
And you have a message! The sender is: Mom.
Later, Stella.
What are you doing here this early?
Breakfast. And I wanted to check that we're still on for flying lessons tonight.
We are. I'm ready.
Good. Now, what should I try today?
I recommend Surprise.
Surprise?
That's a new one, isn't—
Surprise!

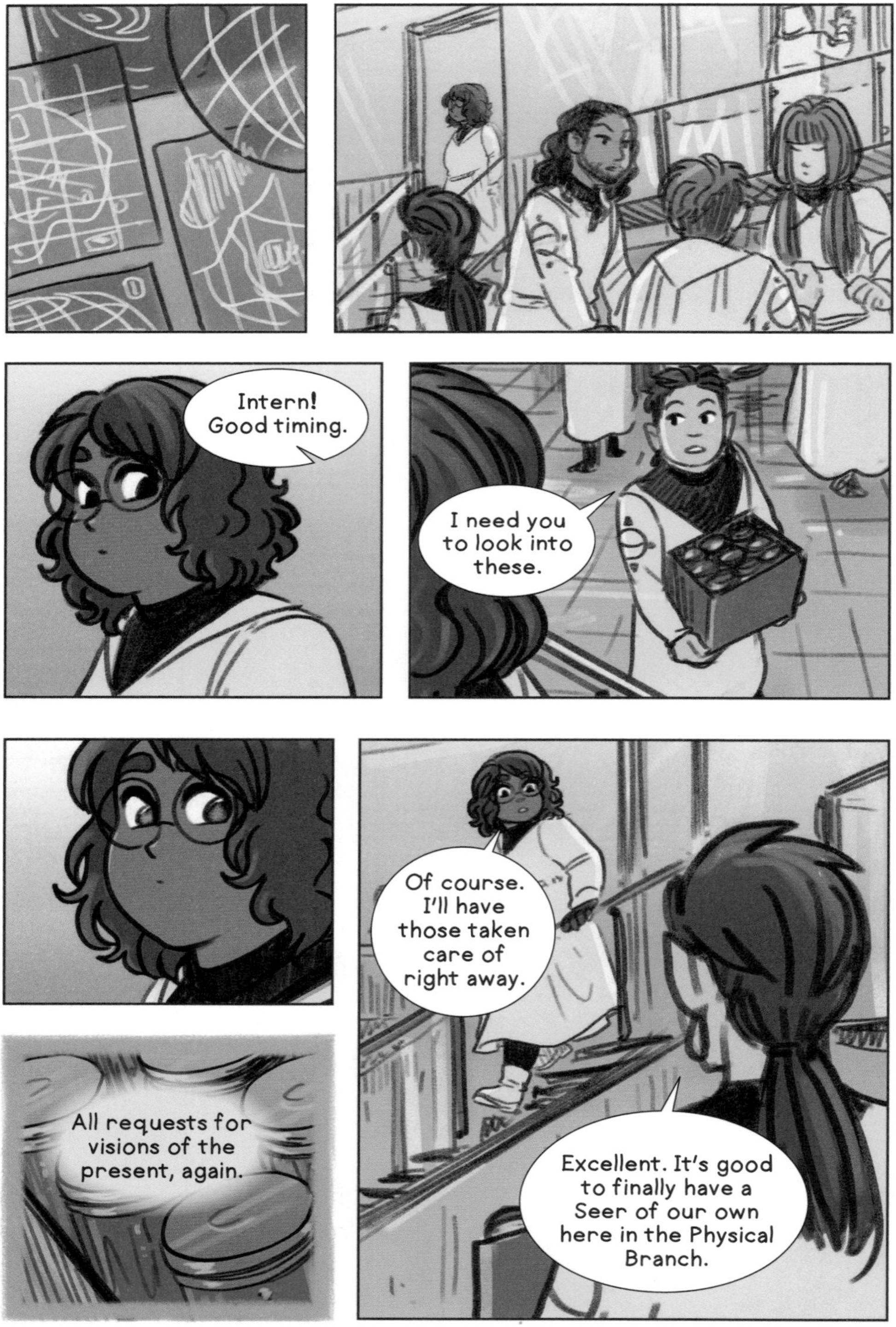
Intern!
Good timing.
I need you to look into these.
Of course. I'll have those taken care of right away.
All requests for visions of the present, again.
Excellent. It's good to finally have a Seer of our own here in the Physical Branch.

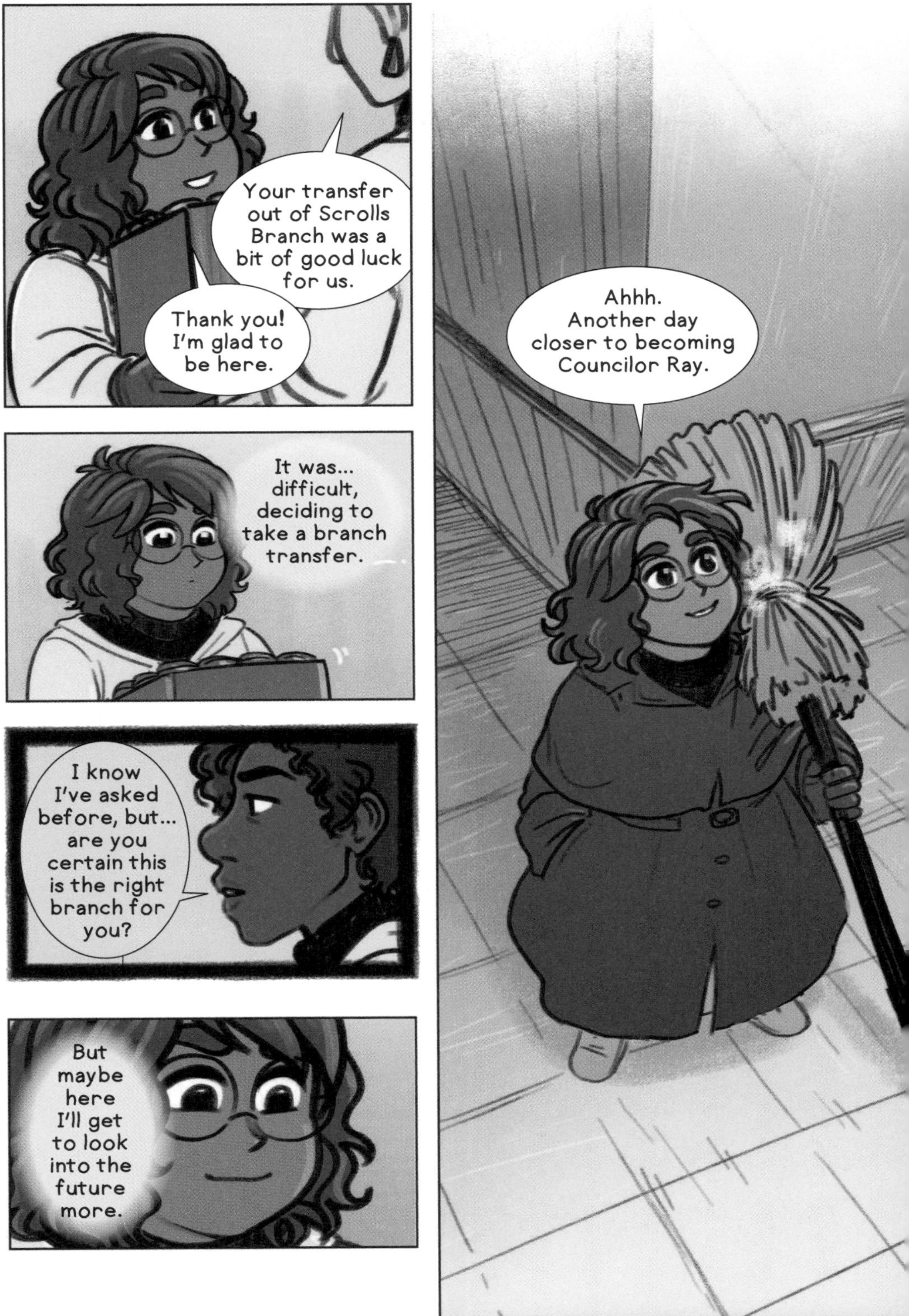
Your transfer out of Scrolls Branch was a bit of good luck for us.
Thank you! I'm glad to be here.
It was... difficult, deciding to take a branch transfer.
I know I've asked before, but... are you certain this is the right branch for you?
But maybe here I'll get to look into the future more.
Ahhh. Another day closer to becoming Councilor Ray.

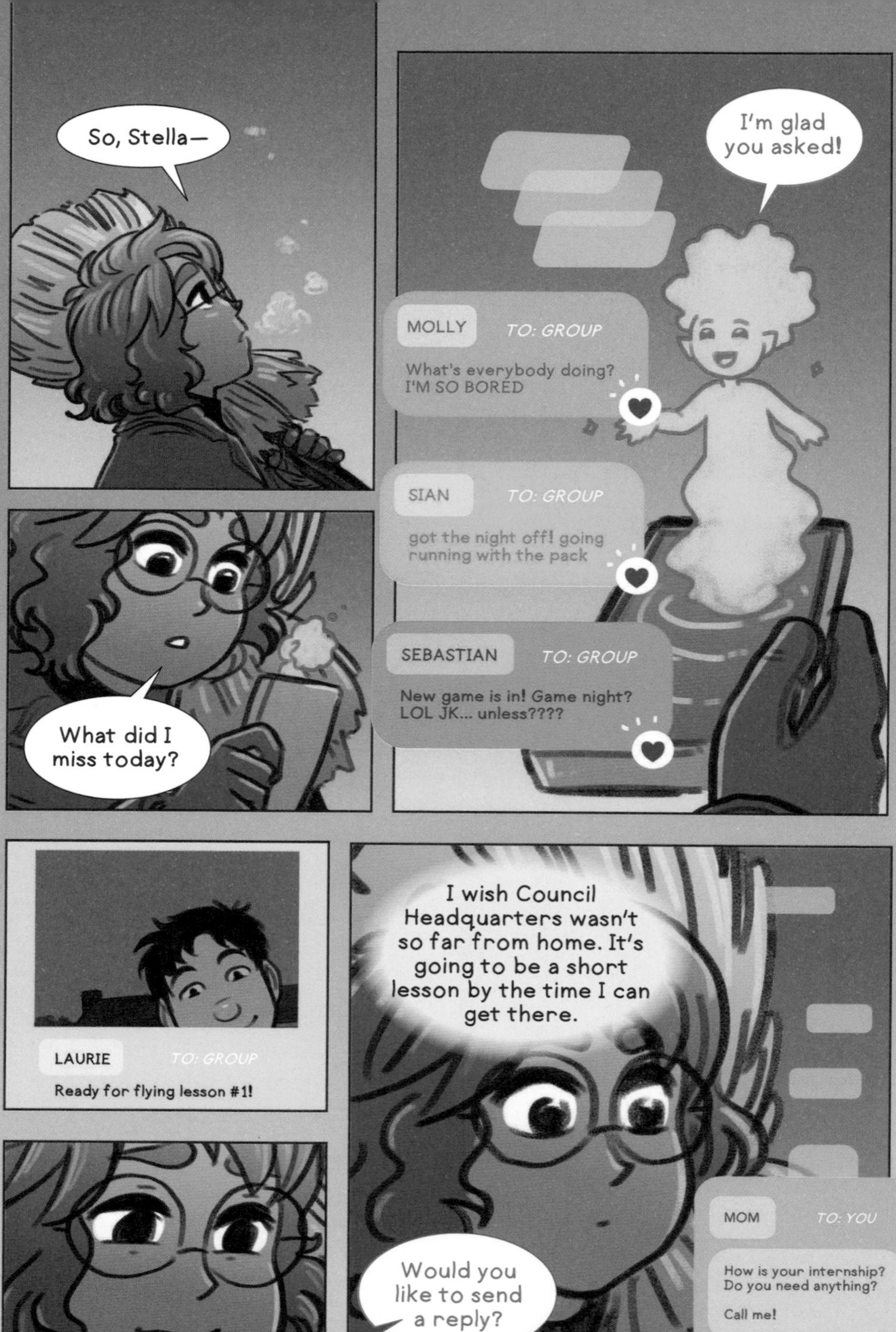
So, Stella—
What did I miss today?
I'm glad you asked!
MOLLY TO: GROUP
What's everybody doing? I'M SO BORED
SIAN TO: GROUP
got the night off! going running with the pack
SEBASTIAN TO: GROUP
New game is in! Game night? LOL JK... unless????
LAURIE TO: GROUP
Ready for flying lesson #1!
I wish Council Headquarters wasn't so far from home. It's going to be a short lesson by the time I can get there.
MOM TO: YOU
How is your internship? Do you need anything?
Call me!
Would you like to send a reply?

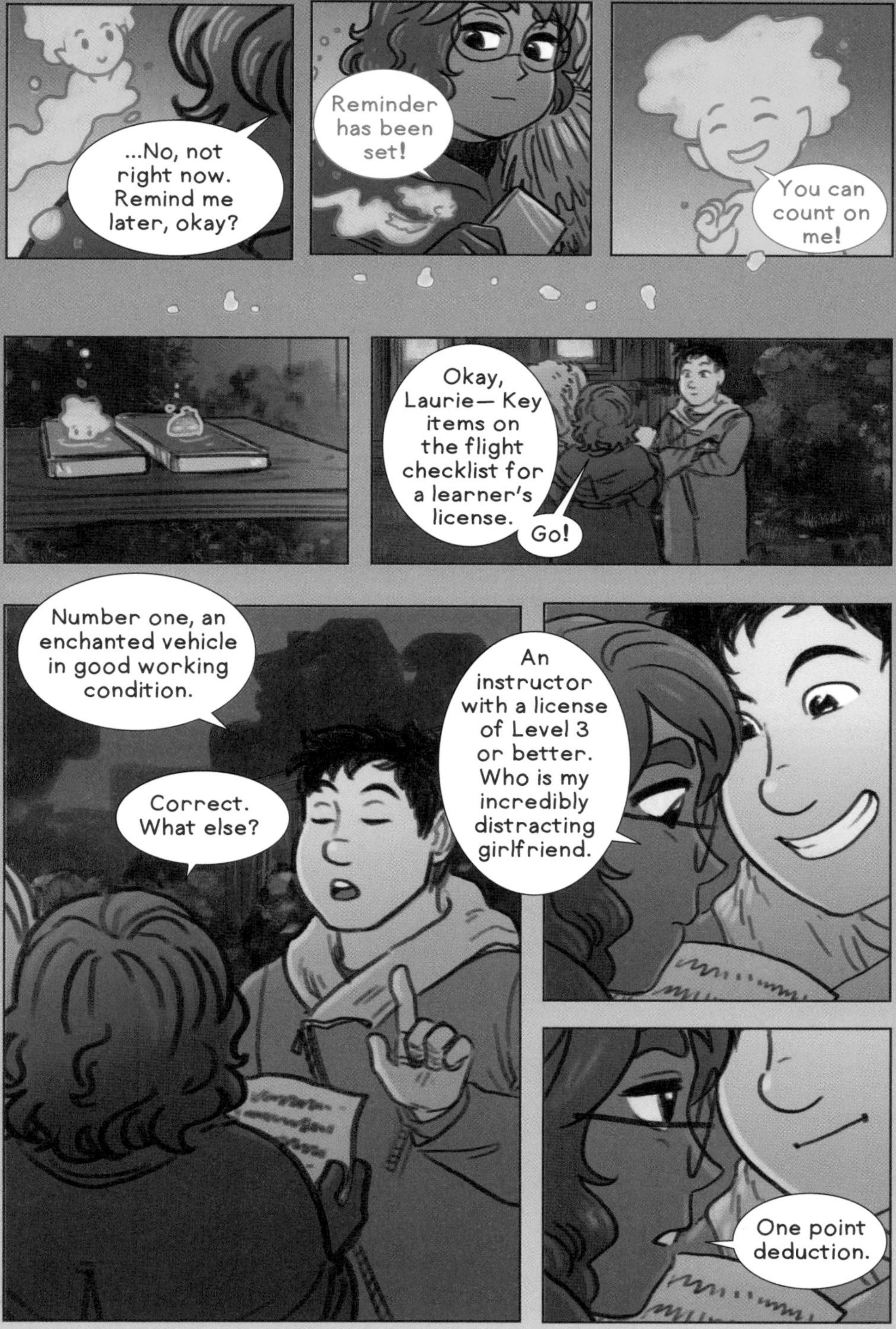
...No, not right now. Remind me later, okay?
Reminder has been set!
You can count on me!
Okay, Laurie— Key items on the flight checklist for a learner's license.
Go!
Number one, an enchanted vehicle in good working condition.
Correct. What else?
An instructor with a license of Level 3 or better. Who is my incredibly distracting girlfriend.
One point deduction.

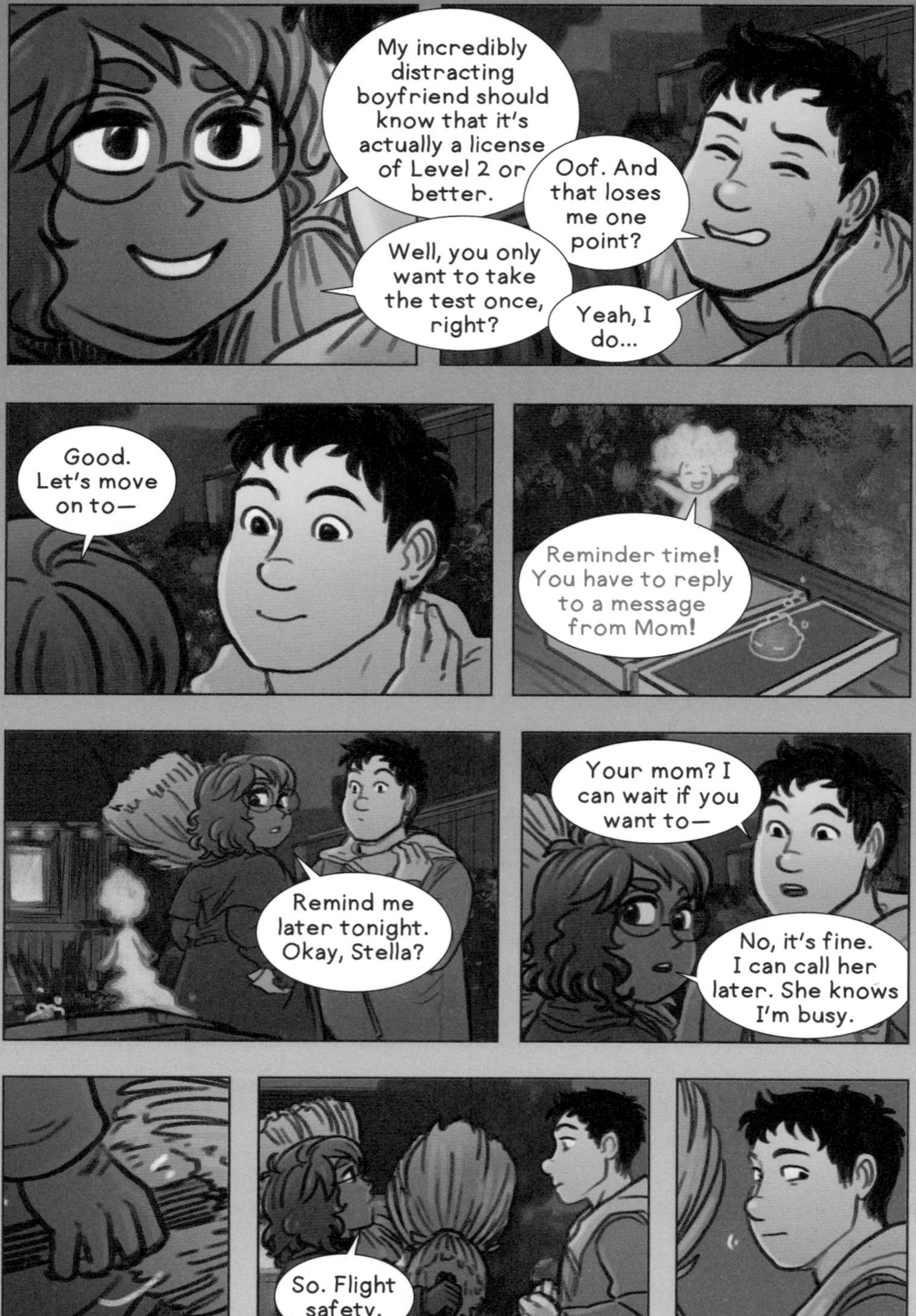

My incredibly distracting boyfriend should know that it's actually a license of Level 2 or better.
Oof. And that loses me one point?
Well, you only want to take the test once, right?
Yeah, I do...
Good. Let's move on to—
Reminder time! You have to reply to a message from Mom!
Remind me later tonight. Okay, Stella?
Your mom? I can wait if you want to—
No, it's fine. I can call her later. She knows I'm busy.
So. Flight safety.

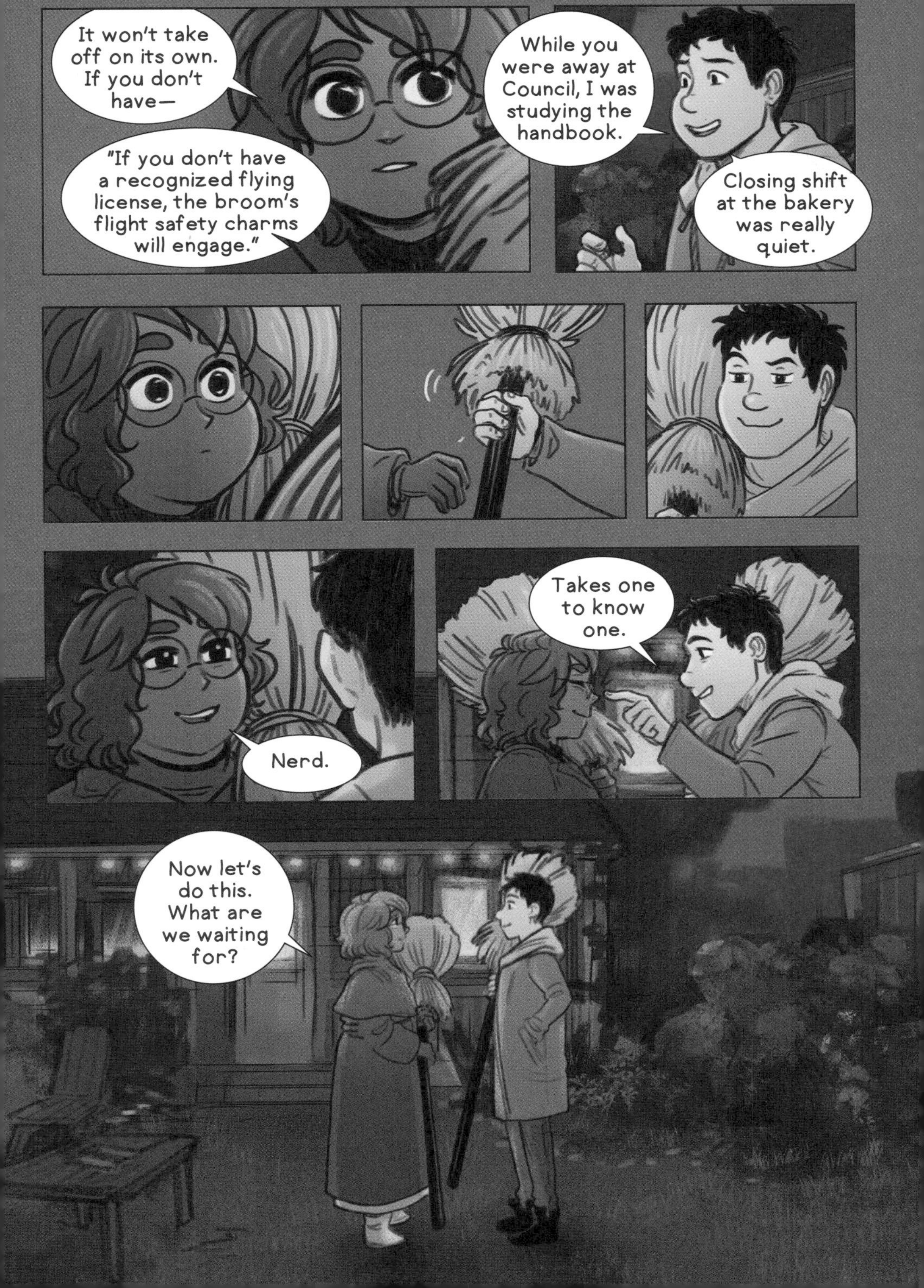
It won't take off on its own. If you don't have—
"If you don't have a recognized flying license, the broom's flight safety charms will engage."
While you were away at Council, I was studying the handbook.
Closing shift at the bakery was really quiet.
Nerd.
Takes one to know one.
Now let's do this. What are we waiting for?

CHAPTER 9

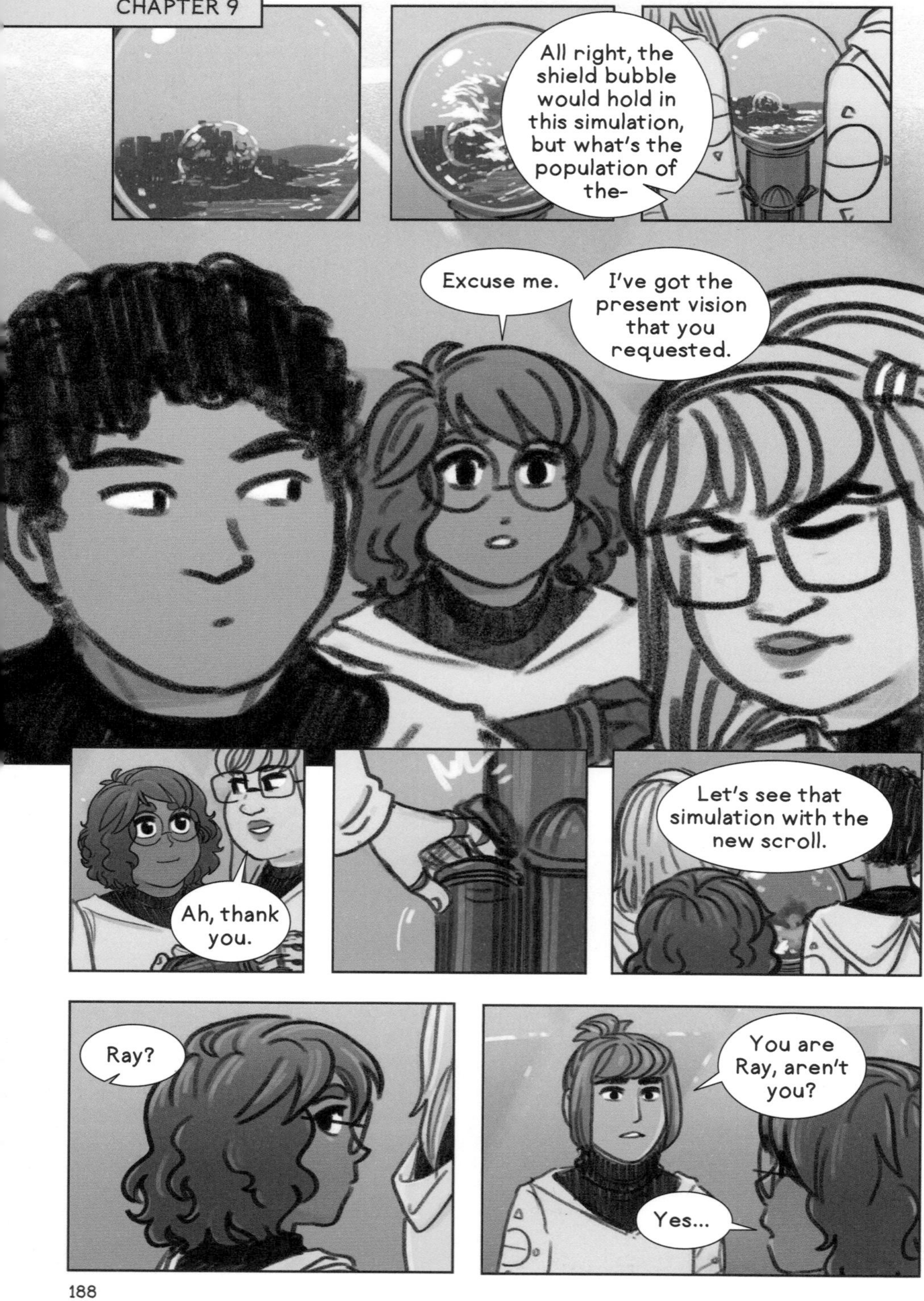
All right, the shield bubble would hold in this simulation, but what's the population of the-
Excuse me.
I've got the present vision that you requested.
Ah, thank you.
Let's see that simulation with the new scroll.
Ray?
You are Ray, aren't you?
Yes...

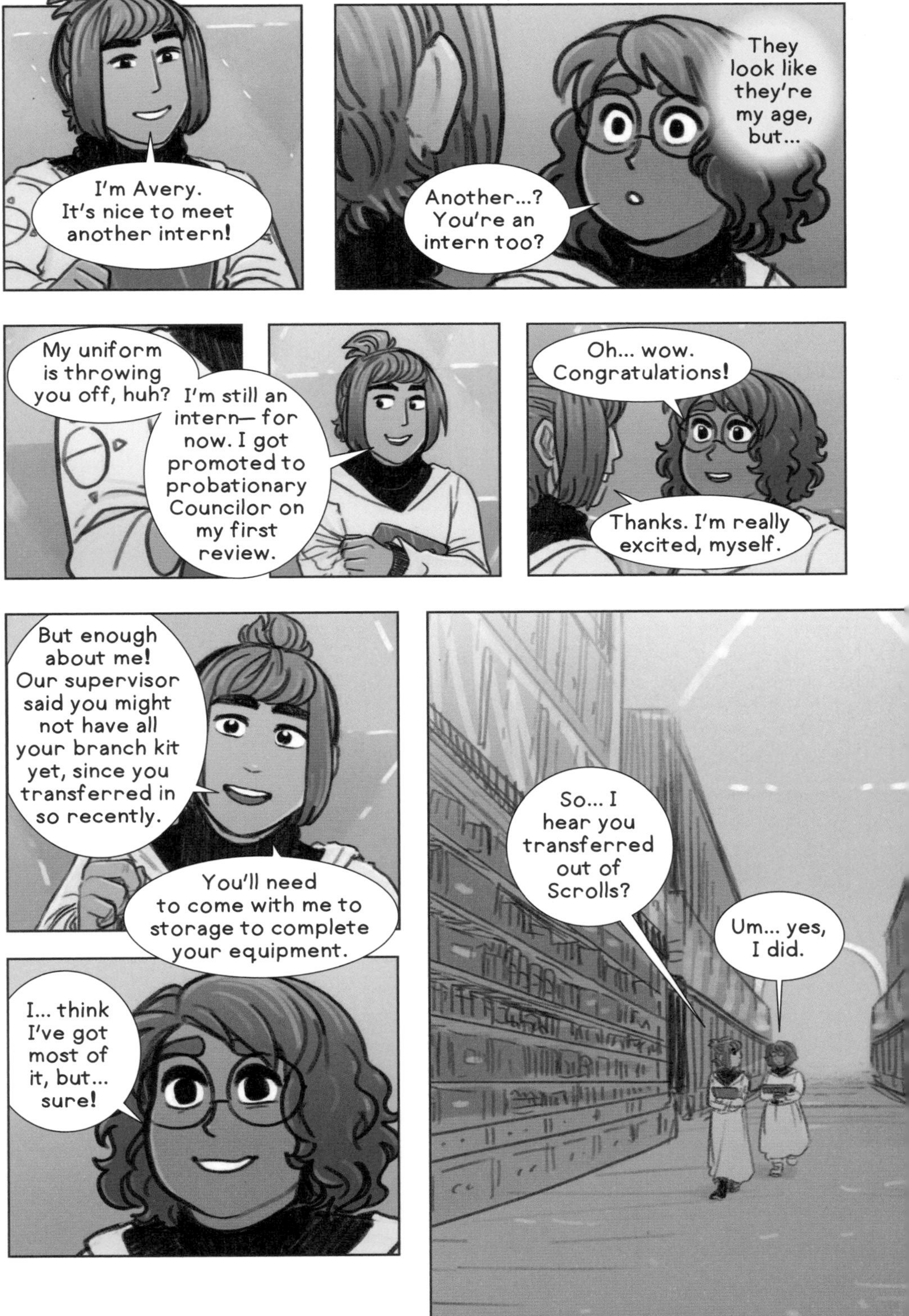
I'm Avery. It's nice to meet another intern!
They look like they're my age, but...
Another...? You're an intern too?
My uniform is throwing you off, huh?
I'm still an intern— for now. I got promoted to probationary Councilor on my first review.
Oh... wow. Congratulations!
Thanks. I'm really excited, myself.
But enough about me! Our supervisor said you might not have all your branch kit yet, since you transferred in so recently.
You'll need to come with me to storage to complete your equipment.
I... think I've got most of it, but... sure!
So... I hear you transferred out of Scrolls?
Um... yes, I did.

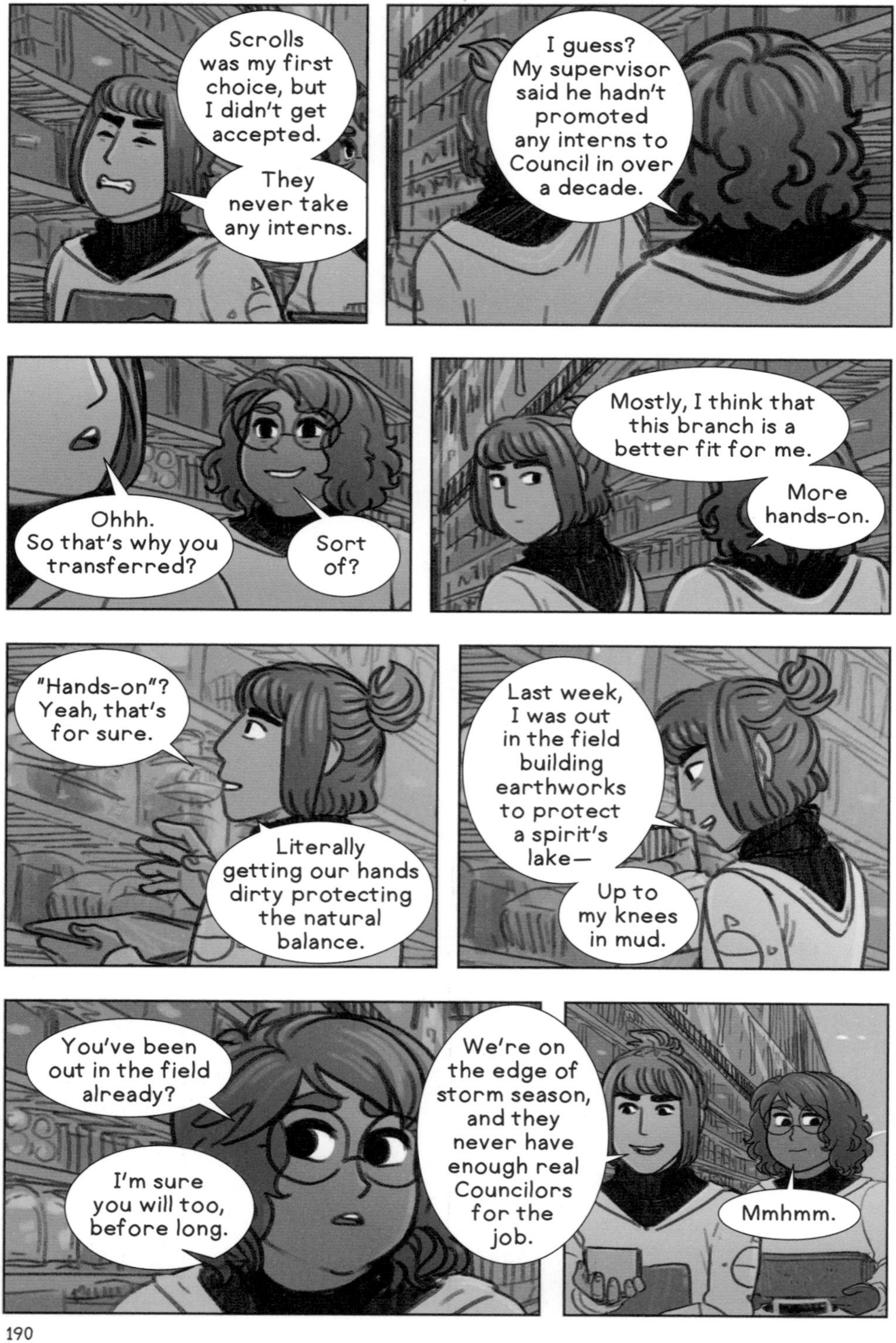
Scrolls was my first choice, but I didn't get accepted.
They never take any interns.
I guess? My supervisor said he hadn't promoted any interns to Council in over a decade.
Ohhh. So that's why you transferred?
Sort of?
Mostly, I think that this branch is a better fit for me.
More hands-on.
"Hands-on"? Yeah, that's for sure.
Literally getting our hands dirty protecting the natural balance.
Last week, I was out in the field building earthworks to protect a spirit's lake—
Up to my knees in mud.
You've been out in the field already?
I'm sure you will too, before long.
We're on the edge of storm season, and they never have enough real Councilors for the job.
Mmhmm.

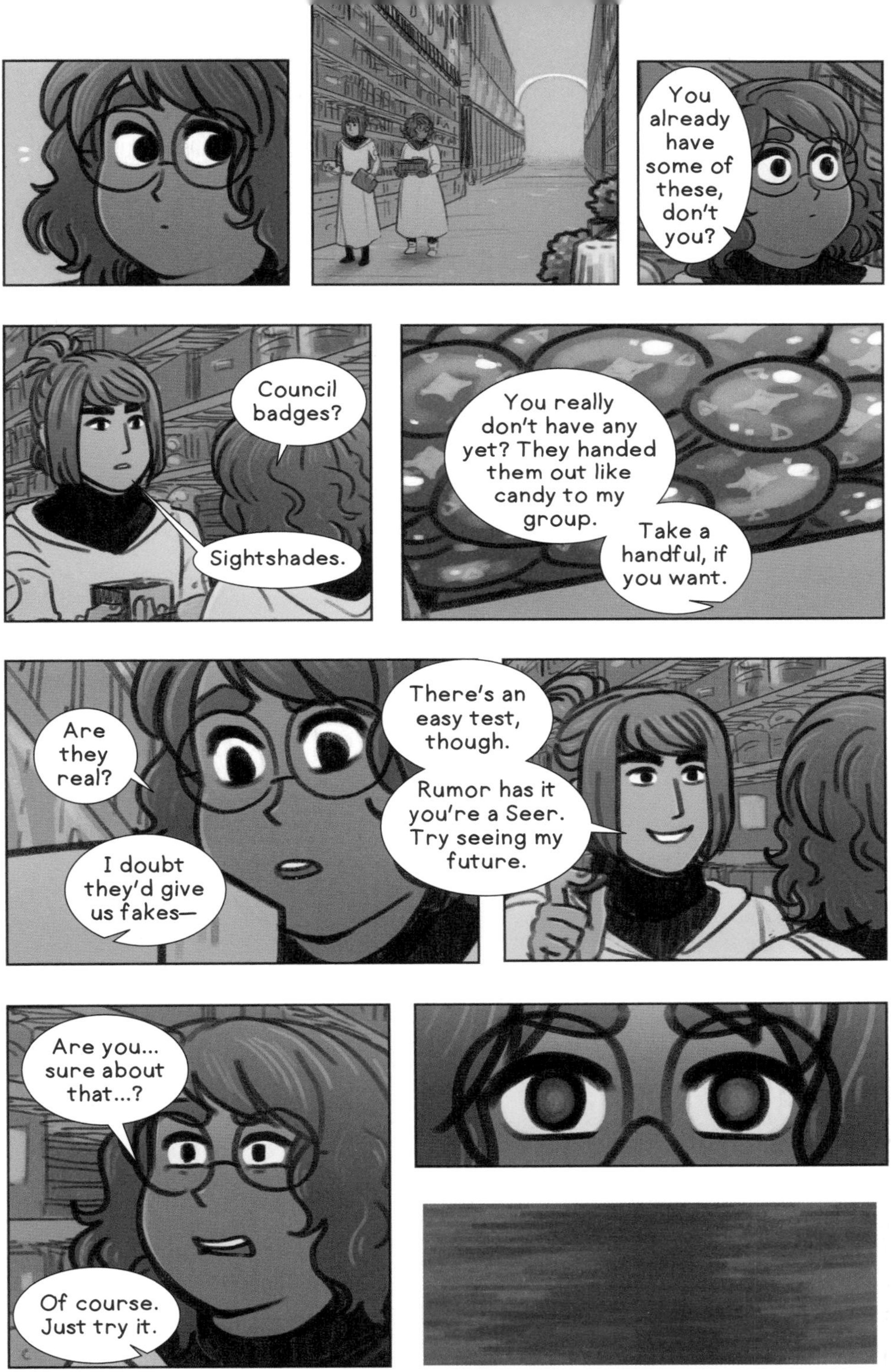

You already have some of these, don't you?
Council badges?
Sightshades.
You really don't have any yet? They handed them out like candy to my group.
Take a handful, if you want.
Are they real?
I doubt they'd give us fakes—
There's an easy test, though.
Rumor has it you're a Seer. Try seeing my future.
Are you... sure about that...?
Of course. Just try it.

They really do work! I can't see anything...

Well, help yourself. That's the last item on the list in the branch guidebook.

Thanks for your help.

Just doing my job!

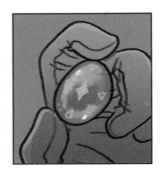

...Why is there a memorial in the storage area?

LONE COUNCILLOR SAVES CITY FROM DESTRUCTION

"Lone Councilor"...

Just imagine being able to make that big a difference in the world...

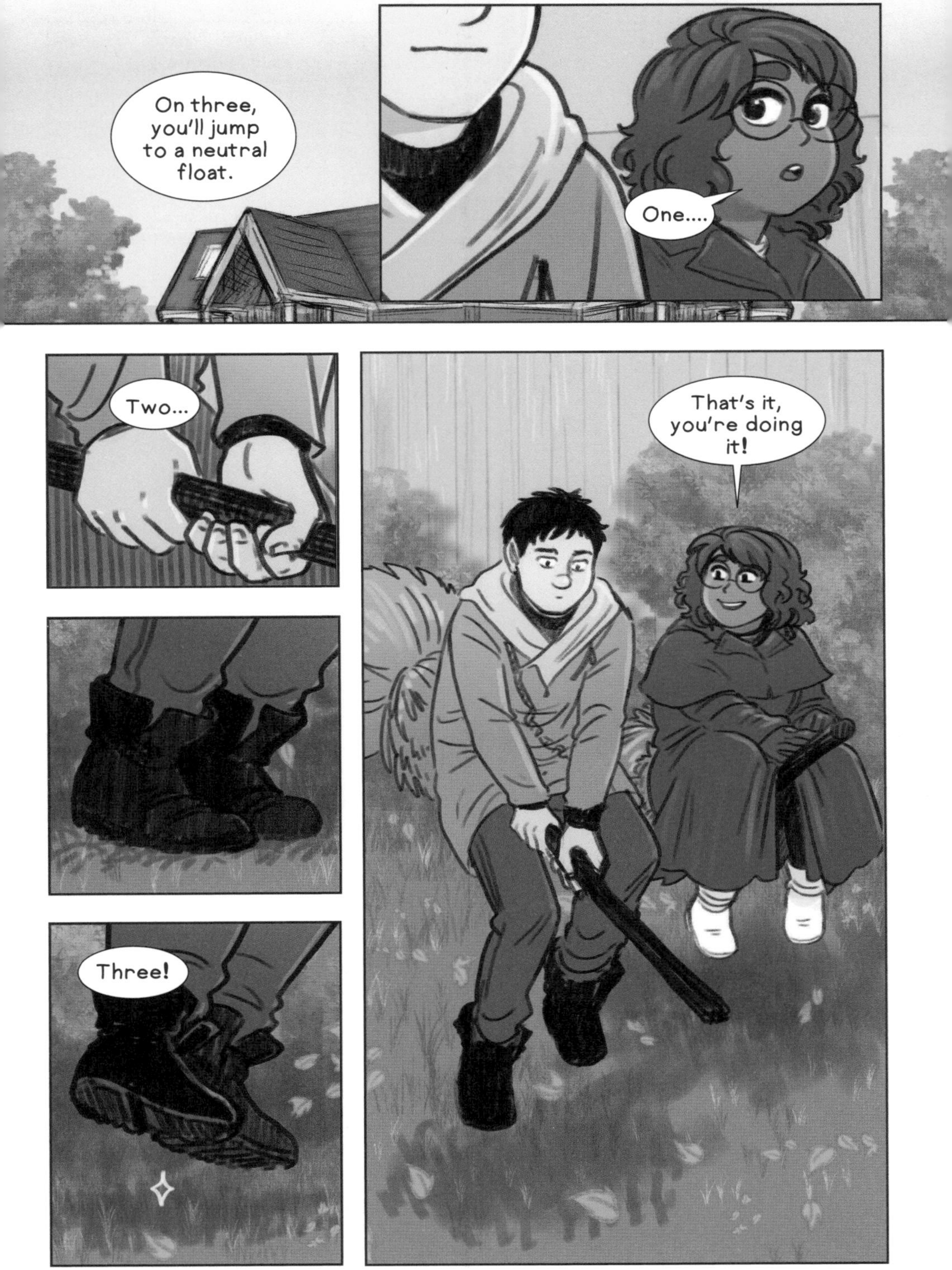
On three, you'll jump to a neutral float.
One....
Two...
Three!
That's it, you're doing it!

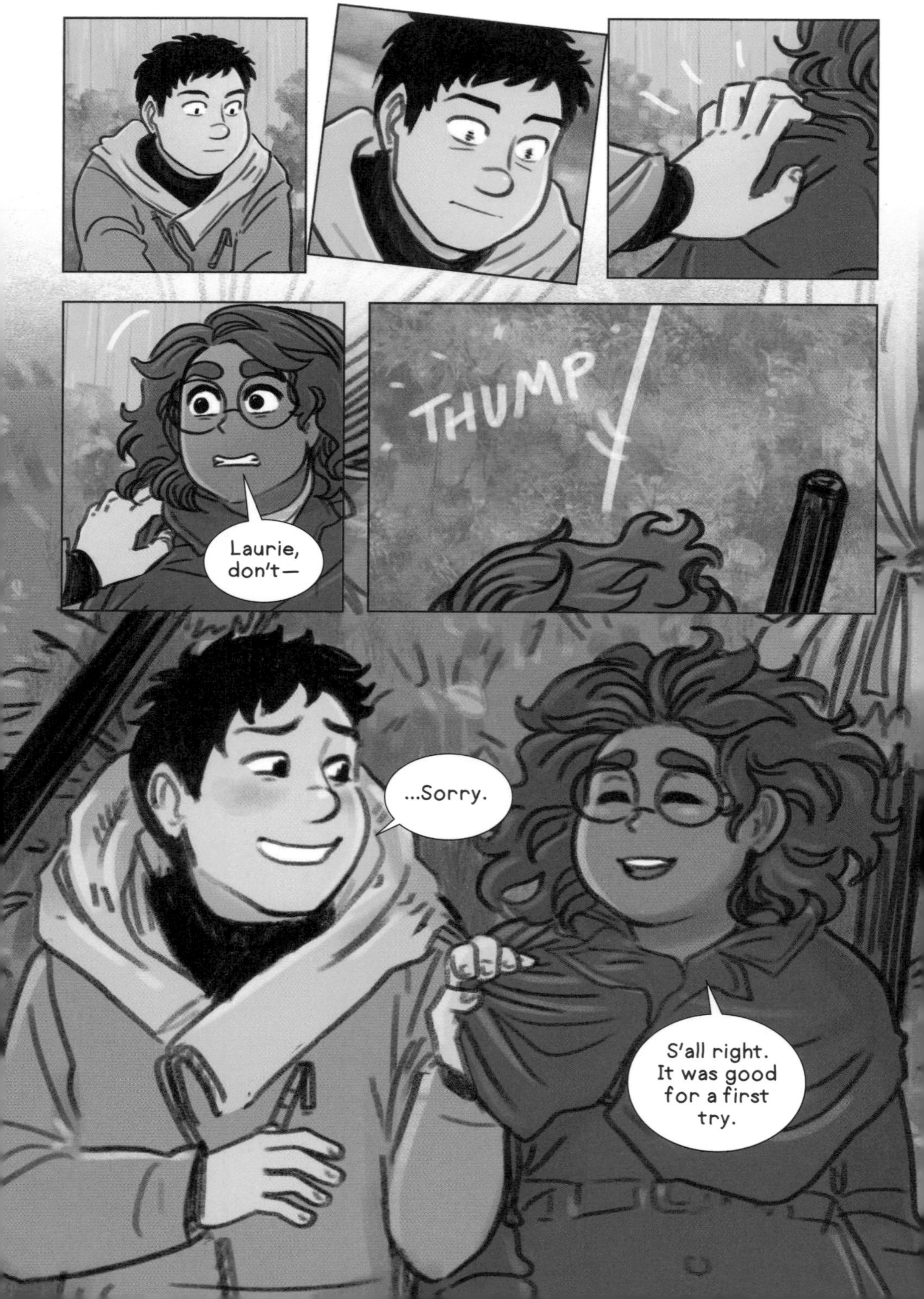
Laurie, don't—
THUMP
...Sorry.
S'all right. It was good for a first try.

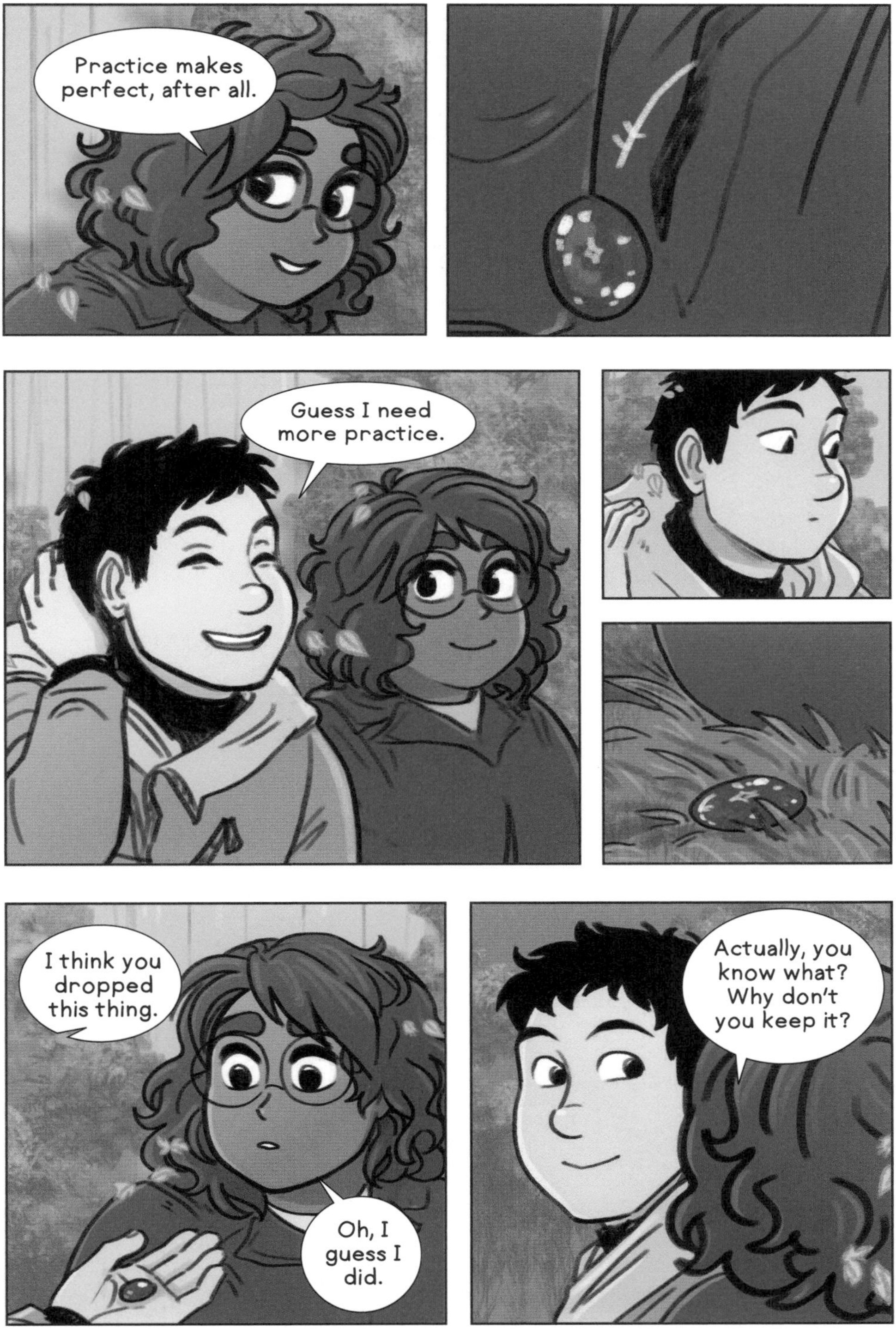
Practice makes perfect, after all.
Guess I need more practice.
I think you dropped this thing.
Oh, I guess I did.
Actually, you know what? Why don't you keep it?

What is it?

Sightshade. Keeps the holder out of a Seer's visions.

Why would I want that?

You tired of looking at me?

I just think you should have the choice.

Can't think I'll want to use it, but thanks.

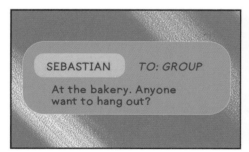

SEBASTIAN   TO: GROUP

At the bakery. Anyone want to hang out?

Want to go?

Yes, but first... one more try. Okay?

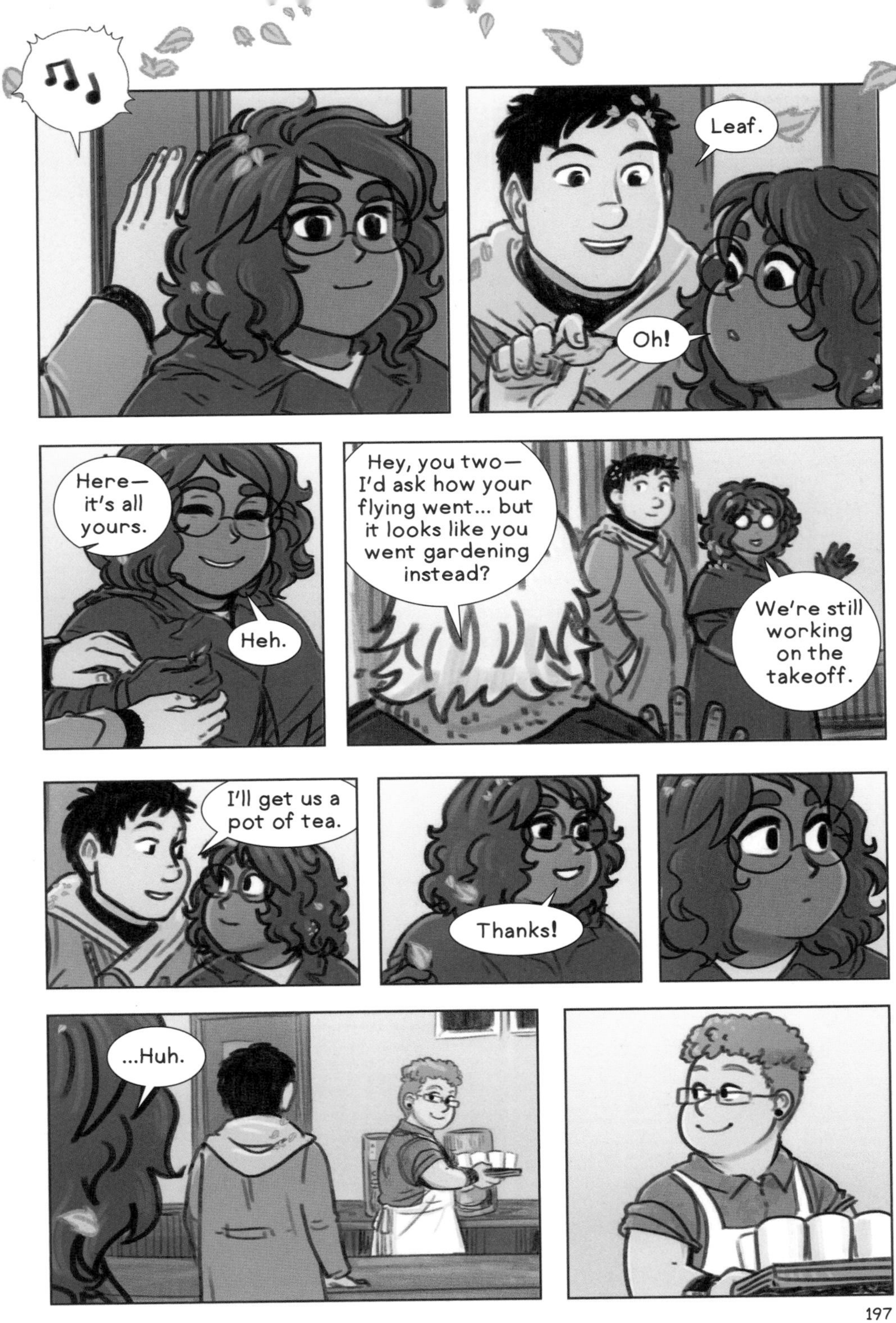
♫♪
Leaf.
Oh!
Here— it's all yours.
Heh.
Hey, you two— I'd ask how your flying went... but it looks like you went gardening instead?
We're still working on the takeoff.
I'll get us a pot of tea.
Thanks!
...Huh.

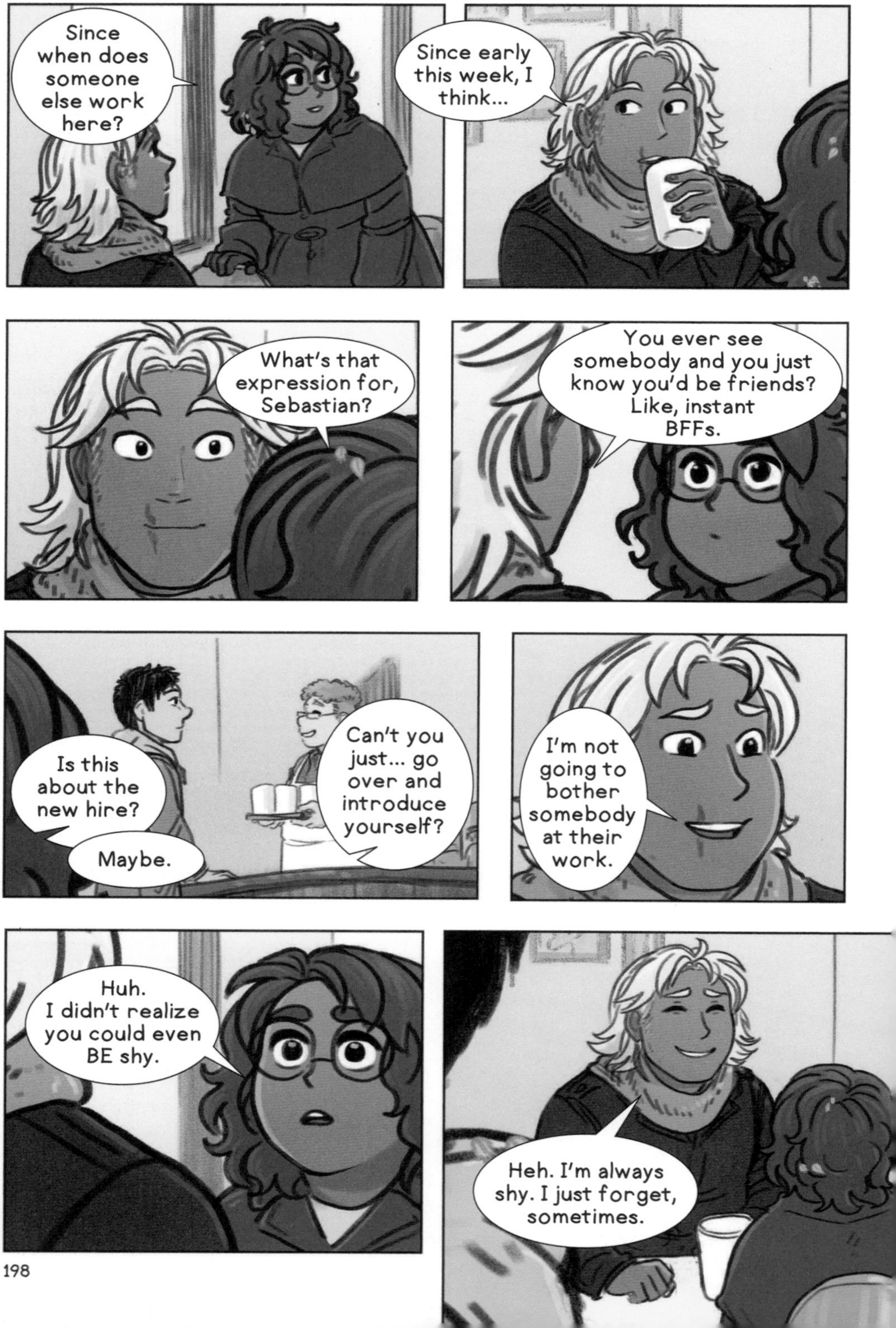
Since when does someone else work here?
Since early this week, I think...
What's that expression for, Sebastian?
You ever see somebody and you just know you'd be friends? Like, instant BFFs.
Is this about the new hire?
Maybe.
Can't you just... go over and introduce yourself?
I'm not going to bother somebody at their work.
Huh. I didn't realize you could even BE shy.
Heh. I'm always shy. I just forget, sometimes.

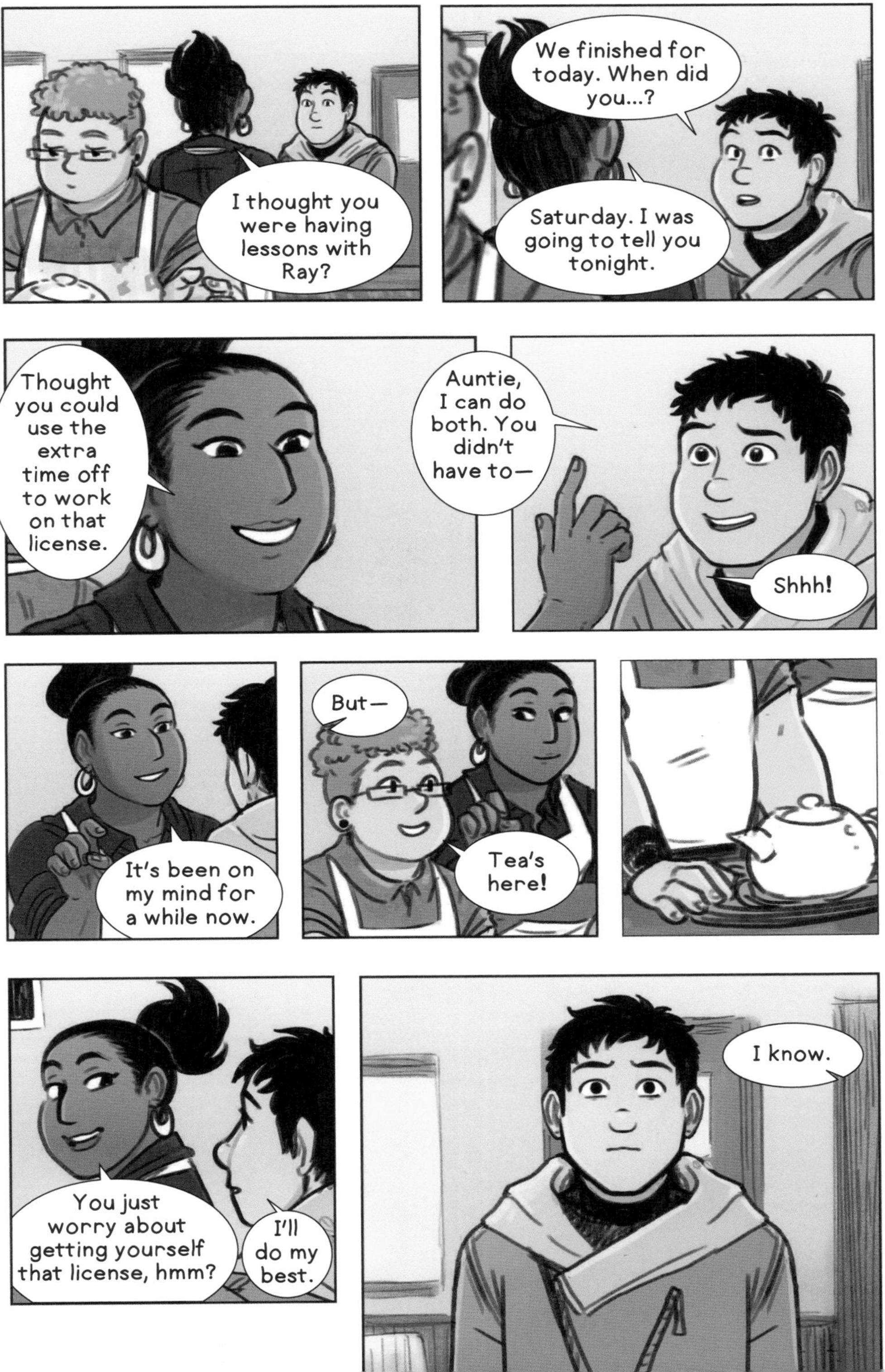
I thought you were having lessons with Ray?
We finished for today. When did you...?
Saturday. I was going to tell you tonight.
Thought you could use the extra time off to work on that license.
Auntie, I can do both. You didn't have to—
Shhh!
It's been on my mind for a while now.
But—
Tea's here!
You just worry about getting yourself that license, hmm?
I'll do my best.
I know.

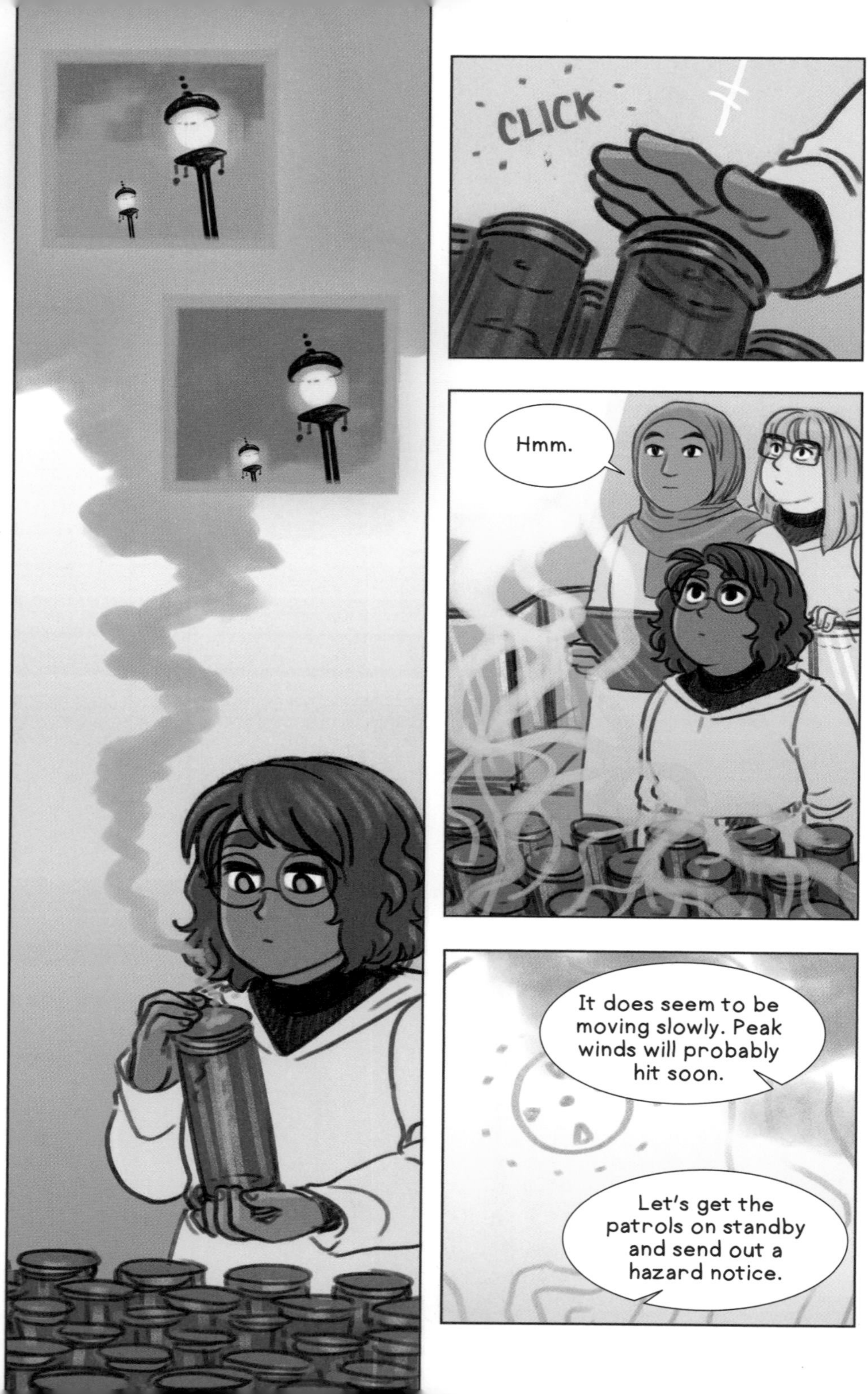
CLICK
Hmm.
It does seem to be moving slowly. Peak winds will probably hit soon.
Let's get the patrols on standby and send out a hazard notice.

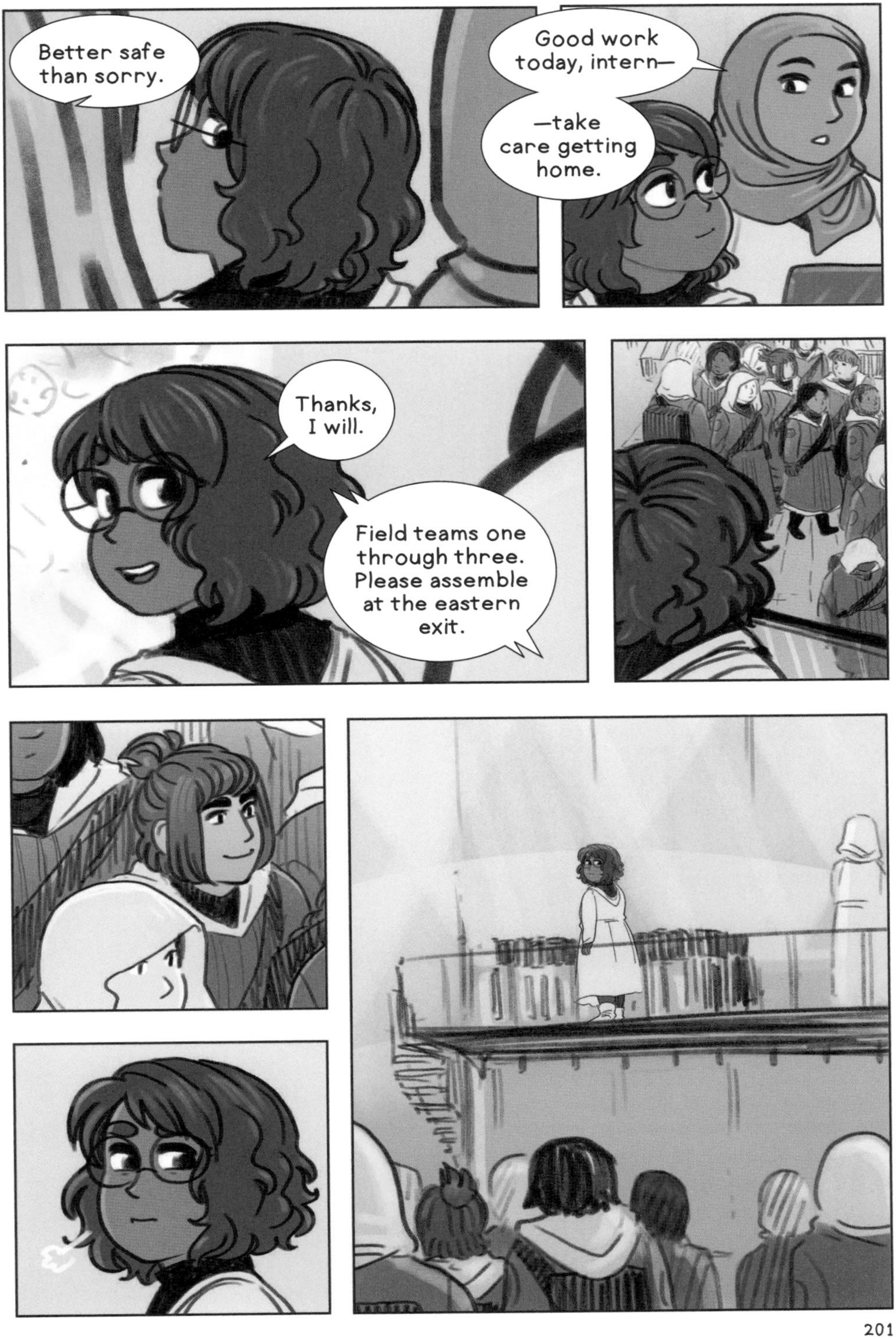
Better safe than sorry.
Good work today, intern—
—take care getting home.
Thanks, I will.
Field teams one through three. Please assemble at the eastern exit.

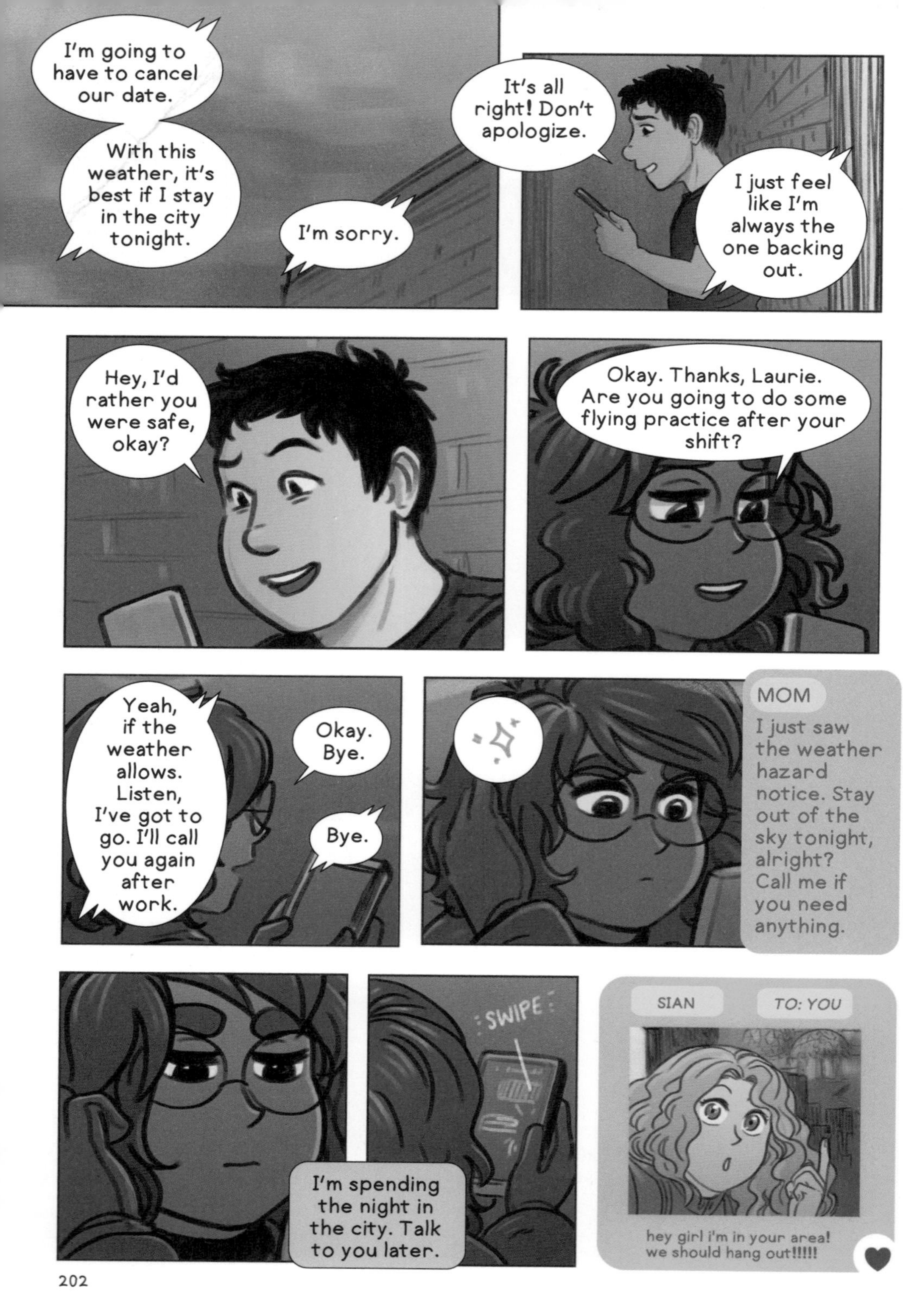

I'm going to have to cancel our date.
With this weather, it's best if I stay in the city tonight.
I'm sorry.
It's all right! Don't apologize.
I just feel like I'm always the one backing out.
Hey, I'd rather you were safe, okay?
Okay. Thanks, Laurie. Are you going to do some flying practice after your shift?
Yeah, if the weather allows. Listen, I've got to go. I'll call you again after work.
Okay. Bye.
Bye.
MOM
I just saw the weather hazard notice. Stay out of the sky tonight, alright? Call me if you need anything.
SWIPE
I'm spending the night in the city. Talk to you later.
SIAN
TO: YOU
hey girl i'm in your area! we should hang out!!!!!

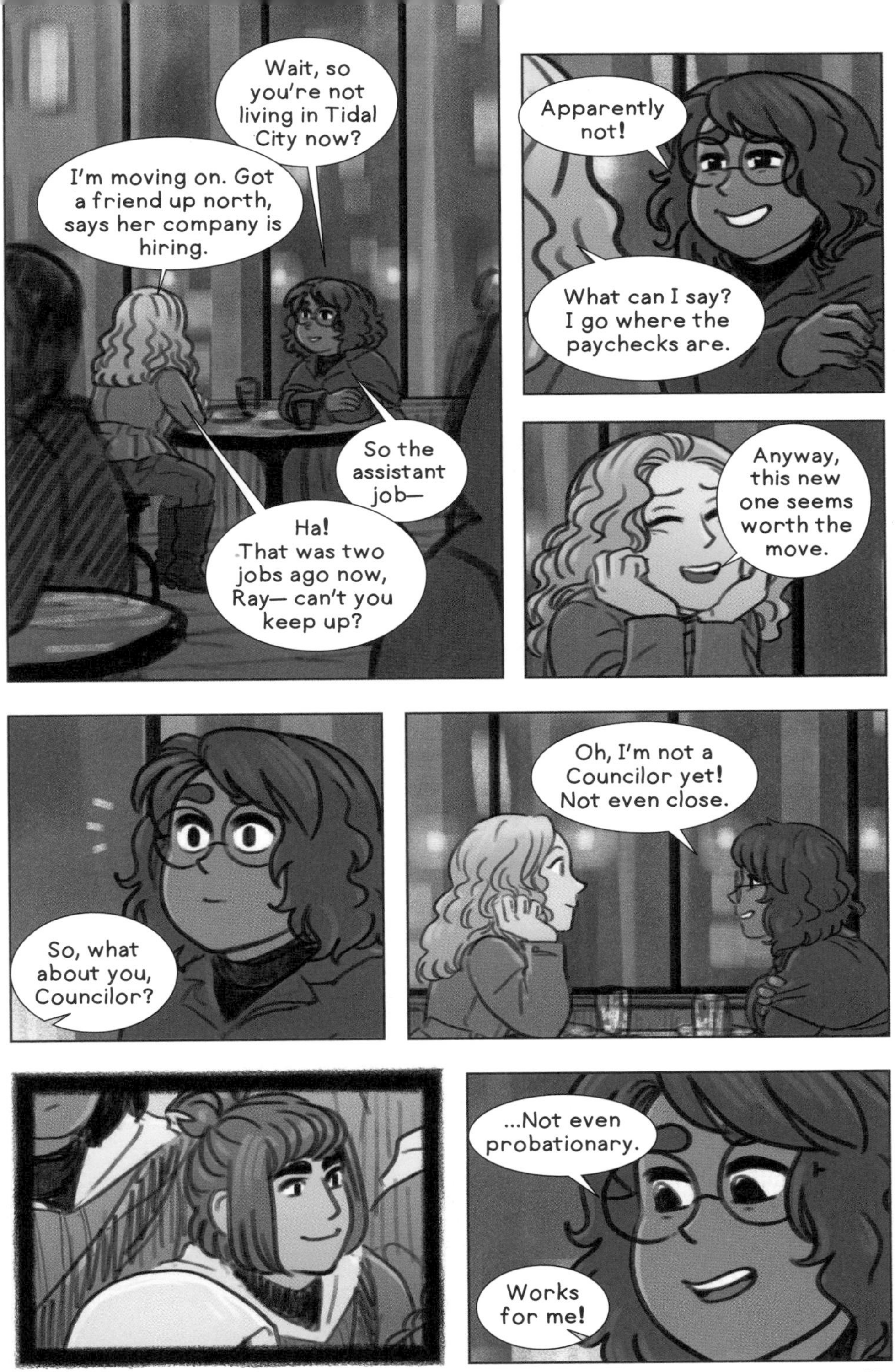
Wait, so you're not living in Tidal City now?
I'm moving on. Got a friend up north, says her company is hiring.
So the assistant job—
Ha! That was two jobs ago now, Ray— can't you keep up?
Apparently not!
What can I say? I go where the paychecks are.
Anyway, this new one seems worth the move.
So, what about you, Councilor?
Oh, I'm not a Councilor yet! Not even close.
...Not even probationary.
Works for me!

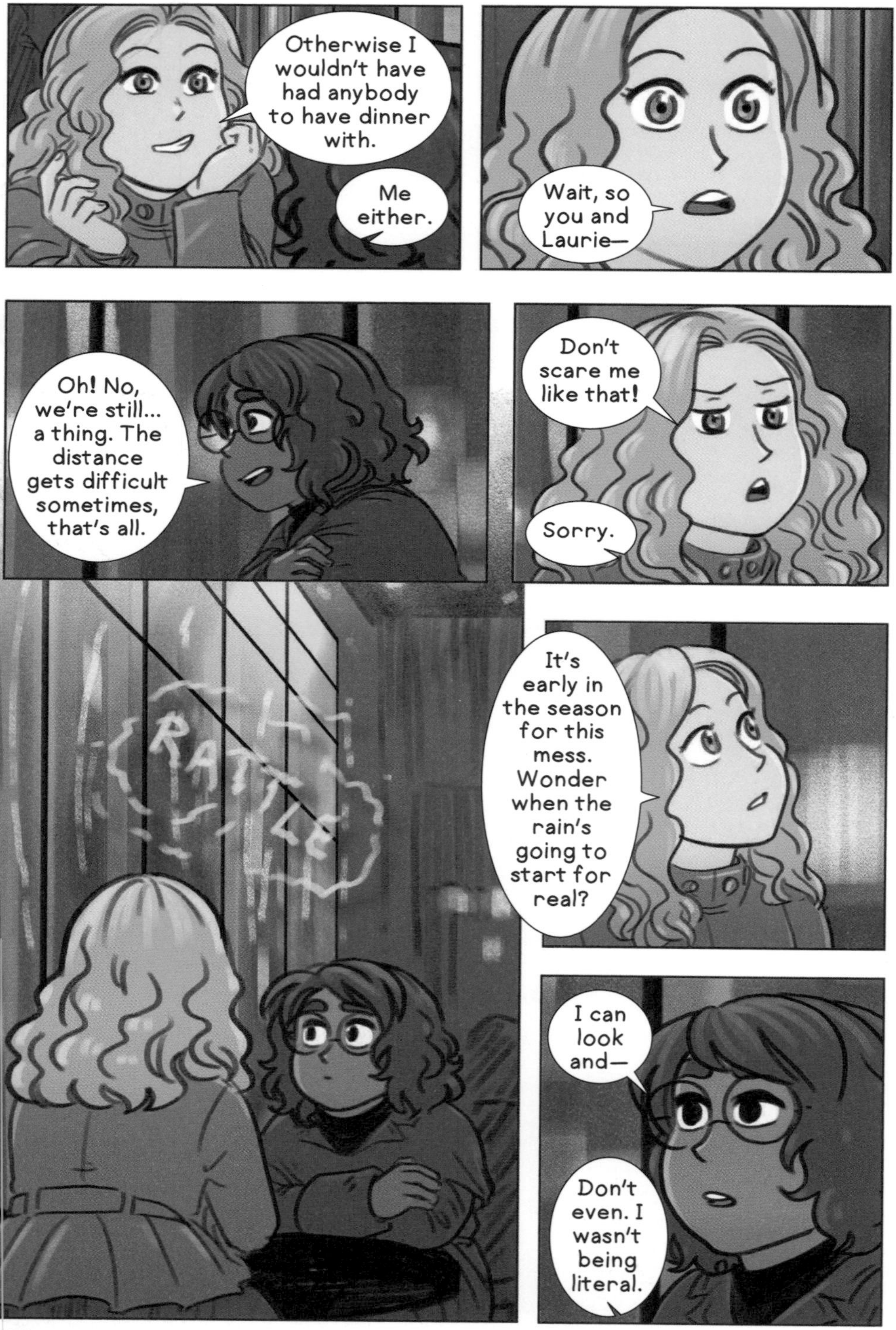
Otherwise I wouldn't have had anybody to have dinner with.
Me either.
Wait, so you and Laurie—
Oh! No, we're still... a thing. The distance gets difficult sometimes, that's all.
Don't scare me like that!
Sorry.
RATTLE
It's early in the season for this mess. Wonder when the rain's going to start for real?
I can look and—
Don't even. I wasn't being literal.

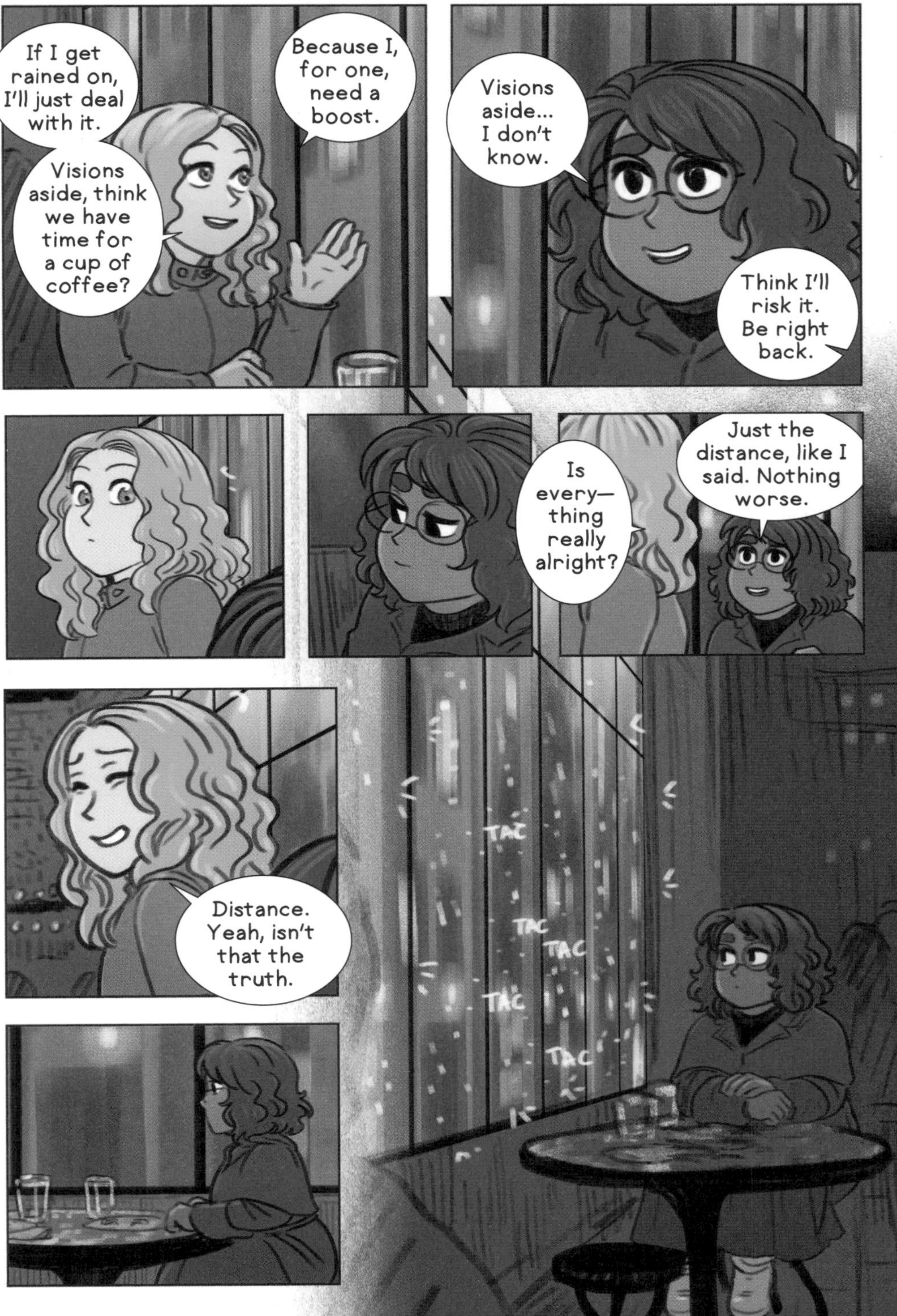
If I get rained on, I'll just deal with it.
Visions aside, think we have time for a cup of coffee?
Because I, for one, need a boost.
Visions aside... I don't know.
Think I'll risk it. Be right back.
Is every—thing really alright?
Just the distance, like I said. Nothing worse.
Distance. Yeah, isn't that the truth.
TAC
TAC
TAC
TAC
TAC

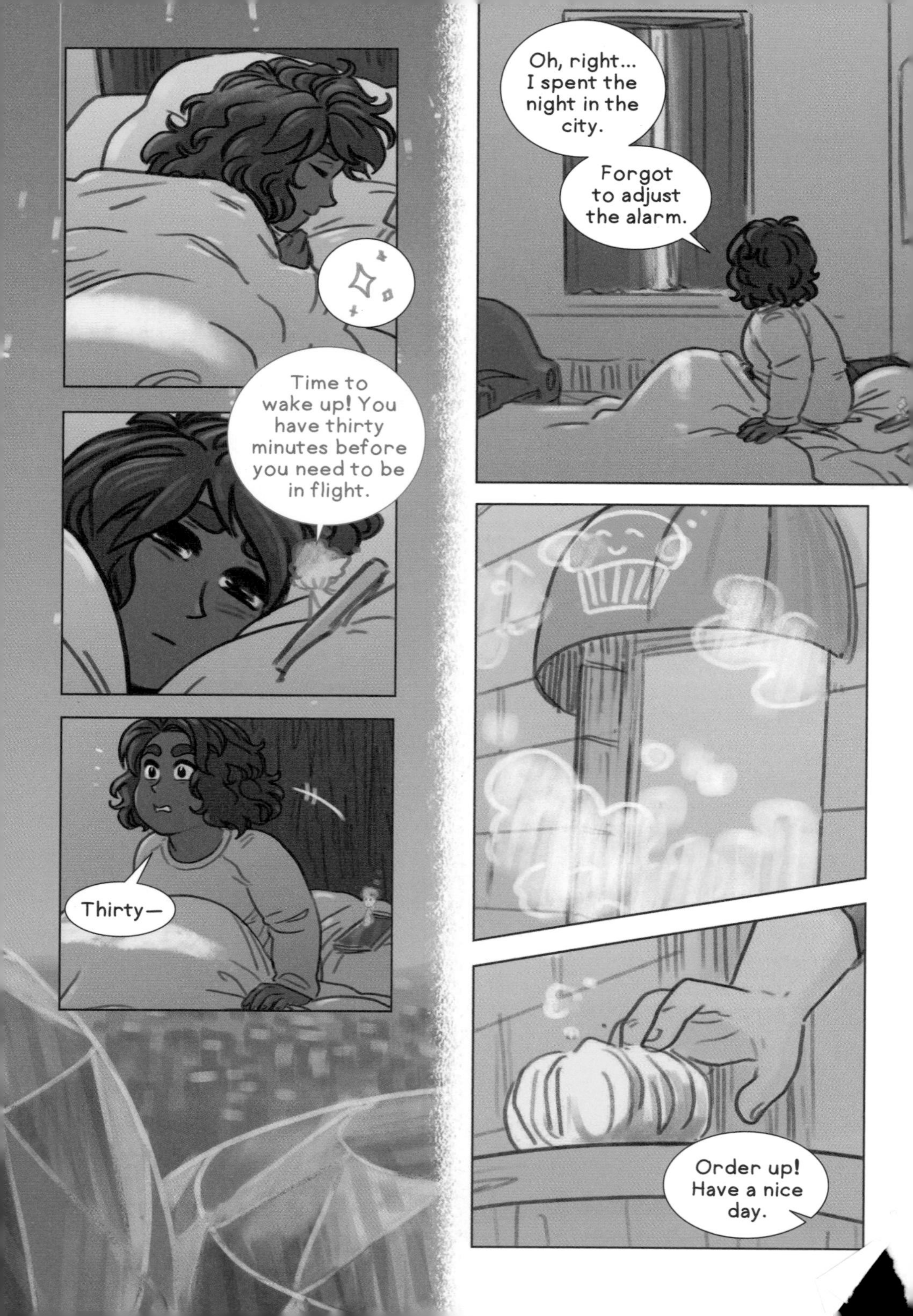
Time to wake up! You have thirty minutes before you need to be in flight.
Thirty—
Oh, right... I spent the night in the city.
Forgot to adjust the alarm.
Order up! Have a nice day.

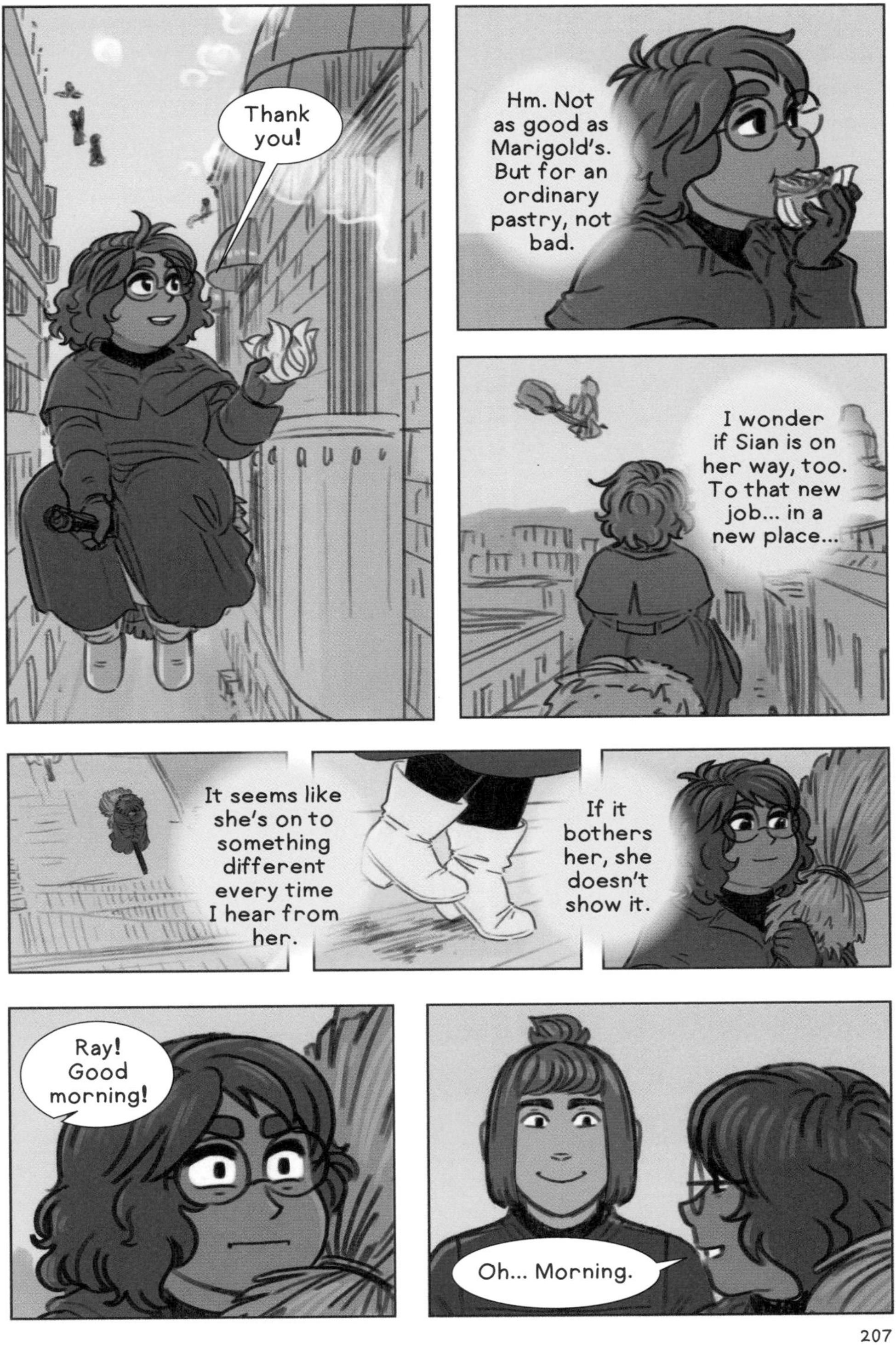
Thank you!
Hm. Not as good as Marigold's. But for an ordinary pastry, not bad.
I wonder if Sian is on her way, too. To that new job... in a new place...
It seems like she's on to something different every time I hear from her.
If it bothers her, she doesn't show it.
Ray! Good morning!
Oh... Morning.

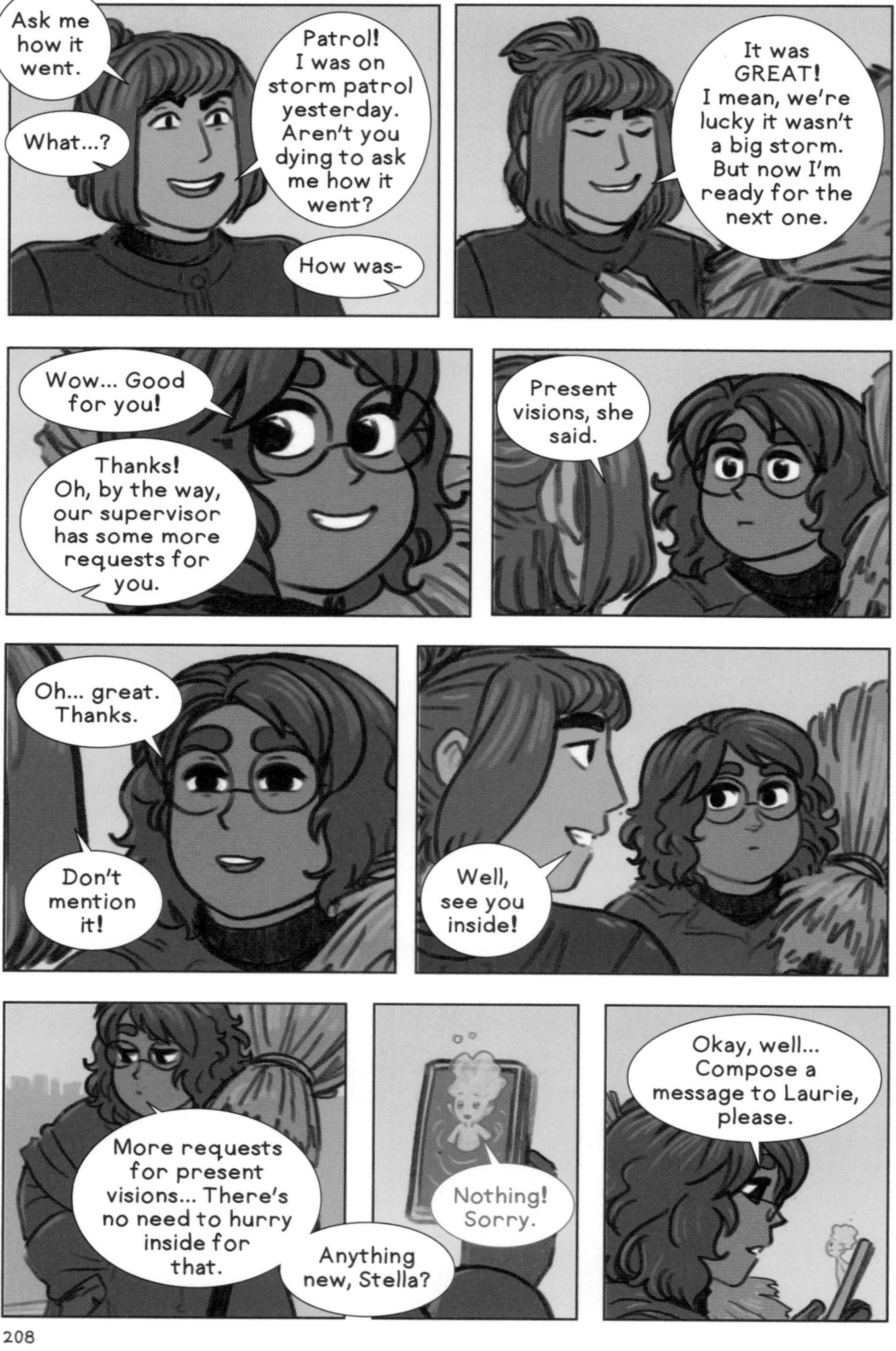
Ask me how it went.
What...?
Patrol! I was on storm patrol yesterday. Aren't you dying to ask me how it went?
How was-
It was GREAT! I mean, we're lucky it wasn't a big storm. But now I'm ready for the next one.
Wow... Good for you!
Thanks! Oh, by the way, our supervisor has some more requests for you.
Present visions, she said.
Oh... great. Thanks.
Don't mention it!
Well, see you inside!
More requests for present visions... There's no need to hurry inside for that.
Anything new, Stella?
Nothing! Sorry.
Okay, well... Compose a message to Laurie, please.

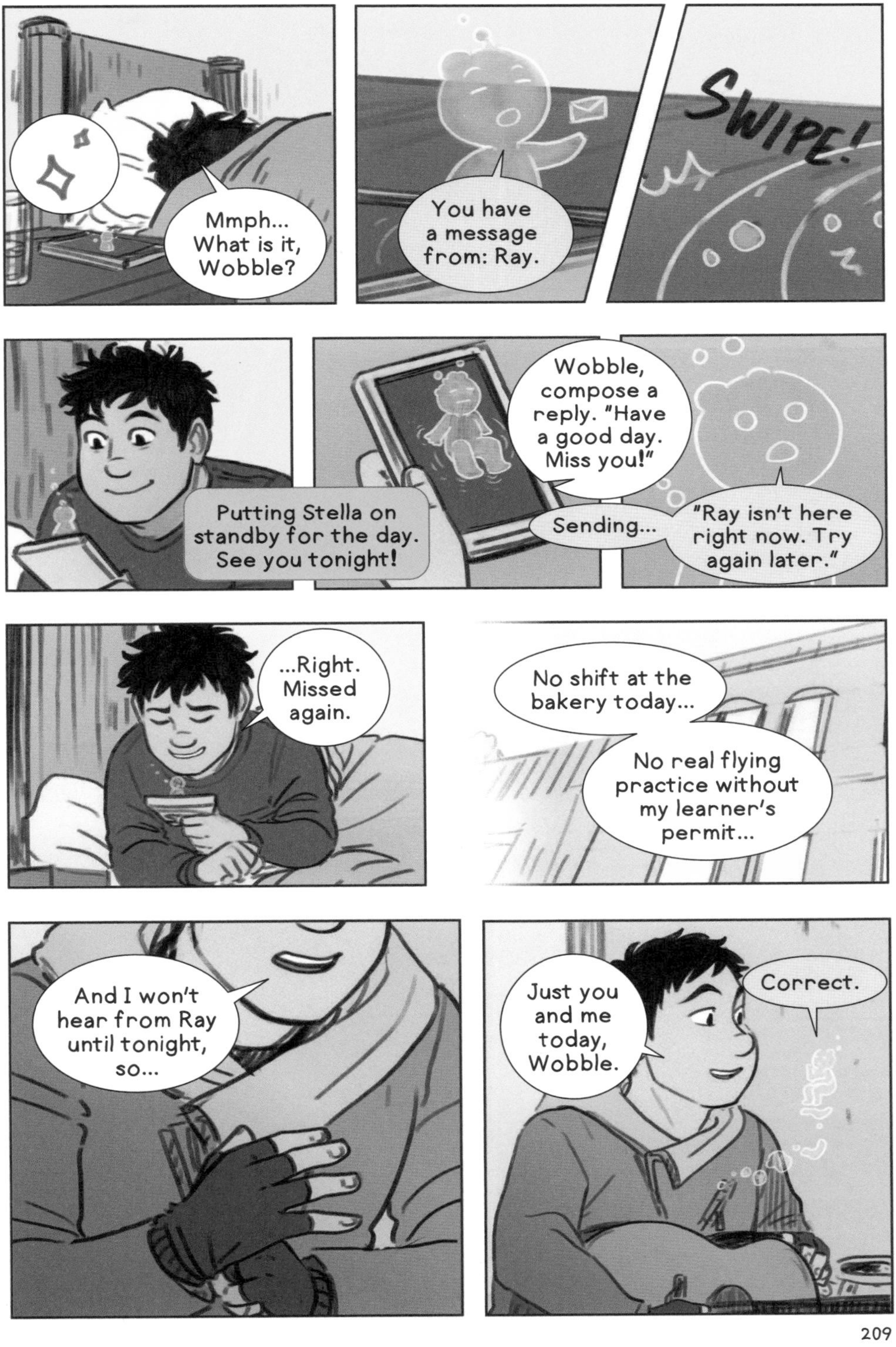
Mmph... What is it, Wobble?
You have a message from: Ray.
SWIPE!
Putting Stella on standby for the day. See you tonight!
Wobble, compose a reply. "Have a good day. Miss you!"
Sending...
"Ray isn't here right now. Try again later."
...Right. Missed again.
No shift at the bakery today...
No real flying practice without my learner's permit...
And I won't hear from Ray until tonight, so...
Just you and me today, Wobble.
Correct.

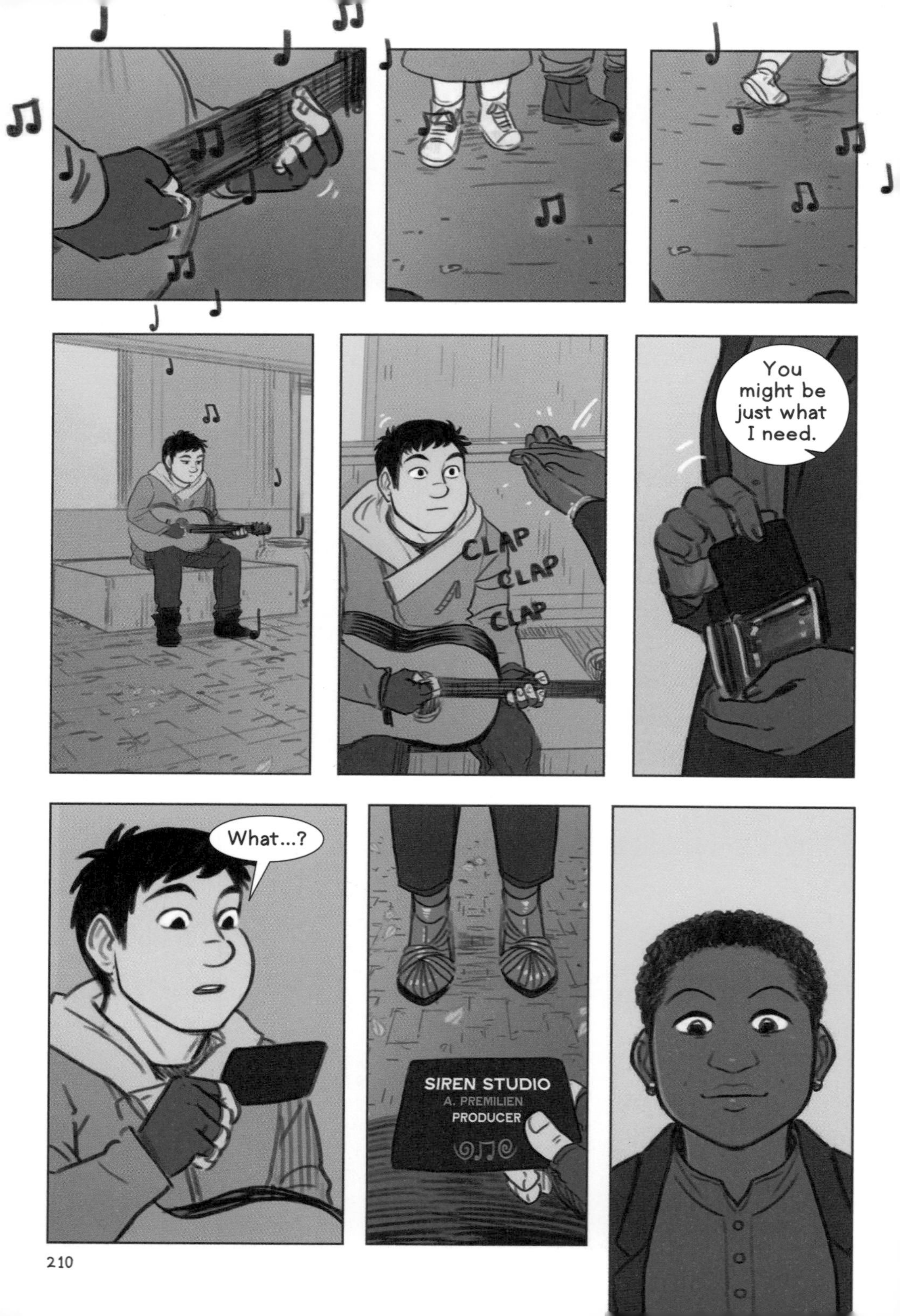
CLAP
CLAP
CLAP
You might be just what I need.
What...?
SIREN STUDIO
A. PREMILIEN
PRODUCER

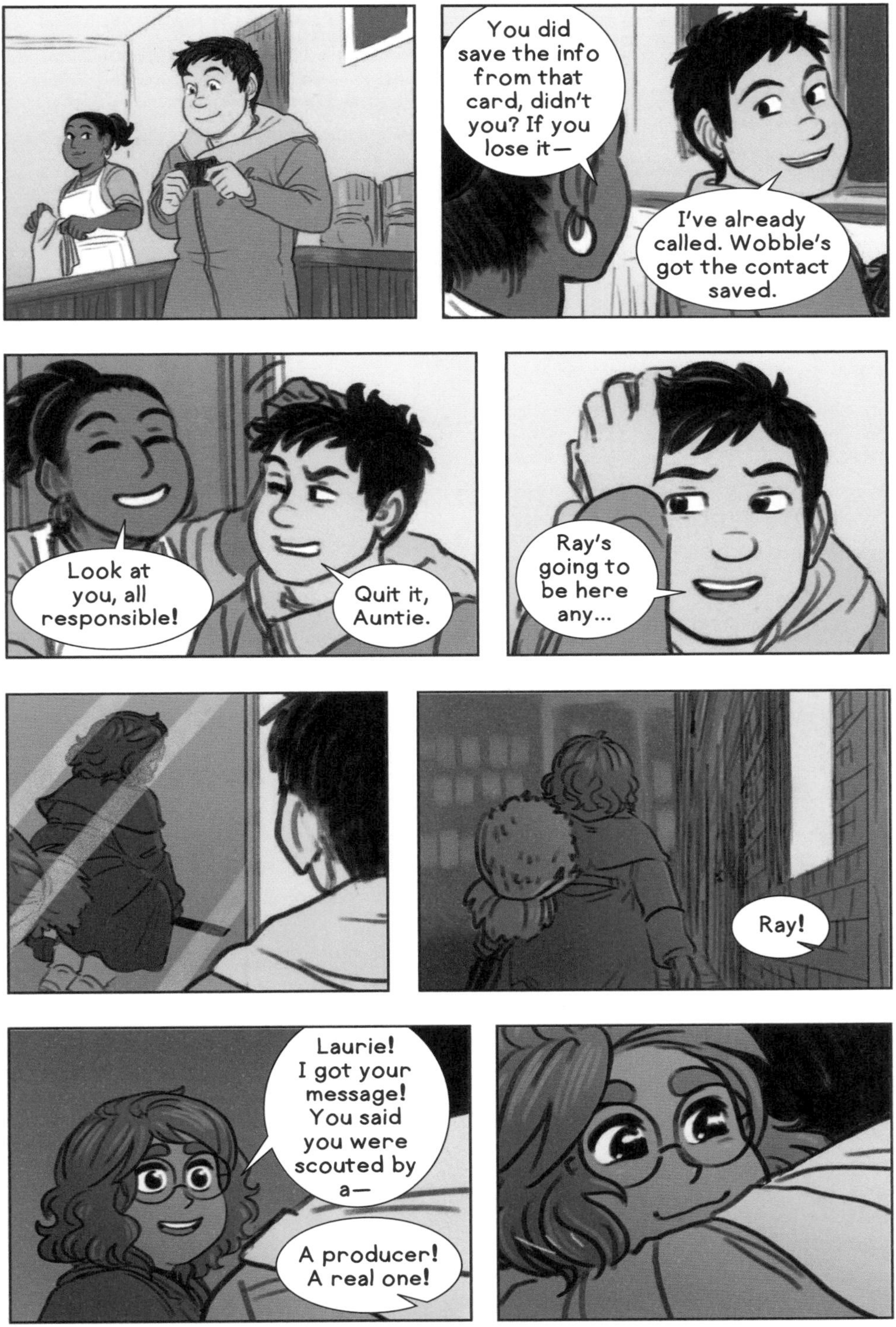
You did save the info from that card, didn't you? If you lose it—
I've already called. Wobble's got the contact saved.
Look at you, all responsible!
Quit it, Auntie.
Ray's going to be here any...
Ray!
Laurie! I got your message! You said you were scouted by a—
A producer! A real one!

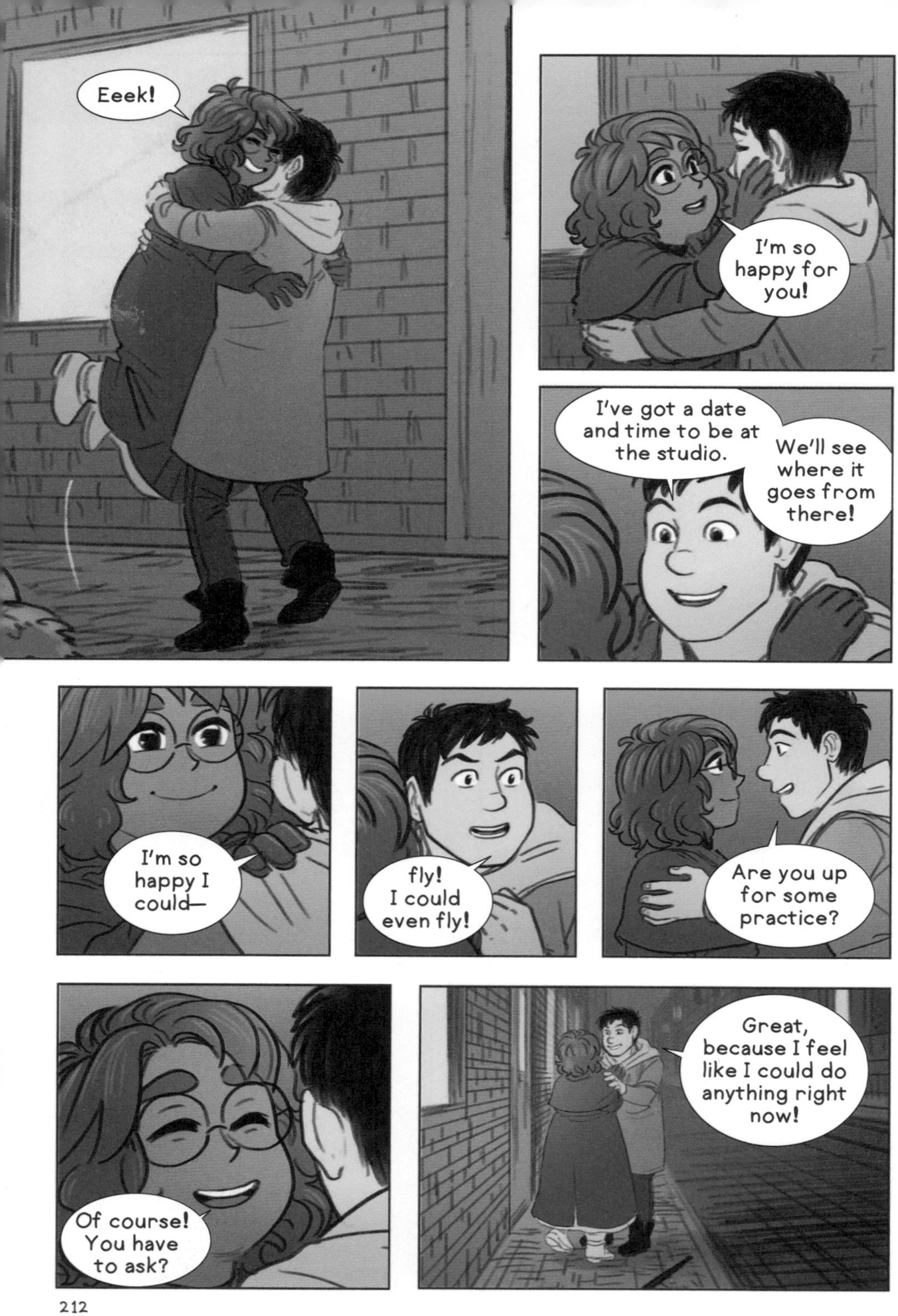
Eeek!
I'm so happy for you!
I've got a date and time to be at the studio.
We'll see where it goes from there!
I'm so happy I could—
fly! I could even fly!
Are you up for some practice?
Of course! You have to ask?
Great, because I feel like I could do anything right now!

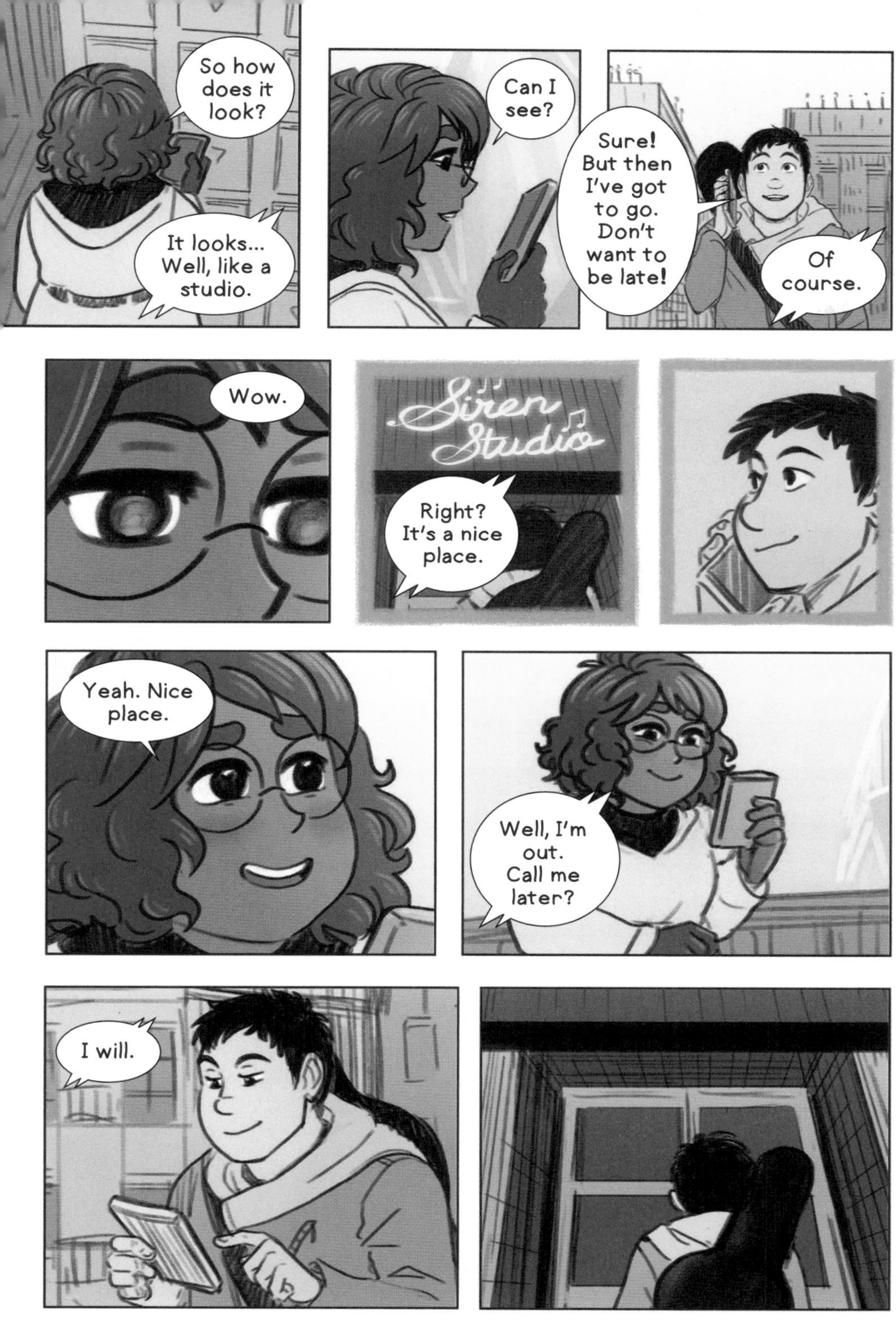
So how does it look?
It looks... Well, like a studio.
Can I see?
Sure! But then I've got to go. Don't want to be late!
Of course.
Wow.
Siren Studio
Right? It's a nice place.
Yeah. Nice place.
Well, I'm out. Call me later?
I will.

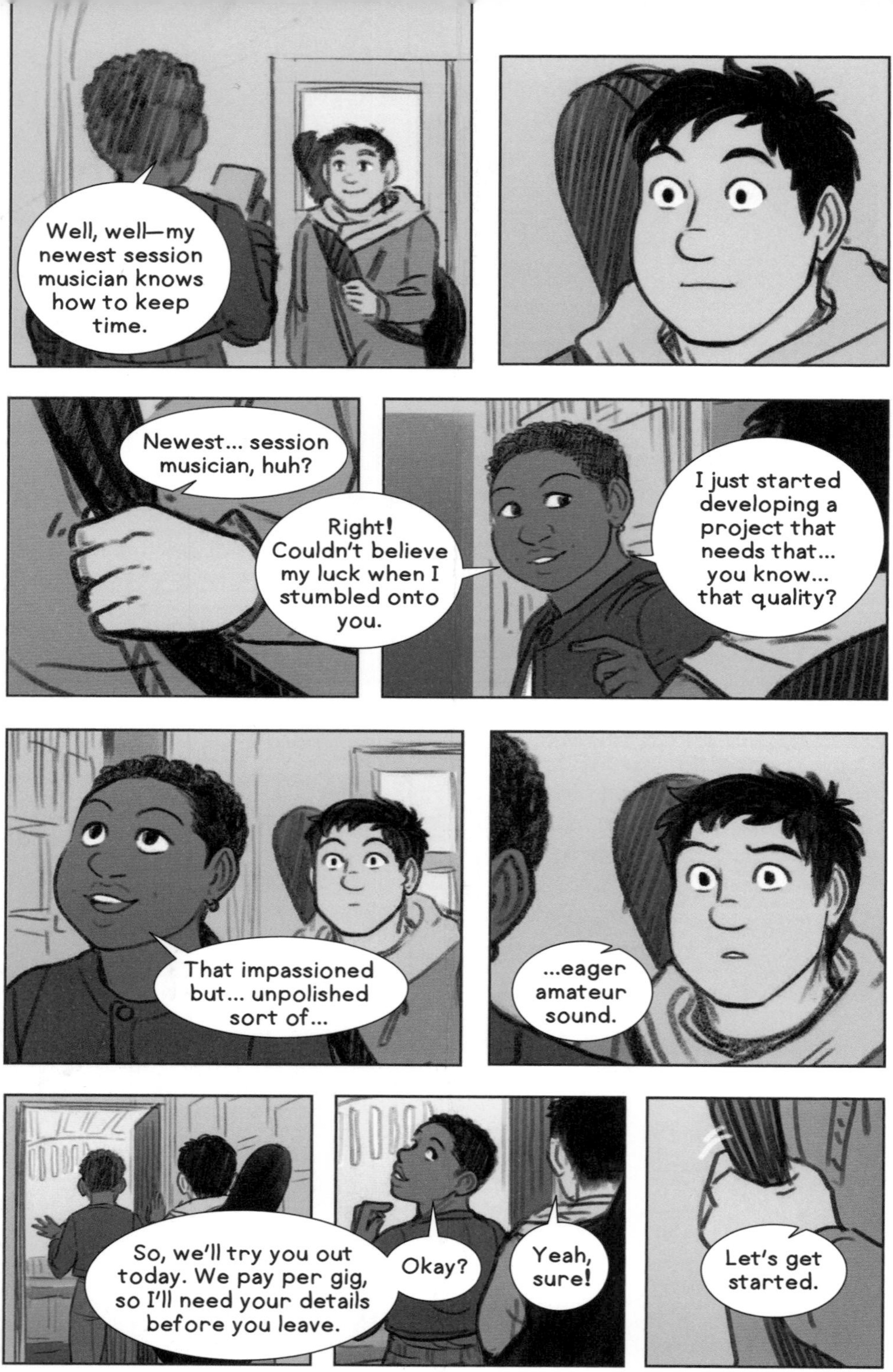
Well, well—my newest session musician knows how to keep time.
Newest... session musician, huh?
Right! Couldn't believe my luck when I stumbled onto you.
I just started developing a project that needs that... you know... that quality?
That impassioned but... unpolished sort of...
...eager amateur sound.
So, we'll try you out today. We pay per gig, so I'll need your details before you leave.
Okay?
Yeah, sure!
Let's get started.

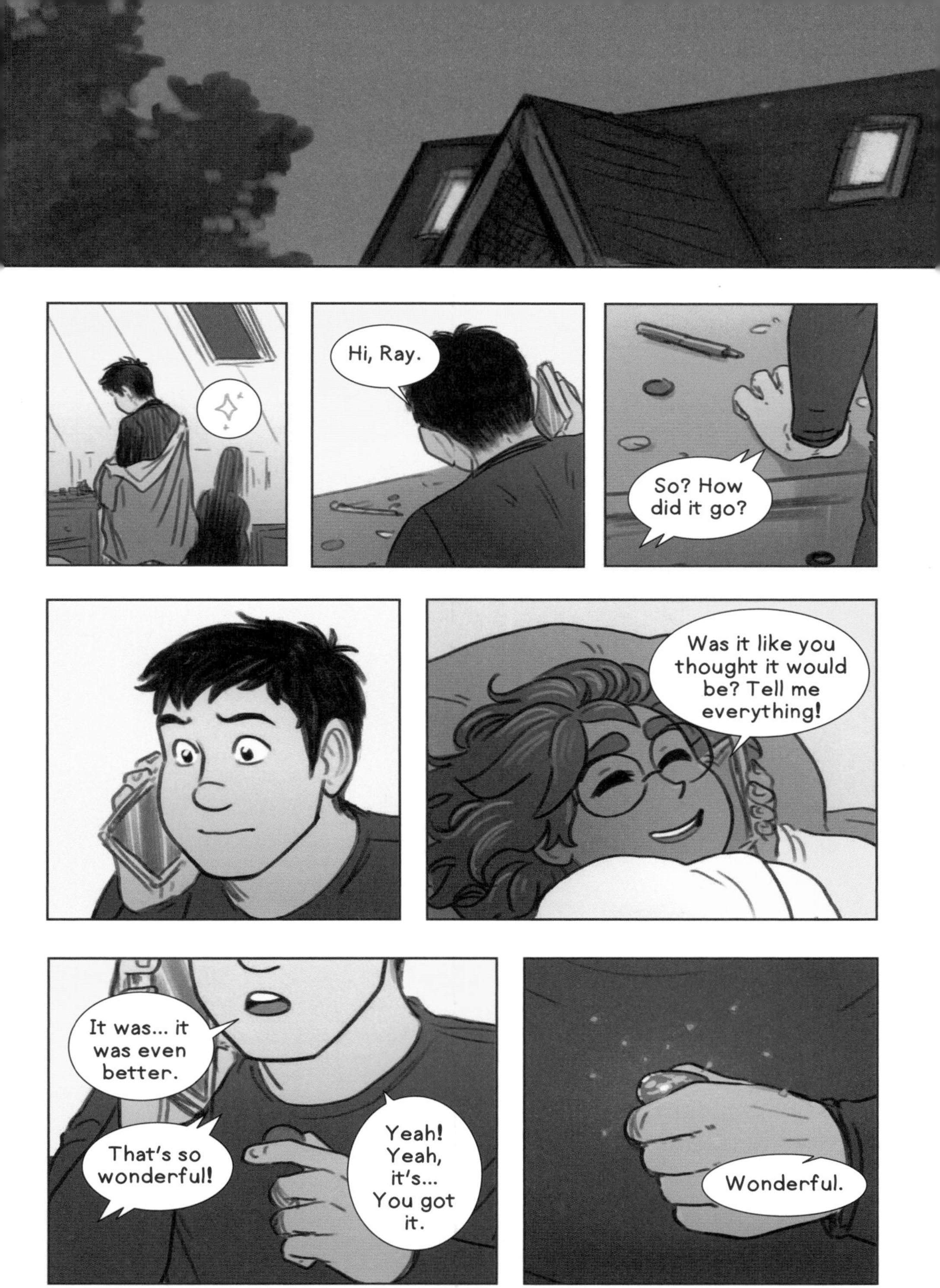

Hi, Ray.
So? How did it go?
Was it like you thought it would be? Tell me everything!
It was... it was even better.
That's so wonderful!
Yeah! Yeah, it's... You got it.
Wonderful.

CHAPTER 10

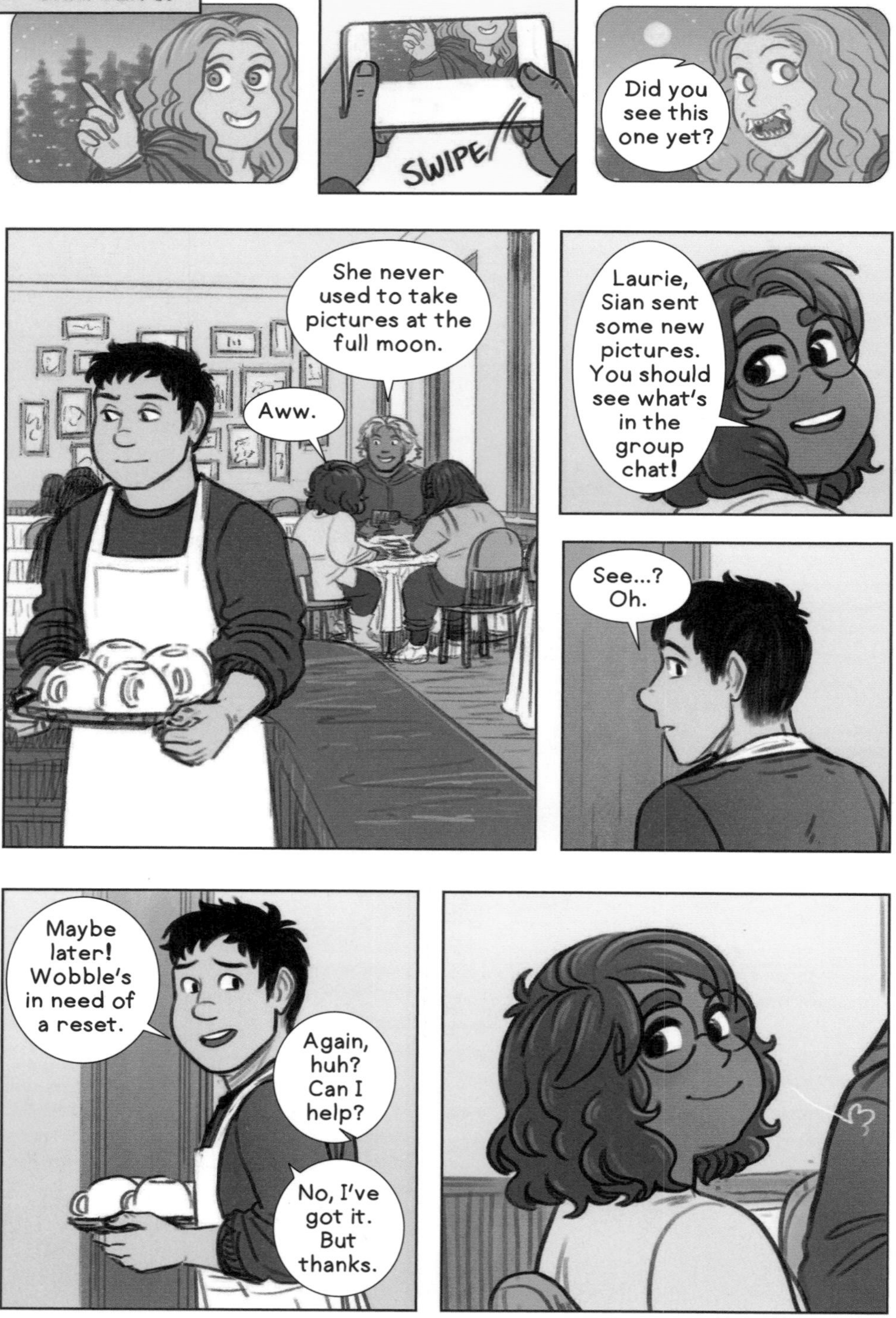
SWIPE
Did you see this one yet?
She never used to take pictures at the full moon.
Aww.
Laurie, Sian sent some new pictures. You should see what's in the group chat!
See...? Oh.
Maybe later! Wobble's in need of a reset.
Again, huh? Can I help?
No, I've got it. But thanks.

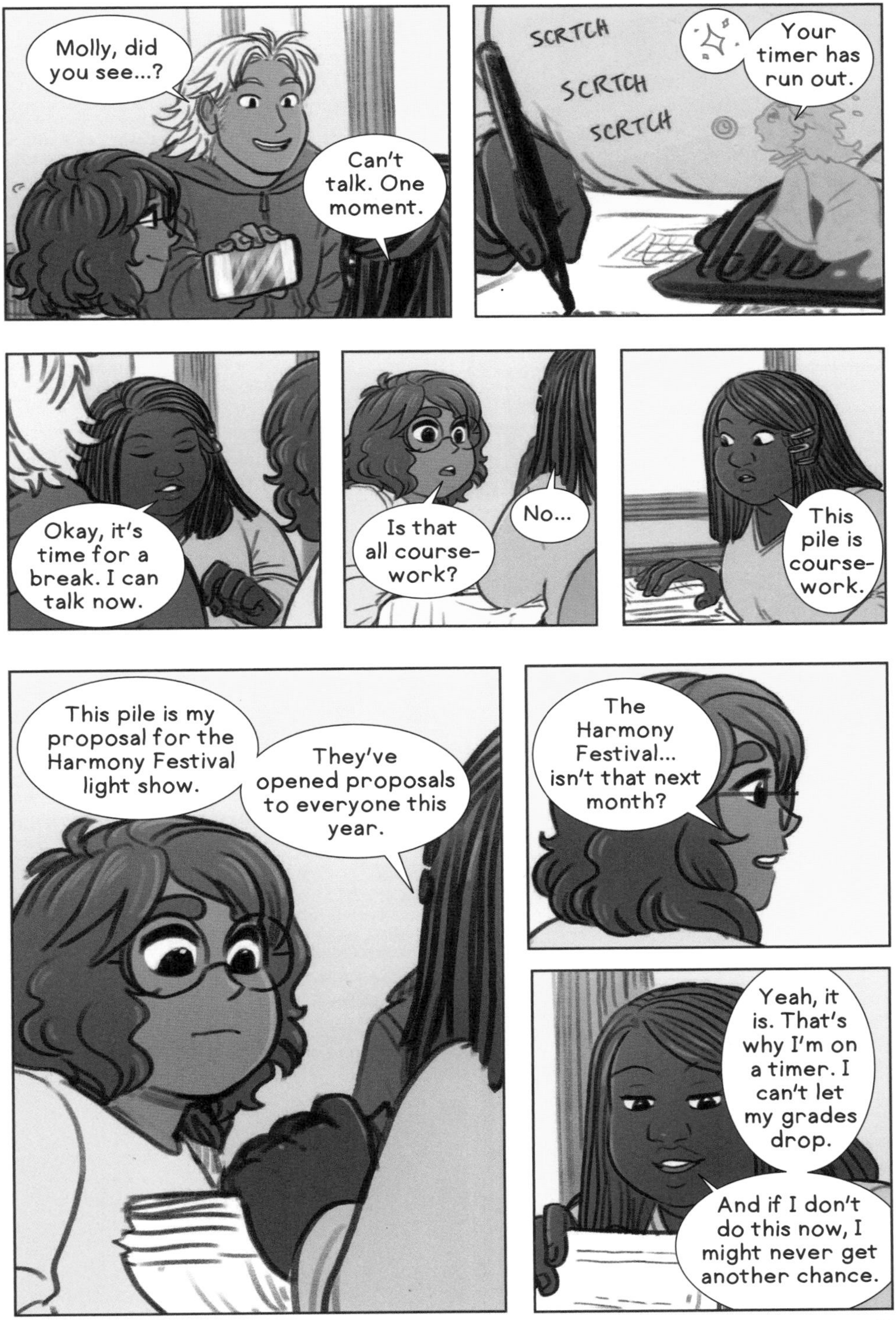
Molly, did you see...?
Can't talk. One moment.
SCRTCH
SCRTCH
SCRTCH
Your timer has run out.
Okay, it's time for a break. I can talk now.
Is that all course-work?
No...
This pile is course-work.
This pile is my proposal for the Harmony Festival light show.
They've opened proposals to everyone this year.
The Harmony Festival... isn't that next month?
Yeah, it is. That's why I'm on a timer. I can't let my grades drop.
And if I don't do this now, I might never get another chance.

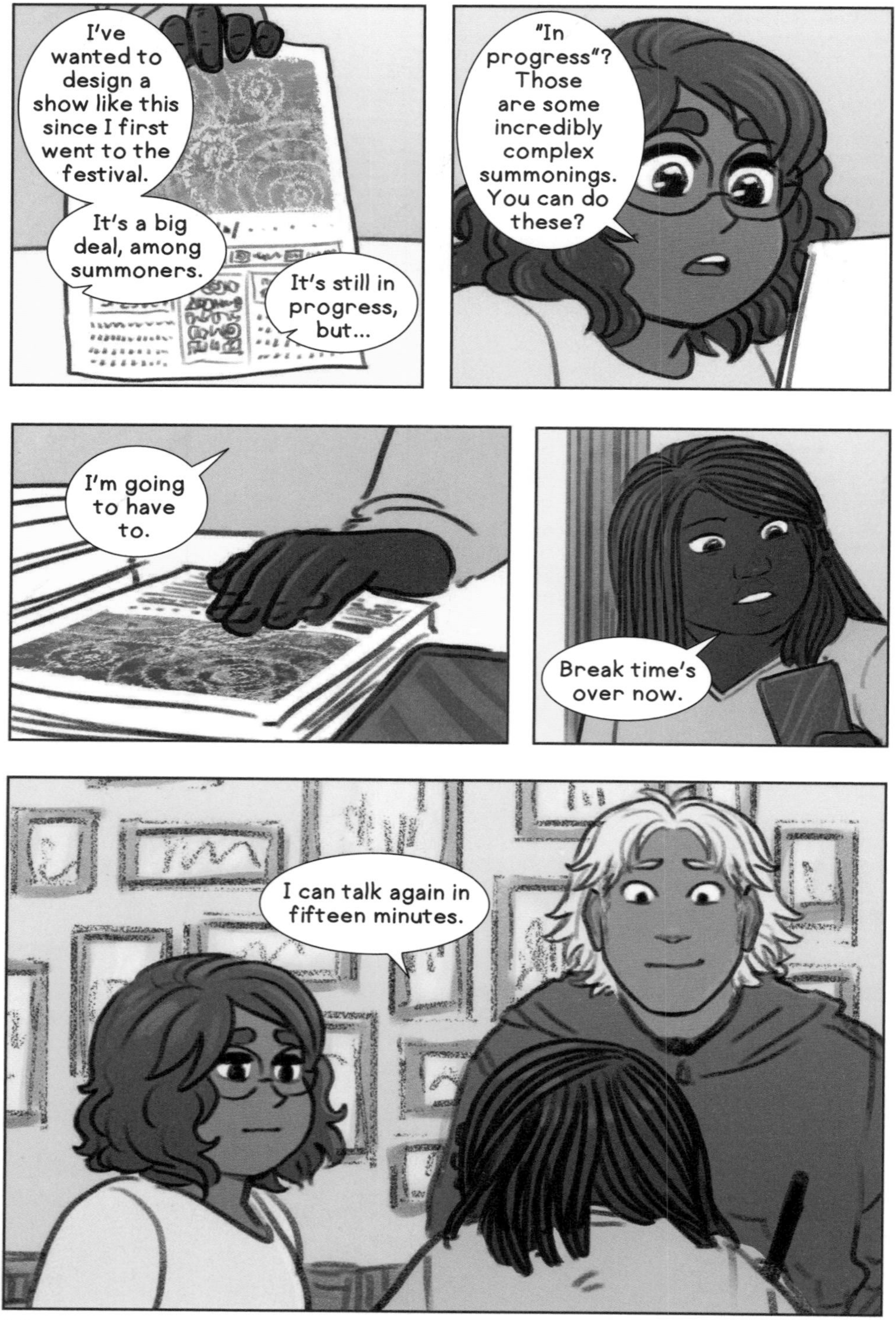
I've wanted to design a show like this since I first went to the festival.
It's a big deal, among summoners.
It's still in progress, but...
"In progress"? Those are some incredibly complex summonings. You can do these?
I'm going to have to.
Break time's over now.
I can talk again in fifteen minutes.

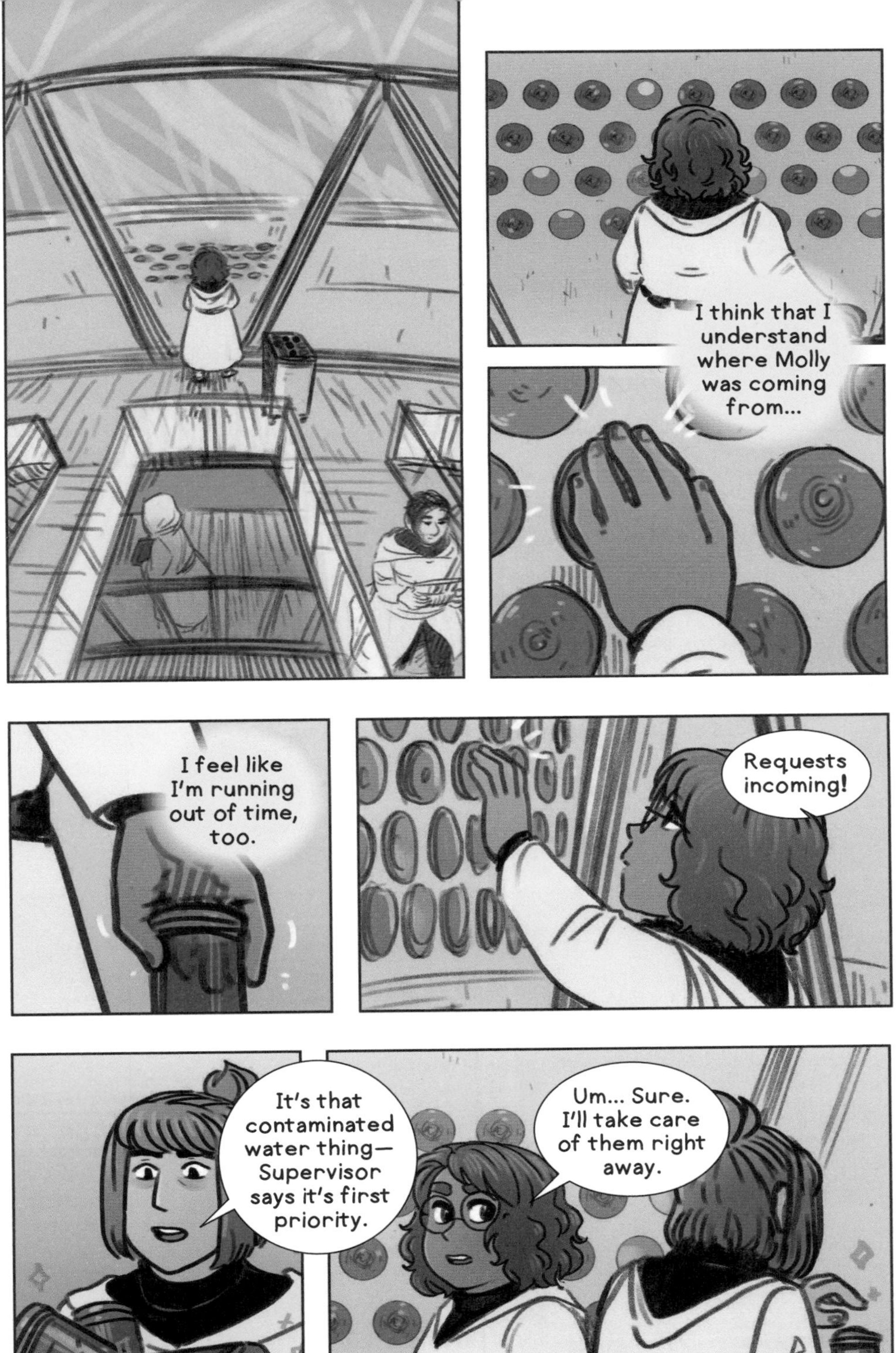
I think that I understand where Molly was coming from...
I feel like I'm running out of time, too.
Requests incoming!
It's that contaminated water thing— Supervisor says it's first priority.
Um... Sure. I'll take care of them right away.

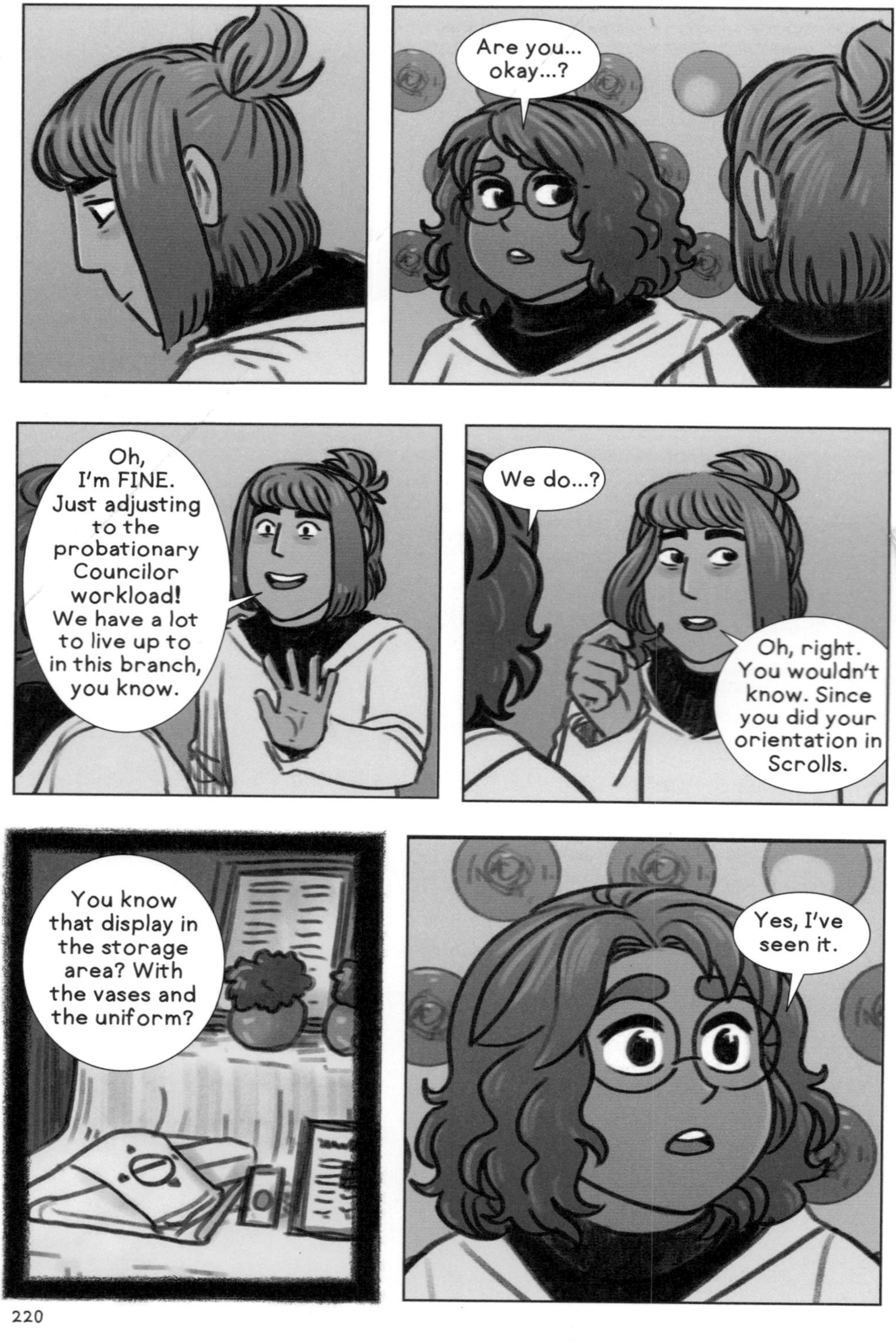
Are you... okay...?
Oh, I'm FINE. Just adjusting to the probationary Councilor workload! We have a lot to live up to in this branch, you know.
We do...?
Oh, right. You wouldn't know. Since you did your orientation in Scrolls.
You know that display in the storage area? With the vases and the uniform?
Yes, I've seen it.

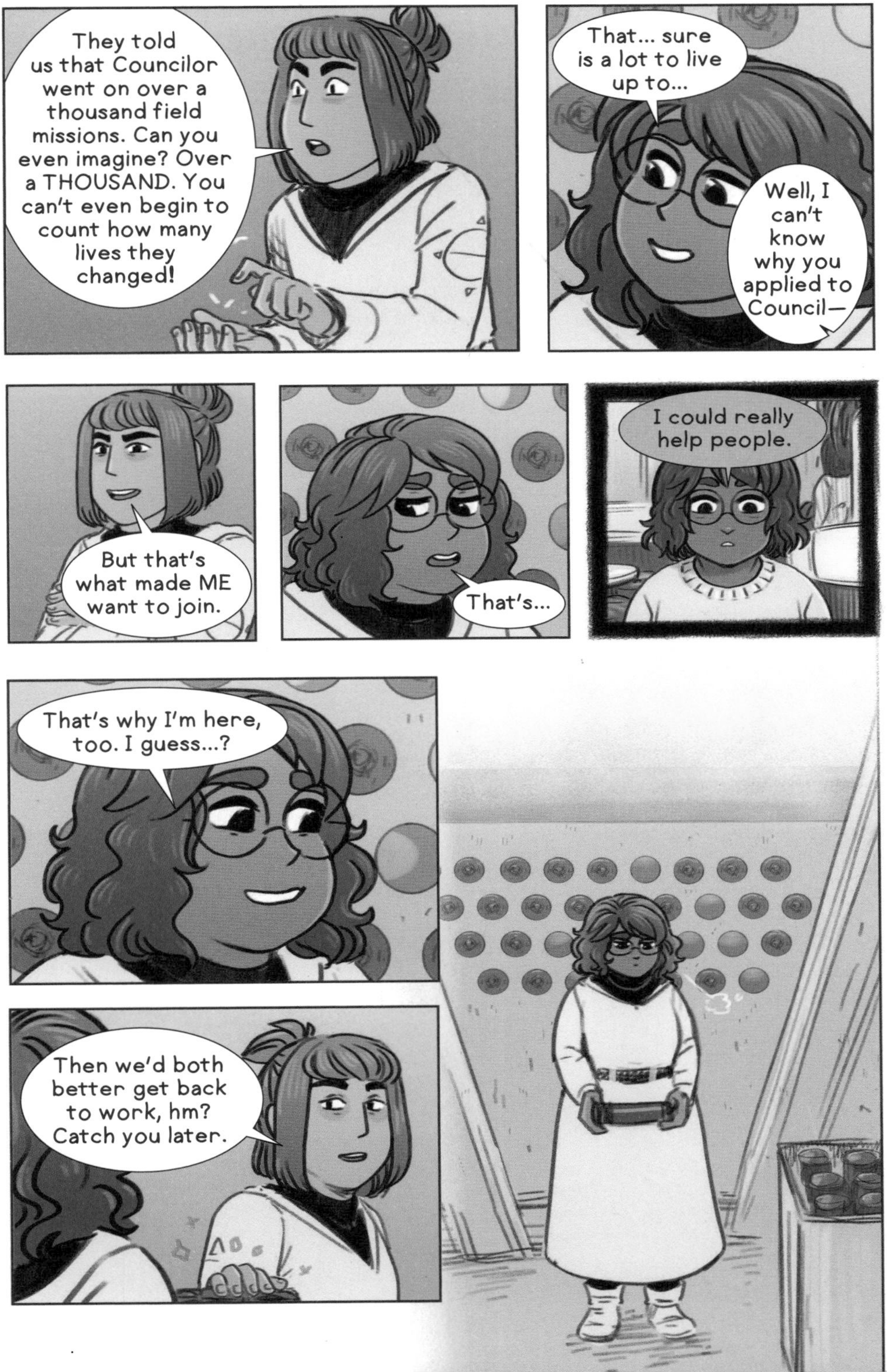
They told us that Councilor went on over a thousand field missions. Can you even imagine? Over a THOUSAND. You can't even begin to count how many lives they changed!
That... sure is a lot to live up to...
Well, I can't know why you applied to Council—
But that's what made ME want to join.
That's...
I could really help people.
That's why I'm here, too. I guess...?
Then we'd both better get back to work, hm? Catch you later.

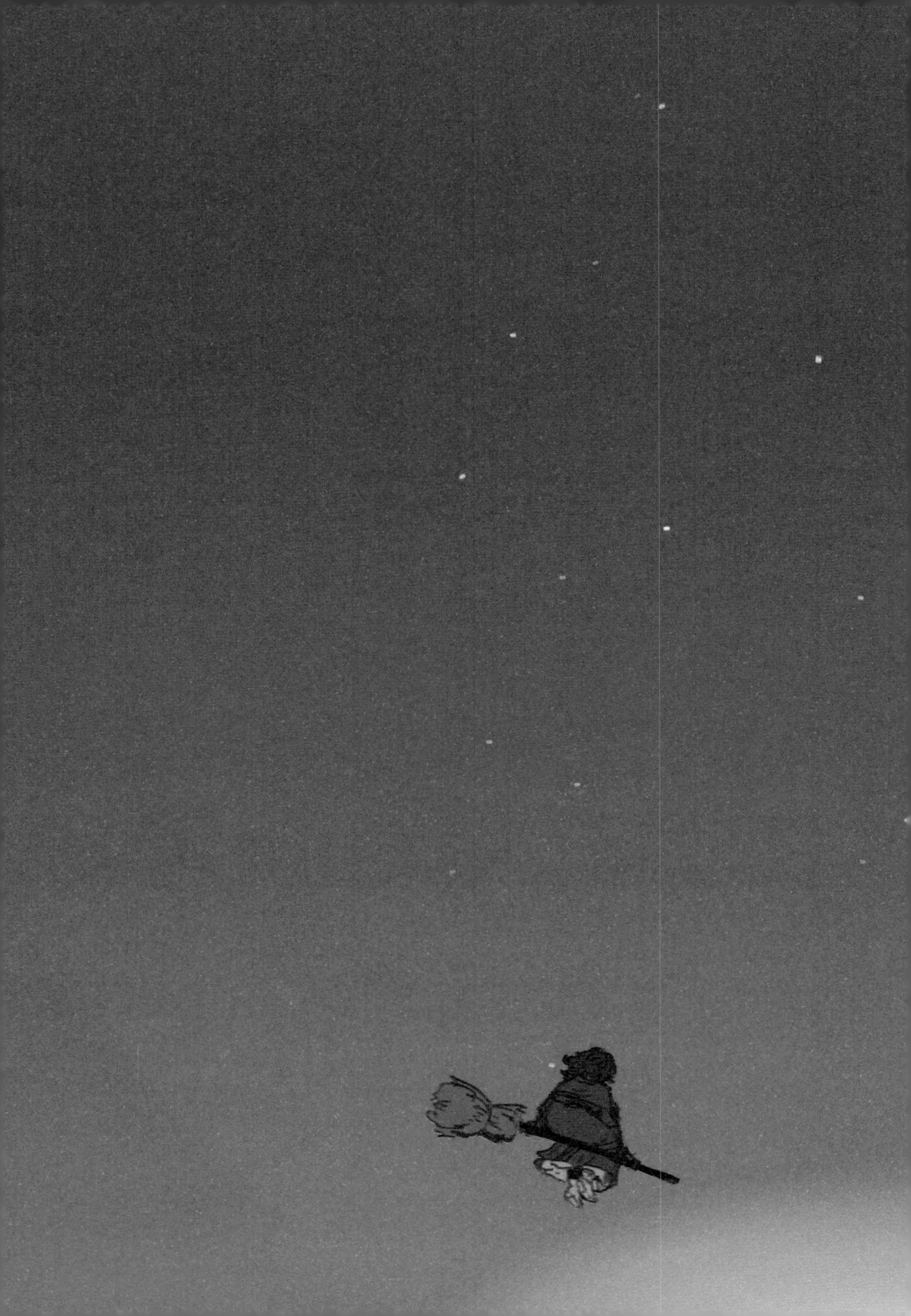

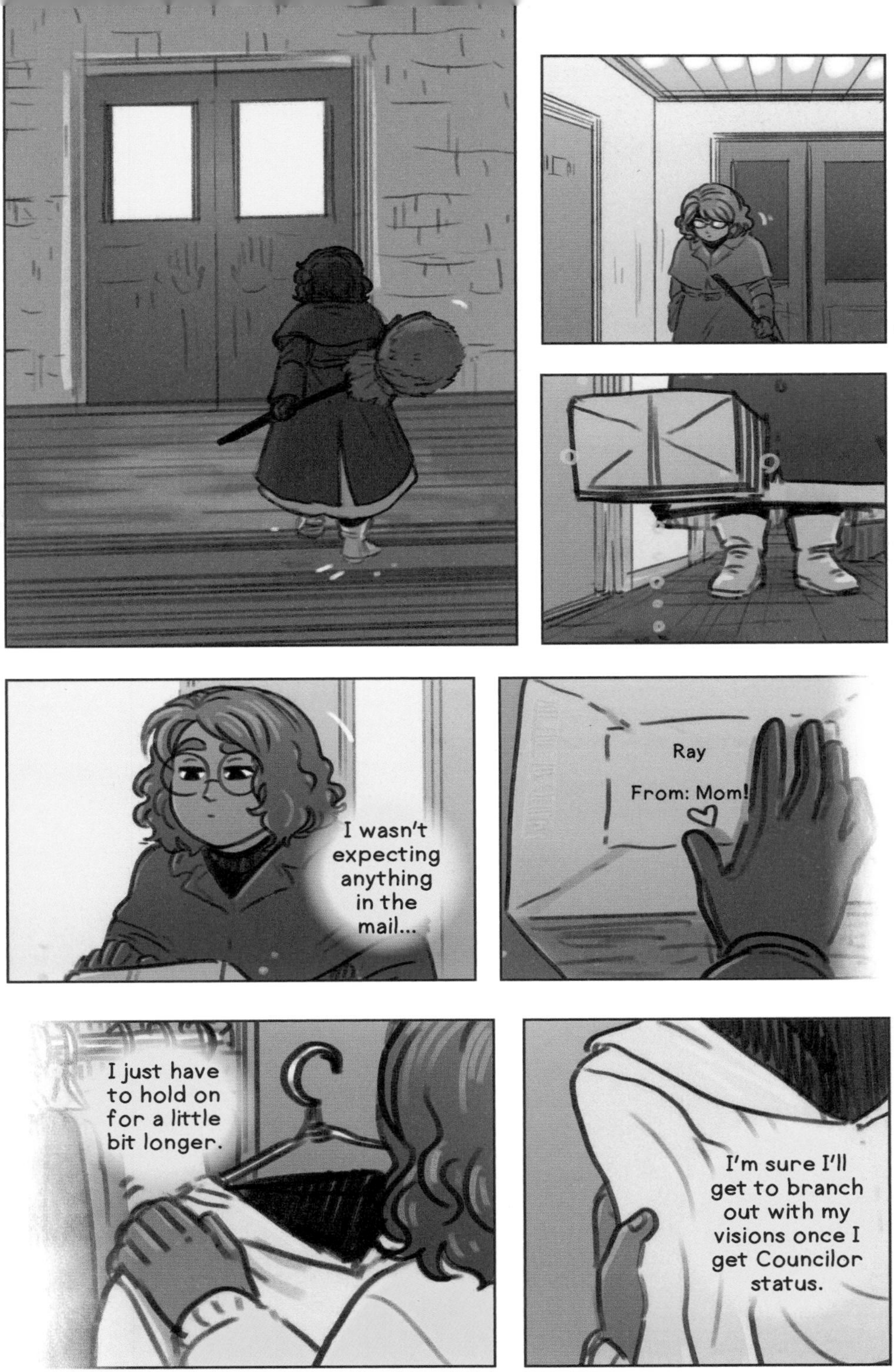
I wasn't expecting anything in the mail...
Ray
From: Mom!
I just have to hold on for a little bit longer.
I'm sure I'll get to branch out with my visions once I get Councilor status.

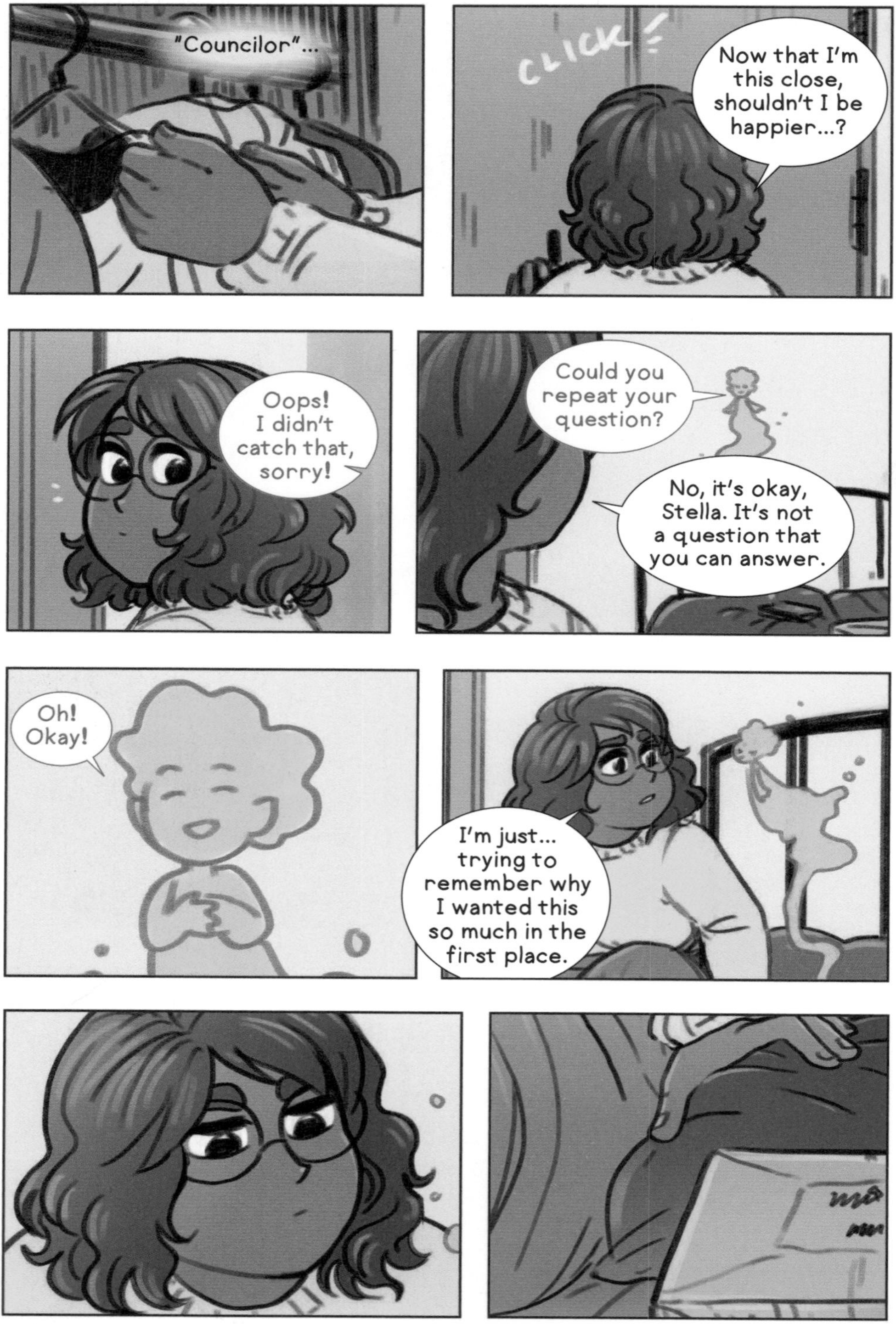

"Councilor"...
CLICK
Now that I'm this close, shouldn't I be happier...?
Oops! I didn't catch that, sorry!
Could you repeat your question?
No, it's okay, Stella. It's not a question that you can answer.
Oh! Okay!
I'm just... trying to remember why I wanted this so much in the first place.

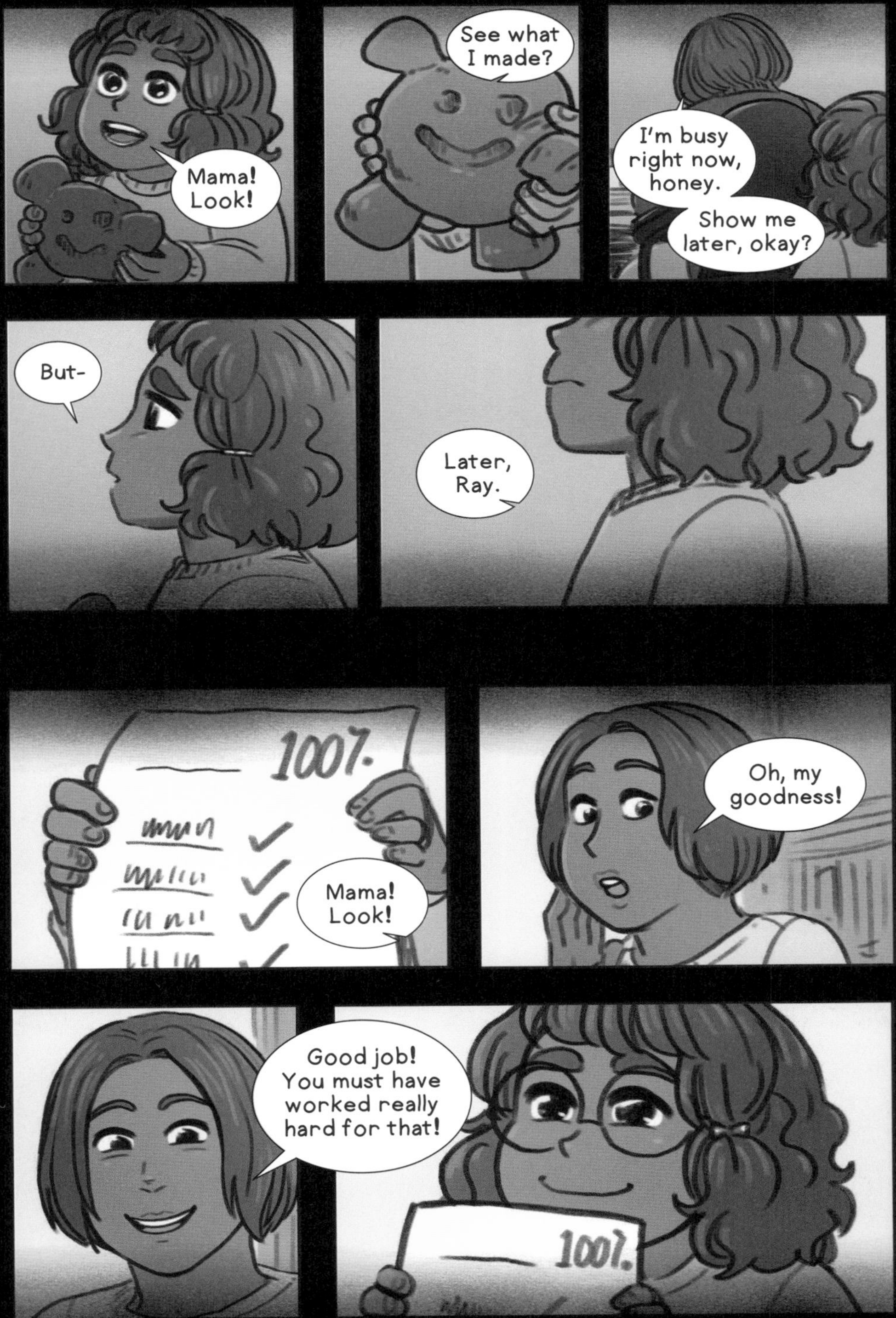
Mama! Look!
See what I made?
I'm busy right now, honey.
Show me later, okay?
But-
Later, Ray.
100%
Mama! Look!
Oh, my goodness!
Good job! You must have worked really hard for that!
100%

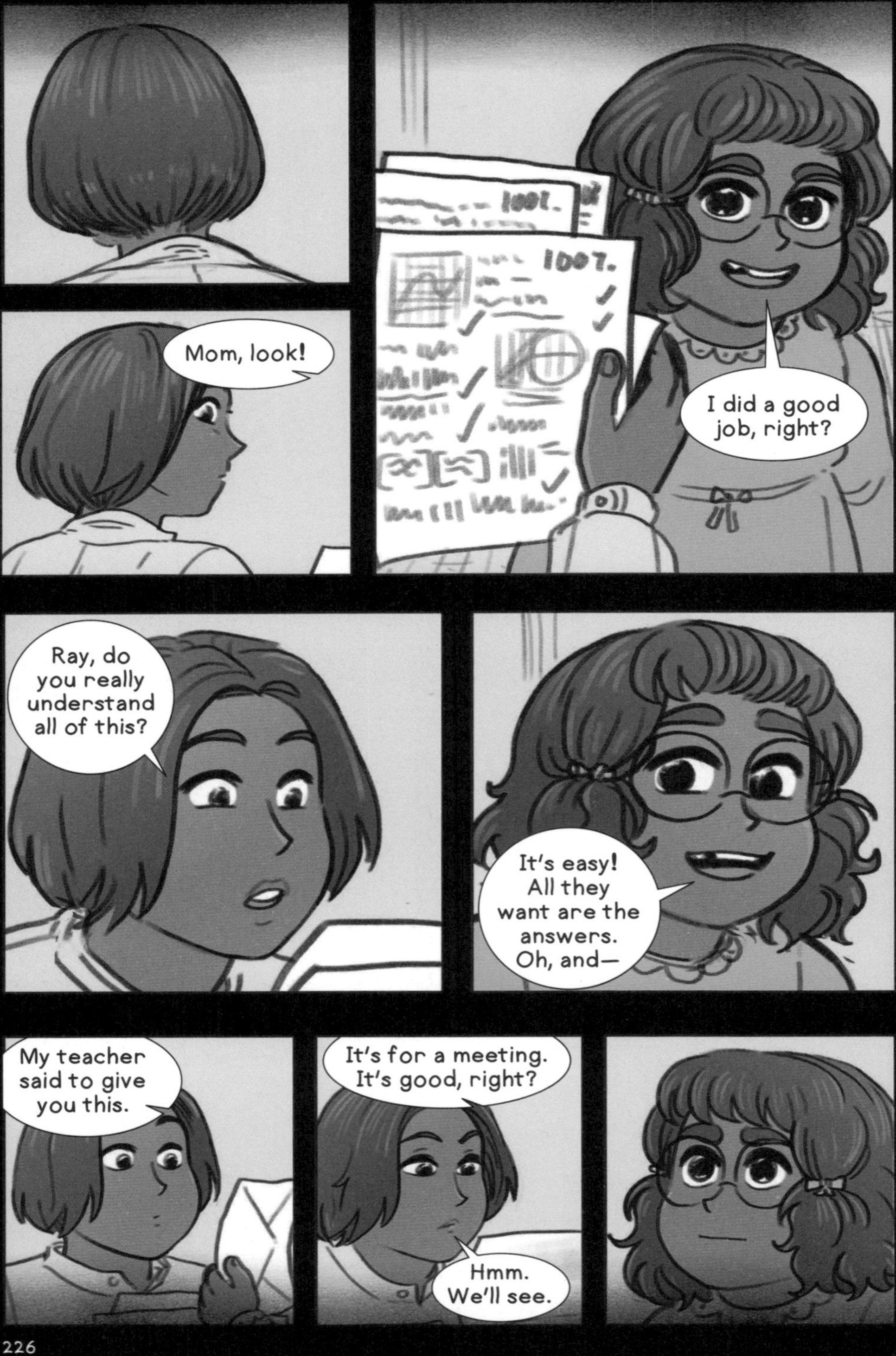
Mom, look!
I did a good job, right?
100%
100%
Ray, do you really understand all of this?
It's easy! All they want are the answers. Oh, and—
My teacher said to give you this.
It's for a meeting. It's good, right?
Hmm. We'll see.

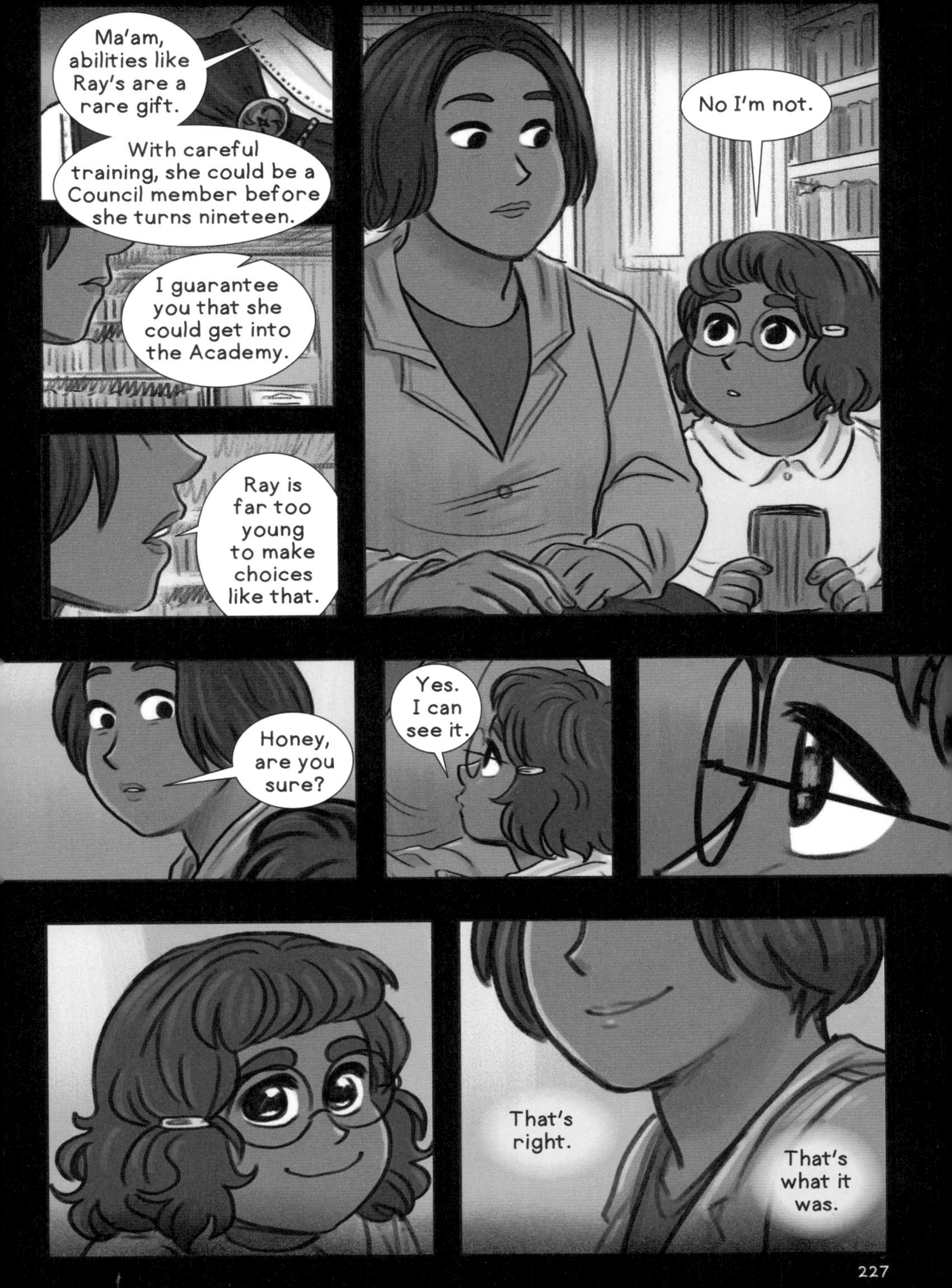

Ma'am, abilities like Ray's are a rare gift.
With careful training, she could be a Council member before she turns nineteen.
I guarantee you that she could get into the Academy.
No I'm not.
Ray is far too young to make choices like that.
Honey, are you sure?
Yes. I can see it.
That's right.
That's what it was.

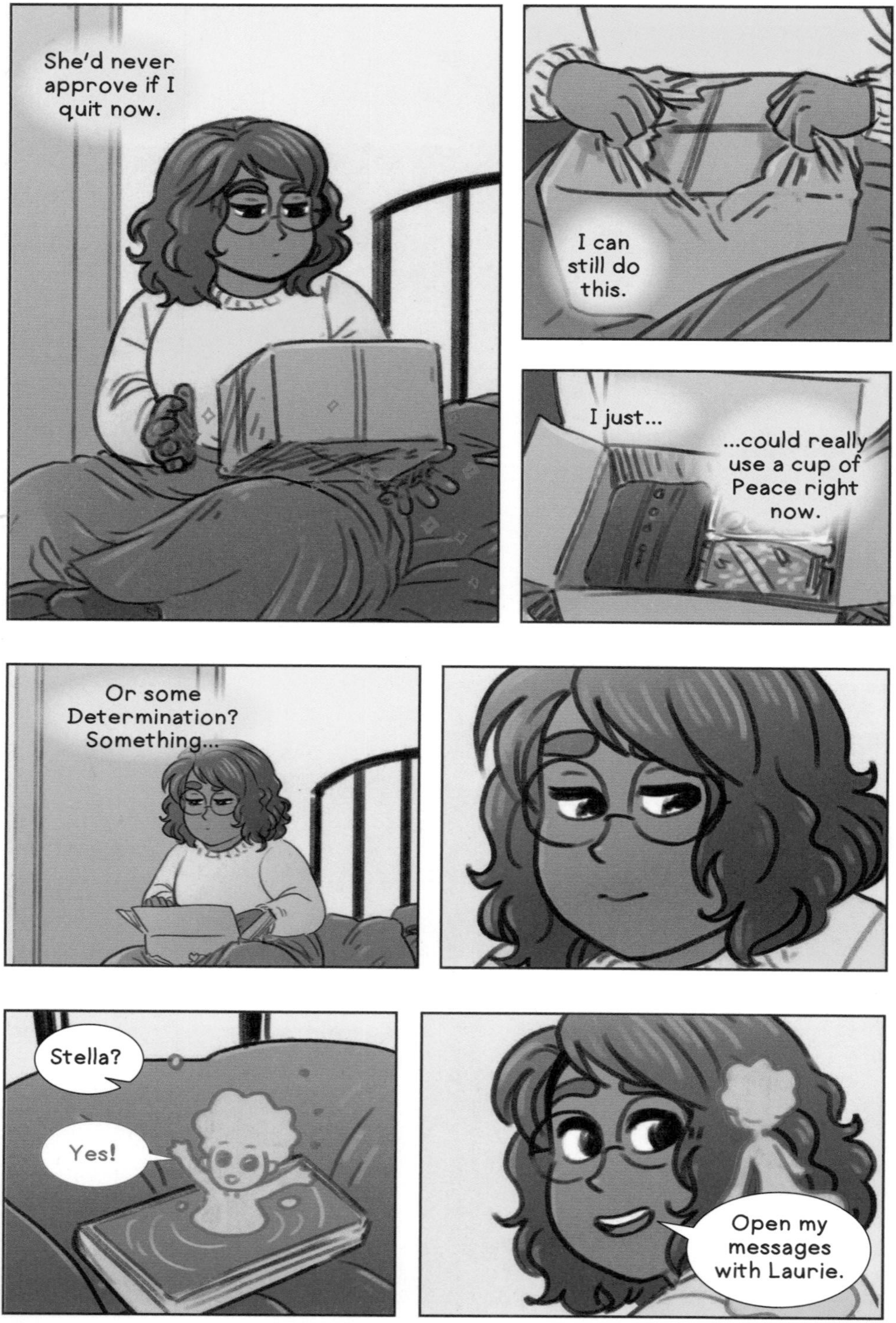
She'd never approve if I quit now.
I can still do this.
I just...
...could really use a cup of Peace right now.
Or some Determination? Something...
Stella?
Yes!
Open my messages with Laurie.

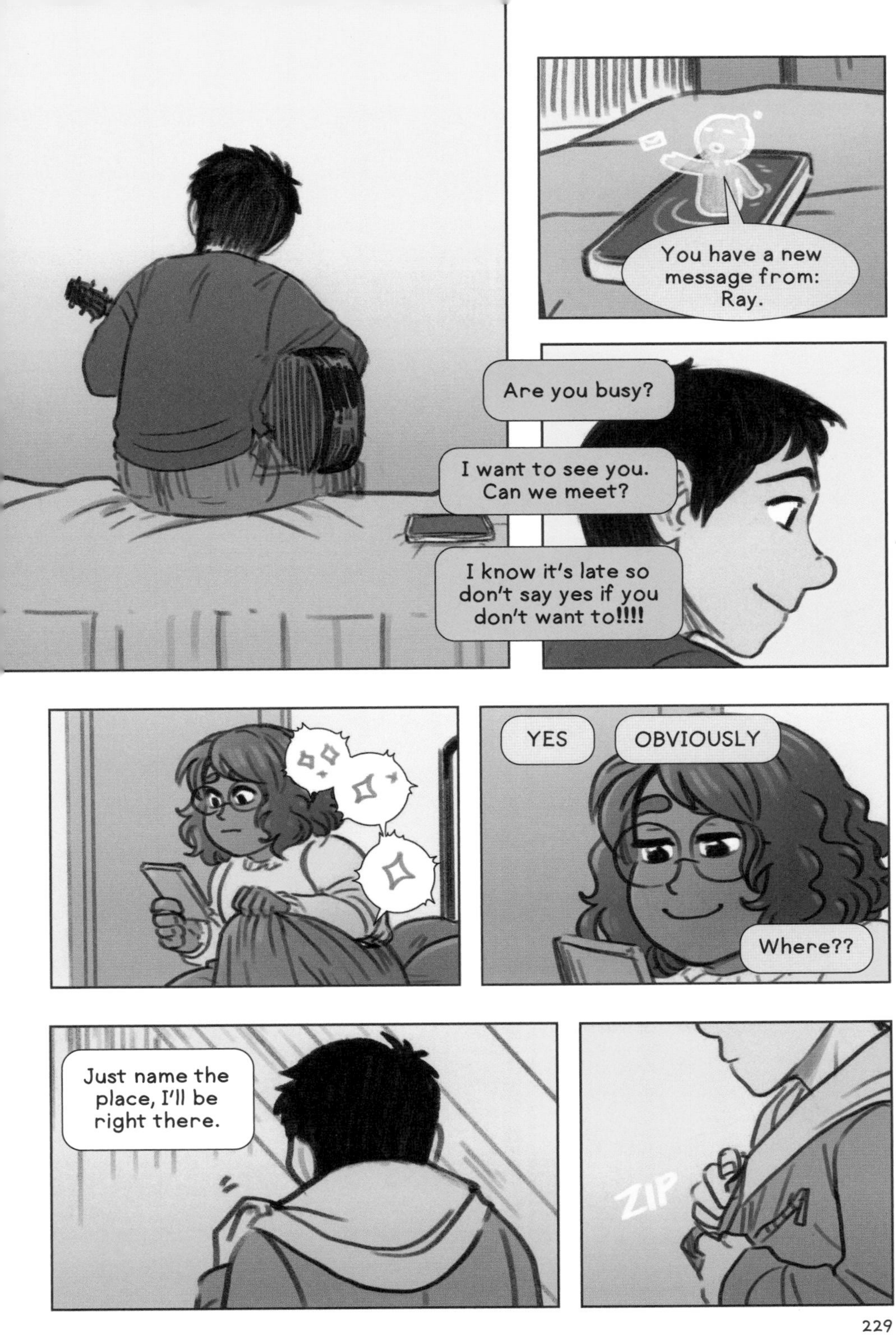

You have a new message from: Ray.
Are you busy?
I want to see you. Can we meet?
I know it's late so don't say yes if you don't want to!!!!
YES
OBVIOUSLY
Where??
Just name the place, I'll be right there.
ZIP

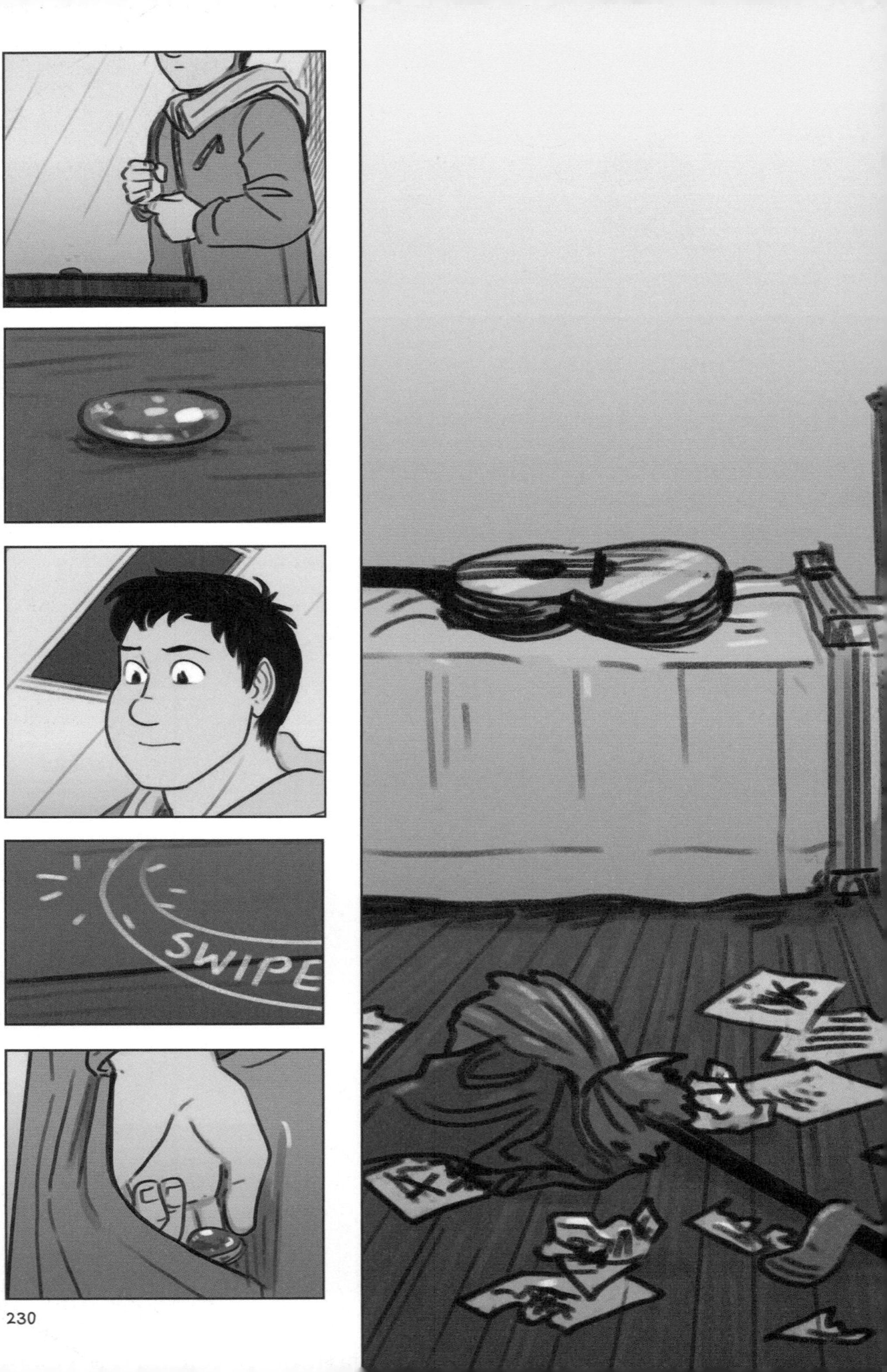
SWIPE

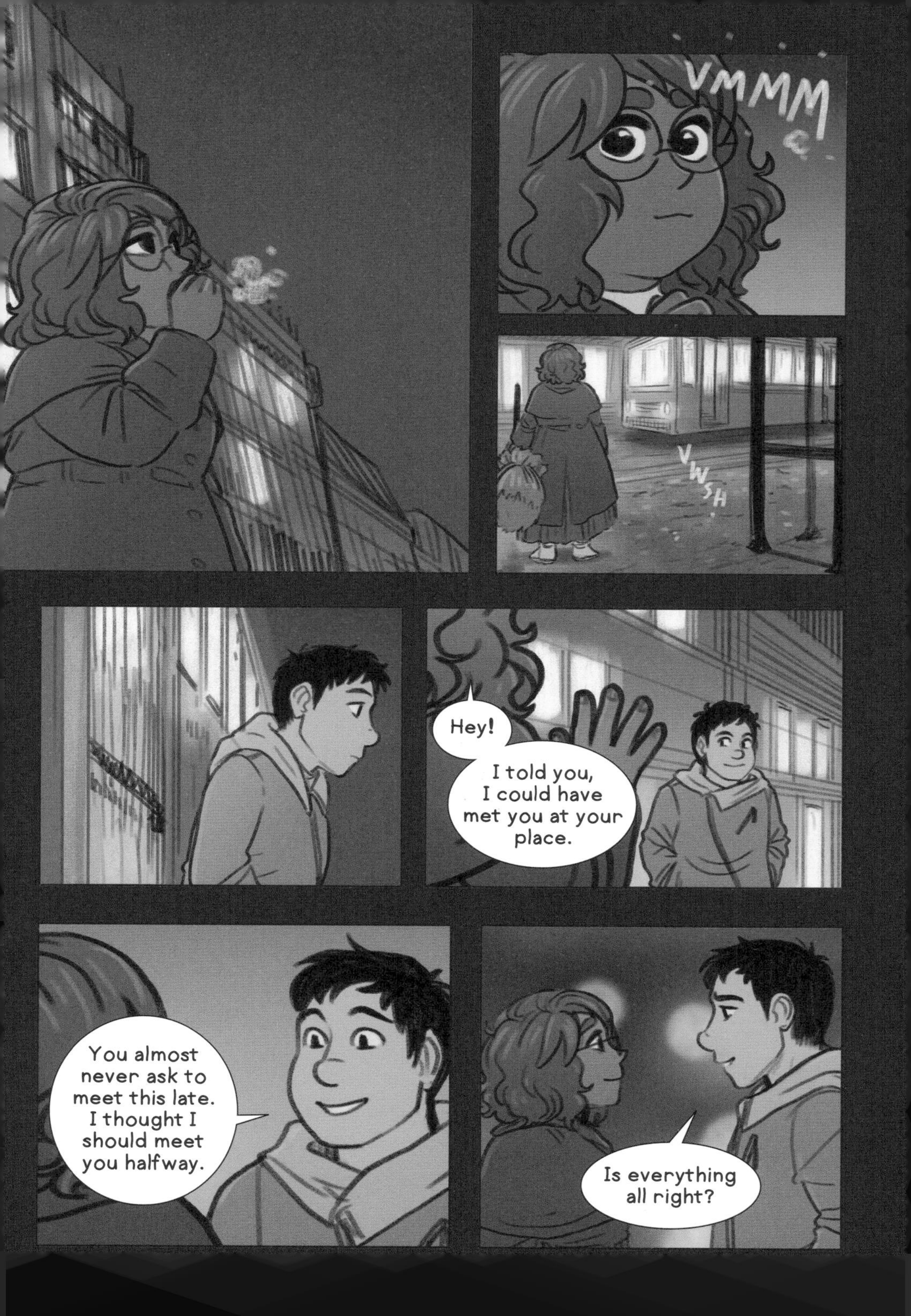
VMMM
VWSH
Hey!
I told you, I could have met you at your place.
You almost never ask to meet this late. I thought I should meet you halfway.
Is everything all right?

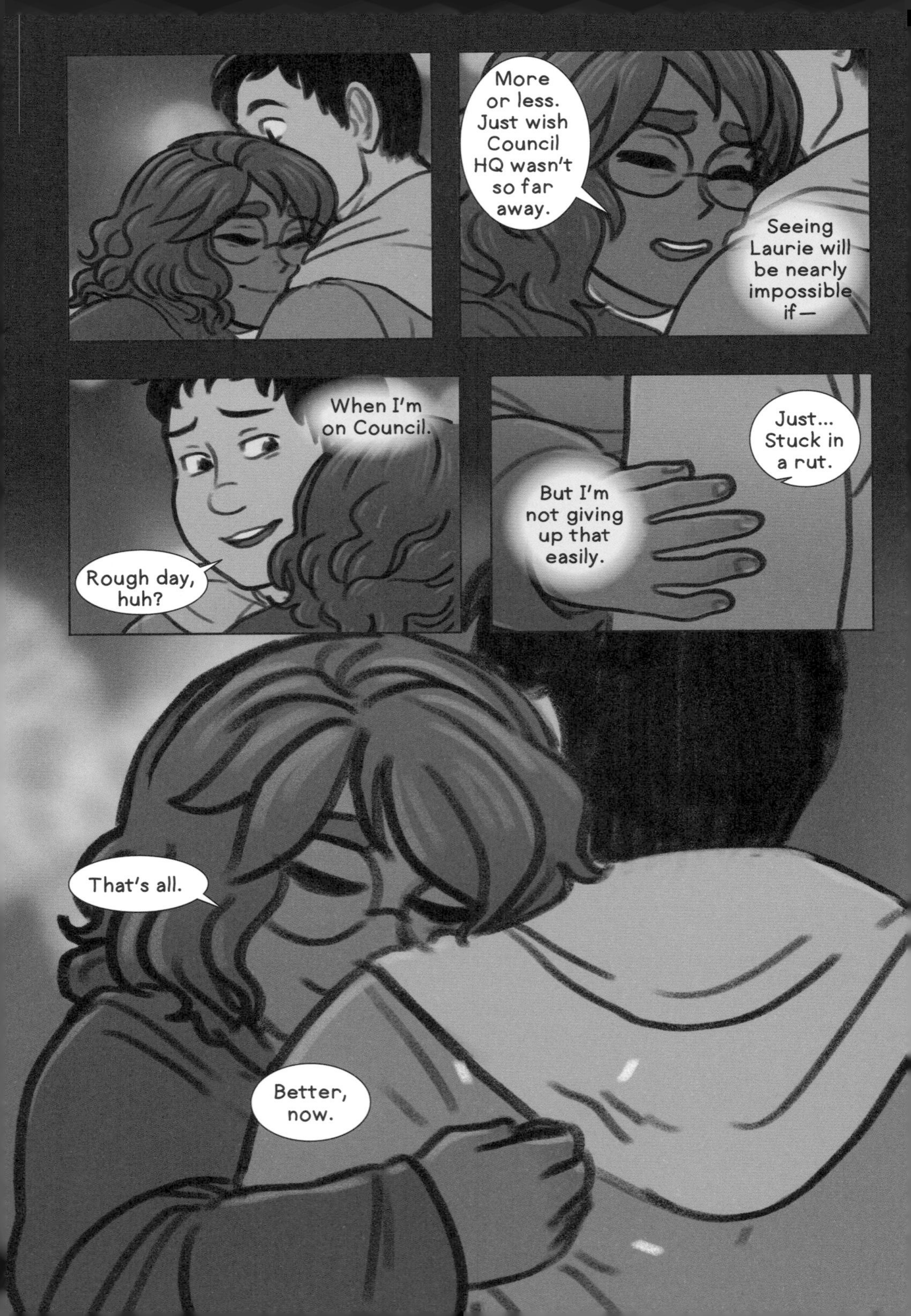
More or less. Just wish Council HQ wasn't so far away.
Seeing Laurie will be nearly impossible if—
When I'm on Council.
Rough day, huh?
Just... Stuck in a rut.
But I'm not giving up that easily.
That's all.
Better, now.

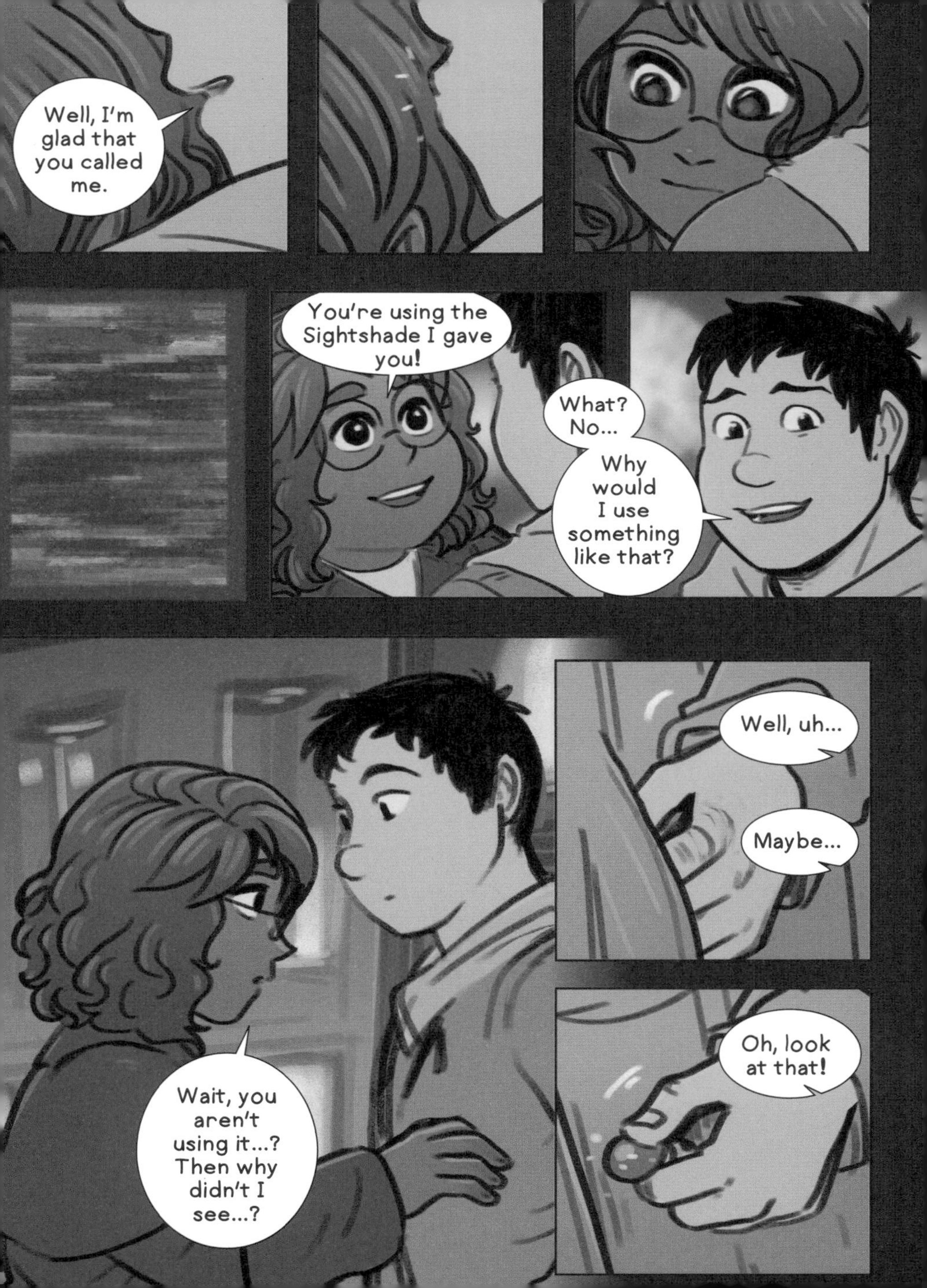
Well, I'm glad that you called me.
You're using the Sightshade I gave you!
What? No...
Why would I use something like that?
Well, uh...
Maybe...
Oh, look at that!
Wait, you aren't using it...? Then why didn't I see...?

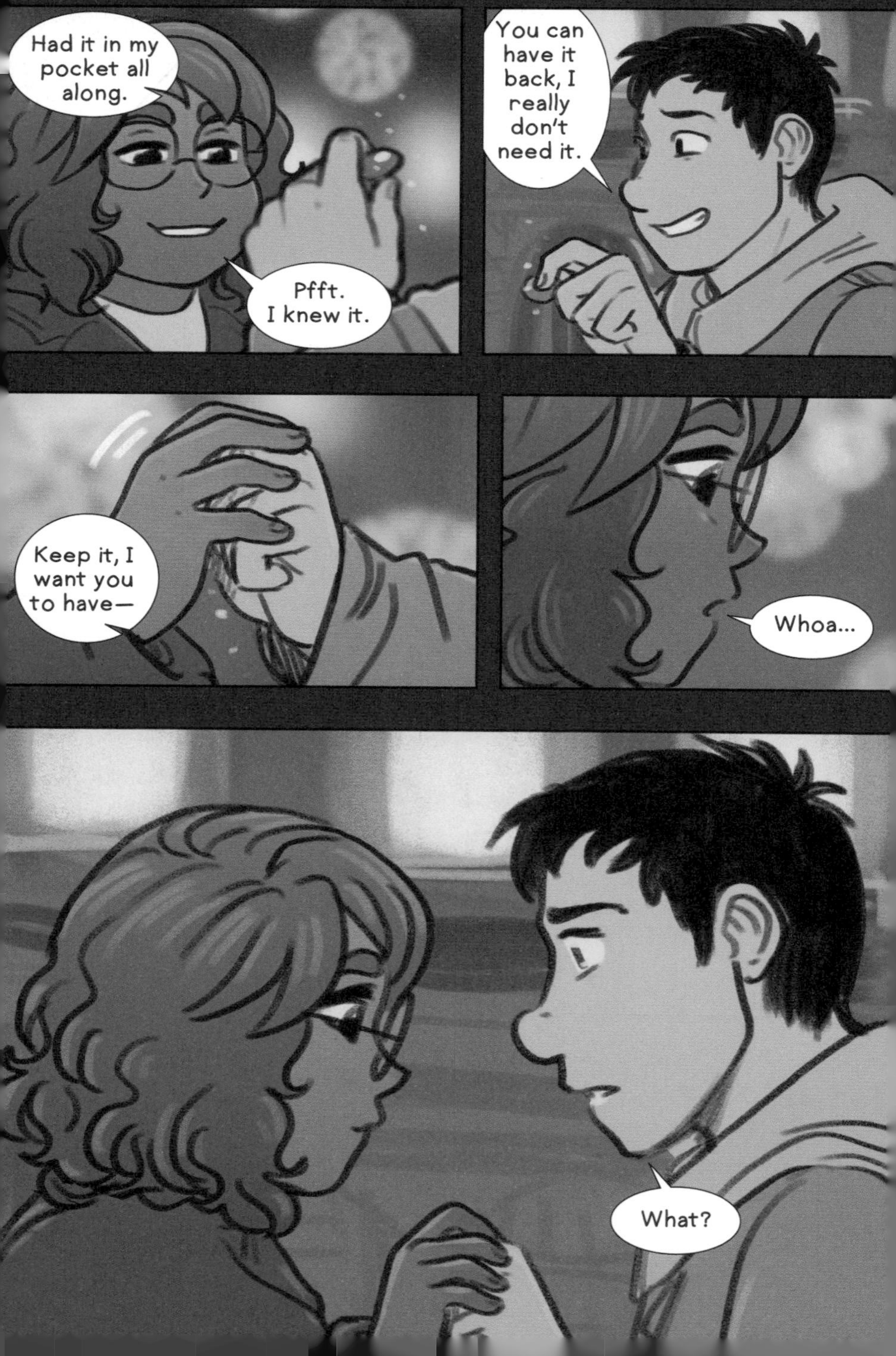
Had it in my pocket all along.
Pfft. I knew it.
You can have it back, I really don't need it.
Keep it, I want you to have—
Whoa...
What?

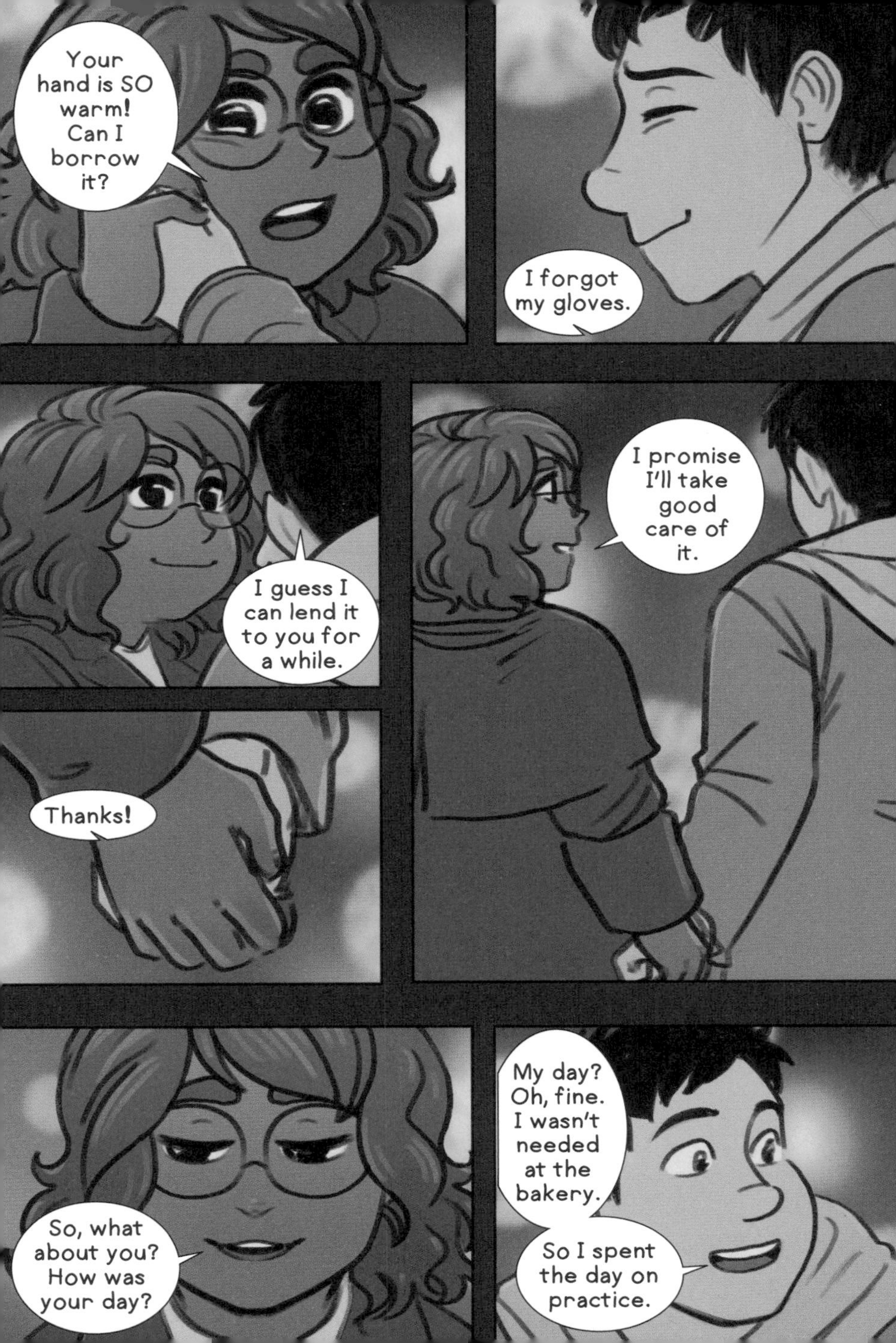
Your hand is SO warm! Can I borrow it?
I forgot my gloves.
I guess I can lend it to you for a while.
Thanks!
I promise I'll take good care of it.
So, what about you? How was your day?
My day? Oh, fine. I wasn't needed at the bakery.
So I spent the day on practice.

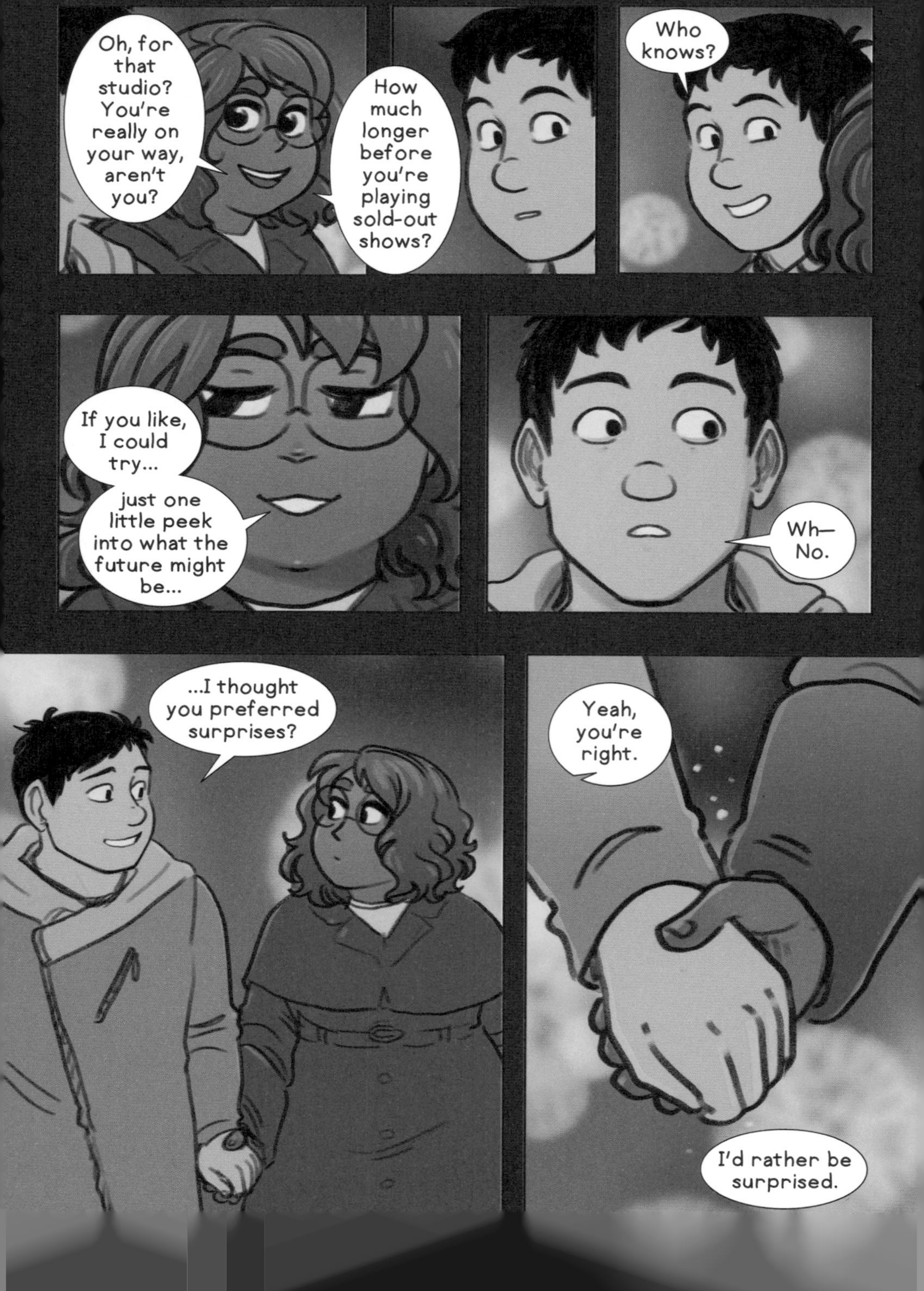
Oh, for that studio? You're really on your way, aren't you?
How much longer before you're playing sold-out shows?
Who knows?
If you like, I could try...
just one little peek into what the future might be...
Wh— No.
...I thought you preferred surprises?
Yeah, you're right.
I'd rather be surprised.

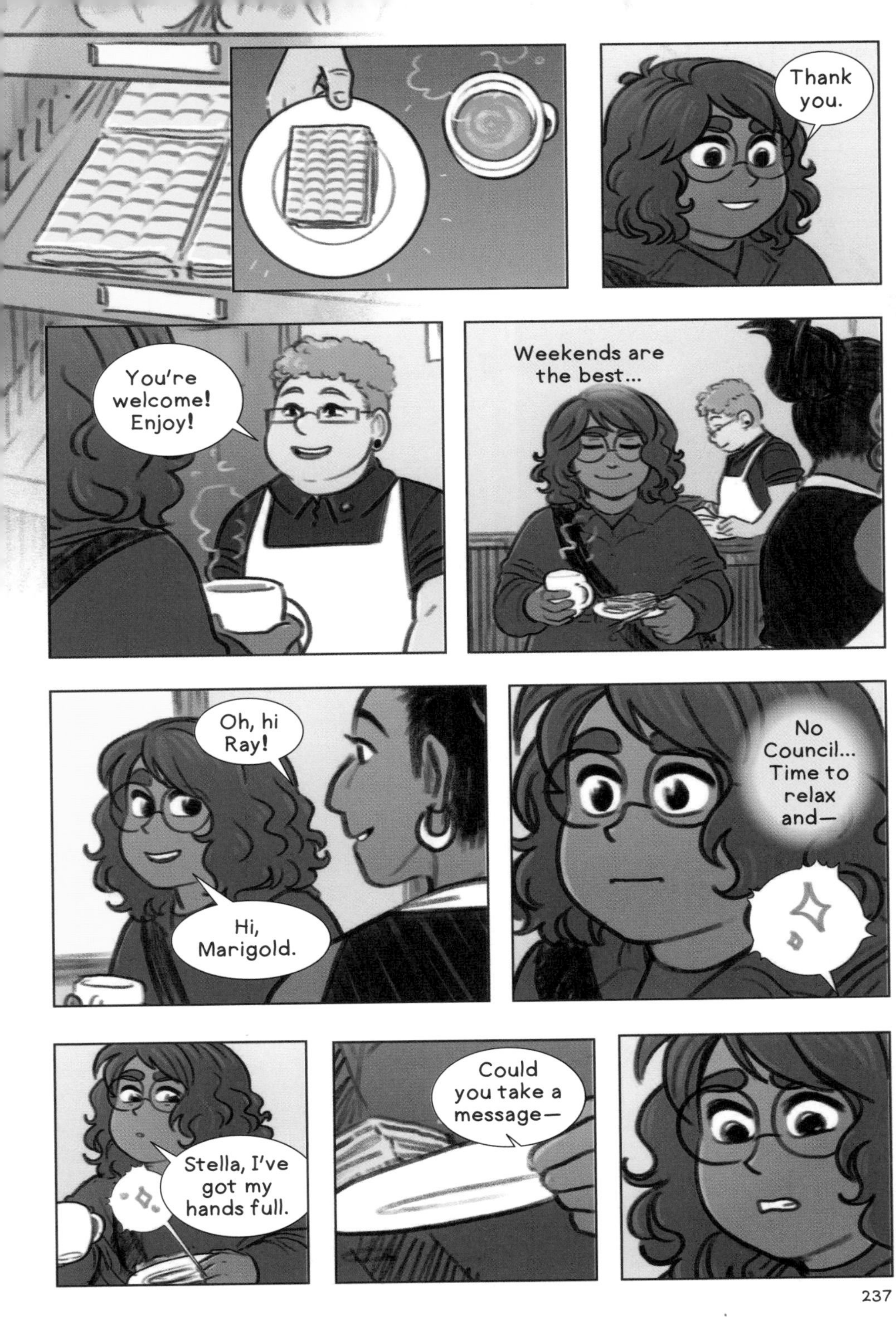
Thank you.
You're welcome! Enjoy!
Weekends are the best...
Oh, hi Ray!
Hi, Marigold.
No Council... Time to relax and—
Stella, I've got my hands full.
Could you take a message—

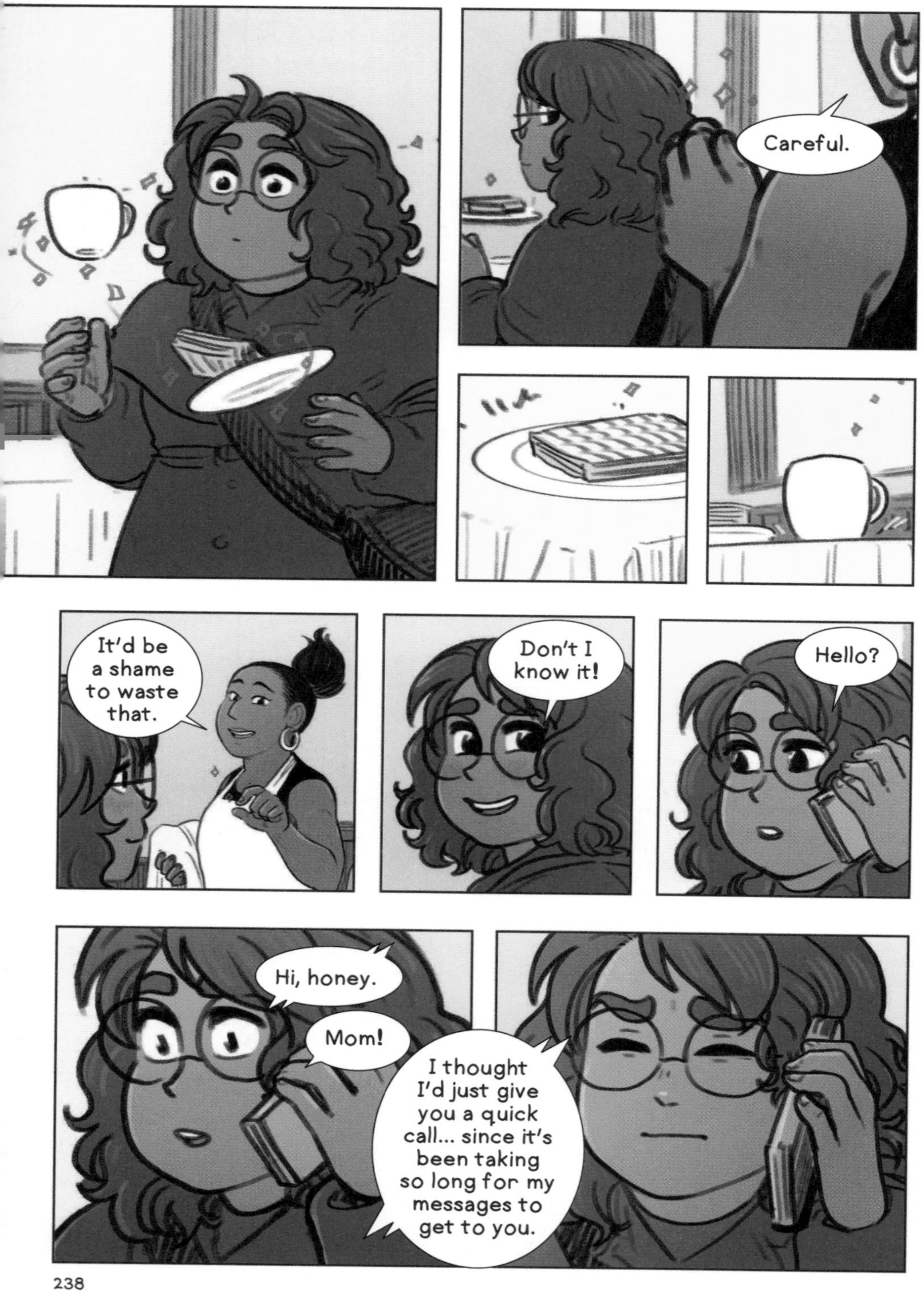
Careful.
It'd be a shame to waste that.
Don't I know it!
Hello?
Hi, honey.
Mom!
I thought I'd just give you a quick call... since it's been taking so long for my messages to get to you.

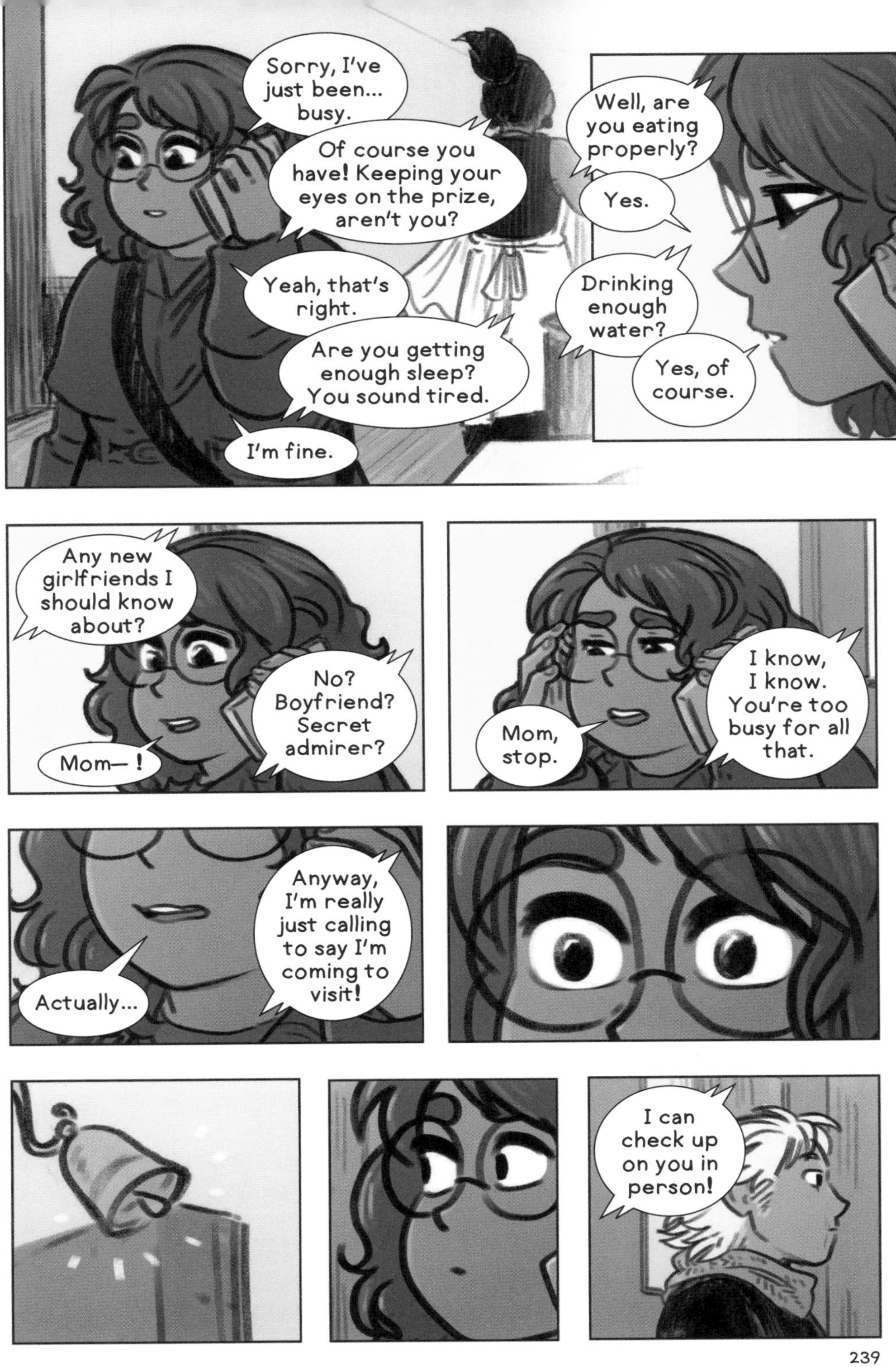

Sorry, I've just been... busy.
Of course you have! Keeping your eyes on the prize, aren't you?
Yeah, that's right.
Are you getting enough sleep? You sound tired.
I'm fine.
Well, are you eating properly?
Yes.
Drinking enough water?
Yes, of course.
Any new girlfriends I should know about?
No? Boyfriend? Secret admirer?
Mom—!
Mom, stop.
I know, I know. You're too busy for all that.
Actually...
Anyway, I'm really just calling to say I'm coming to visit!
I can check up on you in person!

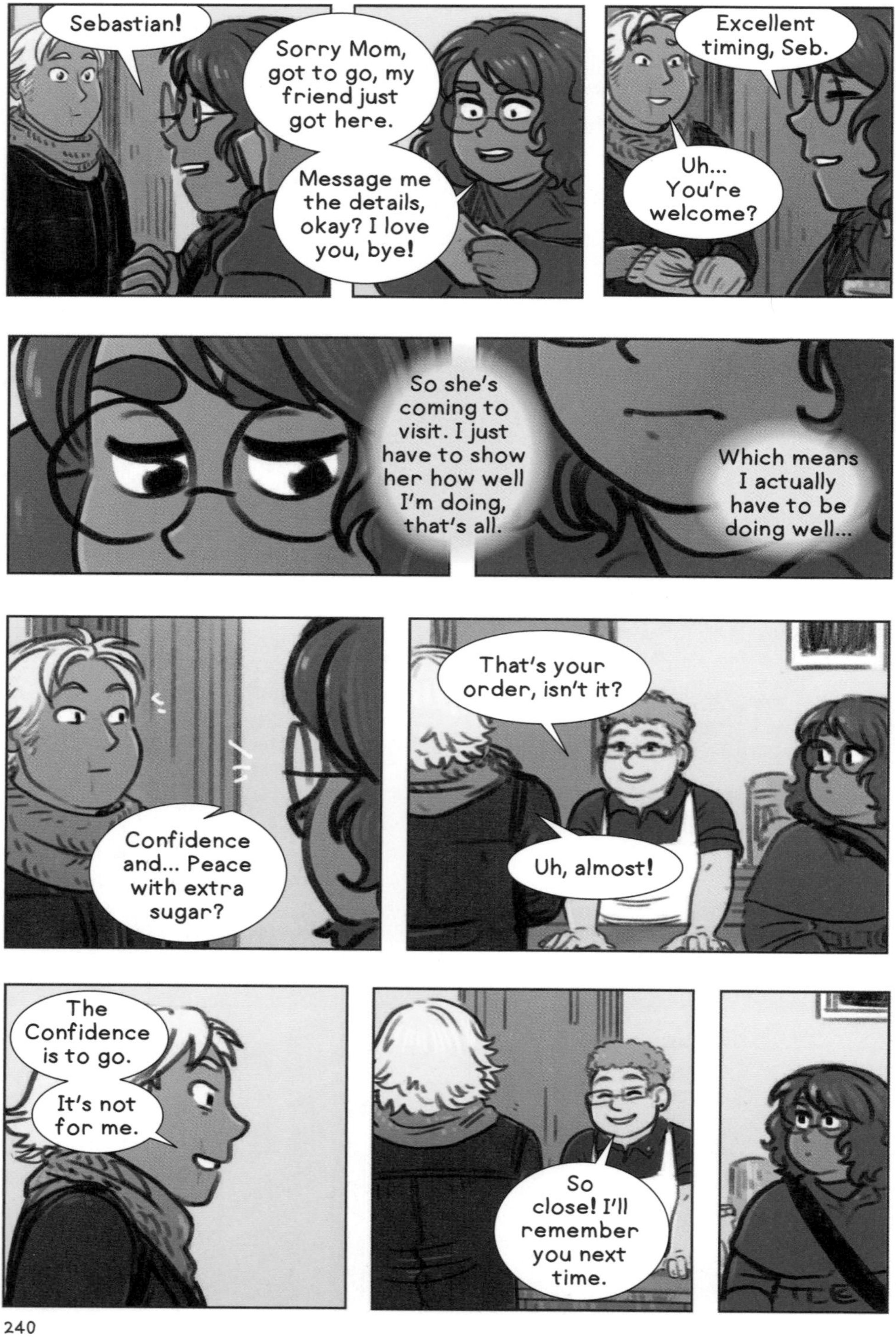
Sebastian!
Sorry Mom, got to go, my friend just got here.
Message me the details, okay? I love you, bye!
Excellent timing, Seb.
Uh... You're welcome?
So she's coming to visit. I just have to show her how well I'm doing, that's all.
Which means I actually have to be doing well...
Confidence and... Peace with extra sugar?
That's your order, isn't it?
Uh, almost!
The Confidence is to go.
It's not for me.
So close! I'll remember you next time.

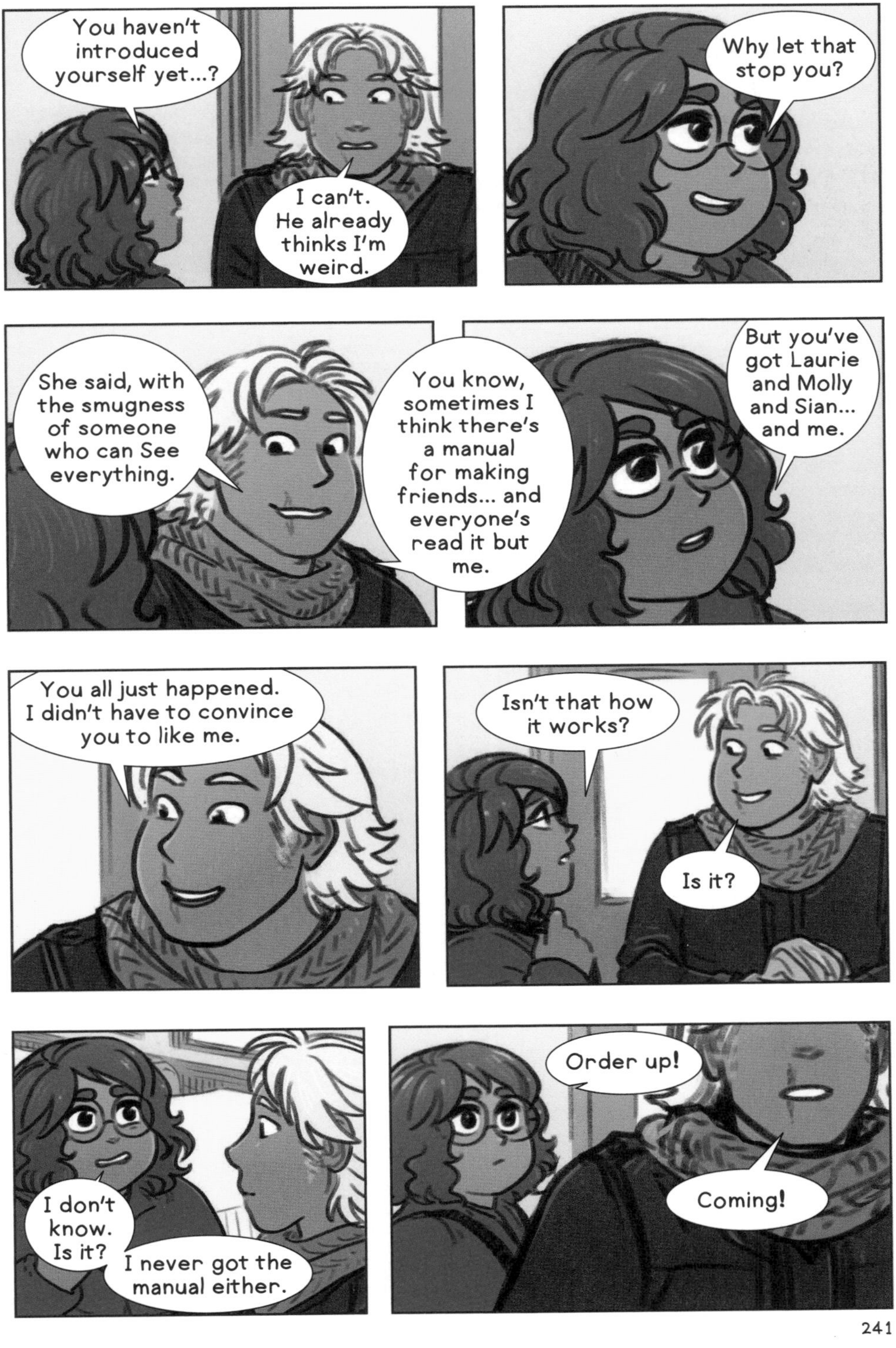

You haven't introduced yourself yet...?
I can't. He already thinks I'm weird.
Why let that stop you?
She said, with the smugness of someone who can See everything.
You know, sometimes I think there's a manual for making friends... and everyone's read it but me.
But you've got Laurie and Molly and Sian... and me.
You all just happened. I didn't have to convince you to like me.
Isn't that how it works?
Is it?
I don't know. Is it?
I never got the manual either.
Order up!
Coming!

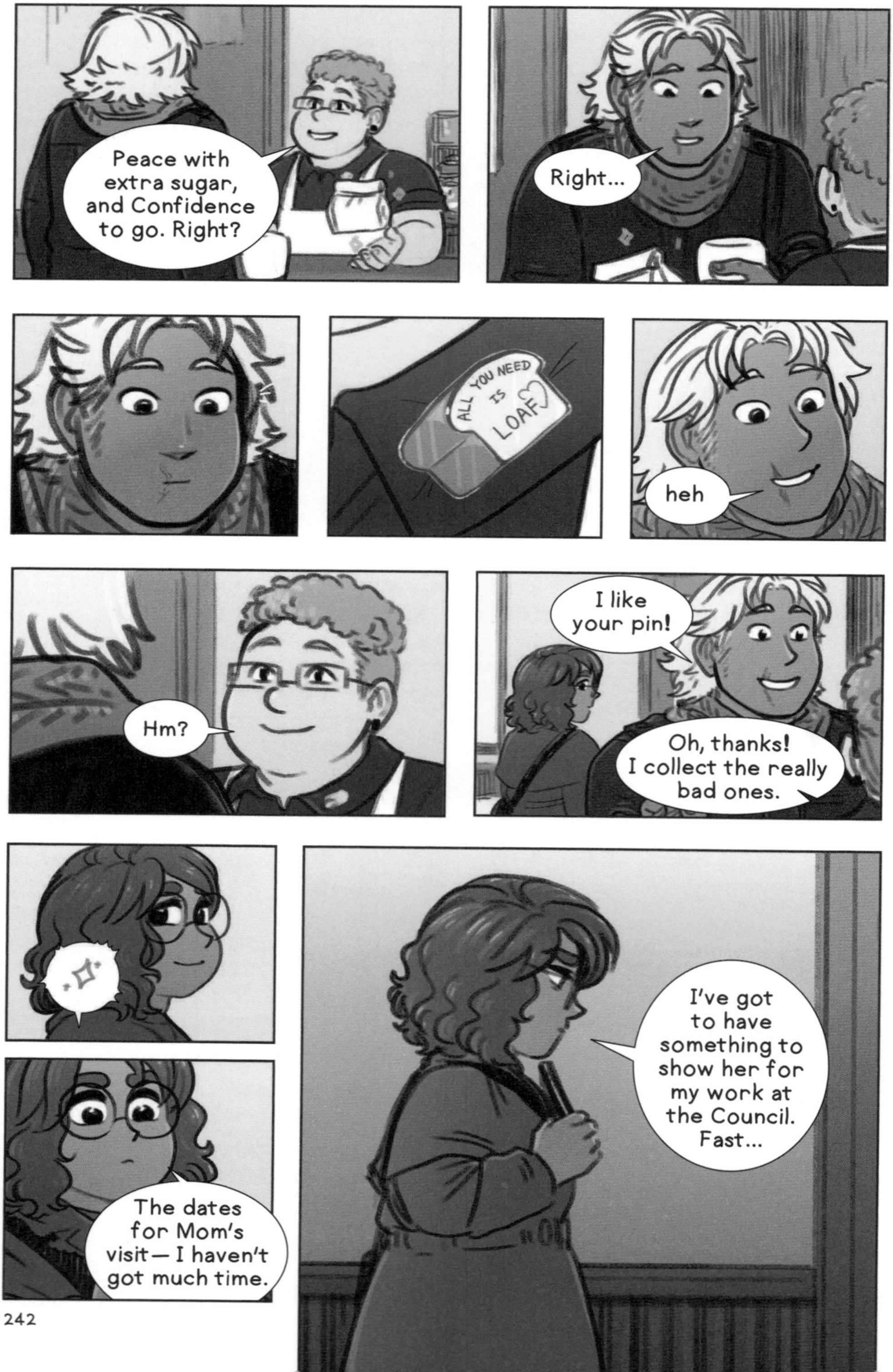
Peace with extra sugar, and Confidence to go. Right?
Right...
ALL YOU NEED IS LOAF
heh
Hm?
I like your pin!
Oh, thanks! I collect the really bad ones.
The dates for Mom's visit— I haven't got much time.
I've got to have something to show her for my work at the Council. Fast...

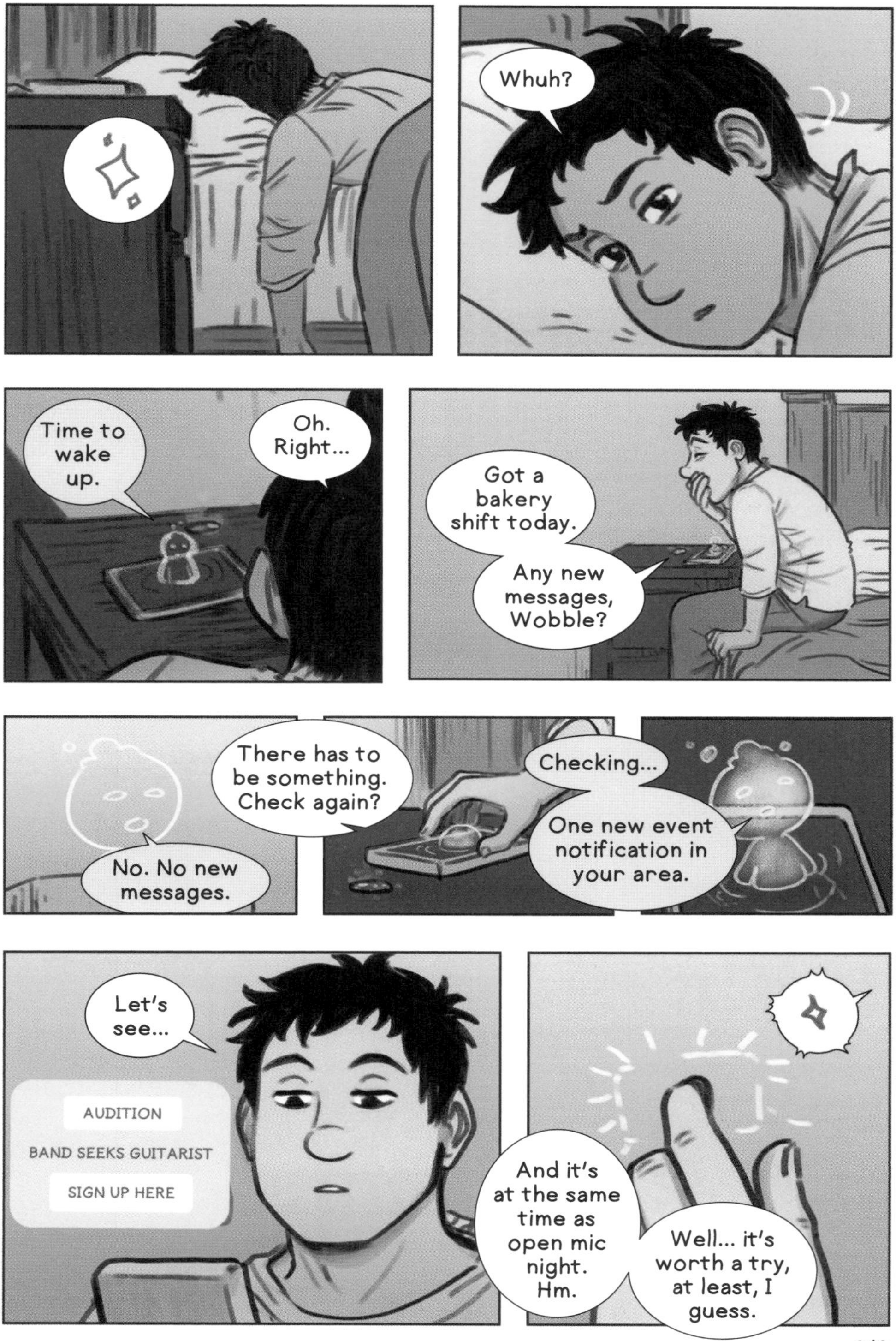

Whuh?
Time to wake up.
Oh. Right...
Got a bakery shift today.
Any new messages, Wobble?
No. No new messages.
There has to be something. Check again?
Checking...
One new event notification in your area.
Let's see...
AUDITION
BAND SEEKS GUITARIST
SIGN UP HERE
And it's at the same time as open mic night. Hm.
Well... it's worth a try, at least, I guess.

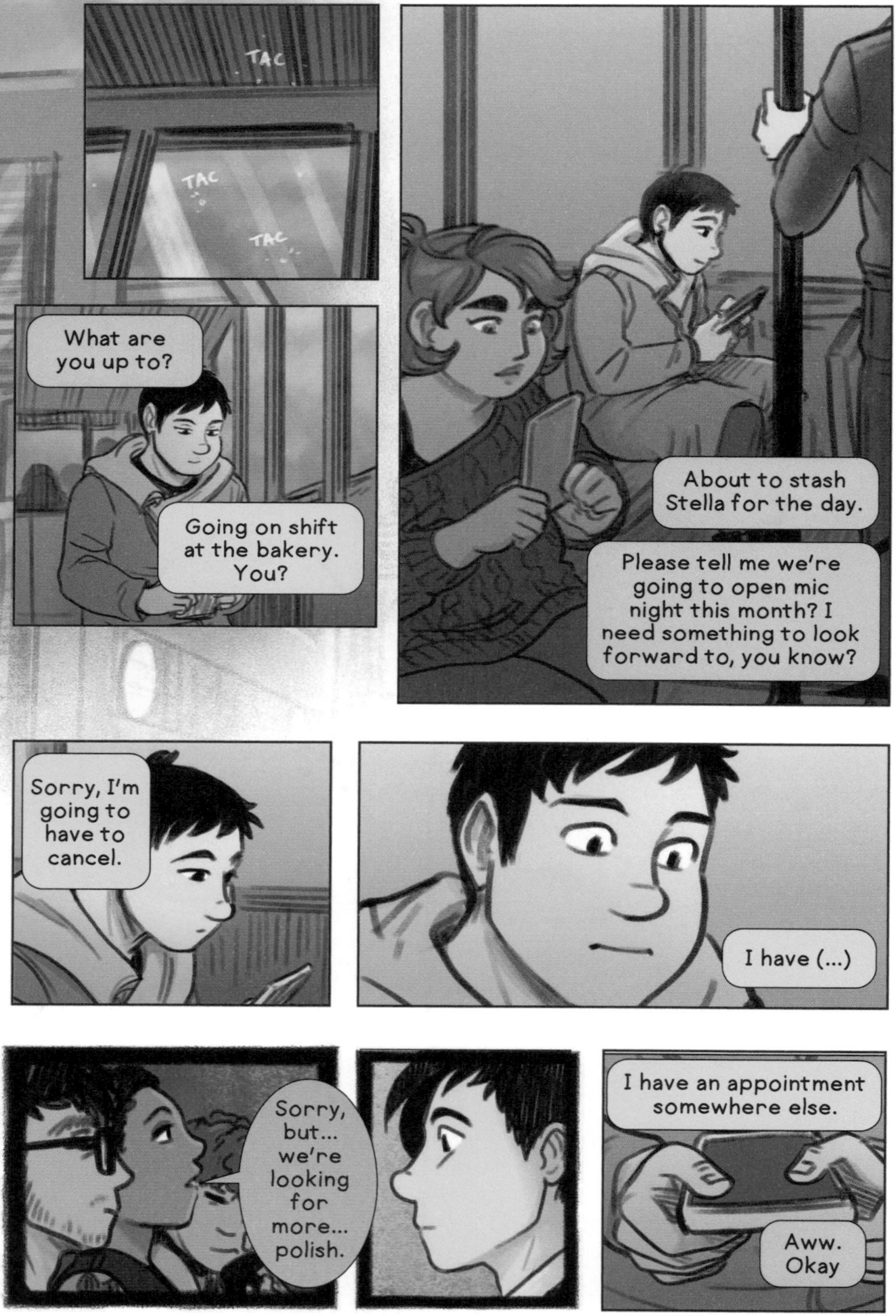
TAC
TAC
TAC
What are you up to?
Going on shift at the bakery. You?
About to stash Stella for the day.
Please tell me we're going to open mic night this month? I need something to look forward to, you know?
Sorry, I'm going to have to cancel.
I have (...)
Sorry, but... we're looking for more... polish.
I have an appointment somewhere else.
Aww. Okay

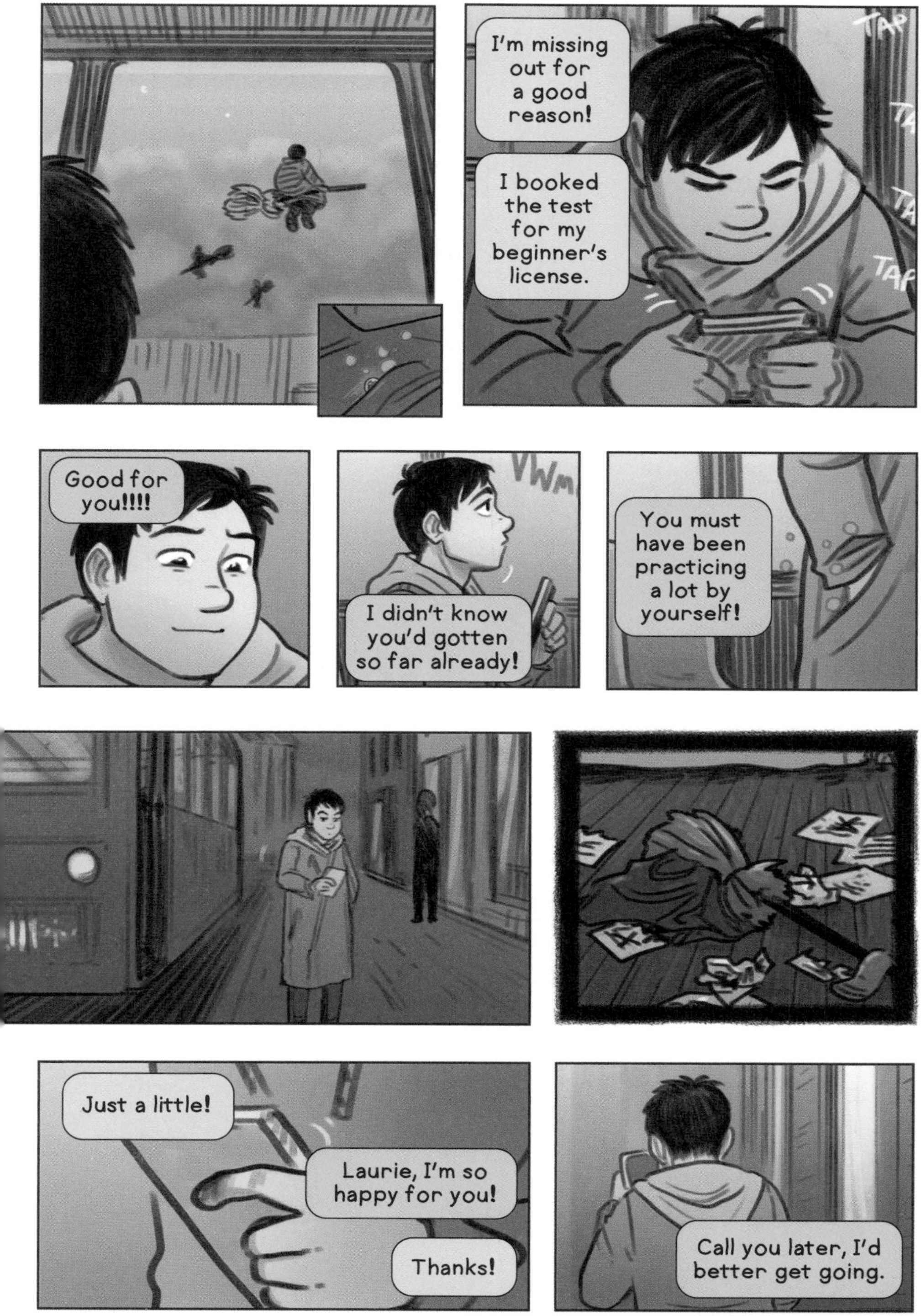

I'm missing out for a good reason!
I booked the test for my beginner's license.
TAP TAP TAP TAP
Good for you!!!!
VWm
I didn't know you'd gotten so far already!
You must have been practicing a lot by yourself!
Just a little!
Laurie, I'm so happy for you!
Thanks!
Call you later, I'd better get going.

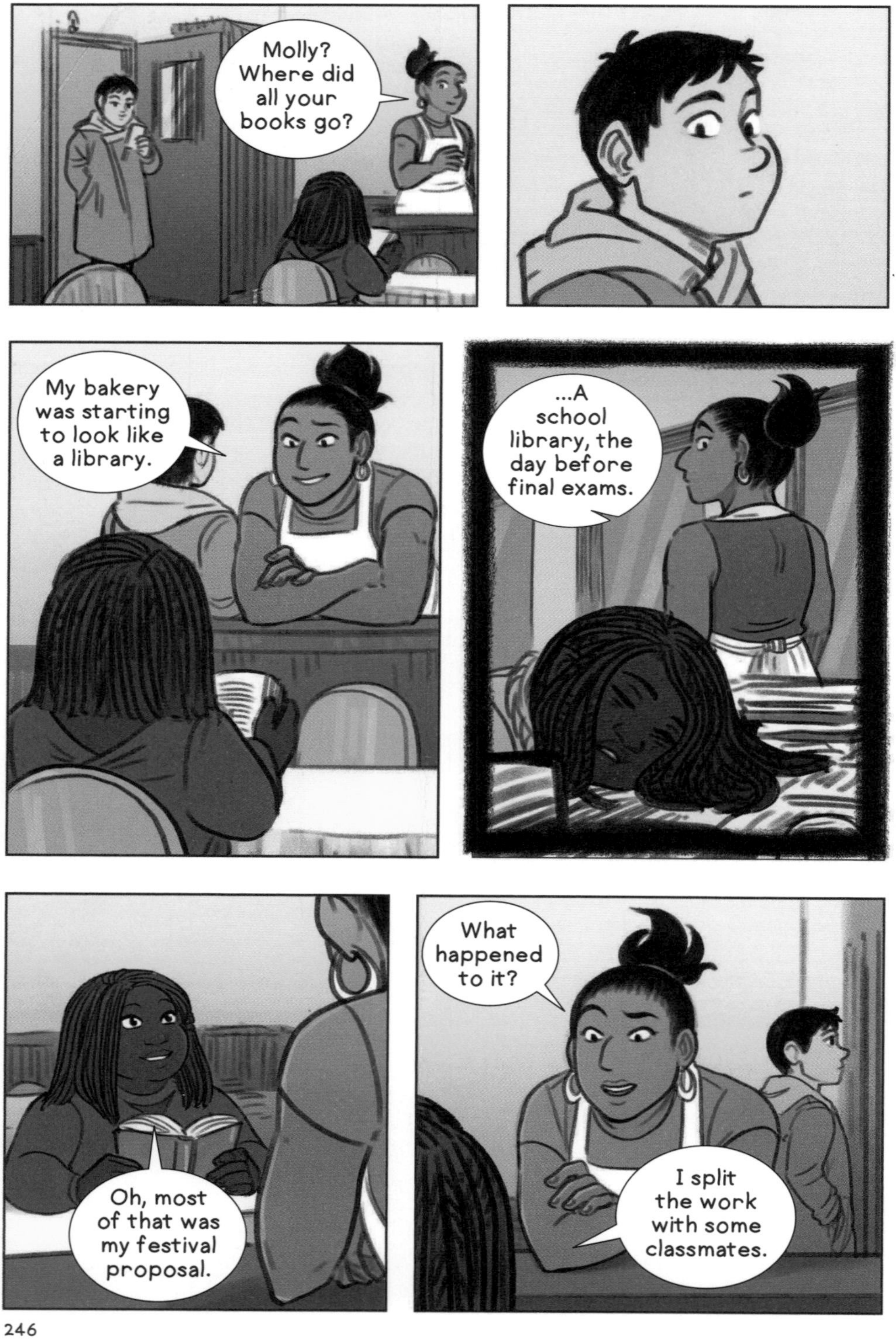
Molly? Where did all your books go?
My bakery was starting to look like a library.
...A school library, the day before final exams.
Oh, most of that was my festival proposal.
What happened to it?
I split the work with some classmates.

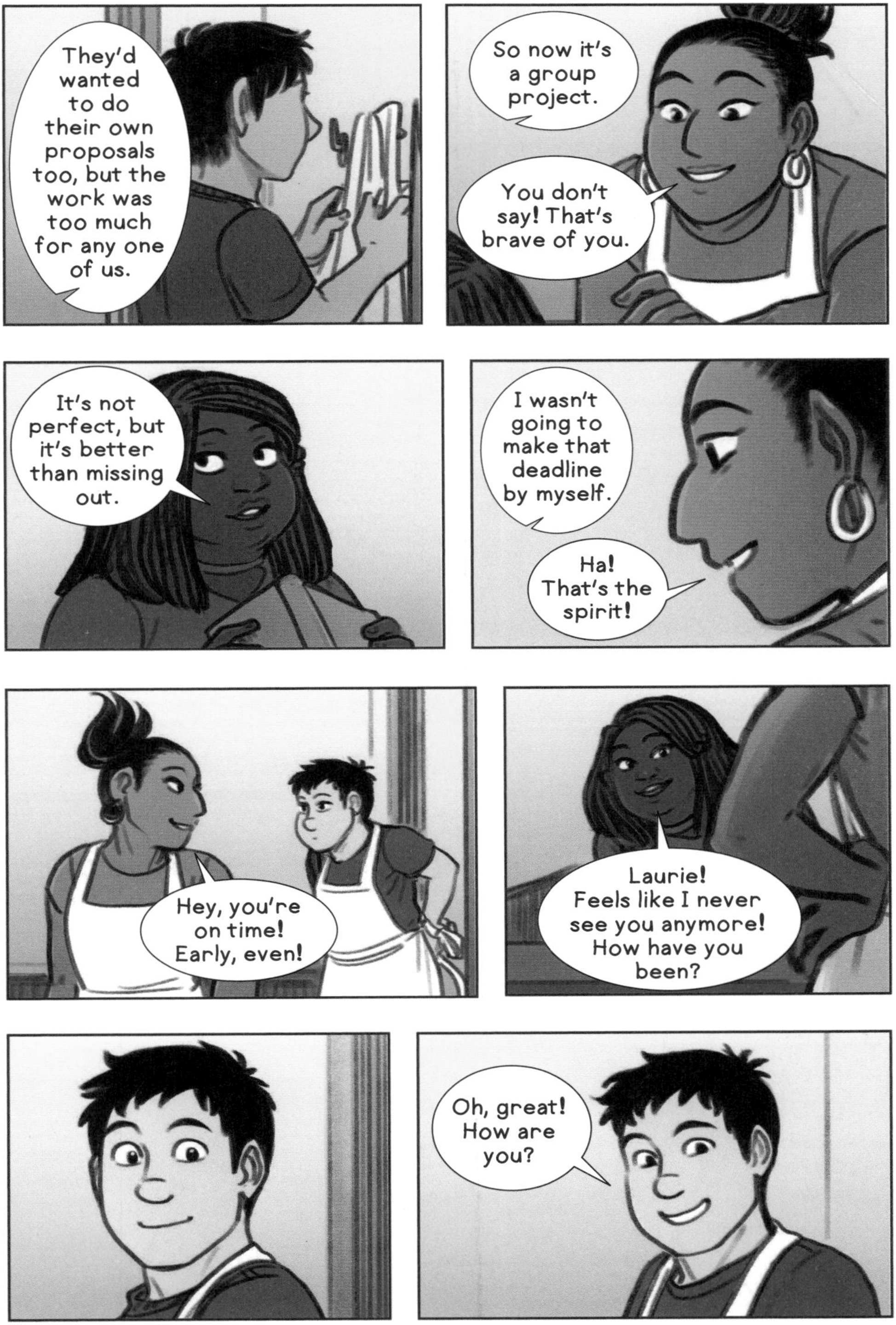
They'd wanted to do their own proposals too, but the work was too much for any one of us.
So now it's a group project.
You don't say! That's brave of you.
It's not perfect, but it's better than missing out.
I wasn't going to make that deadline by myself.
Ha! That's the spirit!
Hey, you're on time! Early, even!
Laurie! Feels like I never see you anymore! How have you been?
Oh, great! How are you?

CHAPTER 11

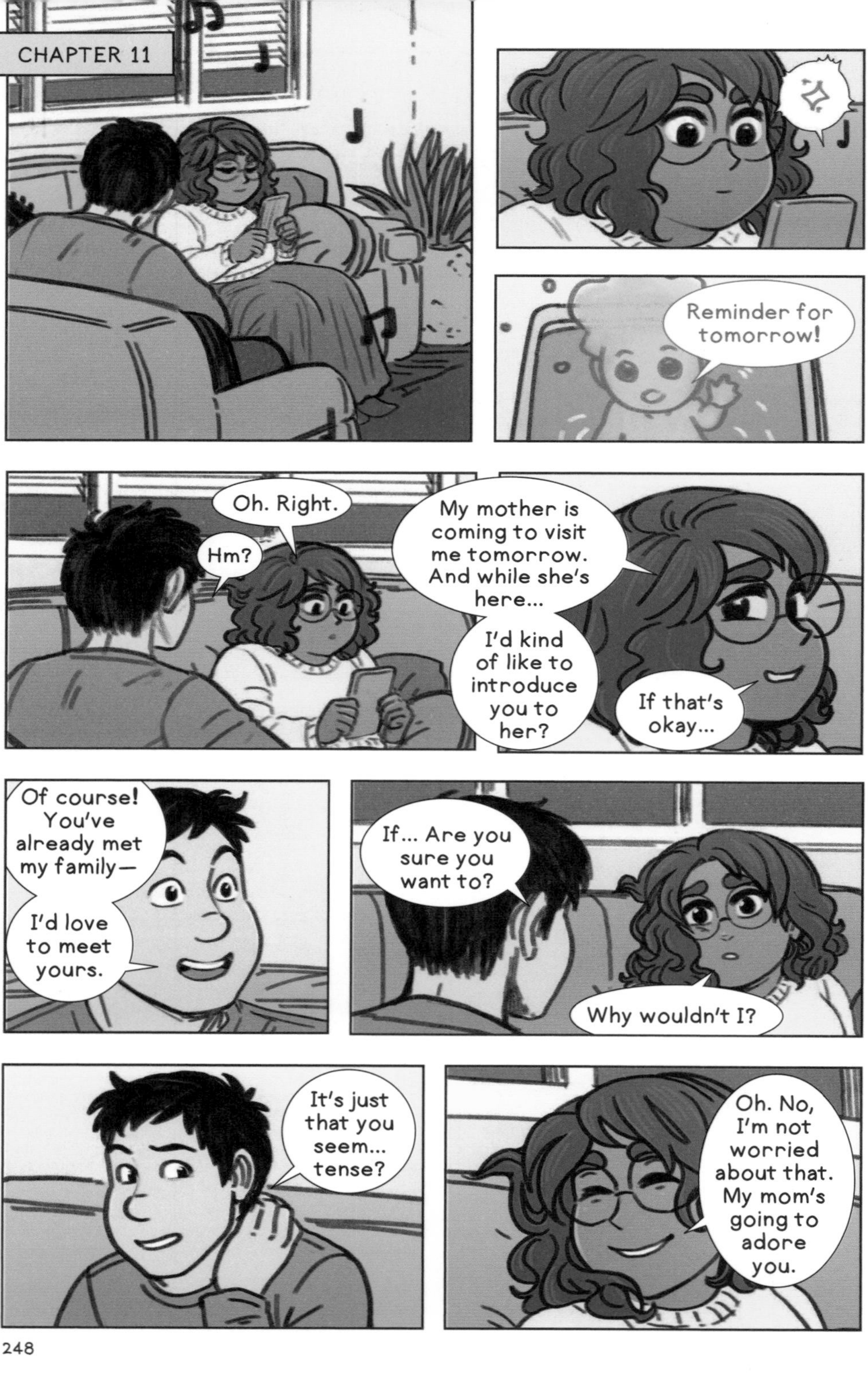
Reminder for tomorrow!
Hm?
Oh. Right.
My mother is coming to visit me tomorrow. And while she's here...
I'd kind of like to introduce you to her?
If that's okay...
Of course! You've already met my family—
I'd love to meet yours.
If... Are you sure you want to?
Why wouldn't I?
It's just that you seem... tense?
Oh. No, I'm not worried about that. My mom's going to adore you.

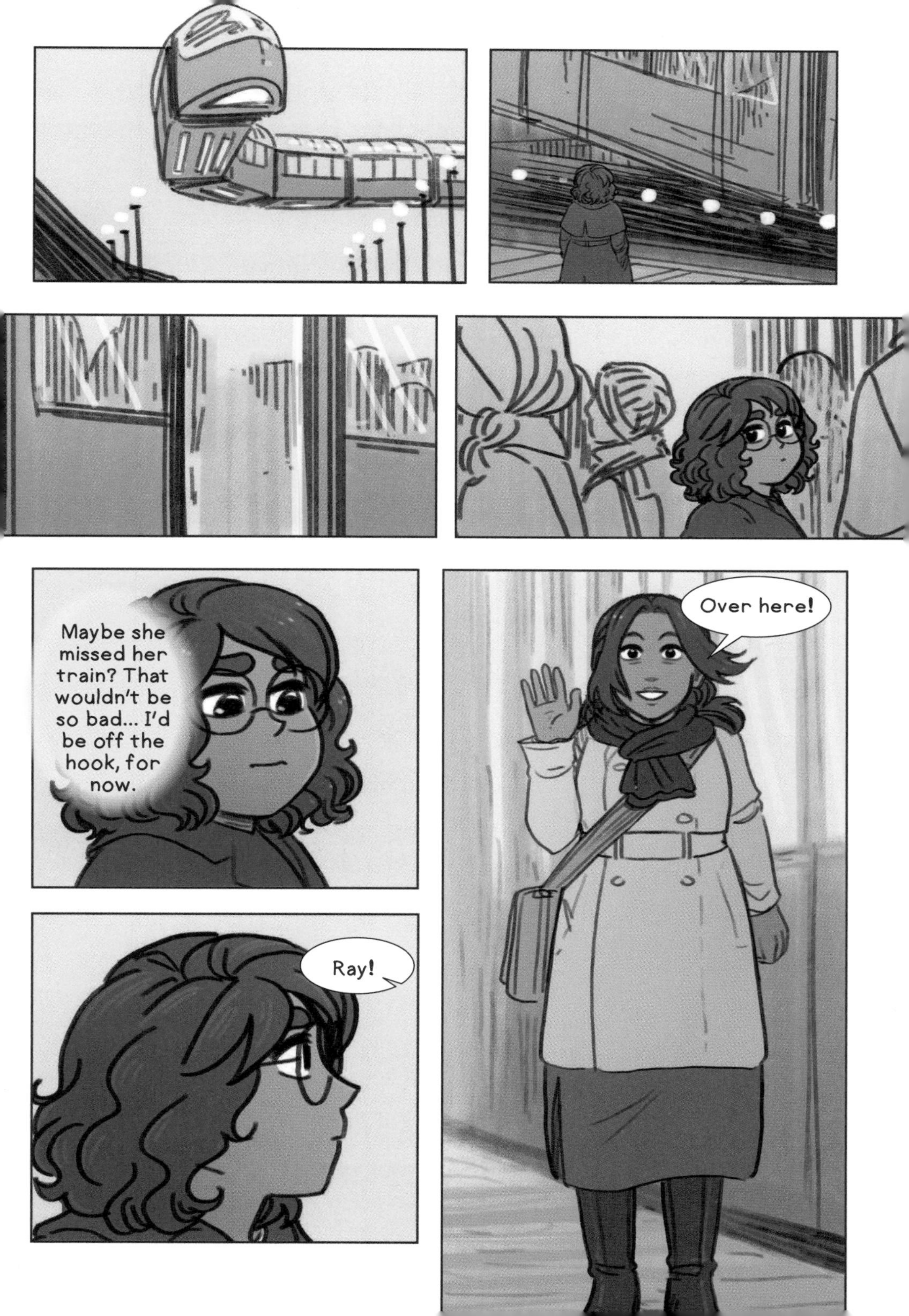
Maybe she missed her train? That wouldn't be so bad... I'd be off the hook, for now.
Over here!
Ray!

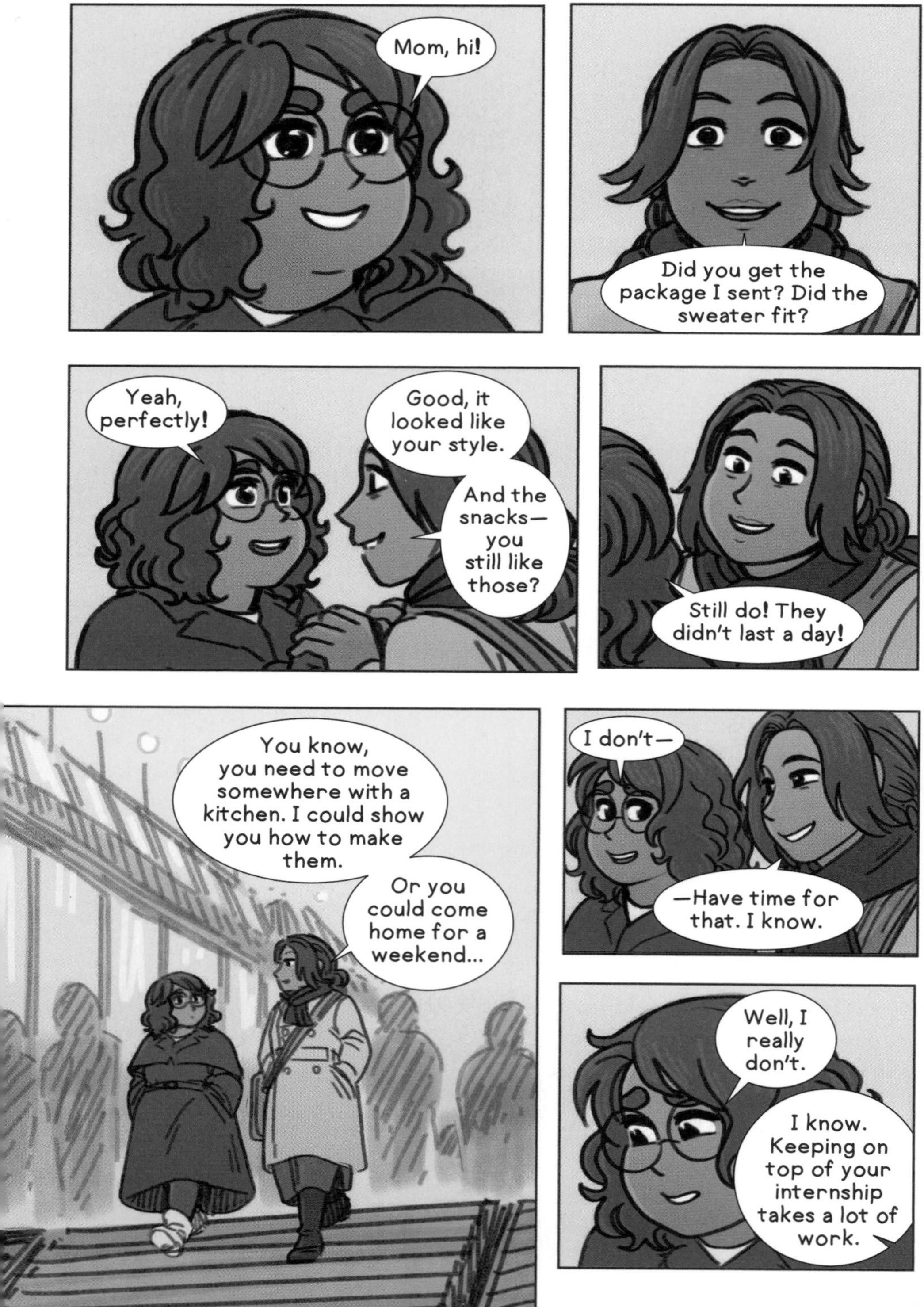

Mom, hi!
Did you get the package I sent? Did the sweater fit?
Yeah, perfectly!
Good, it looked like your style.
And the snacks— you still like those?
Still do! They didn't last a day!
You know, you need to move somewhere with a kitchen. I could show you how to make them.
Or you could come home for a weekend...
I don't—
—Have time for that. I know.
Well, I really don't.
I know. Keeping on top of your internship takes a lot of work.

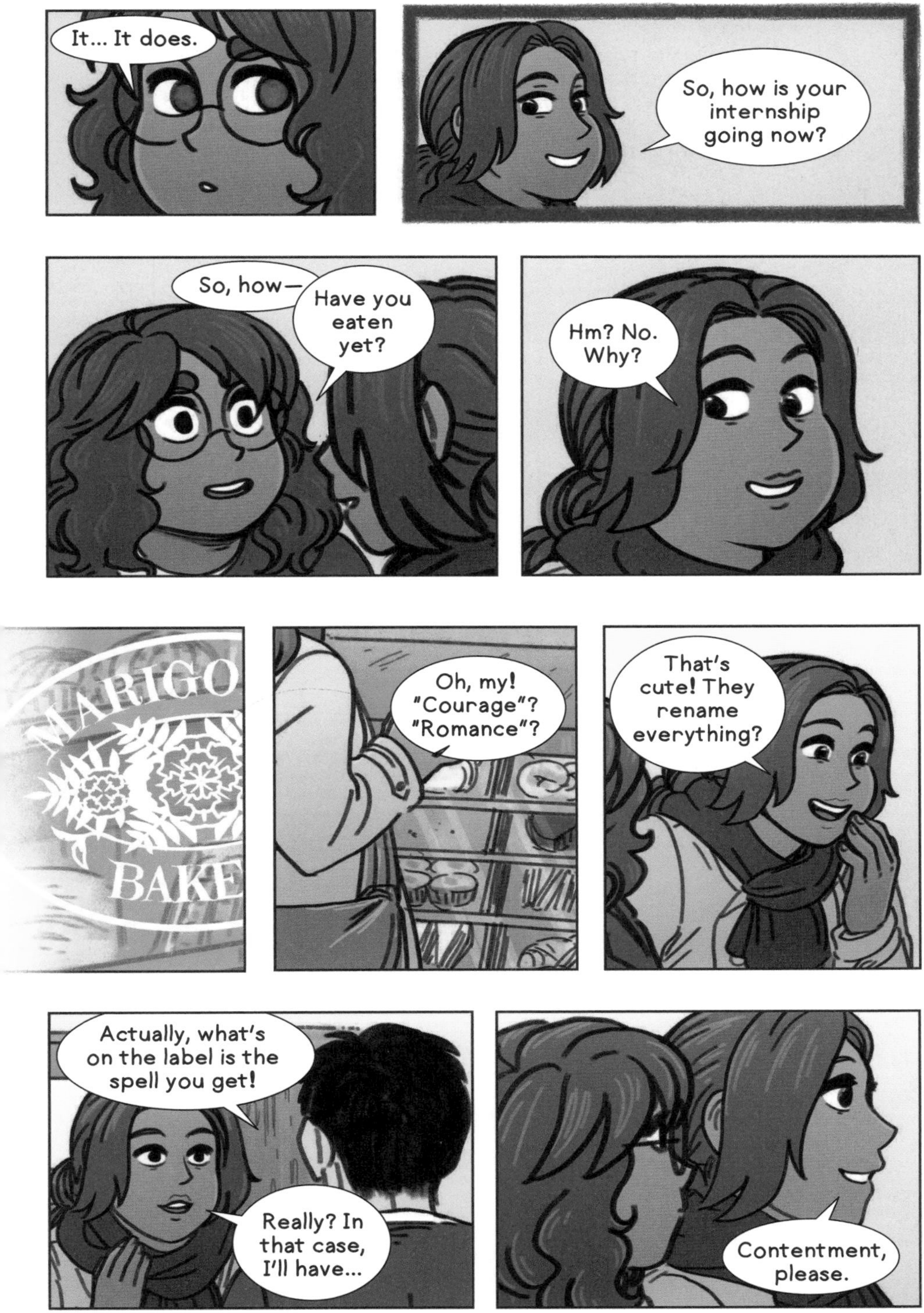
It... It does.
So, how is your internship going now?
So, how—
Have you eaten yet?
Hm? No. Why?
MARIGO
BAKE
Oh, my! "Courage"? "Romance"?
That's cute! They rename everything?
Actually, what's on the label is the spell you get!
Really? In that case, I'll have...
Contentment, please.

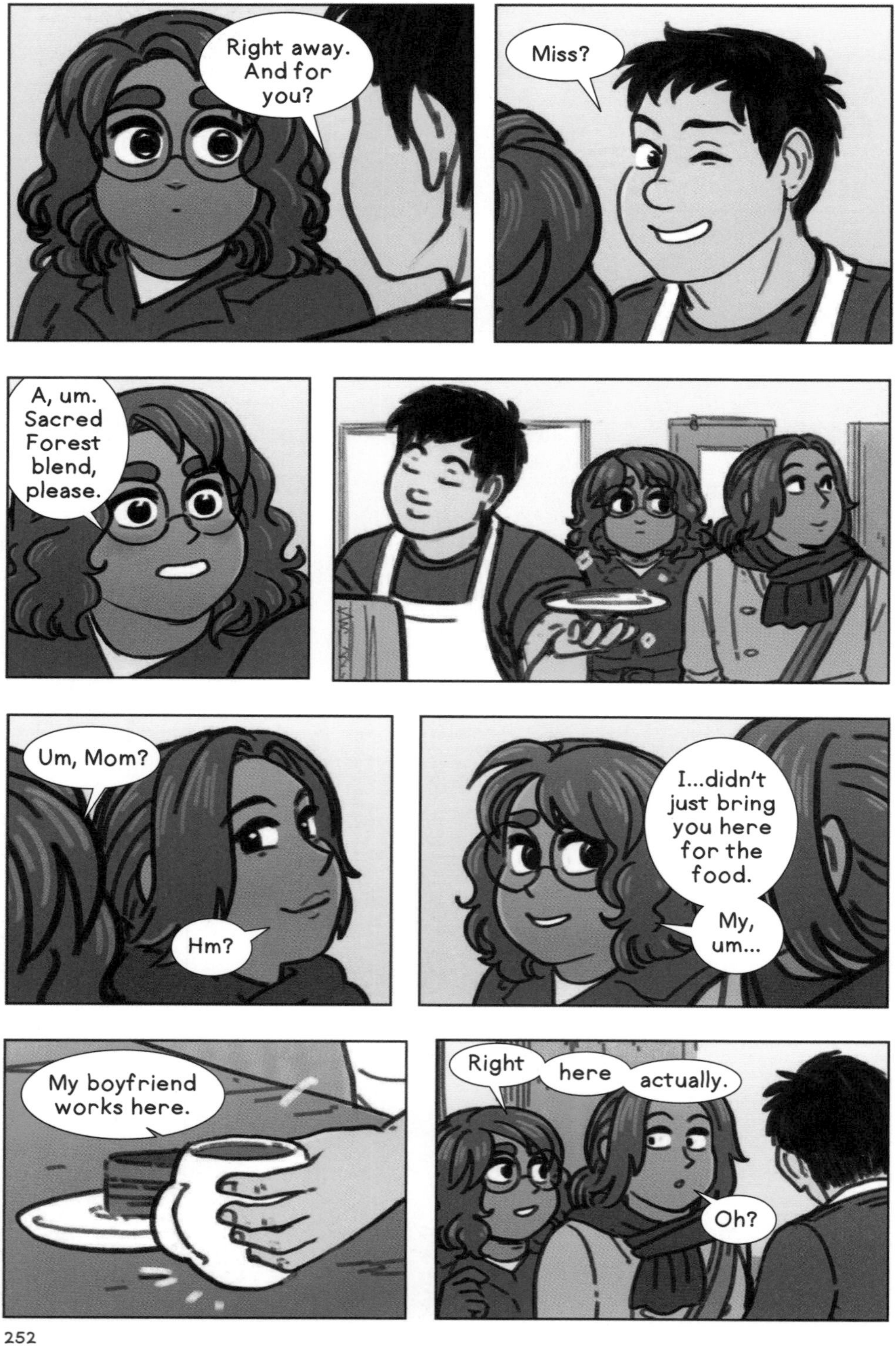

Right away. And for you?
Miss?
A, um. Sacred Forest blend, please.
Um, Mom?
Hm?
I...didn't just bring you here for the food.
My, um...
My boyfriend works here.
Right
here
actually.
Oh?

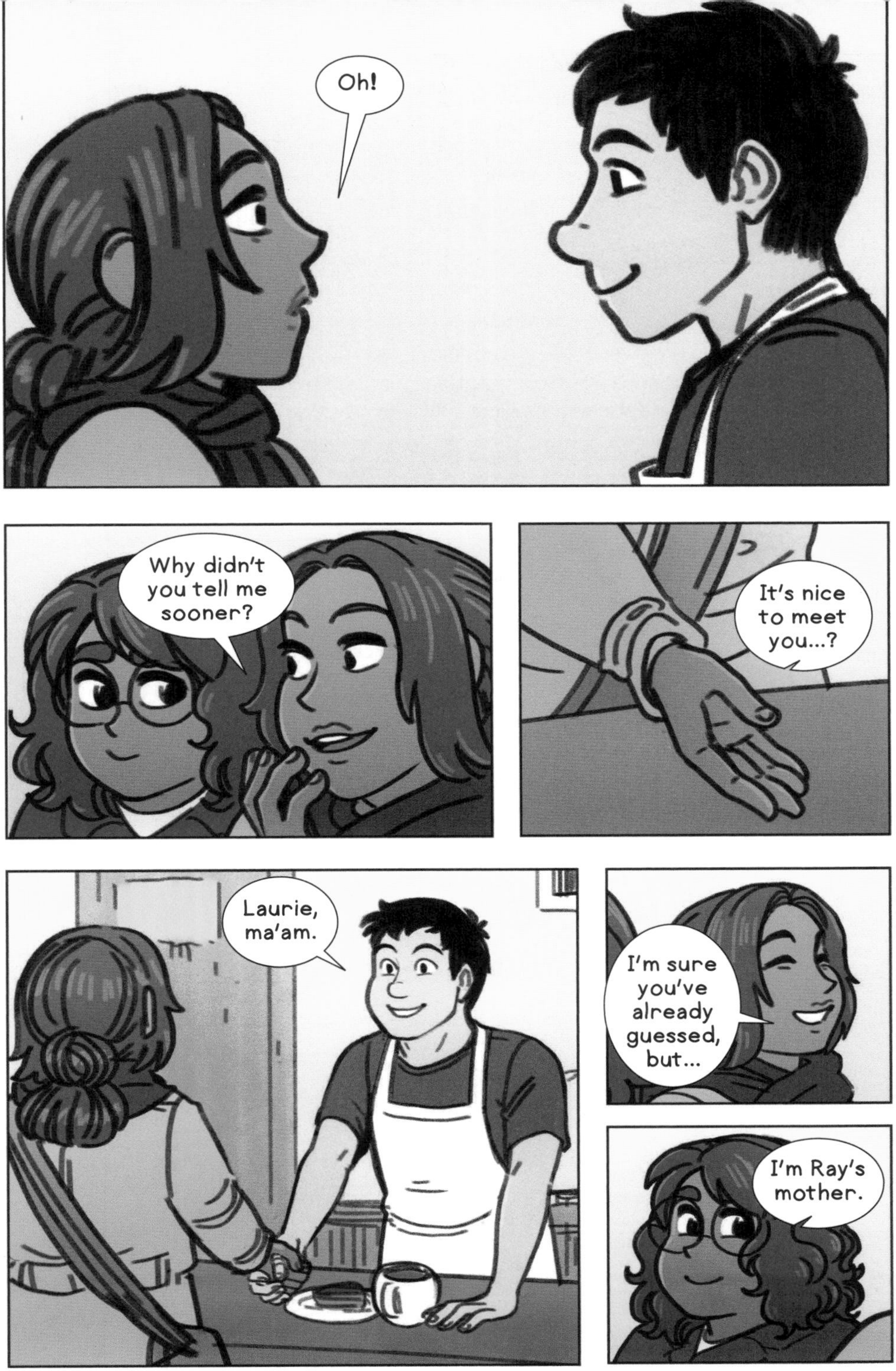
Oh!
Why didn't you tell me sooner?
It's nice to meet you...?
Laurie, ma'am.
I'm sure you've already guessed, but...
I'm Ray's mother.

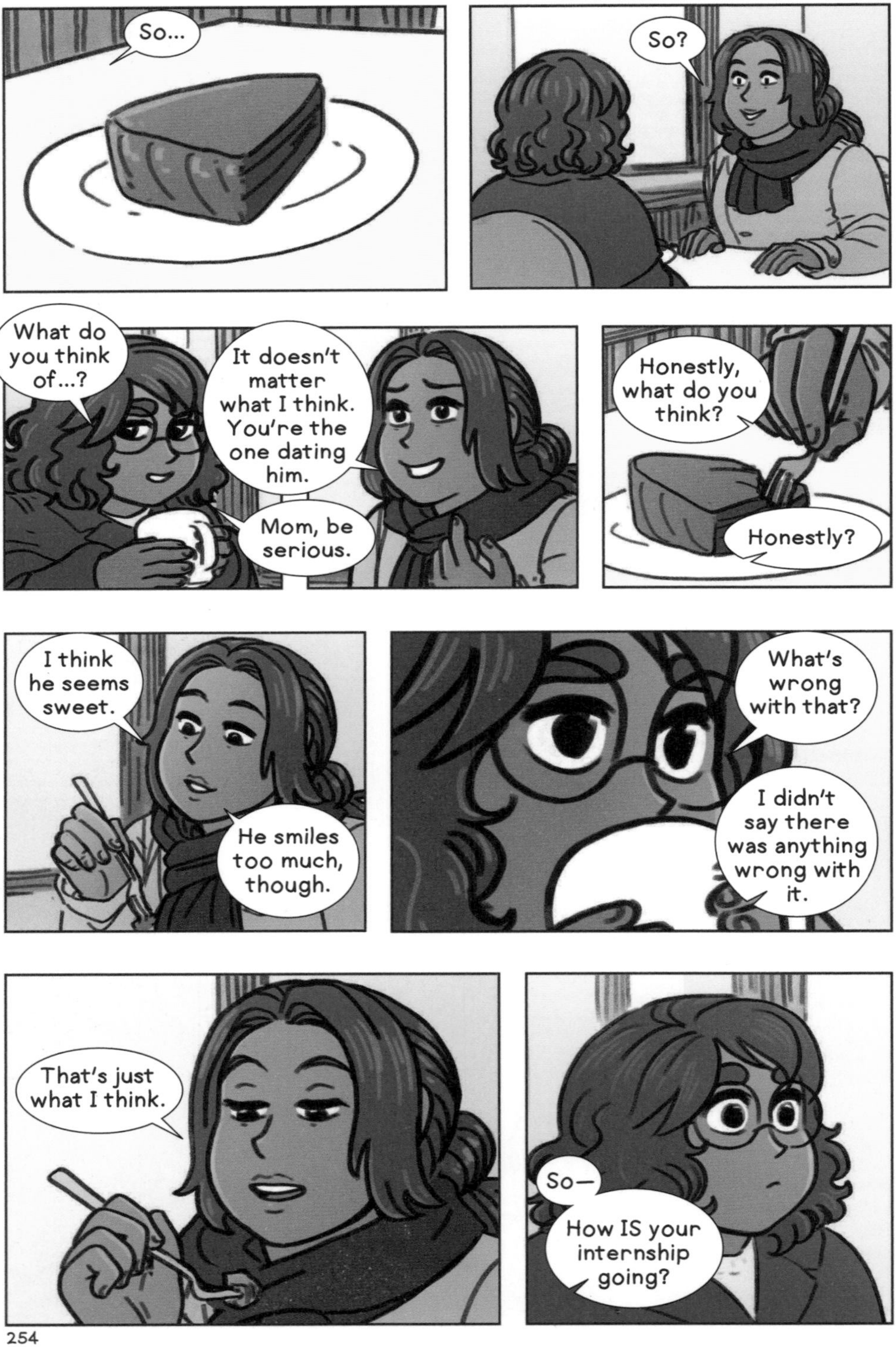
So...
So?
What do you think of...?
It doesn't matter what I think. You're the one dating him.
Mom, be serious.
Honestly, what do you think?
Honestly?
I think he seems sweet.
He smiles too much, though.
What's wrong with that?
I didn't say there was anything wrong with it.
That's just what I think.
So—
How IS your internship going?

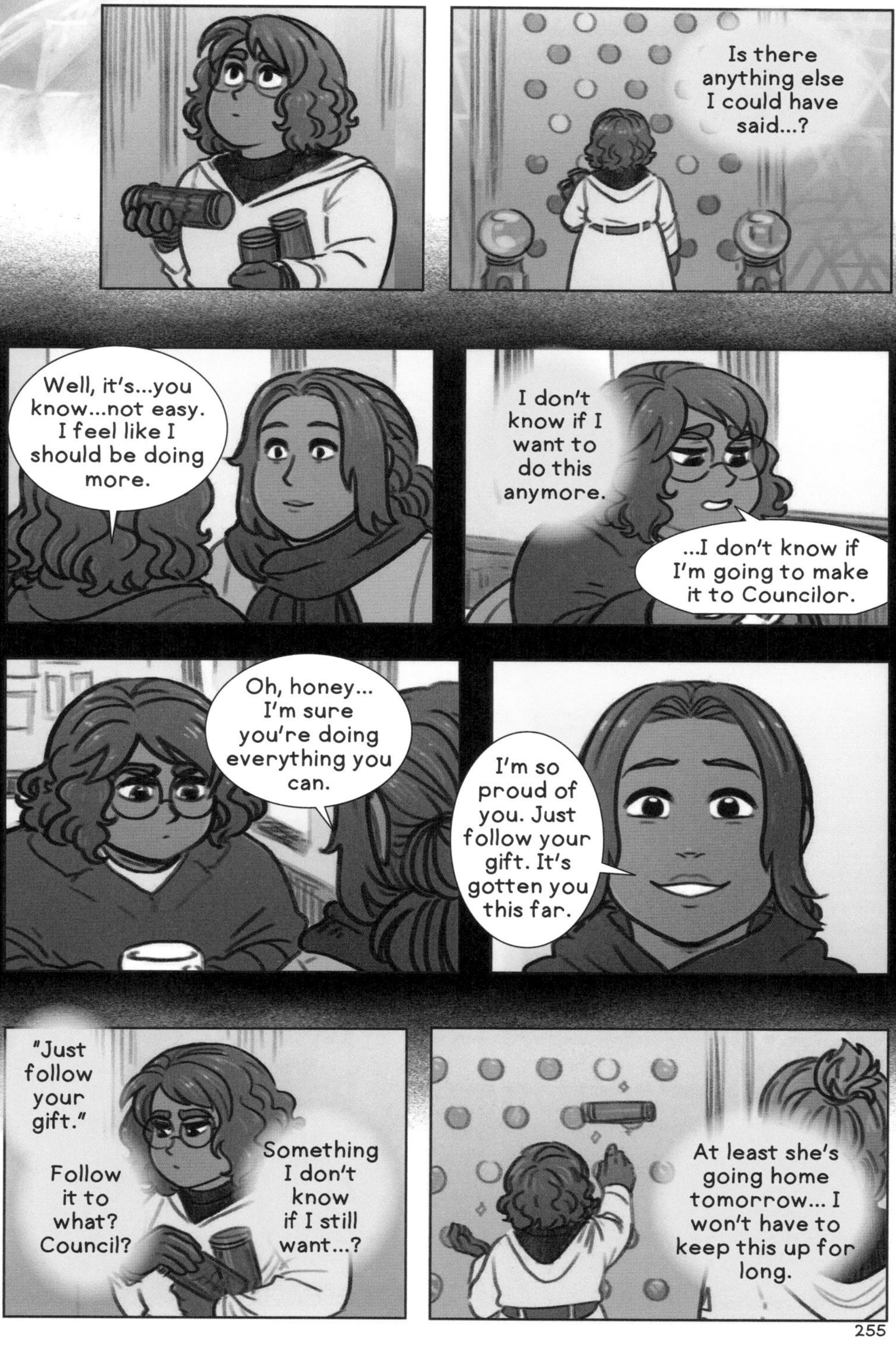
Is there anything else I could have said...?
Well, it's...you know...not easy. I feel like I should be doing more.
I don't know if I want to do this anymore.
...I don't know if I'm going to make it to Councilor.
Oh, honey... I'm sure you're doing everything you can.
I'm so proud of you. Just follow your gift. It's gotten you this far.
"Just follow your gift."
Follow it to what? Council?
Something I don't know if I still want...?
At least she's going home tomorrow... I won't have to keep this up for long.

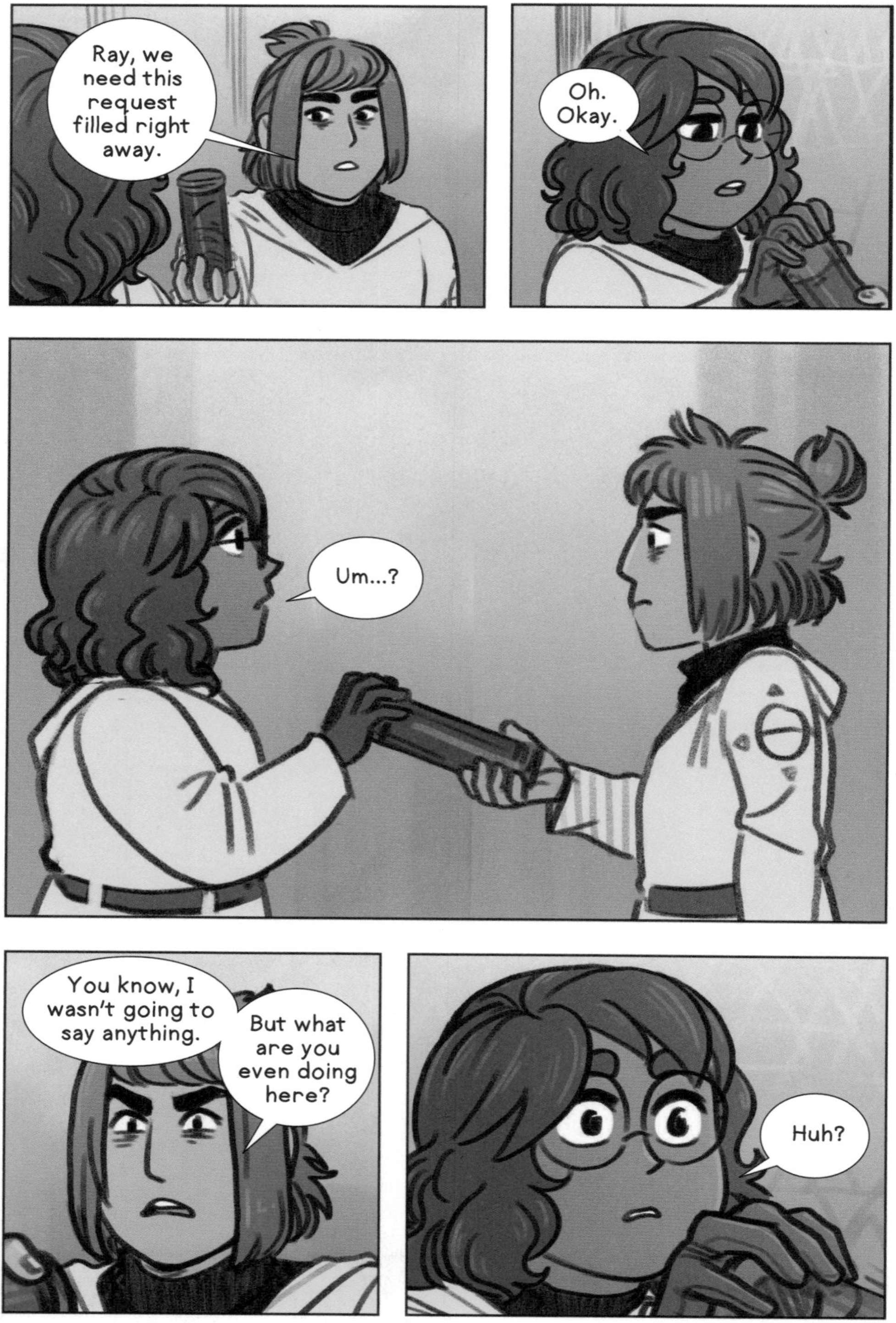
Ray, we need this request filled right away.
Oh. Okay.
Um...?
You know, I wasn't going to say anything.
But what are you even doing here?
Huh?

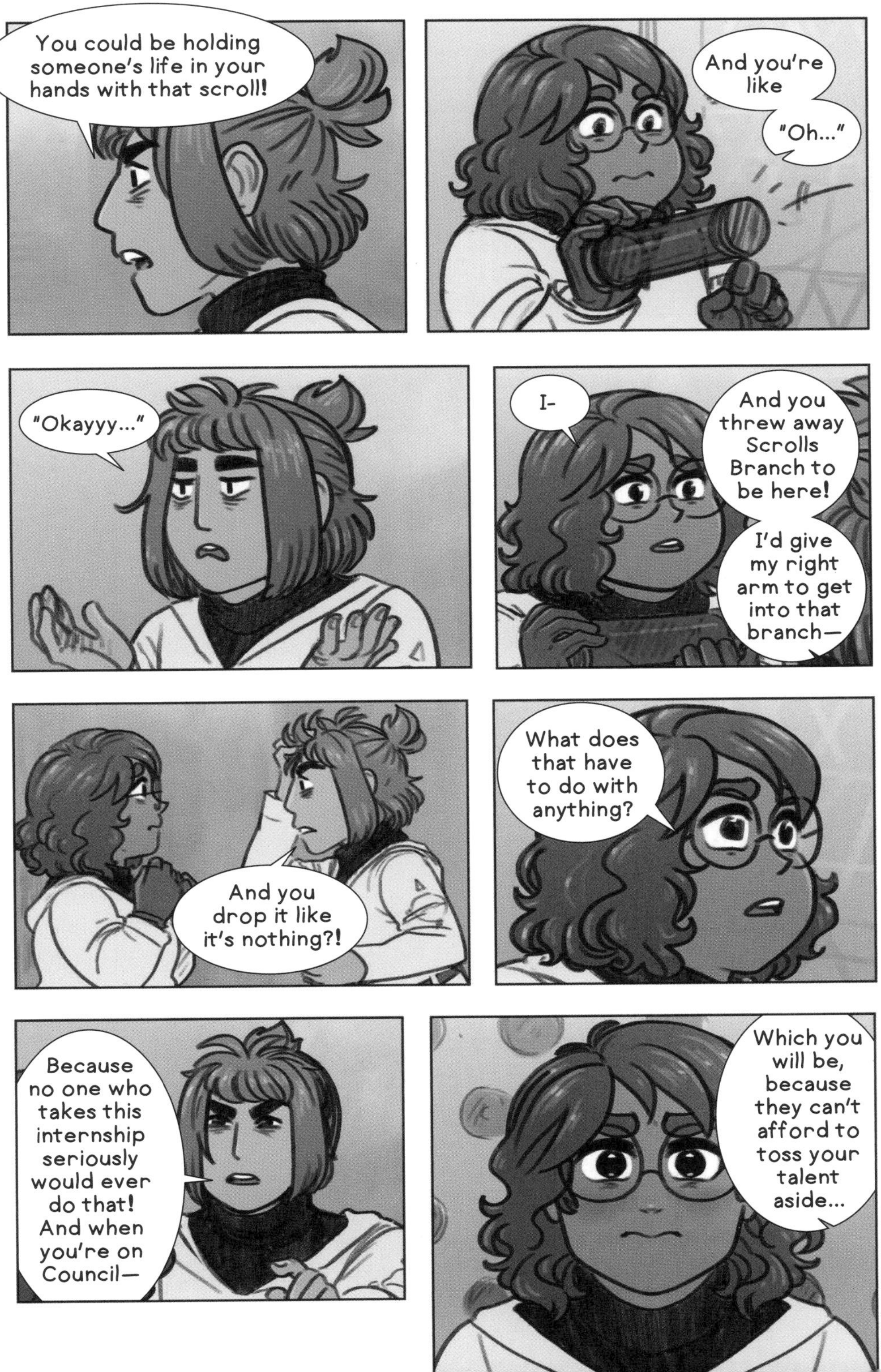
You could be holding someone's life in your hands with that scroll!
And you're like
"Oh..."
"Okayyy..."
I-
And you threw away Scrolls Branch to be here!
I'd give my right arm to get into that branch—
And you drop it like it's nothing?!
What does that have to do with anything?
Because no one who takes this internship seriously would ever do that! And when you're on Council—
Which you will be, because they can't afford to toss your talent aside...

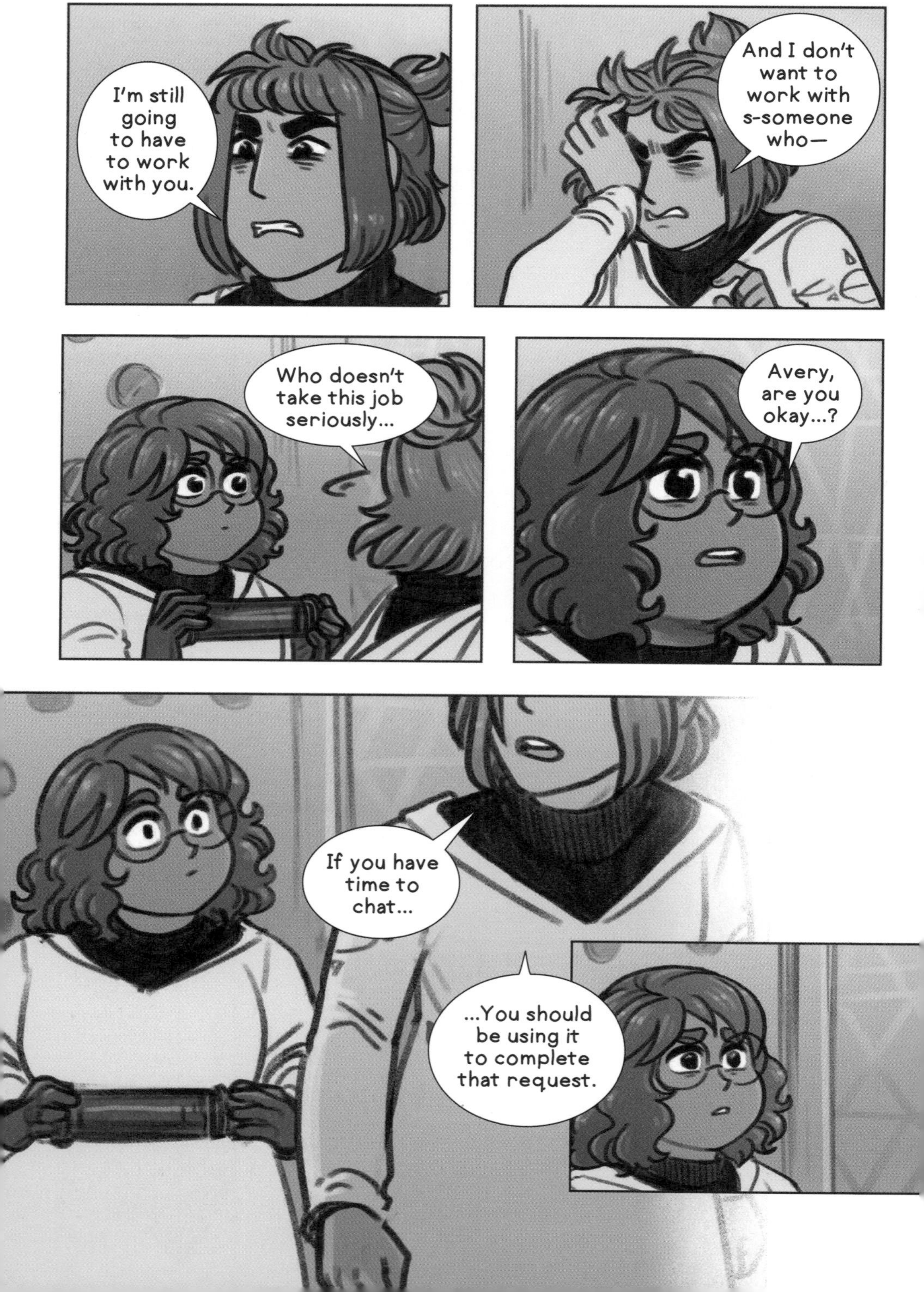
I'm still going to have to work with you.
And I don't want to work with s-someone who—
Who doesn't take this job seriously...
Avery, are you okay...?
If you have time to chat...
...You should be using it to complete that request.

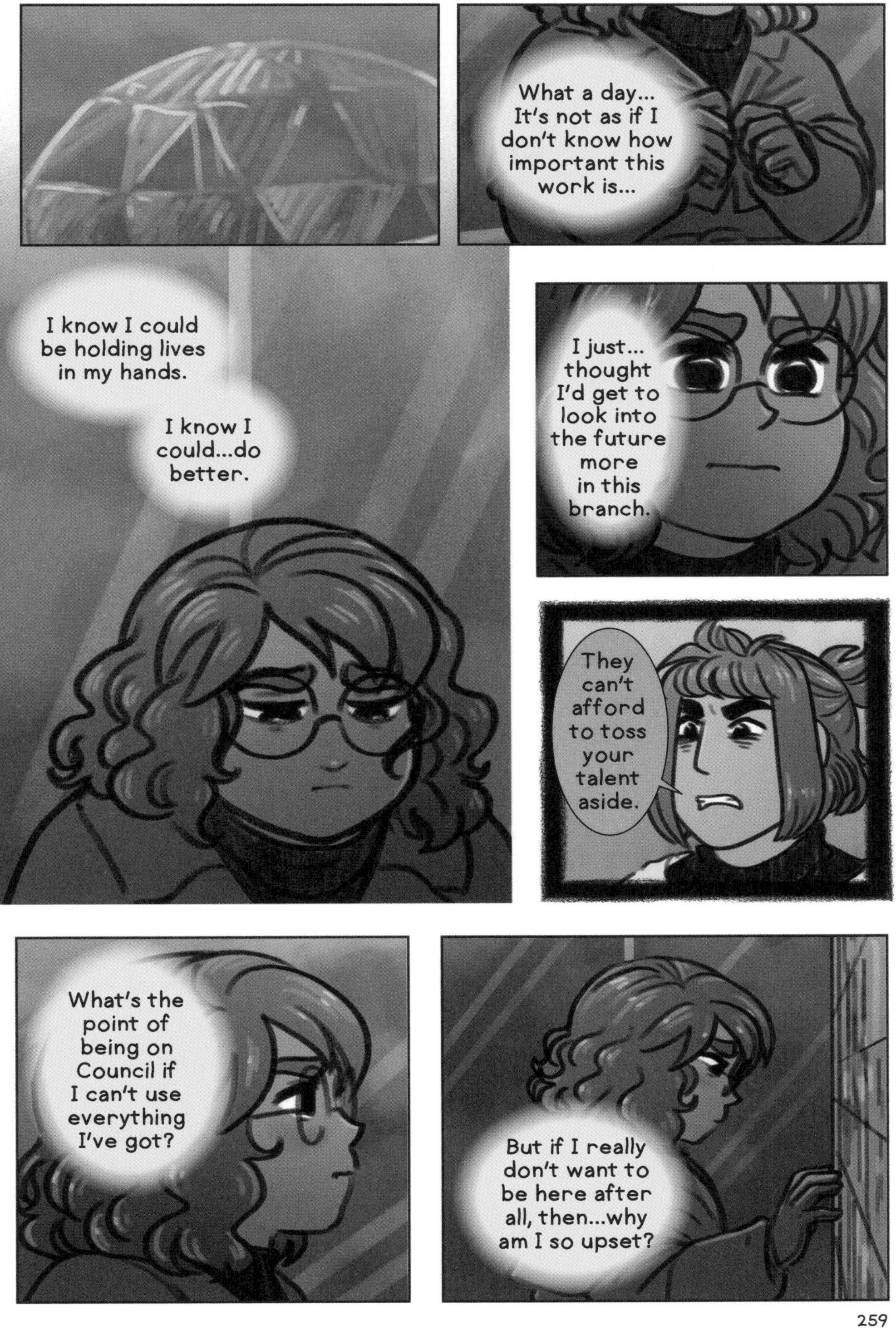
What a day... It's not as if I don't know how important this work is...
I know I could be holding lives in my hands.
I know I could...do better.
I just... thought I'd get to look into the future more in this branch.
They can't afford to toss your talent aside.
What's the point of being on Council if I can't use everything I've got?
But if I really don't want to be here after all, then...why am I so upset?

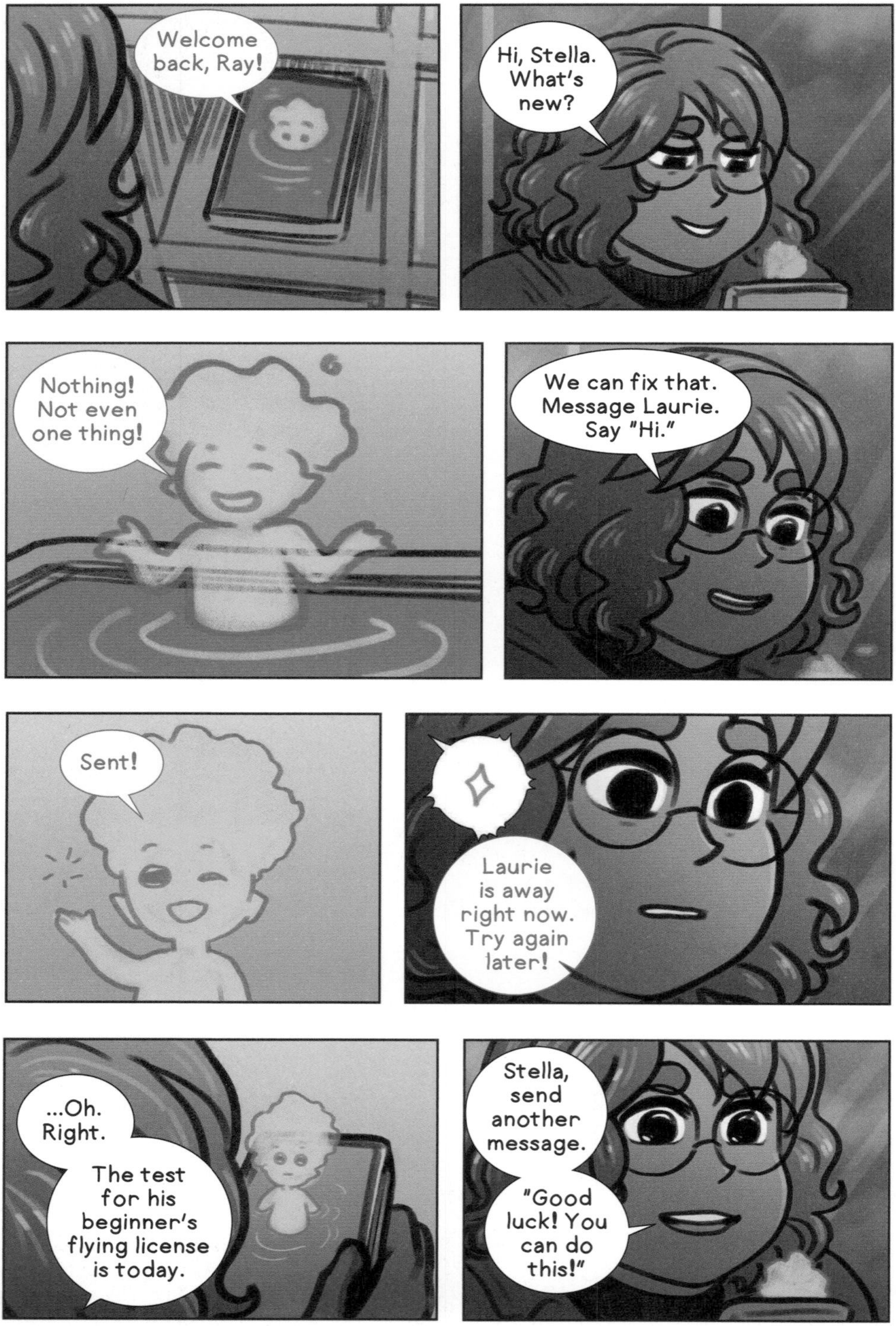
Welcome back, Ray!
Hi, Stella. What's new?
Nothing! Not even one thing!
We can fix that. Message Laurie. Say "Hi."
Sent!
Laurie is away right now. Try again later!
...Oh. Right.
The test for his beginner's flying license is today.
Stella, send another message.
"Good luck! You can do this!"

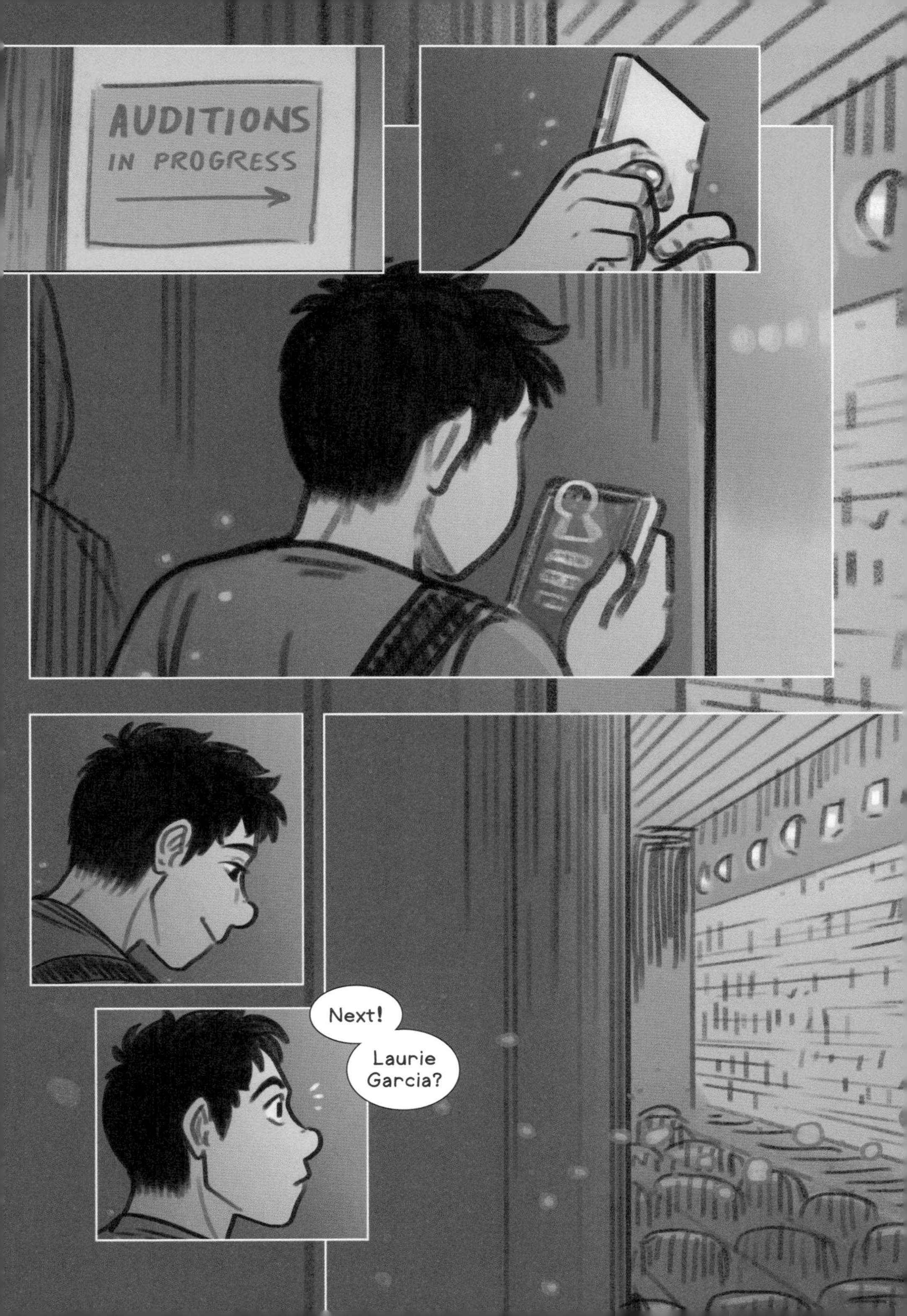
AUDITIONS
IN PROGRESS
Next!
Laurie
Garcia?

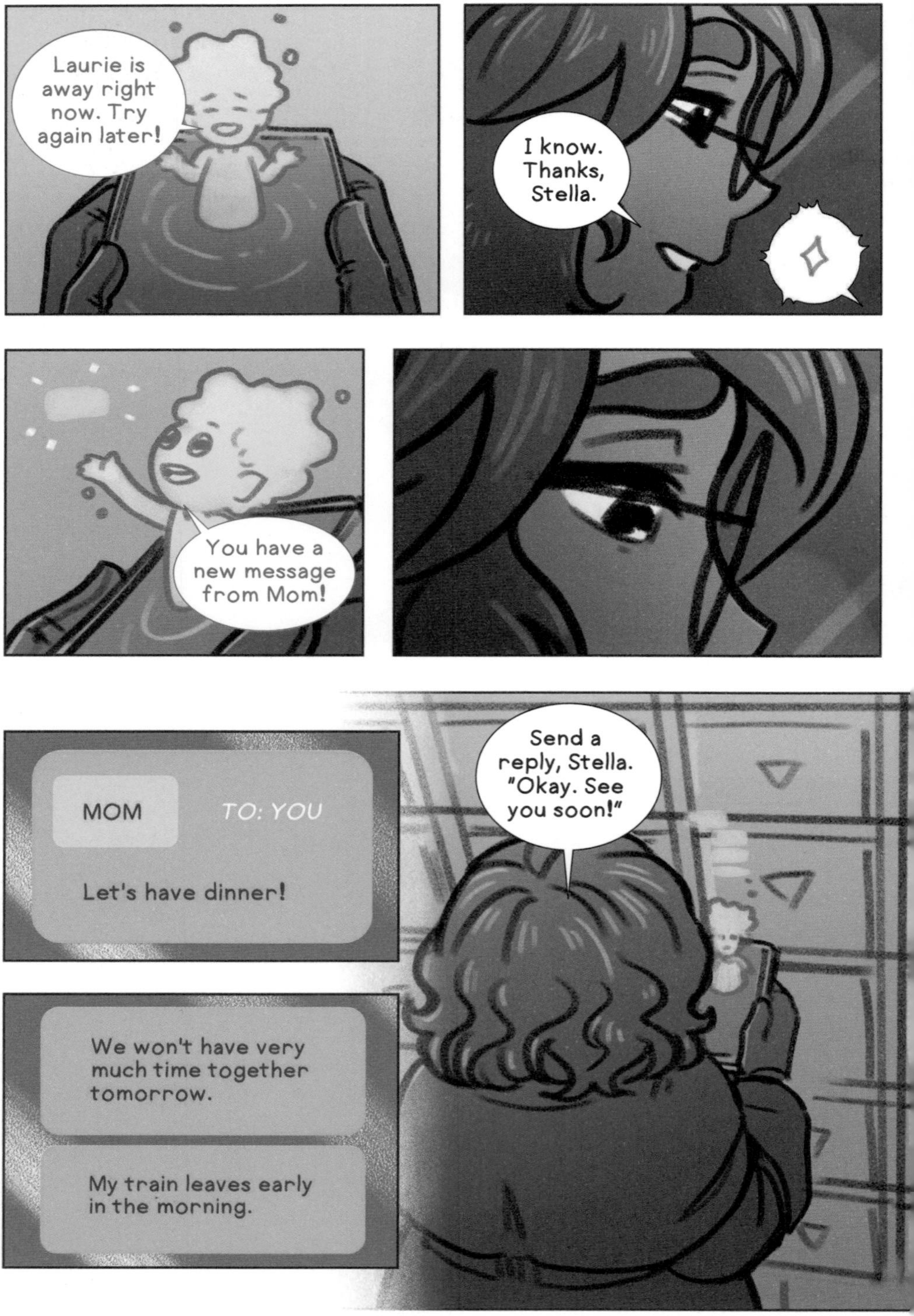
Laurie is away right now. Try again later!
I know. Thanks, Stella.
You have a new message from Mom!
MOM
TO: YOU
Let's have dinner!
Send a reply, Stella. "Okay. See you soon!"
We won't have very much time together tomorrow.
My train leaves early in the morning.

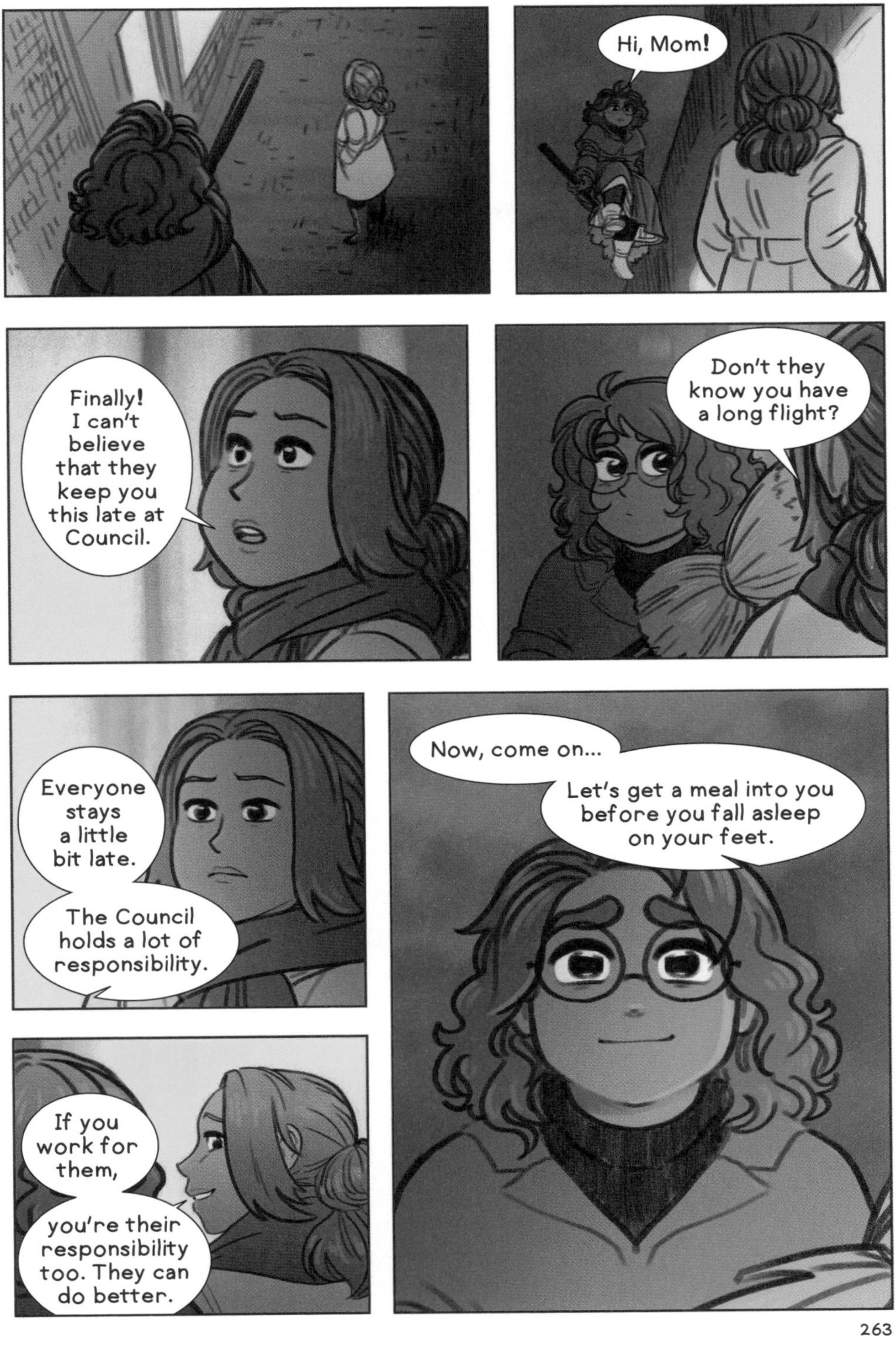
Hi, Mom!
Finally! I can't believe that they keep you this late at Council.
Don't they know you have a long flight?
Everyone stays a little bit late.
The Council holds a lot of responsibility.
If you work for them,
you're their responsibility too. They can do better.
Now, come on...
Let's get a meal into you before you fall asleep on your feet.

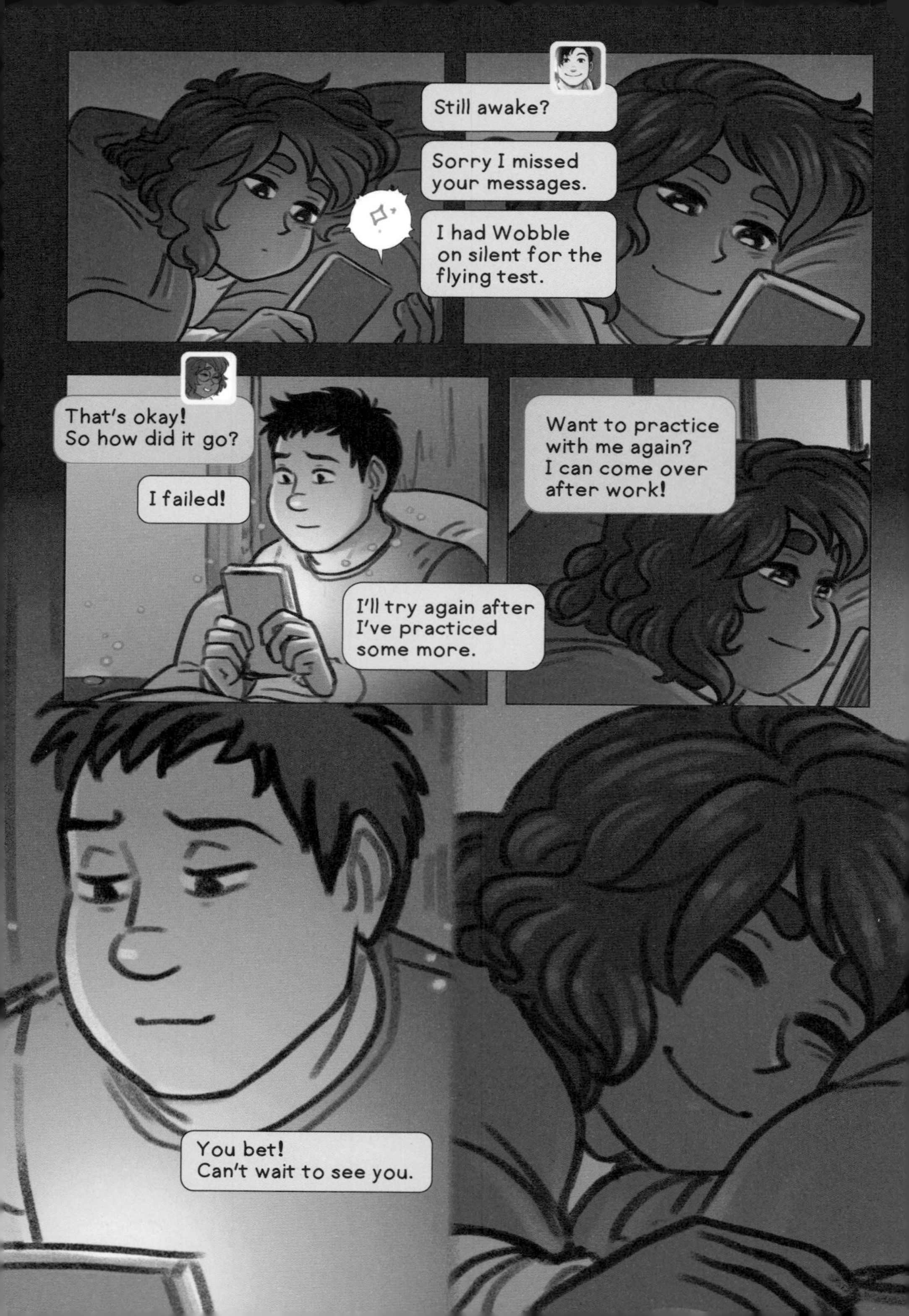
Still awake?
Sorry I missed your messages.
I had Wobble on silent for the flying test.
That's okay! So how did it go?
I failed!
I'll try again after I've practiced some more.
Want to practice with me again? I can come over after work!
You bet! Can't wait to see you.

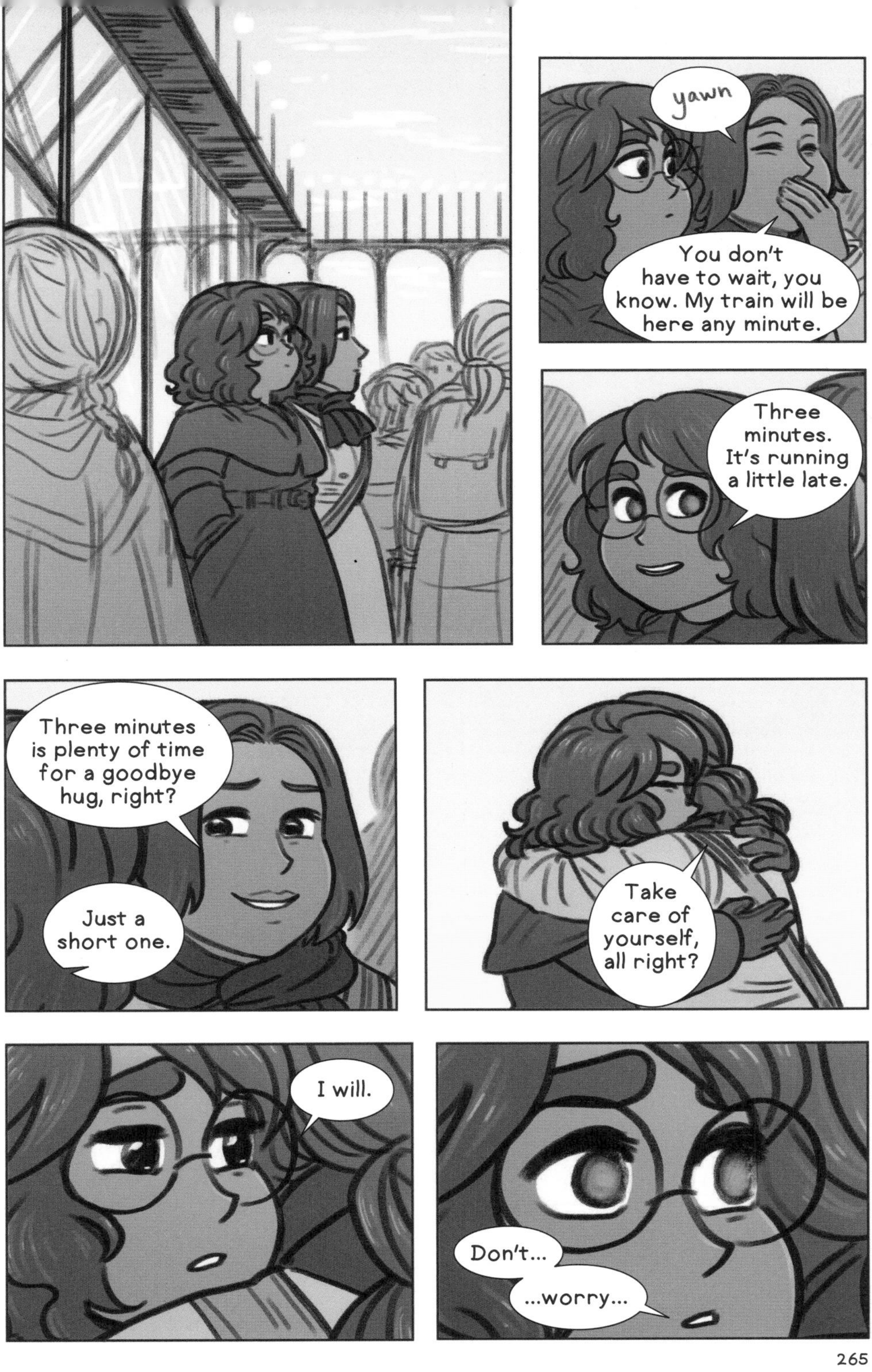
yawn
You don't have to wait, you know. My train will be here any minute.
Three minutes. It's running a little late.
Three minutes is plenty of time for a goodbye hug, right?
Just a short one.
Take care of yourself, all right?
I will.
Don't...
...worry...

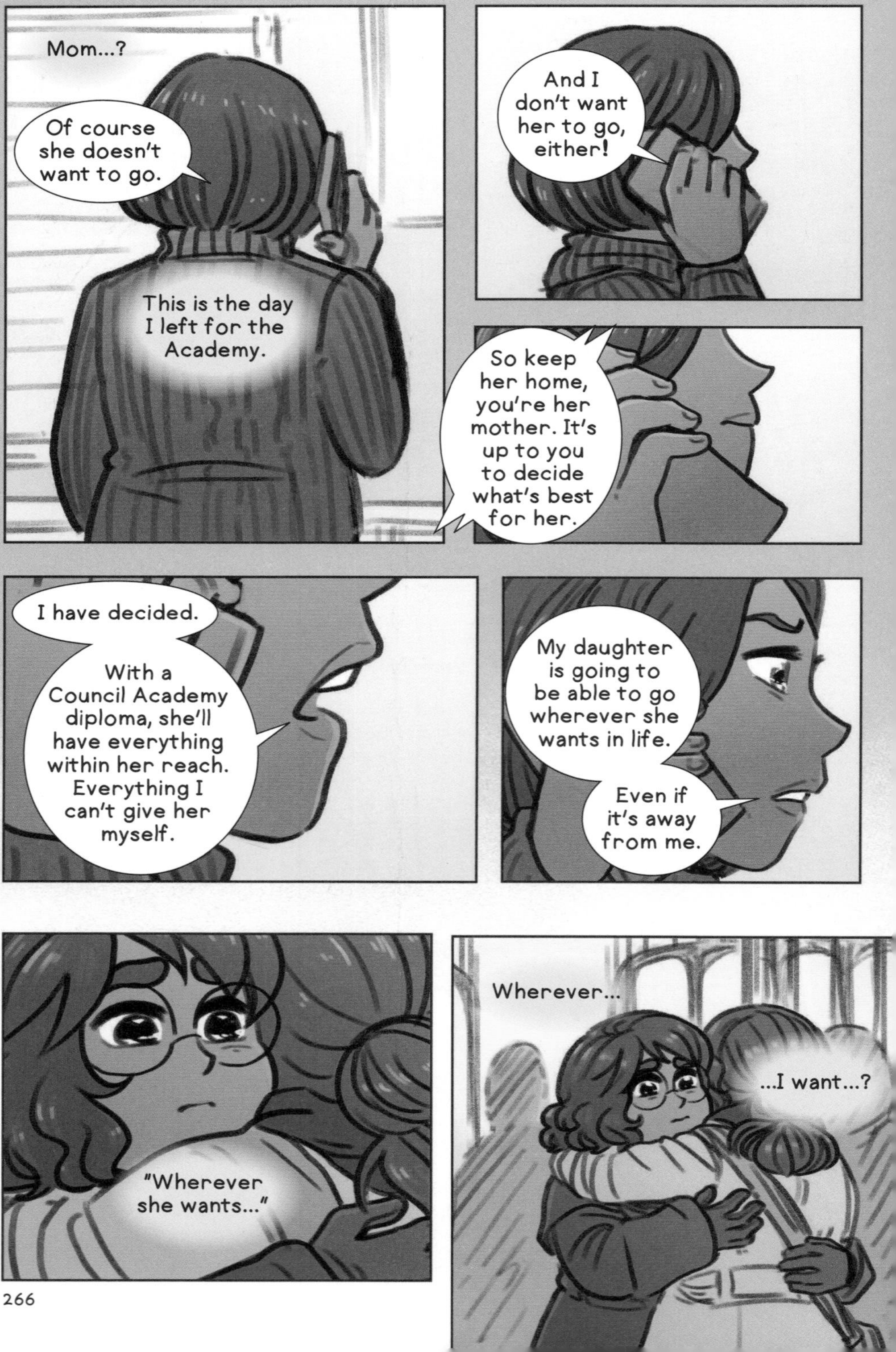
Mom...?
Of course she doesn't want to go.
This is the day I left for the Academy.
And I don't want her to go, either!
So keep her home, you're her mother. It's up to you to decide what's best for her.
I have decided.
With a Council Academy diploma, she'll have everything within her reach. Everything I can't give her myself.
My daughter is going to be able to go wherever she wants in life.
Even if it's away from me.
"Wherever she wants..."
Wherever...
...I want...?

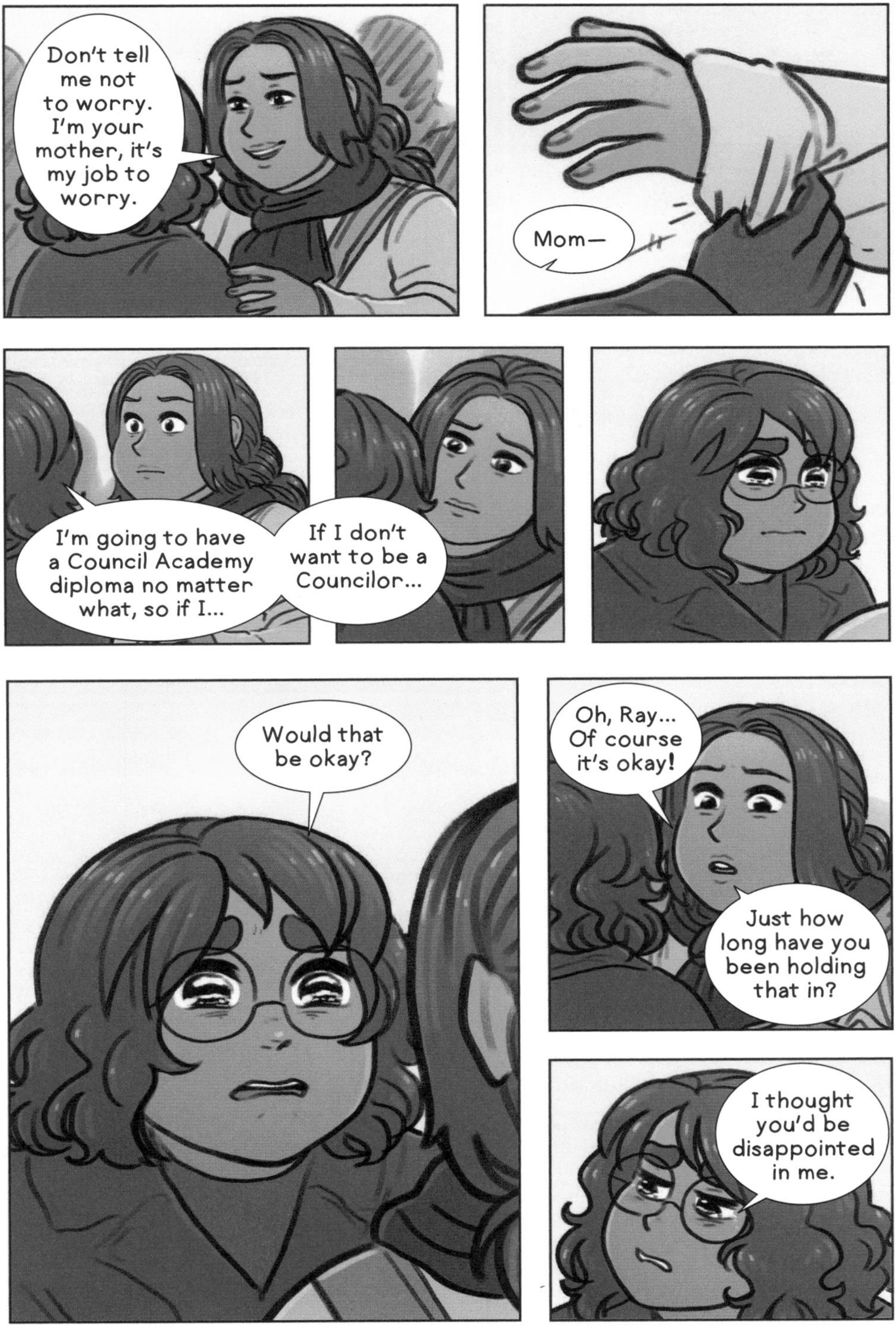
Don't tell me not to worry. I'm your mother, it's my job to worry.
Mom—
I'm going to have a Council Academy diploma no matter what, so if I...
If I don't want to be a Councilor...
Would that be okay?
Oh, Ray... Of course it's okay!
Just how long have you been holding that in?
I thought you'd be disappointed in me.

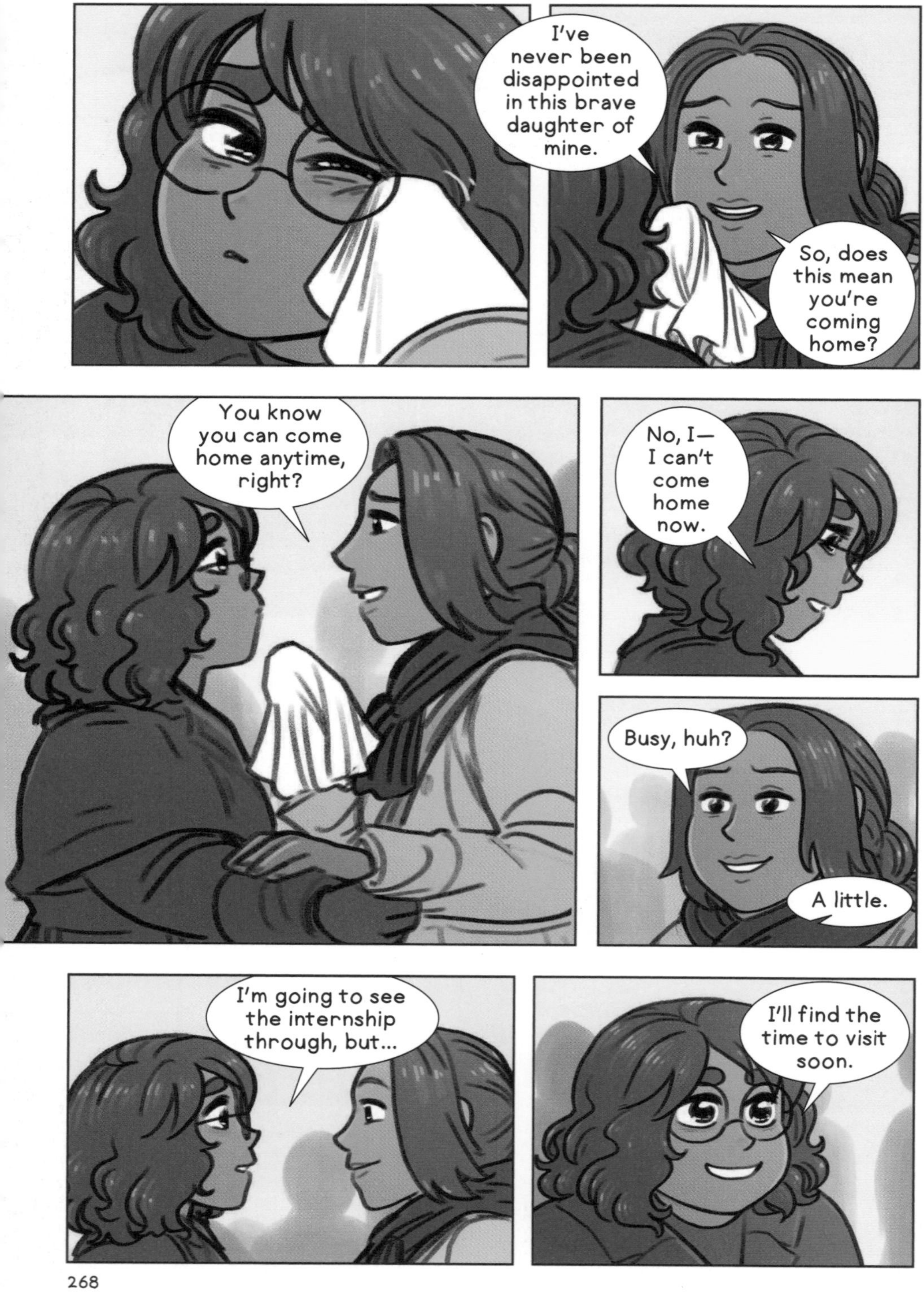
I've never been disappointed in this brave daughter of mine.
So, does this mean you're coming home?
You know you can come home anytime, right?
No, I— I can't come home now.
Busy, huh?
A little.
I'm going to see the internship through, but...
I'll find the time to visit soon.

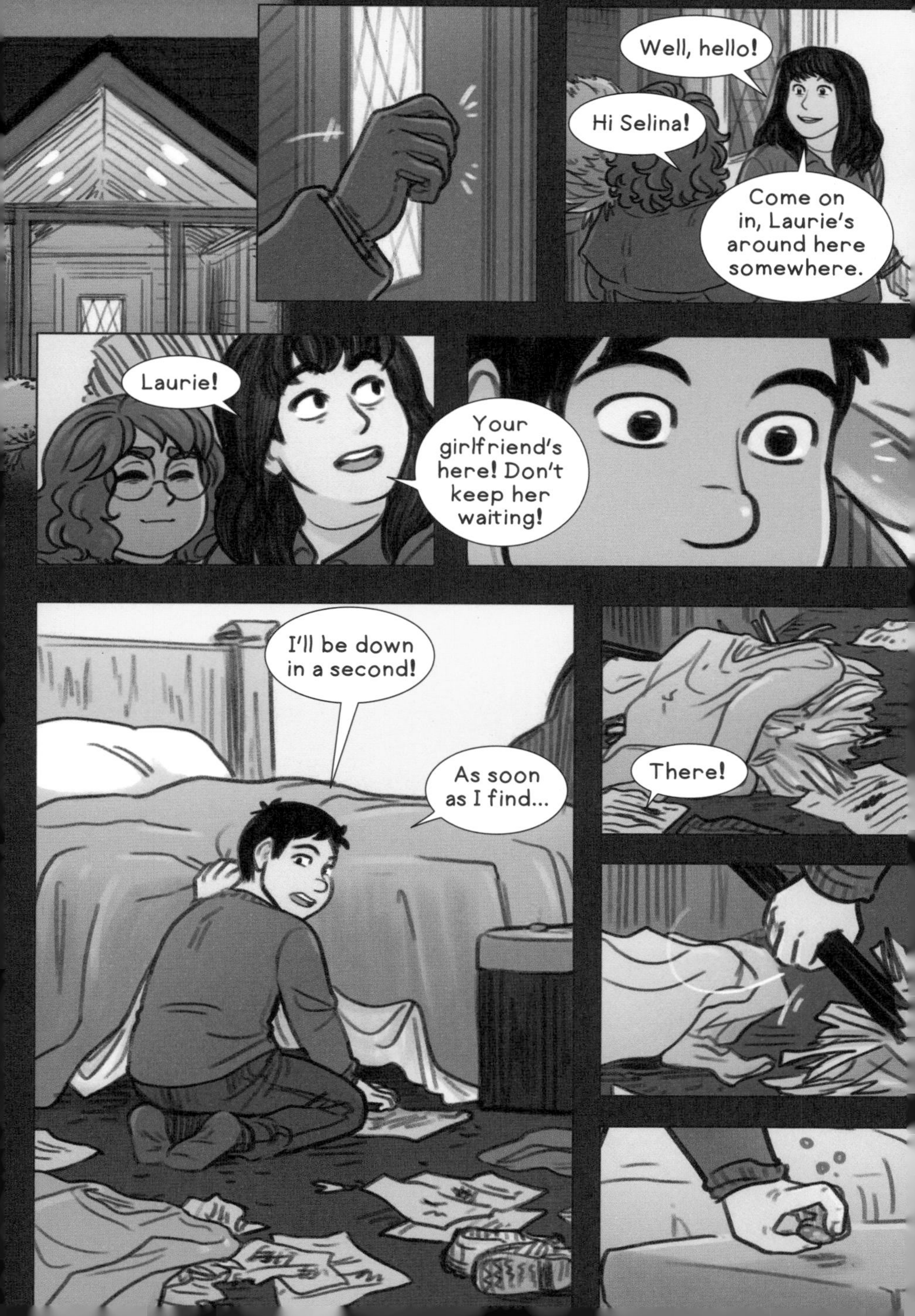
Well, hello!
Hi Selina!
Come on in, Laurie's around here somewhere.
Laurie!
Your girlfriend's here! Don't keep her waiting!
I'll be down in a second!
As soon as I find...
There!

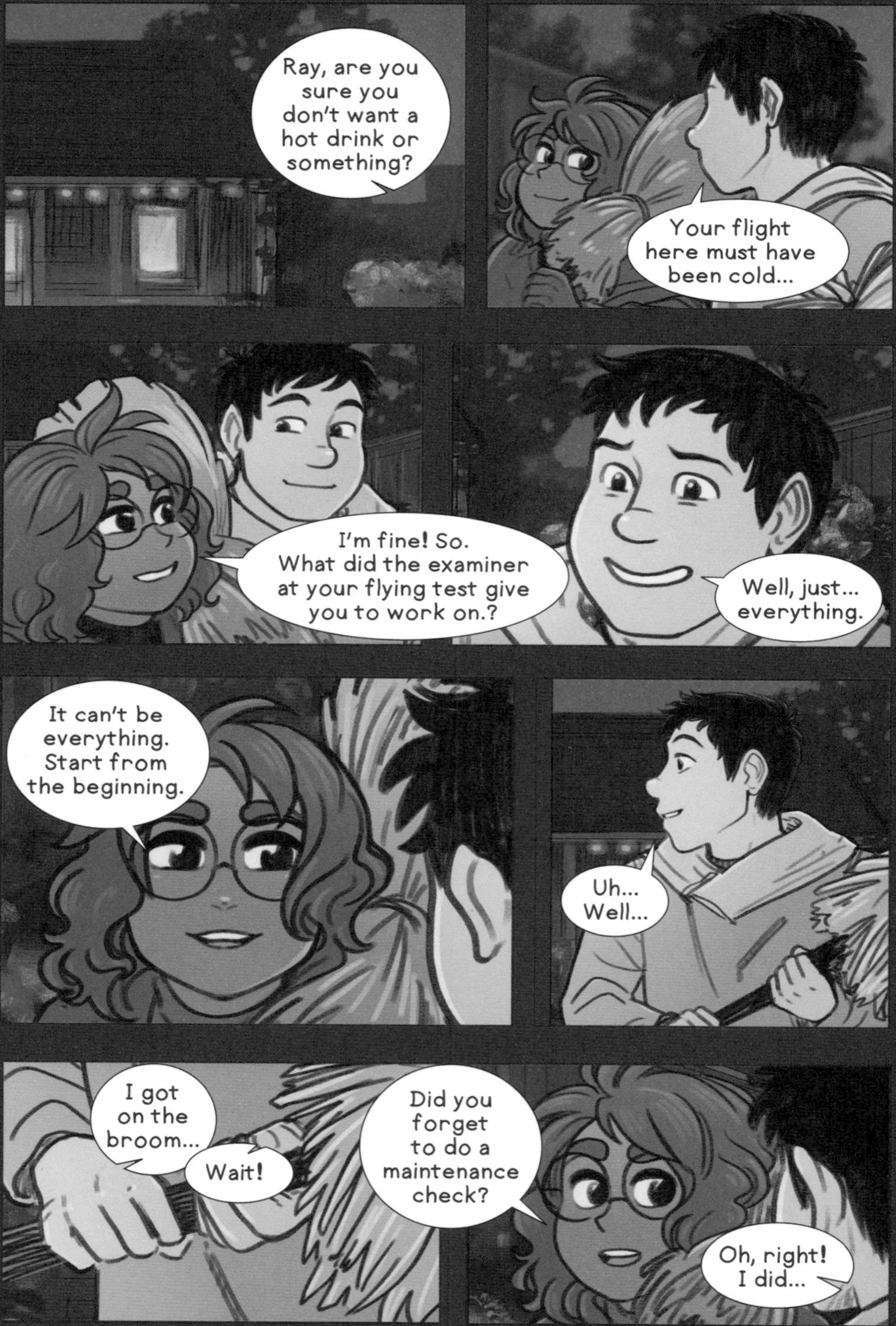
Ray, are you sure you don't want a hot drink or something?
Your flight here must have been cold...
I'm fine! So. What did the examiner at your flying test give you to work on.?
Well, just... everything.
It can't be everything. Start from the beginning.
Uh... Well...
I got on the broom...
Wait!
Did you forget to do a maintenance check?
Oh, right! I did...

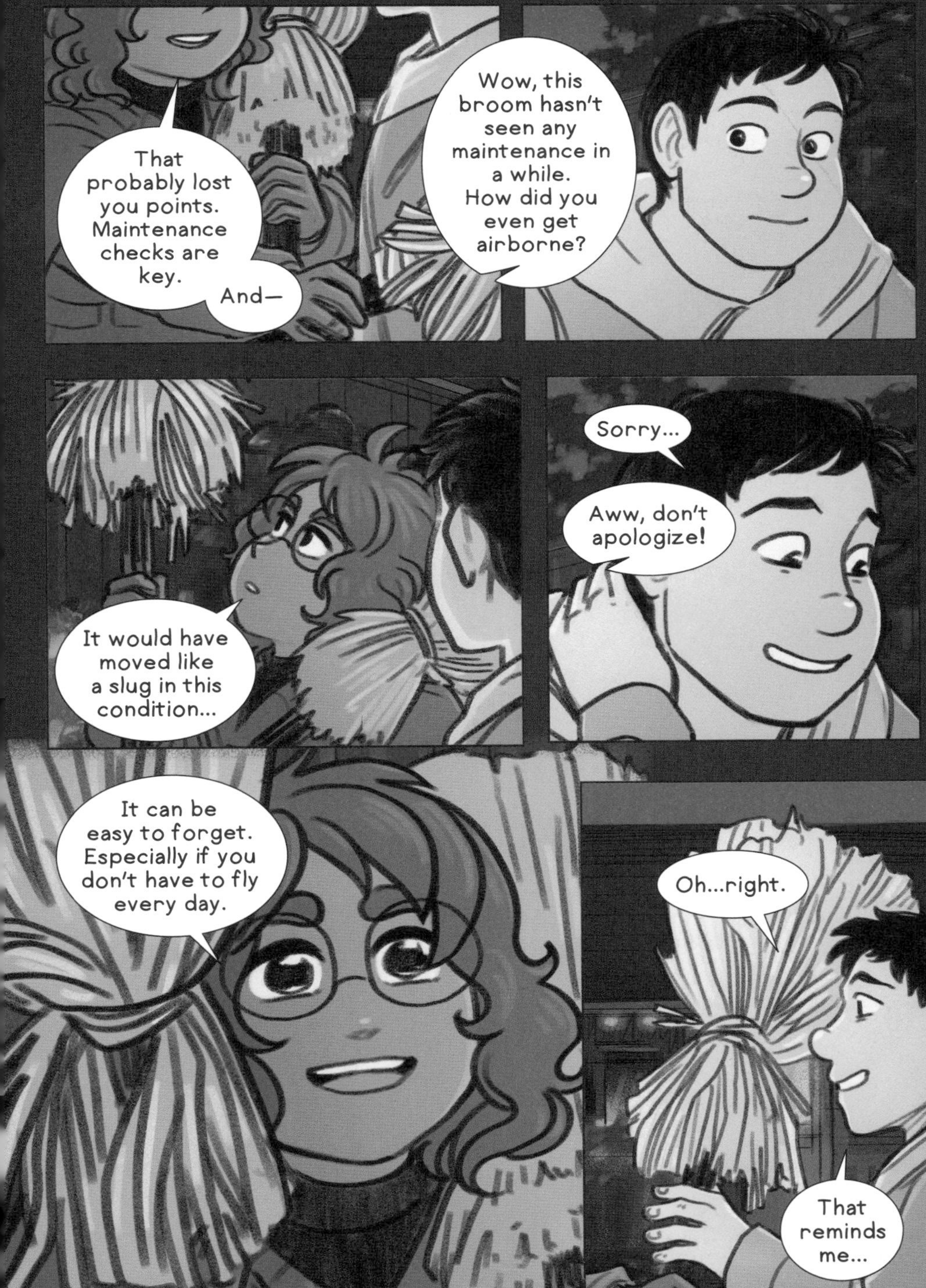
That probably lost you points. Maintenance checks are key.
And—
Wow, this broom hasn't seen any maintenance in a while. How did you even get airborne?
It would have moved like a slug in this condition...
Sorry...
Aww, don't apologize!
It can be easy to forget. Especially if you don't have to fly every day.
Oh...right.
That reminds me...

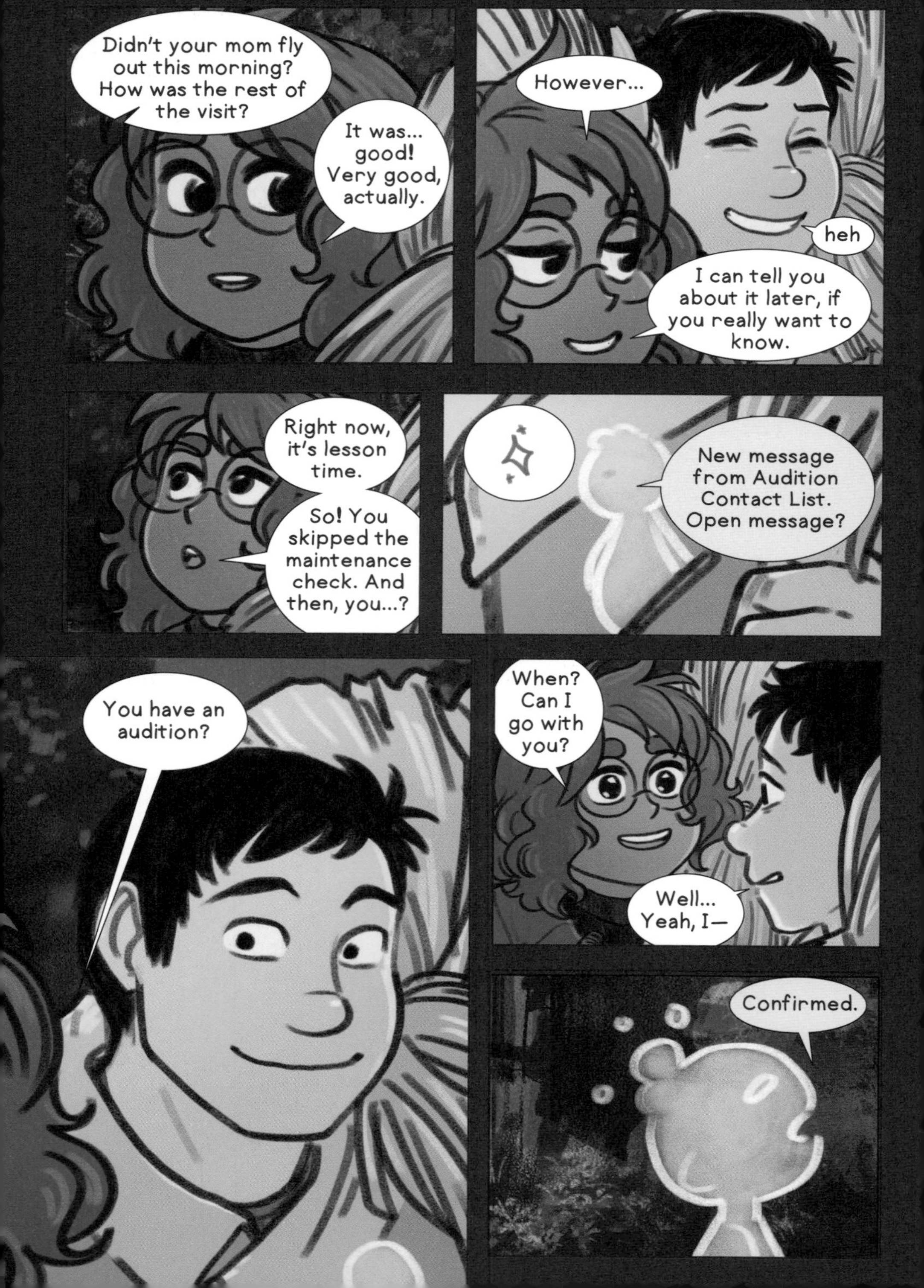
Didn't your mom fly out this morning? How was the rest of the visit?
It was... good! Very good, actually.
However...
heh
I can tell you about it later, if you really want to know.
Right now, it's lesson time.
So! You skipped the maintenance check. And then, you...?
New message from Audition Contact List. Open message?
You have an audition?
When? Can I go with you?
Well... Yeah, I—
Confirmed.

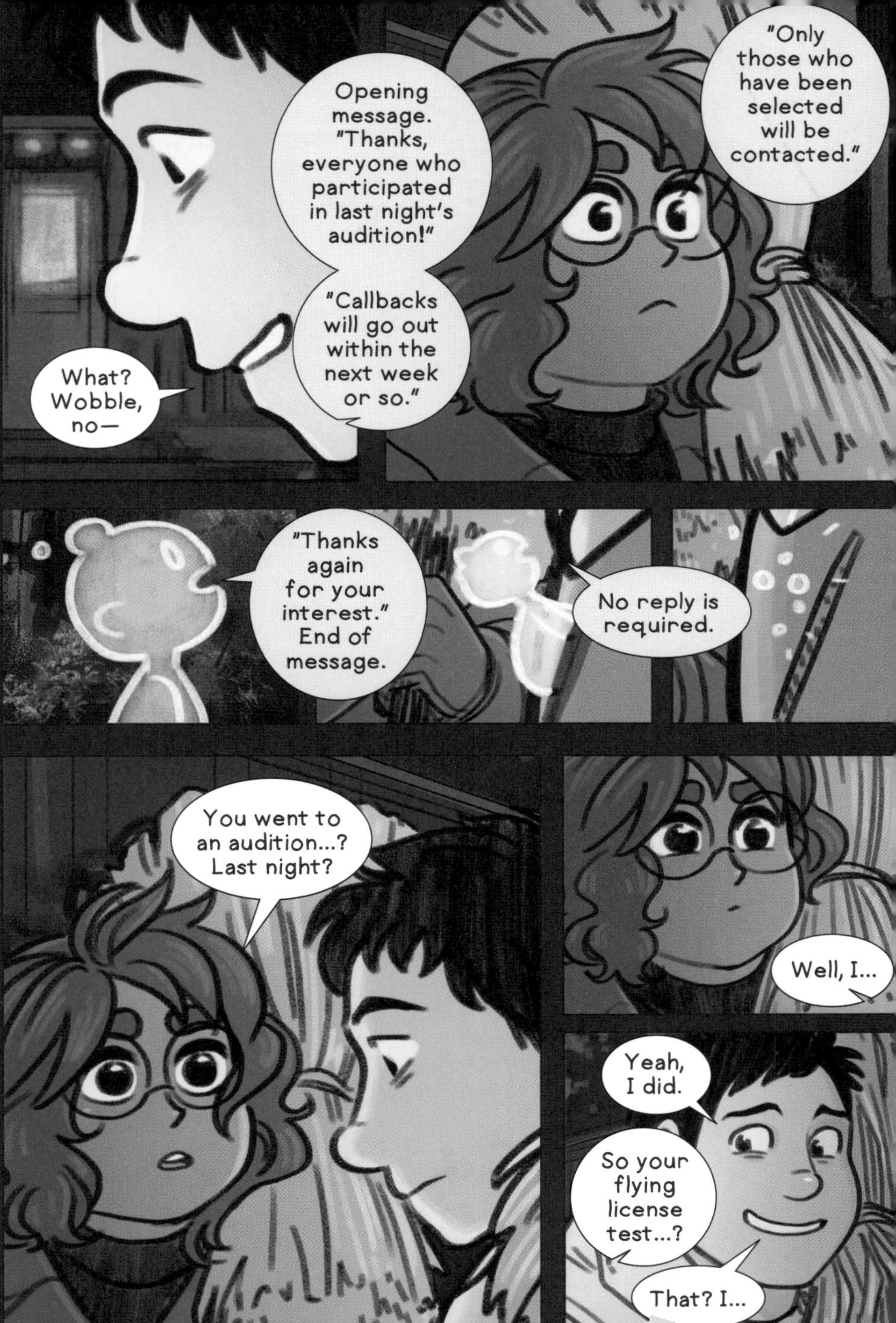
Opening message. "Thanks, everyone who participated in last night's audition!"
"Callbacks will go out within the next week or so."
What? Wobble, no—
"Only those who have been selected will be contacted."
"Thanks again for your interest." End of message.
No reply is required.
You went to an audition...? Last night?
Well, I...
Yeah, I did.
So your flying license test...?
That? I...

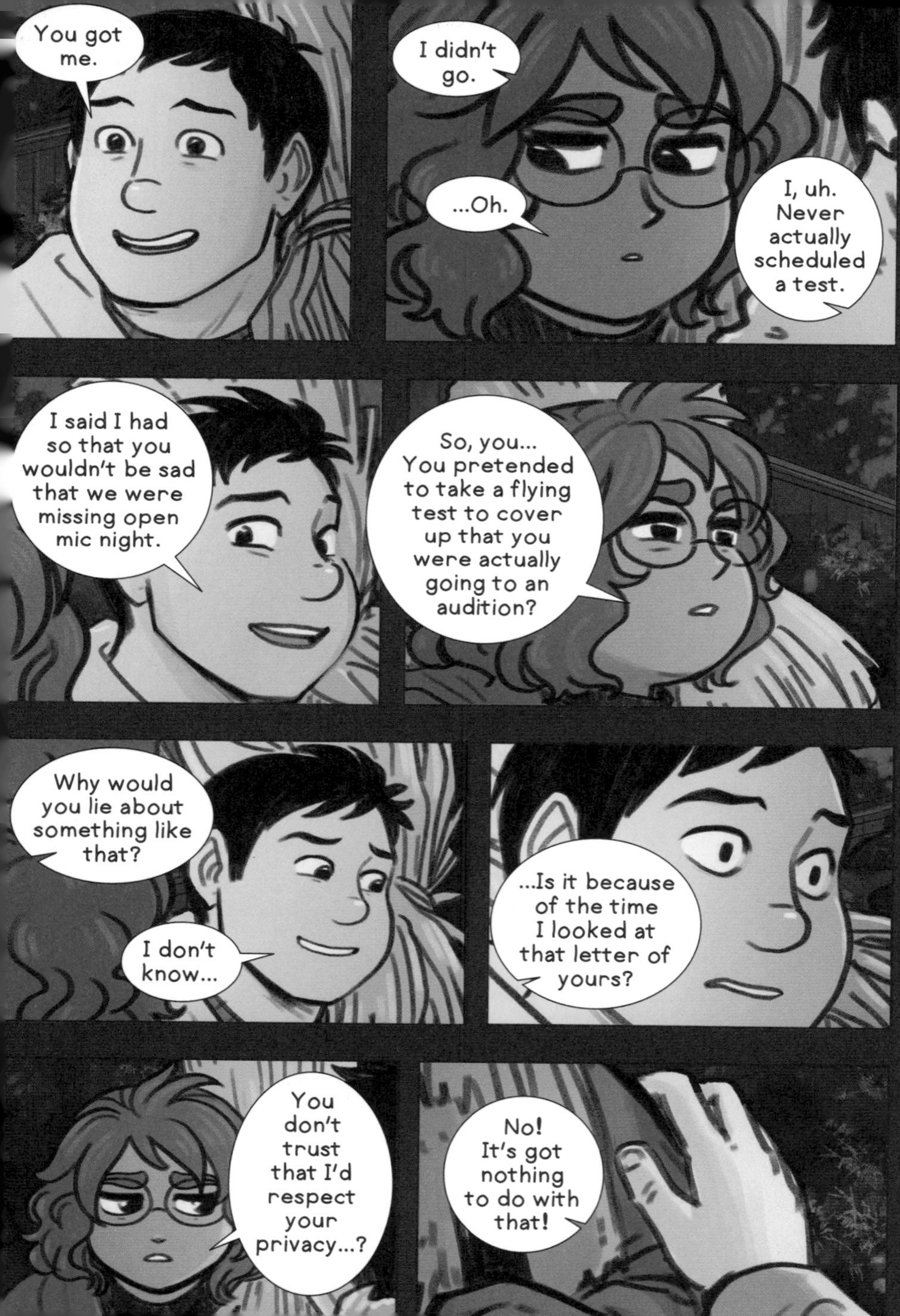
You got me.
I didn't go.
...Oh.
I, uh. Never actually scheduled a test.
I said I had so that you wouldn't be sad that we were missing open mic night.
So, you... You pretended to take a flying test to cover up that you were actually going to an audition?
Why would you lie about something like that?
I don't know...
...Is it because of the time I looked at that letter of yours?
You don't trust that I'd respect your privacy...?
No! It's got nothing to do with that!

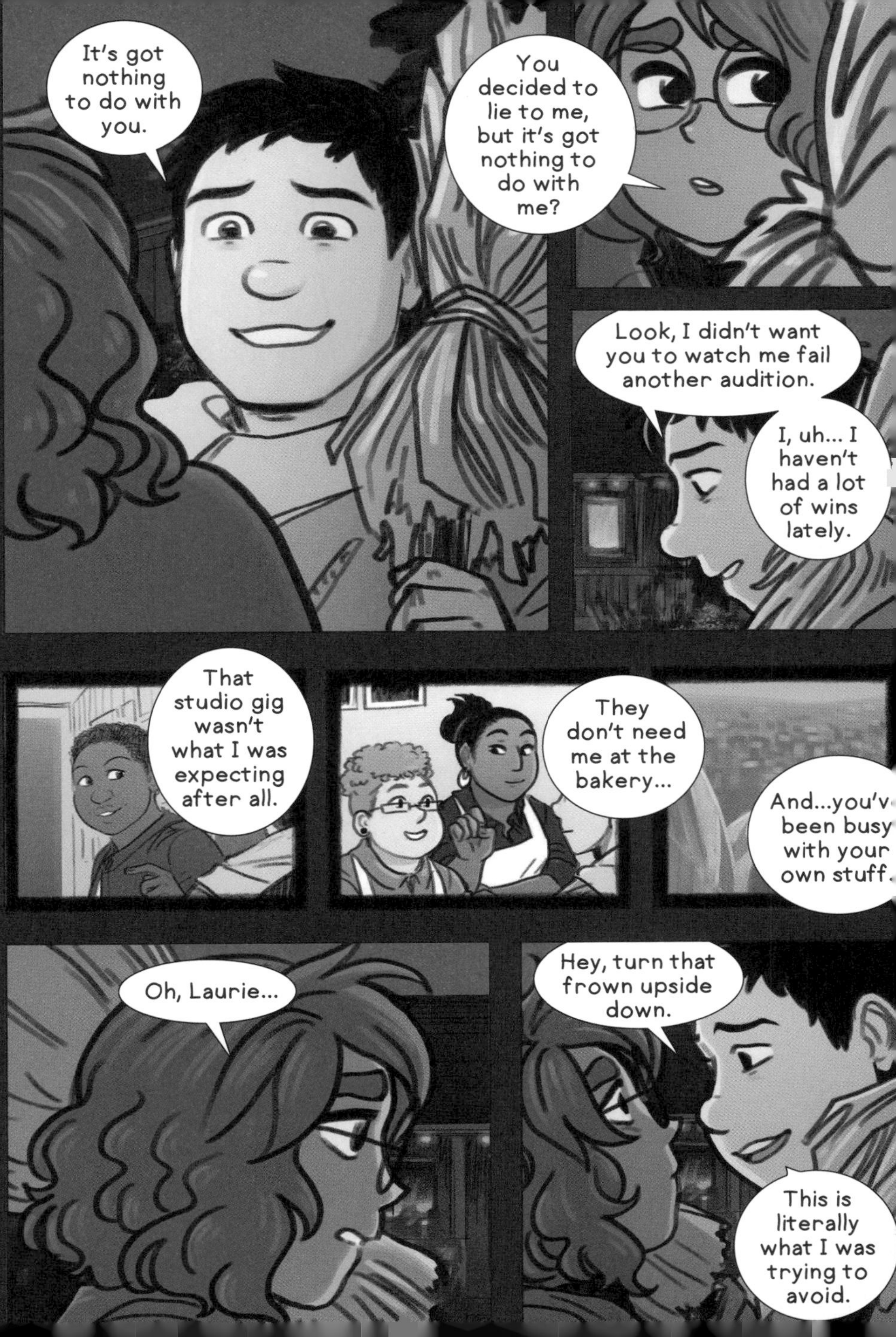
It's got nothing to do with you.
You decided to lie to me, but it's got nothing to do with me?
Look, I didn't want you to watch me fail another audition.
I, uh... I haven't had a lot of wins lately.
That studio gig wasn't what I was expecting after all.
They don't need me at the bakery...
And...you'v been busy with your own stuff.
Oh, Laurie...
Hey, turn that frown upside down.
This is literally what I was trying to avoid.

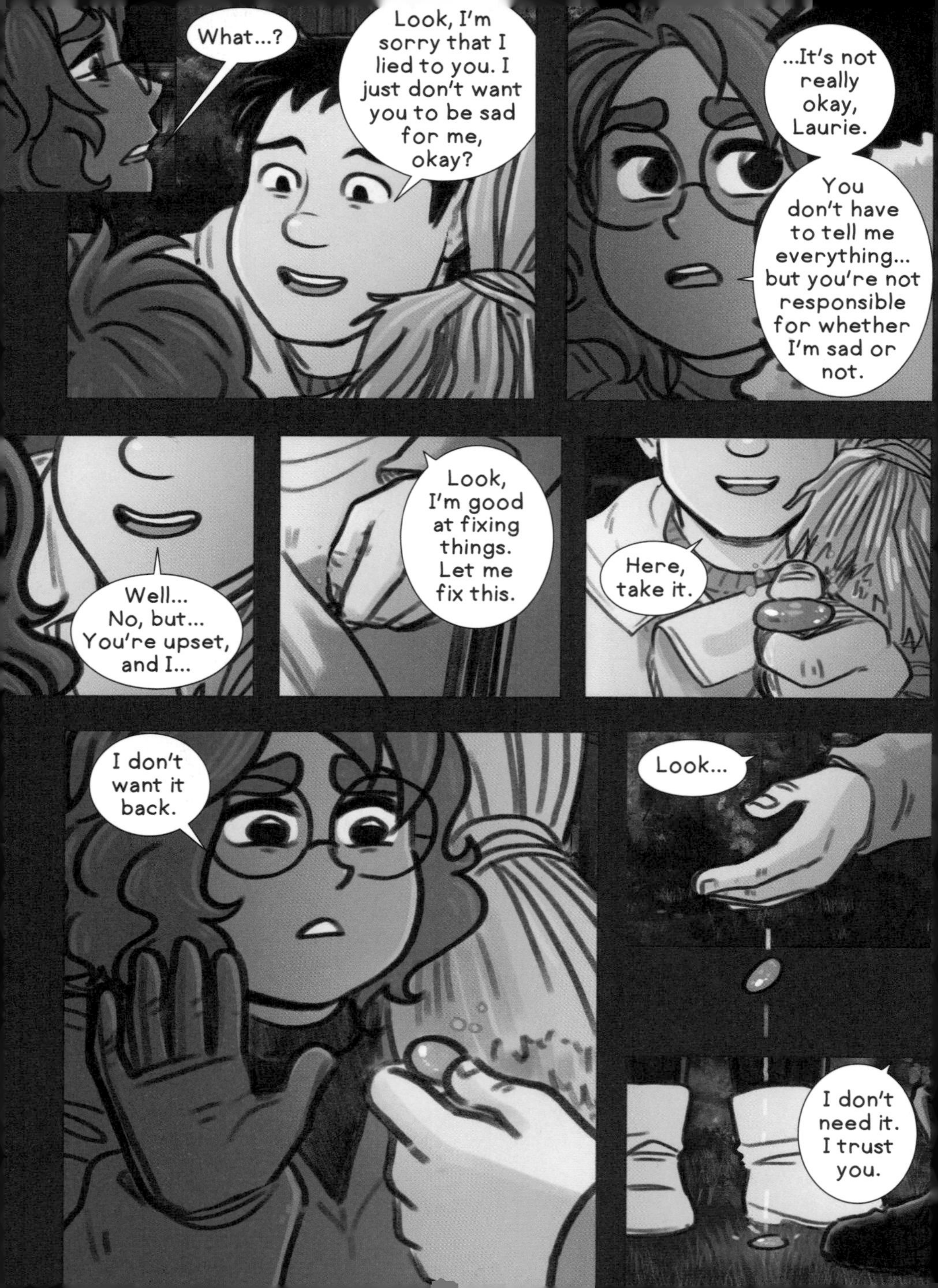
What...?
Look, I'm sorry that I lied to you. I just don't want you to be sad for me, okay?
...It's not really okay, Laurie.
You don't have to tell me everything... but you're not responsible for whether I'm sad or not.
Well... No, but... You're upset, and I...
Look, I'm good at fixing things. Let me fix this.
Here, take it.
I don't want it back.
Look...
I don't need it. I trust you.

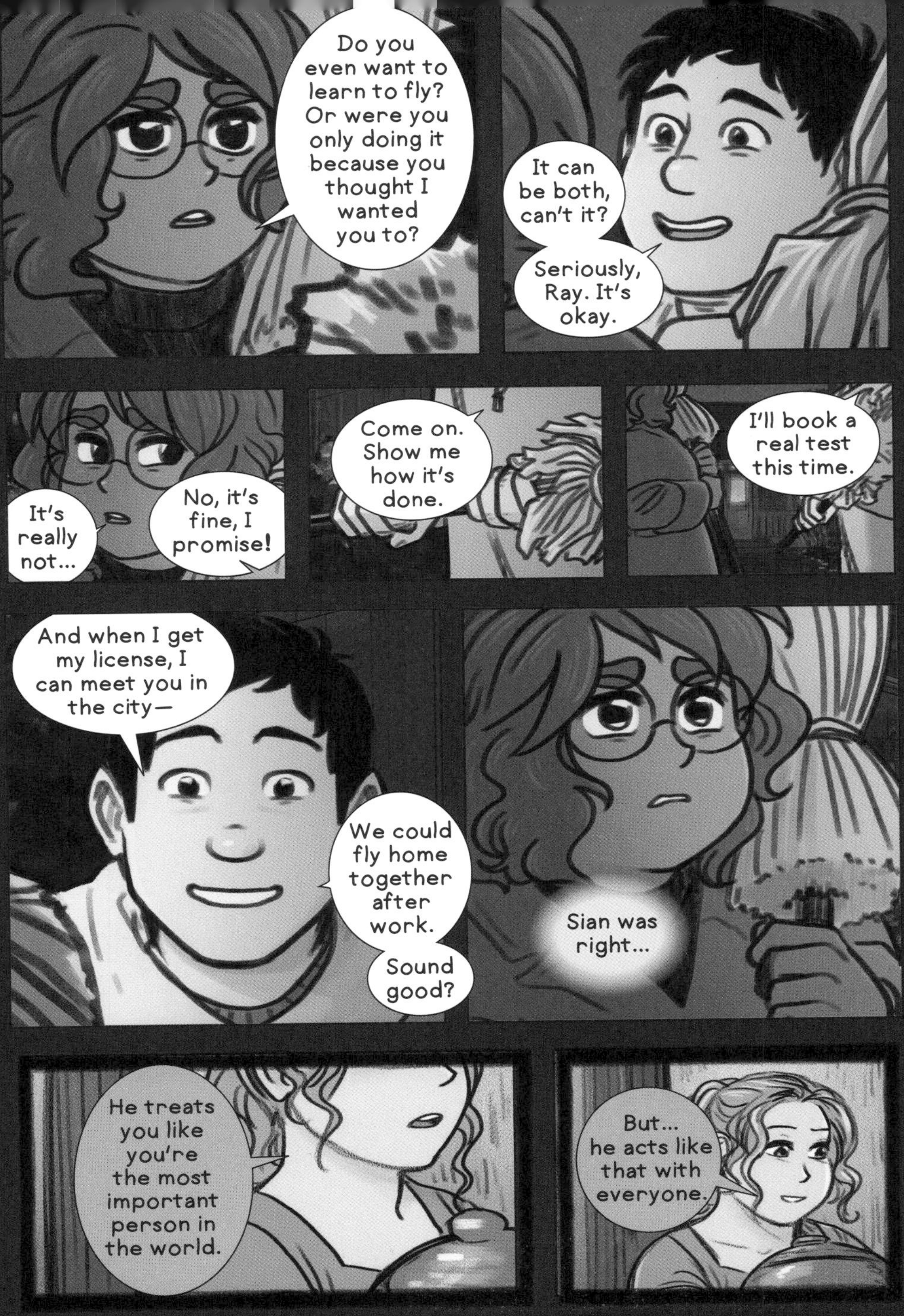
Do you even want to learn to fly? Or were you only doing it because you thought I wanted you to?
It can be both, can't it?
Seriously, Ray. It's okay.
It's really not...
No, it's fine, I promise!
Come on. Show me how it's done.
I'll book a real test this time.
And when I get my license, I can meet you in the city—
We could fly home together after work.
Sound good?
Sian was right...
He treats you like you're the most important person in the world.
But... he acts like that with everyone.

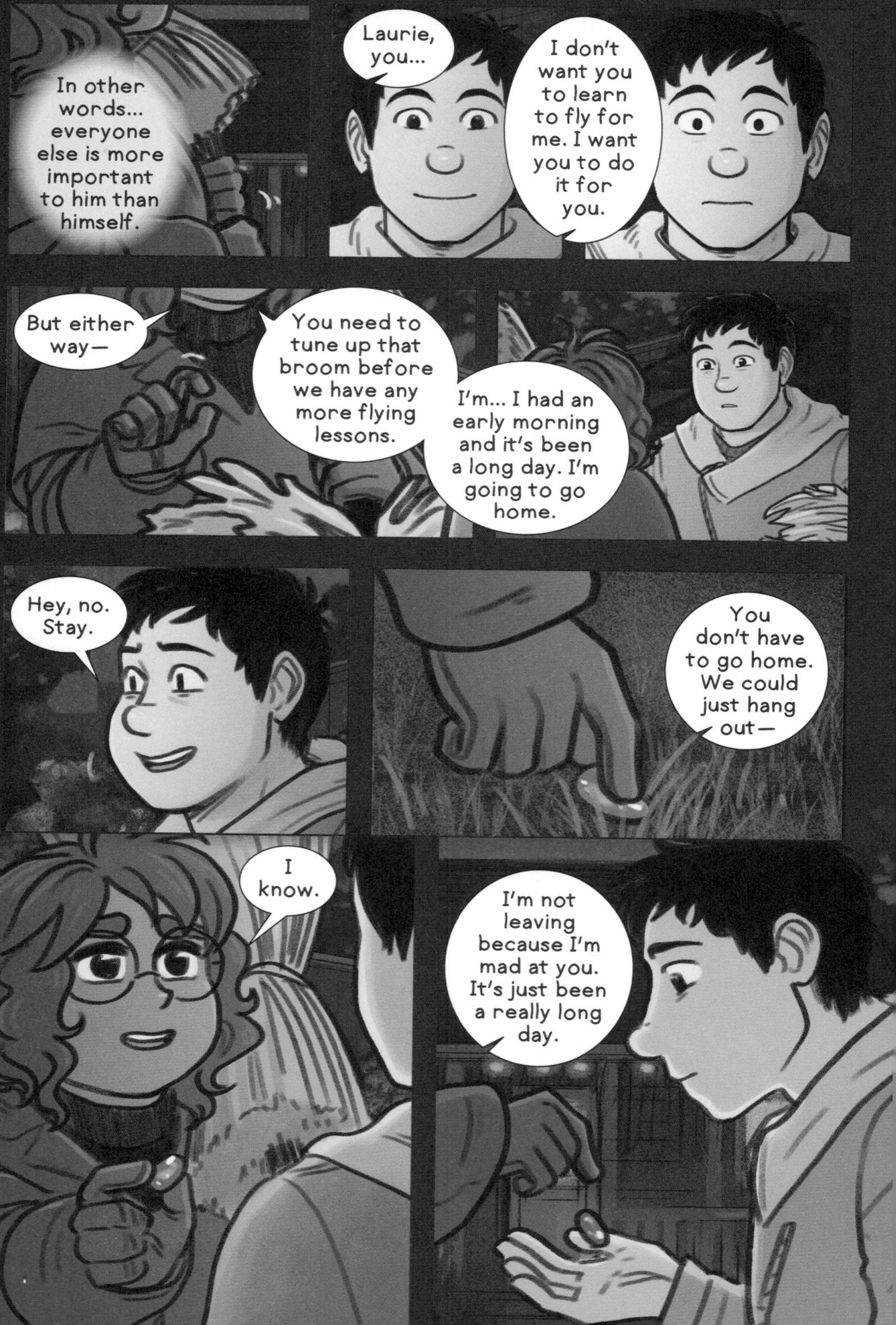
In other words... everyone else is more important to him than himself.
Laurie, you...
I don't want you to learn to fly for me. I want you to do it for you.
But either way—
You need to tune up that broom before we have any more flying lessons.
I'm... I had an early morning and it's been a long day. I'm going to go home.
Hey, no. Stay.
You don't have to go home. We could just hang out—
I know.
I'm not leaving because I'm mad at you. It's just been a really long day.

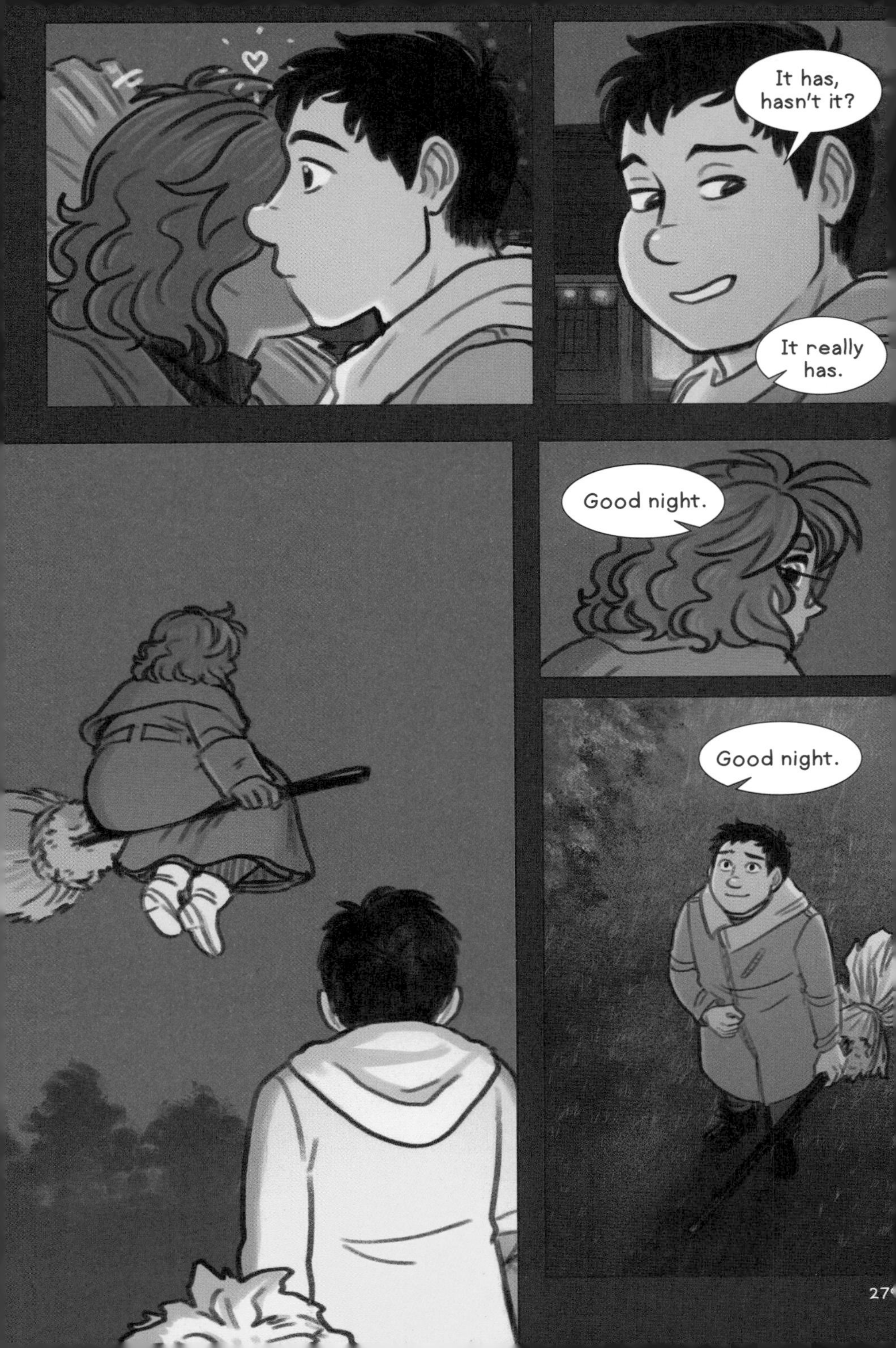
It has, hasn't it?
It really has.
Good night.
Good night.

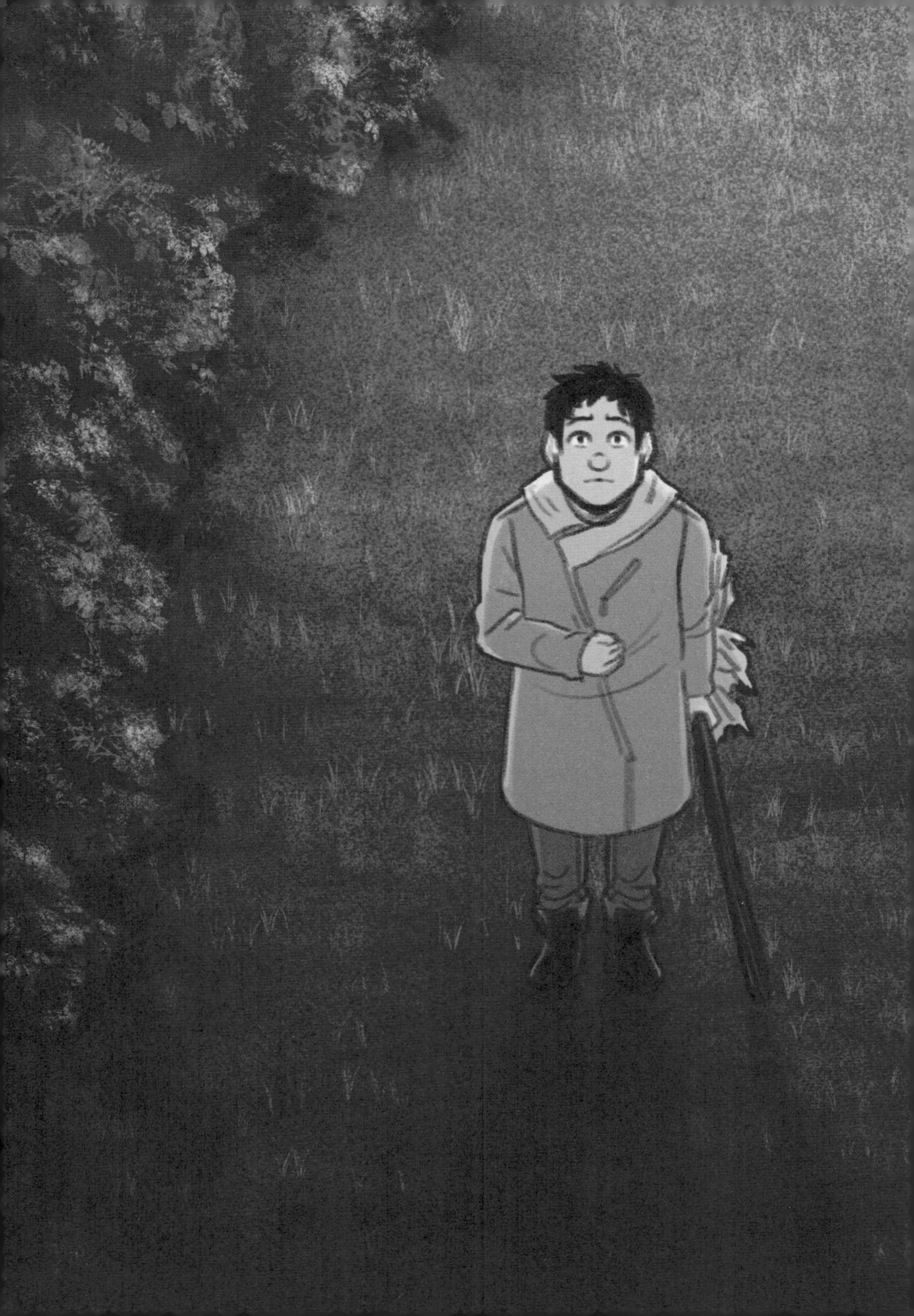

CHAPTER 12

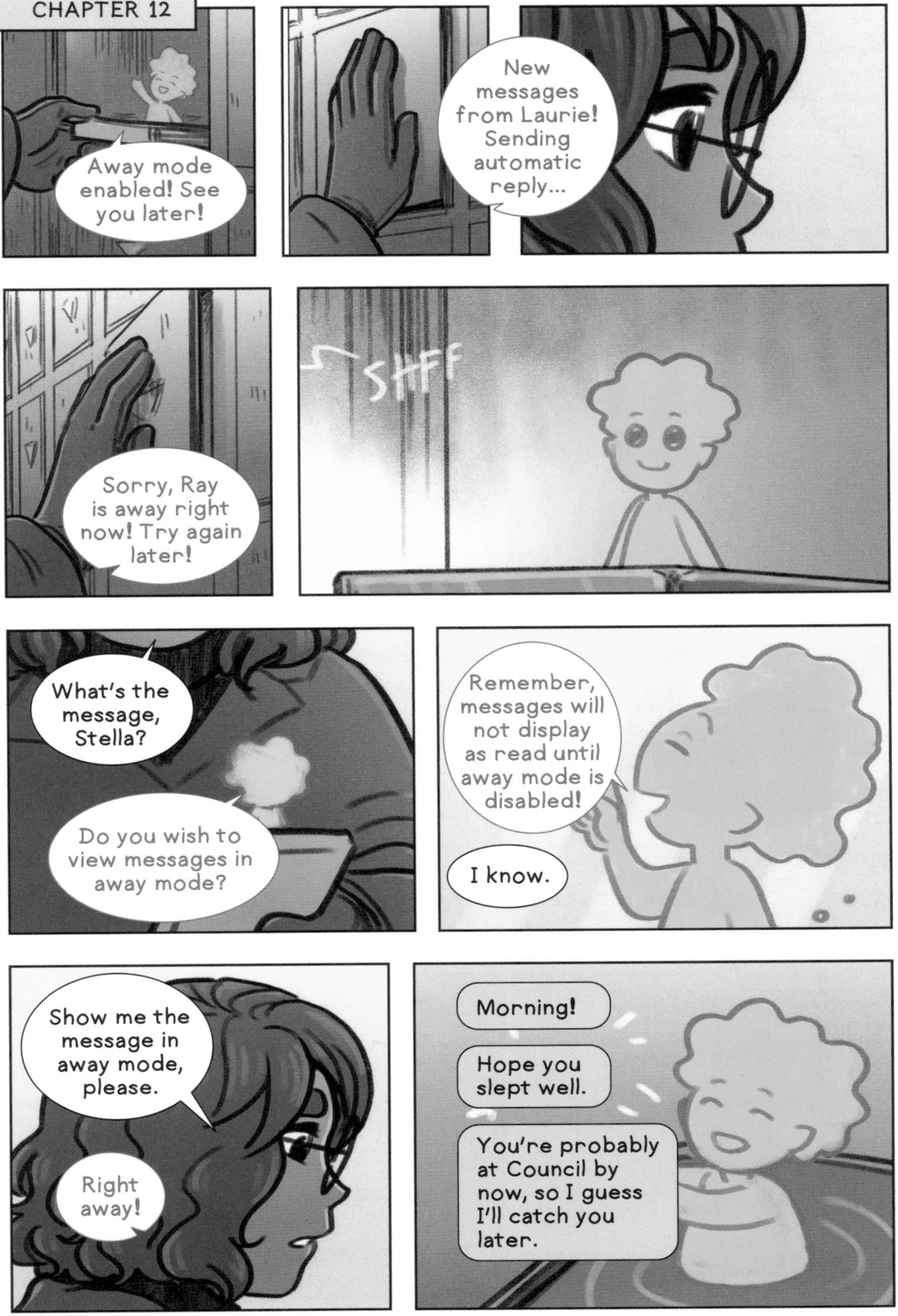
Away mode enabled! See you later!
New messages from Laurie! Sending automatic reply...
Sorry, Ray is away right now! Try again later!
SHFF
What's the message, Stella?
Do you wish to view messages in away mode?
Remember, messages will not display as read until away mode is disabled!
I know.
Show me the message in away mode, please.
Right away!
Morning!
Hope you slept well.
You're probably at Council by now, so I guess I'll catch you later.

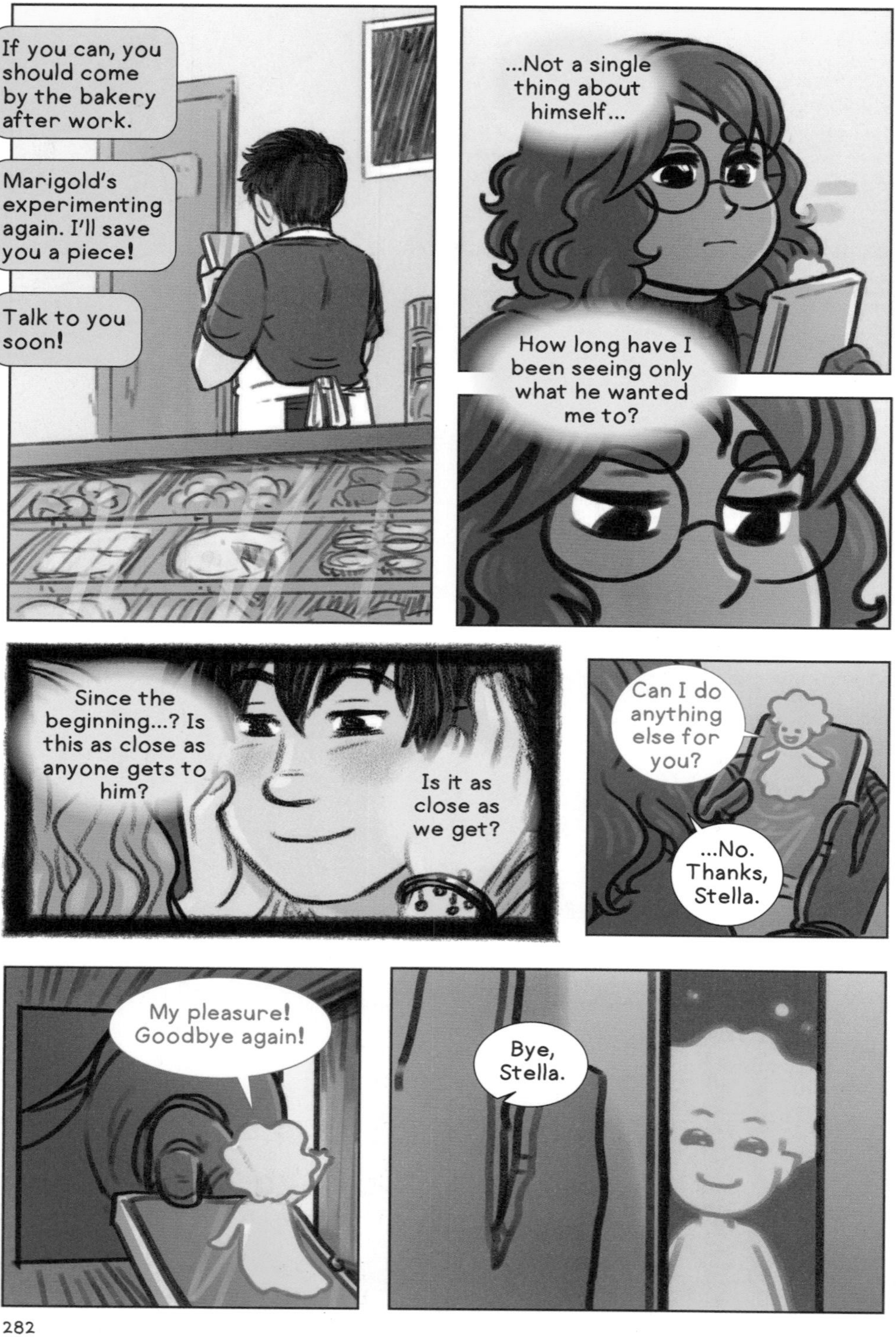
If you can, you should come by the bakery after work.
Marigold's experimenting again. I'll save you a piece!
Talk to you soon!
...Not a single thing about himself...
How long have I been seeing only what he wanted me to?
Since the beginning...? Is this as close as anyone gets to him?
Is it as close as we get?
Can I do anything else for you?
...No. Thanks, Stella.
My pleasure! Goodbye again!
Bye, Stella.

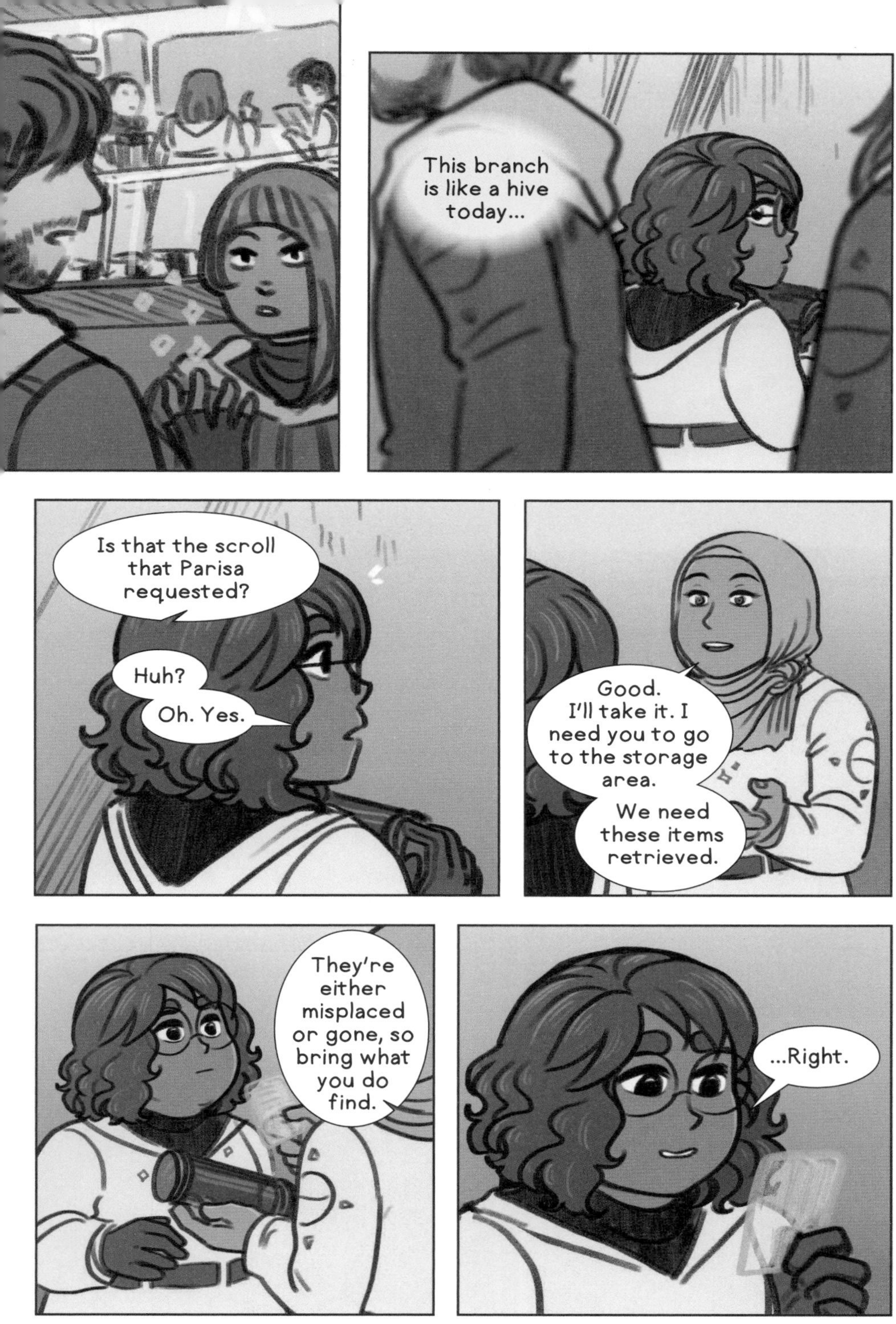
This branch is like a hive today...
Is that the scroll that Parisa requested?
Huh?
Oh. Yes.
Good. I'll take it. I need you to go to the storage area.
We need these items retrieved.
They're either misplaced or gone, so bring what you do find.
...Right.

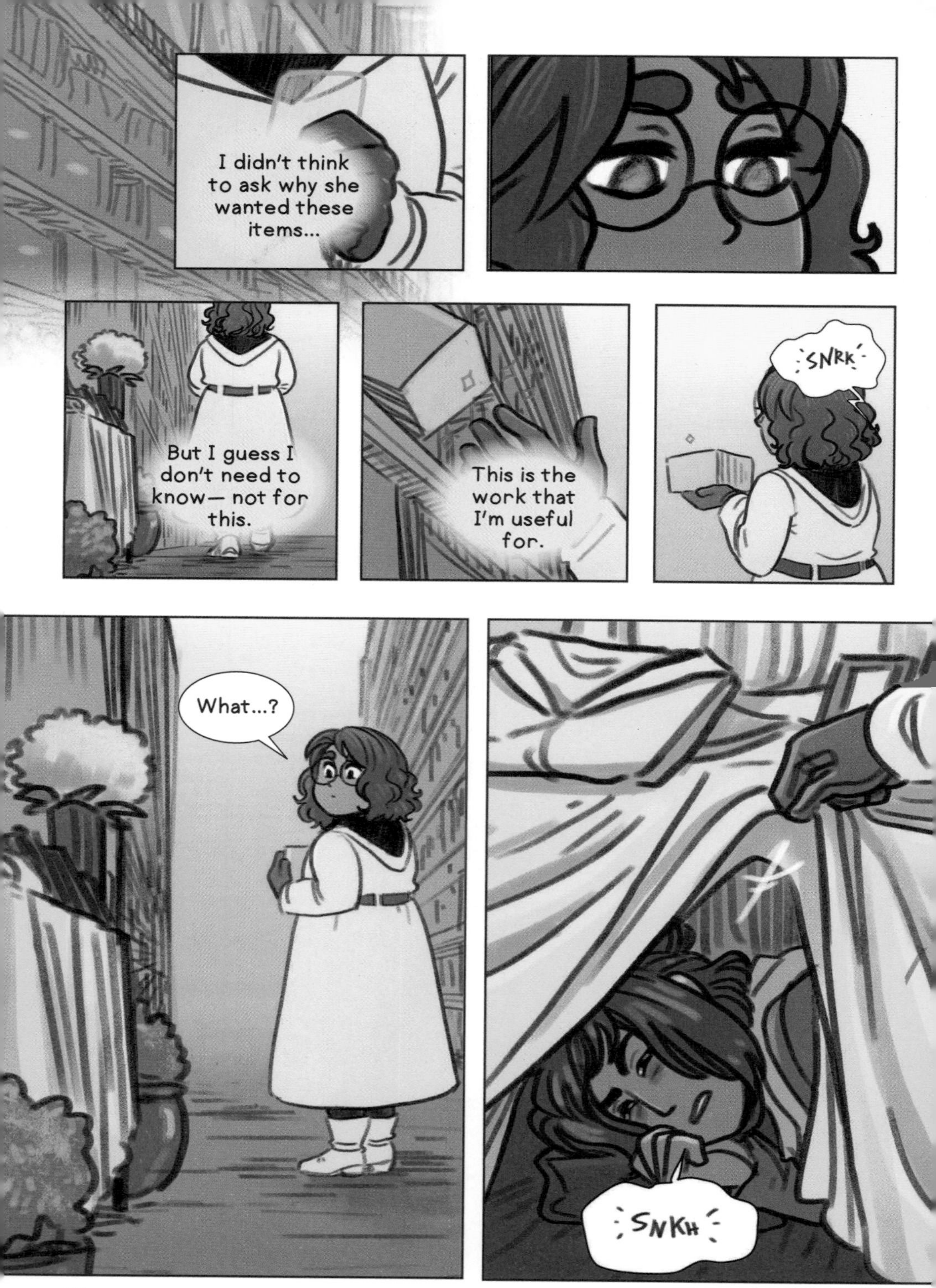

I didn't think to ask why she wanted these items...
But I guess I don't need to know— not for this.
This is the work that I'm useful for.
SNRK
What...?
SNKH

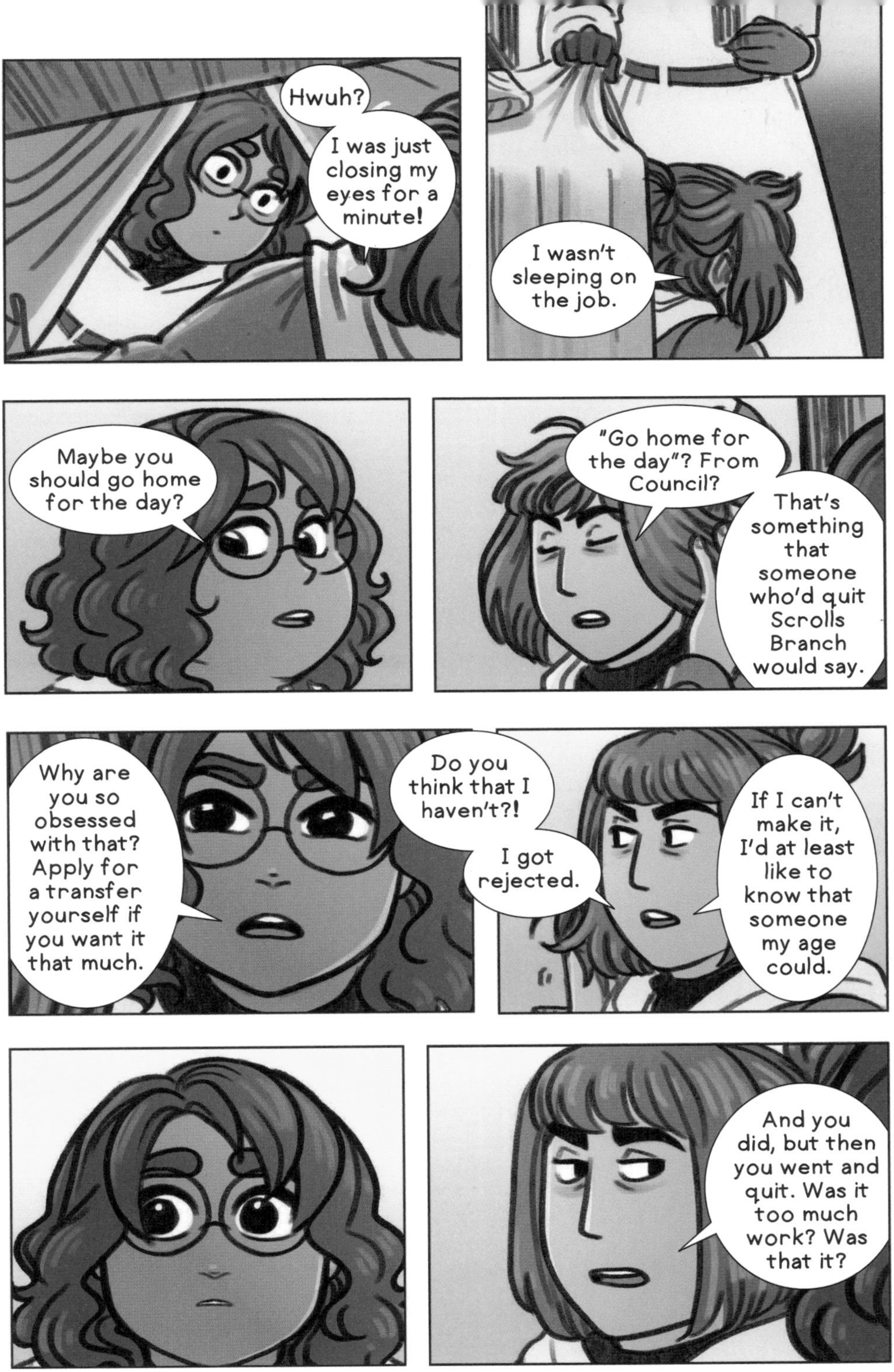
Hwuh?
I was just closing my eyes for a minute!
I wasn't sleeping on the job.
Maybe you should go home for the day?
"Go home for the day"? From Council?
That's something that someone who'd quit Scrolls Branch would say.
Why are you so obsessed with that? Apply for a transfer yourself if you want it that much.
Do you think that I haven't?!
I got rejected.
If I can't make it, I'd at least like to know that someone my age could.
And you did, but then you went and quit. Was it too much work? Was that it?

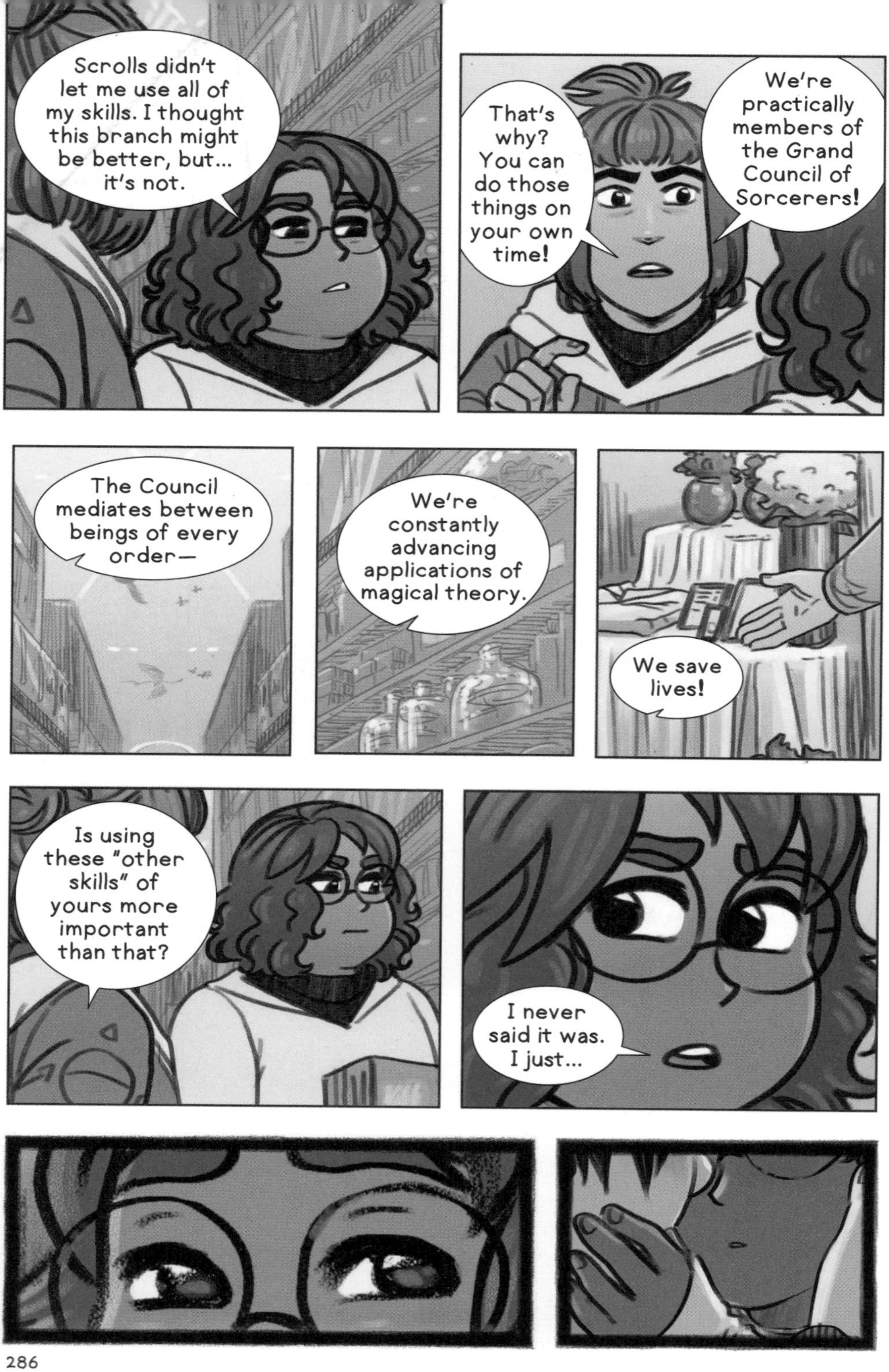
Scrolls didn't let me use all of my skills. I thought this branch might be better, but... it's not.
That's why? You can do those things on your own time!
We're practically members of the Grand Council of Sorcerers!
The Council mediates between beings of every order—
We're constantly advancing applications of magical theory.
We save lives!
Is using these "other skills" of yours more important than that?
I never said it was. I just...

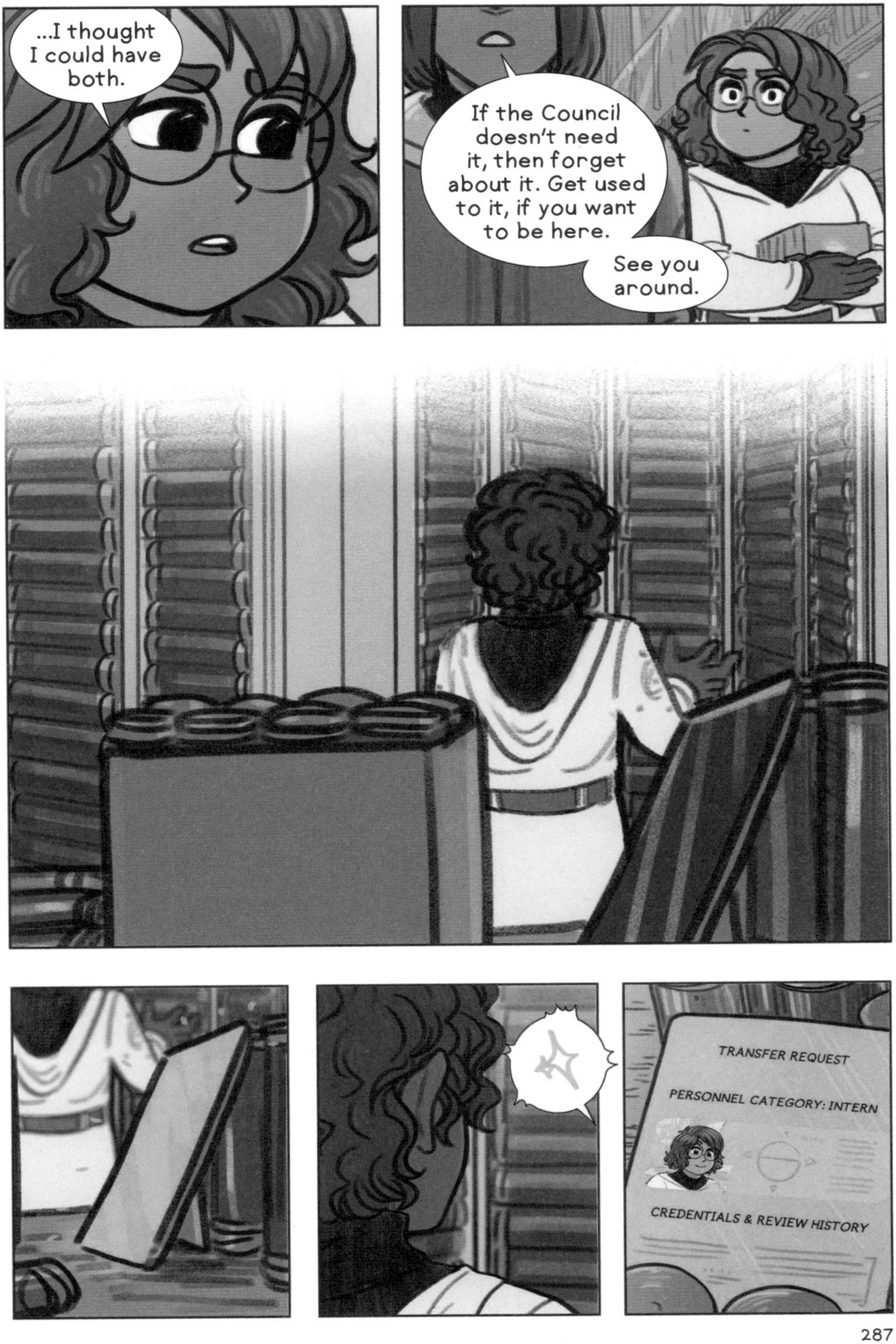
...I thought I could have both.
If the Council doesn't need it, then forget about it. Get used to it, if you want to be here.
See you around.
TRANSFER REQUEST
PERSONNEL CATEGORY: INTERN
CREDENTIALS & REVIEW HISTORY

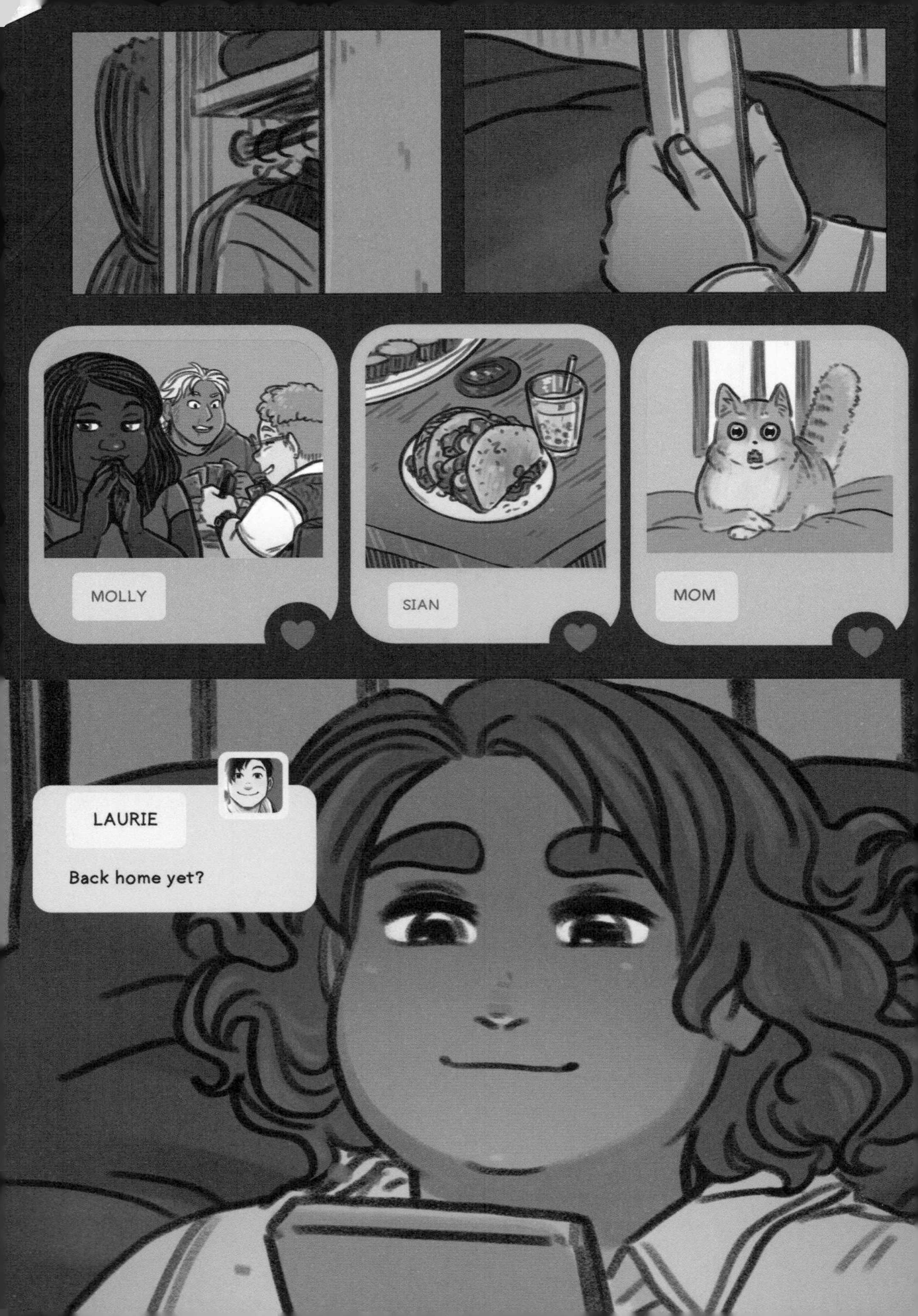
MOLLY
SIAN
MOM
LAURIE
Back home yet?

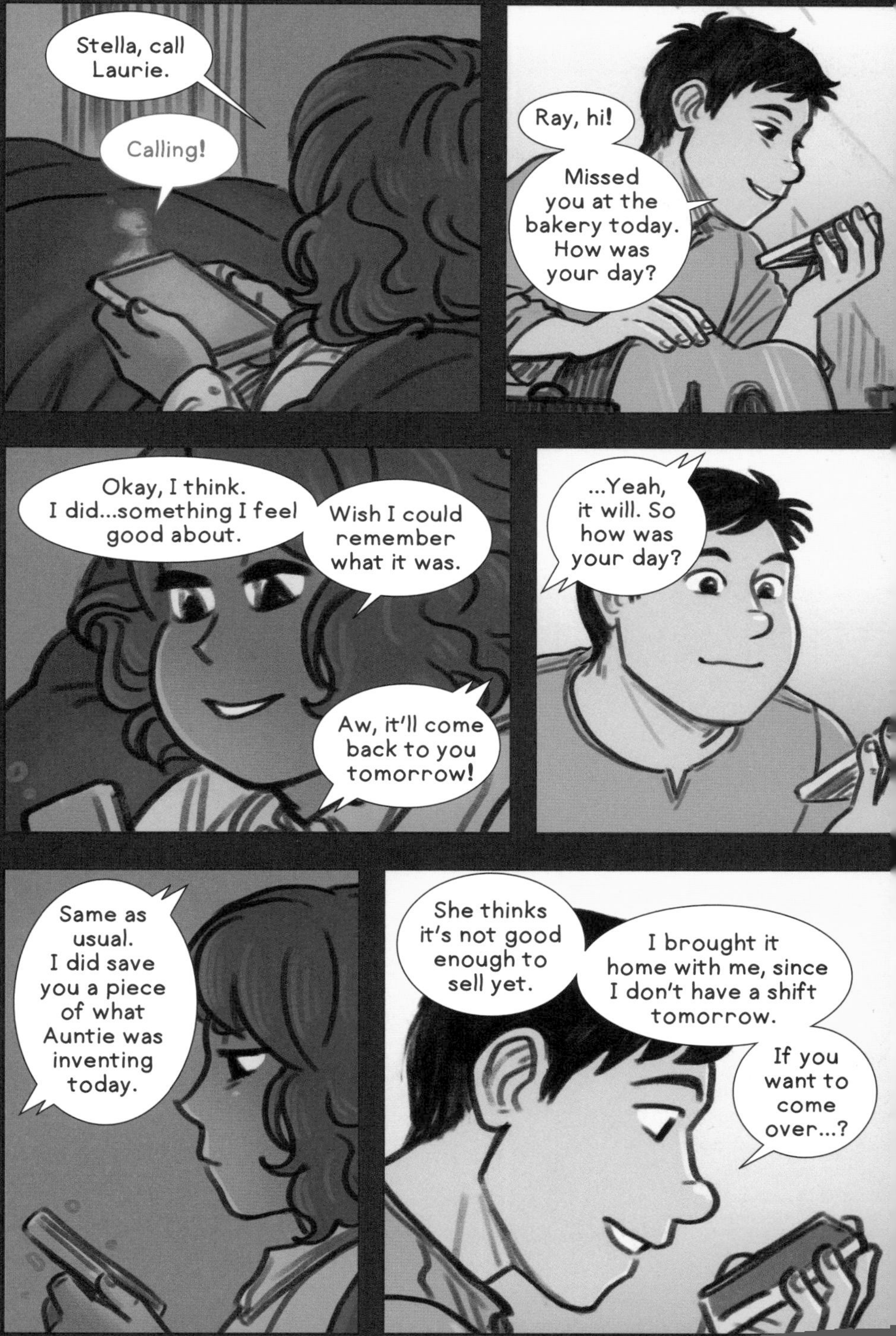
Stella, call Laurie.
Calling!
Ray, hi!
Missed you at the bakery today. How was your day?
Okay, I think. I did...something I feel good about.
Wish I could remember what it was.
Aw, it'll come back to you tomorrow!
...Yeah, it will. So how was your day?
Same as usual. I did save you a piece of what Auntie was inventing today.
She thinks it's not good enough to sell yet.
I brought it home with me, since I don't have a shift tomorrow.
If you want to come over...?

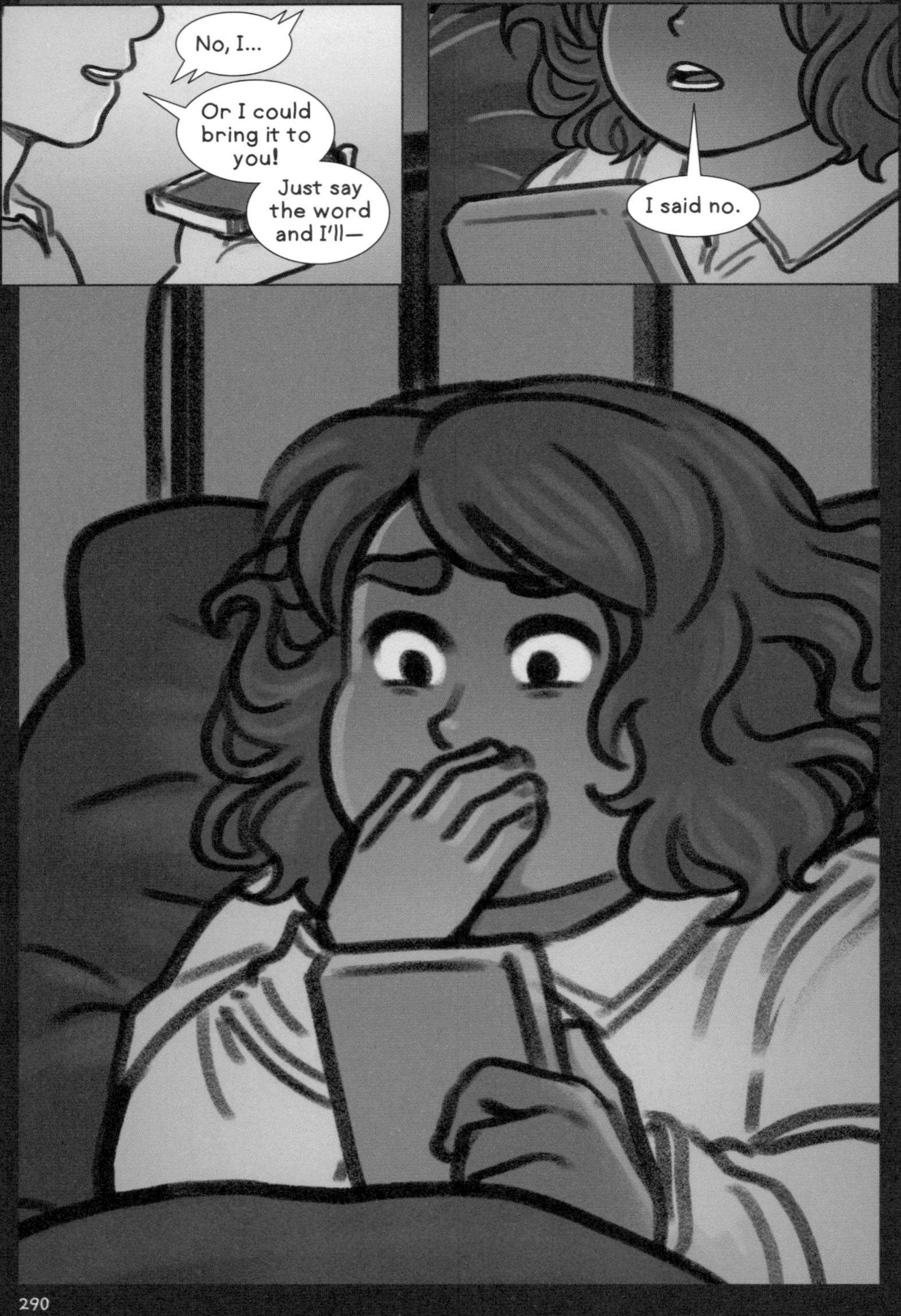
No, I...
Or I could bring it to you!
Just say the word and I'll—
I said no.

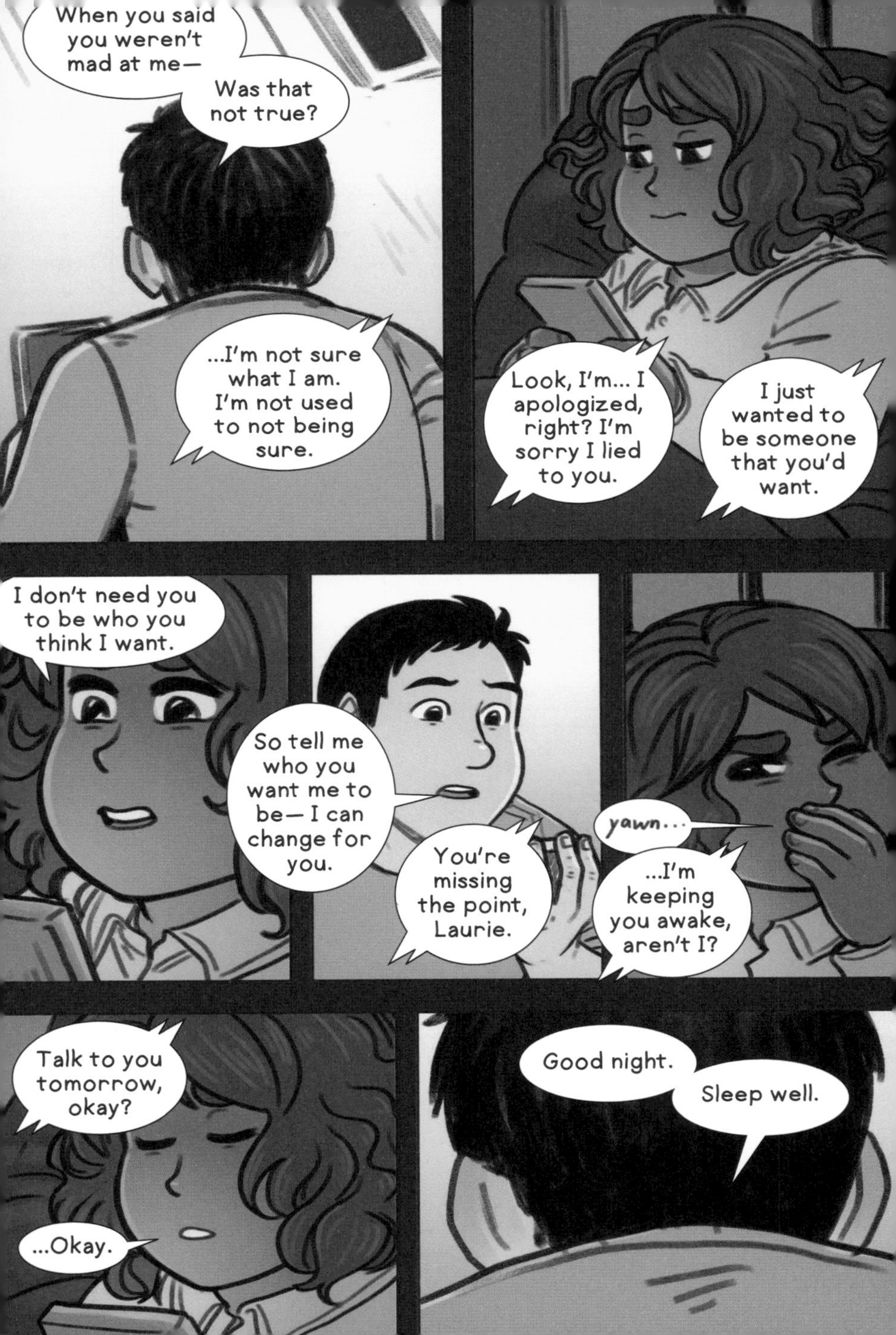
When you said you weren't mad at me—
Was that not true?
...I'm not sure what I am. I'm not used to not being sure.
Look, I'm... I apologized, right? I'm sorry I lied to you.
I just wanted to be someone that you'd want.
I don't need you to be who you think I want.
So tell me who you want me to be—I can change for you.
You're missing the point, Laurie.
yawn...
...I'm keeping you awake, aren't I?
Talk to you tomorrow, okay?
...Okay.
Good night.
Sleep well.

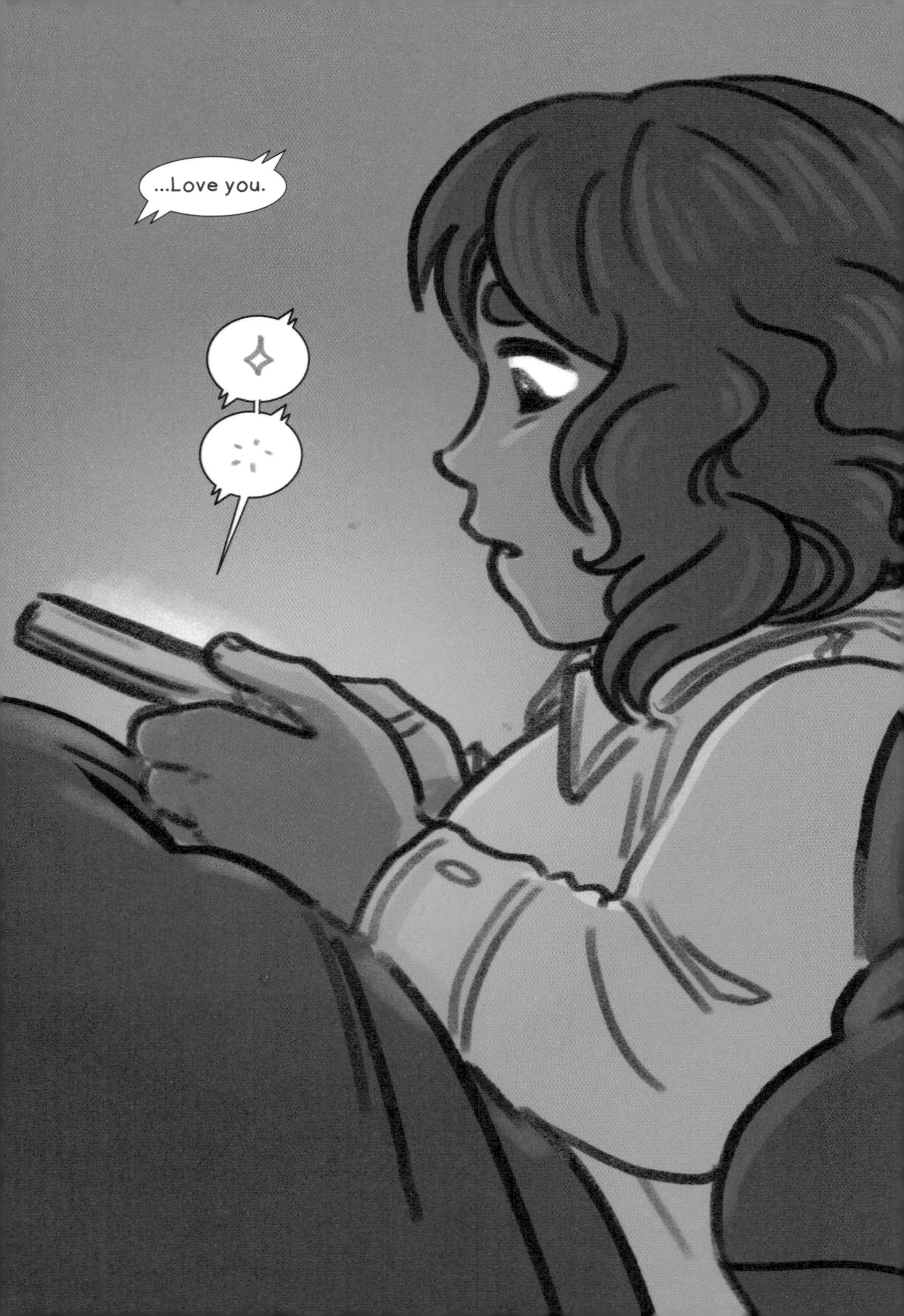
...Love you.

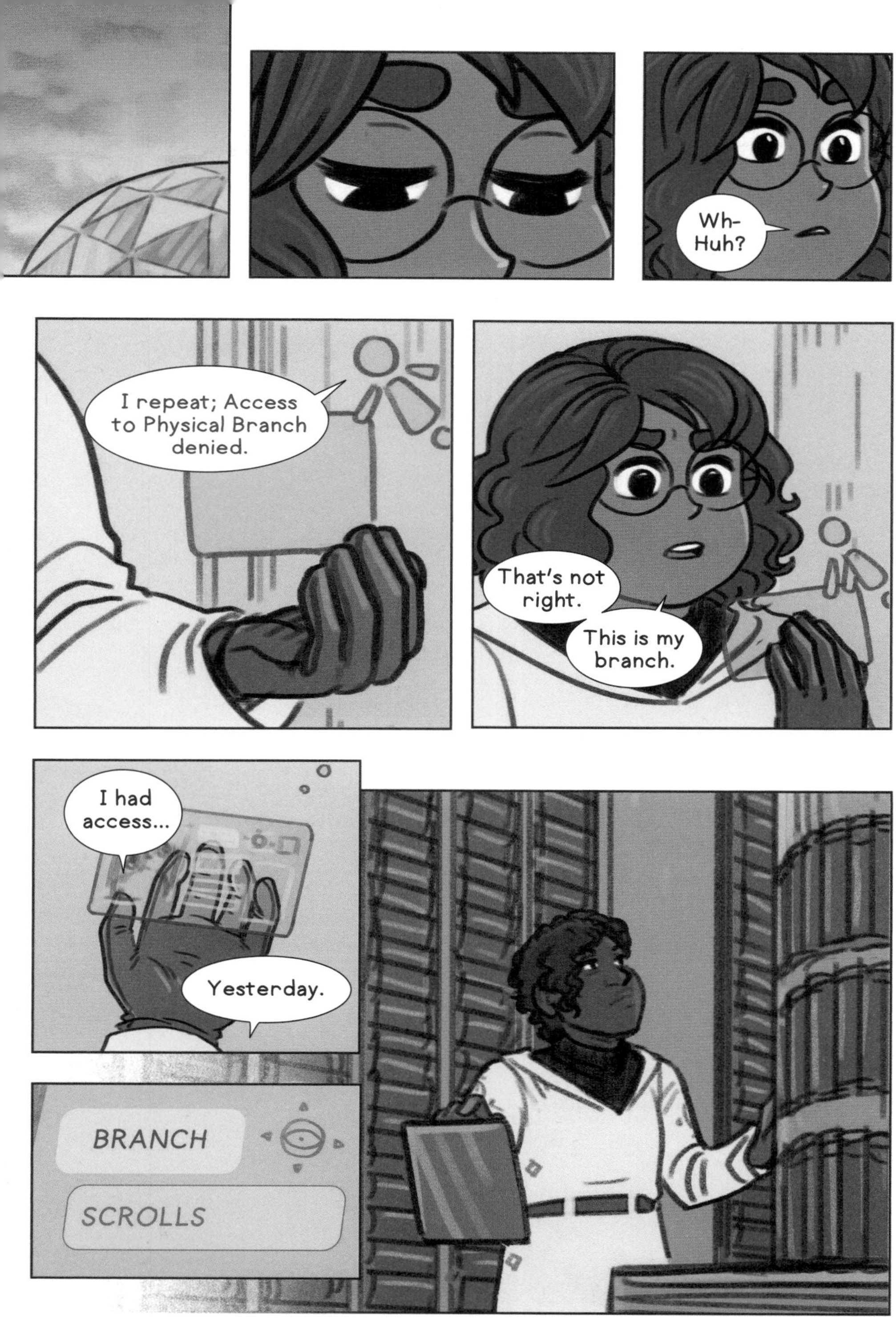
Wh-
Huh?
I repeat; Access to Physical Branch denied.
That's not right.
This is my branch.
I had access...
Yesterday.
BRANCH
SCROLLS

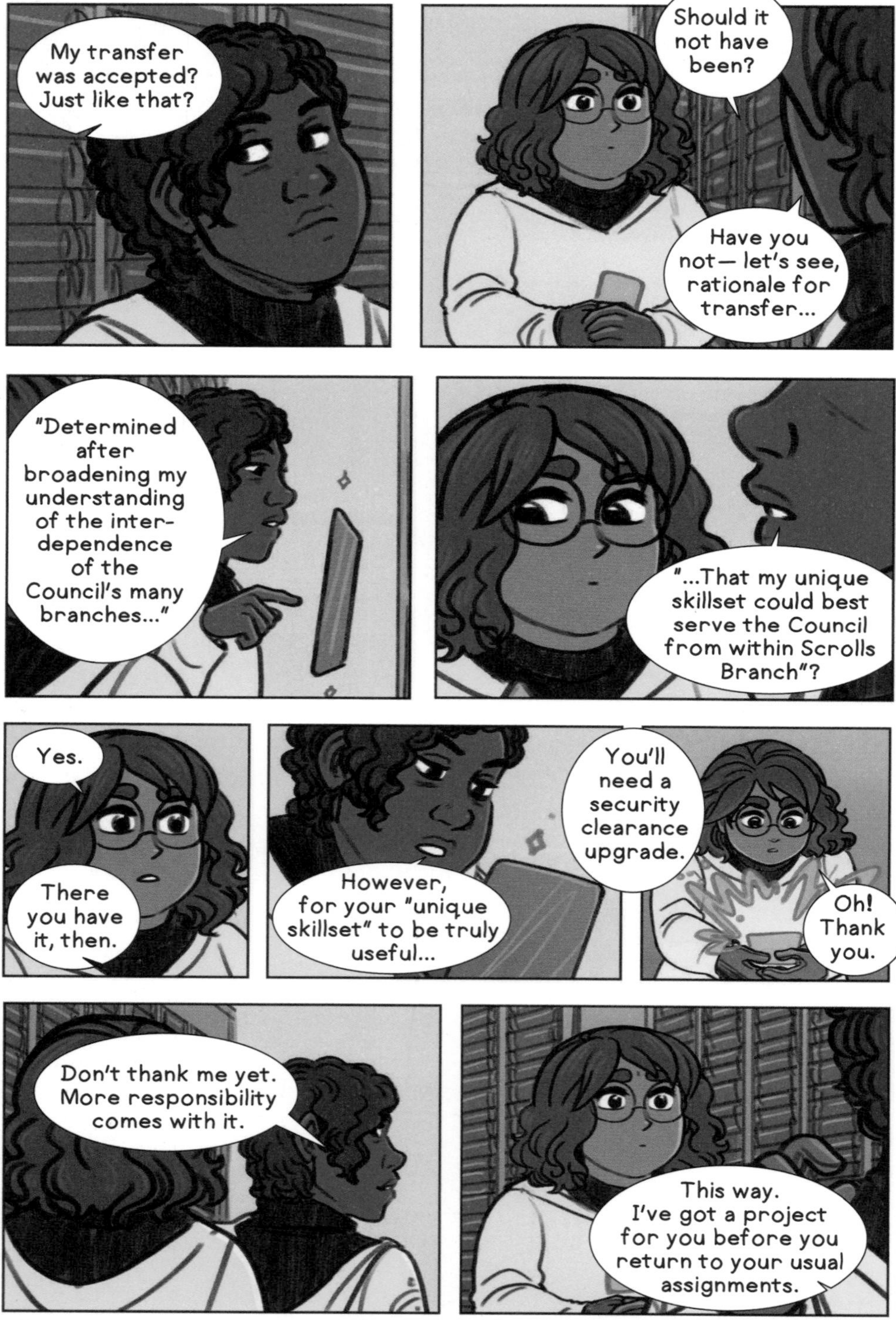
My transfer was accepted? Just like that?
Should it not have been?
Have you not— let's see, rationale for transfer...
"Determined after broadening my understanding of the inter-dependence of the Council's many branches..."
"...That my unique skillset could best serve the Council from within Scrolls Branch"?
Yes.
There you have it, then.
However, for your "unique skillset" to be truly useful...
You'll need a security clearance upgrade.
Oh! Thank you.
Don't thank me yet. More responsibility comes with it.
This way. I've got a project for you before you return to your usual assignments.

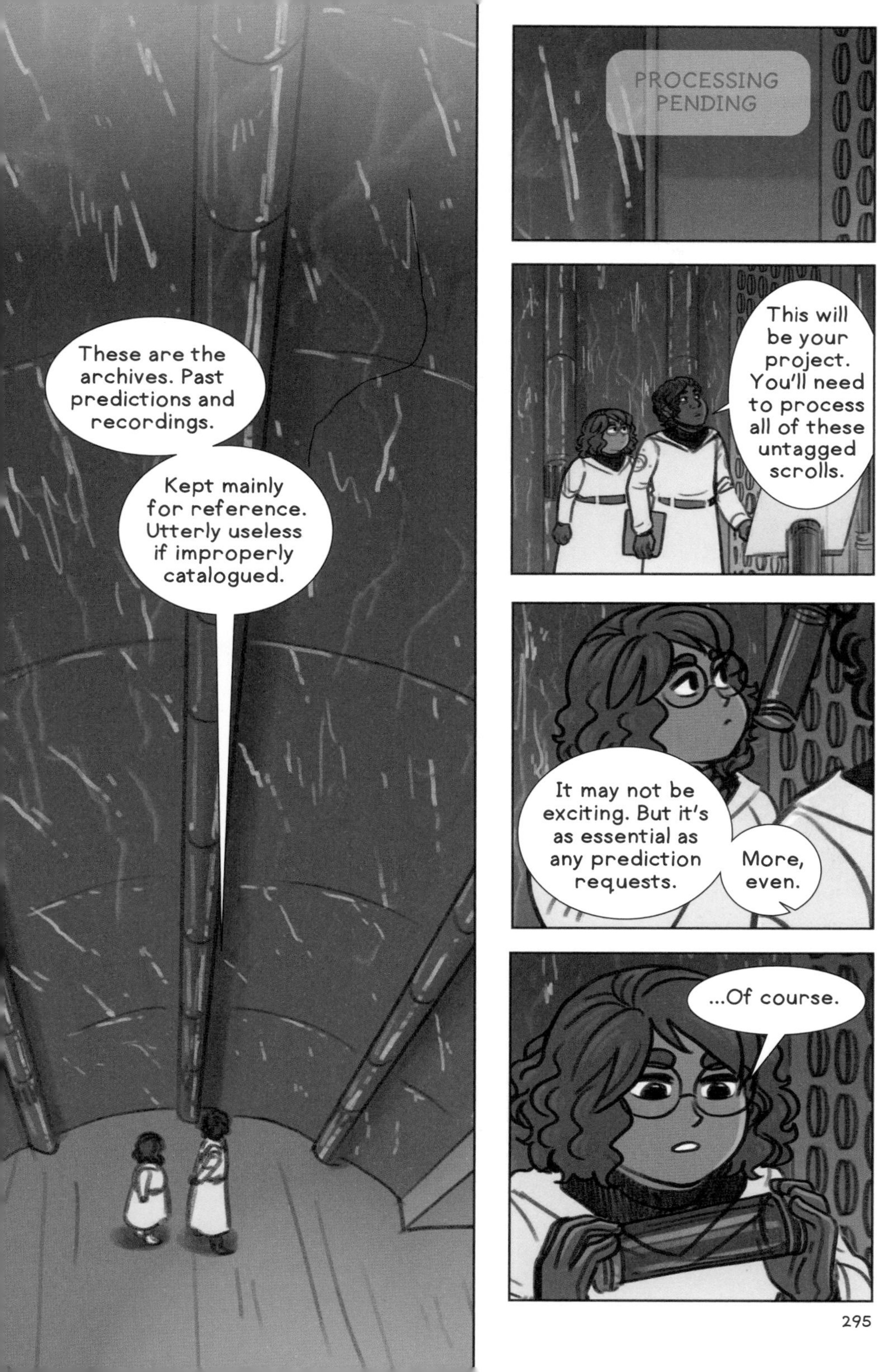
These are the archives. Past predictions and recordings.
Kept mainly for reference. Utterly useless if improperly catalogued.
PROCESSING PENDING
This will be your project. You'll need to process all of these untagged scrolls.
It may not be exciting. But it's as essential as any prediction requests.
More, even.
...Of course.

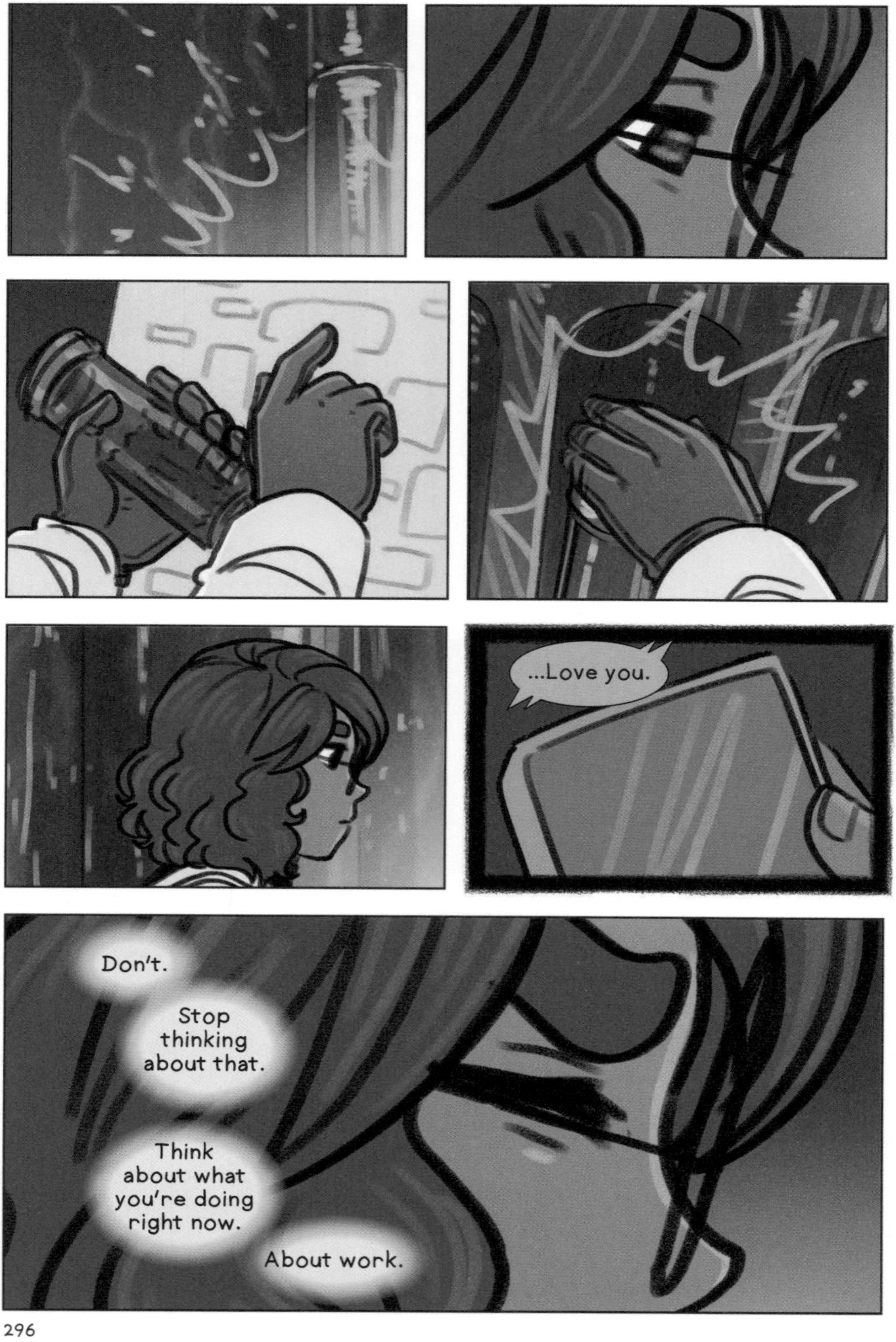
...Love you.
Don't.
Stop thinking about that.
Think about what you're doing right now.
About work.

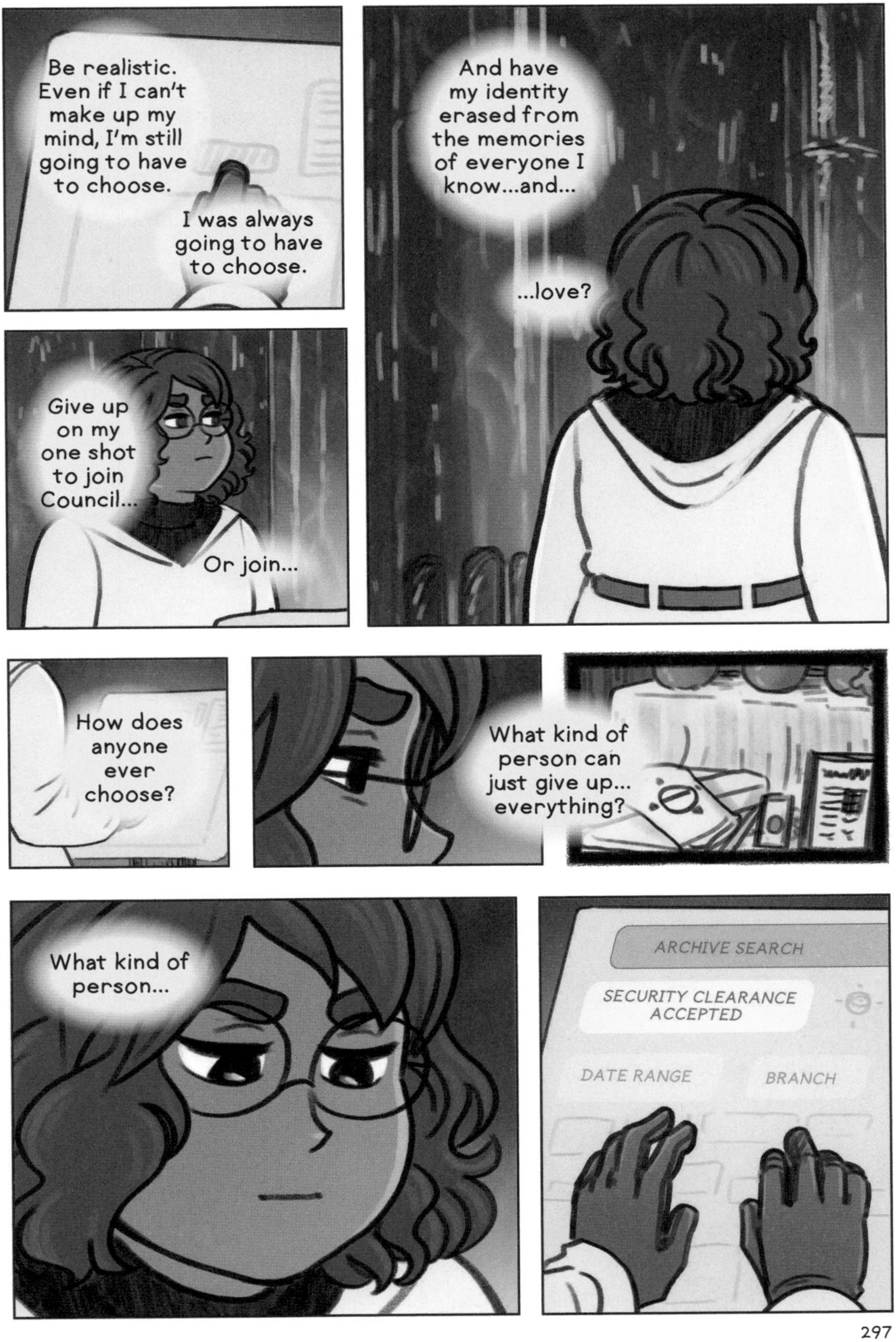
Be realistic. Even if I can't make up my mind, I'm still going to have to choose.
I was always going to have to choose.
And have my identity erased from the memories of everyone I know...and...
...love?
Give up on my one shot to join Council...
Or join...
How does anyone ever choose?
What kind of person can just give up... everything?
What kind of person...
ARCHIVE SEARCH
SECURITY CLEARANCE ACCEPTED
DATE RANGE
BRANCH

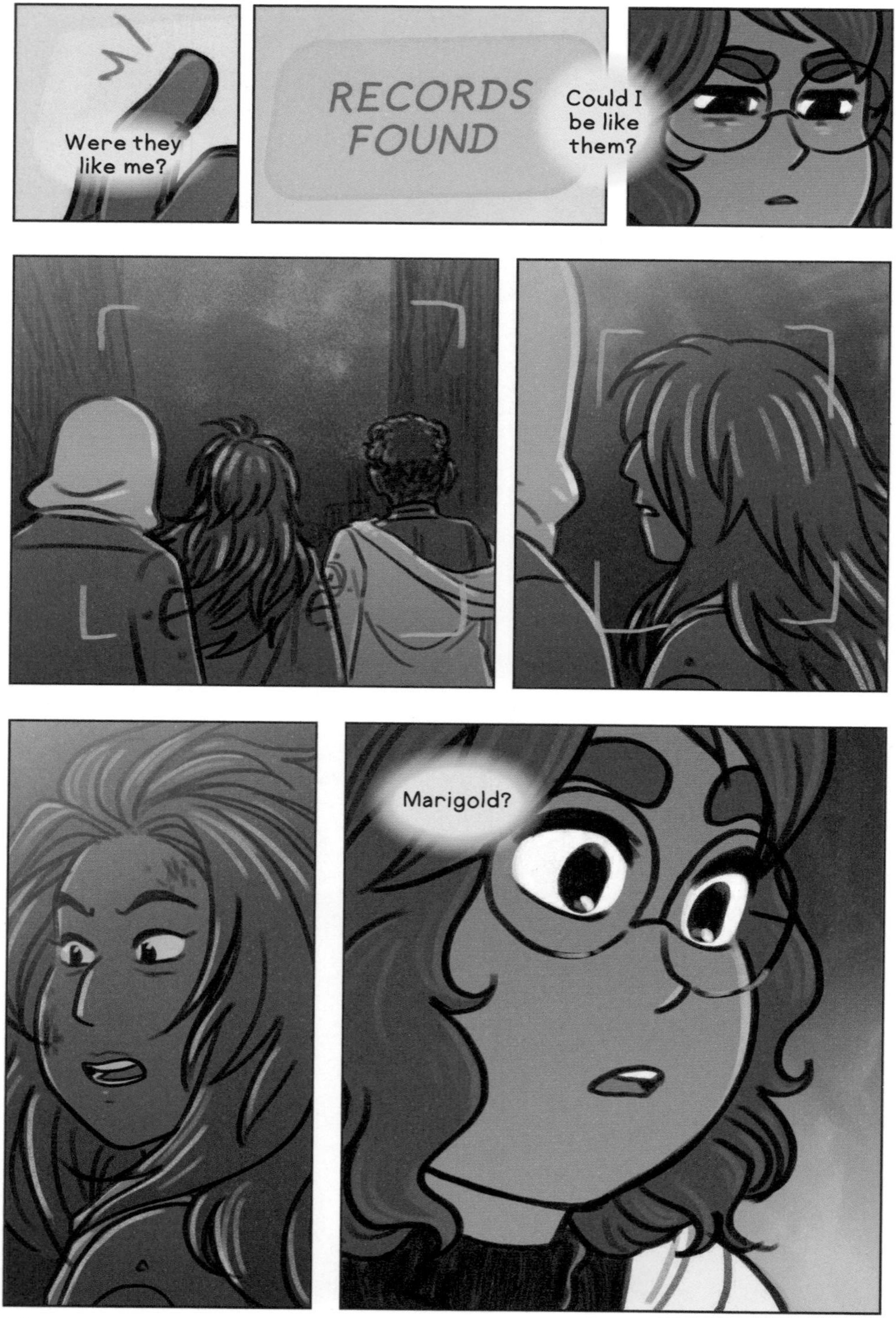
Were they like me?
RECORDS FOUND
Could I be like them?
Marigold?

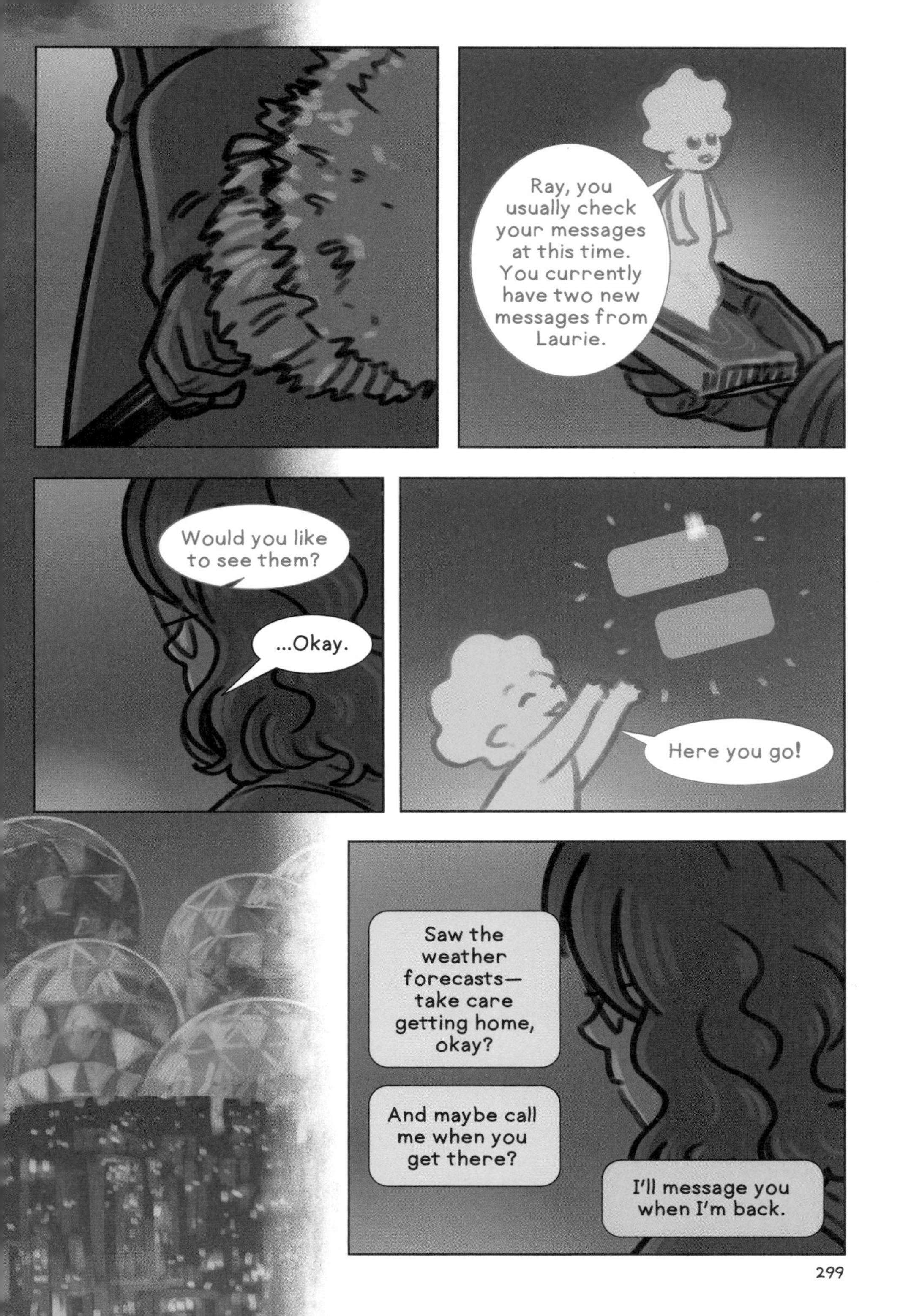

Ray, you usually check your messages at this time. You currently have two new messages from Laurie.
Would you like to see them?
...Okay.
Here you go!
Saw the weather forecasts— take care getting home, okay?
And maybe call me when you get there?
I'll message you when I'm back.

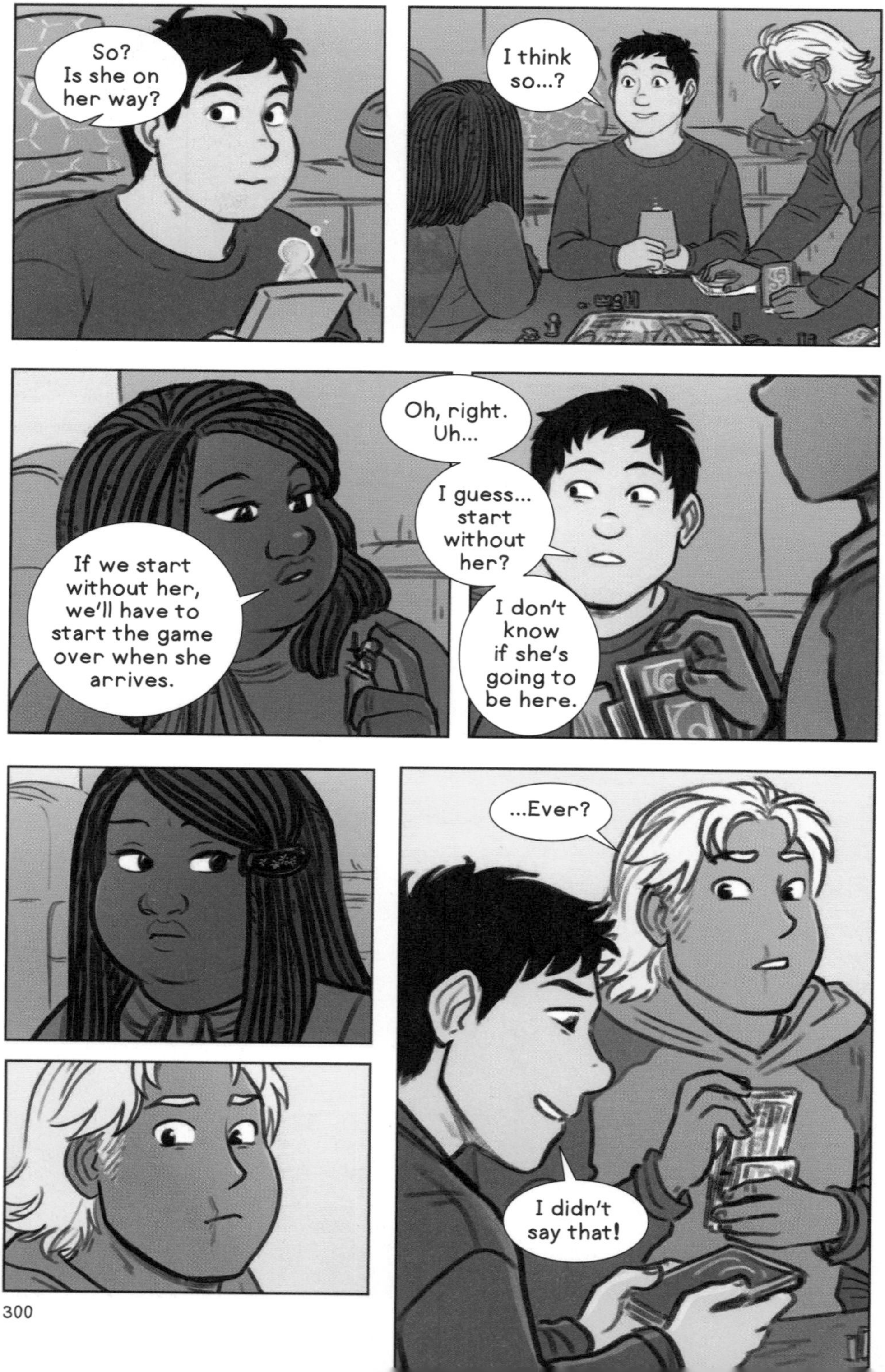
So? Is she on her way?
I think so...?
If we start without her, we'll have to start the game over when she arrives.
Oh, right. Uh...
I guess... start without her?
I don't know if she's going to be here.
...Ever?
I didn't say that!

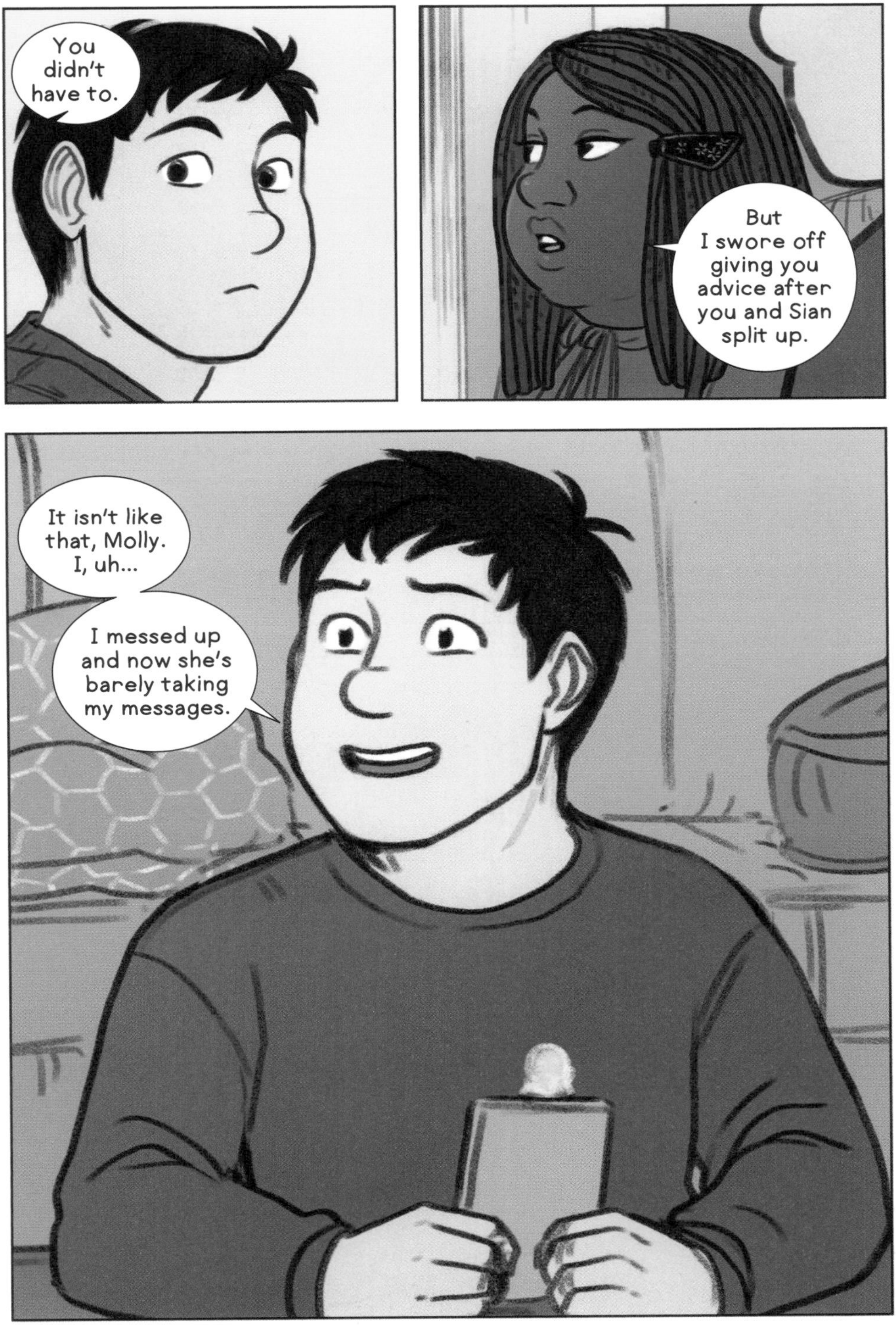
You didn't have to.
But I swore off giving you advice after you and Sian split up.
It isn't like that, Molly. I, uh...
I messed up and now she's barely taking my messages.

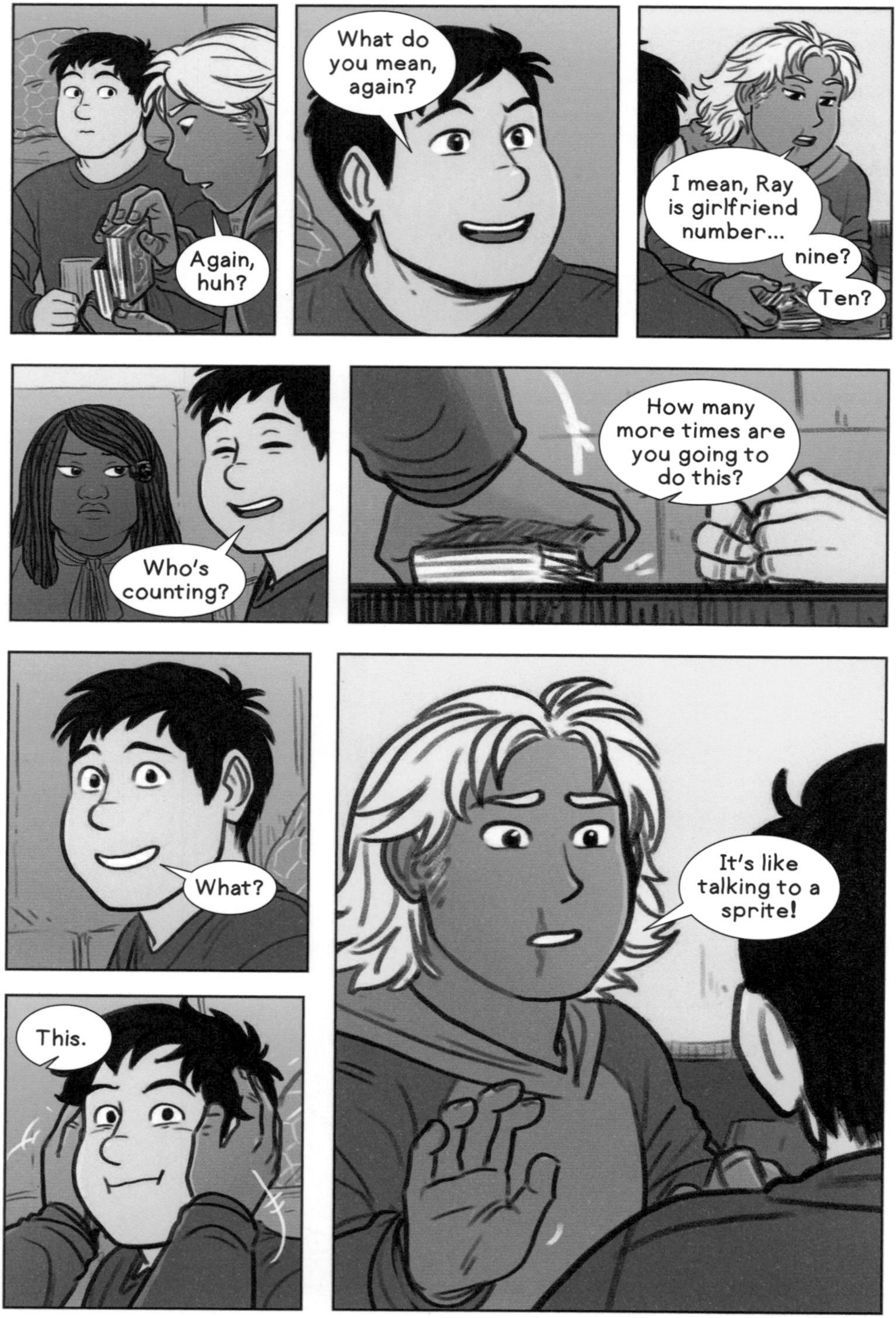
Again, huh?
What do you mean, again?
I mean, Ray is girlfriend number...
nine?
Ten?
Who's counting?
How many more times are you going to do this?
What?
This.
It's like talking to a sprite!

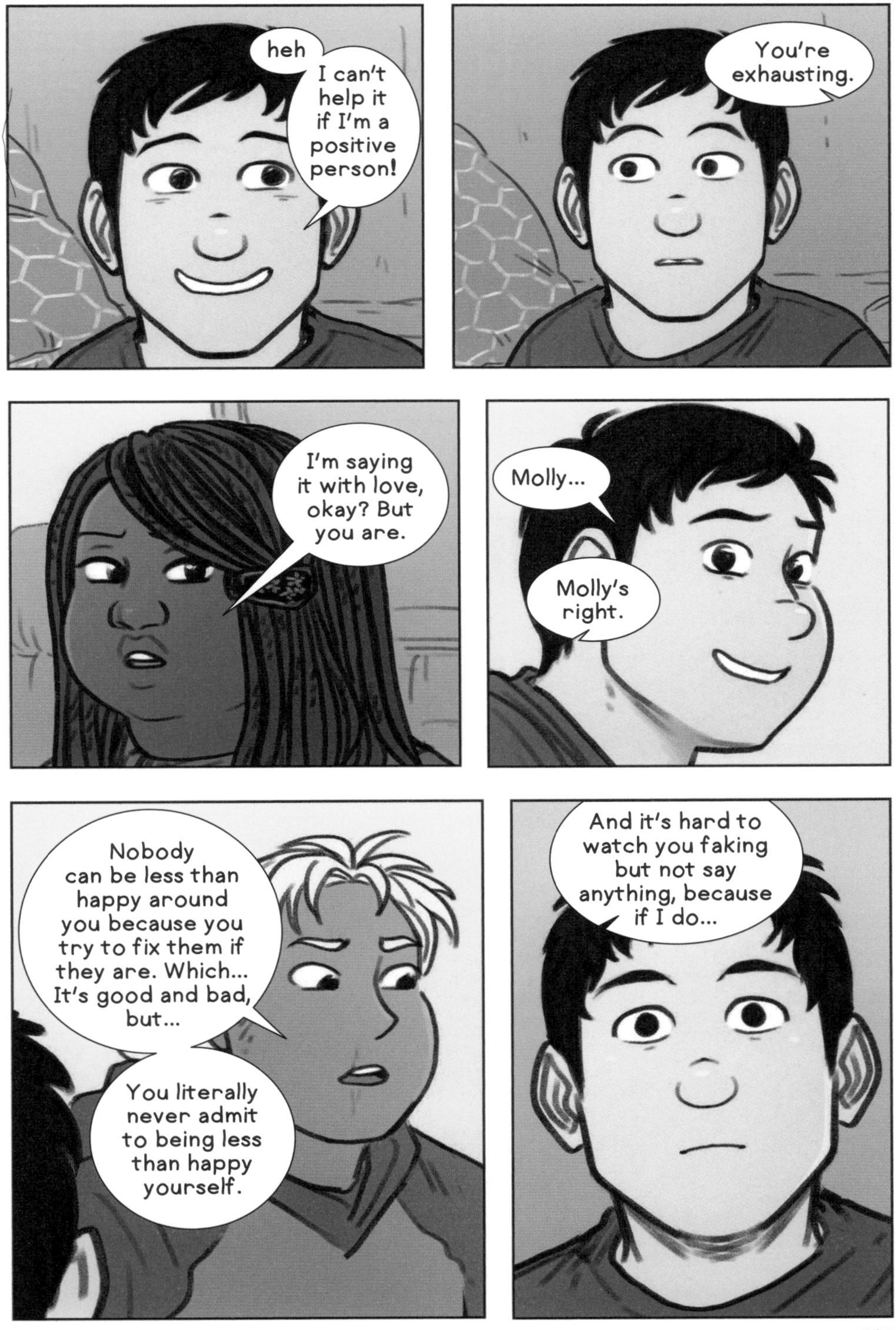
heh
I can't help it if I'm a positive person!
You're exhausting.
I'm saying it with love, okay? But you are.
Molly...
Molly's right.
Nobody can be less than happy around you because you try to fix them if they are. Which... It's good and bad, but...
You literally never admit to being less than happy yourself.
And it's hard to watch you faking but not say anything, because if I do...

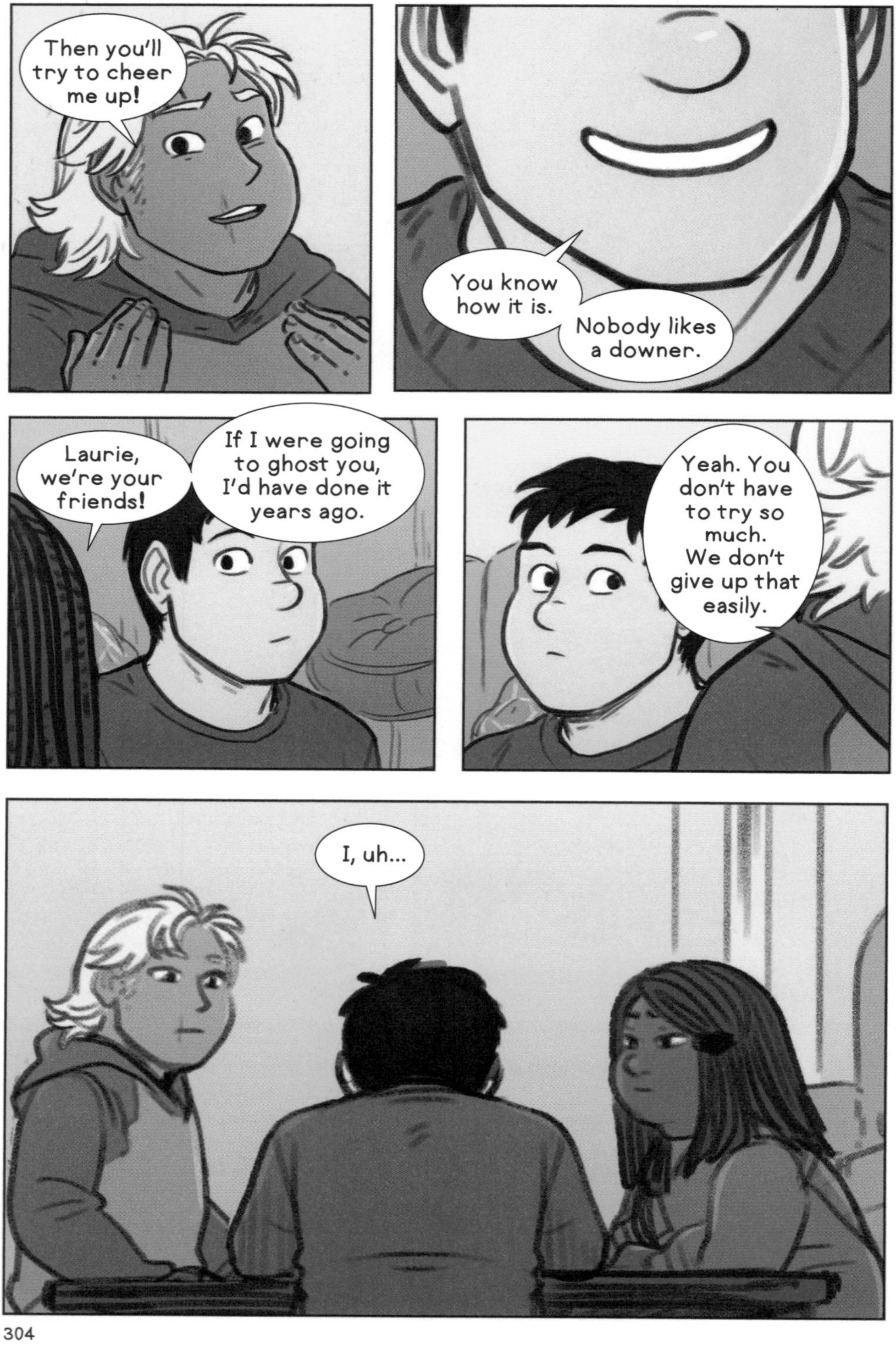
Then you'll try to cheer me up!
You know how it is.
Nobody likes a downer.
Laurie, we're your friends!
If I were going to ghost you, I'd have done it years ago.
Yeah. You don't have to try so much.
We don't give up that easily.
I, uh...

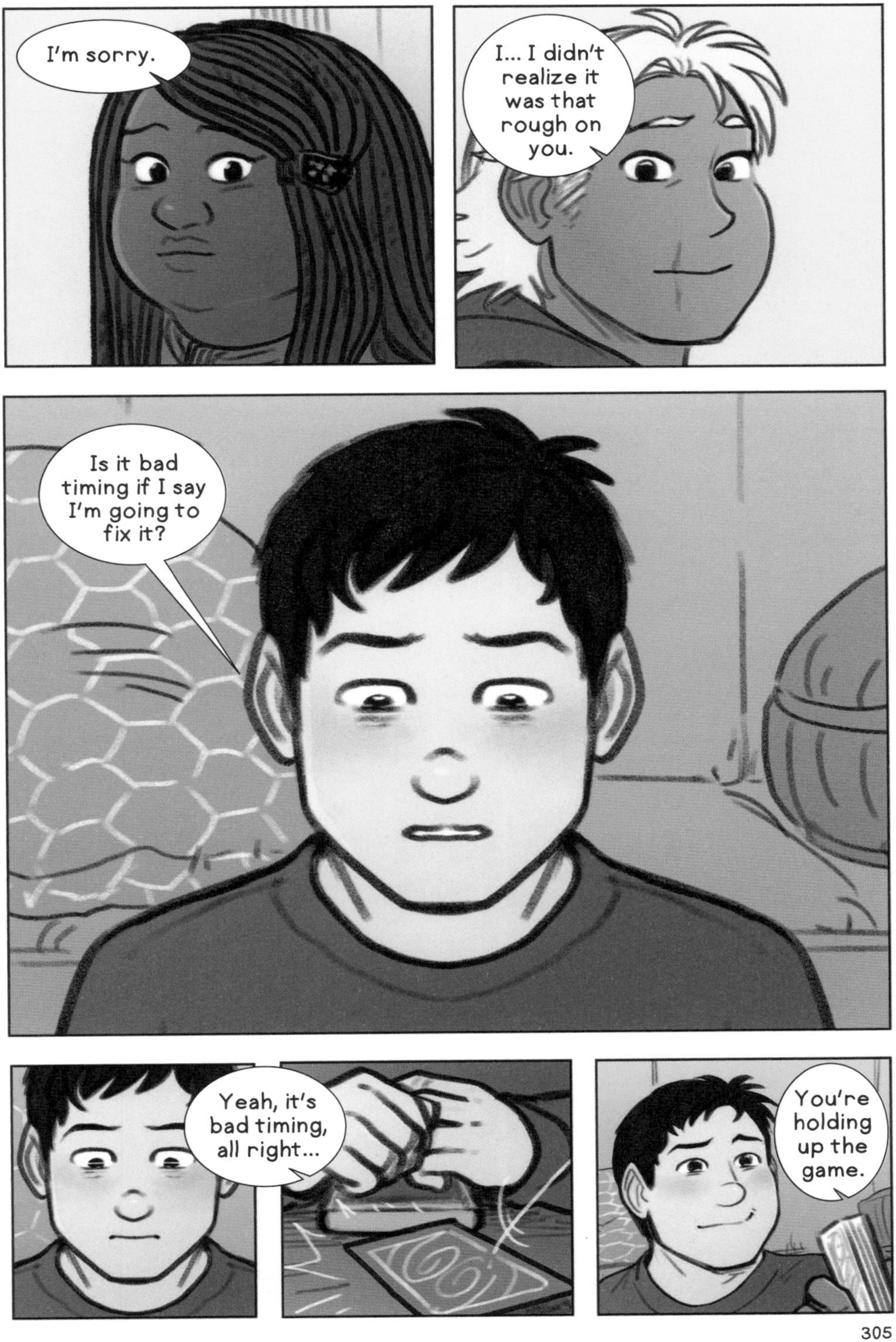
I'm sorry.
I... I didn't realize it was that rough on you.
Is it bad timing if I say I'm going to fix it?
Yeah, it's bad timing, all right...
You're holding up the game.

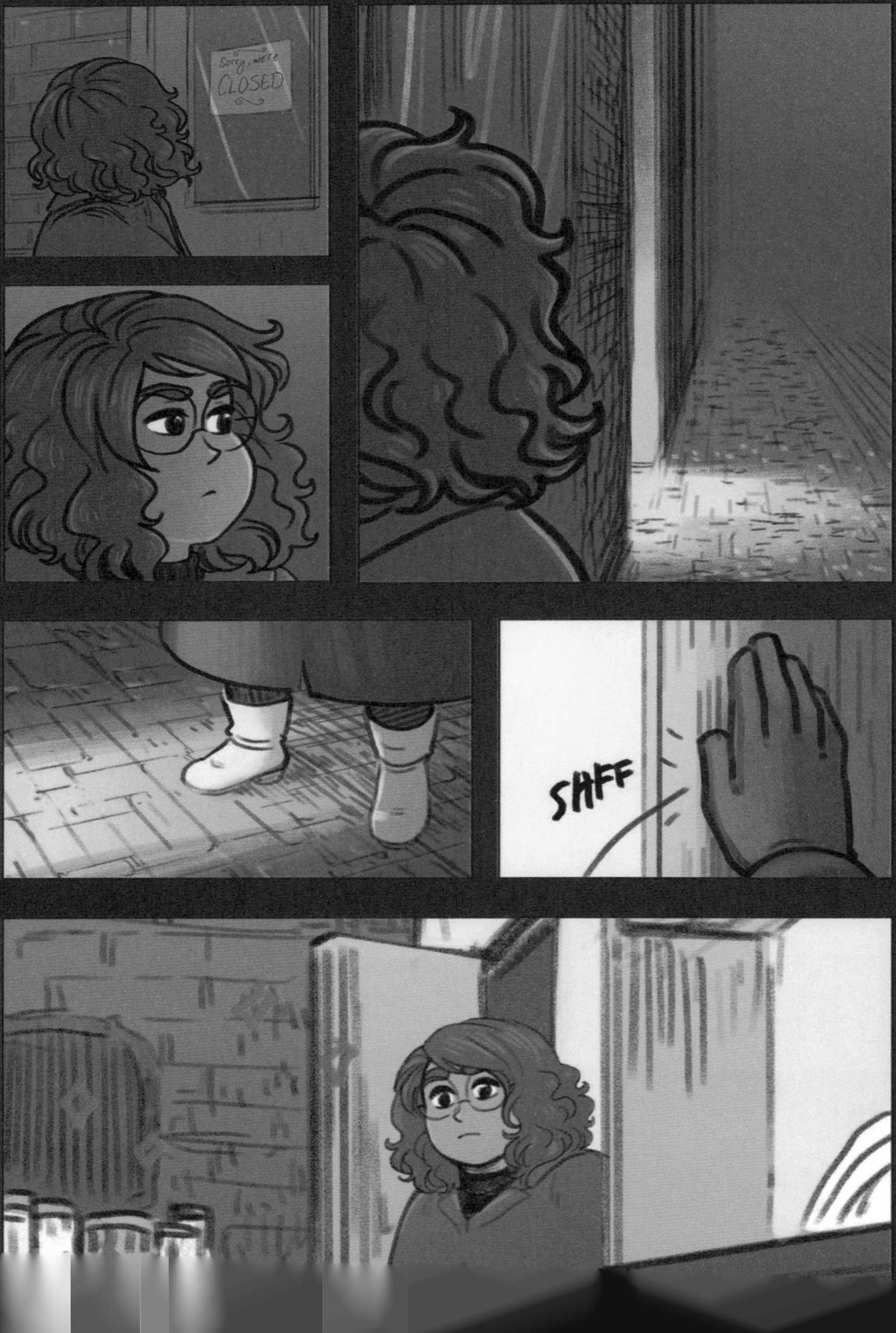

Sorry, we're CLOSED
SHFF

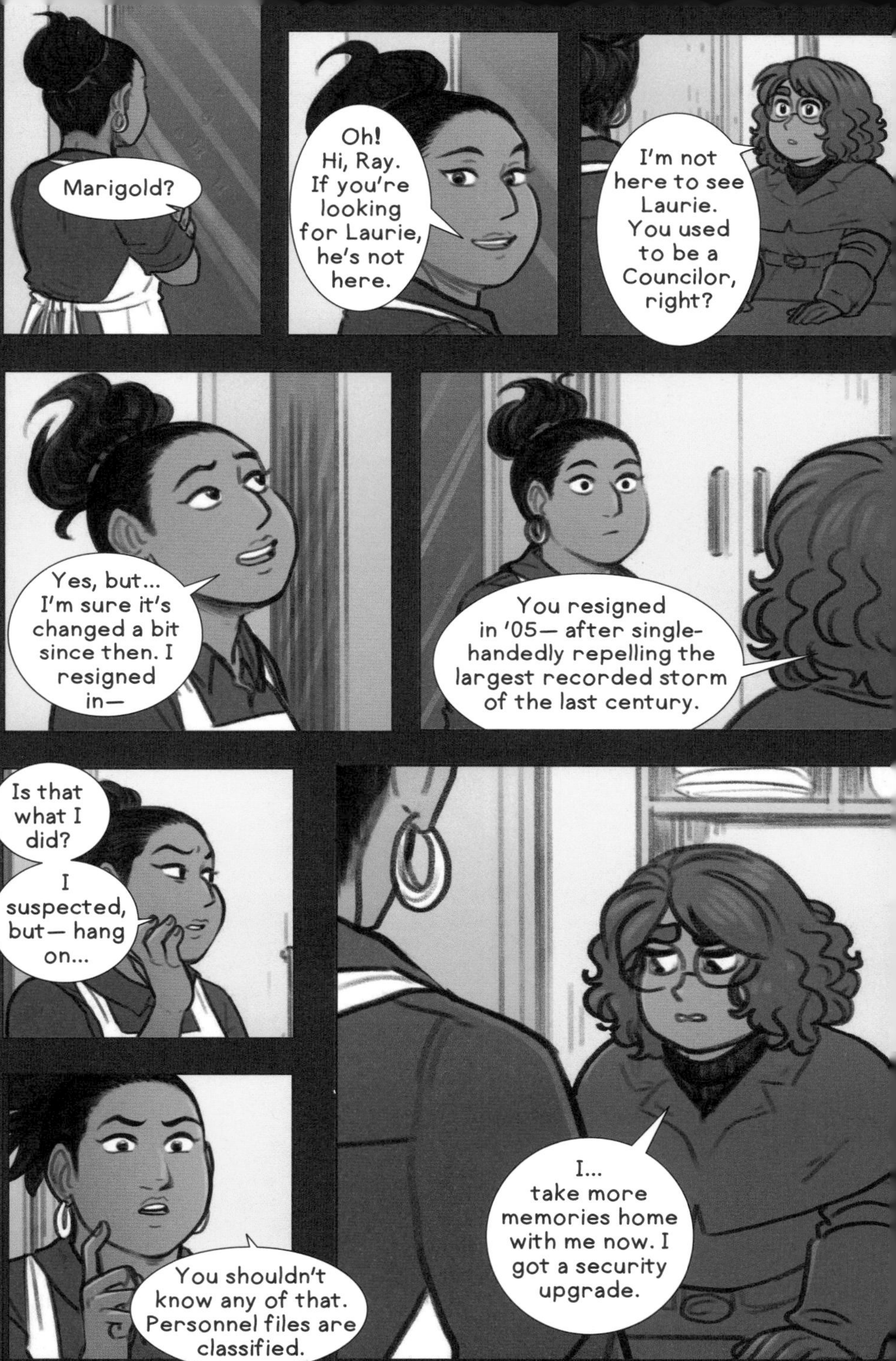
Marigold?
Oh! Hi, Ray. If you're looking for Laurie, he's not here.
I'm not here to see Laurie. You used to be a Councilor, right?
Yes, but... I'm sure it's changed a bit since then. I resigned in—
You resigned in '05— after single-handedly repelling the largest recorded storm of the last century.
Is that what I did?
I suspected, but— hang on...
You shouldn't know any of that. Personnel files are classified.
I... take more memories home with me now. I got a security upgrade.

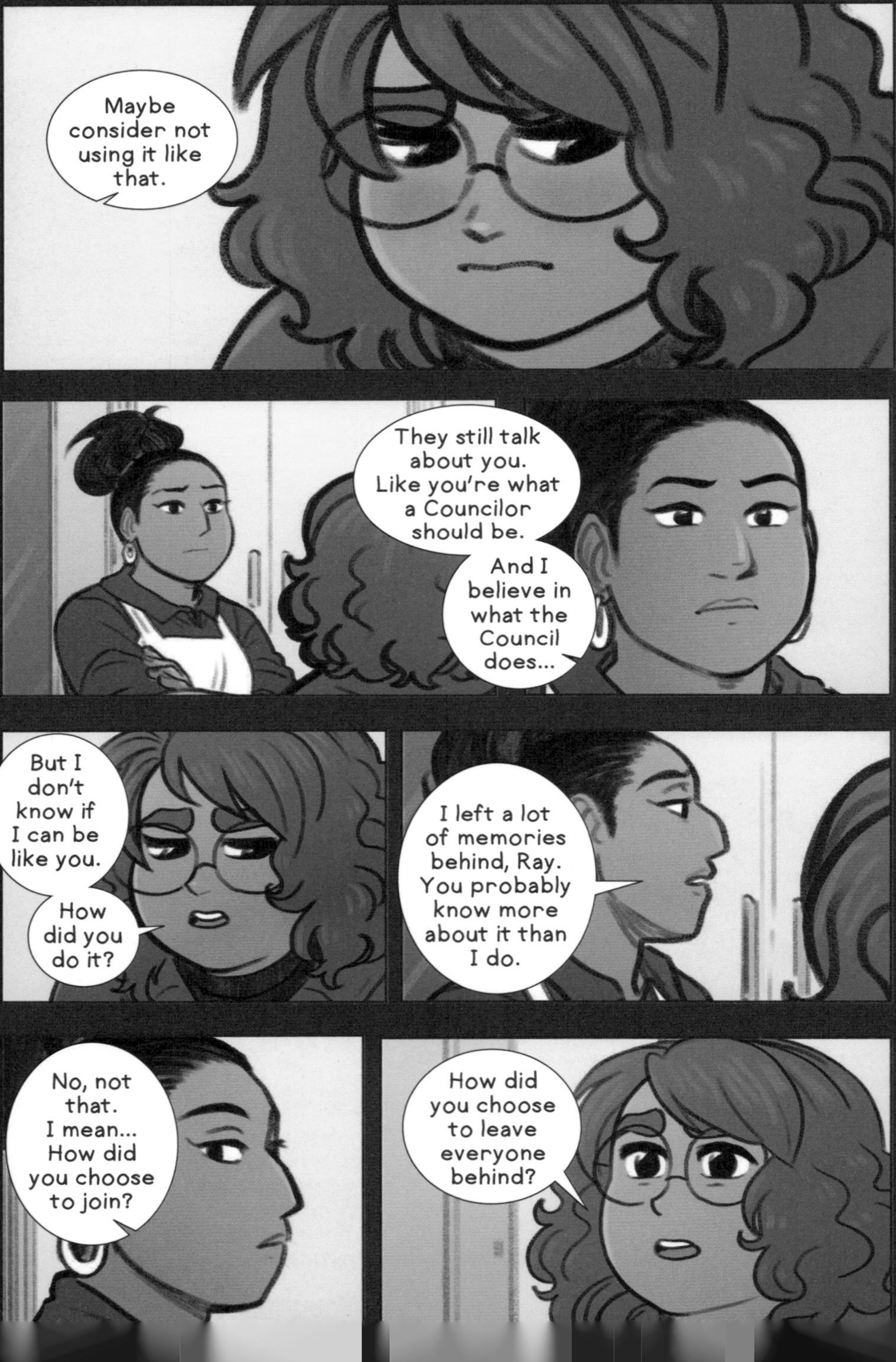
Maybe consider not using it like that.
They still talk about you. Like you're what a Councilor should be.
And I believe in what the Council does...
But I don't know if I can be like you.
How did you do it?
I left a lot of memories behind, Ray. You probably know more about it than I do.
No, not that. I mean... How did you choose to join?
How did you choose to leave everyone behind?

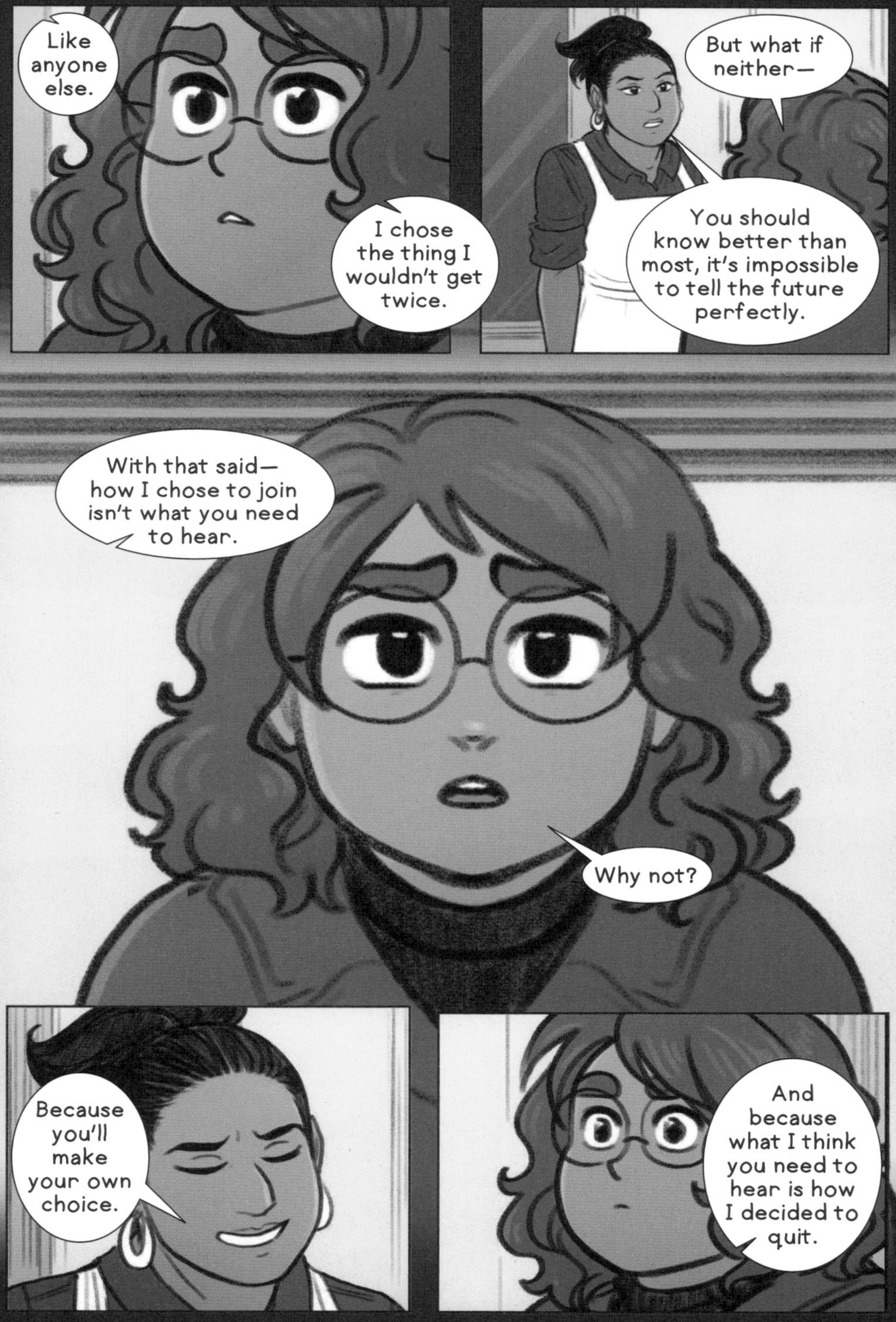
Like anyone else.
I chose the thing I wouldn't get twice.
But what if neither—
You should know better than most, it's impossible to tell the future perfectly.
With that said— how I chose to join isn't what you need to hear.
Why not?
Because you'll make your own choice.
And because what I think you need to hear is how I decided to quit.

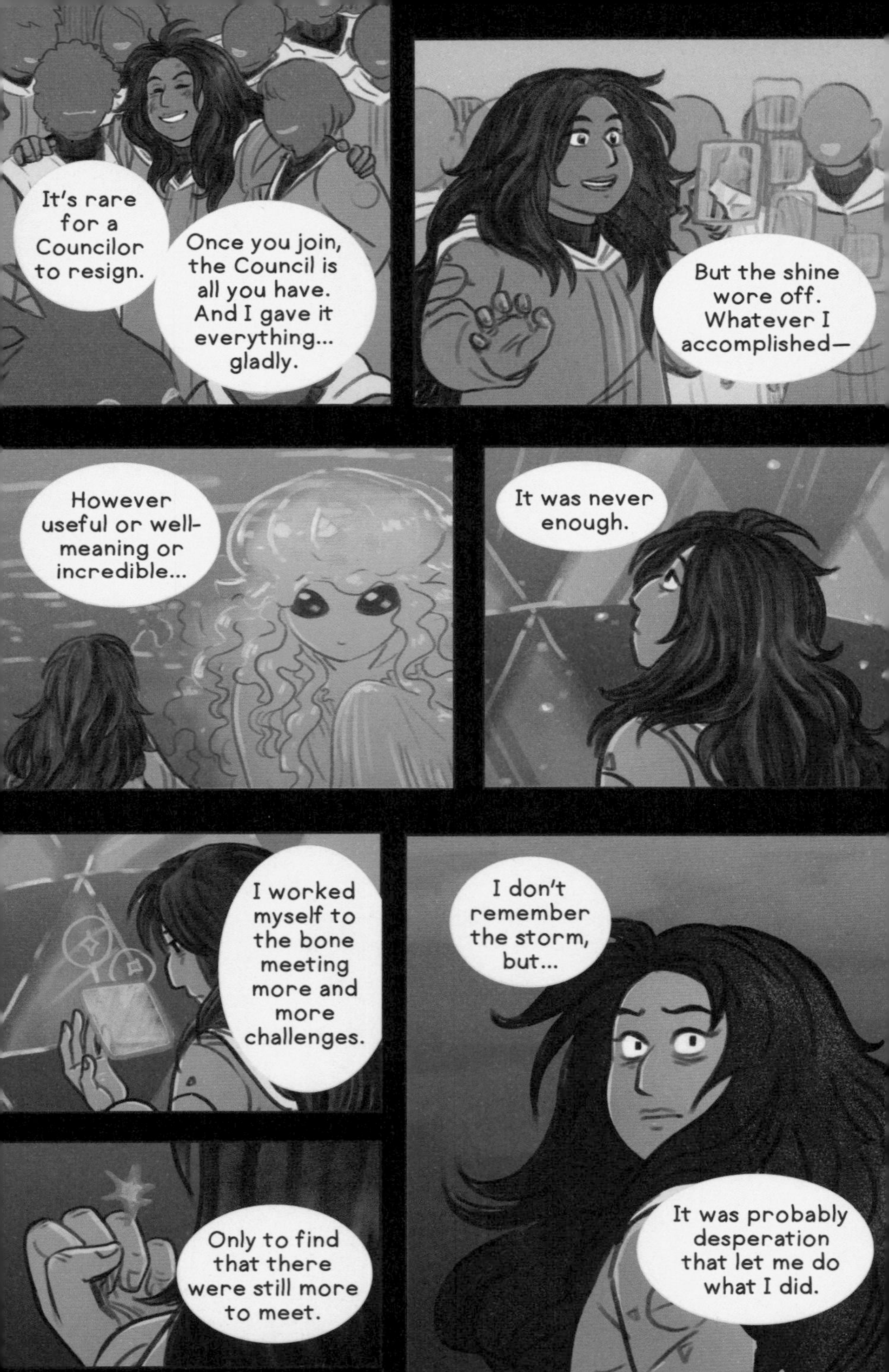
It's rare for a Councilor to resign.
Once you join, the Council is all you have. And I gave it everything... gladly.
But the shine wore off. Whatever I accomplished—
However useful or well-meaning or incredible...
It was never enough.
I worked myself to the bone meeting more and more challenges.
Only to find that there were still more to meet.
I don't remember the storm, but...
It was probably desperation that let me do what I did.

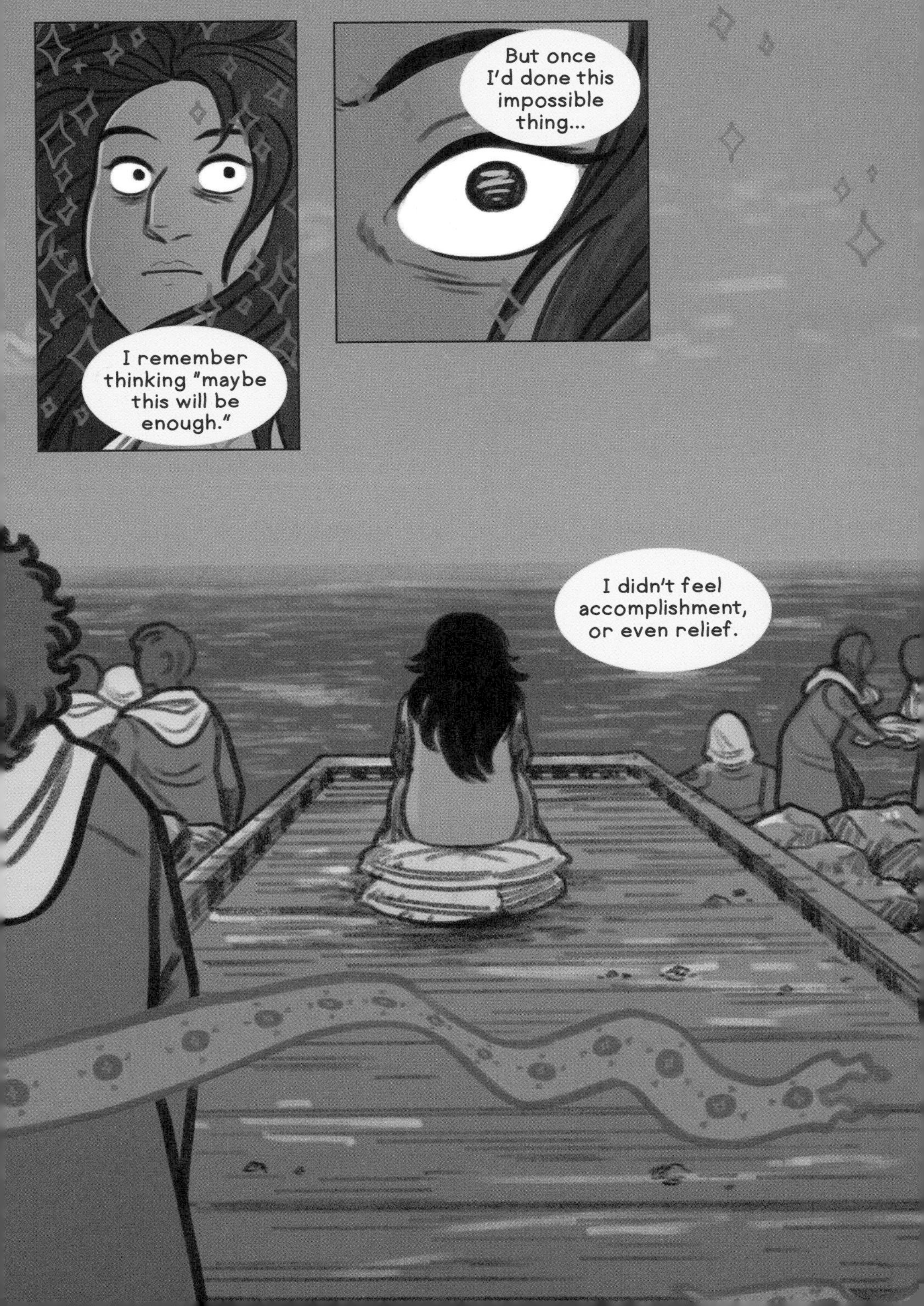
I remember thinking "maybe this will be enough."
But once I'd done this impossible thing...
I didn't feel accomplishment, or even relief.

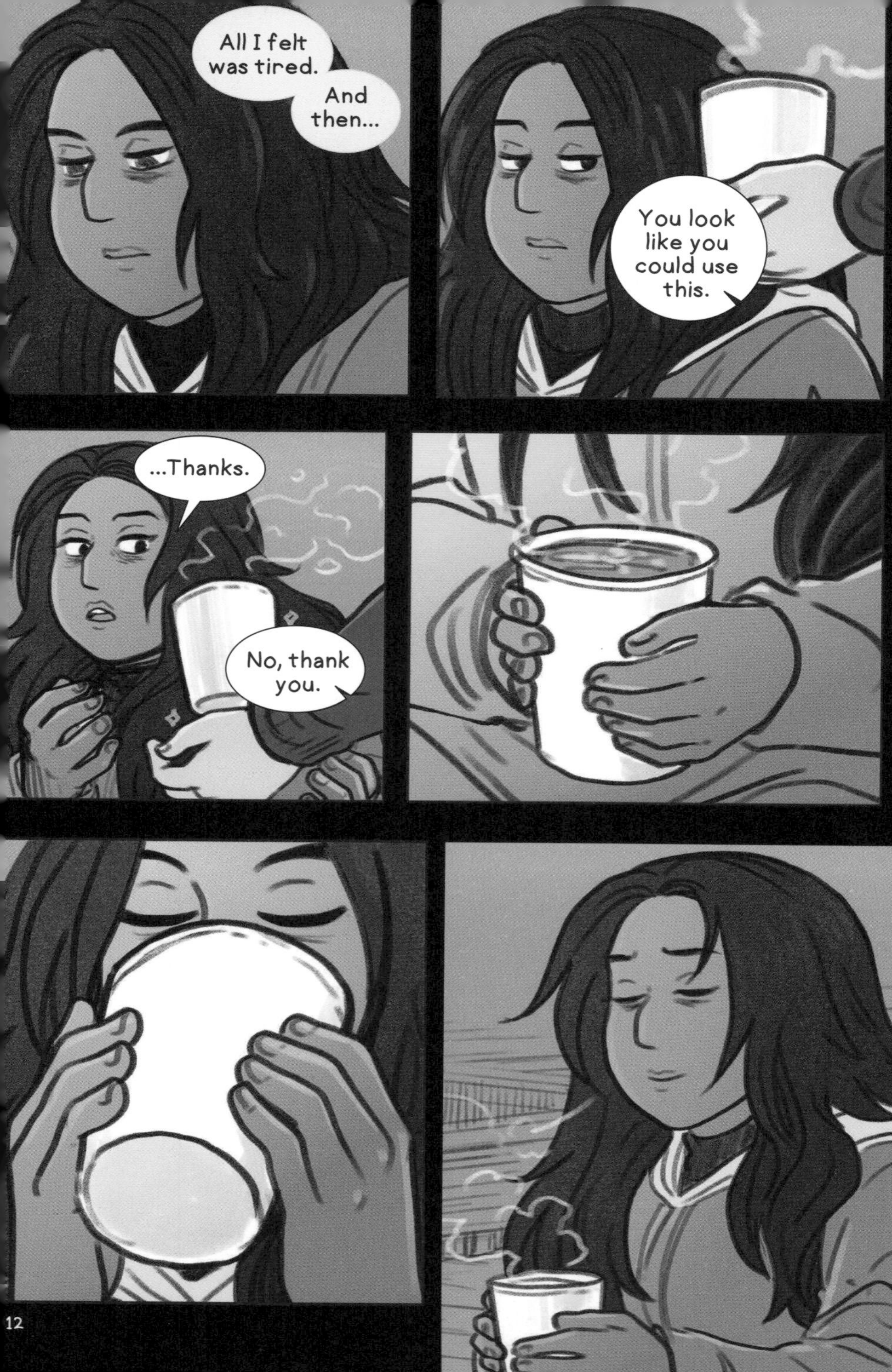
All I felt was tired.
And then...
You look like you could use this.
...Thanks.
No, thank you.

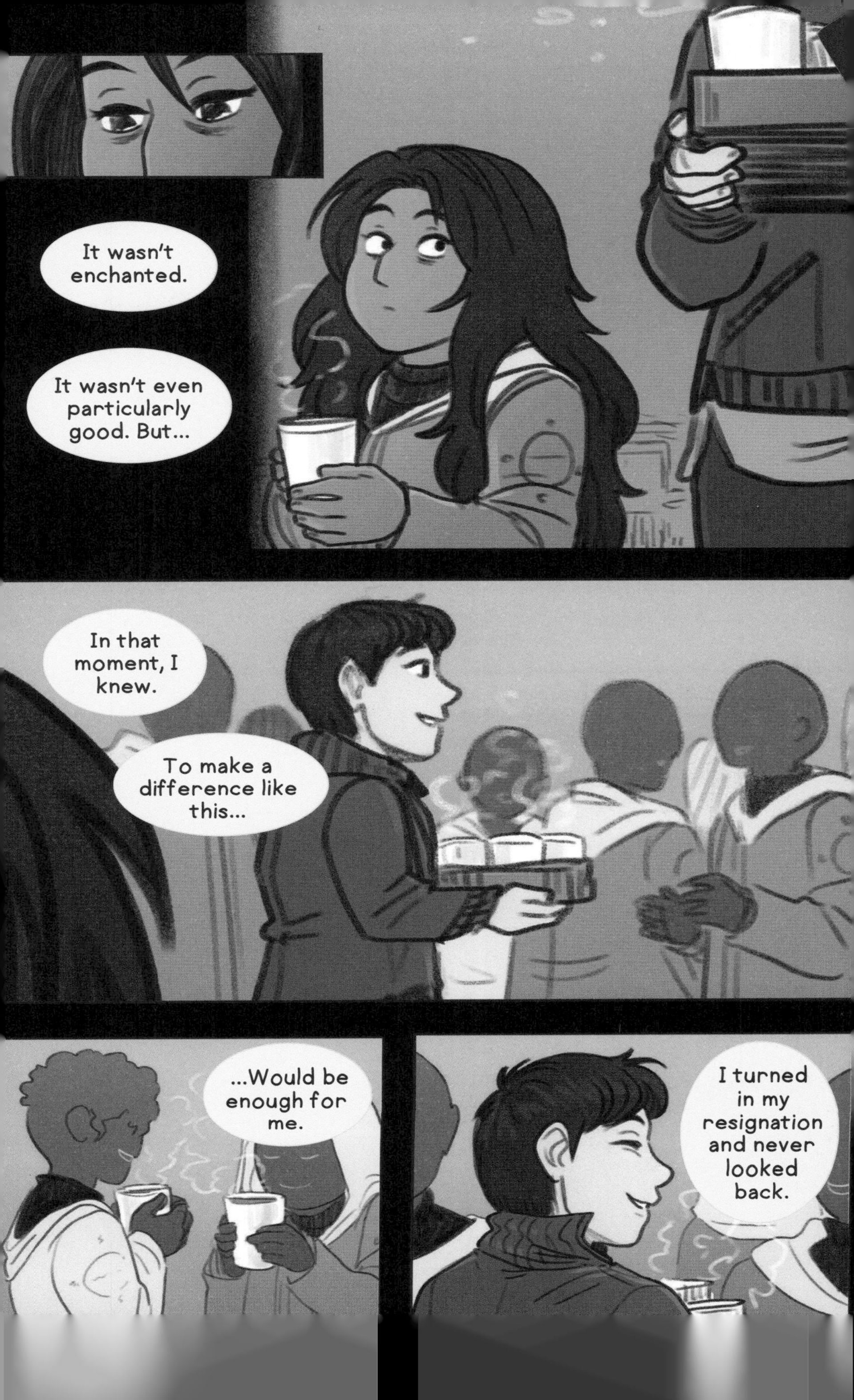
It wasn't enchanted.
It wasn't even particularly good. But...
In that moment, I knew.
To make a difference like this...
...Would be enough for me.
I turned in my resignation and never looked back.

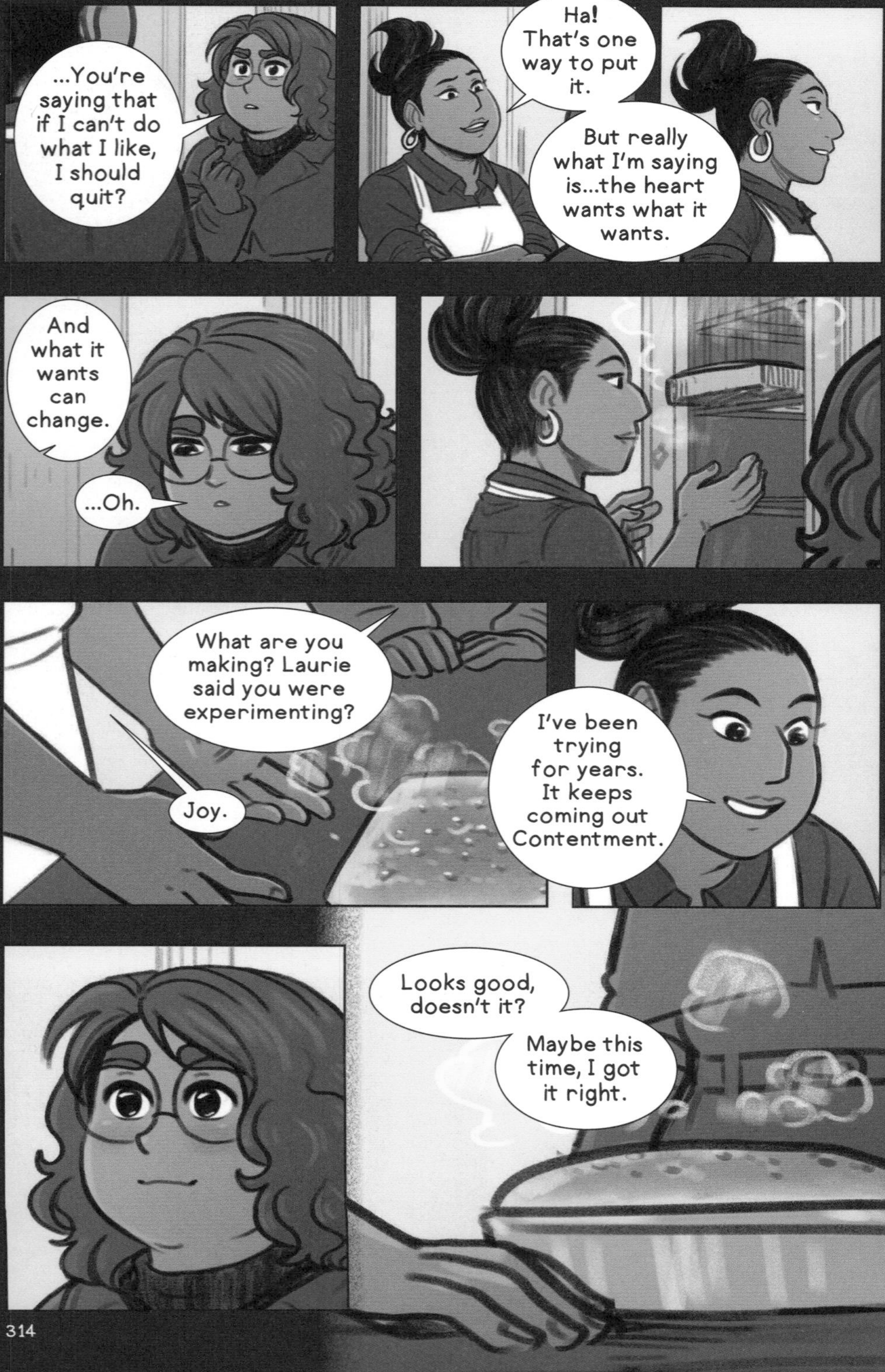
...You're saying that if I can't do what I like, I should quit?
Ha! That's one way to put it.
But really what I'm saying is...the heart wants what it wants.
And what it wants can change.
...Oh.
What are you making? Laurie said you were experimenting?
Joy.
I've been trying for years. It keeps coming out Contentment.
Looks good, doesn't it?
Maybe this time, I got it right.

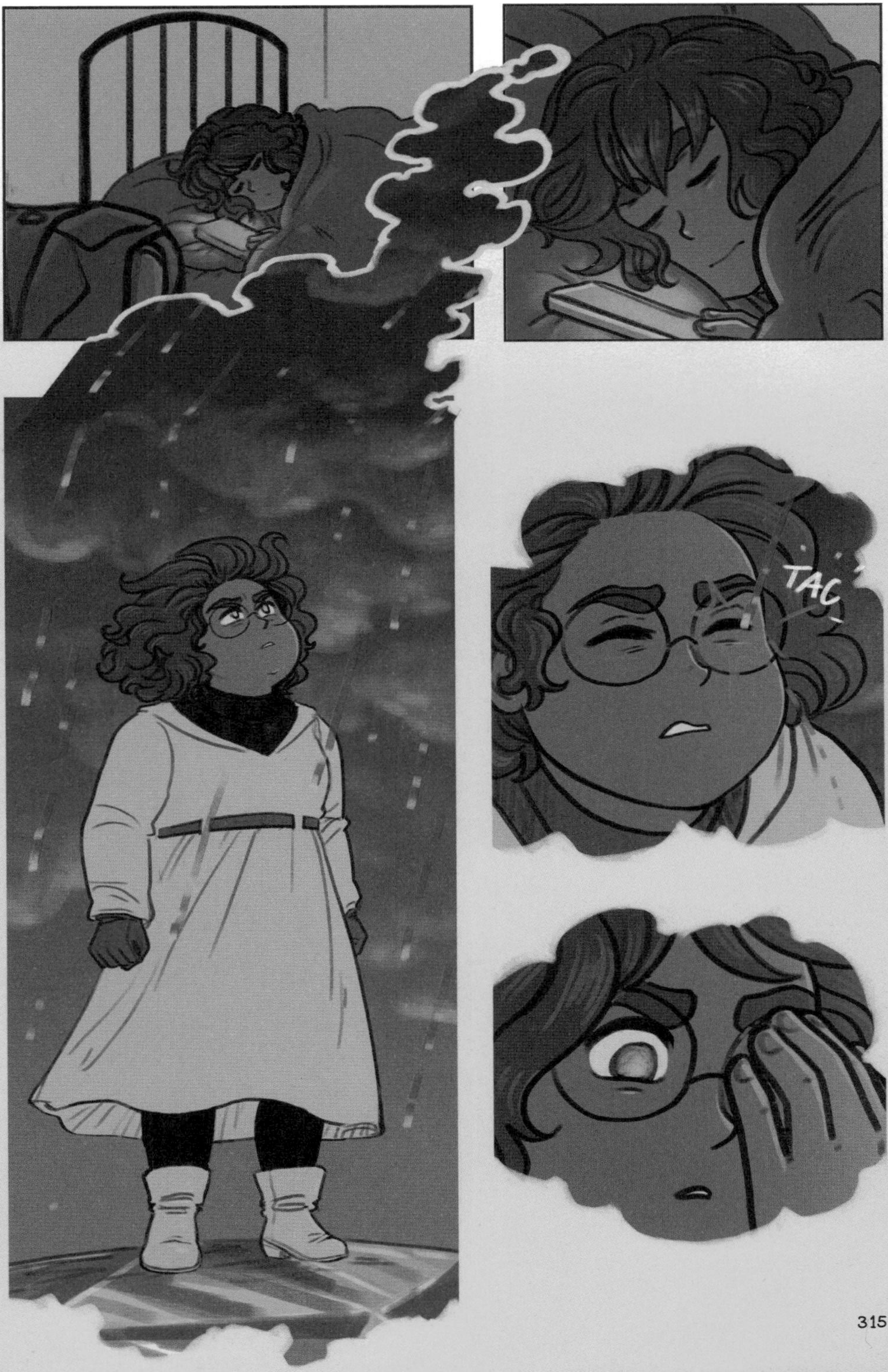
TAC

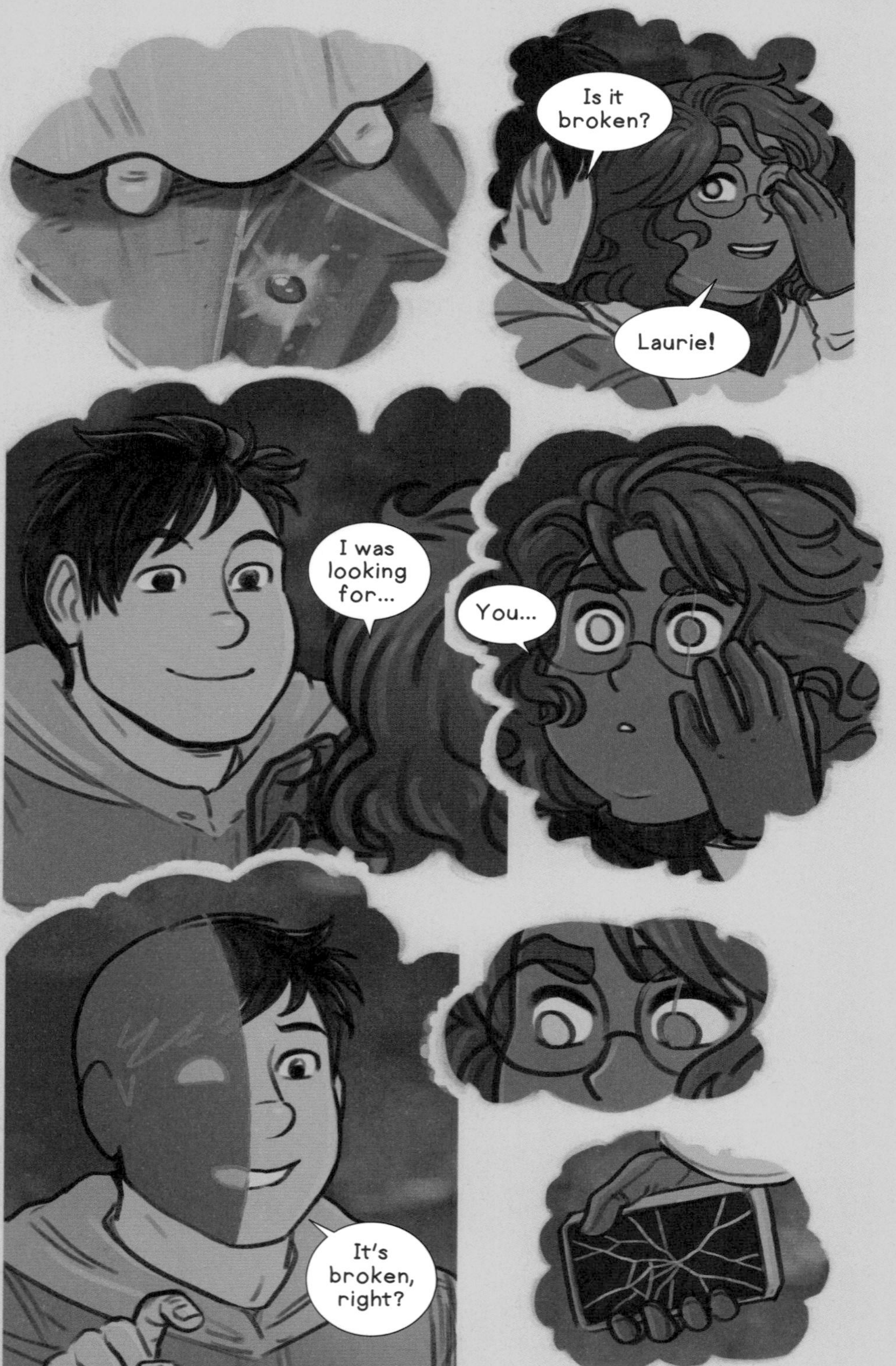
Is it broken?
Laurie!
I was looking for...
You...
It's broken, right?

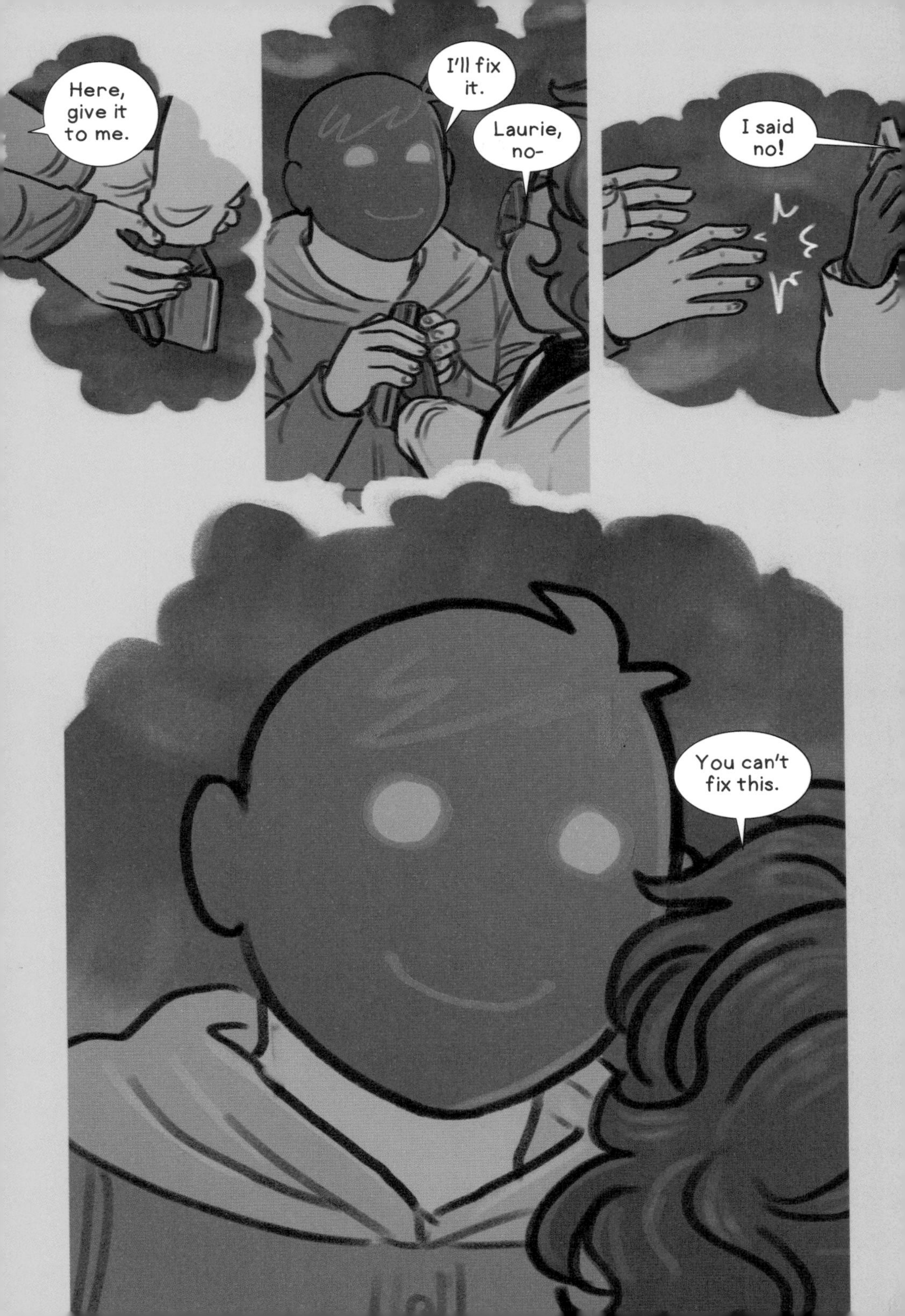
Here, give it to me.
I'll fix it.
Laurie, no-
I said no!
You can't fix this.

You can't...

...?

MOM
Even cuter than the last one, look!

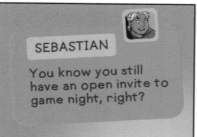
SIAN
Do you want me to fly over there? BECAUSE I WILL!!! Just say the word

SEBASTIAN
You know you still have an open invite to game night, right?

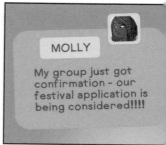
MOLLY
My group just got confirmation - our festival application is being considered!!!!

That's so exciting! You absolutely deserve it. Good luck!!!!!!!

POP

318

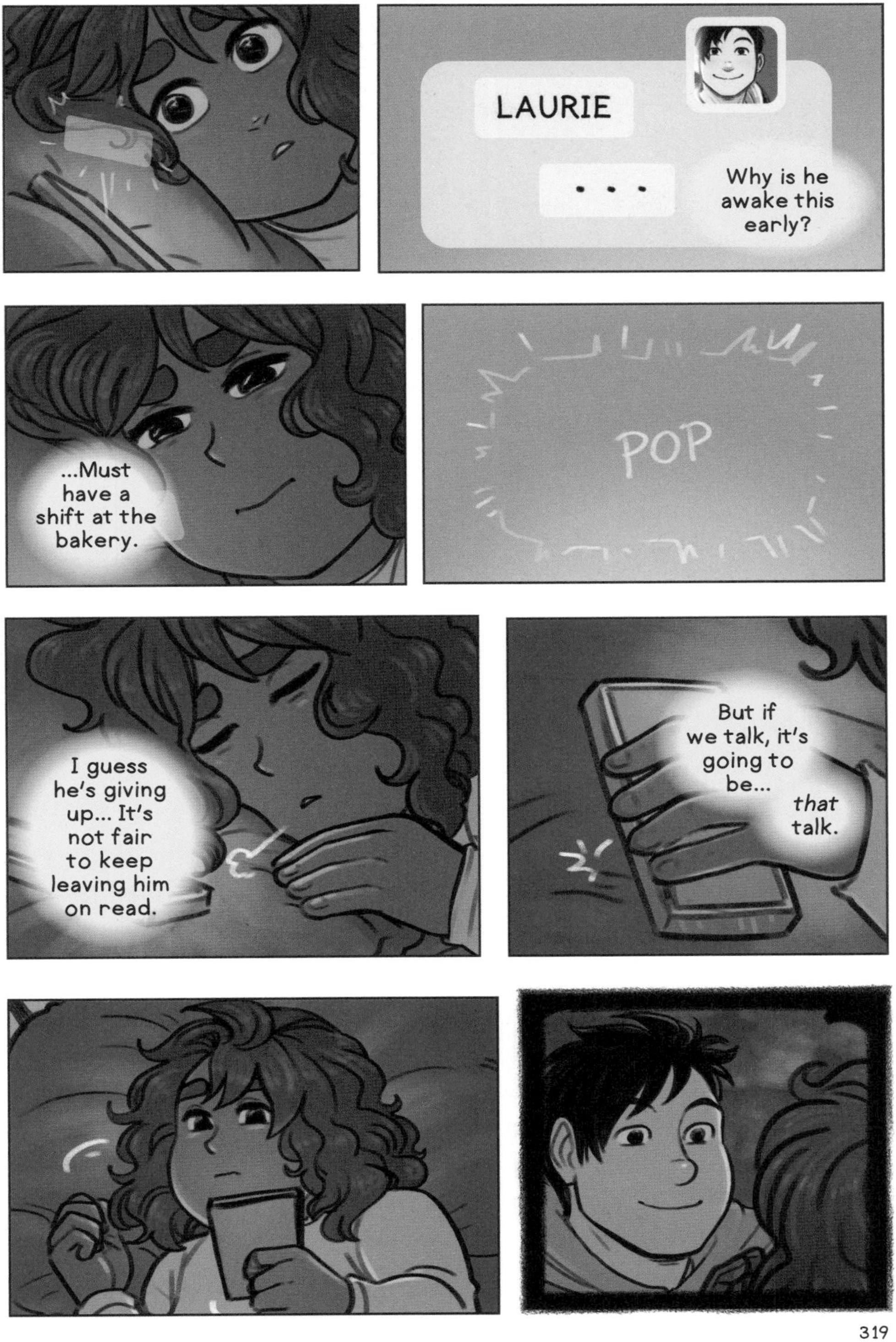
LAURIE
...
Why is he awake this early?
...Must have a shift at the bakery.
POP
I guess he's giving up... It's not fair to keep leaving him on read.
But if we talk, it's going to be... *that* talk.

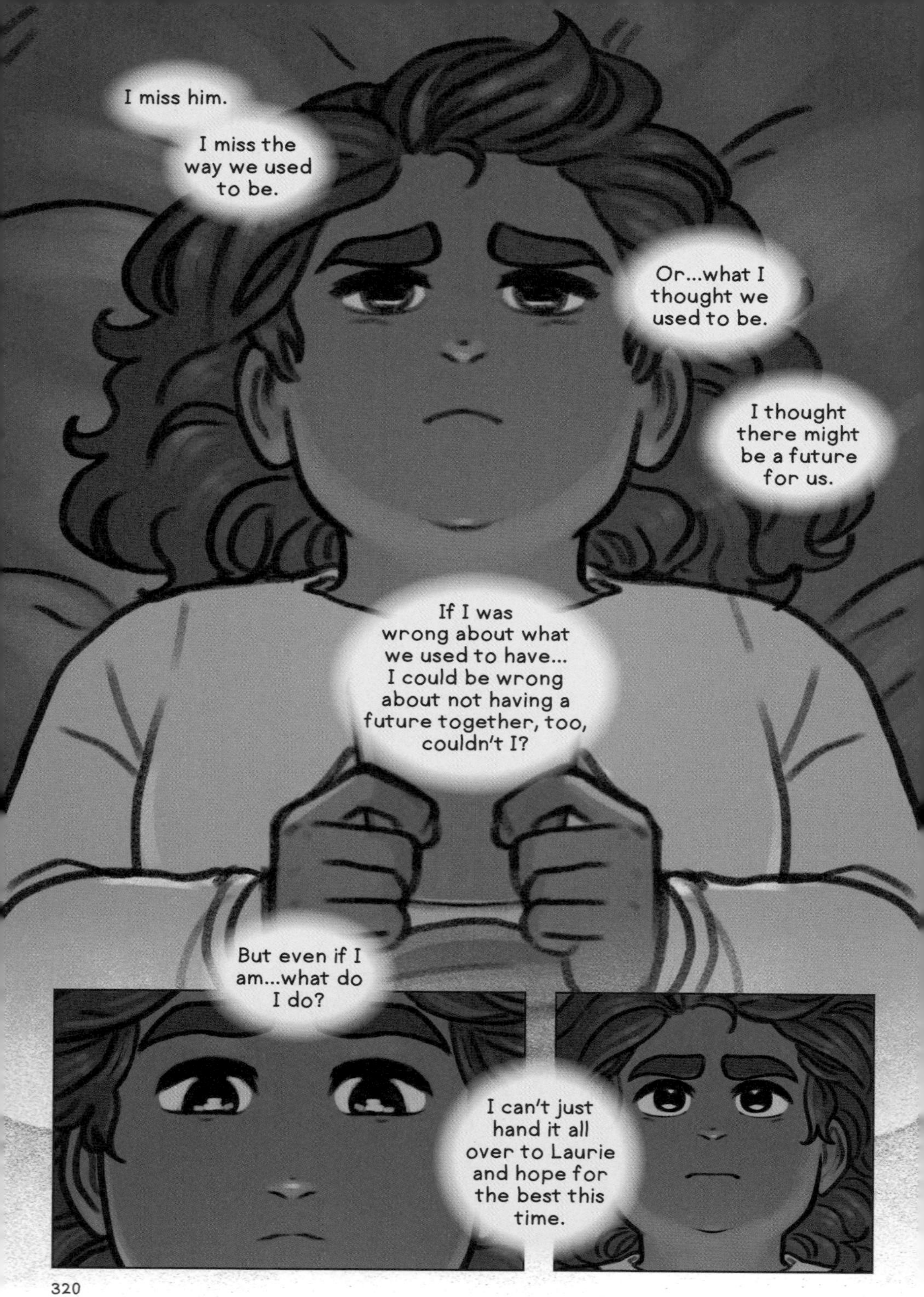
I miss him.
I miss the way we used to be.
Or...what I thought we used to be.
I thought there might be a future for us.
If I was wrong about what we used to have... I could be wrong about not having a future together, too, couldn't I?
But even if I am...what do I do?
I can't just hand it all over to Laurie and hope for the best this time.

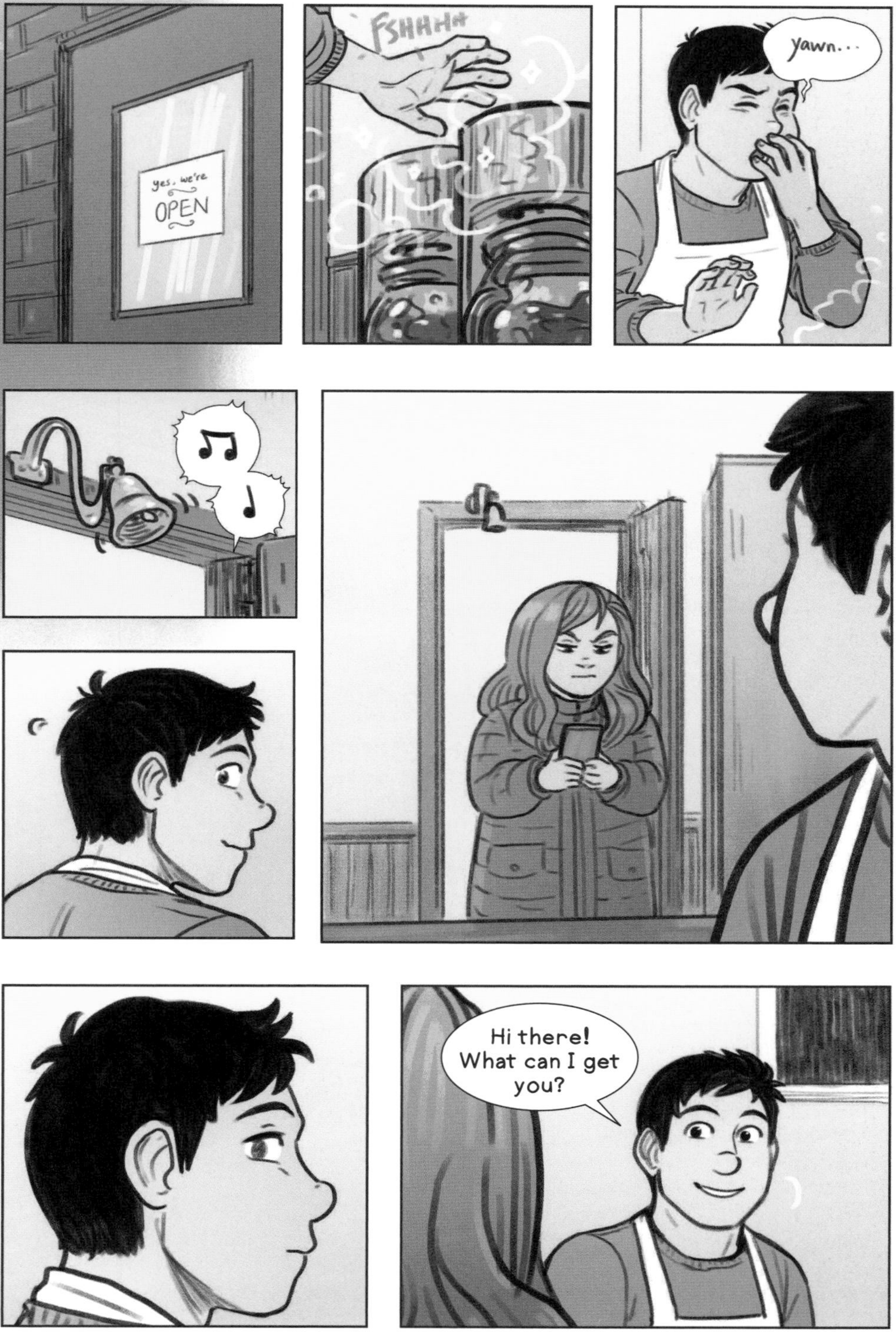
yes, we're
OPEN
FSHHHH
yawn...
Hi there! What can I get you?

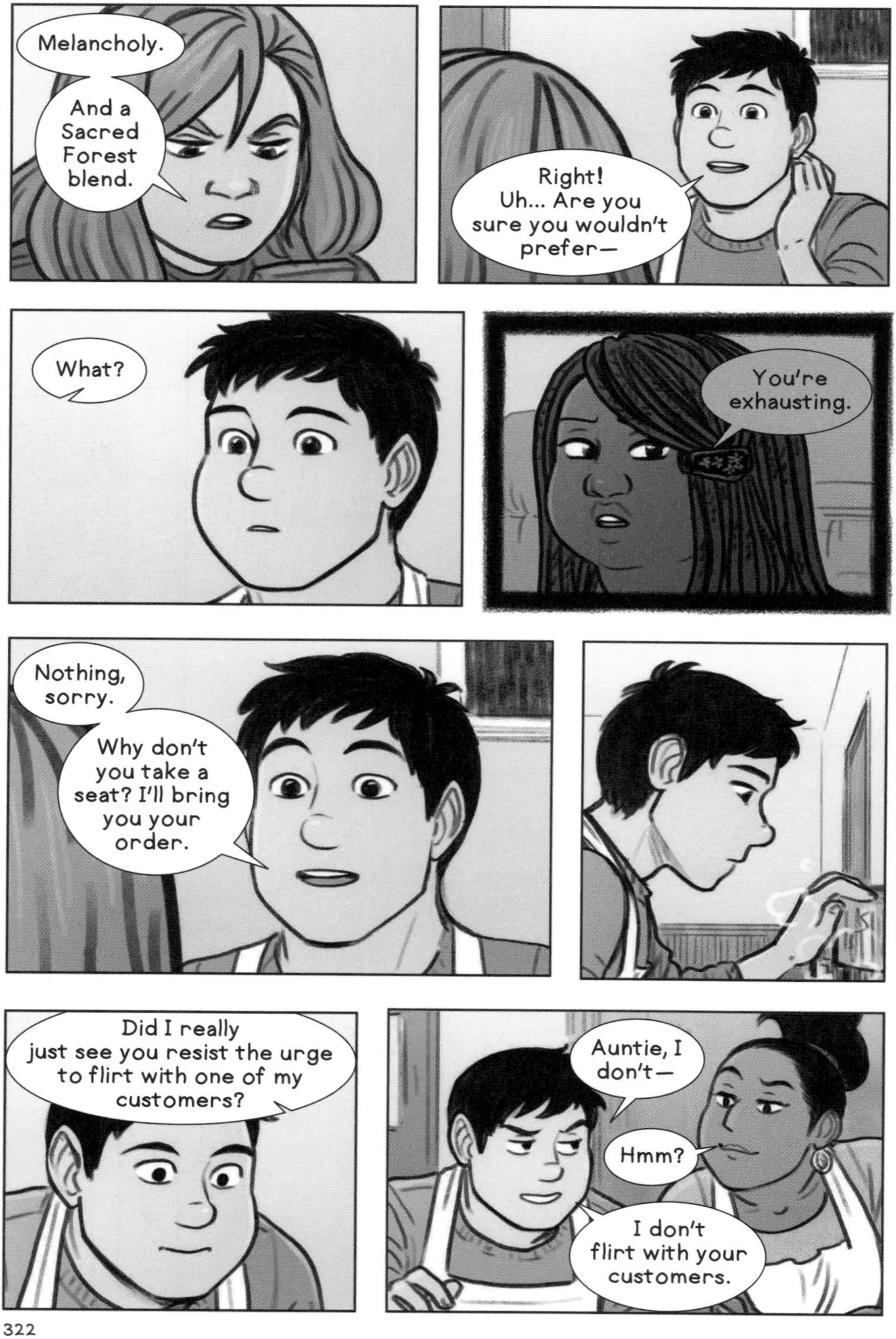
Melancholy.
And a Sacred Forest blend.
Right! Uh... Are you sure you wouldn't prefer—
What?
You're exhausting.
Nothing, sorry.
Why don't you take a seat? I'll bring you your order.
Did I really just see you resist the urge to flirt with one of my customers?
Auntie, I don't—
Hmm?
I don't flirt with your customers.

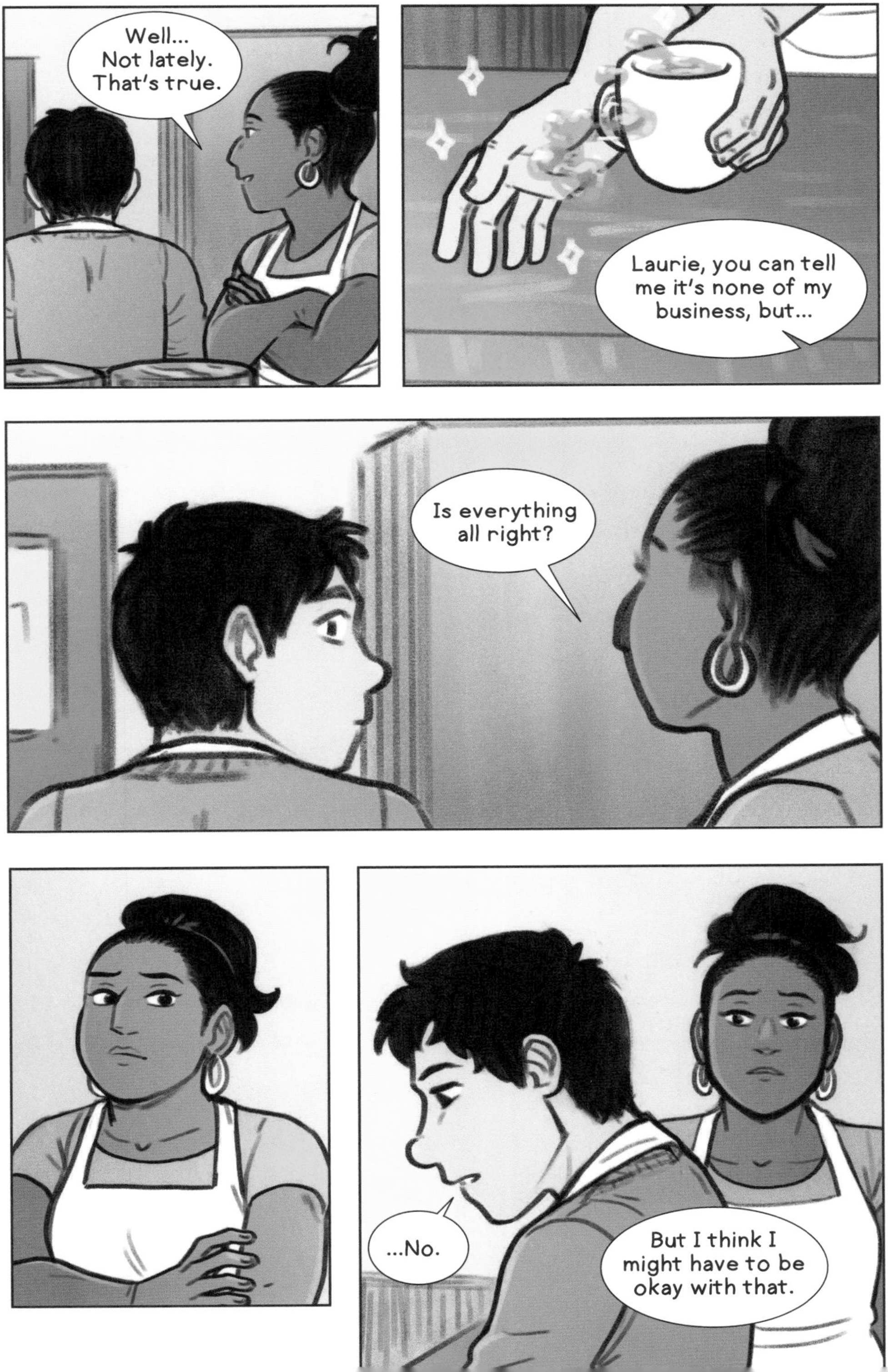
Well... Not lately. That's true.
Laurie, you can tell me it's none of my business, but...
Is everything all right?
...No.
But I think I might have to be okay with that.

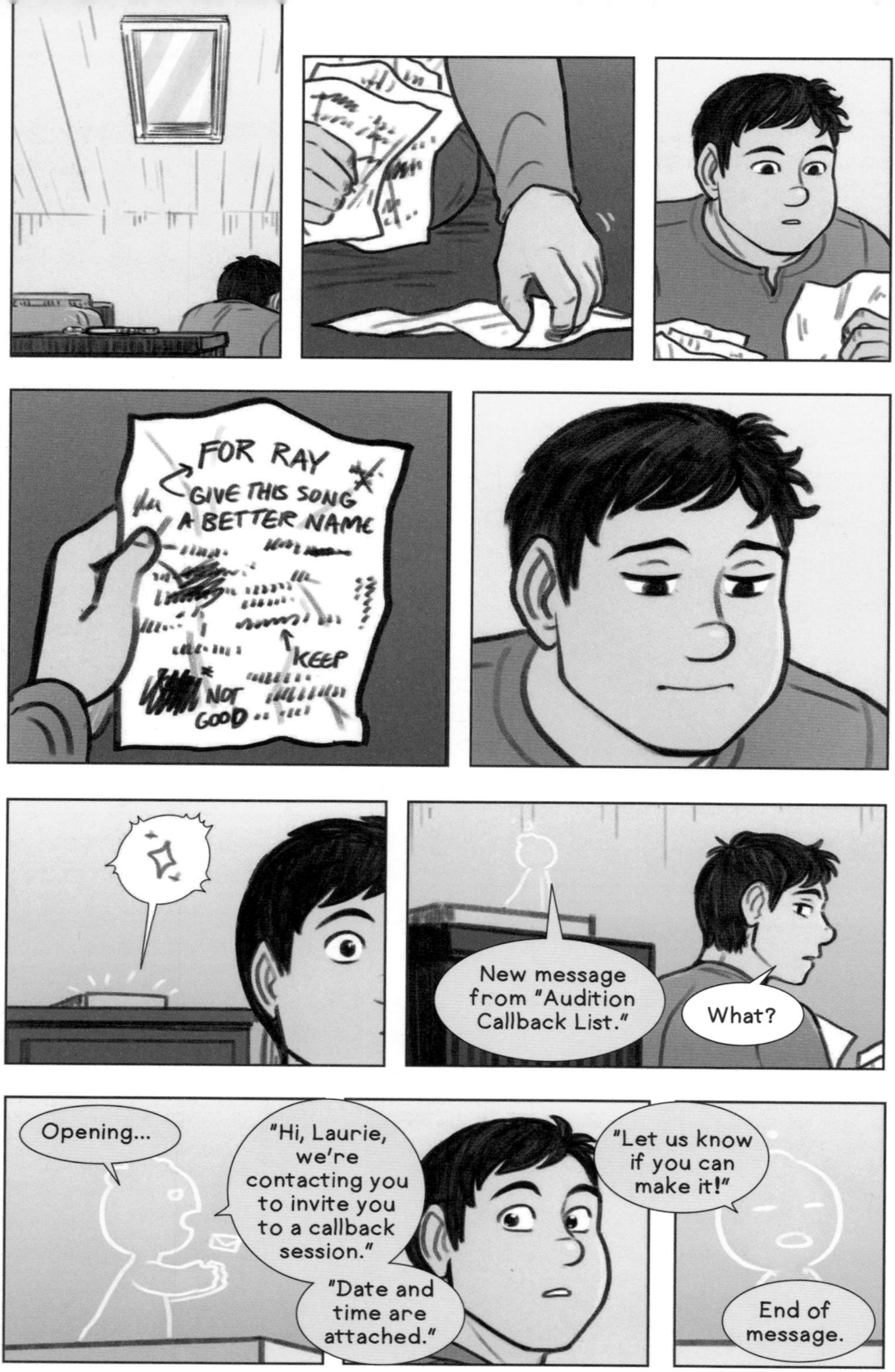
FOR RAY
GIVE THIS SONG A BETTER NAME
KEEP
NOT GOOD
New message from "Audition Callback List."
What?
Opening...
"Hi, Laurie, we're contacting you to invite you to a callback session."
"Date and time are attached."
"Let us know if you can make it!"
End of message.

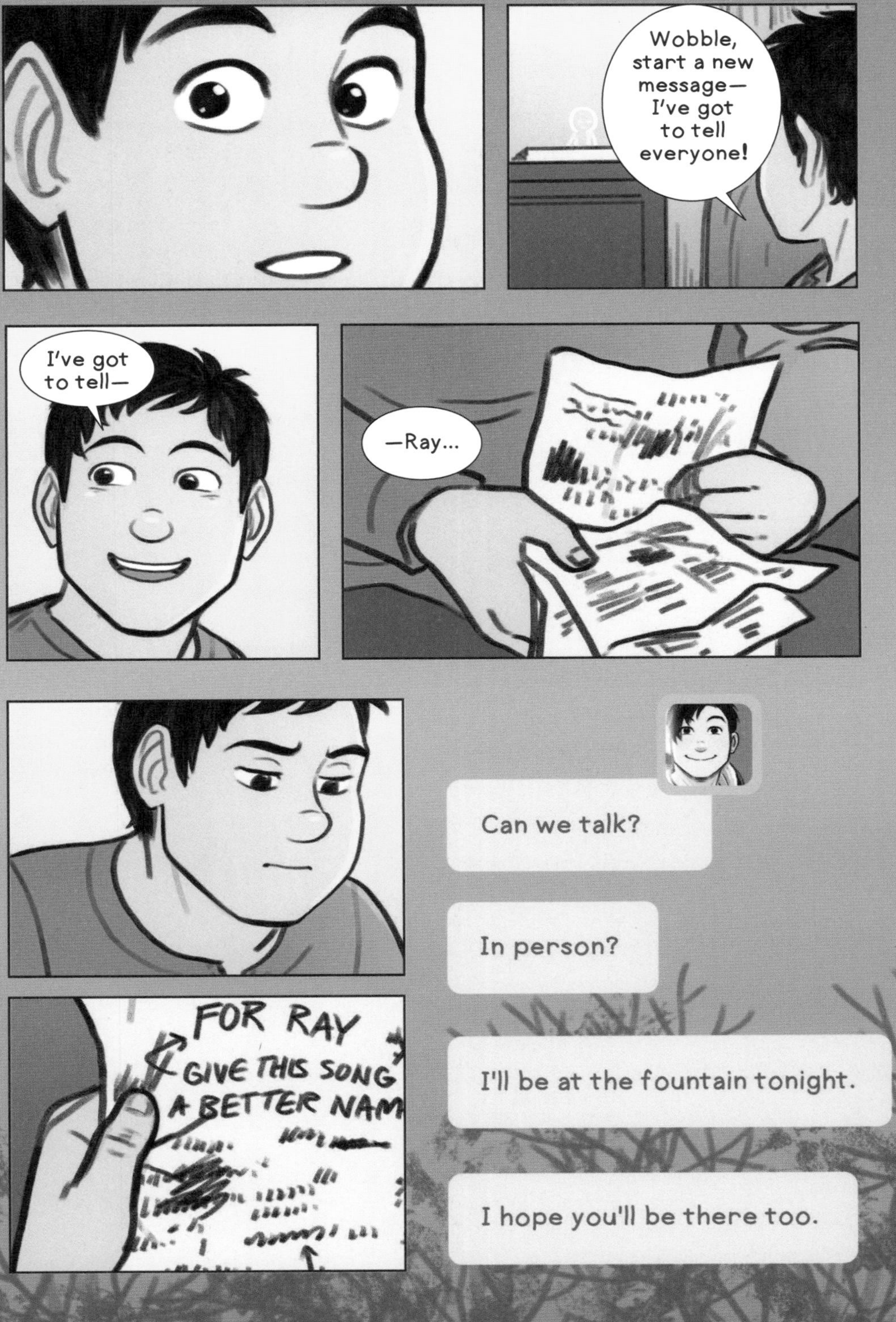

Wobble, start a new message— I've got to tell everyone!
I've got to tell—
—Ray...
Can we talk?
In person?
FOR RAY
GIVE THIS SONG A BETTER NAM
I'll be at the fountain tonight.
I hope you'll be there too.

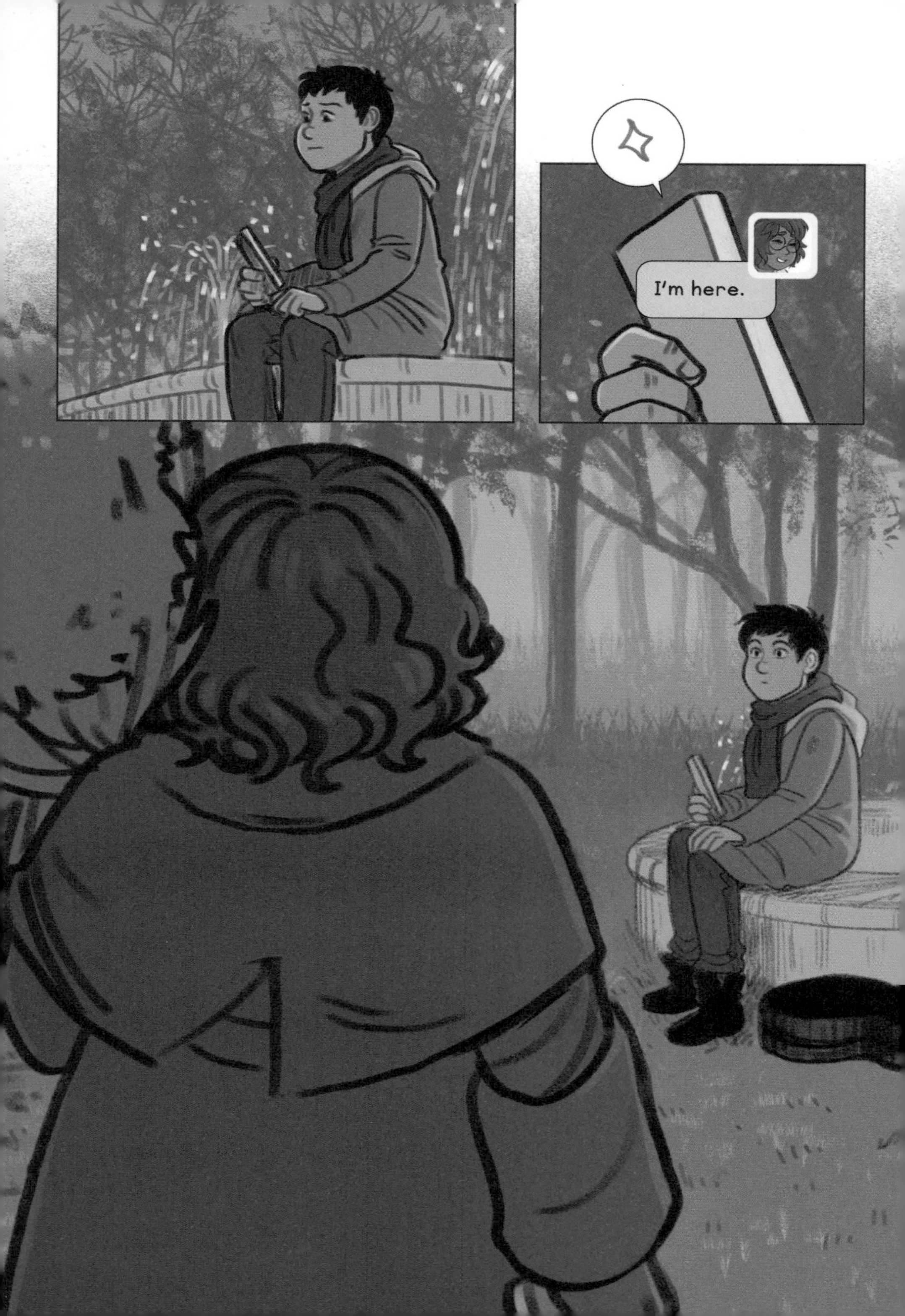
I'm here.

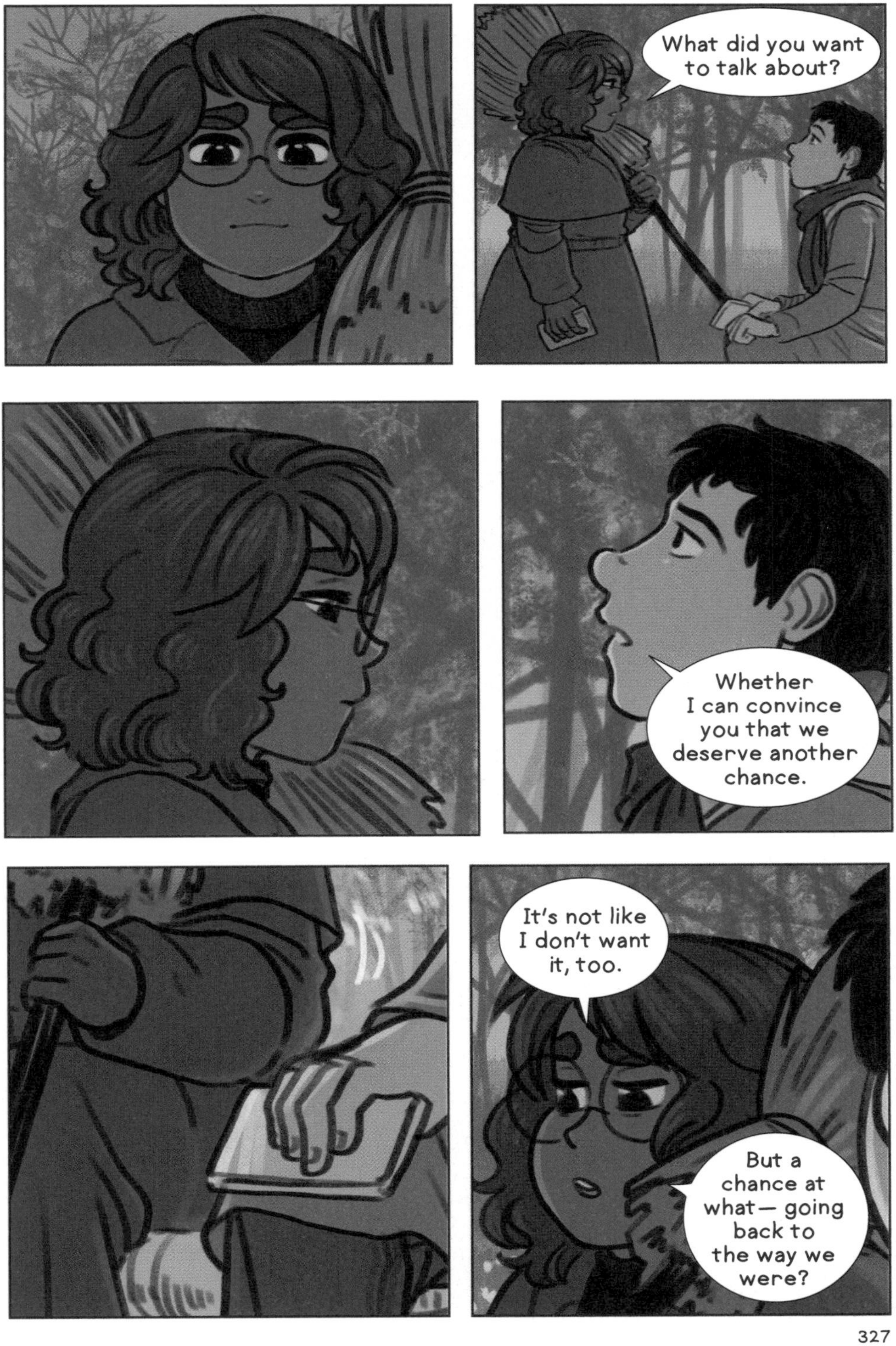
What did you want to talk about?
Whether I can convince you that we deserve another chance.
It's not like I don't want it, too.
But a chance at what— going back to the way we were?

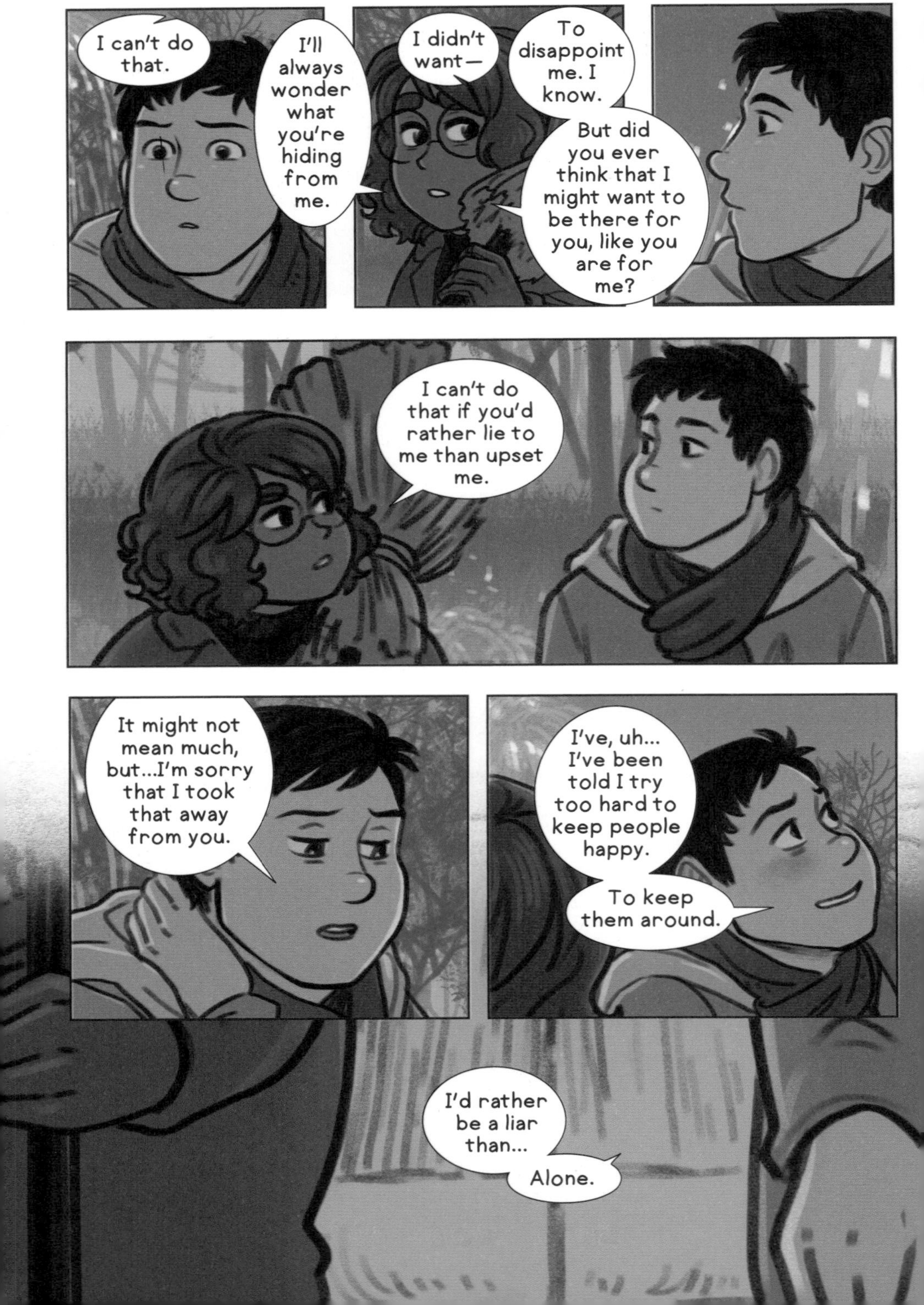
I can't do that.
I'll always wonder what you're hiding from me.
I didn't want—
To disappoint me. I know.
But did you ever think that I might want to be there for you, like you are for me?
I can't do that if you'd rather lie to me than upset me.
It might not mean much, but...I'm sorry that I took that away from you.
I've, uh... I've been told I try too hard to keep people happy.
To keep them around.
I'd rather be a liar than...
Alone.

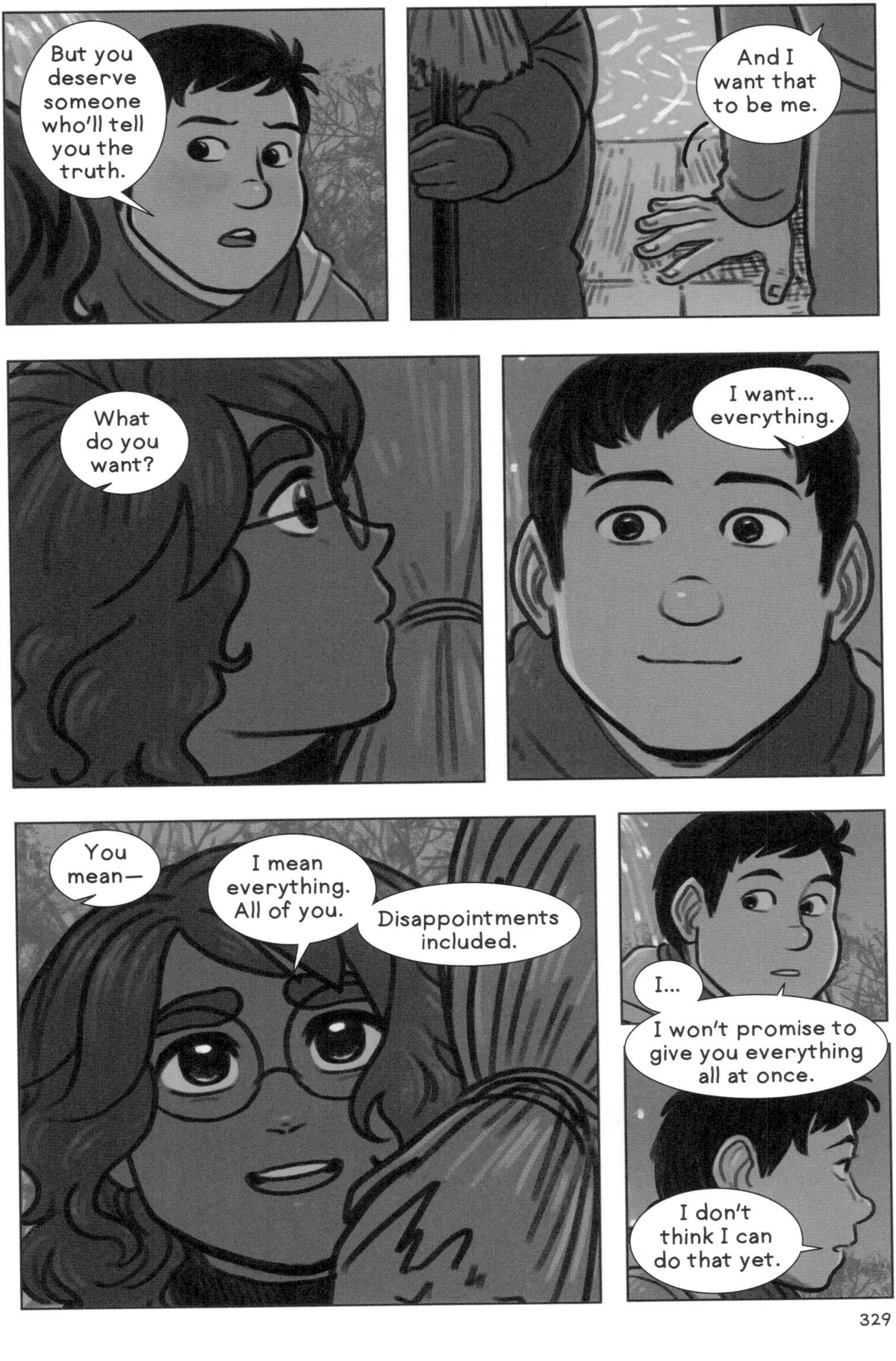
But you deserve someone who'll tell you the truth.
And I want that to be me.
What do you want?
I want... everything.
You mean—
I mean everything. All of you.
Disappointments included.
I...
I won't promise to give you everything all at once.
I don't think I can do that yet.

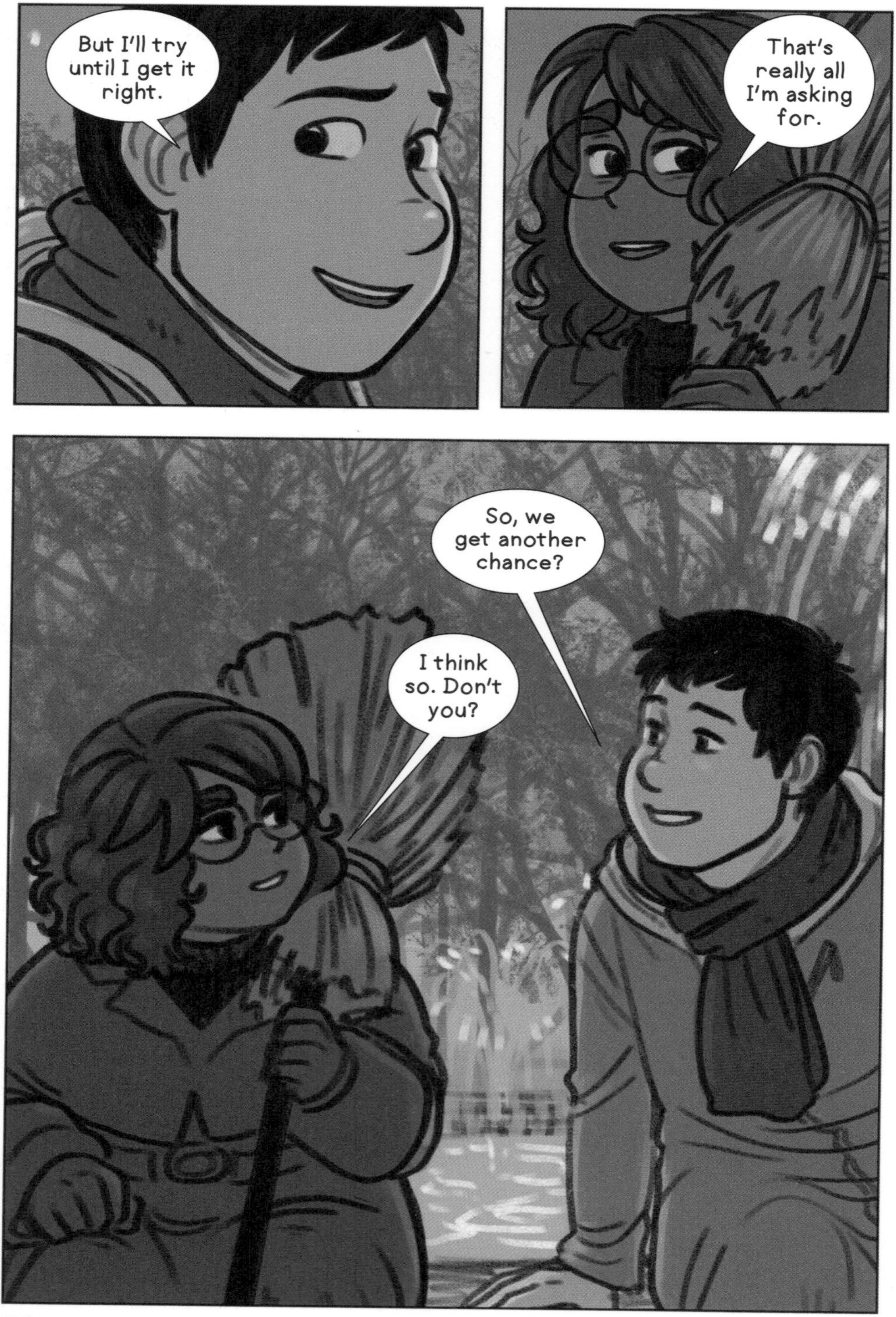
But I'll try until I get it right.
That's really all I'm asking for.
So, we get another chance?
I think so. Don't you?

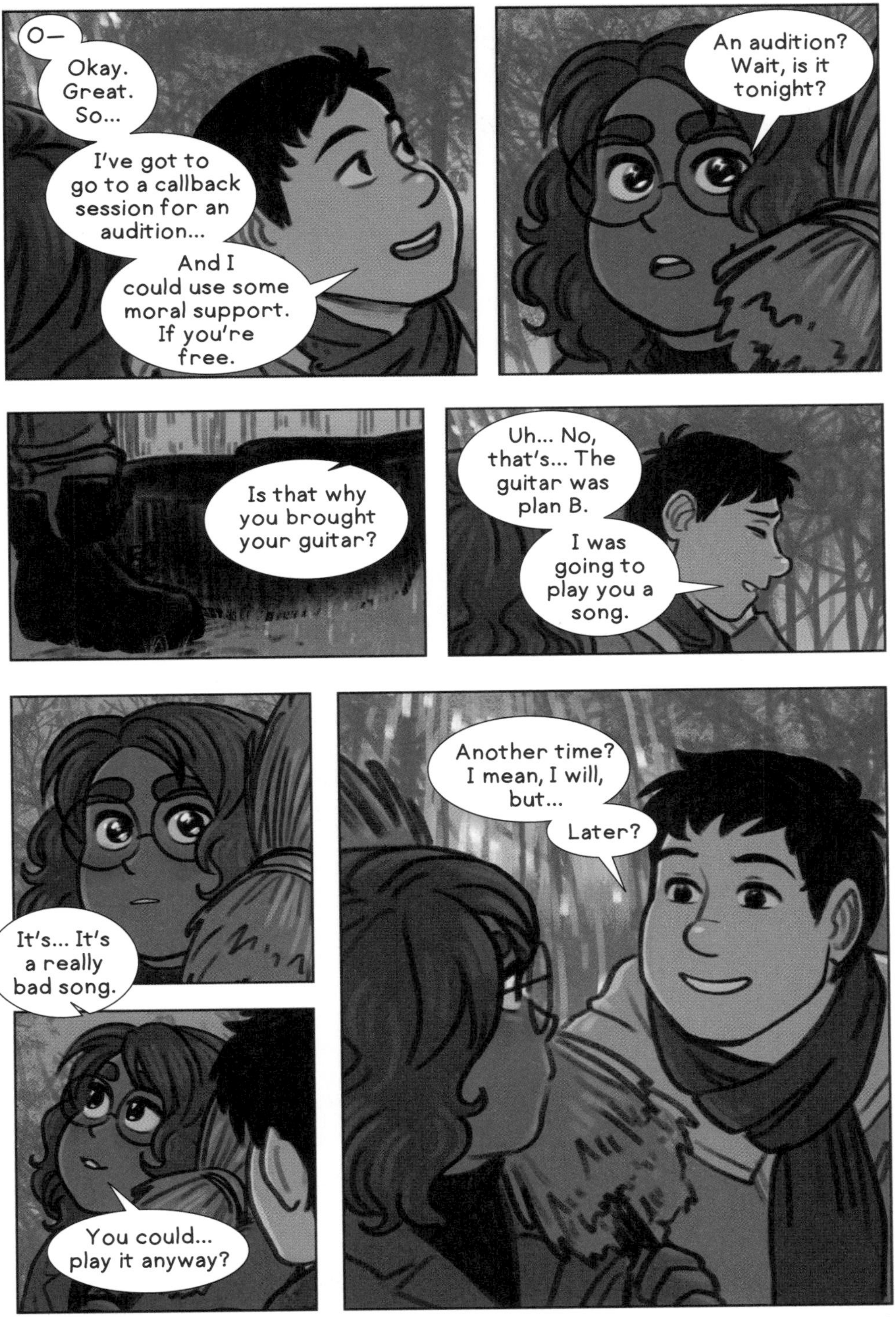
O—
Okay. Great. So...
I've got to go to a callback session for an audition...
And I could use some moral support. If you're free.
An audition? Wait, is it tonight?
Is that why you brought your guitar?
Uh... No, that's... The guitar was plan B.
I was going to play you a song.
It's... It's a really bad song.
You could... play it anyway?
Another time? I mean, I will, but...
Later?

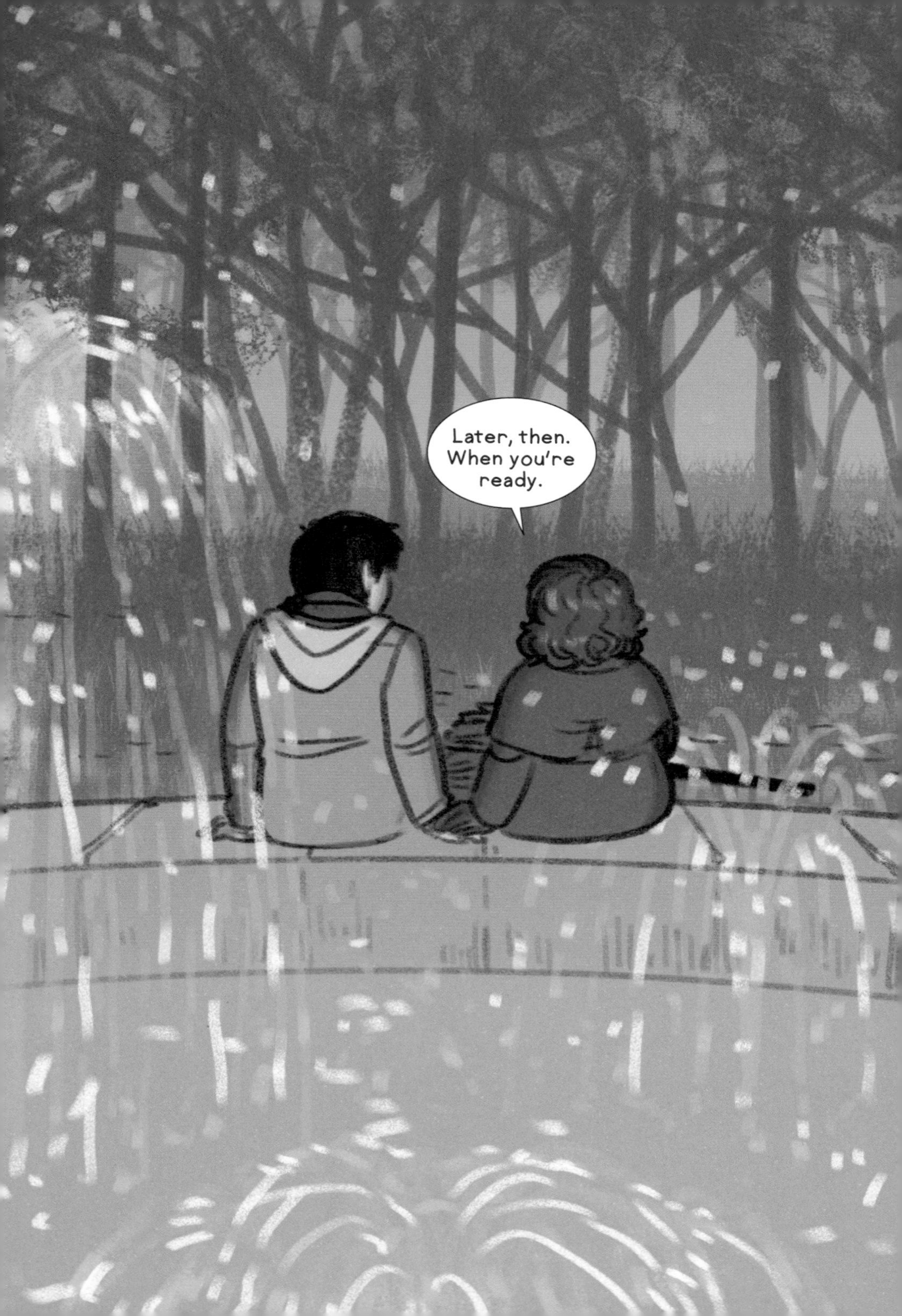
Later, then. When you're ready.

CHAPTER 13

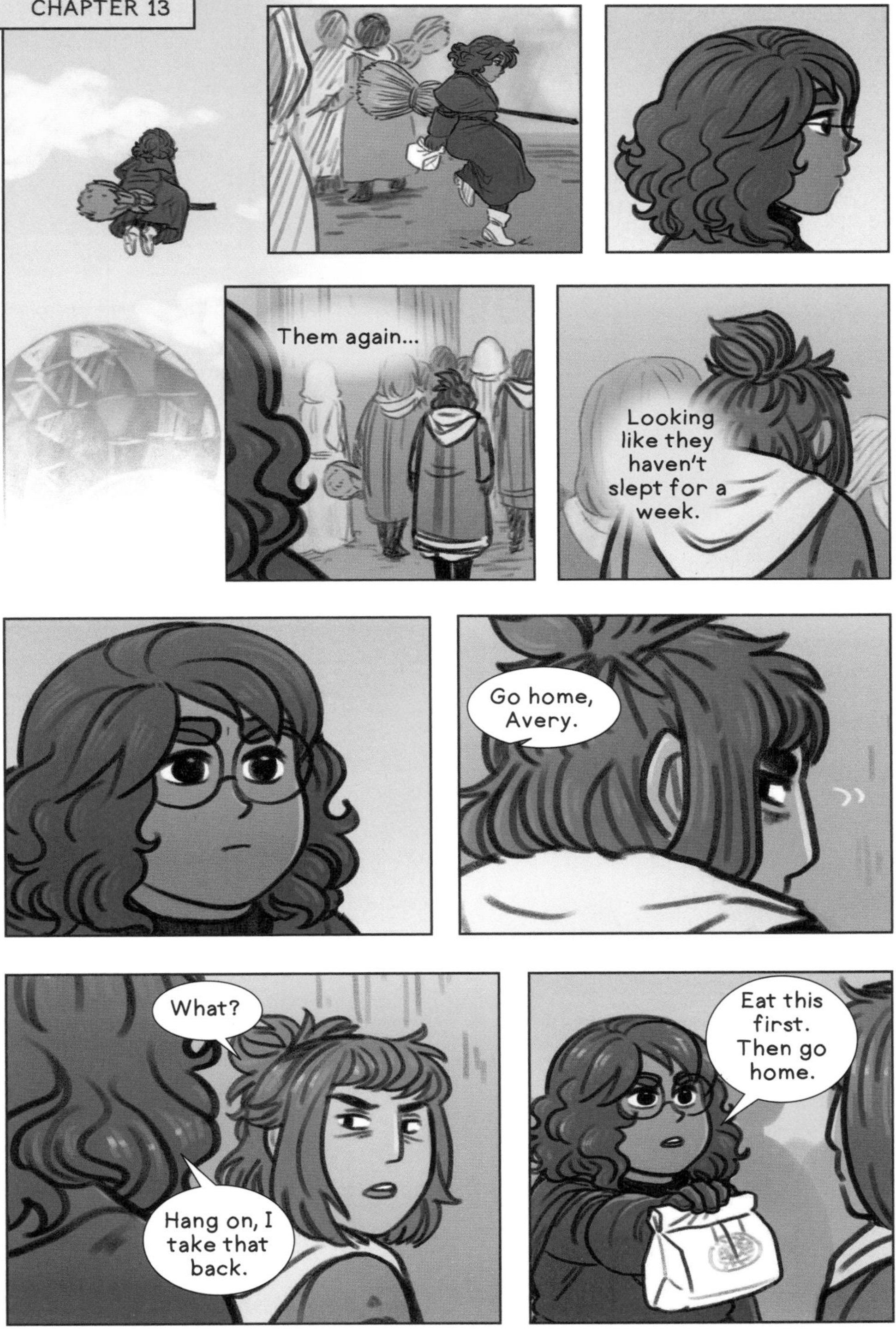
Them again...
Looking like they haven't slept for a week.
Go home, Avery.
What?
Hang on, I take that back.
Eat this first. Then go home.

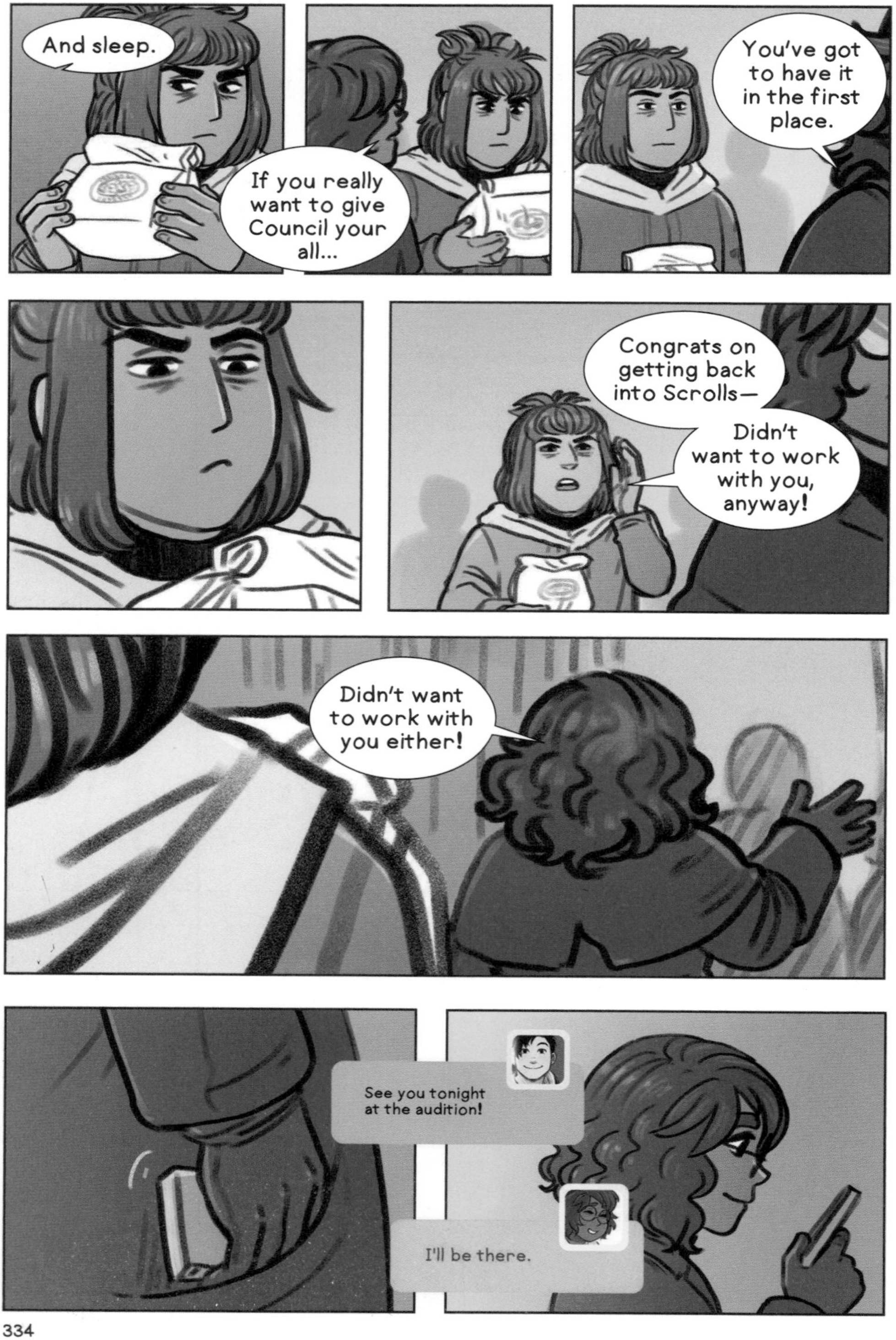
And sleep.
If you really want to give Council your all...
You've got to have it in the first place.
Congrats on getting back into Scrolls—
Didn't want to work with you, anyway!
Didn't want to work with you either!
See you tonight at the audition!
I'll be there.

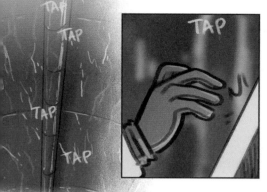

TAP TAP TAP TAP TAP

TAP

There!

Last one!

Better get back to my supervisor. Requests must be piling up.

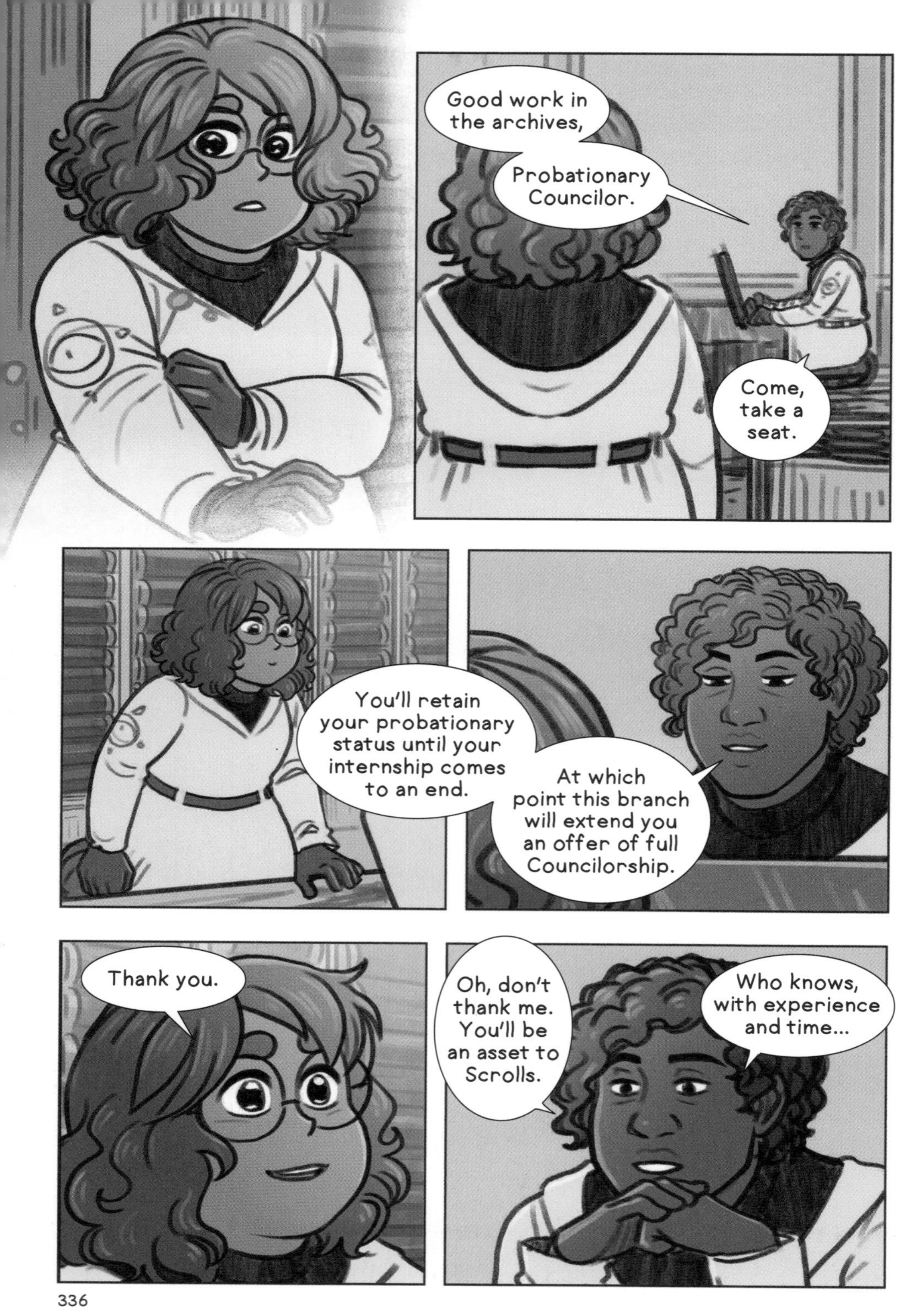
Good work in the archives,
Probationary Councilor.
Come, take a seat.
You'll retain your probationary status until your internship comes to an end.
At which point this branch will extend you an offer of full Councilorship.
Thank you.
Oh, don't thank me. You'll be an asset to Scrolls.
Who knows, with experience and time...

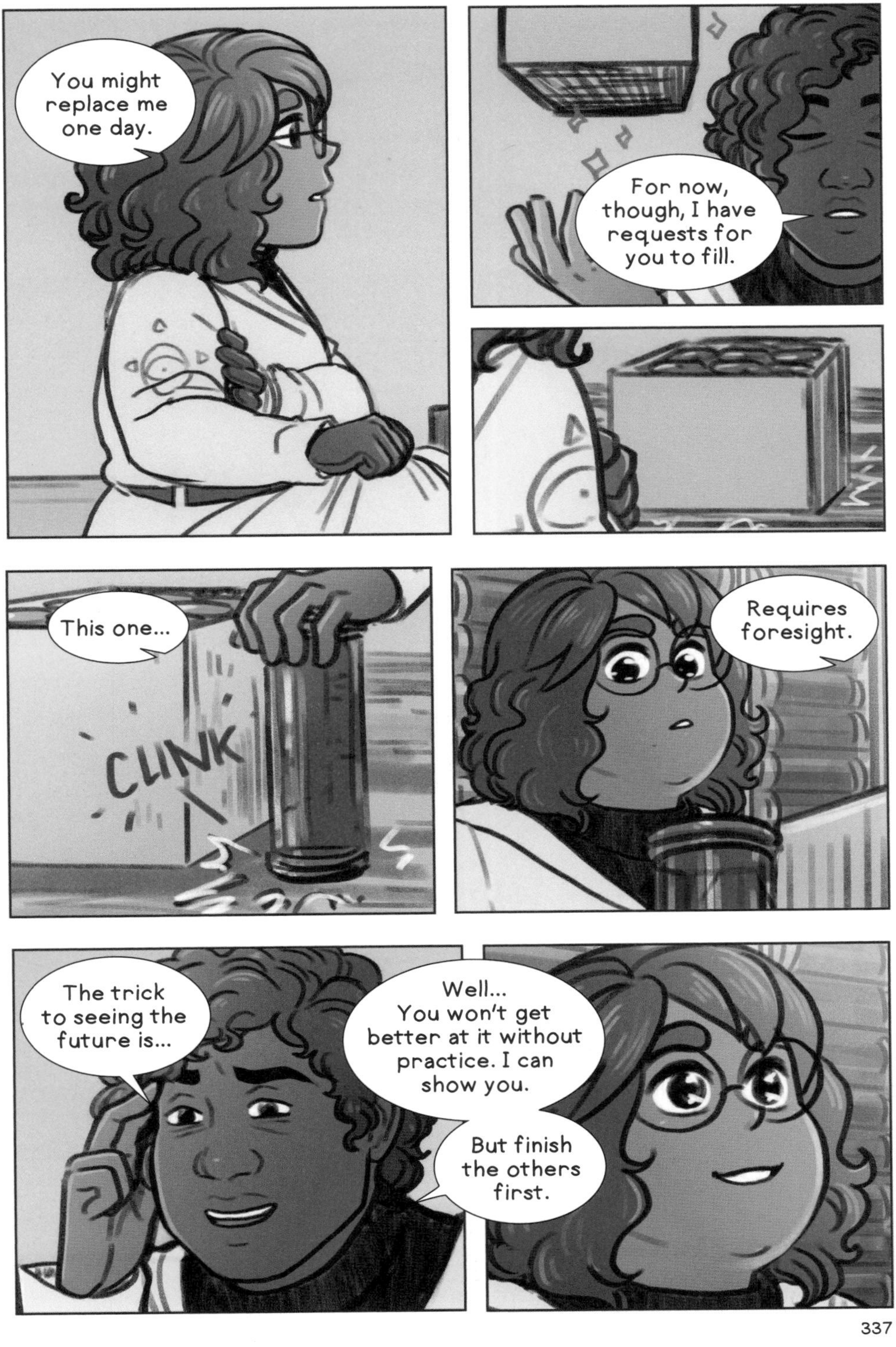
You might replace me one day.
For now, though, I have requests for you to fill.
This one...
CLINK
Requires foresight.
The trick to seeing the future is...
Well... You won't get better at it without practice. I can show you.
But finish the others first.

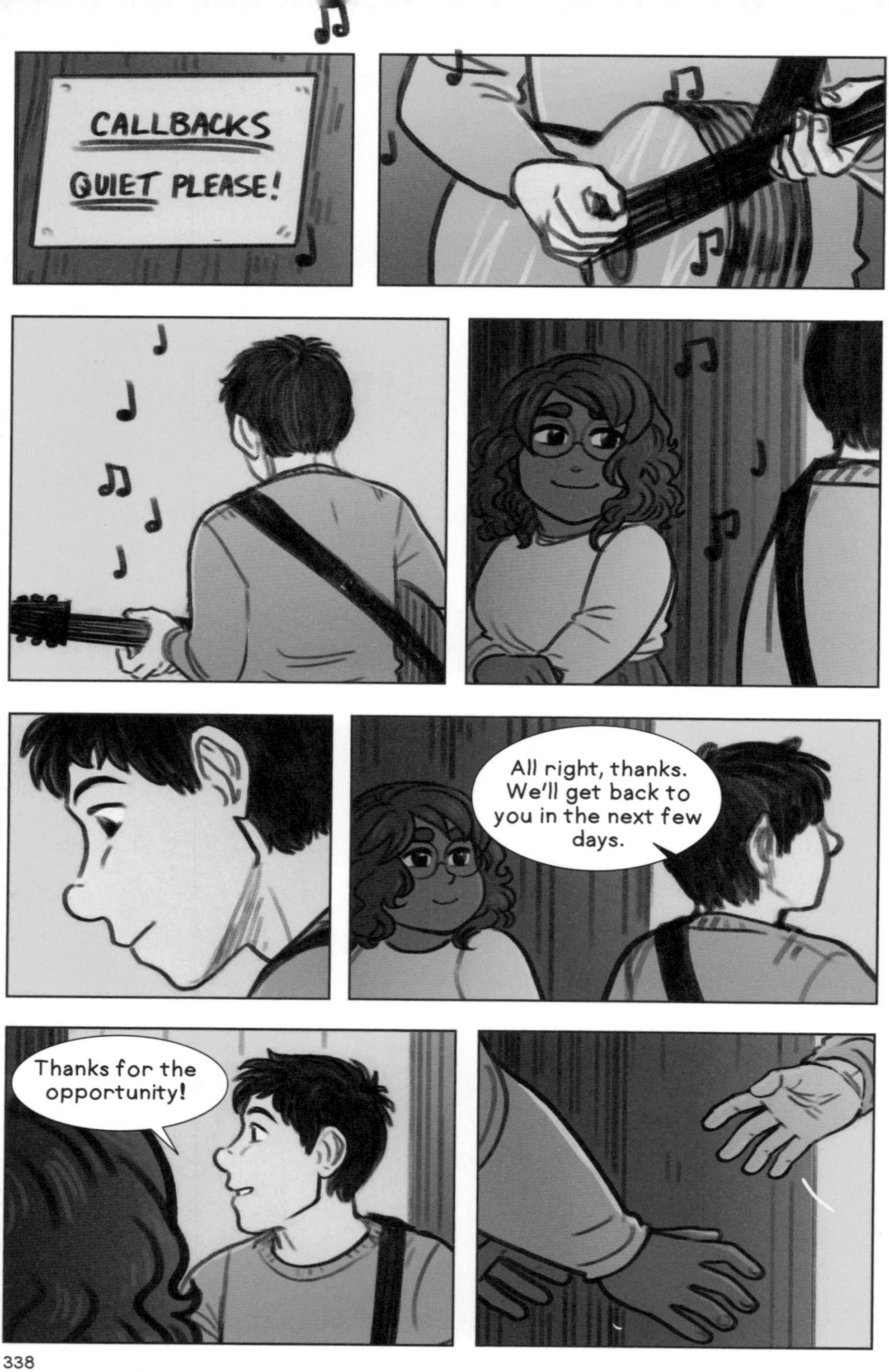

CALLBACKS
QUIET PLEASE!
All right, thanks. We'll get back to you in the next few days.
Thanks for the opportunity!

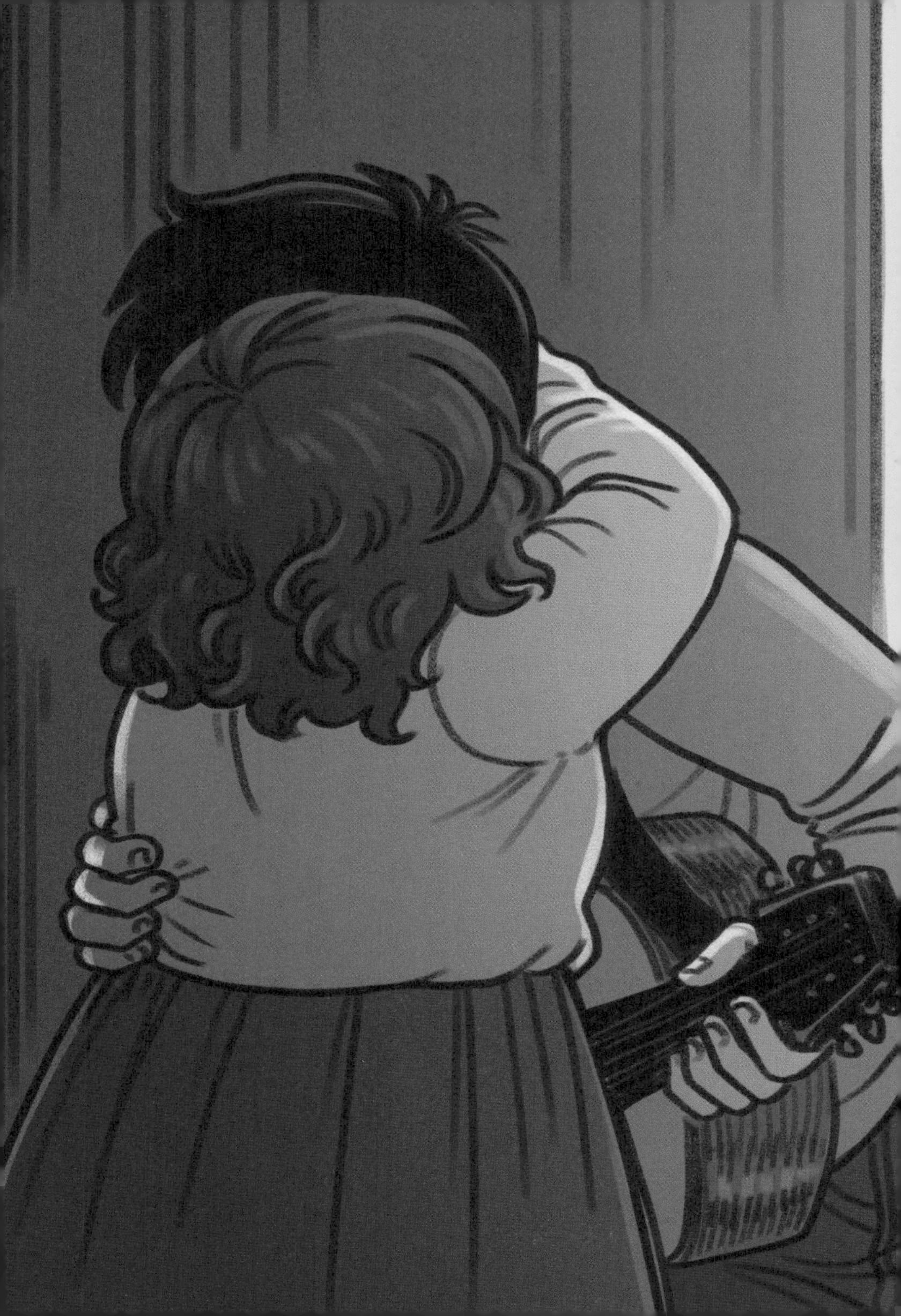

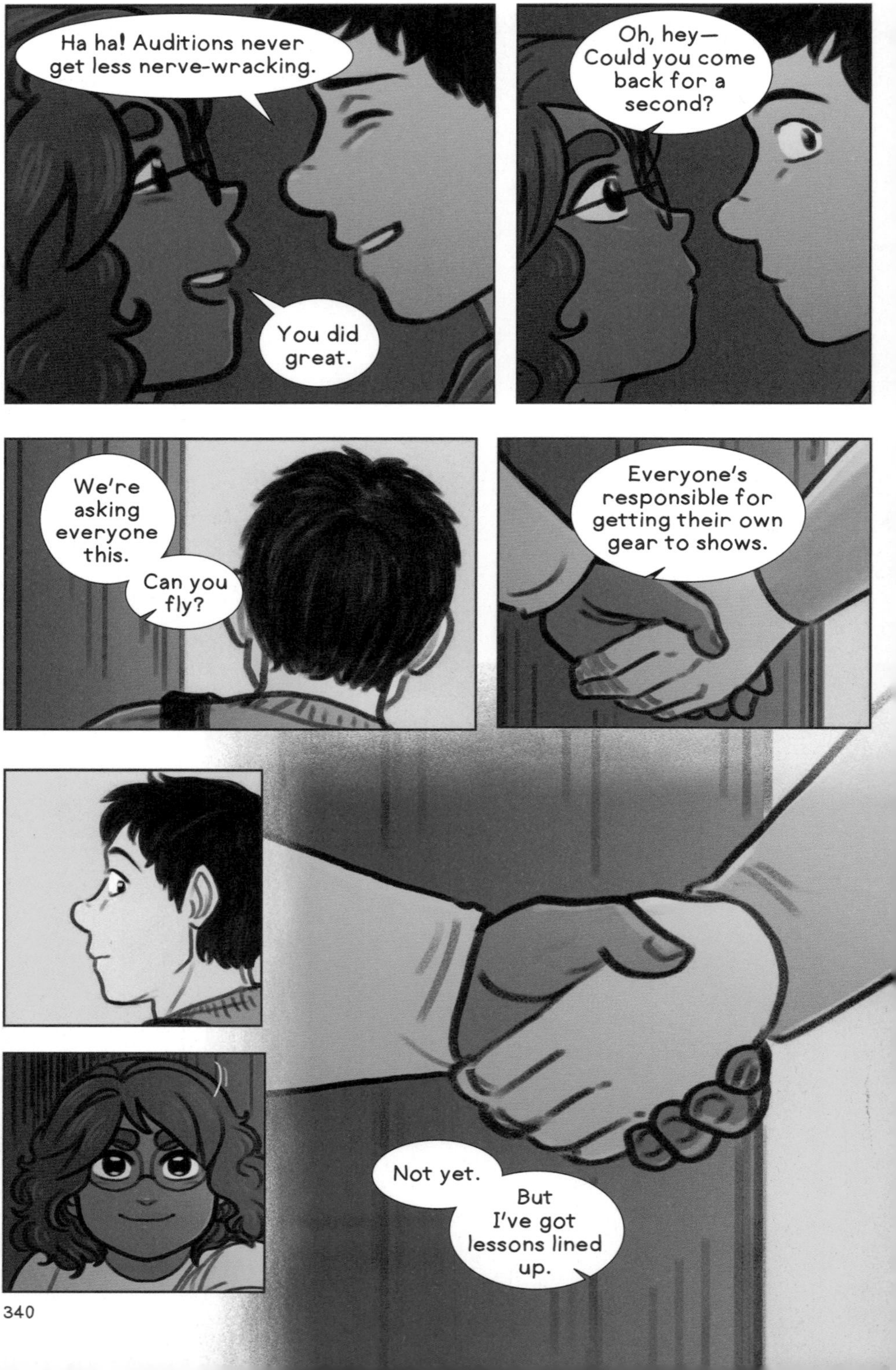
Ha ha! Auditions never get less nerve-wracking.
You did great.
Oh, hey— Could you come back for a second?
We're asking everyone this.
Can you fly?
Everyone's responsible for getting their own gear to shows.
Not yet.
But I've got lessons lined up.

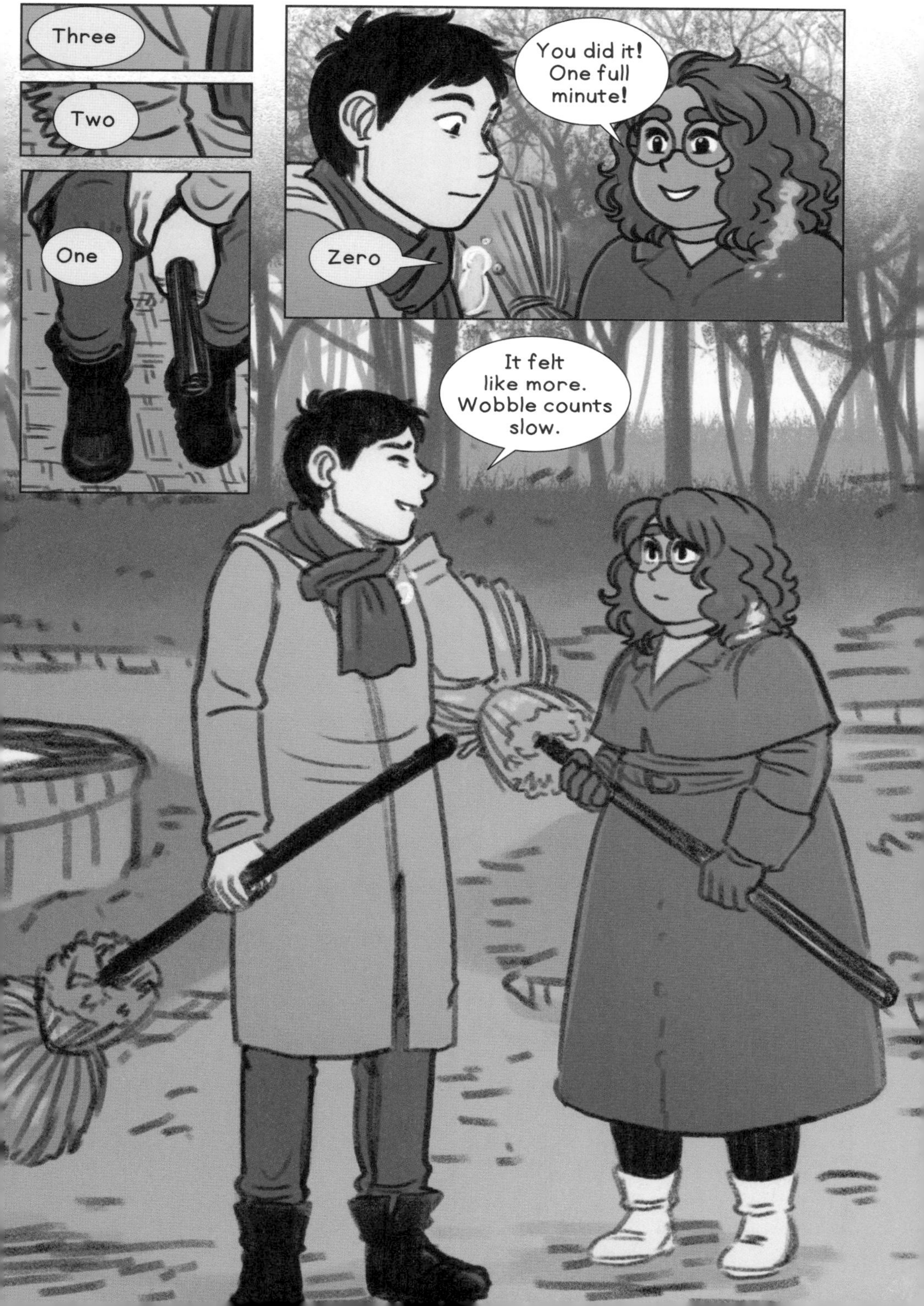
Three
Two
One
Zero
You did it! One full minute!
It felt like more. Wobble counts slow.

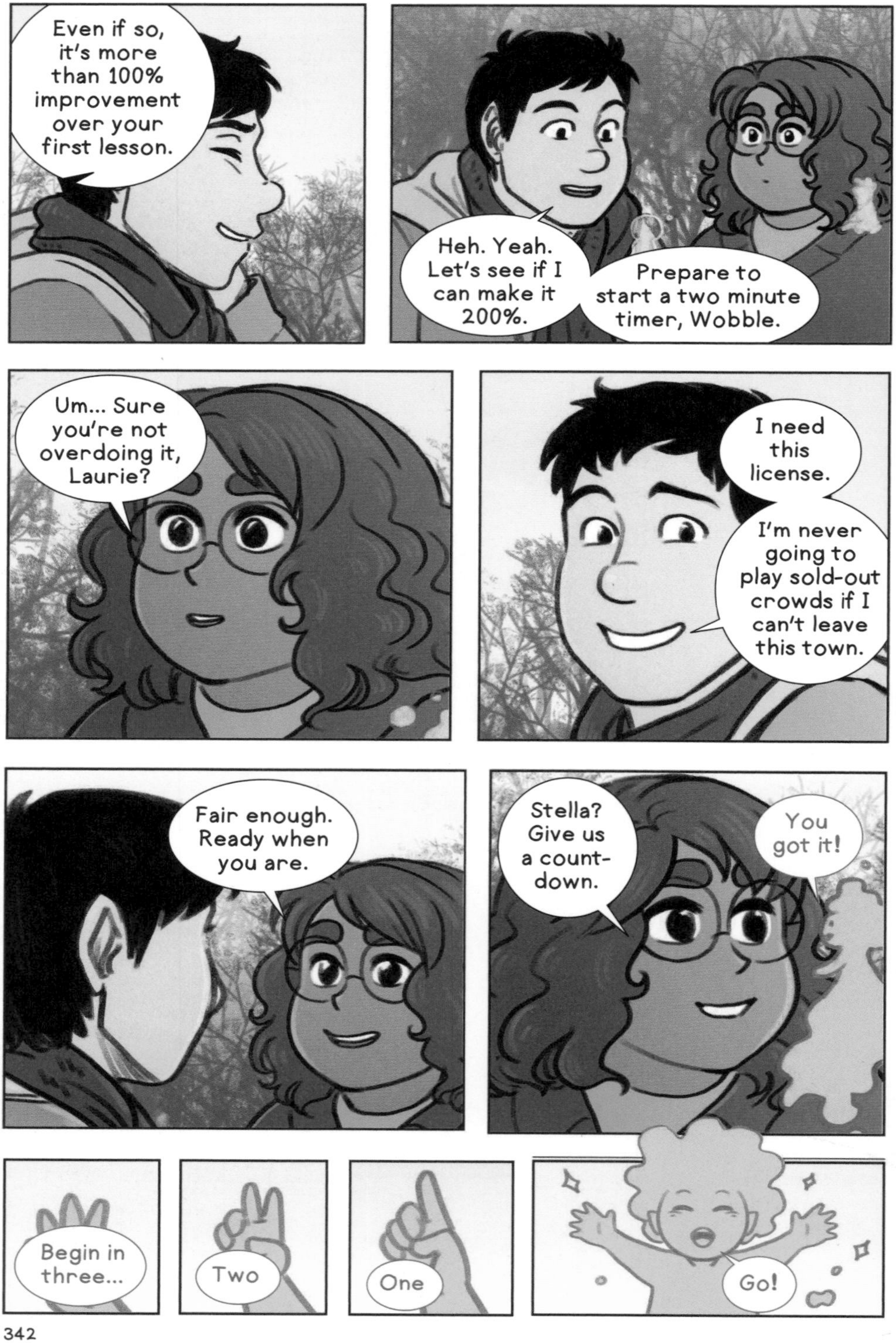
Even if so, it's more than 100% improvement over your first lesson.
Heh. Yeah. Let's see if I can make it 200%.
Prepare to start a two minute timer, Wobble.
Um... Sure you're not overdoing it, Laurie?
I need this license.
I'm never going to play sold-out crowds if I can't leave this town.
Fair enough. Ready when you are.
Stella? Give us a count-down.
You got it!
Begin in three...
Two
One
Go!

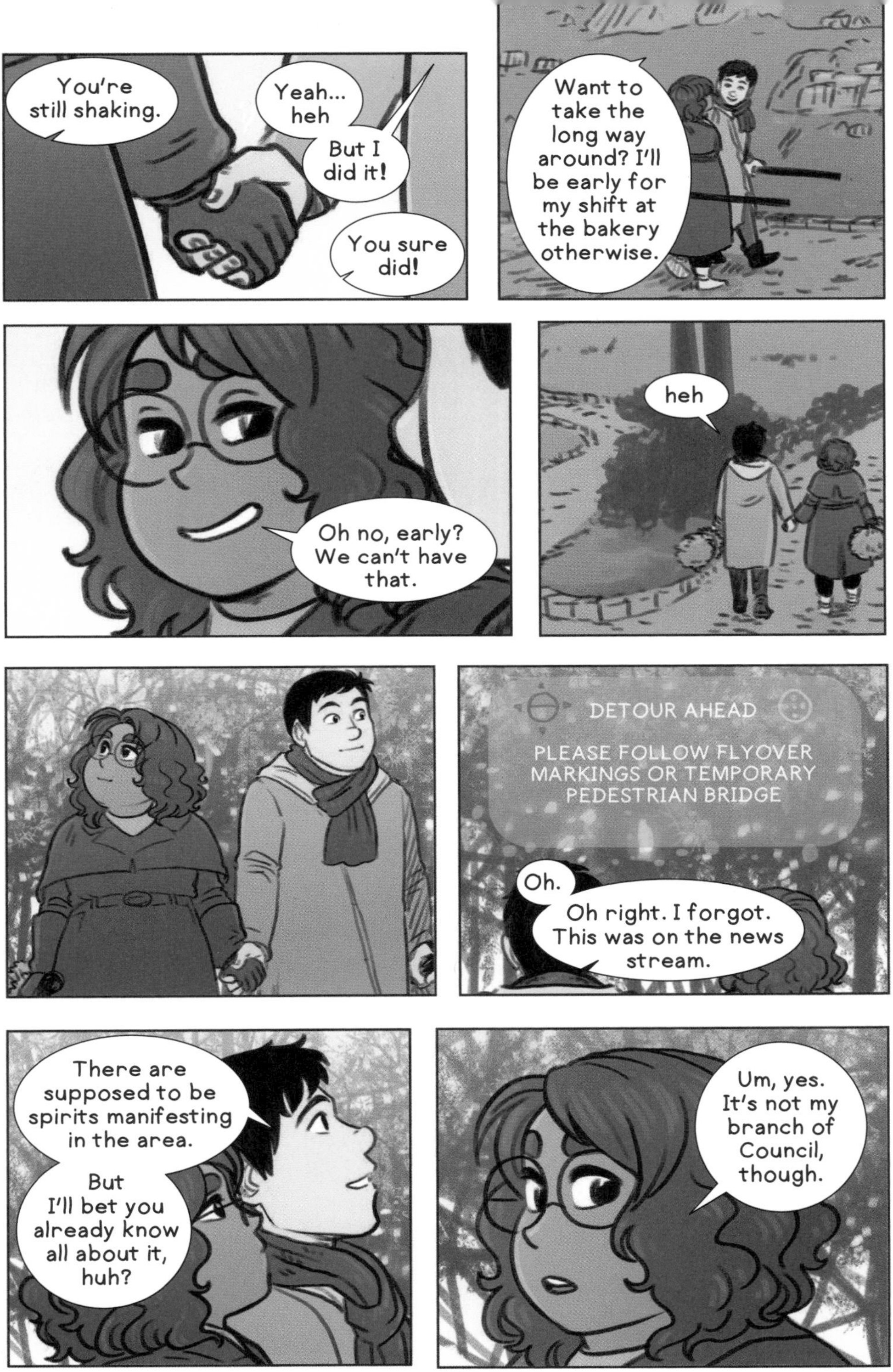
You're still shaking.
Yeah... heh
But I did it!
You sure did!
Want to take the long way around? I'll be early for my shift at the bakery otherwise.
Oh no, early? We can't have that.
heh
DETOUR AHEAD
PLEASE FOLLOW FLYOVER MARKINGS OR TEMPORARY PEDESTRIAN BRIDGE
Oh.
Oh right. I forgot. This was on the news stream.
There are supposed to be spirits manifesting in the area.
But I'll bet you already know all about it, huh?
Um, yes. It's not my branch of Council, though.

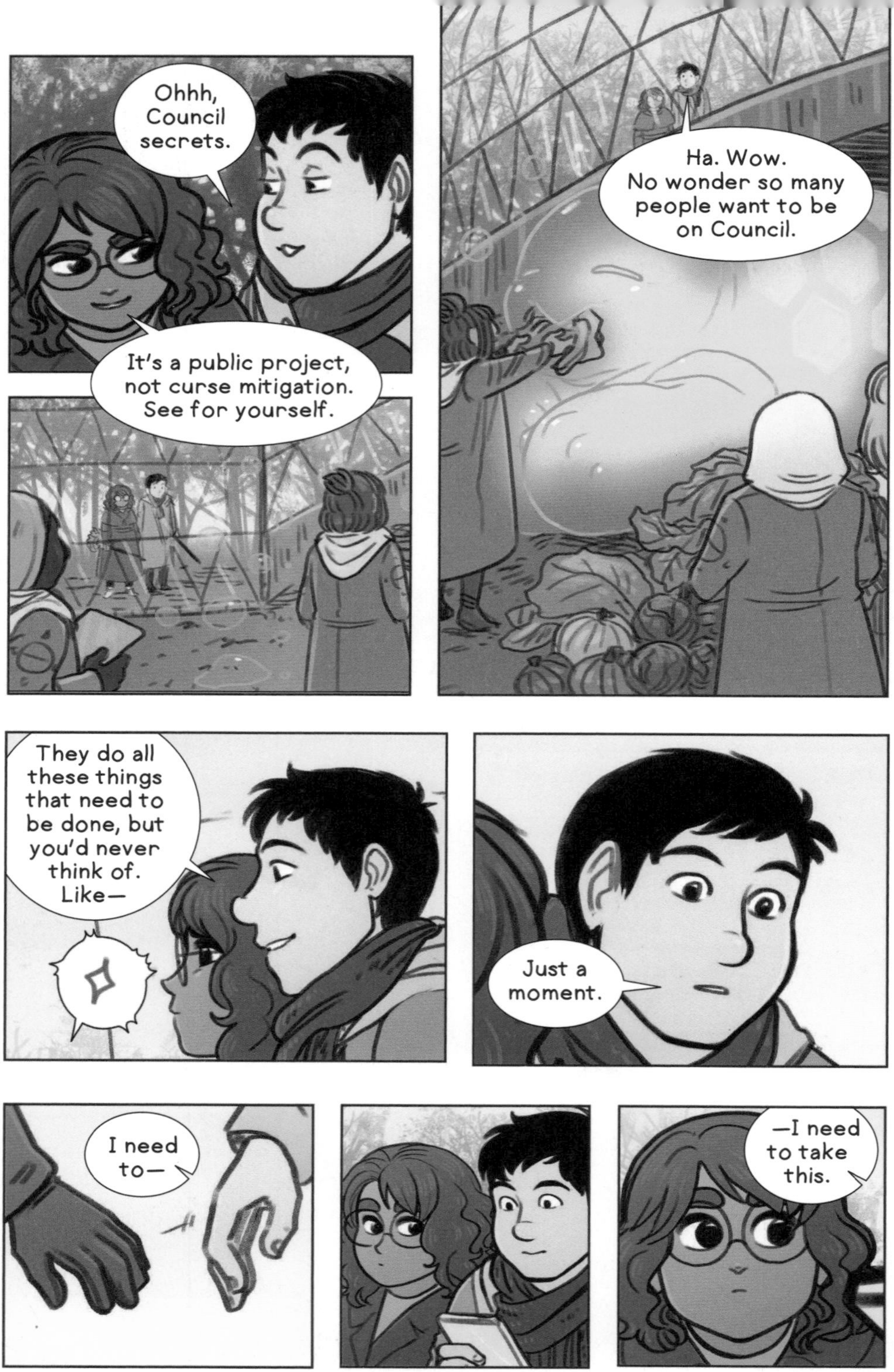
Ohhh, Council secrets.
It's a public project, not curse mitigation. See for yourself.
Ha. Wow. No wonder so many people want to be on Council.
They do all these things that need to be done, but you'd never think of. Like—
Just a moment.
I need to—
—I need to take this.

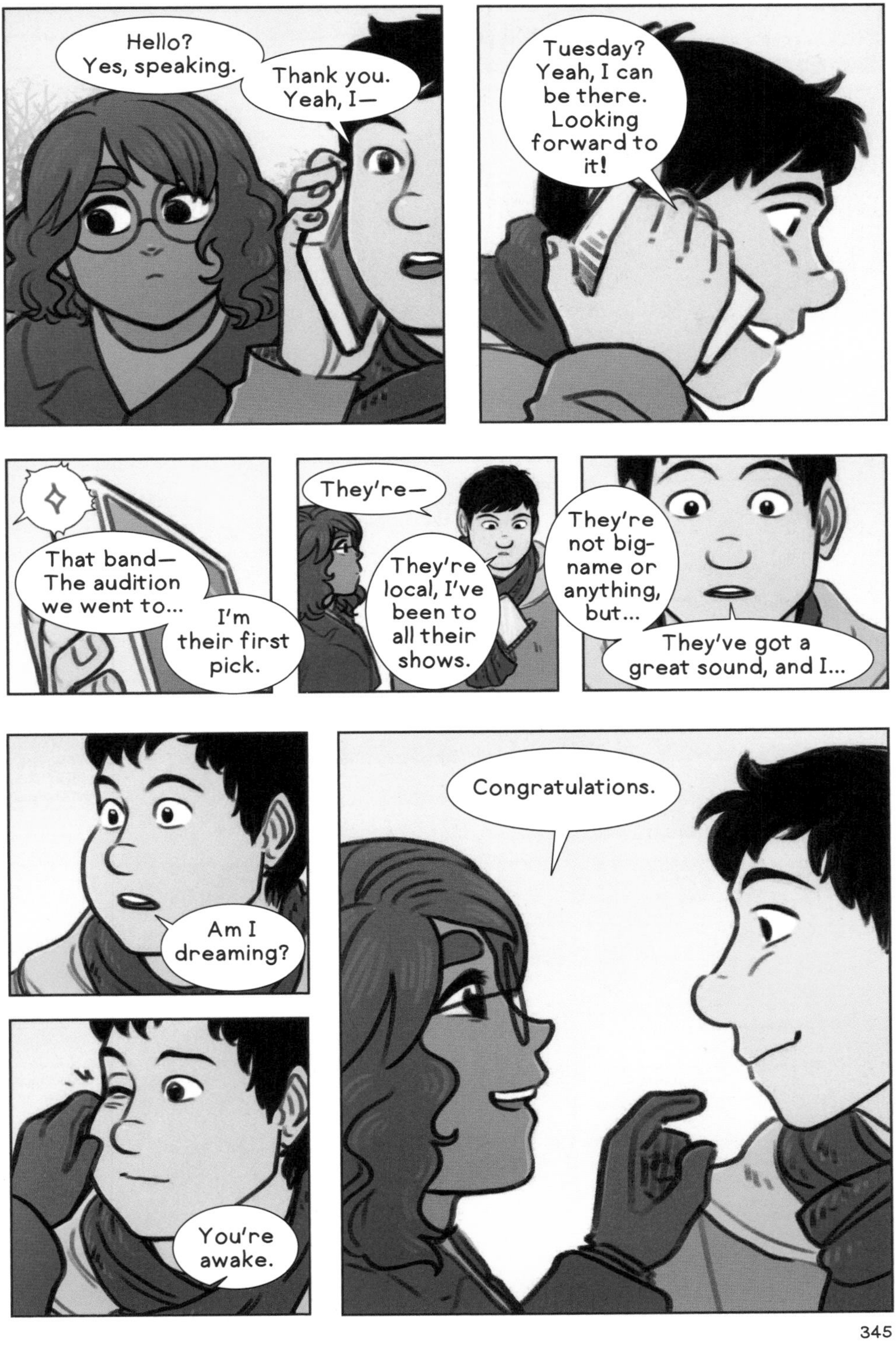
Hello?
Yes, speaking.
Thank you.
Yeah, I—
Tuesday?
Yeah, I can be there.
Looking forward to it!
That band—
The audition we went to...
I'm their first pick.
They're—
They're local, I've been to all their shows.
They're not big-name or anything, but...
They've got a great sound, and I...
Am I dreaming?
You're awake.
Congratulations.

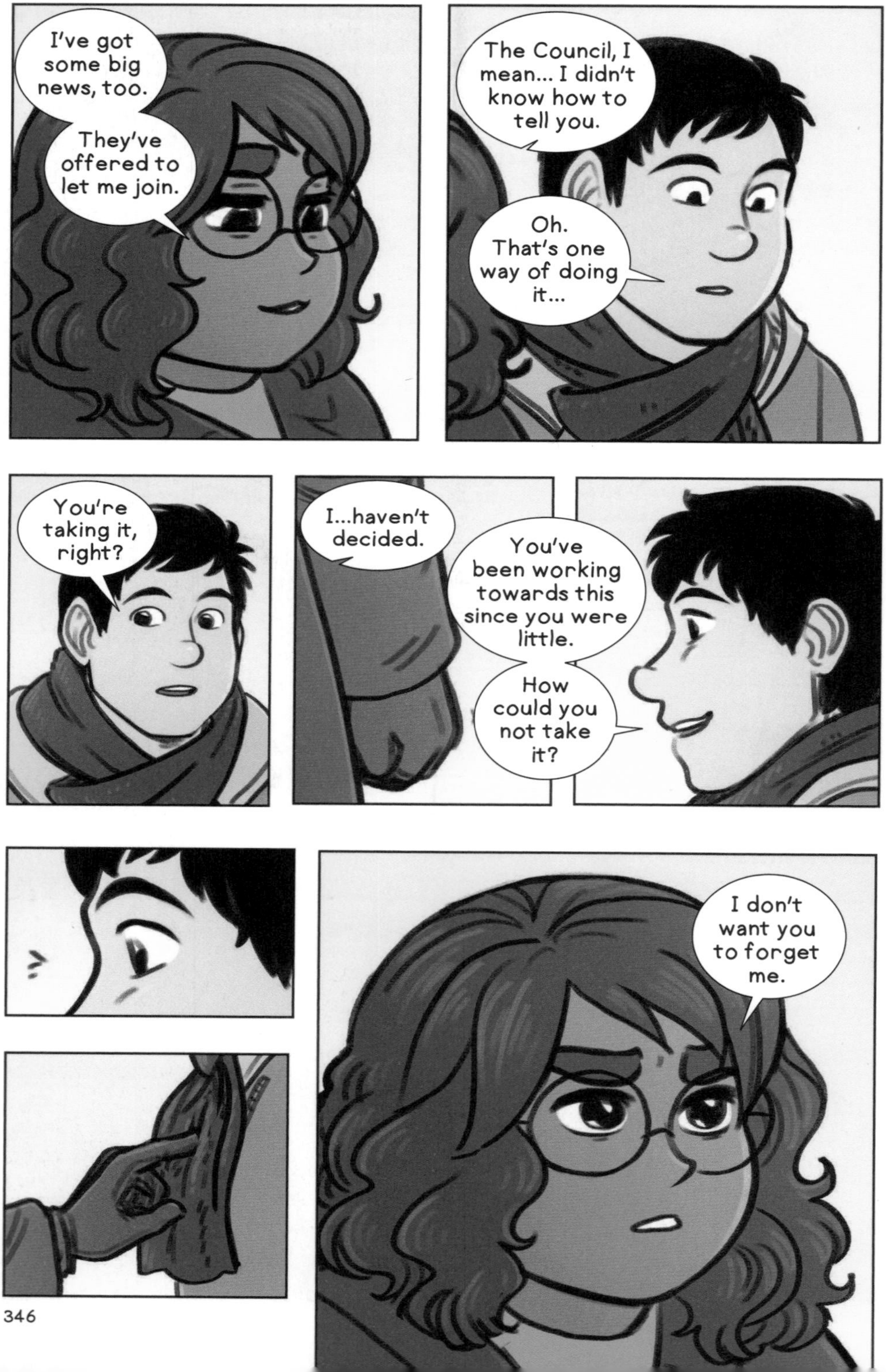
I've got some big news, too.
They've offered to let me join.
The Council, I mean... I didn't know how to tell you.
Oh. That's one way of doing it...
You're taking it, right?
I...haven't decided.
You've been working towards this since you were little.
How could you not take it?
I don't want you to forget me.

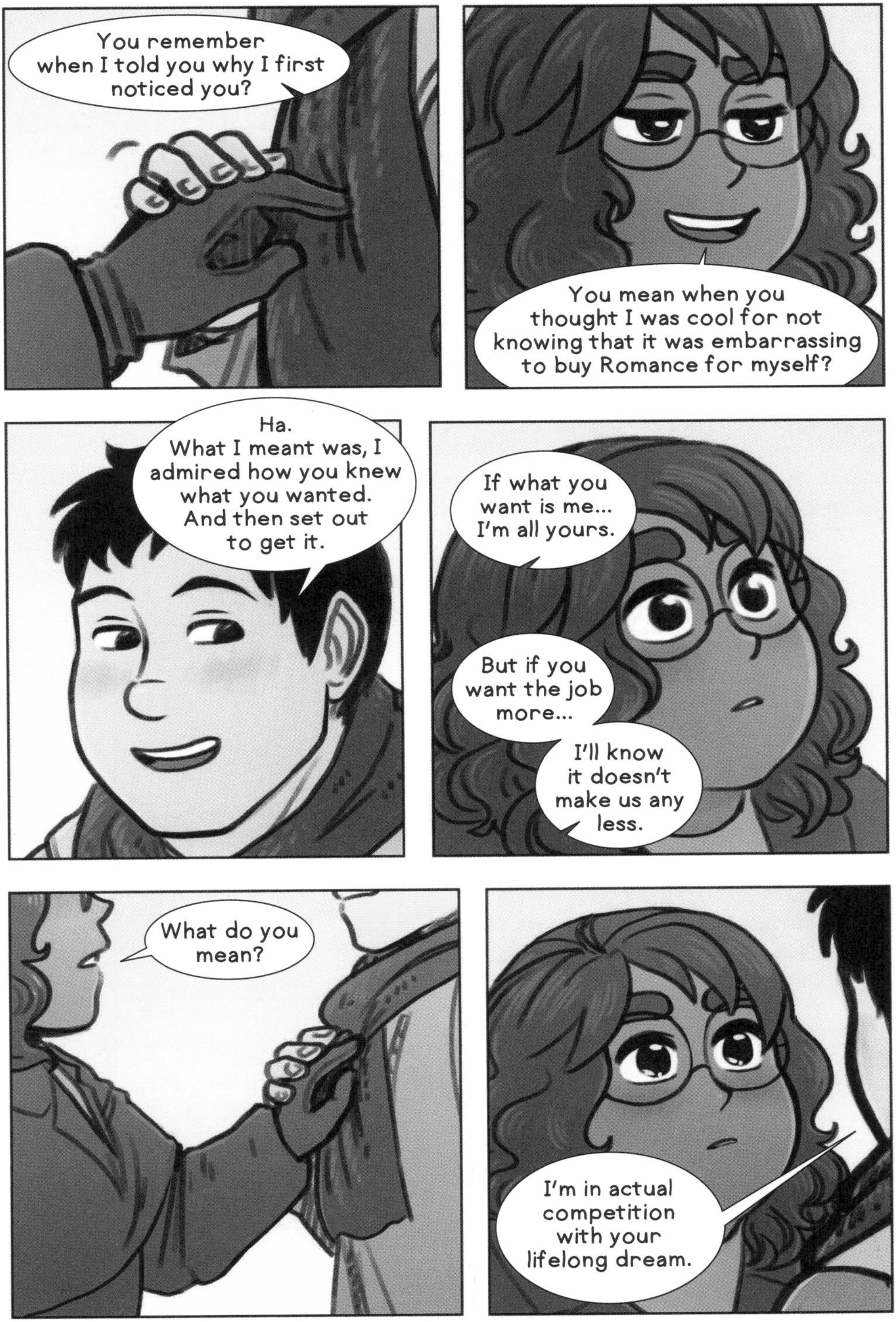

You remember when I told you why I first noticed you?
You mean when you thought I was cool for not knowing that it was embarrassing to buy Romance for myself?
Ha. What I meant was, I admired how you knew what you wanted. And then set out to get it.
If what you want is me... I'm all yours.
But if you want the job more...
I'll know it doesn't make us any less.
What do you mean?
I'm in actual competition with your lifelong dream.

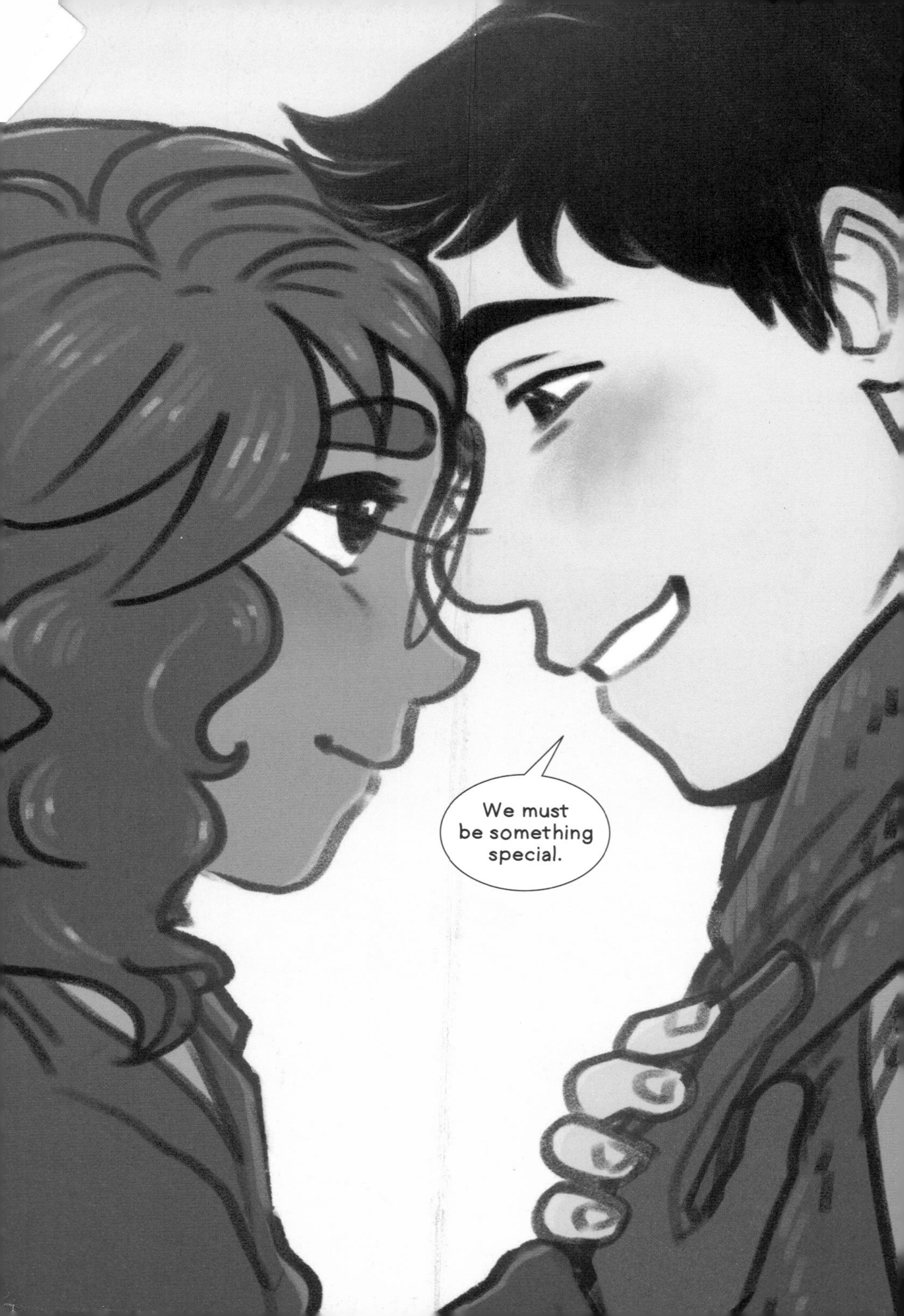
We must be something special.

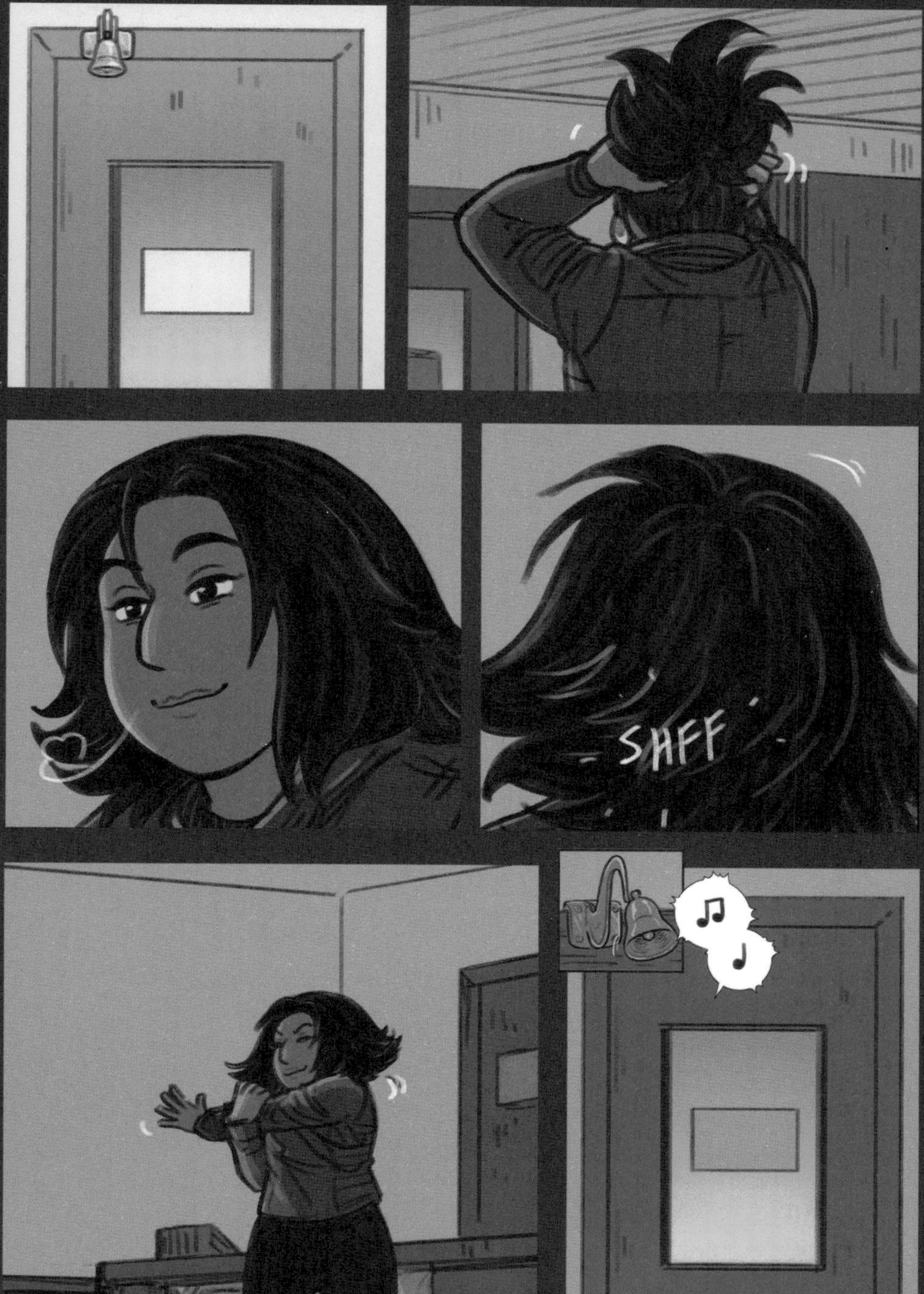
SAFF

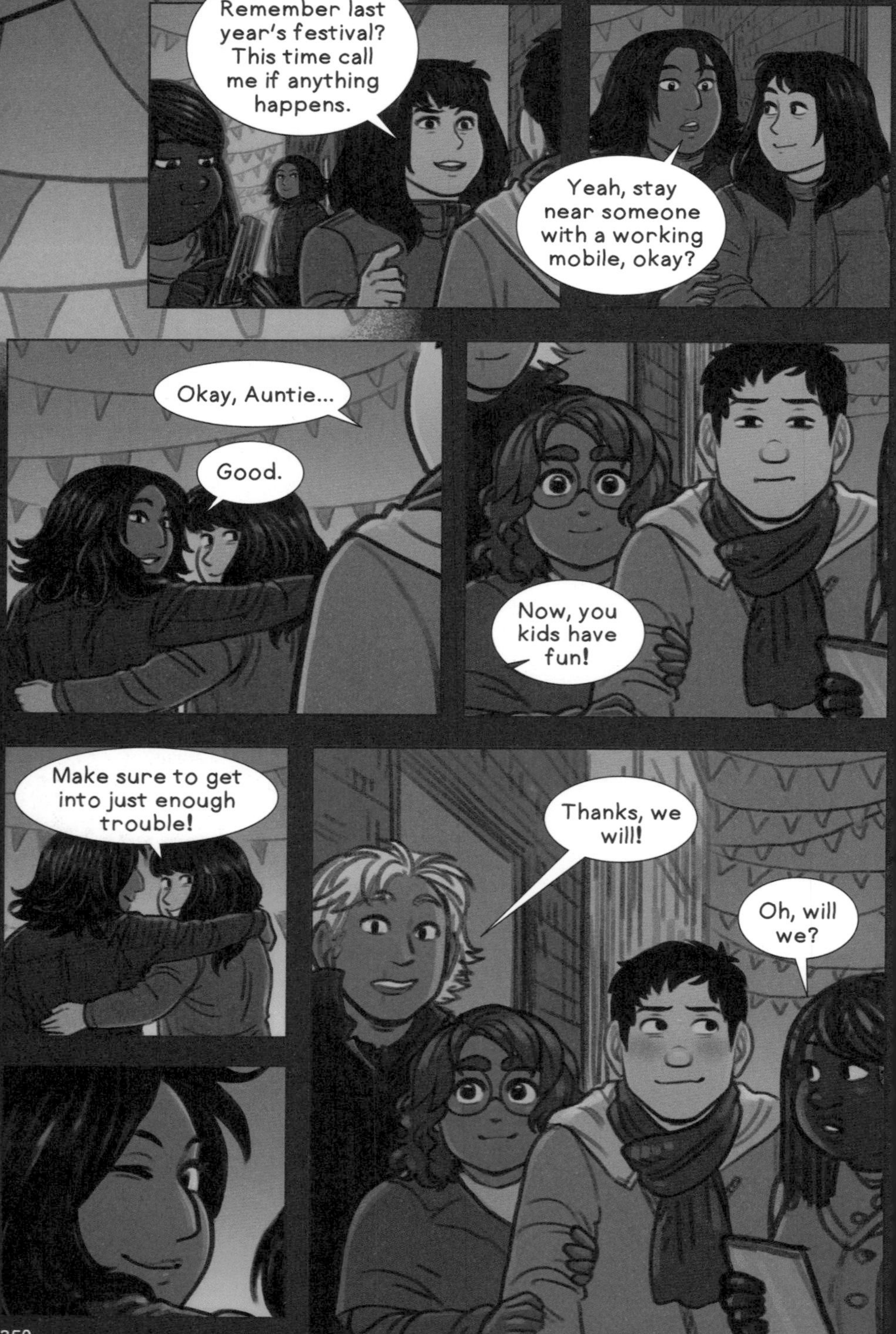
Remember last year's festival? This time call me if anything happens.
Yeah, stay near someone with a working mobile, okay?
Okay, Auntie...
Good.
Now, you kids have fun!
Make sure to get into just enough trouble!
Thanks, we will!
Oh, will we?

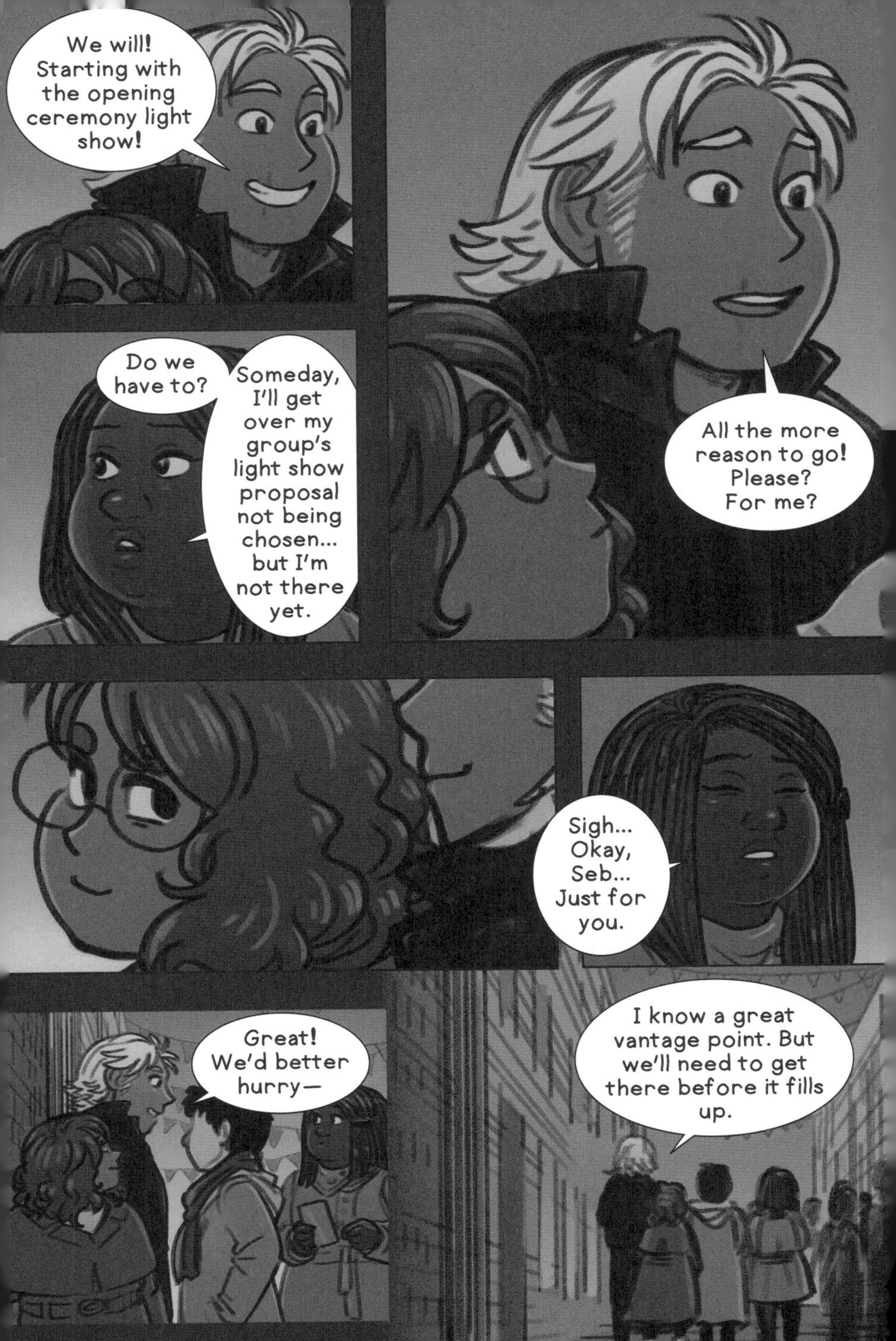
We will! Starting with the opening ceremony light show!
Do we have to?
Someday, I'll get over my group's light show proposal not being chosen... but I'm not there yet.
All the more reason to go! Please? For me?
Sigh... Okay, Seb... Just for you.
Great! We'd better hurry—
I know a great vantage point. But we'll need to get there before it fills up.

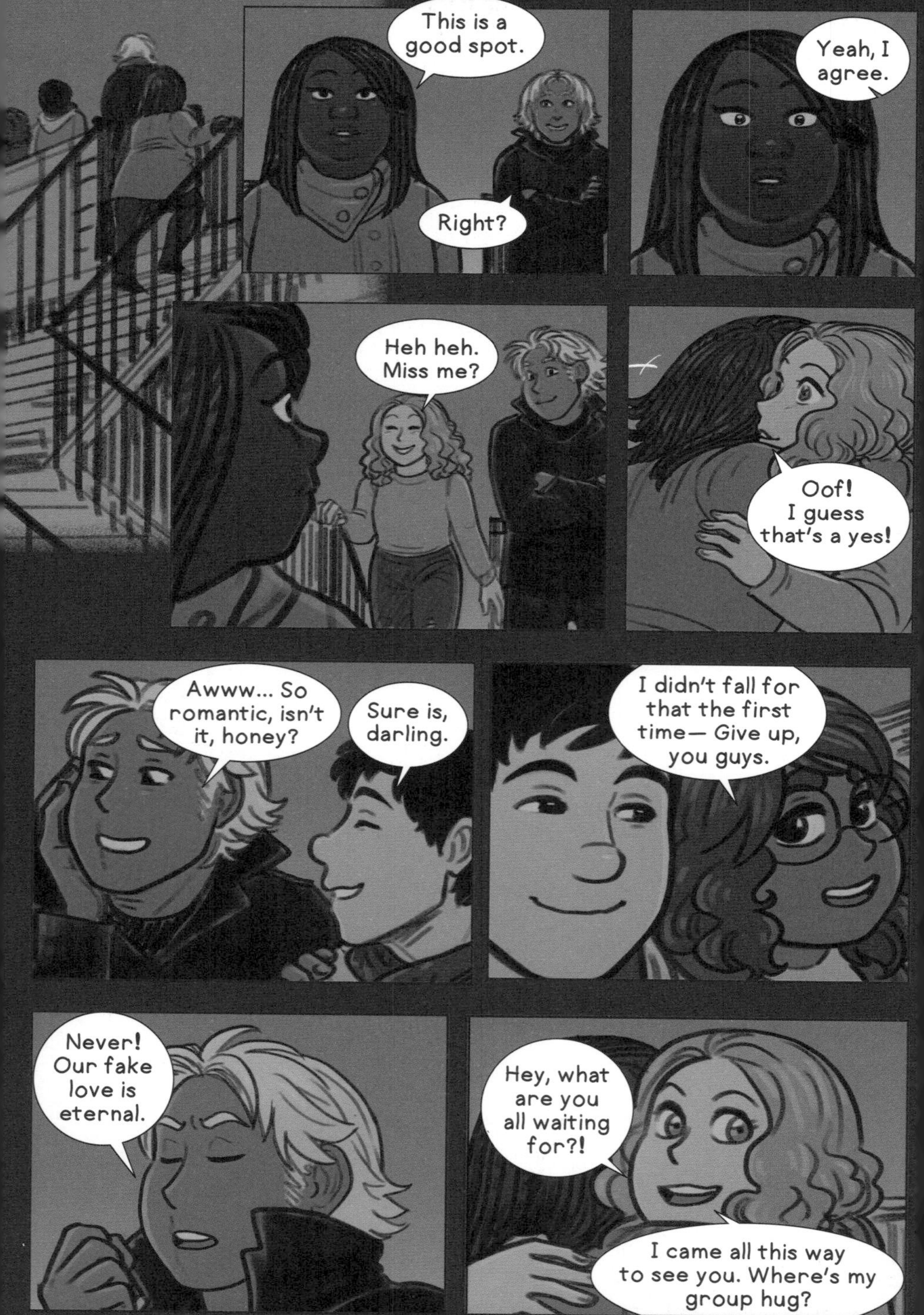
This is a good spot.
Right?
Yeah, I agree.
Heh heh. Miss me?
Oof! I guess that's a yes!
Awww... So romantic, isn't it, honey?
Sure is, darling.
I didn't fall for that the first time— *Give up*, you guys.
Never! Our fake love is eternal.
Hey, what are you all waiting for?!
I came all this way to see you. Where's my group hug?

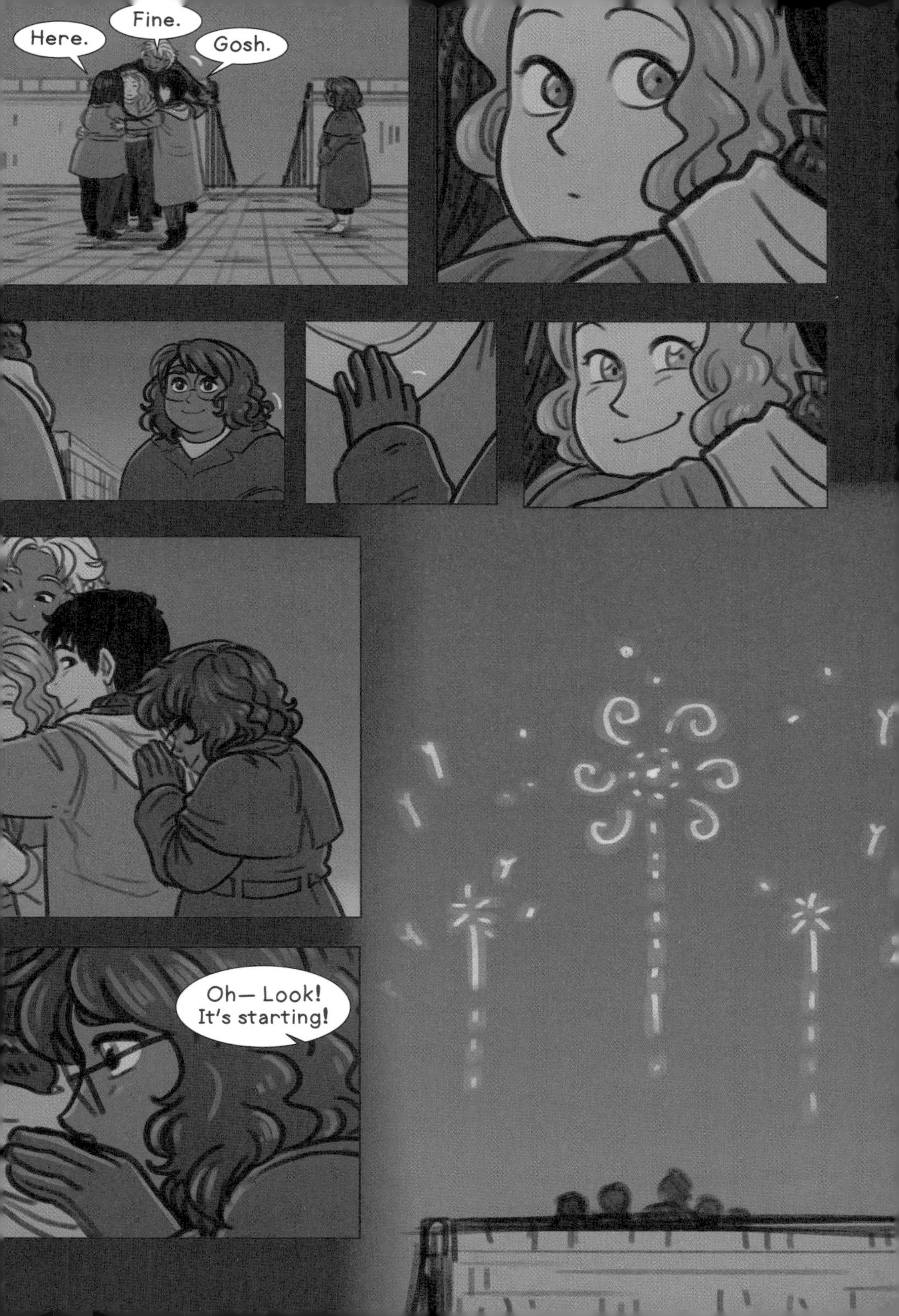
Here.
Fine.
Gosh.
Oh— Look! It's starting!

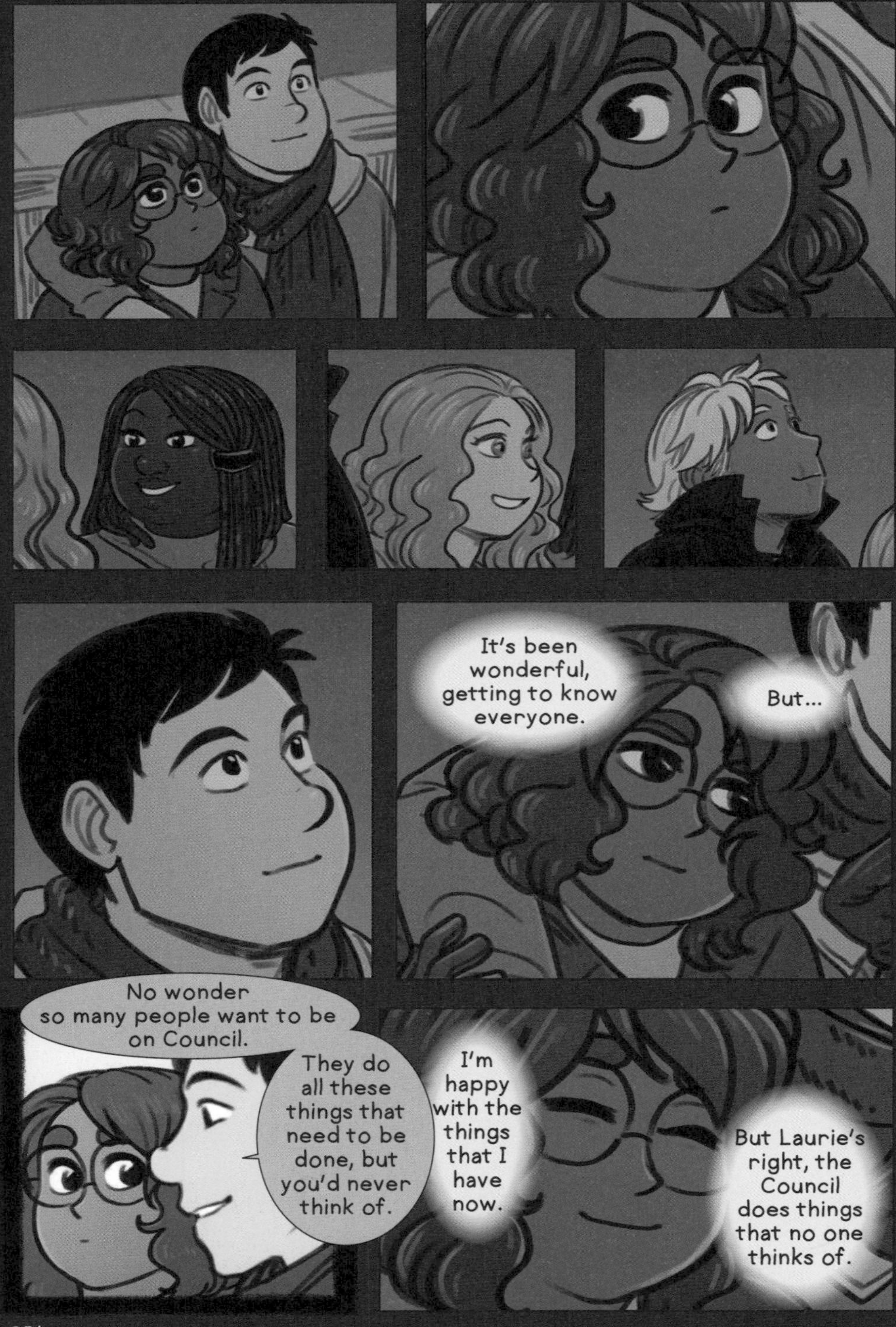

It's been wonderful, getting to know everyone.
But...
No wonder so many people want to be on Council.
They do all these things that need to be done, but you'd never think of.
I'm happy with the things that I have now.
But Laurie's right, the Council does things that no one thinks of.

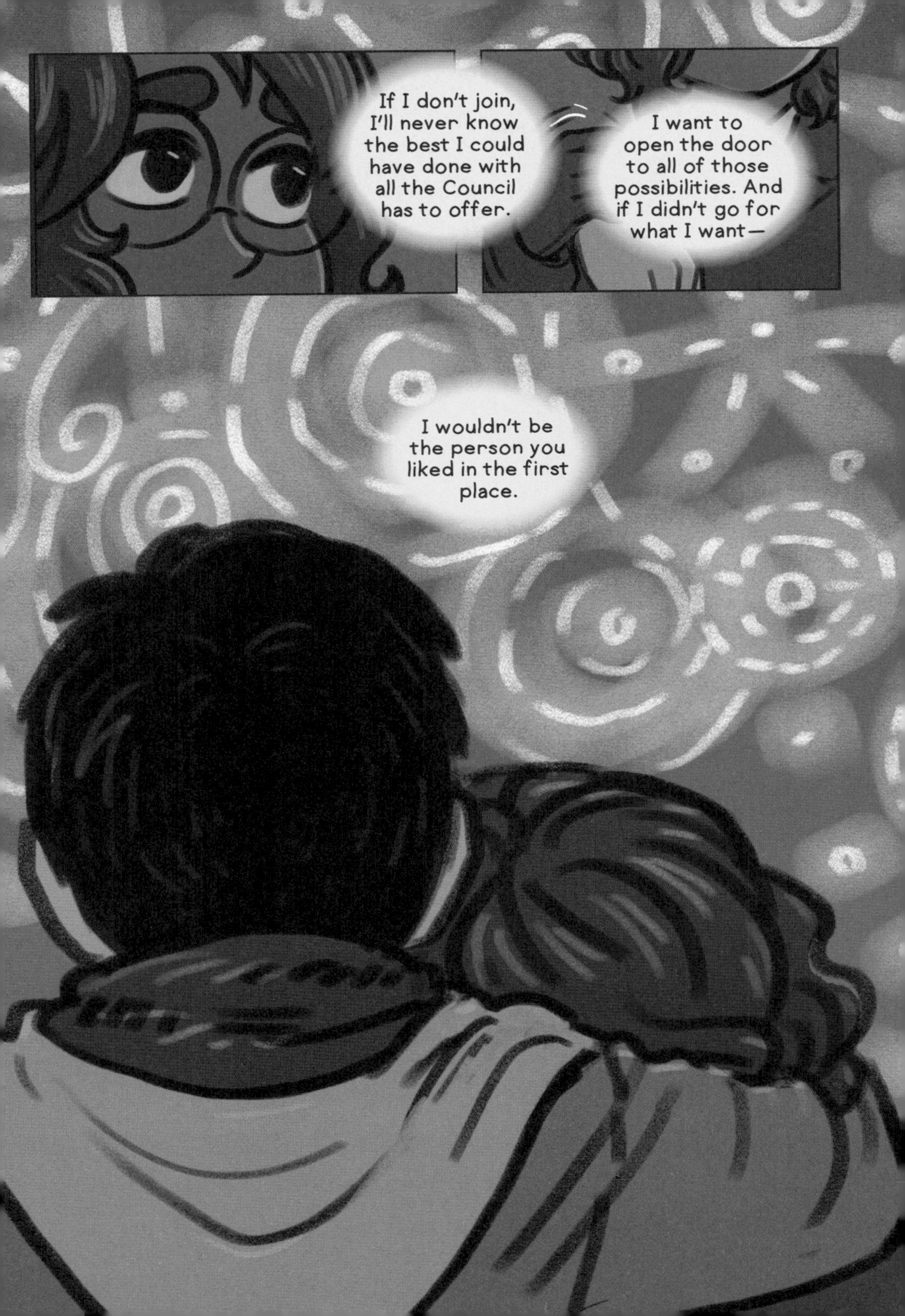
If I don't join, I'll never know the best I could have done with all the Council has to offer.
I want to open the door to all of those possibilities. And if I didn't go for what I want—
I wouldn't be the person you liked in the first place.

CHAPTER 14

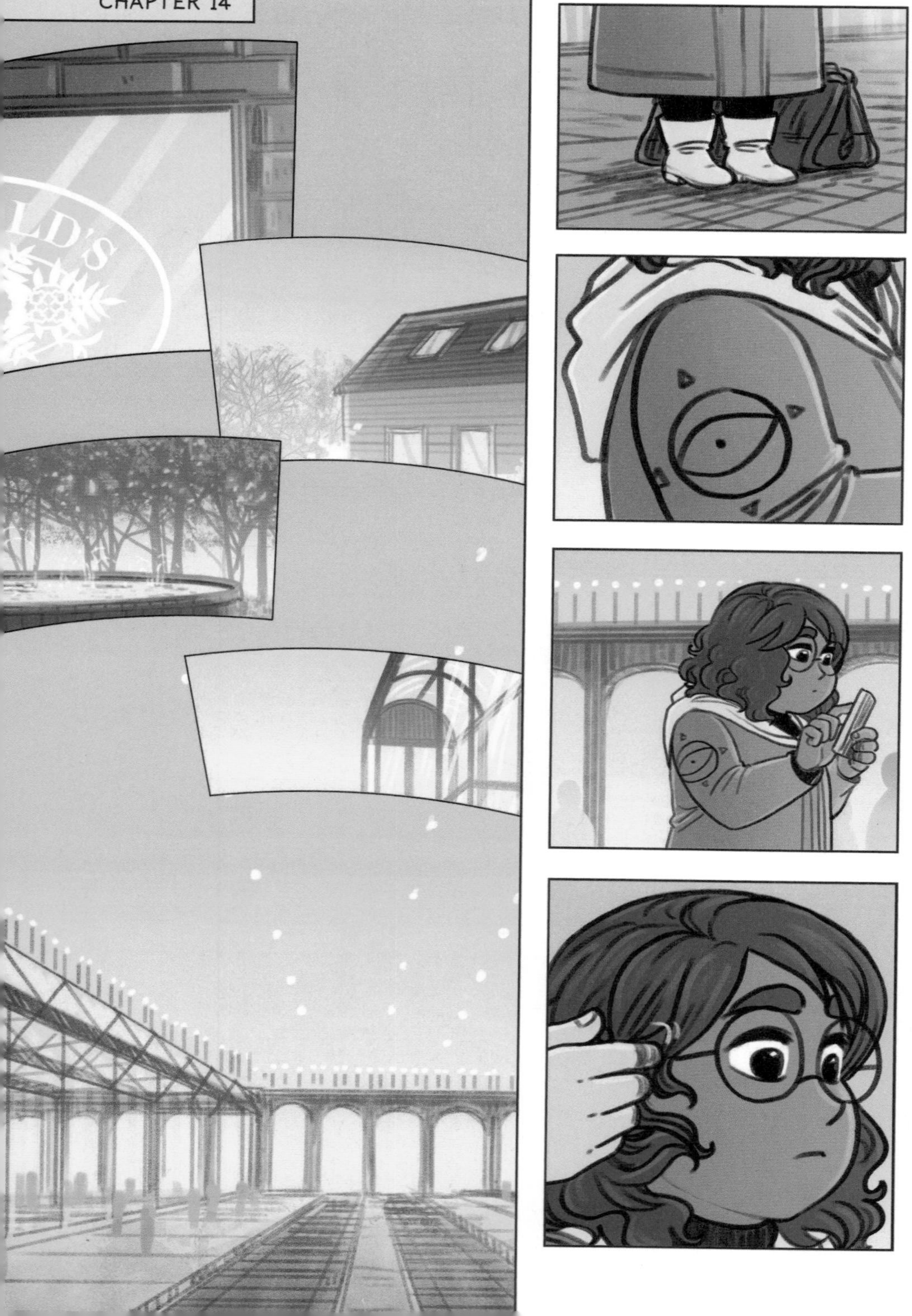

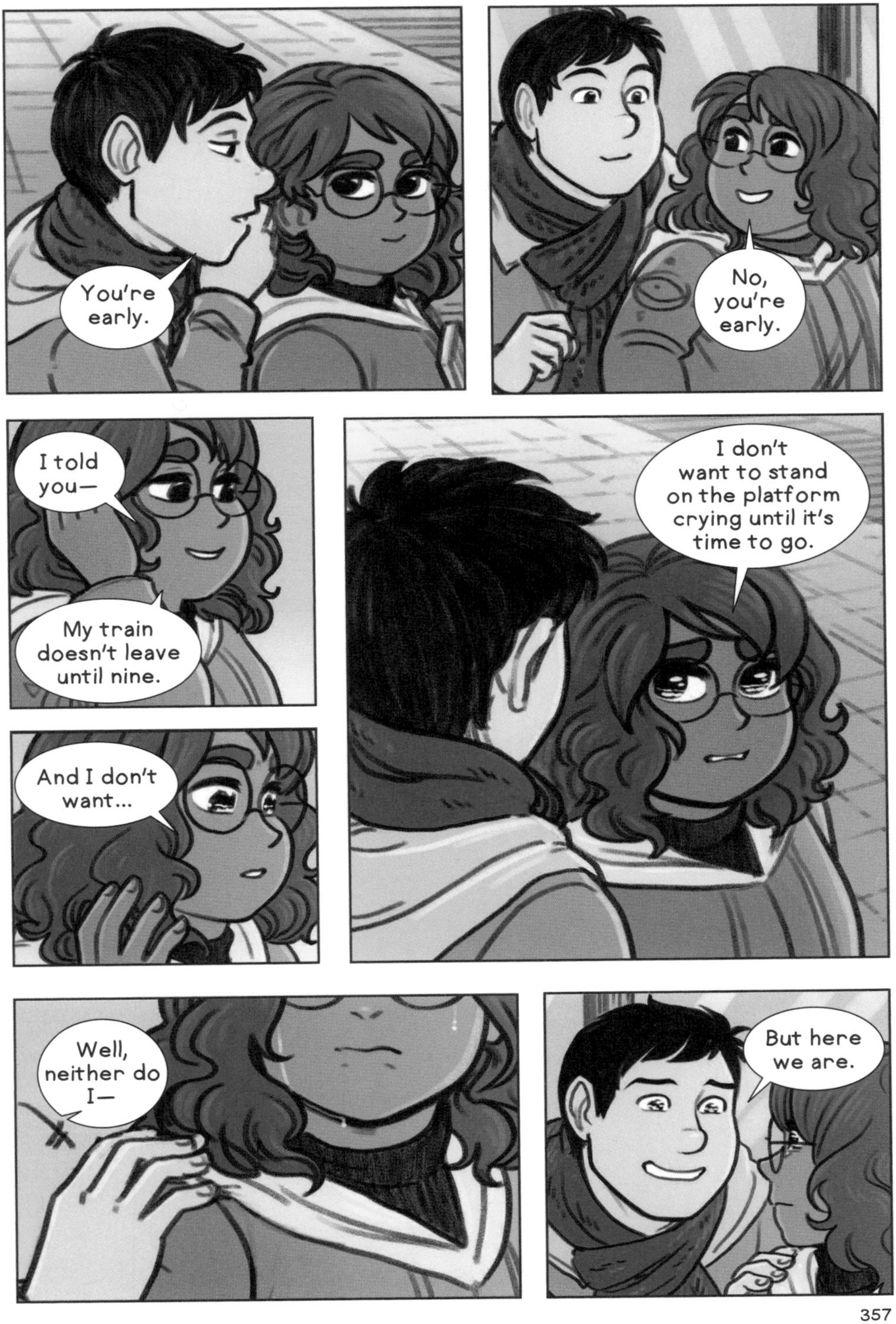
You're early.
No, you're early.
I told you—
My train doesn't leave until nine.
And I don't want...
I don't want to stand on the platform crying until it's time to go.
Well, neither do I—
But here we are.

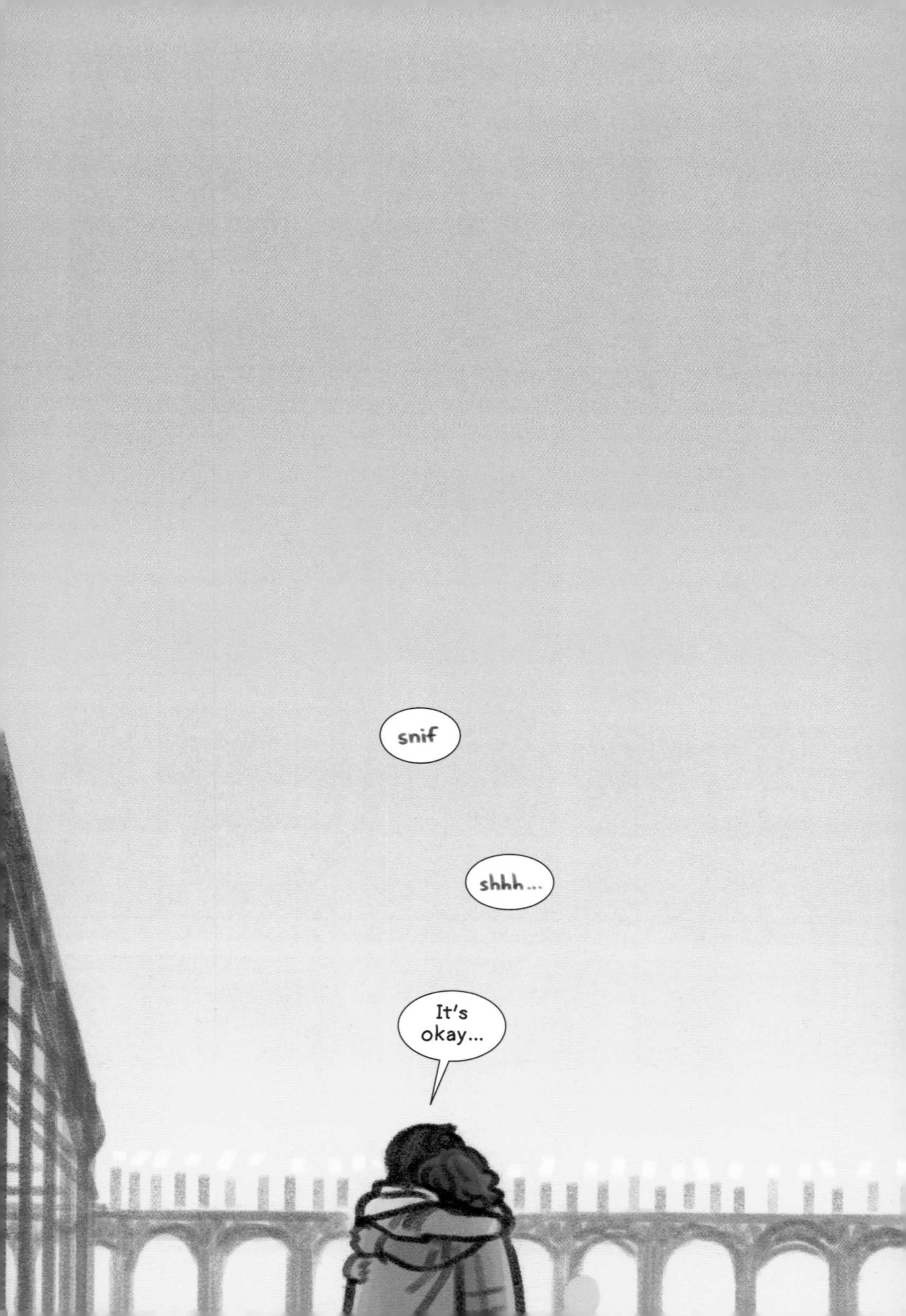
snif
shhh...
It's okay...

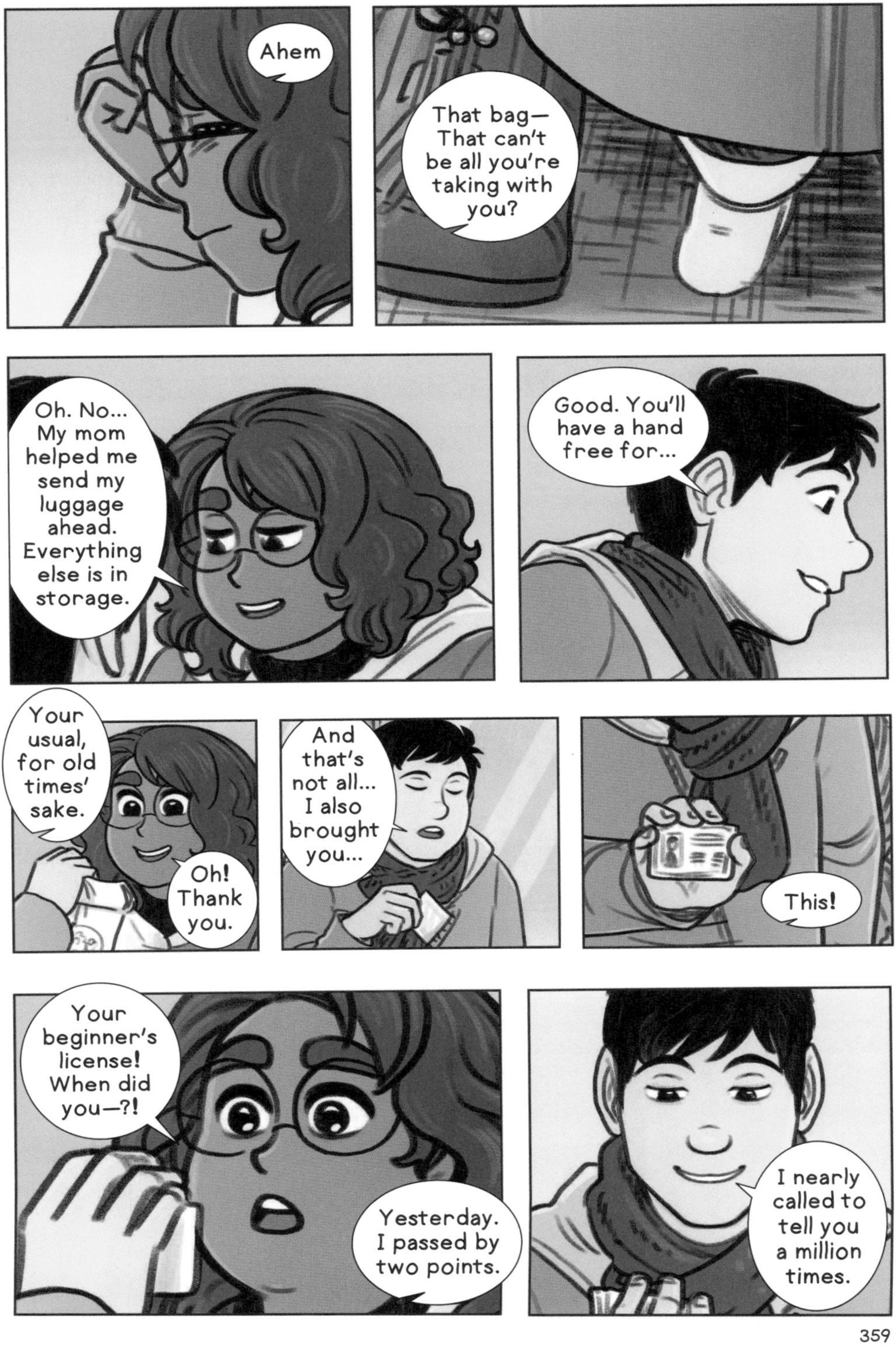
Ahem
That bag— That can't be all you're taking with you?
Oh. No... My mom helped me send my luggage ahead. Everything else is in storage.
Good. You'll have a hand free for...
Your usual, for old times' sake.
Oh! Thank you.
And that's not all... I also brought you...
This!
Your beginner's license! When did you—?!
Yesterday. I passed by two points.
I nearly called to tell you a million times.

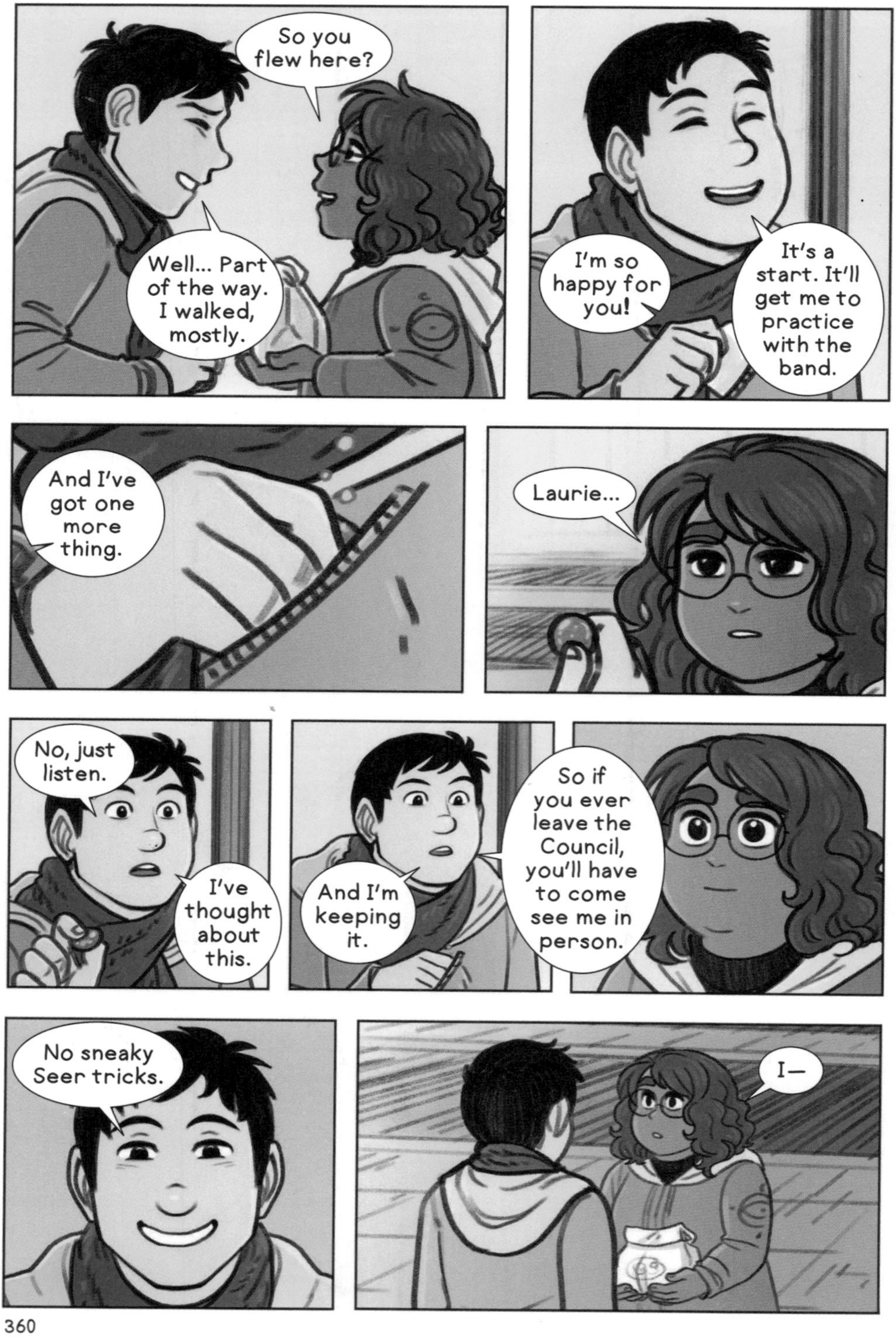
So you flew here?
Well... Part of the way. I walked, mostly.
It's a start. It'll get me to practice with the band.
I'm so happy for you!
And I've got one more thing.
Laurie...
No, just listen.
I've thought about this.
And I'm keeping it.
So if you ever leave the Council, you'll have to come see me in person.
No sneaky Seer tricks.
I—

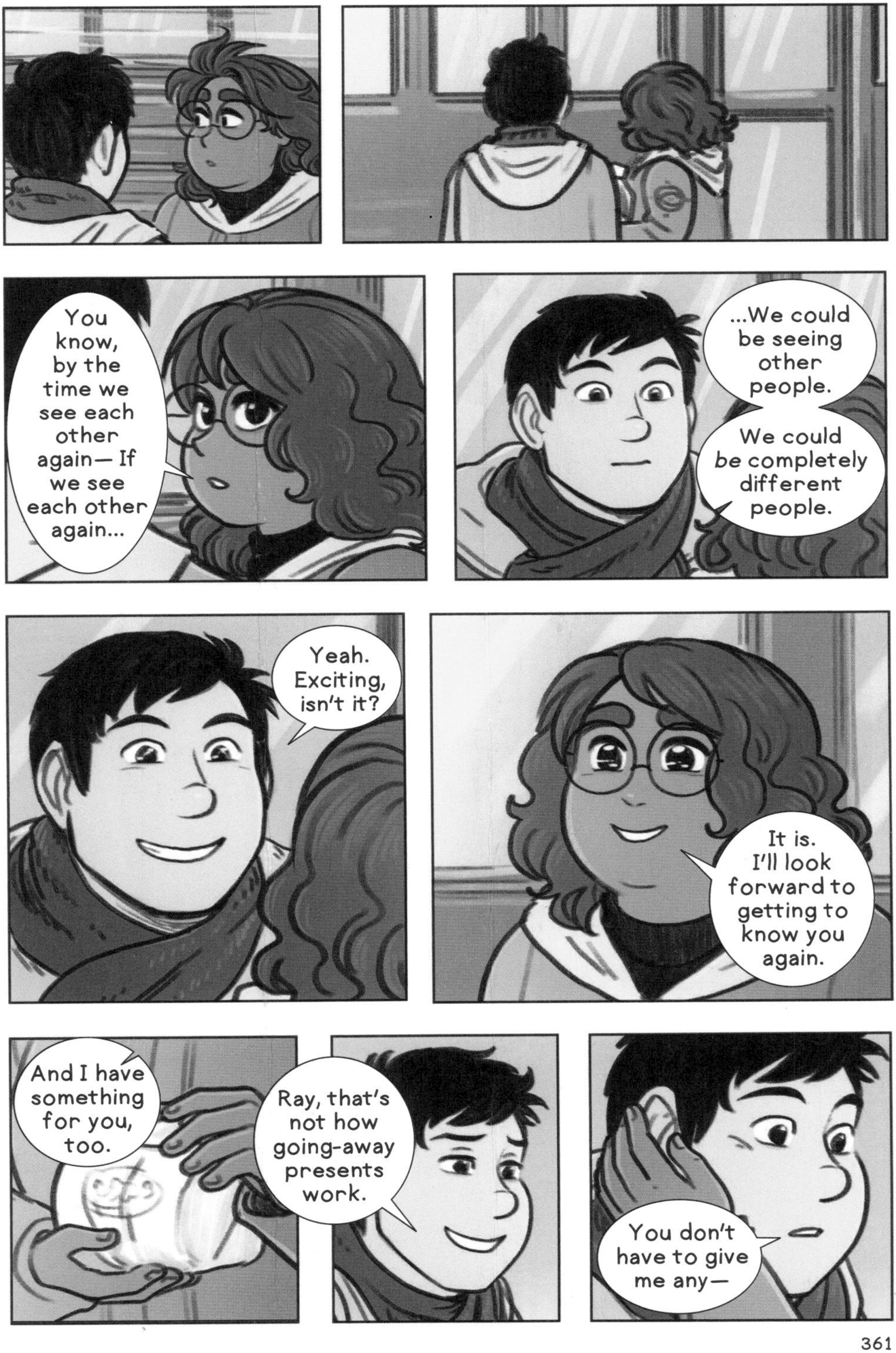
You know, by the time we see each other again— If we see each other again...
...We could be seeing other people.
We could *be* completely different people.
Yeah. Exciting, isn't it?
It is. I'll look forward to getting to know you again.
And I have something for you, too.
Ray, that's not how going-away presents work.
You don't have to give me any—

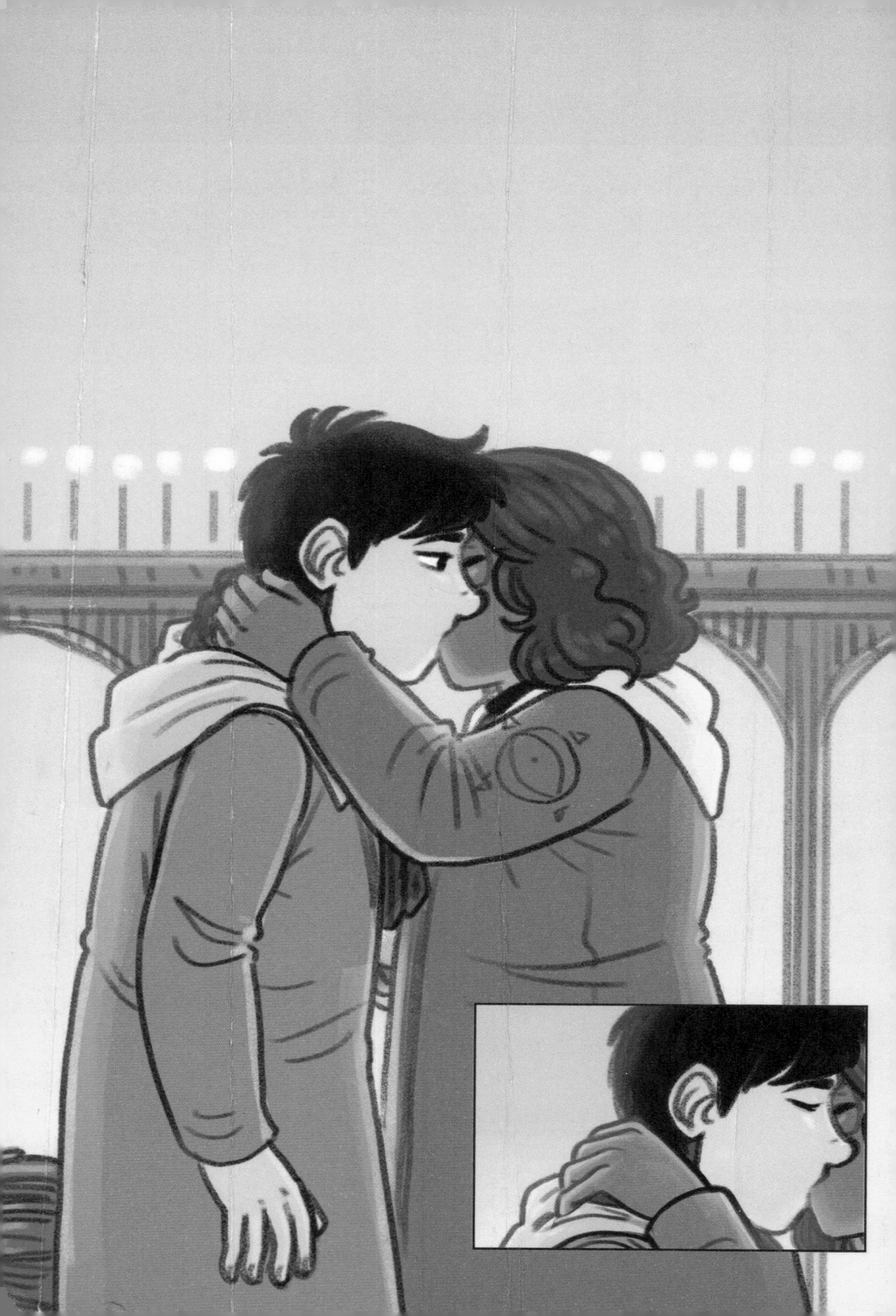

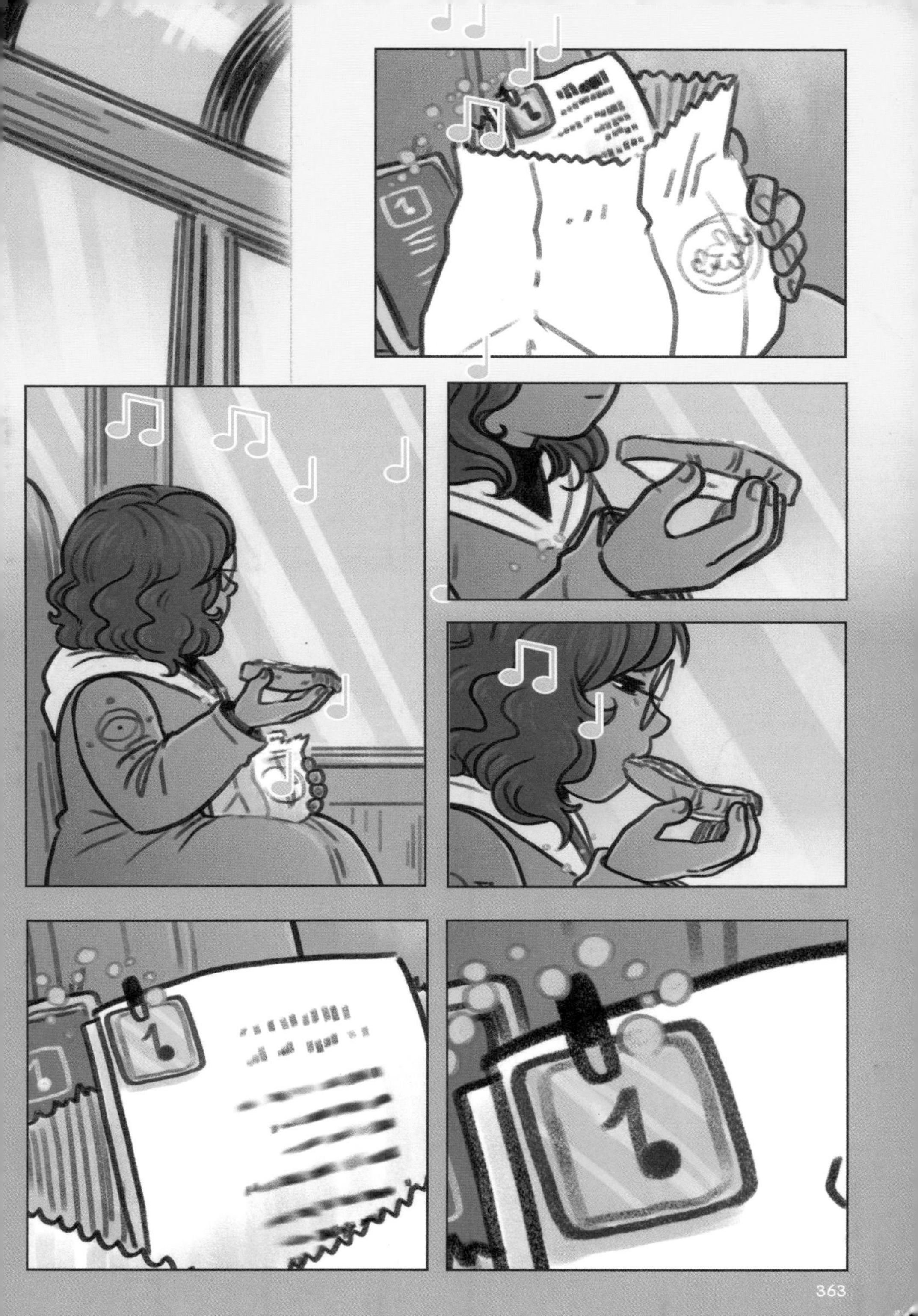

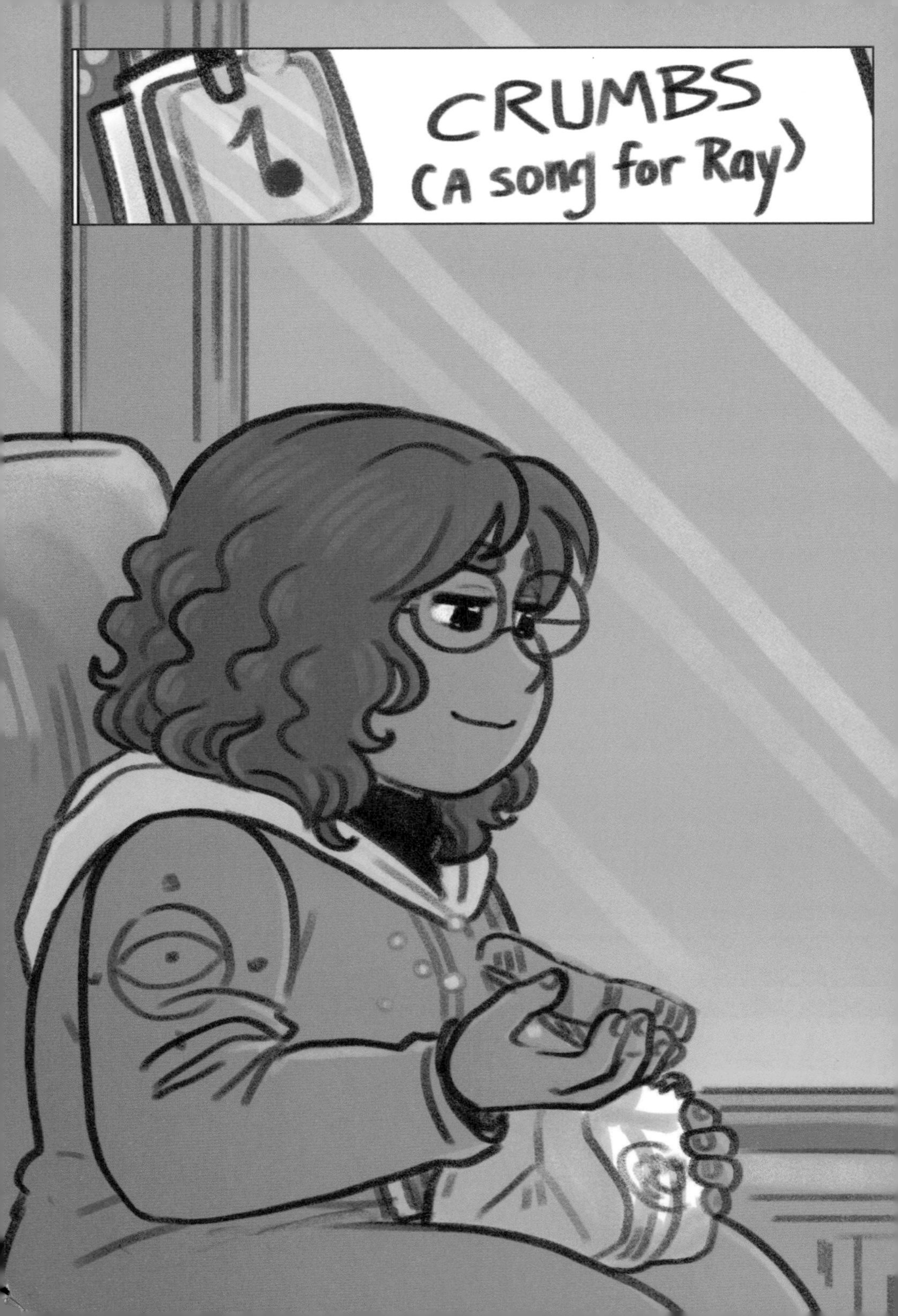
1
CRUMBS
(A song for Ray)

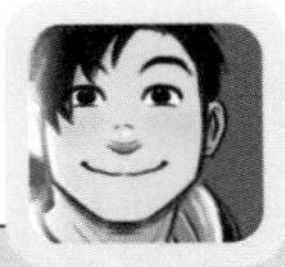

EPILOGUE

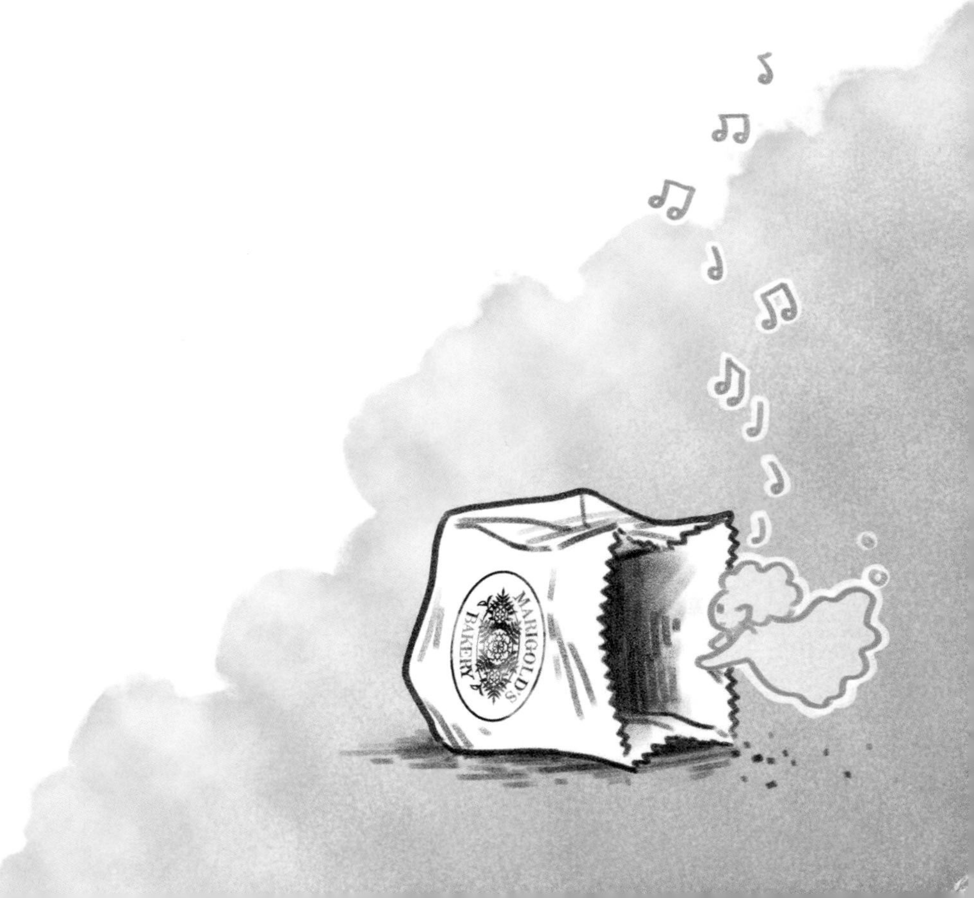
MARIGOLD'S
BAKERY

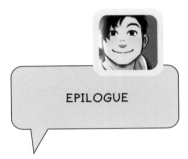

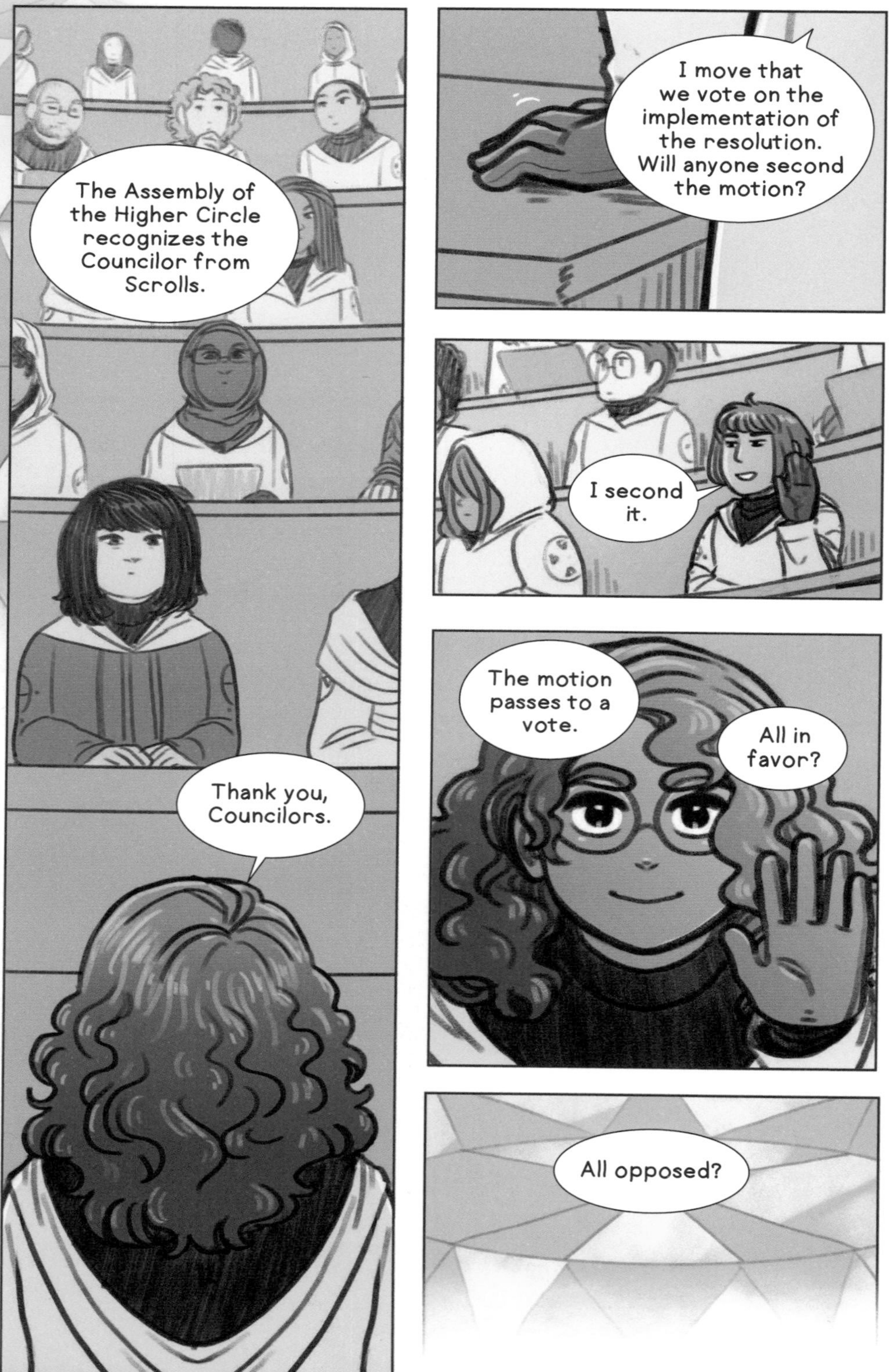
The Assembly of the Higher Circle recognizes the Councilor from Scrolls.
Thank you, Councilors.
I move that we vote on the implementation of the resolution. Will anyone second the motion?
I second it.
The motion passes to a vote.
All in favor?
All opposed?

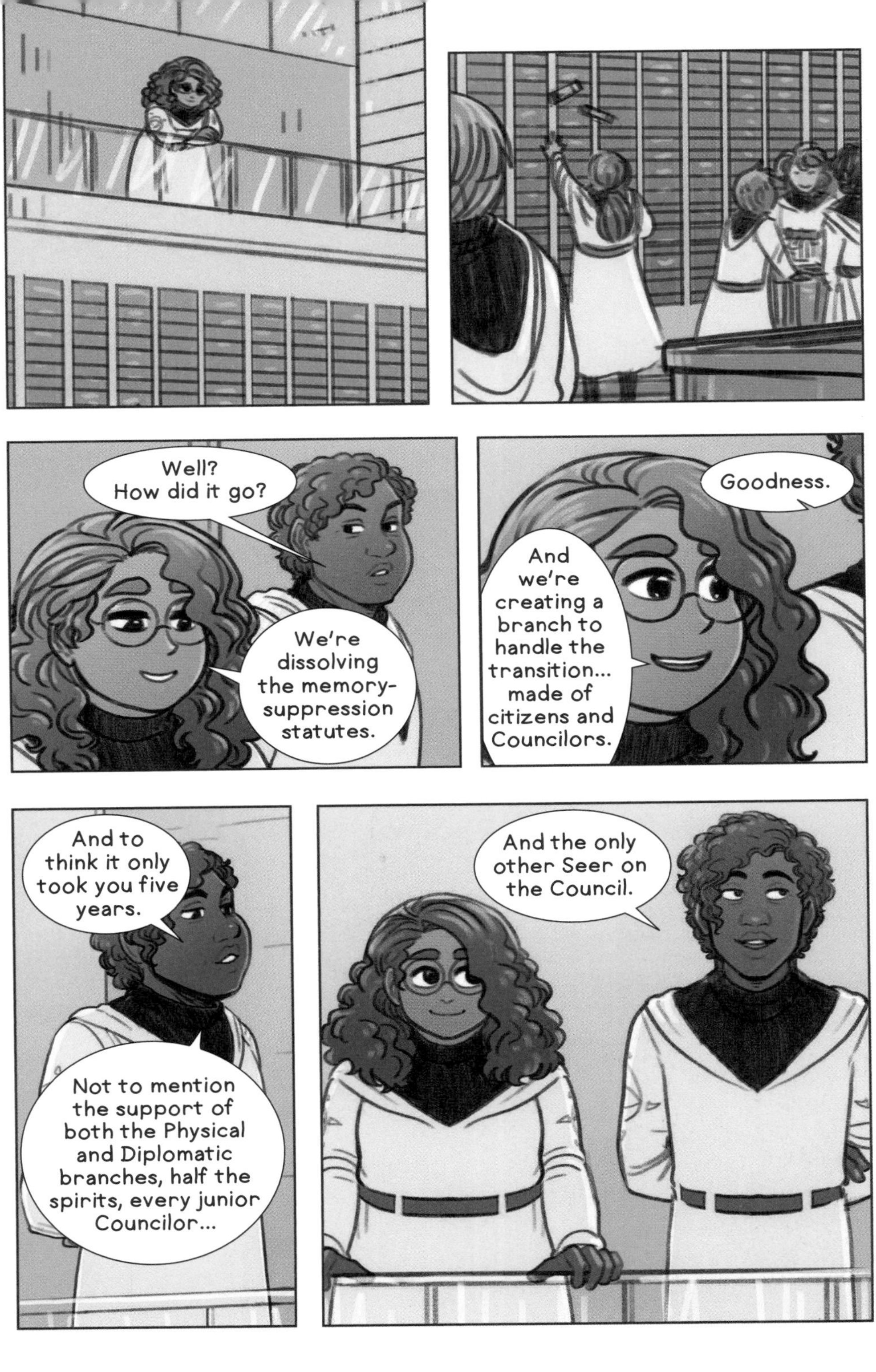
Well? How did it go?
We're dissolving the memory-suppression statutes.
Goodness.
And we're creating a branch to handle the transition... made of citizens and Councilors.
And to think it only took you five years.
Not to mention the support of both the Physical and Diplomatic branches, half the spirits, every junior Councilor...
And the only other Seer on the Council.

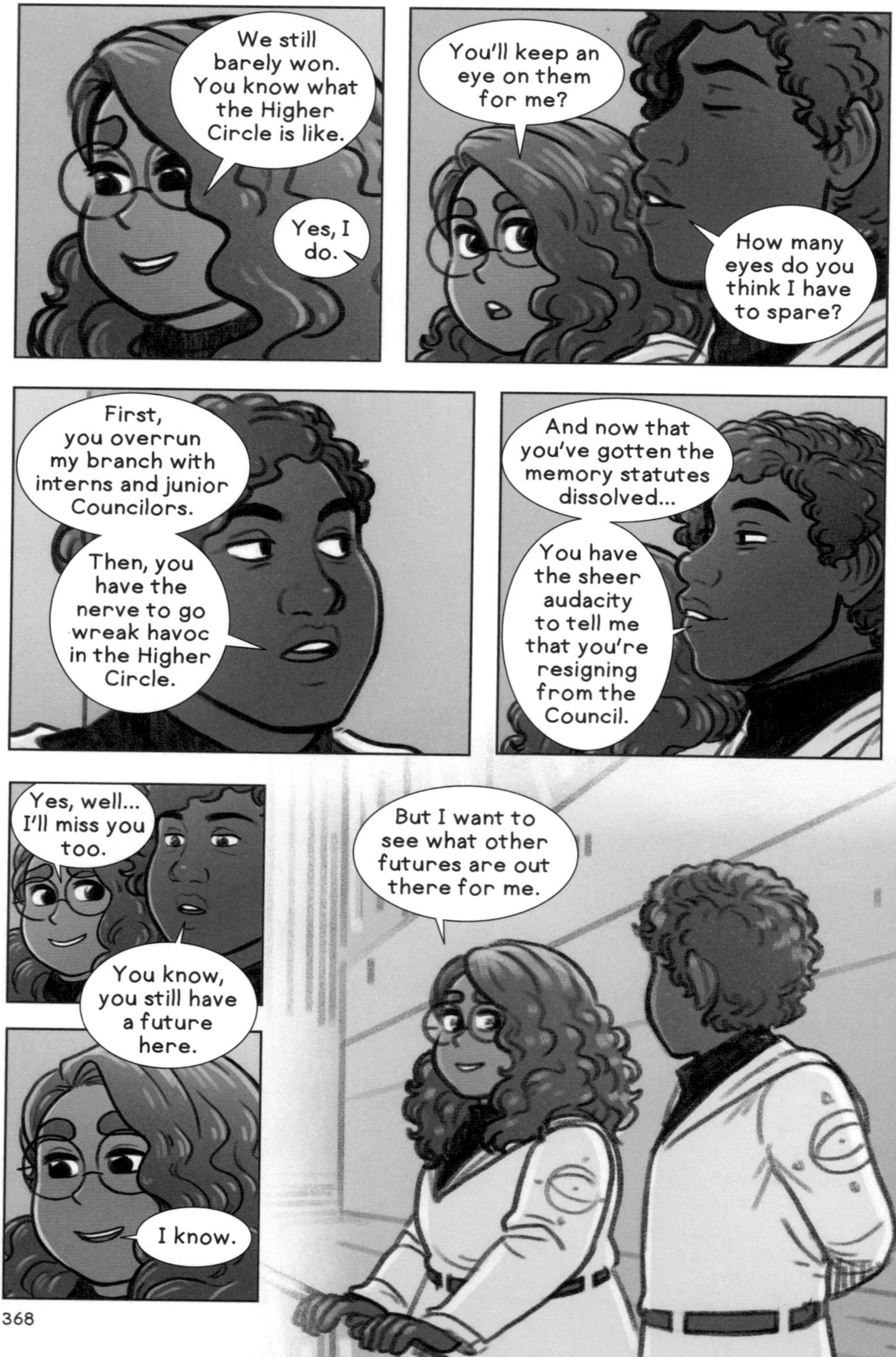
We still barely won. You know what the Higher Circle is like.
Yes, I do.
You'll keep an eye on them for me?
How many eyes do you think I have to spare?
First, you overrun my branch with interns and junior Councilors.
Then, you have the nerve to go wreak havoc in the Higher Circle.
And now that you've gotten the memory statutes dissolved...
You have the sheer audacity to tell me that you're resigning from the Council.
Yes, well... I'll miss you too.
You know, you still have a future here.
I know.
But I want to see what other futures are out there for me.

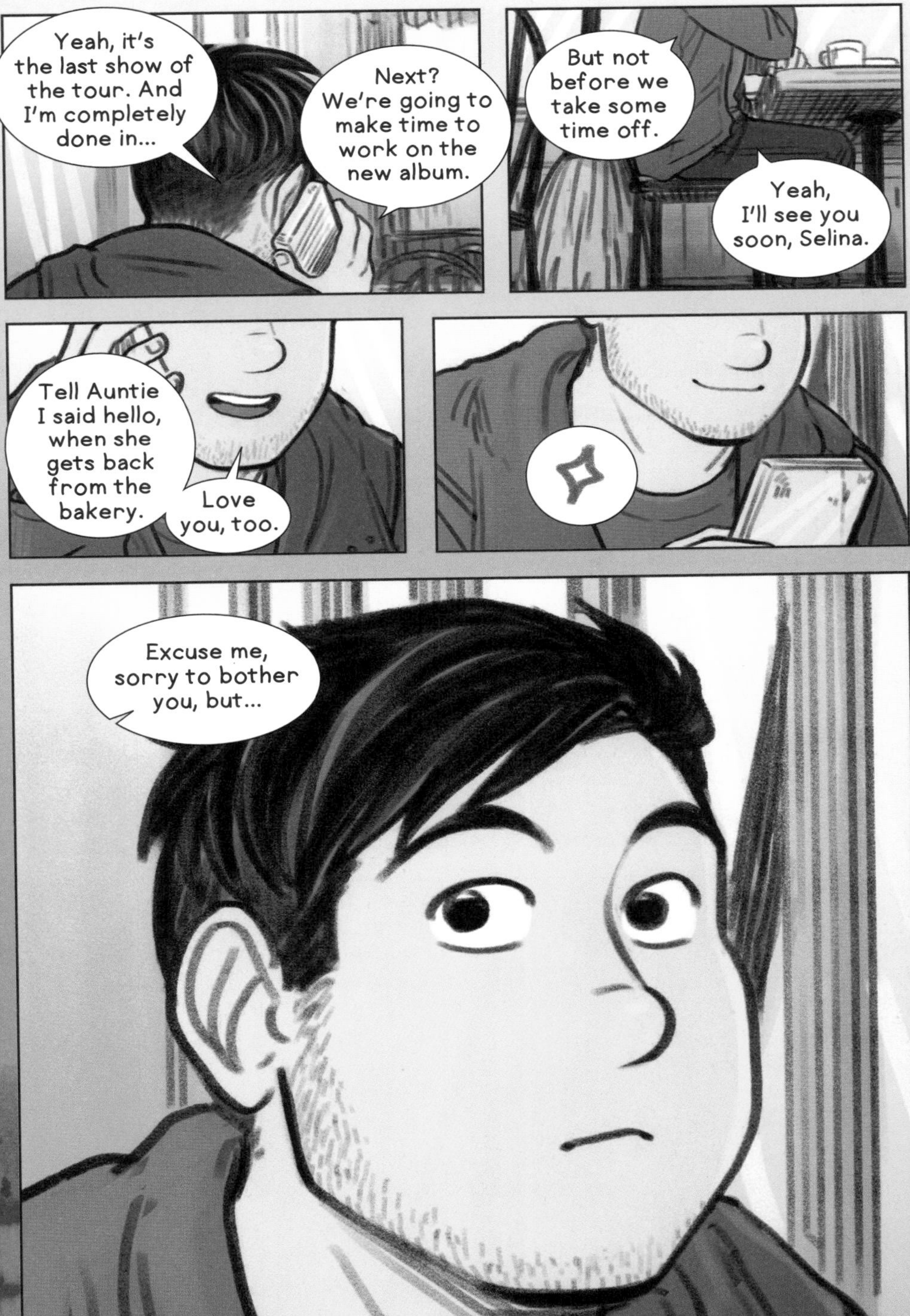
Yeah, it's the last show of the tour. And I'm completely done in...
Next? We're going to make time to work on the new album.
But not before we take some time off.
Yeah, I'll see you soon, Selina.
Tell Auntie I said hello, when she gets back from the bakery.
Love you, too.
Excuse me, sorry to bother you, but...

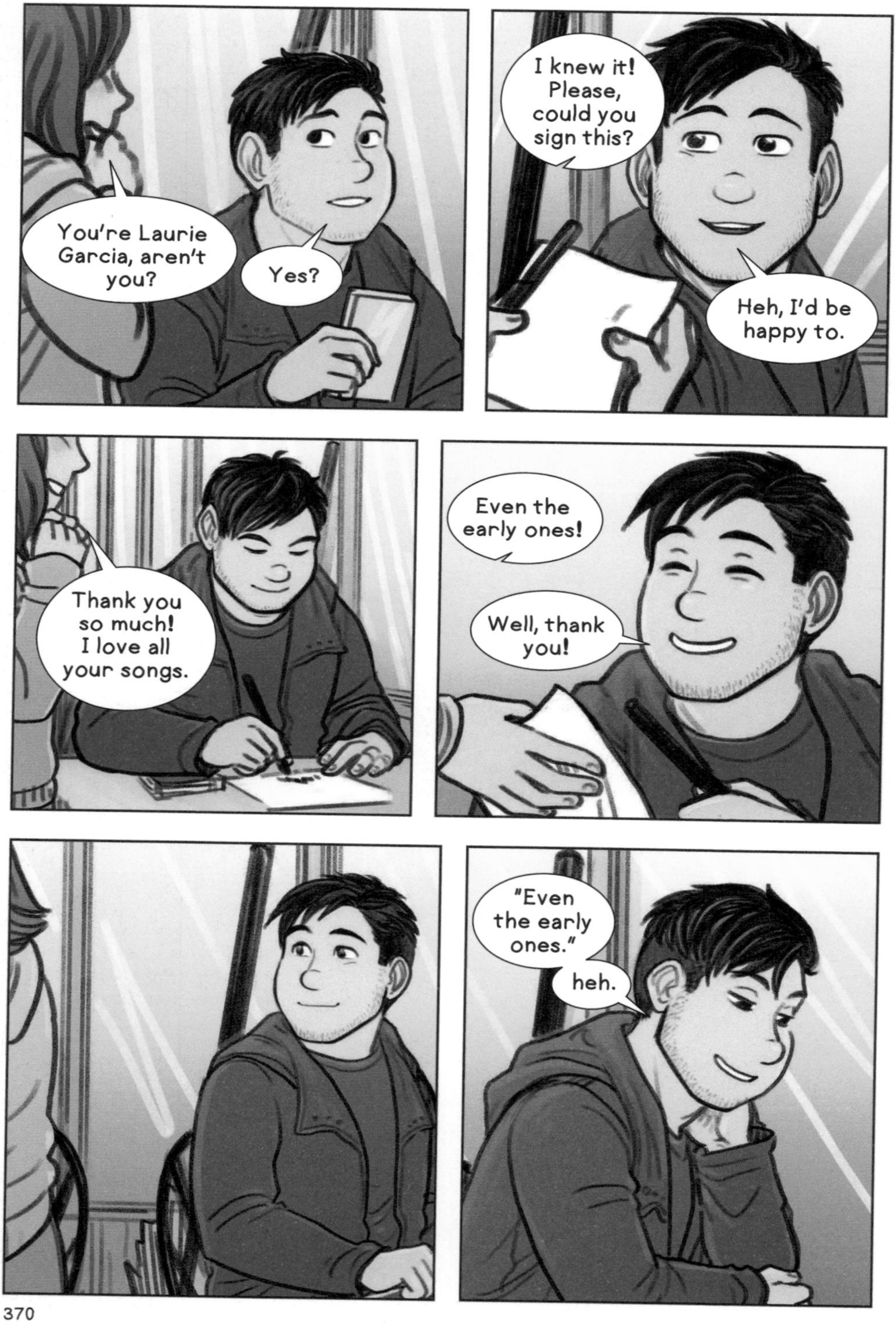
You're Laurie Garcia, aren't you?
Yes?
I knew it! Please, could you sign this?
Heh, I'd be happy to.
Thank you so much! I love all your songs.
Even the early ones!
Well, thank you!
"Even the early ones."
heh.

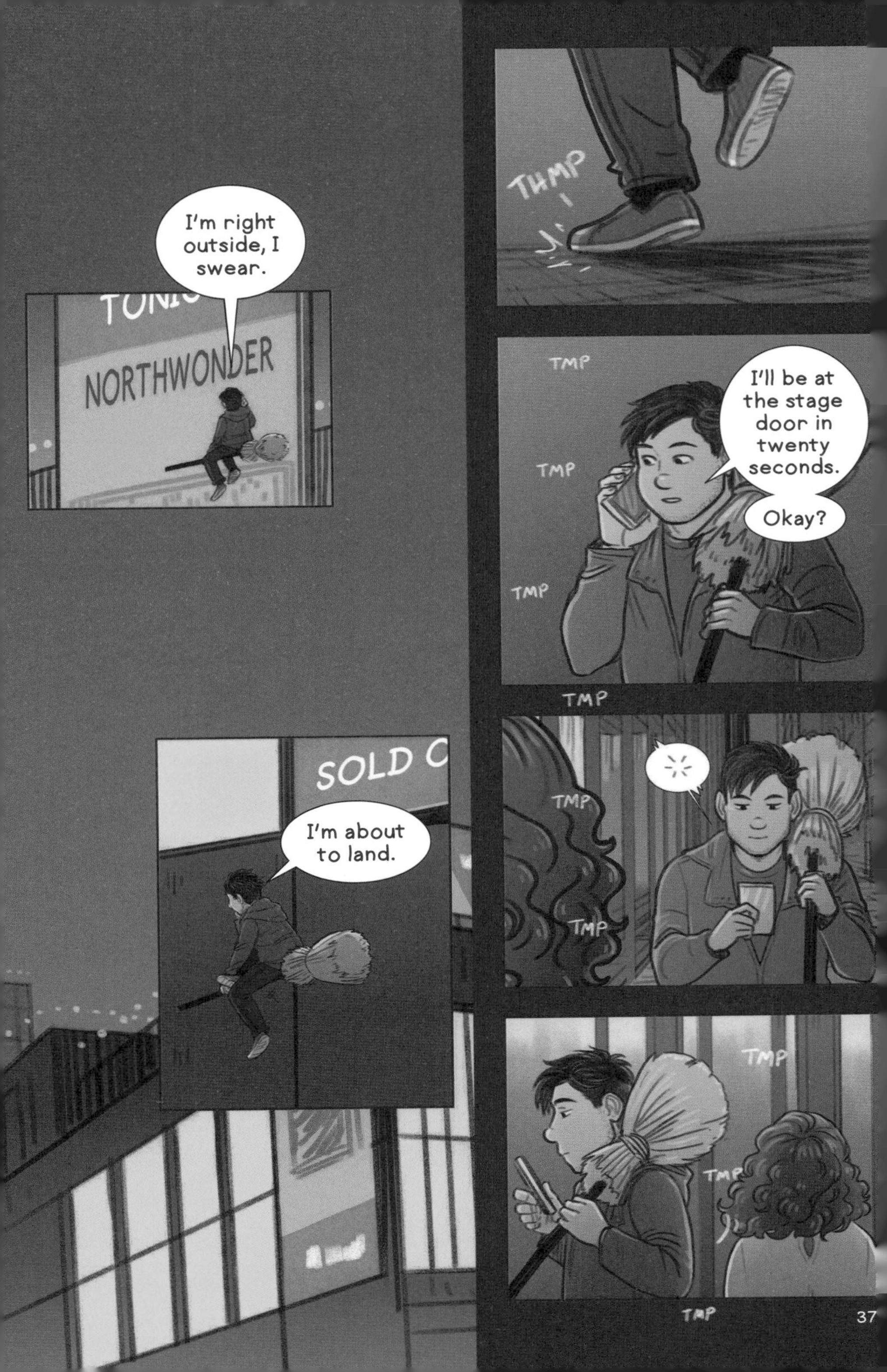

I'm right outside, I swear.
TONIC
NORTHWONDER
SOLD O
I'm about to land.
THMP
TMP
TMP
TMP
I'll be at the stage door in twenty seconds.
Okay?
TMP
TMP
TMP
TMP
TMP
TMP

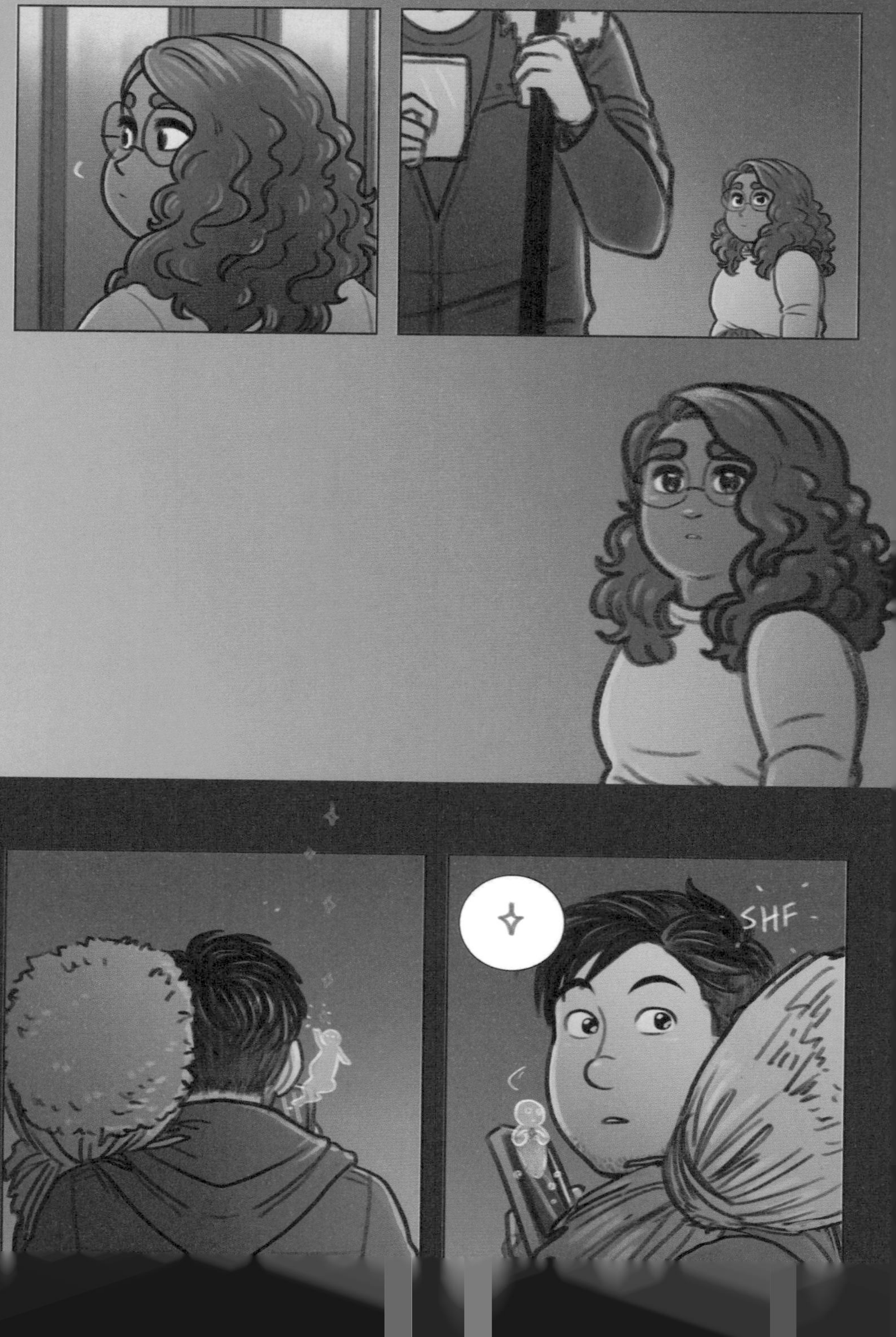
SHF

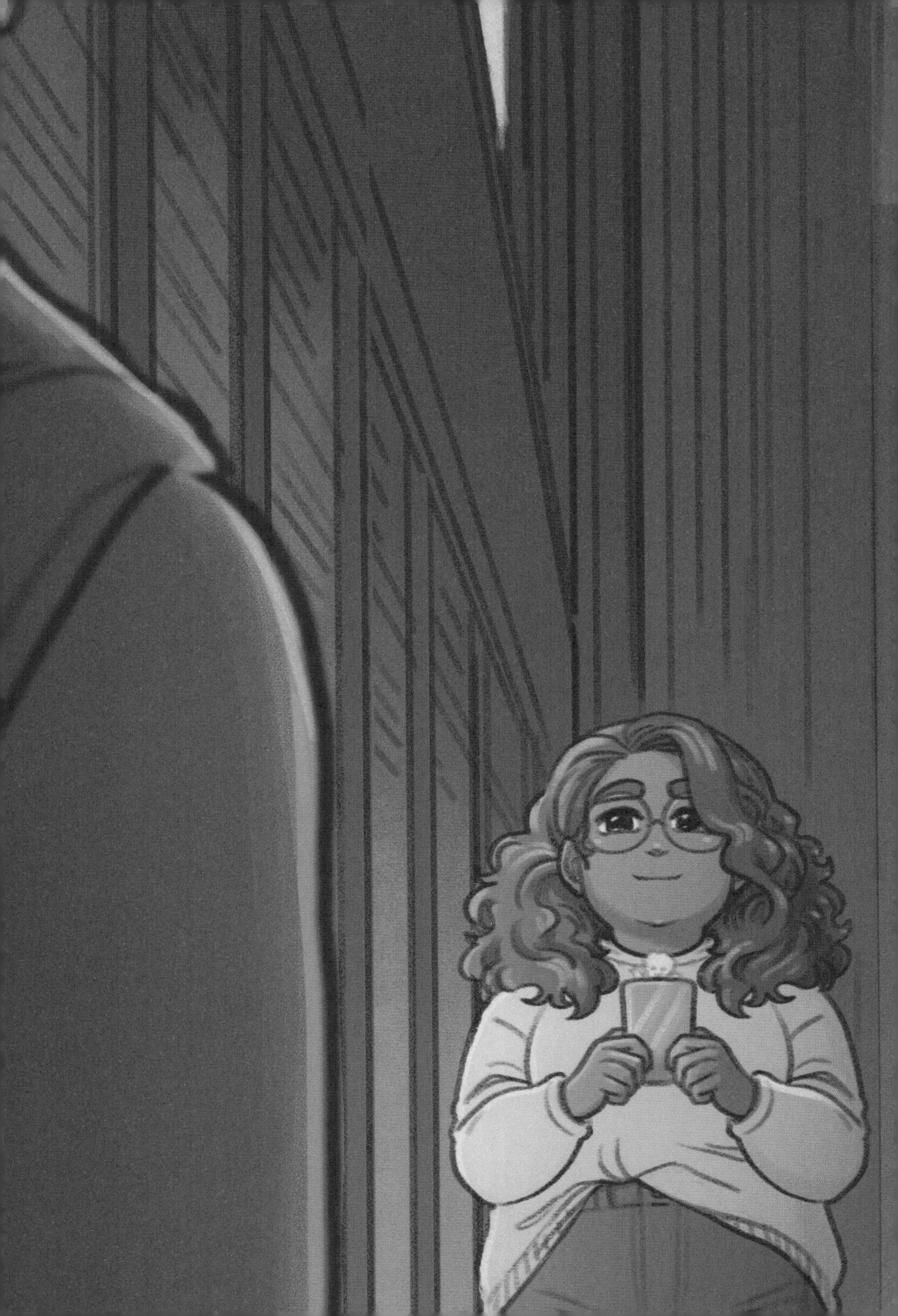

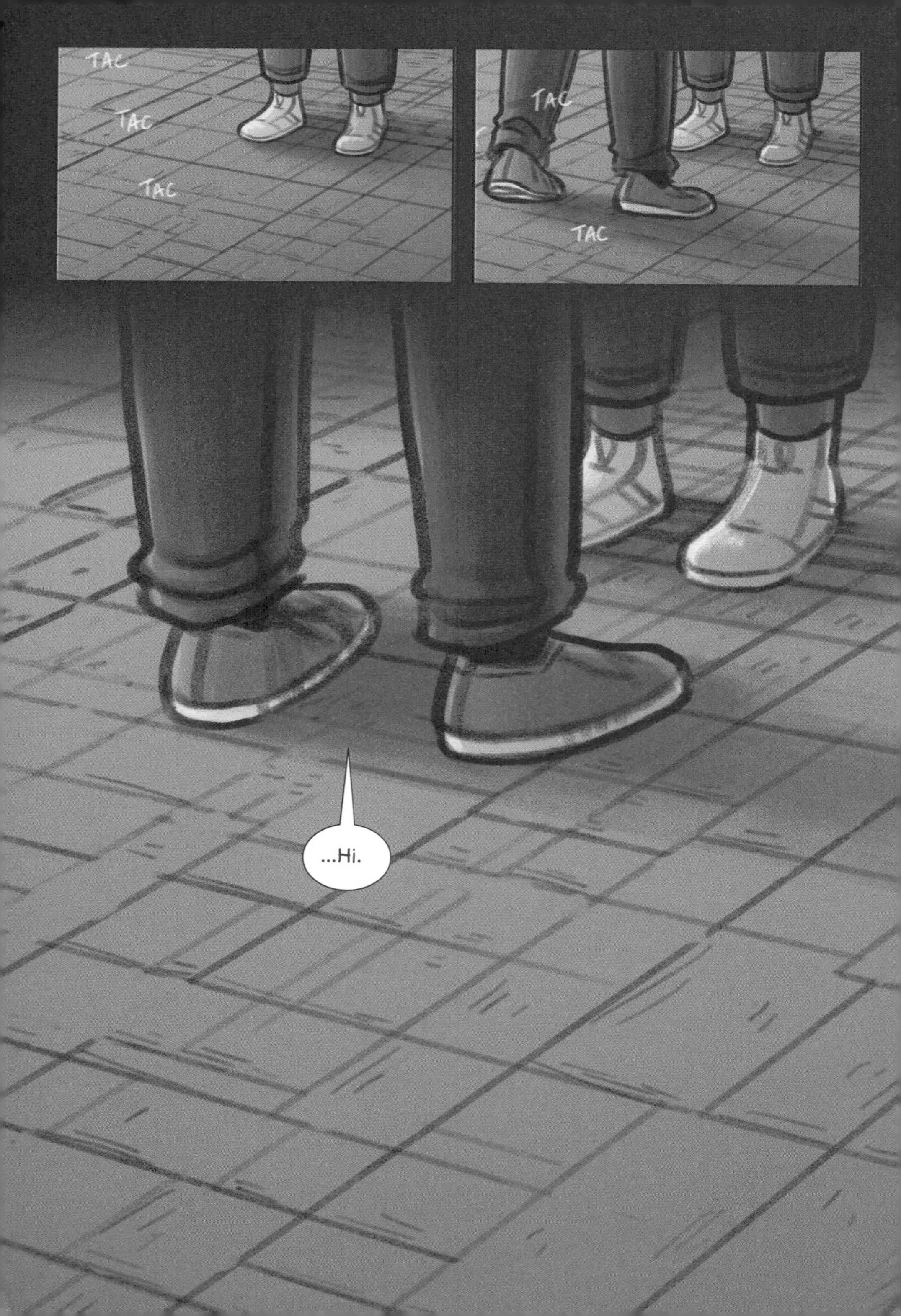
TAC
TAC
TAC
TAC
TAC
...Hi.

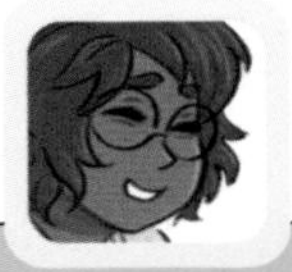

EXTRAS

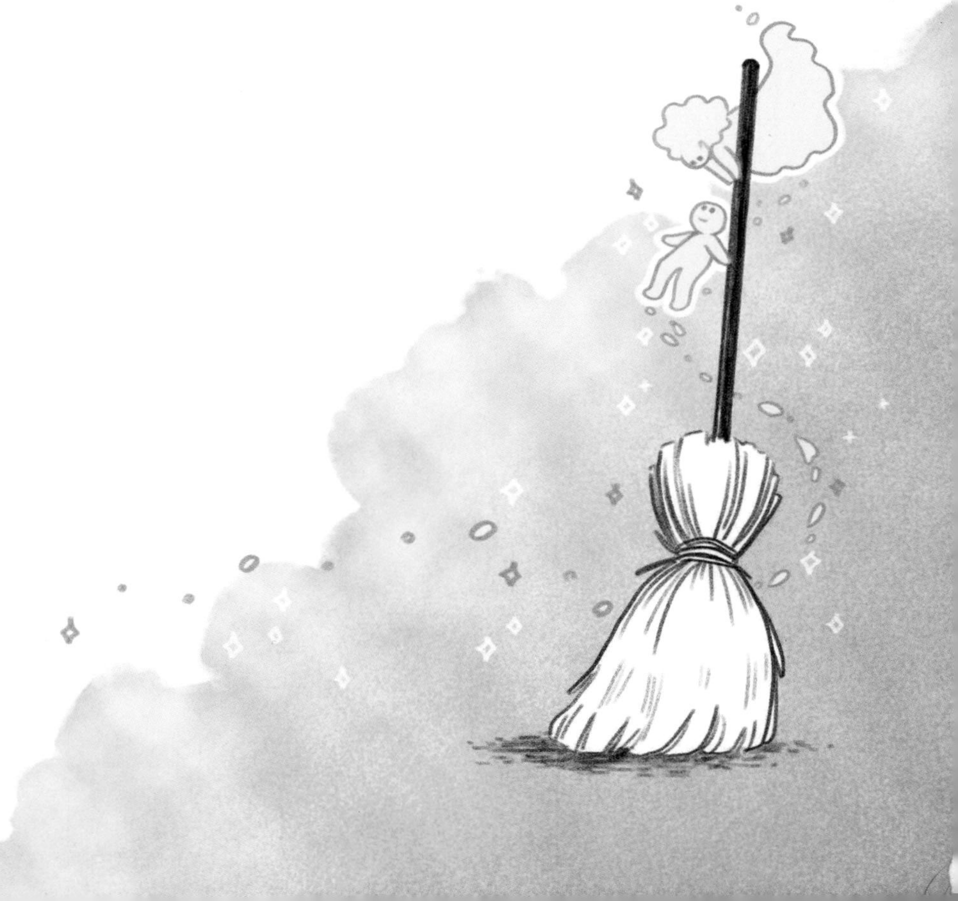

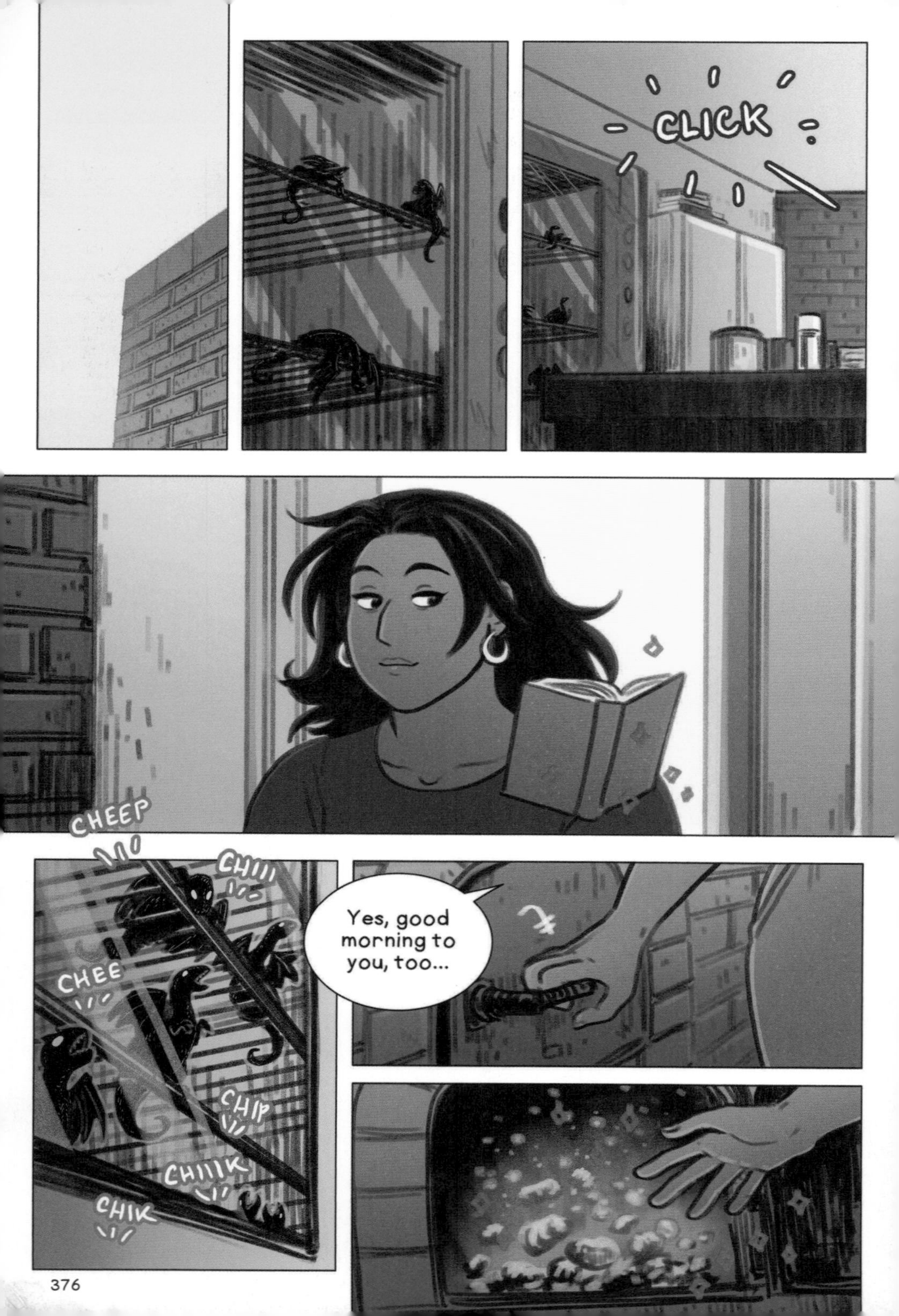
CLICK
CHEEP
CHIII
CHEE
CHIP
CHIIIK
CHIK
Yes, good morning to you, too...

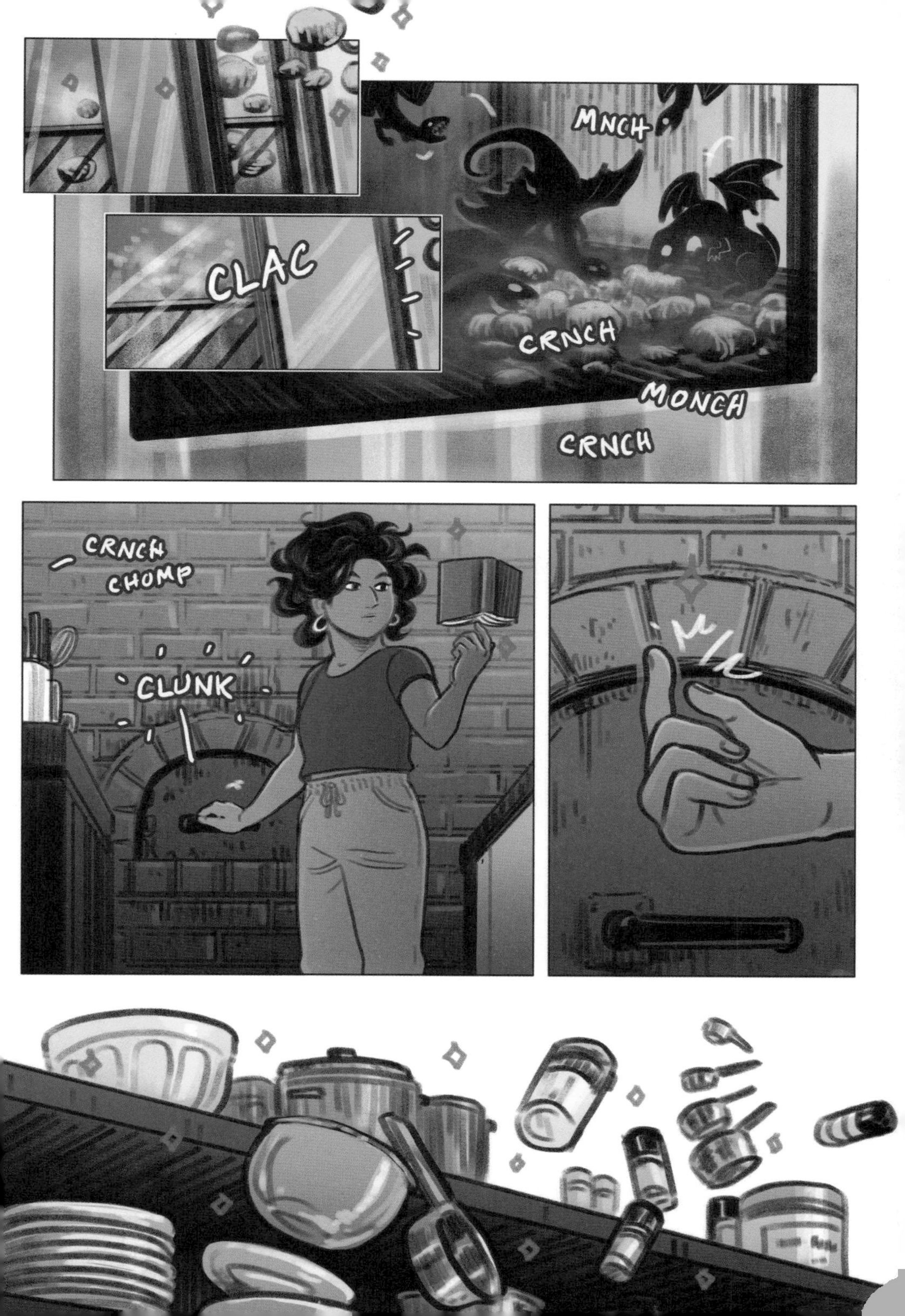
CLAC
MNCH
CRNCH
MONCH
CRNCH
CRNCH
CHOMP
CLUNK

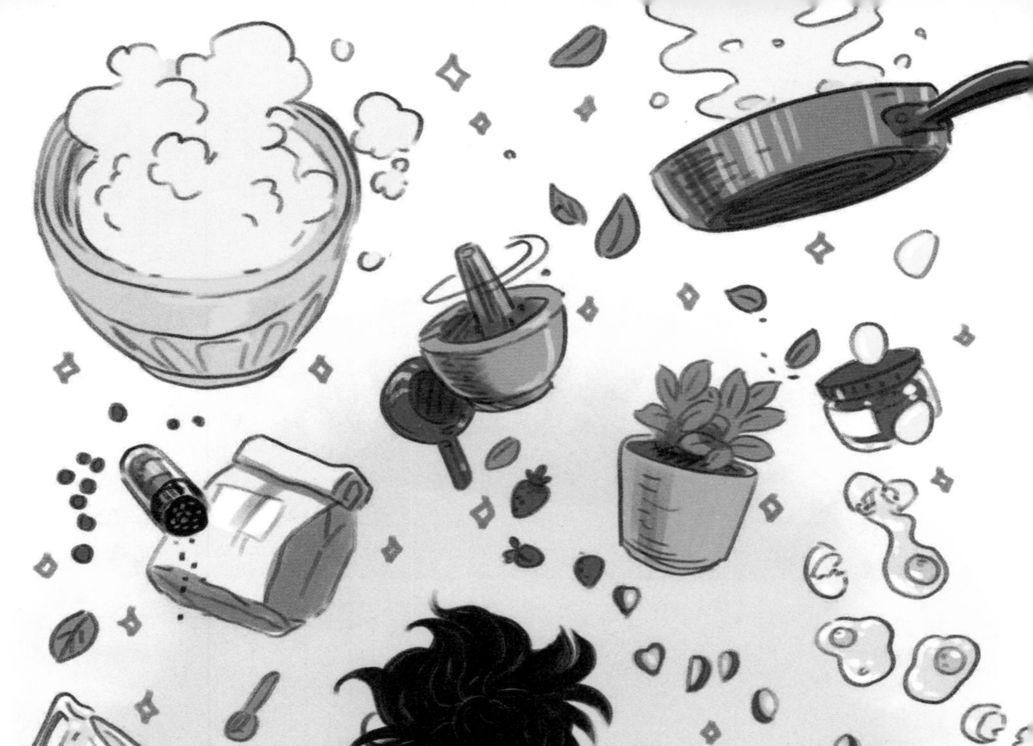

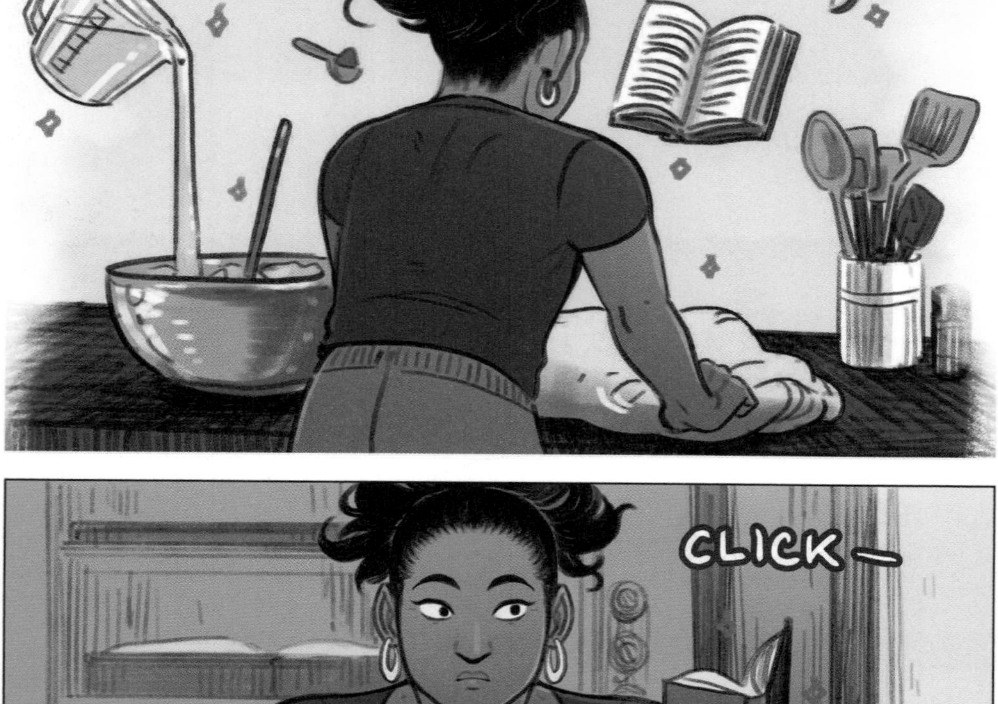
CLICK—

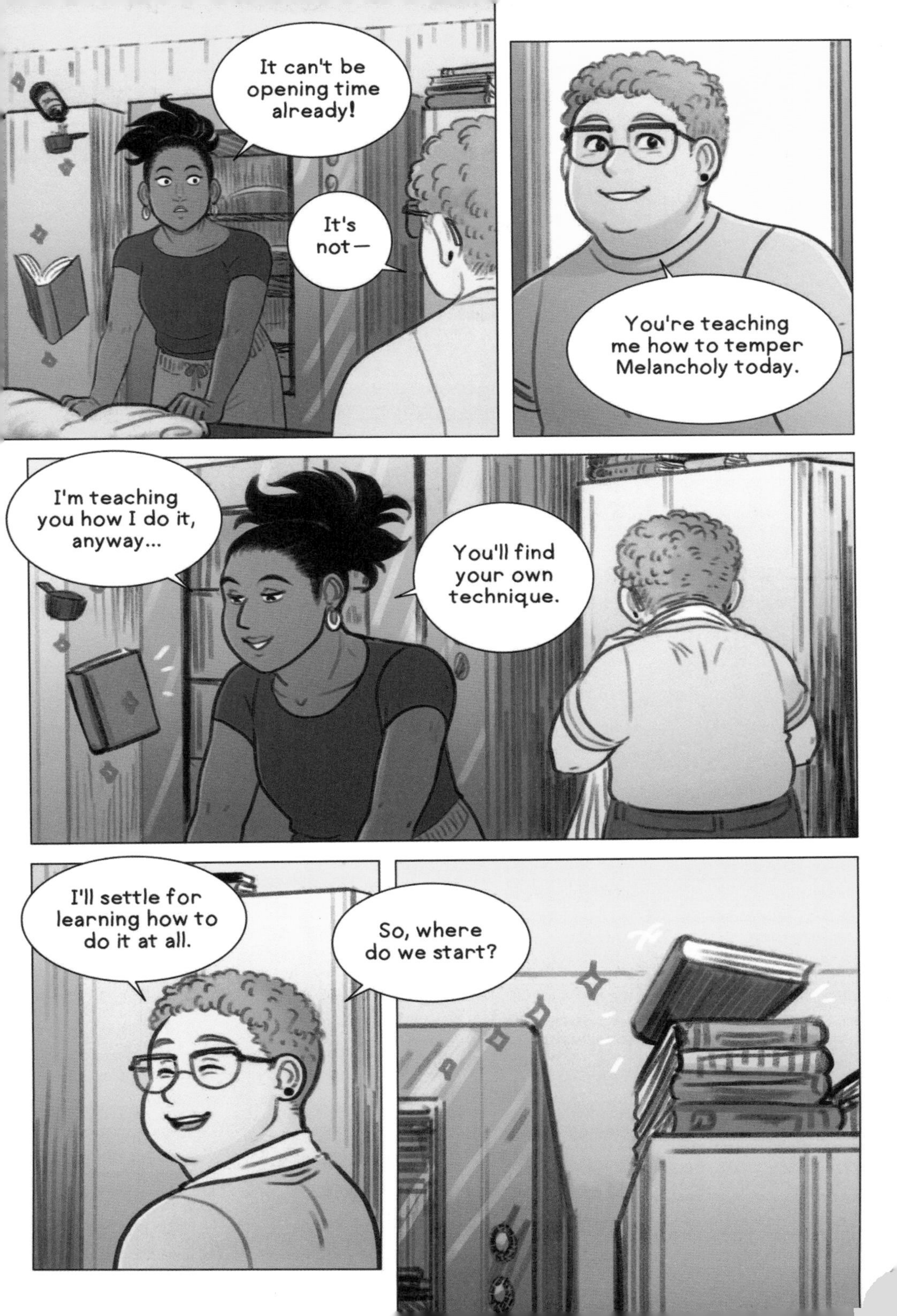
It can't be opening time already!
It's not—
You're teaching me how to temper Melancholy today.
I'm teaching you how I do it, anyway...
You'll find your own technique.
I'll settle for learning how to do it at all.
So, where do we start?

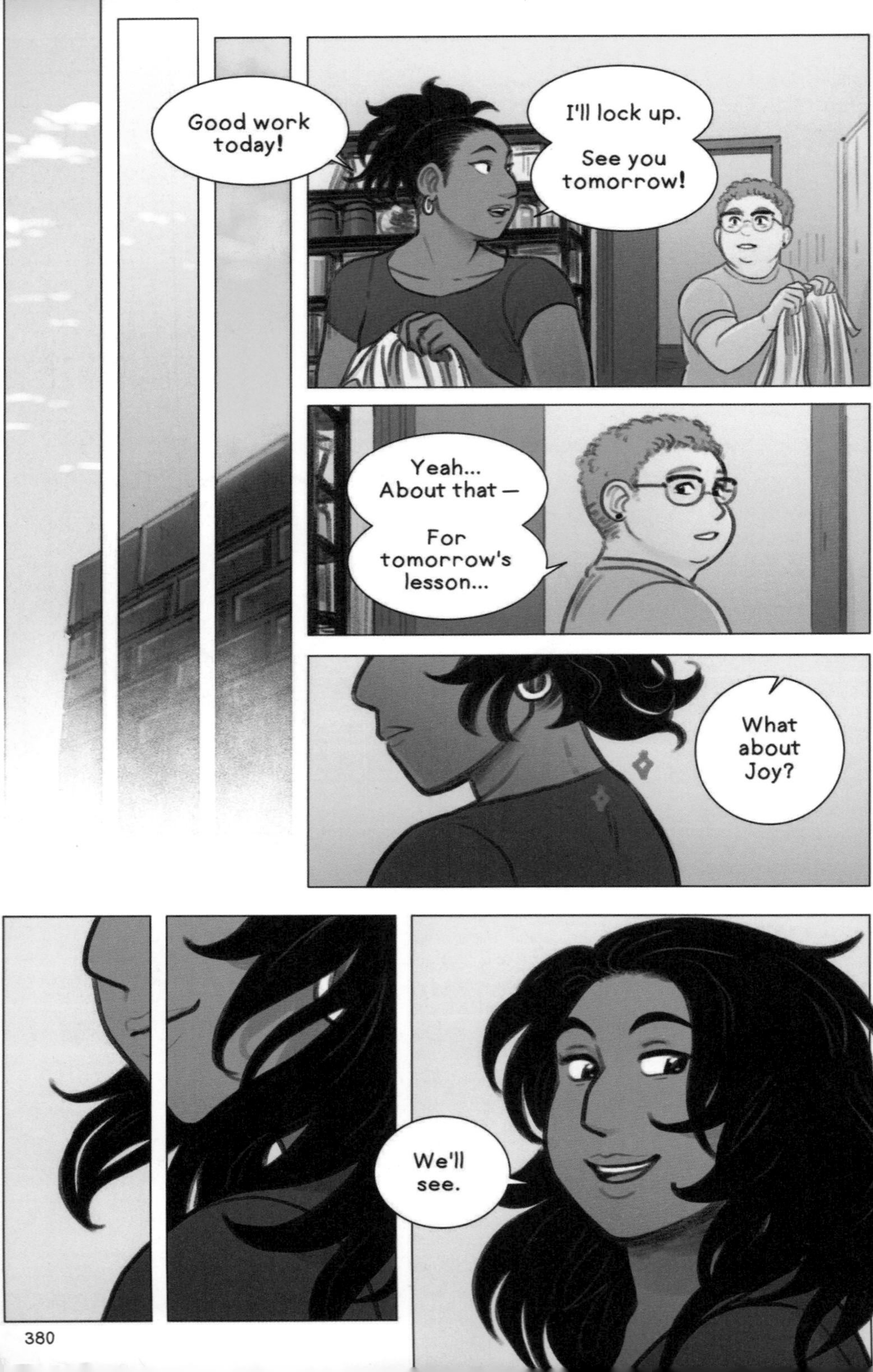
Good work today!
I'll lock up.
See you tomorrow!
Yeah... About that —
For tomorrow's lesson...
What about Joy?
We'll see.

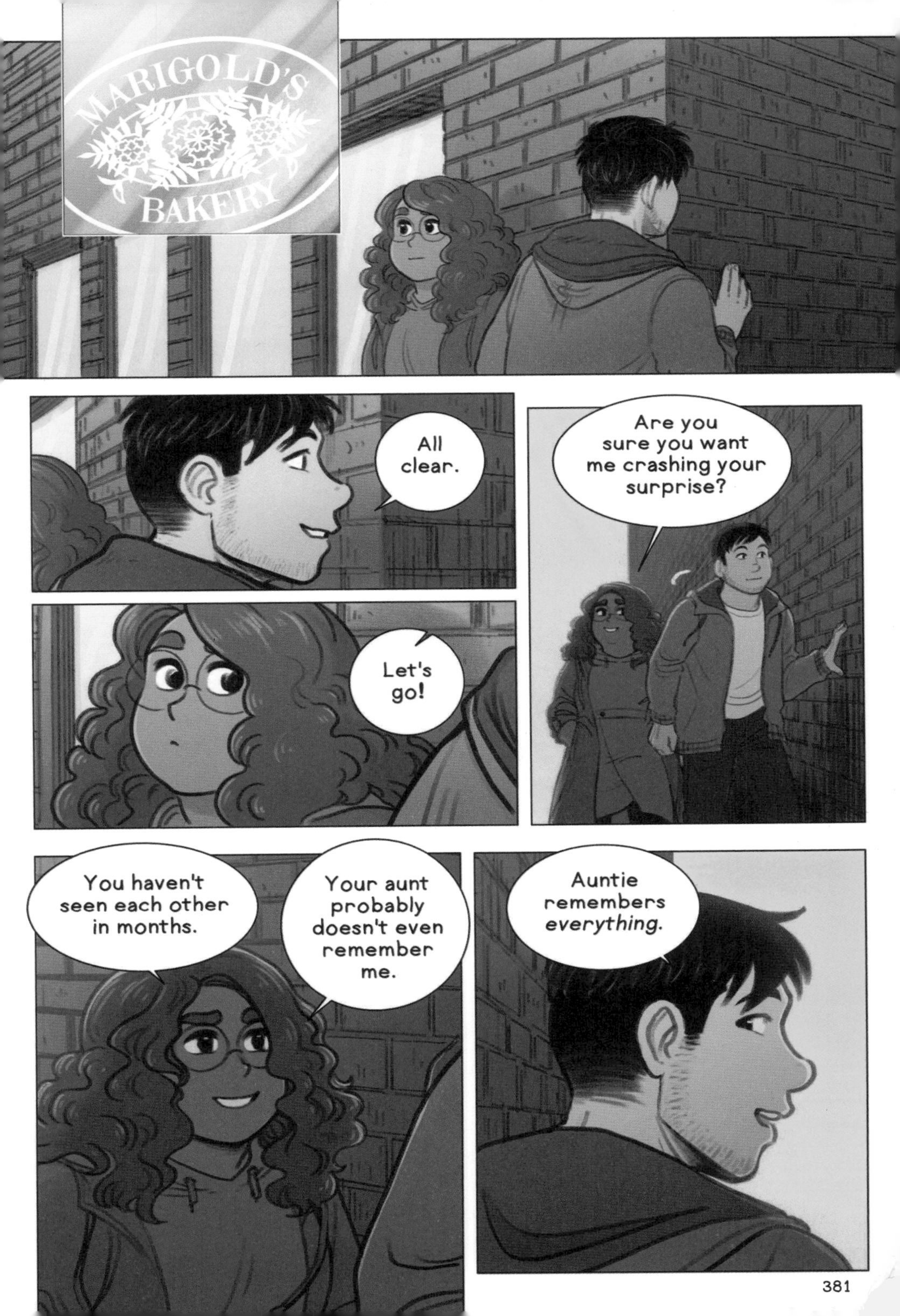
MARIGOLD'S BAKERY
All clear.
Are you sure you want me crashing your surprise?
Let's go!
You haven't seen each other in months.
Your aunt probably doesn't even remember me.
Auntie remembers *everything*.

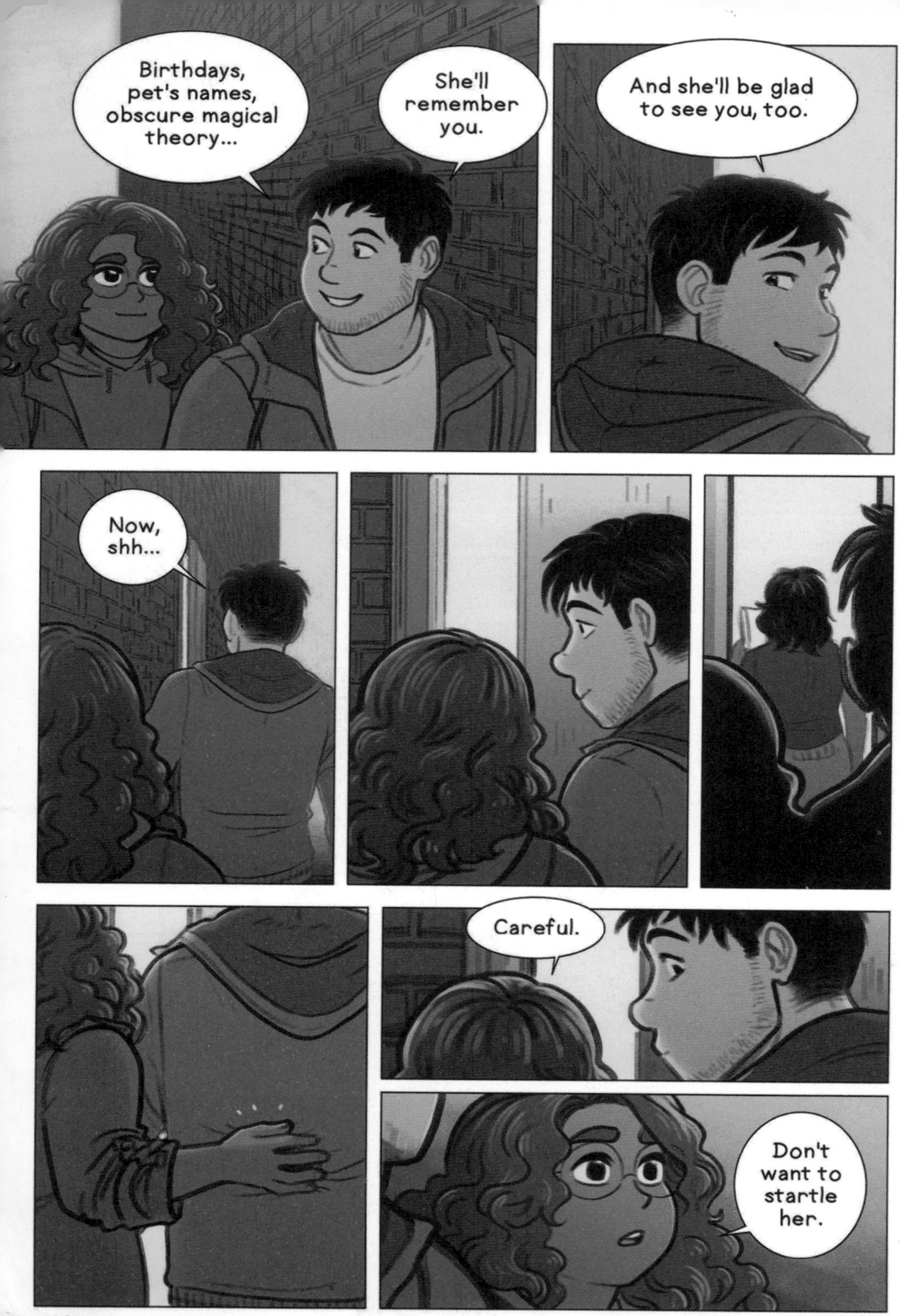
Birthdays, pet's names, obscure magical theory...
She'll remember you.
And she'll be glad to see you, too.
Now, shh...
Careful.
Don't want to startle her.

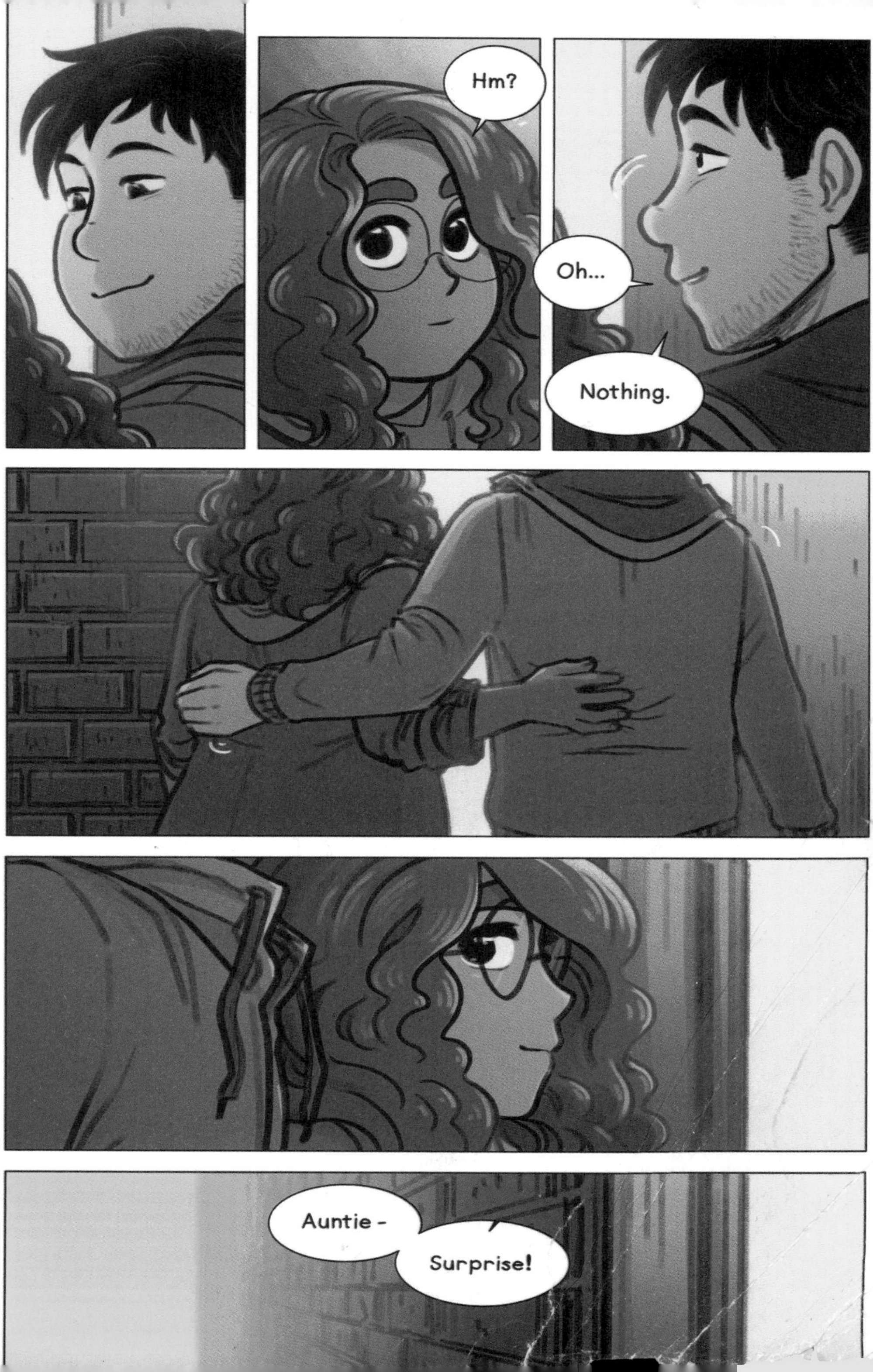
Hm?
Oh...
Nothing.
Auntie -
Surprise!

Acknowledgments

Maybe in some other enchanted world, books can be charmed into existence with a wish. In this world, it takes a bit more magic:

My family, who believed in and supported my comics, sight unseen.

H.B. Klein and my colleagues in webcomics, with their wealth of advice and their friendship.

Alakotila, who saved Crumbs from tripping on deadlines more times than I'd like to count.

And last but not least, Emilia Rhodes, Juliet Goodman, Celeste Knudsen, Alice Wang, Bones Leopard and the team at Etch, who did the heavy lifting of transforming over two thousand digital panels into these hundreds of pages.

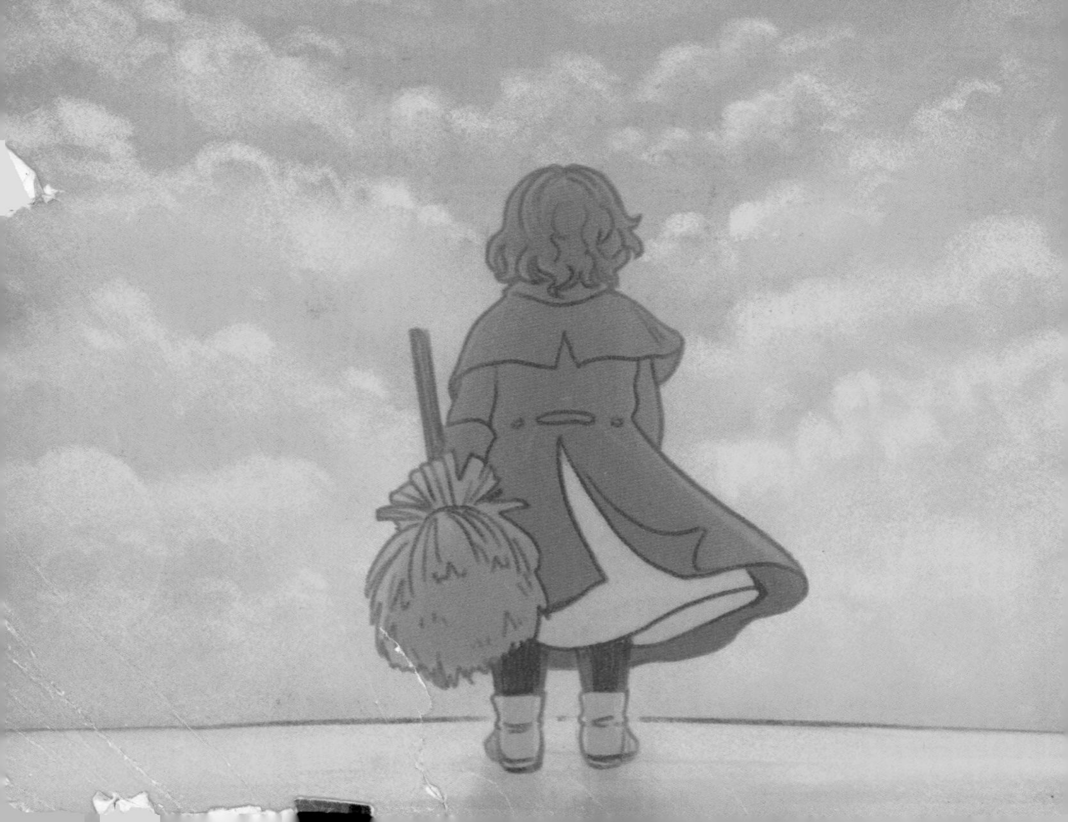